THE ARRIVAL

The sky glowed. Harry was an Angeleno; he judged the mistiness of the night by that glow, the glow of the Los Angeles lights reflected from the undersides of the clouds. The glow wasn't bright tonight, and stars showed through.

Something brighter than a star showed through, a dazzling pinpoint that developed a tail and vanished, all in a moment.

A long blue-white flame formed, and held for several seconds, while narrow lines of light speared down from one end. Other lights pulsed slowly, like beating hearts.

On another night Harry might have taken it for a meteor shower. Tonight . . . He'd read a hundred versions of the aliens conquering Earth, and they all sounded more spectacular than this flaring and dying of stars and smudges of lights. Any movie would have had sound effects too. But it looked so *real*.

Also by Larry Niven in Orbit:

Also by Larry Niven, Jerry Pournelle and Steven Barnes in Orbit:

Footfall
LARRY NIVEN AND
JERRY POURNELLE

ORBIT

An Orbit Book

First published in Great Britain by Victor Gollancz Ltd 1985
Published by Sphere Books Ltd 1986
Reprinted 1986 (twice), 1988, 1989
Reprinted in Orbit 1990, 1991

Reproduced printed and bound in Great Britain by
BPCC Hazell Books
Aylesbury, Bucks, England
Member of BPCC Ltd.

ISBN 0 7088 8376 1

Sphere Books Ltd
A Division of
Macdonald & Co (Publishers) Ltd
165 Great Dover Street
London SE1 4YA

A member of Maxwell Macmillan Publishing Corporation

To Robert Gleason

CONTENTS

DRAMATIS PERSONAE

THE DISCOVERERS

Linda Crichton Gillespie – *a Washington debutante*
Jeanette Crichton – *her sister*
Dr. Richard Owen – *astronomer*
Dr. Mary Alice Mouton – *astronomer*
Major General Edmund Gillespie, USAF – *astronaut*

WASHINGTON

David Coffey – *President of the United States*
Mrs. Jeanne Coffey – *First Lady*
Mrs. Carlotta Trujillo Dawson
Roger Brooks – *Special Assignments Reporter, Washington Post*
James Frantz – *White House Chief of Staff*
Henry Morton – *Vice President*
Dr. Arthur Hart – *Secretary of State*
Hap Aylesworth – *Special Assistant to the President for Political Affairs*
Ted Griffin – *Secretary of Defense*
Admiral Thorwald Carrell – *National Security Advisor*
Peter McCleve – *Attorney General*
Alan Rosenthal – *Secretary of the Treasury*
Connie Fuller – *Secretary of Commerce*
Arnold Biggs – *Secretary of Agriculture*
Jack Clybourne – *Presidential Protection Unit, Secret Service*

THE SOVIETS

Academician Pavel Aleksandrovich Bondarev –
Director, Lenin Institute
Lorena Polinova – *his secretary and mistress*
Marina Nikolayevna Bondarev – *his wife*
Boris Ogarkov – *Party Secretary at the Institute*
Andrei Pyatigorskiy – *Assistant Director, Lenin
Institute*
General Nikolai Nikolayevich Narovchatov –
Party Third Secretary, later First Party Secretary
Chairman Anatoliy Vladimirovich Petrovskiy –
Chairman of the Supreme Soviet
Ilya Trusov – *Chairman of the KGB*
Dmitri Parfenovich Grushin – *KGB officer*
Marshal Leonid Edmundovich Shavyrin –
Marshal of the Long Range Strategic Rocket Forces

SURVIVORS AND OTHERS

Harry Reddington – *unemployed minstrel*
Jeri Wilson – *Senior Editor, Harris Wickes Press*
Melissa Wilson – *her daughter*
William Adolphus Shakes
Kelvin Shakes
Miranda Shakes
Isadore and Clara Leiber
George and Vicki Tate-Evans
Jack and Harriet McCauley
Martin Carnell – *Show-dog breeder*
Ken Dutton – *Bookstore manager*
Cora Donaldson
Sarge Harris
Patsy Clevenger } *friends of Ken Dutton*
Anthony Graves
Maximilian Rohrs – *general contractor, Bellingham*

Evelyn Rohrs – *former Washington socialite*
Ben Lafferty – *Sheriff, Whatcom County, Washington*
Leigh Young – *Deputy Sheriff*
Whitey Lowenthal – *welder*
Carol North } *citizens of Lauren, Kansas*
Rosalee Pinelli)

KOSMOGRAD

Colonel Arvid Pavlovich Rogachev – *Commander of Kosmograd*
Nikolai – *onetime Sergeant, Red Air Force*
Aliana Aleksandrovna Tutsikova – *Deputy Commander*
Dr. Giselle Beaumont – *French scientist*
The Honorable Giorge N'Bruhna – *Nigerian politician*
Captain John Greeley, USAF – *astronaut*

THE FITHP

Herdmaster Pastempeh-keph
Advisor Fathisteh-tulk
K'turfookeph – *the Herdmaster's mate*
Chowpeentulk – *Advisor's mate*
Fookerteh – *the Herdmaster's son*
Attackmaster Koothfektil-rusp
Defensemaster Tantarent-fid
Breaker-Two Takpussch (later Takpusseh-yamp)
Breaker-One Raztupisp-minz
Fistarteh-thuktum – *priest and historian*
Koolpooleh – *male assistant to Fistarteh-thuktun*
Paykurtank – *female assistant to Fistarteh-thuktun*
Octuple leader Pretheeteh-damb
Tashayamp – *female assistant to Takpusseh (later his mate)*
Octuple Leader Chintithpit-mang (sleeper)
Shreshleemang – *Chintithpit-mang's mate*

Eight-cubed Leader Harpanet
Eight-cubed Leader Siplisteph
Rashinggith – *warrior (Year Zero Fithp)*
Birithart-yamp – *warrior in Africa*
Pheegorun – *warrior in Africa, died by spear*
Thirparteth-fuft – *guard officer*

COLORADO SPRINGS

Sergeant Ben Mailey – *U.S. Army*
Sherry Atkinson ⎫
Robert and Virginia Anson ⎪
Nat Reynolds ⎬ *the Threat Team*
Joe Ransom ⎪
Wade and Jane Curtis ⎪
Bob Burnham ⎭
Lieutenant General Harvey Toland – *U.S. Army*
The Honorable Joe Dayton – *Speaker of the House*
Senator Alexander Haswell – *President Pro Tem of the Senate*
Senator Raymond Carr of Kansas

JAYHAWKS

Juana Trujillo Morgan
Lieutenant Colonel Joe Halverson
Major David Morgan ⎫
Captain Evan Lewis ⎬ *Kansas National Guard*
Corporal Jimmy Lewis ⎪
Captain George Mason ⎭

WARRIORS AND PRISONERS

John Woodward
Carrie Woodward ⎫ *prisoners*
Alice McLennon
Gary Capehart

Ensign Jeff Franklin
Hamilton Gamble ⎫ *crewmen,*
Dr. Arthur Grace "Tiny" Pelz Michael
Jason Daniels
Samuel Cohen

Roy Culzer ⎫ *Shuttle pilots*
Jay Hadley

Commander Anton Villars – *Captain, USNS Ethan Allen*
Colonel Julius Carter – *U.S. Special Forces*
Lieutenant Jack Carruthers – *U.S. Special Forces*
Lieutenant Ivan Semeyusov – *Soviet Expeditionary Force*
Brant Chisholm – *South African farmer*
Katje Chisholm – *his wife*
Mvubi – *Zulu warrior*
Niklaus Van Der Stel – *Afrikaaner Commando*

PROLOGUE

Where are they?

– Enrico Fermi

The Fifth Part of the Year Three

Within its broad array of nested rings, the planet was a seething storm. It had always been so. Patterns chased themselves across its brown-on-brown face in bands and curlicues. The space around it churned with activity: billions of icy particles in a broad array of nested rings; eights of moons; streamers of dust whipped by powerful magnetic fields; all whirling around at terrific velocities, at several makasrupkithp per breath. *Message Bearer* maneuvered within that storm.

The Herdmaster's Advisor, gazing raptly through the thick double window, seemed to notice only the beauty of the scene.

The Herdmaster found that irritating. His own domain included collisions, industrial operations, internal quarrels, and the peaceful integration of sleepers with spaceborn. He had quite enough problems without . . . that.

Message Bearer's main telescope was the equal of any astronomical installation on the world they had left behind. The alien probe was close now, by astronomical standards, and the screen showed it in fine detail.

A circular antenna. A pod at the tip of a long boom radiated infrared warmth. That would be the power supply. Two more booms thrust instruments outward. *Clasp digits with me, that I may know your herd!* One extension held what had to be cameras, the other some kind of electronic sensing device.

Sixty-four sleepers, the Breaker's team, were working now to infer what they could about the creatures who had built that machine. They hadn't told the Herdmaster anything useful. When the camera platform began to turn, the Herdmaster's digits flexed restlessly.

'You made your decision half a year ago,' Advisor Fathisteh-tulk said placidly. 'You did not destroy it then. How can you destroy it now?'

'Here is where their fragile spy probe must pass through endless orbiting debris. It must survive collisions, radiation, orbital fluctuations, and any unreal danger the prey may imagine. Here is where some mischance is most likely to smash it!'

'We agreed that the probe will find no trace of us. *Message Bearer* is tiny on this scale. Surely the probe is not seeking us: it was launched long before we arrived. But if there were something to see, yonder camera might have seen it by now. Some evidence of our presence, vivid in their receivers . . . and *now* comes a flash of light, then silence from the probe, ever after. Would that tickle your suspicions?'

'If you were Herdmaster, would you continue to worry?'

That was cruel. At the beginning of things, Fathisteh-tulk had been Herdmaster. He had entered his death-sleep expecting to be Herdmaster again. In his present subservient position the concerns of a Herdmaster seemed not to bother him at all. Sometimes Herdmaster Pastempch-keph wondered if he was being mocked.

'Were I Herdmaster,' the Advisor said placidly, 'I would do as you have done. Rest quiet while the probe passes through. Make no attempt to move the ship, send no message to our work force on the Foot. Let the probe pass. When the second probe comes, we will be established on the Foot. Let them try to distinguish us against an unknown background.'

And he turned from the telescope screen, perhaps

pointedly, to gaze on the great brown-patterned world and its vast rings.

The Herdmaster said, 'I worry. For much of their history the prey must have studied this . . . great gaudy ornament in their sky. They would know what to expect better than we do after less than a year. What have we missed?'

Outside the broad main ring system, a narrower ring still roiled from the wake of *Message Bearer*'s drive.

November 1980

As she closed the gate and automatically picked up a scrap of paper that had blown into the yard, Linda Gillespie realized that she was beginning to think of this house – a typical California development split-level – as home. That would make the second *home* since she was married. There had been three other places they hadn't stayed in long enough to think about as homelike at all. Five moves in four years. The Air Force was a mobile service, especially for hot fighter pilots. The best place had been in Texas, when Edmund had been with the astronaut office, and they'd lived in El Lago.

But this couldn't really be home. It was just a rented house, a place to stay during Edmund's tour at the Space and Missiles Systems Organization in Los Angeles. Now that he'd been assigned as a shuttle pilot, they'd move again. Back to Houston! That would be nice. Houston treated astronauts and their families very well indeed.

It was a gloomy Los Angeles November morning, chilly even through her cashmere sweater, with low clouds and fog. The air smelled damp, with a trace of the odor of smog. There was no sunshine, although by noon there would be. It wasn't pleasant outside.

Inside was better. She poured coffee and sat at the kitchen table. Too early for Ed to call. He wouldn't anyway. He never did when he was out of town. *It's all very well to be married to an astronaut hero, but it would be nice to have a husband at home once in a while.* The *Los*

Angeles Times lay on the table, and she thumbed through it.

She didn't like to be alone at home, but she didn't want to go anywhere, either. Ed could assure her she was perfectly safe, much safer, much safer than in Washington, where she'd grown up, and she could believe him – but she knew Washington, and Los Angeles was a mystery. One San Francisco columnist kept teasing Los Angeles about being invisible.

There was also the Hollywood Strangler, and a man alleged to be the Freeway Killer was on trial for the torture sex murders of a dozen young boys. Great place to raise children. She folded the paper.

Time to wax the kitchen floor, she decided. Ed didn't care much, but his colonel would come to dinner next week, and Colonel McReady's wife was inclined to snoop. Besides, it wasn't that hard to do floors.

Ed wouldn't approve. Not now. She grinned and looked down at her stomach. Didn't show a bit. She wasn't sick, either, and if it hadn't been for the missed periods and medical reports there'd be no reason to suspect she was pregnant. Even so, Ed treated her like she was made of Dresden china. He carried out the garbage, did all the lifting, and worried about hurting her during sex.

That thought made her frown. Ed went all gooey over her pregnancy, but it turned him off! *Maybe I'll lose interest in a month or so. I sure hope so, the way he acts.*

Linda poured more coffee. The telephone rang, startling her so that she dropped the cup. It was Corningware and didn't break, but it clattered loudly on the floor, spilling coffee everywhere.

'Hello?'

'Linda?'

'Yes?'

'By golly, it is you! It's Roger.'

'Oh. How are you, Roger?'

'Great. Glad you haven't forgotten me.'

'No, I haven't forgotten.' You don't forget your first, she thought. First love, first sex experience, first – a lot of firsts with Roger, back in high school and just after. And what should I say? That he hasn't called in a long time, but that's all right because I didn't want him to? 'Roger, how did you get our number?'

'We reporters have our ways. Hey, I'd like to see you. What about a really unusual experience?'

She giggled. 'Roger, I'm a married woman.'

'Sure. Happily?'

'Yes, of course —'

'Good. Good for you and Edmund, anyway. What I have in mind is in Edmund's line. JPL. The Saturn encounter. Voyager is out there getting pictures nobody understands, and we can see them firsthand.' He paused a moment. 'It's this way, I'm here in Los Angeles covering the Saturn story. Not exactly Pulitzer Prize material, but I took the assignment to get away from Washington for a while. So I'm out at the Jet Propulsion Laboratory where the pictures come in. We get briefings from the scientists, and there's science-fiction writers, and it's a hell of a show. Let me pick you up on my way out, you're almost on the way. I'll have you home by dinnertime, and I won't try to seduce you.'

And Ed was gone for a week. 'It's tempting. It really is, but I can't.'

'Sure you can.'

'Roger, my sister is staying here —'

'So what? I'll have you home before dinner.'

Linda thought about that. Jenny was off somewhere for the day. Saturn pictures. Reporters. It might be fun. 'You said science-fiction writers. Is Nat Reynolds there?'

'Yeah, I think so. Just a second, there's a list – yeah, he's there. Know him?'

'No, but Edmund likes his books. I bought one for his birthday. Think I could get it autographed?'

'An astronaut's wife? Hell, those sci-fi types will turn flips to meet you.'

Nat Reynolds was hung over, and it was far too early to be up. It was a miracle he'd made it up the arroyo to the Jet Propulsion Laboratory parking lot and got the Porsche into the tiny slot the JPL guard had showed him.

There were cars parked for a half a mile along the road leading to where JPL nestled in what had once been a lonely arroyo. The street immediately outside the press center was nearly blocked by TV vans, and a thick web of cables spanned the sidewalk to vanish through open loading doors. The press corps had turned out in force, bringing almost as many cameras and crews as they'd send to the site of a bank robbery in progress.

The Von Karman Auditorium was a madhouse. Nearly every square foot of floor space was covered by someone: scientist, public relations, press corps, most holding coffee cups or carrying bulky objects.

The press corps was divided. There were the working press and there were the science-fiction writers, and no doubt about who was who. The press was there to work. Some had fun, but all had deadlines. The SF types were there to gawk, and be part of the scene, and absorb the atmosphere, and maybe someday it would get into a story and maybe not. Their world was being created and they were here to see it happen.

This is Saturn!

Huge TV screens showed pictures as they came in from the Voyager. Every few minutes a picture changed. A close view of the planet, black-and-white streamlines and whorls. Rings, hundreds of them, like a close-up of a phonograph record. Saturn again, in color, with his rings in wide angle. Sections of the rings in close-up. Shots of moons. All just as it came in, so that the press saw it as soon as the scientists.

At the Jupiter passings the pictures had come in faster,

in vivid swirls and endless storms, God making merry with an airbrush, and four moons that turned out to be worlds in their own right. But to balance that they'd soon see Titan, which was known to have an atmosphere. Sagan and the other scientists weren't saying they hoped to find life on Titan – but they were certainly interested in the giant moon, which had so far been disappointingly featureless.

The screens shifted, and the babble in the room fell off for a moment. A moon like a giant eyeball: one *tremendous* crater of the proportions of an iris, with a central peak for the pupil. Anything bigger, Nat thought, would have shattered the whole moon. He heard a female voice say, 'Well, we've located the Death Star,' and he grinned without turning around.

What do the newspeople think of us? He could picture himself: the idiot grin, mouth slightly open, drifting down the line of screens without looking where he was going, tripping over cables . . . Nat couldn't make himself care. A screen changed to show something like a dry riverbed or three twined plumes of smoke or . . . *F-ring*, the printout said. Nat said, 'What the hell . . .'

'You'd know if you'd been here last night.'

'I've got to get *some* sleep.' Nat didn't need to look around. He'd written two books with Wade Curtis; he expected to recognize that voice in Hell, when they planned their escape. Wade Curtis talked like he had an amplifier in his throat, turned high. Partly that was his military training, partly the deafness he'd earned as an artillery officer.

He also had a tendency to lecture. 'F-ring,' he said. 'You know, like A, B, C, rings, only they're named in order of discovery, not distance from the planet, so the system's all screwed up. The F-ring is the one just outside the big body of rings. It's thin. Nobody ever saw it until the space probes went out there, and Pioneer didn't get much of a picture even then.'

Nat held up his hand, *I know*, I know, the gesture said. Curtis shrugged and was quiet.

But the F-ring didn't look normal at all. It showed as three knotted streamers of gas or dust or God knows what all braided together. 'Braided,' Nat said. 'What does that?'

'None of the astronomers wanted to say.'

'Okay, I can see why. Catch me in a mistake, I shrug it off. A scientist, he's betting his career.'

'Yeah. Well, I know of no law of physics that would permit *that*!'

Nat didn't either. He said, 'What's the matter, haven't you ever seen three earthworms in love?' and accepted Wade's appreciative chuckle as his due. 'I'd be afraid to write about it. Someone would have it explained before I could get the story into print.'

The press conference was ready to start. The JPL camera crew unlimbered its gear to broadcast the press conference all over the laboratory grounds, and one of the public relations ladies went around turning off the screens in the conference room.

'Hmm. Interesting stuff still coming,' Curtis said. 'And there aren't any seats. I had a couple but I gave them to the *Washington Post*. Front-row seats, too.'

'Too bad,' Nat said. 'What the hell, let's watch the conference from the reception area. Jilly's out there already.'

On the morning of November 12, 1980, the pressroom at Jet Propulsion Laboratories was a tangled maze of video equipment and moving elbows. Roger and Linda had come early, but not early enough to get seats. A science-fiction writer in a bush jacket gave up his, two right in the front row.

'Sure it's all right?' Roger asked.

The sci-fi man shrugged. 'You need 'em more than I do. Tell Congress the space program's *important*, that's all I ask.'

Roger thanked the man and sat down. Linda Gillespie

was trapped near the life-size spacecraft model, fending off still another reporter who was trying to interview her: what had it been like, marooned on Earth while her husband was aboard Skylab?

She looked great. He hadn't seen her since – since when? Only twice since she'd married Edmund. And of course he'd been at her wedding. Linda's mother had cried. Damn near cried myself, Roger thought. How did I let her get out of circulation? But I wasn't ready to marry her myself. Maybe I should have . . .

And maybe I'm just feeling mellow about things that happened four years ago. It's easy to remember the good times. He squirmed uncomfortably. They had been good. He glanced sideways at her, but she was looking at the model. Best forget all that anyway.

The trouble was, he wasn't getting any story he could understand. People were excited, but they didn't say why. The regular science press people weren't telling. They all knew each other, and they resented outsiders at big events like this.

Roger doodled, looking up when anyone called a greeting, hoping nobody would want his attention. He hadn't asked for this assignment.

He heard, 'Haven't you ever seen three earthworms in love?' and looked. A clump of science-fiction writers stood beneath a screen that showed . . . yeah, three earthworms in love, or a bad photo of spaghetti left on a plate, or just noise. He wrote, 'F ring: Three earthworms in love,' and tapped Linda's shoulder. 'Linda? Save my seat?'

'Where're you going?'

'Maybe I can get something from the science-fiction writers.' Nobody else was trying that; it might get him a new slant. At least they'd talk English.

'It looks like things are starting.'

Frank Bristow, the JPL newsroom manager, had taken his place at the podium. Roger had met him briefly when signing in. The regular press corps all seemed to know him as well as each other. Roger didn't know anyone.

Bristow was about to make his opening statement. The Voyager project manager and four astrophysicists were taking their seats at a raised table. Brooks sat down again. He wished he were somewhere else.

Roger Brooks was approaching thirty, and he didn't like it. There were temptations in his job: too much free food and booze. He took care to maintain the muscle tone when his lifestyle didn't. His straight blond hair was beginning to thin, and that worried him a little, but his jaw was still square, with none of the softening he saw in his friends. He had given up smoking three years ago, flatly, and suffered through horrid withdrawal symptoms. His teeth were white again, but the scars between the index and middle fingers of his right hand would never go away. He'd been taken drunk one night in Vietnam, and a cigarette had burned out there.

Roger Brooks had been just old enough to cover some of the frantic last days in Vietnam, but he had been too late to get anything juicy. He had missed Watergate: his suspicions were right, but he was too junior to follow them up. Other reporters got Pulitzer prizes.

Something had changed in him after that. It was as if there were a secret somewhere, calling to him. Little assignments couldn't hold his interest.

'He missed one chance to be played by Robert Redford,' one of his ladies had been heard to say. 'He isn't about to miss another.'

This was a little assignment. He wondered if he should have taken it, even for the chance to get to California, even though half the Washington newsroom staff would have sold fingers and toes for the chance. But nobody was keeping secrets here. Whatever Voyager One told them, they would shout it to the world, to the Moon if they could. The trick was to understand them.

No big story, maybe, but the trip was worth it. He glanced at Linda and thought: definitely worth it. He twisted uncomfortably as old memories came back. They'd been so inexperienced! But they'd learned, and no sex had ever been as good as his memory of Linda that last time. Maybe he'd edited that memory. Maybe not. *I've got to stop thinking about that! It'll show . . . What in hell am I going to write about?*

Another group was clumped beneath the full-size model of the Voyager spacecraft. They had to be scientists, because most of them were men and they all wore suits. A couple of the science-fiction writers stood with them, more like colleagues than press. No reporters did that. Would that make an interesting angle? The sci-fi people didn't pretend to be neutral. They were enthusiasts and didn't care who knew it, while the reporters tried to pout on this smug air of impartiality.

The briefing began. The Program Director talked about the spacecraft. Mission details, spacecraft performing well. Some data lost because it was raining in Spain where were located the high-gain antennae – was that a joke? No, nobody was laughing.

'Three billion miles away, and they're getting pictures,' somebody said on his right. A pretty girl, long legs, slim ankles, short bobbed hair. Badge said Jeri Wilson, some geological magazine. Wedding ring, but that didn't always mean anything. Maybe she'd be here the rest of the week. She seemed to be alone.

The mission planning people left the podium and the scientists, Brad Smith and Ed Stone and Carl Sagan, came up to tell what they thought they were learning. Roger listened, and tried to think of an interesting question. In a situation like this, the important thing was get yourself noticed, for future reference, then try for an exclusive. He jotted useful phrases:

'New moons are going to get dull pretty soon.'

'Not dozens of rings. Hundreds. We're still counting.'

Long pause. 'Some of them are eccentric.'

'What does that mean?' someone whispered.

The sci-fi man in the khaki bush jacket answered in what he probably thought was a whisper. 'The rings are supposed to be perfect circles with Saturn at the center. All the theory says they *have* to be. Now they've found some that aren't circles, they're ellipses.'

Other scientists spoke:

'. . . May be the largest crater in the solar system in relation to the body it's on . . .'

'There isn't any Janus. There are two moons where we thought Janus was. They share the same orbit, and they change places every time they pass. Oh, yes, we've known for some time those orbits were possible. It's a textbook exam question in celestial mechanics. It's just that we never found anything like it in the real universe —'

Brooks jotted down details on that one; it was definitely worth a mention. Janus was the moon named for the two-faced god of beginnings!

He whispered that to Linda, and got an appreciative nod. The Wilson girl wrote something too.

'The radial spokes in the rings seem to be caused by very tiny particles, around the size of a wavelength of light. Also the process seems to be going on above the ring, not in it.'

Radial spokes in the rings! They ought to disappear as the rings turned, because the inner rings were moving faster than the outer rings. They didn't disappear. Weird news from everywhere in Saturn system. Some of Brooks' colleagues would understand the explanations, when they came . . .

Yet the press conference offered more than Brooks had expected. He had interviewed scientists before. It was the lack of answers that was interesting here.

'We don't know what that means.'

'We wouldn't like to say yet.'

'The more we learn from Voyager, the less we know about rings.'

'If we fiddle with the numbers a little we can pretty well explain why Cassini's Divide is so much bigger than it ought to be.' Dramatic pause. 'Of course that doesn't explain why there are five faint rings inside it!'

'If I'd had to make a long list of things we *wouldn't* see, eccentric rings would have been the first item.'

'Brad, what about braided rings?'

'That would have been off the top of the paper.'

Everyone up there looked happy, Brooks noted. Fun things were going on here. If Brooks didn't have the background to appreciate them, who did?

A newsperson asked, 'Have you got any more on the radial spokes? I'd have thought that violated the laws of physics.'

David Morrison from Hawaii answered, 'I'm sure the rings are doing everything right. We just don't understand it yet.' Brooks jotted it down.

'Where I want to be,' Roger said, 'is in a motel room with you.' They were walking the grounds of JPL: lawn, fountains, vaguely Oriental rock gardens, a bridge, all very nice.

'That was years ago,' Linda said. 'And it's all over.'

'Sure?'

'Yes, Roger, I'm sure. Now be good. You promised you would. Don't make me sorry I came with you.'

'No, of course I won't,' Roger said. 'It really is good to see you again. And I'm glad you're happy with Edmund.'

Are you? Linda wondered. And am I? Of course I am. I'm very happy *with* Edmund. It's when he goes off and leaves me to take care of everything and I'm alone all the time and I see these goddam romantic perfume ads and things like that I get unhappy about Major Edmund Gillespie. I wonder if the feminists did us any favors, letting us admit we get horny just like men?

She grinned broadly.

'Yeah?' Roger demanded.

'Nothing.' Nothing I'd tell you. But it's nice to see I could have some company if I wanted . . .

Lunch was in the JPL cafeteria. Roger and Linda were made welcome at the science-fiction writers' table, but the writers didn't *know* any more than Roger did. They were having fun with not knowing.

Someone passed a cartoon down the table. It showed hanging off to one side, either the *Star Wars* Death Star or Saturn's moon Mimas, Saturn huge across the background. In the foreground a spacecraft used mechanical arms to twist the F-ring into a braid. The caption. 'You've a wicked sense of humor, Darth Vader!'

Another writer looked up and yawned.'Oh, it's just another goddam spectacular picture of Saturn.' That earned him appreciative laughter.

But no one *knew*, which made it a frustrating lunch. Saturn had secrets, maybe, but he wasn't telling them, and the writers didn't have any logical guesses about the strange pictures.

Halfway through the lunch Linda called to someone. 'Wes. We didn't expect to see you here —'

He was a trim athletic man in a faded baseball cap. Linda introduced him around the table.'Wes married Carlotta,' she told Roger. 'You remember Carlotta. She was my best friend in school —'

'Sure,' Roger said. 'How are you?'

One of the writers looked thoughtful. 'Wes Dawson . . . You're running for Craig Hosmer's old seat.'

'Right.'

'Wes has always been for the space program,' Linda said. 'Maybe you fellows will vote for him —'

'Not our district,' Wade Curtis said. 'We live north of there. But maybe we can help. We're always interested in people who'll promote space.'

*　　*　　*

It was late afternoon when they got back to the house. Roger pulled into the driveway.

'You might as well come in and meet Jenny,' Linda said. 'Remember her?'

'Sure I remember The Brat. I had to bribe her to leave us alone —'

'Well, she's grown a bit now.' Linda led the way to the house and unlocked the door. It was strangely silent inside. She went to the kitchen and found a note held to the refrigerator by a tomato-shaped magnet. Roger was standing behind her, scanning over her shoulder, as she read it.

SIS: Had to run down to San Diego. Beach party, Charlene's with me. Back tomorrow. Jenny.

Linda frowned at the note.

'Beach party?' Roger asked.

'She's a freshman at Long Beach State. Anthropology. But she took up scuba diving in a big way. Her current boyfriend is at Scripps.' Linda shook her head in dismay. 'Mother will kill me if she finds out I let her go to an all-night party.'

Roger shook his head. 'The Brat's in college? Jeez, Linda, she can't be more than – what, fifteen?'

'Seventeen.'

Roger sighed. 'I guess it's been longer than I thought.'

'Yes, it has been. Want some coffee?'

'Sure.'

She got out the filters and put water on. Roger hadn't said anything, hadn't done anything, but she could feel the vibes. Had Jenny planned this? But no, she didn't know Roger was in town, and she wouldn't if she had. She'd always liked Roger, but she liked Edmund more. No, Jenny wouldn't have deliberately arranged to leave her alone with a lover from the past . . .

It had been a long time, but she remembered every

detail. Pampered Georgetown University freshman dating the reporter from the *Washington Post*. They'd planned it, a weekend together in her parents' Appalachian cabin. It had been summer, and no one was using the place. The weather in the mountains had been perfect. There'd been a delicious thrill of anticipation as they drove up the twisting highway. She hadn't had that feeling since.

Edmund was different. Edmund was older too, and more glamorous. Fighter pilot. Astronaut. Everything a hero should be. *Everything but a great lover . . . That's not fair, not fair at all.*

There'd been anticipation when she met Edmund. It lasted all during their courtship – and died on their wedding night.

I'd forgotten all this, but I feel it now. Just as I did then. But —

The coffee machine was set up and there wasn't any reason to watch it any longer. She turned. Roger was standing very close to her. She didn't have to move far to be in his arms.

PART ONE

The Rogues

CHAPTER ONE
DISCOVERY

'When you have eliminated the impossible, whatever remains, *however improbable*, must be the truth.'

— SHERLOCK HOLMES in *The Sign of Four*

COUNTDOWN: H MINUS SIX WEEKS

The lush tropical growth of the Kona Coast ended abruptly. Suddenly the passionflower vines and palm trees were gone, and Jenny was driving through barren lava fields. 'It looks like the back side of the Moon,' she said.

Her companion nodded and pointed toward the slopes off to their right. 'Mauna Loa. They said it's terrible luck to take any of the lava home.'

'Who says?'

'The Old Hawaiians, of course. But a surprising number of tourists, too. They take the stuff home, and later they mail it back.' He shrugged. 'Bad luck or no, so far as anyone knows, she — Mauna Loa is always she to the Old Ones – she's never taken a life.'

Captain Jeanette Crichton expertly downshifted the borrowed TR-7 as the road began another steep ascent. The terrain was deceptive. From the beach the mountains looked like gentle slopes until you tried climbing them. Then you realized just how *big* the twin volcanoes were. Mauna Kea rose nearly 14,000 feet above the sea – and plunged 20,000 feet downward to the sea bottom, making it a bigger mountain than Everest.

3

'You'll turn left at the next actual road,' Richard Owen said. 'It'll be a way. Mind if I doze off? I had a late night.'

'All right by me,' she said. She drove on.

Not very flattering, she thought. Picks me up in Kona, gets me to drive him up the side of a volcano, and goes to sleep. Romantic . . .

She ran her fingers along her shoulder-length hair. It was dark brown with a trace of red, and at the moment it couldn't be very attractive since it was still damp from her morning swim. She hadn't much of a tan, either. Sometimes her freckles ran together to give the illusion of a tan, but it was too early in the spring for that. Damp hair, no tan. Not really the popular image of a California girl.

Her figure was all right, if a bit athletic; the Army encouraged officers to run four miles a day, and she did that although she could get out of the requirement if she really wanted to. The medium-length skirt and T-shirt showed her off pretty well. Still, it couldn't be looks that attracted this astronomer to her, any more than she was overwhelmed by his appearance. All the same, there'd been some electricity earlier. Now it was nearly gone.

He was up all night, she thought. And will be again tonight. Let him sleep. That should liven him up. God knows what I'd be like if I had to live on a vampire's schedule.

They drove through alternate strips of pasture and lava fields. At irregular intervals someone had made crude stacks of lava rocks. Three or four rocks, each smaller than the one below, the bottom one perhaps two feet across, piled in a stack; she'd been told they were religious offerings made by the Old Hawaiians. If so, they couldn't be very old; Mauna Loa erupted pretty often, and certainly this field had been overflowed several times during the twentieth century.

She turned left at the intersection, and the way became even steeper. The TR-7 laboured through the climb. There were fewer fresh lava fields here; now they were on the side

4

of Mauna Kea. 'She' was supposed to be pretty thoroughly dormant. They drove through endless miles of ranchlands given by King Kamehameha to a British sailor who'd become the king's friend.

Richard Owen woke just as they reached the 'temporary' wooden astronomy base station. 'We stop here,' he said. 'Have some lunch.'

There wasn't much there. Long one-story wooden barracks in a sea of lava and mud, with a few straggly trees trying to live in the lava field. She pulled in alongside several GMC Jimmy four-wheel-drive vehicles. 'We could go on up,' she said. 'I don't really need lunch —'

'Regulations. Acclimatization. It's nearly fourteen thousand feet at the top. Pretty thin air. Thin enough here at ten thousand. It's not easy to do anything, even walk, until you get used to it.'

By the time they reached the clapboard barracks buildings she was ready to agree.

There were half a dozen observatories on the lip of the volcano. Richard parked the Jimmy in front of the NASA building. It looked liked an observatory in a Bugs Bunny cartoon: a square concrete building under a shiny metal dome.

'Do I get to look through the telescope?' she asked.

He didn't laugh. Maybe he had answered that one too often. 'No one looks through telescopes anymore. We just take pictures.' He led the way inside, through bare-walled corridors and down an iron stairway to a lounge furnished with chrome-steel office tables and chairs.

There was a woman in the lounge. She was about Jeanette's age, and she would have been pretty if she'd washed her face and put on some lipstick. She was frowning heavily as she drank coffee.

'Mary Alice,' Owen said, 'this is Jeanette Crichton. Captain Crichton, Army Intelligence. Not a spook, she does photo reconnaissance and that sort of thing.

Dr. Mary Alice Mouton. She's an asteroid specialist.'

'Hi,' Mary Alice said. She went on frowning.

'Problem?' Owen asked.

'Sort of.' She didn't seemed to notice Jeanette at all. 'Rick, I wish you'd come look at this —'

'Sure.'

Dr. Mouton led the way and Rick Owen followed. Jeanette shook her head and tagged after them, through another corridor and up some stairs, past an untidy computer room. All mad, she thought. But what did I expect?

She hadn't known what to expect at all. This was her first trip to Hawaii, courtesy of an engineering association meeting that invited her to speak on satellite observation. That conference was over and she was taking a couple of days' leave, swimming the Big Island's reefs and enjoying the sun. She didn't know anyone in Hawaii, and it had been pretty dull. Jeanette began to make plans to visit Linda and Edmund before going back to Fort Bragg.

Then Richard Owen had met her at the reef. They'd had breakfast after their swim, and he'd invited her to come up to see the observatory. She'd brought a sleeping bag; she didn't know whether Owen expected to share it with her, but from little things he'd said at lunch and on the drive up after lunch she was pretty sure he'd make the offer. She'd been trying to decide what to do when he did.

Now it was as if she weren't there at all.

She followed them into a small, cluttered room. There was a big view-screen in one corner. Dr. Mouton did things to the controls and a field of stars showed on the screen. She did something else, and the star field blinked on and off; as it did, one star seemed to jump back and forth.

'New asteroid?' Owen asked.

'That's what I thought,' Dr. Mouton said. 'Except – take a good look, Rick. And think about what you're seeing.'

He stared at the screen. Jeanette came closer. She

6

couldn't see anything strange. You take the pictures on two different nights and do a blink comparison. The regular stars won't have moved enough to notice, but anything that moves against the background of the 'fixed stars,' like a planet or an asteriod, will be in two different places on the two different photos. Blink back and forth between the two plates: the 'moving' body would seem to jump back and forth. That was how Clyde Tombaugh discovered Pluto. It was also a standard photo reconnaissance technique, to see what had changed in the interval between two satellite photos.

'What's the problem?' Owen asked.

'That's moving too far for the interval.'

'It's close —'

'Not that close,' she said. 'I got the plates from a few weeks ago. Rick, I had to trace back damn near night by night, it's moving so fast! It's in a hyperbolic orbit.'

'Come on, it can't be!'

'It is,' Dr. Mouton said.

'Excuse me,' Jeanette said. They both turned to look at her. They'd obviously forgotten she was there. 'What's a hyperbolic orbit?'

'Fast,' Owen said. 'Moving too fast for the sun's gravity. Objects in a hyperbolic orbit can escape from the solar system altogether.'

She frowned. 'How could something be moving that fast?'

'Big planets can make it happen,' Richard said. 'Disturb something's orbit —'

'It's under power,' Mary Alice Mouton said.

'Aw, come on.'

'I know it's silly, but it's the only explanation I can think of. Rick, I've followed that thing backward for weeks, and it has *decelerated* most of the way.'

'But —'

'Jupiter can't do that. Nothing can.'

'No, of *course* it . . . Mary Alice?'

7

'The computer plot fits perfectly if you assume it's a powered spacecraft.' Dr. Mouton's voice had taken on a flat, dry note. 'And nothing else does.'

An hour later. Two more astronomers had come in, looked at the plates, and left shaking their heads. One had insisted that whatever else they found, the early plates were genuine; he'd taken them himself. The other hadn't even admitted seeing anything.

Owen used the telephone to call Arizona. 'Laura? Rick Owen. We've got something funny here. Did any of your people happen to get pictures looking south of Leo the past few weeks?' He read off a string of coordinates and waited for a few moments.

'Good! Looked at them? Could you please go look? Yes, now. I know it's not convenient, but believe me, it's important.'

'You don't really believe that's a powered ship, do you?' Jeanette asked.

Mary Alice looked at her with haunted eyes. 'I've tried everything else, and nothing fits the data. And *yes*, I remember the pulsars!' which meant nothing to Jeanette.

They drank coffee while Owen talked. Finally he put down the phone. He looked frightened. 'Kitt Peak has seen it,' he announced. 'Chap named Tom Duff, a computer type, spotted it. They didn't believe it. It's just where we saw it. Mary Alice, you may have a problem about credit for discovery.'

'Bother the credit, what is it?' Dr. Mouton demanded.

'Rick, it's *big* and it's under power, and it's coming *here*.'

———

In California it would be three in the morning. Jeanette heard the phone ring three times, then the sleepy voice. 'Yes?'

'Linda, this is Jenny.'

'Jenny? But – well, hello, is something wrong?'

'Kind of, Sis. I need to talk to your husband. Fast.'

'What?' There was a pause. 'All right.'

'And get him some coffee,' Jenny said.'He's going to need it.'

Presently she heard the newly awakened voice of Major General Edmund Gillespie. 'Jenny? What's wrong?'

'General, I have something strange to report —'

'General. Are you being official?'

'Well – formal. Yes, sir. I've already called my colonel, and he agreed that it would be a good idea to call you.'

'Just a second, Jenny. Linda, where's that coffee? Ah. Thanks. Okay, shoot.'

'Yes, sir.' As she spoke, she tried to imagine the scene. General Gillespie sitting on the edge of the bed, growing more and more awake. His hair probably looks like his head is exploding. Linda pacing back and forth wondering what in the world is going on. Maybe Joel had been awakened. Well, there wasn't any help for that. A lot of people were going to be losing sleep.

'Jenny, are you seriously suggesting that this is – an *alien* ship? Men from Mars and all that?'

'Sir, we both know there can't be any men from Mars. Or anywhere else in the solar system. But this is a large object, it's moving faster than anything that could stay inside the solar system, it has been decelerating for weeks, and it appears to be coming here. Those are facts, confirmed by three different observatories.' Suddenly she giggled. 'Ed, you're an astronaut. What do *you* think it is?'

'Damned if I know,' Gillespie said.'Russian?'

'No,' Jeanette said.

There was a long silence from the other end. 'You'd know, wouldn't you? But are you that sure?'

'Yes, sir. I'm that sure. It is not a Soviet ship.' *It's my job to know things like that.* 'I've been monitoring the Soviet space program for ten years, and they can't build anything like that. Neither can we . . .'

'Jenn – Captain, if this is a joke we're all going to be in trouble.'

'For God's sake, General, why would I joke about this?' she demanded. 'I told you, I already got my colonel out of bed! He's going through channels, but you can imagine what's going to happen to a UFO report —'

'I can think of people to call,' Gillespie said. 'I'm just having trouble believing it.'

'Yes, sir,' Jenny said dryly.

'Yeah, I know, so must you,' Ed Gillespie said. 'But I see your point. If it's an alien ship, we've got some preparing to do. Jenny, who is your C.O.?'

'Colonel Robert Hartley G-2 Strategic Army Command, Fort Bragg. Here's the phone number.'

Linda watched as her husband put the phone down. He looked worried. 'What's my kid sister done now?'

'Maybe earned herself a medal,' Edmund said. He lifted the phone and began dialing.

'Who are you calling now?' Linda asked. 'This is crazy —'

'Hello, Colonel Hartley? General Ed Gillespie here. Captain Crichton said you'd be expecting my call . . . Yeah. Yeah, she's always had a level head. Yeah. Yeah, I believe her too. Okay, so what do we do about it?'

This is crazy, Linda thought. Absolutely crazy. My kid sister discovers flying saucers. I don't believe it. I will not believe it. Only —'

Only Jenny never pulled a practical joke in her life. She doesn't drink, she doesn't take drugs, and —'

Aliens? An alien ship approaching Earth?

She saw that Edmund had put the phone down. 'So now what?' she asked.

'I don't know. Hard to think. Have to let people know. Have to let the President know. I'm not sure how to do that.'

10

'Wes Dawson could do it,' Linda said.

'By God!' He looked at his watch. 'After six in Washington. Wes might be up. I'll *wake* him up. You got his home number handy?'

David Coffey had always thought of himself as a night person, but that wasn't possible now. The President of the United States couldn't sleep late. It just wasn't done.

He couldn't even insist on being left alone for breakfast, although he tried. As he sat down on the terrace to enjoy the lovely spring day in Washington, the Chief of Staff said, 'Wes Dawson. California —'

'I know who he is.'

'Insists on joining you for breakfast.'

'Insists?'

'He didn't put it that way, but yes. Said he was calling in any favours he had coming. Vital, he said.'

David Coffey sighed. He felt the pressure of his belt. There was a cabinet meeting at eleven, and he'd hoped to get in a half-hour swim before then. Tighten up the gut a bit. 'Tell Congressman Dawson I'm flattered,' he said. 'And ask the housekeeper please to set another place at the table.'

Flying saucers. Spaceships. Silly, the President thought. The sort of stuff the midwestern papers ran when there wasn't any other news. Fakery. Or insanity. Except that Wes Dawson wasn't crazy, had never been crazy, and even though he was acting manic, he wasn't crazy now.

'Let me get this straight, Wes,' Coffey said. 'The astronomers have seen a spaceship approaching Earth. It will be here next month. You want to go meet it.'

'Yes, Mr. President.'

'Wes, do you know – scratch that. Of course you know how goofy this sounds. All right, assume it's all true. Why not?'

'Somebody has to,' Dawson said. 'And the fact that I used up all my favors to be the first to tell you about it ought to show I'm interested.'

'Yeah, I give you that.'

'I'm on both Space and Foreign Relations. You ought to have somebody from the Congress when we go out to meet them.'

'Why go out to meet them at all?'

'Because – it's more fitting, sir,' Dawson said. 'Think about it. Mr. President, they came from a *long* way off. From another star —'

'Sure about that?' the Chief of Staff asked. 'Why not from another planet?'

'Because we've seen all the likely planets close up, and there's no place for a civilization,' Dawson said patiently. 'Anyway. Mr. President, they came from a long way off. Even so, they'll recognize that the first step is the hard one. We want to meet them in orbit, not wait for them to come here.

'Let me try to put it in perspective,' he said. 'Would the history of the Pacific Islands have been different if the first time the Europeans encountered Hawaiians, the Polynesians had been well out at sea in oceangoing boats? Mightn't they have been treated with more respect?'

'I see,' the President said. 'You know, Wes, you just may be right. That's assuming there's anything to this.'

'If there is, do I get to go?' Dawson asked.

David Coffey laughed. 'We'll see about that,' he said. He turned to the Chief of Staff. 'Jim, get hold of General Gillespie. Get him on a plane for Washington. And the Army captain who discovered this thing.' He sighed. 'And get it on the agenda for the cabinet meeting today. Let's see what the Secretary of State has to say about welcoming the Men from Mars . . .'

―――――――

Wes Dawson walked back from the White House to his offices in the Rayburn Building. He didn't really have time to do that, but it was a fine morning, and the walk would do him good, and he was too excited to work anyway.

The President hadn't said no!

Wes strolled quickly through the Federal Triangle and along Independence Avenue. He'd done that often, but he still tended to gawk at the great public buildings along the way. It was all there. Government granite, magnificent buildings in the old classic stype, built to last back when America had craftsmen able to compete with the great builders of old Greece and Rome. And more than that. The Archives, with the original Constitution and Declaration of Independence to make you misty-eyed and silent and remind you that we'd done things even the Romans couldn't, we'd invented a stable government of free citizens. Beyond that was the Smithsonian, old castle and new extension.

The President hadn't said no! I'm going to space! Only – only would President Coffey remember? It wasn't an ironclad promise. No one had heard it but Jim Frantz. If the President forgot, the Chief of Staff would forget too, because Coffey might have had a reason to forget. Or —

It's too fine a morning to think that way. Coffey didn't say no! I really could go to space!

Ahead was the Space Museum, with its endless traffic, the only building in Washington that drew crowds during weekend blizzards. Wes wanted to look in. Just for a moment. There was work to do, and Carlotta would be waiting in the office to hear what happened in his meeting with the President, and he ought to hurry, but dammit . . .

Across from the museum was NASA itself.

Wes grinned from ear to ear, startling passersby who weren't used to people looking happy. A couple of runners came past and returned the grin, although they couldn't know what made him so cheerful.

'I know a secret,' he said aloud as he looked up toward the eighth-floor corner office of the Administrator. Have they told him by now? Maybe they'll even have him at the Cabinet meeting. But I'm the one who told the President, and I've got my claim staked . . .

And I'm the right man. I've been waiting for this day all my life. I'm in good shape – well, reasonably good. I'll be in better. I'll run every day —

He ran a couple of steps, realized that wasn't practical for a man in a dark pinstripe three-piece suit, and grinned again. Starting this afternoon, he thought. And I'll get to Houston for training. Real training. I've been there before. Good thing, being on the space committee —

Aliens! The full force of it hit him just as he reached the Capitol reflecting pool. They're really here. Aliens. This is where human history breaks into two pieces. The search for extraterrestrial intelligence is over, the aliens are coming . . . Take that, Bill Proxmire!

He climbed the hill to the Rayburn building and walked between the two monstrous statues that faced each other across the granite steps. They were the ugliest statues in Washington, crude attempts to portray the majesty and compassion of the law in Greek classical style but done by a very bad sculptor who hadn't understood what the Greeks were trying to do – and who hadn't known much about human anatomy either. Wes grinned as he passed them. It was obvious what had happened. Someone had insisted on statues, and some forgotten congressman had said 'Al, my cousin Cindy Lou married a guy who makes statues . . .'

His aides hurried to intercept him as he entered his suite of offices. Wes knew he was late, but dammit! Now here came Larry with a fistful of messages. Wes waved him aside and went past the receptionist and into his office, bursting to tell Carlotta —

She was seated in his chair. A dozen Boy Scouts from

his district were draped on the other chairs and couches.

Oh, damn, Wes thought, and put on his best smile.

Carlotta saw the fixed political grin on her husband's face, but she could see beyond it to the glow of enthusiasm in Wes's eyes. He didn't need to say anything. After all, they'd lived together nearly twenty-five years, and had been married for twenty-two. She could tell.

Wes has a chance. A chance to be the ambassador of the human race. No, make that consul or whatever the hell they call the second in charge of an embassy. The Russians are likely to provide the ambassador. Thank God I made Wes learn some Russian. Her bed would be empty now, and that wouldn't be so good, but he sure looked happy. Couldn't wait to tell her about it.

But the Scouts were here. Bad timing, but the appointment was made weeks ago. How could anyone know Congressman Dawson would eat his breakfast at the White House?

The boys swarmed around Wes. He seemed friendly enough. Not too friendly. He wasn't making many political points with this visit. Why couldn't the damn kids go away?

That wasn't really fair. She'd encouraged them to come herself. Carlotta liked boys. All congressmen welcomed visiting Boy Scouts, but Wes and Carlotta were happier than most when they came to Washington. Not just Scouts. All boys.

If Simon had lived . . . Carlotta thought. But he hadn't. Simon Dawson, age three months, dead of whatever it was that killed babies in their first year: Silent Killer, Crib Death.

The doctors had told her she couldn't have more children. She'd gambled anyway, and very nearly died in childbirth. It was a month before she could hold her daughter in her arms, and another before she recovered, and it was obvious that Sharon would be the only child of the Dawson family, the only heir to two long and respectable lines. That was almost twenty years ago. Sharon was enrolled at Radcliffe now, and didn't think much of her father's career. Carlotta had never been able quite to understand why.

Doesn't matter. All colleges teach nonsense. She'll outgrow it. Carlotta got up and went to Wes. He was bursting to tell her, but he had control of his face now. 'Hi,' she said. 'This is Troop 112. Johnny Braisicku is the Senior Patrol Leader. Johnny, this is my husband, Congressman Dawson.'

They were nice boys, and they came from the district. Wes shook hands with each one of them. When he'd finished he gave Carlotta a rueful grin. She winked at him.

The most important news we've ever heard, she thought. Possibly the most important thing *anyone* ever heard. And here we're chatting with Boy Scouts while the staff decides what we ought to think and how Wes ought to vote, and there's nothing we can do about it. If congressmen spent any time *being* congressmen and thinking about the job, they wouldn't *have* the job. It's a strange way to run a country.

CHAPTER TWO
ANNOUNCEMENTS

Suspicion is the companion of mean souls, and the bane of all good society.

– THOMAS PAINE, *Common Sense*

COUNTDOWN H: MINUS SIX WEEKS

'I really don't think you should do that,' Jeanette Crichton said.

Richard Owen paused with his hand on the telephone, then snorted. 'Nothing you can do about it. The Army doesn't have any jurisdiction over me.'

'I never said we did,' Jeanette said. 'And why be paranoid? But you ought to think it over.'

'I already did,' Owen said. 'The Soviets have to know. They may already, in which case it's better if they know that *we* know about it. And you're nice and friendly, but somehow I've got the feeling that if I wait very long a *real* spook might show up.' He lifted the receiver and dialed.

And now what? Jeanette thought. He's right, the Army doesn't have any jurisdiction, and the Russians probably know all about it anyway. If they don't now, they'll learn soon enough. They have a lot more in space than we do, with their big manned station.

'Academician Pavel Bondarev,' Owen said. 'Da. Bondarev.' His fingers drummed against the desk. 'Pavel? Richard Owen in Hawaii. Uh —yes, of course, I'll wait.' He put his hand over the transmitter. 'They have

17

a policy,' he told Jeanette. 'They're not allowed to talk to Americans unless there are three of them together. Even somebody as high as Bondarev. Talk about paranoid, these guys own the copyright . . . Ah. Academician Bondarev? Your colleagues are there? Excellent. This is Professor Richard Owen, University of Hawaii. We've turned up something interesting I think you better know about . . .'

——————

Pavel Aleksandrovich Bondarev put down the telephone and stared thoughtfully at the ceiling.

'Is it real?' Boris Ogarkov's flat peasant face was twisted into an inquiring frown, which made him look very unpleasant.

'Yes,' Bondarev said absently. Boris was the Institute Party Secretary. He was not well educated. Boris was from the working class. Uninspired but tireless Party activities had brought him to the attention of his superiors. He was one of those raised to a position of power, who knew that loyalty to the system was the only way he would ever be more than a menial. He had cunning enough to know that the Institute was important to the Soviet Union, and so not to interfere with its work. Instead he busied himself with seeing that there was a portrait of Lenin in every office, and that *everyone*, scientist, secretary, clerk, or janitor, voted in every election. 'I know this American well,' Bondarev continued. 'We have published two papers together, and worked together when I was in the United States. He would not call me for a hoax.'

'Not as a hoax,' Andrei Pyatigorskiy said. 'But could he be mistaken? We have seen no evidence of this.'

'Perhaps we have,' Bondarev said. 'And perhaps not. As a favor, Andrei, will you please call Dr. Nosov at the observatory, and ask his staff to examine all the photographs that might be relevant?'

18

'Certainly.'

'Thank you. I need not say that Nosov must not speak of this to anyone. No matter what he finds.'

'I can call the Party Secretary at the observatory,' Boris Ogarkov said. 'He will help to keep this secret.'

Bondarev nodded agreement.

'But, Pavel Aleksandrovich, do you believe this story? Alien spacecraft coming to Earth?' Pyatigorskiy gestured helplessly. 'How can you believe it?'

Bondarev shrugged. 'If you agree that they did not lie, we have no choice but to believe it. The Americans have excellent equipment, and enough so that every observatory has comparators and computers. As you well know —'

'If we had half so much —' Pyatigorskiy said. Half the time he had to build his own equipment, because the Institute could not get the foreign exchange credits to obtain electronics and optics from the West, and unless it had been built for the military, Russian laboratory equipment did not work well.

Bondarev shrugged again. 'Certainly. But there are many reasons why the Americans would see it first.'

'Perhaps it has been seen from Kosmograd,' Boris Ogarkov said.

Pyatigorskiy nodded agreement. 'Their telescopes are much better than those we have here.'

'I will ask,' Bondarev said. And perhaps get an answer, perhaps not. Reports from the Soviet space station were closely guarded. Often Bondarev did not get them for months.

'We should see their photographs,' Pyatigorskiy said. 'Instantly when they come in. And you should be able to call Rogachev and tell him where to point his instruments.'

'Perhaps,' Bondarev said. He looked significantly at his subordinate. Andrei Pyatigorskiy was an excellent development scientist, but his career would not be aided by criticizing policy in front of Boris Ogarkov. Boris probably

19

would not report this, but he would remember . . .

'It is vital,' Andrei continued. He sounded stubborn. 'If aliens are coming, we must make preparations.'

'Is it not likely that they know in Moscow?' Ogarkov asked. 'Perhaps they have heard from Kosmograd, and already know.'

'I think not,' Bondarev said quietly. 'It is of course possible. They know much in Moscow. But I think we here would have heard, if not what they know, that they have learned *something* of importance. In the meantime, it is vital that we look at our own photographs. If this object shows, then we know it is no hoax.' He looked thoughtful. 'No ordinary hoax, at all events.'

'So that's that,' Richard Owen said. 'They hadn't seen it.' He walked over to the window overlooking the road up Mauna Kea.

'Or said they hadn't,' Jeanette said.

'Yeah, that's right.' He glanced at his watch. 'Next thing is a press conference.' He looked at her defiantly.

She shook her head. 'Richard, there's nothing I can do to stop you. I think you're wrong, though.'

'Don't the people have a right to know?'

'I suppose so,' she said. 'Do you think the Russians believe you?'

'Why shouldn't they?' Owen demanded.

'They don't often believe anything we say. They see plots everywhere,' Jeanette said.

'Not Bondarev,' Owen protested. 'I've known him a long time. He'll believe me.'

'Yes. But will his superiors believe him? Anyway, it's not my problem.'

'Sure about that?'

'What?'

'There's a mess of cars coming up the road,' Owen said.

'State police, and an Army staff car. I never saw anything like that up here before . . .'

Lieutenant Hall Brassfield was nervous. He couldn't have been more than twenty years old, and he wasn't sure who Jeanette was.

Small wonder, she thought.

'Captain,' he said, 'I don't really know any more than that. The orders said to get you to Washington by first available transportation, highest priority, and we arranged that. A chopper will meet us down at the five-thousand-foot level. He'll get you to Pearl. There's a Navy jet standing by there.'

Jeanette frowned. 'Isn't that a bit unusual?'

'You bet your sweet – yes, ma'am, that's unusual. Leastwise *I* never did anything like this before.'

She looked at the sheet of orders. They'd been hastily typed from telephone dictation, and looked nothing like standard military orders. She'd never seen anything like them. Come to that, she thought, not very many officers had. At the bottom it said 'By order of the President of the United States,' and below that was 'For the President, James F. Frantz, Chief of Staff.'

'Those came in about an hour ago,' the lieutenant said. 'And it's all I know. We're a training command, Captain.'

'All right, Lieutenant, but someone will have to go to my hotel. I have things there, and the bill has to be paid.'

'Yes, ma'am, Major Johnston said I'd have to take care of that. I'll send your bags on to you, only I don't know where to send them.' He chuckled. 'I wouldn't think the White House would be the right address for a captain. But that's the only place listed on those orders.'

Jeanette nodded, more to herself than to the lieutenant. Whenever she was in Washington, she stayed at Flintridge with her aunt and uncle, so that was no problem. Only it was probably a 'hurry up and wait' situation. There wasn't any need for her at the White House. Not that urgently, and probably not at all. The President would want to confirm the sighting, but before she could get to Washington he'd have a dozen others to tell him about the mysterious – what? She giggled.

'Penny for your thoughts,' Richard Owen said.

'What do we call it?' she asked. 'UFO? But it isn't *flying*.'

Lieutenant Brassfield looked puzzled. 'UFO? All this is over a *flying saucer*?'

'Yes,' Jeanette said.

'Hey, now wait a minute —'

'It's all true,' Richard Owen said. 'We've spotted an alien spaceship. It's on its way to Earth. Captain Crichton called the Army.'

'Maybe I better not know any more about this,' Brassfield said.

Jeanette thought of Richard Owen's upcoming press conference and laughed. 'It won't hurt. Lieutenant, do you have anyone in Kona? Or somebody who can get there fast?'

'Yes, ma'am.'

'Good. Have him go to the Kamehameha Hotel and collect my bags. He's to be careful with my uniform, but get it packed. All my stuff. Then drive like hell to meet us where that helicopter is picking us up. If I'm going to the White House, I am damned if I'll go bare-legged!'

KGB Headquarters was across the city square from the Institute. It was a drab brick building, in contrast to the Institute's pillars and marble facade. Pavel Bondarev walked briskly across the square. It was a pleasant day, warm enough that he did not need an overcoat.

A new man sat at the reception desk in KGB headquarters. He looked very young. Pavel Bondarev grimaced, then shrugged. What cannot be cured must be endured. He had learned patience, and he forced himself to be still, although he was bursting with the news.

A long line of citizens waited in front of the reception desk. Men in ill-fitting suits, women in stained skirts and scarves, farmers, workers, minor factory officials – they all held forms to be signed, permission slips of one kind or another. Today there were not so many farmers; in fall there would be hundreds wanting to sell the produce from their tiny private plots.

Bondarev shook his head. Absurd, he thought. They should be working, not standing in lines here. But it is typically Russian, and if they didn't stand in lines they wouldn't work anyway. They'd just get drunk.

If there were not residency controls, everyone would live in Moscow. Once while visiting Washington he'd heard a song at an American's party: 'How you going to keep them down on the farm?' It was evidently a problem for the Americans as well as the Russians.

He walked past the line. A man at the head of the line, round-faced like Boris Ogarkov, glared at him sullenly but didn't say anything. Bondarev stood at the desk. Two men were at another desk nearby. He thought he recognized the one who was typing a report on a battered machine of German make. Bondarev wondered idly if the typewriter had been brought to Russia by the Wehrmacht. It was certainly old enough. Provincial establishments, even KGB, did not often get new equipment.

The reception officer ignored him as long as possible, then looked up insolently. 'Yes?'

You will be that way, will you? Bondarev thought. Very well. Bondarev spoke quietly, but loud enough so he was certain that the men at the next desk could overhear him. 'I am Bondarev. I wish to see the duty officer.'

The desk officer frowned. The man at the next desk ceased typing.

'What is the nature of your business?'

'If I had meant for you to know, I would have told you,' Bondarev said. 'Now you will please inform the senior officer present that Academician Bondarev, Director of the Lenin Research Institute of Astrophysics and Cosmography, wishes to see him and that the matter is urgent.'

The receptionist's frown deepened, but his face lost the insolent look. A full Academician would have powerful friends, and the Institute was important in the provincial city. The officer who had been typing got up from the desk and came over. 'Certainly, Comrade Academician,' he said. 'I will go and tell Comrad Orlov at once.' He looked down sideways at the receptionist, then left.

'I am required to ask,' the receptionist said. His voice was sullen.

He has not long held his commission as an officer of the KGB, Bondarev thought. And he has rather enjoyed having everyone act respectful, even fearful. He did not expect to find someone to fear.

'This way, Comrade Academician.' The other agent indicated a doorway.

As Bondarev passed through, the receptionist was saying 'How should I know he was an Academician? He did not say so.'

Bondarev smiled.

The office was not large. The desk was cluttered. Bondarev did not recognize the officer at the desk, but he was certain he had seen him before.

'Yes, Comrade Academician?'

'I must use your scrambler telephone to call Moscow, Comrade Orlov. Party Third Secretary Narovchatov in the Kremlin. It is urgent. No one must listen.It is a matter of state security.'

'If it is a matter of state security, we must record —'

'Yes, but not to listen,' Bondarev said. 'Comrade, believe me, you do not *want* to listen to this call.'

*   *   *

It took nearly an hour to complete the call. Then General Narovchatov's voice came on the line. 'Pavel Aleksandrovich! It is good to hear from you.' The hearty gravel voice changed. 'All is well?'

'Da, Comrade General. Marina is well, your grandchildren are well.'

'Ah. Another year, Pavel. Another year and you may return to Moscow. But hard as it is, you must stay there now. Your work is needed.'

'I know,' Bondarev said. 'Marina will be grateful that it is only one more year. That, however, is not why I have called.'

'Then?'

'I have called from the KGB station in order to use the scrambler telephone. The officer on duty is watching to see that no one listens. It is a matter of great importance, Nikolai Nikolayevich. The greatest importance.'

General Nikolai Nikolayevich Narovchatov put down the telephone and carefully finished writing his notes in the leather-bound book on his desk. Once in Paris a wealthy lady had given him a score of the leather books, full of blank pages of excellent paper. That had been long ago, long enough that his baggage had been searched when he returned, and the border guards had wondered what sinister messages were written on the blank paper until the superiors he traveled with had become impatient and the guards wordlessly passed him through. Each book lasted nearly a year, and now only two were left.

He stared at his notes. Aliens. An alien spaceship was coming to Earth. Nonsense.

But it is *not* nonsense, he thought. Pavel Bondarev would not have been my ideal of a son-in-law. I would have preferred that Marina marry a diplomat. Still, there is no questioning that the Academician is intelligent. Intelligent

25

and cautious. He would not call if he were not certain. The Americans have seen this object —

The Americans *say* they have seen this object. An American scientist calls a Soviet scientist. A friendly gesture, one scientist to another.

Could this be? Narovchatov stared at his notebook as if the notes he had taken could tell him something he didn't know. Pavel Bondarev was intelligent, he knew this American, and he believed that this was real. But of course he would. The CIA was clever. Almost as clever as the KGB.

And more to the point – the KGB would *not* believe the Americans. He thought of the problems a provincial KGB officer would have in trying to notify Moscow of a development like this, and nodded in satisfaction. It would be hours before the senior officials of the KGB would know.

The Americans have seen something, or say they have. More important, now that they knew where to look, Russian astronomers at the Urals Observatory have seen it as well.

Not nonsense. It is real. Something is there. Could the *Americans* have done something like this? It didn't seem likely, but the Americans had surprised them before.

I must do something. I do not know what.

Narovchatov's ornately carved desk stood at one end of a long, high-ceilinged room. The inevitable portrait of Lenin dominated one wall, but the others held tapestries from Mongolia. Persian rugs covered the floor. The room was comfortable, full of quiet elegance, tasteful and restful, a room where he could work; but it was also a room where he could relax, as was necessary more and more often now.

He had first seen this room as a very young soldier at the beginning of the Great Patriotic War. His special regiment had been assigned to guard duty in the Kremlin just before the Germans were driven away. It was not a long tour of duty. The OMSBON were sent to chase Germans soon after.

It had been long enough, and he had seen enough. Nikolai

Nikolayevich Narovchatov would never return to Kirov, where his father worked in the hammer mill. Communism had been kind enough to Nikolai Narovchatov. It had taken him from the villages to Kirov, from the stolid peasant misery of a Russian winter to the comparative warmth of the city and industrial life. It had made his children literate. Nikolai never wanted more, but his son did. If that office came from Communism, then Communism was worth studying.

It took him thirty years, but he never doubted that he would arrive. Party work in the Army, then Moscow University, where he studied engineering and always took excellent marks in the political courses. He could have had better grades in his academic subjects, but he did not want to show up his friends, for he always sought out the relatives of high party officials. If you wish power, it is best to have friends in high places; and if you know no one in high places, meet their children.

Great Stalin died, and Khrushchev began his slow rise to power. Those were not easy years, for it was difficult to tell who would win in the inevitable struggle. Beria had fallen, and with him fell the NKVD, to be divided into the civil militia and the KGB . . . Nikolai Narovchatov chose his friends carefully, and kept his ties with the Party. Eventually he married the daughter of the Party Secretary of the Russian Soviet Federated Socialist Republic, largest of the fifteen republics that together made up the USSR. Shortly after, Khrushchev fell, and the Party men became even more dominant.

From then on his rise was rapid. He became a 'political general.' Mostly he despised that group, but the title was useful. It paid well, and gave him ties within the Army and the Rocket Forces; and unlike many political generals, he had fought in the Great Patriotic War, and elsewhere. He had earned his medals.

As I have earned my place, he thought. Party work, ass kissing, yes, enough of that, but I have also built factories

27

that actually produce goods. I have helped keep the Germans helpless, cannot the Americans understand why we must? I have dismissed corrupt officials where I could, and minimized the damage of those I could not do without. I have been a good manager, and I have earned my place. A good place, with my son safely established in the Ministry of Trade, and my daughters well married, one grandchild in Moscow's Institute of International Relations . . .

And now this.

At least I shall be the first to inform the Chairman. Marina, Marina, I did not approve your choice of a husband, but I see I was wrong. It was a good day.

He pushed back his chair and stood, and feeling very weary, went down the ornate hall to the office of the Chairman.

The biggest story in history, and David Coffey was President when it happened. Aliens, coming here!

He sat at the center of the big table in the Cabinet Room. The others had stood when he entered, and didn't take their seats until he was settled. It upset David, but he'd become used to it. They didn't stand for David Coffey, but for the President of the United States.

Coffey was aware that at least half the people in the room thought they could do the job better than he could, and one or two might be right. They'd never get the chance. Not even Henry Morton. *The political writers all like to talk about Henry being 'a heartbeat away from the Presidency,' but I never felt better in my life. The Party wanted Morton as Vice President, but he'll never have a clear shot at this chair.*

David was a little in awe of the Secretary of State. Dr. Arthur Hart had written a best-seller on diplomacy, made a fortune trading in overseas commodities, and was a favorite guest on the TV talk shows. Hart's face was probably better known to the average citizen than the President's.

But he'll never sit here either. Hasn't enough fire in his belly. He'd like to be President, but he hasn't the killer instinct it takes to get high elective office.

David looked around the table at the others. Certainly Hart was the most distinguished man in the room. It wasn't an overwhelmingly distinguished Cabinet.

'I don't think I have it in me to be a great President,' David had told his wife the night he was elected. When Jeanne protested, David shook his head. 'But then I don't think the country *wants* a great President just now. The nation's about worn out with great this and great that. I can't be a great President, so I'll just have to settle for being a damned good one – and that I can manage.'

And so far I have. It's not a great cabinet, but it's a damned good one.

'Gentlemen. And ladies,' he added for the benefit of the Secretary of Commerce and the Secretary of the Interior. 'In place of our regular agenda, there is a somewhat pressing item which the Chief of Staff will explain to you. Jim, if you will —'

'It's just plain damned crazy,' Peter McCleve said. 'Mr. President, I will not believe it.' He turned toward the President in his place at the center of the big conference table. 'I simply do not believe it.'

'You can believe it,' Ted Griffin said. The Secretary of Defense spoke directly to the Attorney General, but he talked mostly for the President's benefit. 'Peter, I heard it just before I came over.'

'Sure, from the same people who told Dawson,' McCleve said.

'They do seem to have checked it thoroughly.' Ted Griffin was a big man, tall and beefy and built like the football player he'd been. He looked as if he might shout a lot, but in fact he almost never did.

'You accept the story, then?' the Secretary of State asked.

'Yes.'

'I see.' Arthur Hart put the tips of his fingers together in a gesture he'd made famous on *Meet the Press*. Constitutionally, the Secretary of State was the senior Cabinet officer. In fact he was the fourth most important man in the room, counting the President as top. Numbers two and three (the order was uncertain) were Hap Aylesworth, Special Assistant to the President for Political Affairs, and Admiral Thorwald Carrell.

'Assume it's true,' Hart continued. 'I do. So the important thing is, what do we do now?'

'I suppose you want to tell the Russians,' Alan Rosenthal said.

Arthur Hart looked at the Secretary of the Treasury with amusement. Rosenthal couldn't always contain his dislike of Russians. 'I think someone must,' Hart said.

'Someone did,' Ted Griffin announced. When everyone was looking at him, he nodded for emphasis. 'I got that news just before I came over here. That astronomer guy in Hawaii called someone . . .' – he glanced at a note on the table in front of him – 'a Pavel Bondarev at the Astrophysics Institute near Sverdlovsk. Yeah, well, who could stop him? He dialed direct.'

'How long do you suppose it takes a story like that to get from Sverdlovsk to the Kremlin?' the Attorney General asked.

'It could be quite a while,' Arthur Hart said. 'I was thinking that the President might call the Chairman —'

'Moscow already knows,' Admiral Carrell said. His gravelly voice stopped all the extraneous chatter in the room. 'Pavel Bondarev is the son-in-law of General Narovchatov. Narovchatov's been with Chairman Petrovskiy for twenty years.'

'Hmm.'

Everyone turned to look at the Chief of Staff. Jim

Frantz almost never said anything in Cabinet meetings.

'What prompted that, Jim?' Arthur Hart asked.

Frantz smiled softly. 'The way *we* heard was that this Captain Crichton who found out about it was General Gillespie's sister-in-law. His wife knew Carlotta Dawson in college, and Congressman Dawson was here for breakfast.'

'I often wonder if any country in the world could operate if communications went only through channels,' Ted Griffin said. 'So. The Russians know, and by the time we leave this meeting, the country will know.' He smiled at the startled looks that caused. 'Yes, Captain Crichton said this astronomer chap was calling a press conference.'

'So we have to decide what to tell the public.' Hap Aylesworth was short and beefy, perpetually fighting a weight problem. His necktie was always loosened and his collar unbuttoned. He seldom appeared in photographs; when cameras came out, Aylesworth would usually urge someone else forward. As Special Assistant he was the President's political advisor, but for the past nine years he'd given David Coffey political advice. The *Washington Post* called him the Kingmaker.

'There may be a more pressing problem,' Admiral Carrell said.

Aylesworth raised a bushy eyebrow.

'The Russians. I don't know it would be such a good idea for the President to call Chairman Petrovskiy, but I think I'd better get on the horn to General Narovchatov.'

'Why?' Ted Griffin asked.

'Obvious, isn't it?' Carrell said. He pushed back a gray pinstripe sleeve to glance at his watch. 'One of the first things they'll do once they're sure of this is start mobilizing. Military, civil defense, you name it. Ted, I'd hate for your military people to get all upset —'

'Are you certain of this?' David Coffey asked.

'Yes, sir,' Admiral Carrell said. 'Sure as anything, Mr. President.'

'Why would they assume this . . .' – Attorney General McCleve had trouble getting the words out – 'this alien spacecraft is hostile?'

'Because they think *everything* is hostile,' Carrell said.

'Afraid he's right, Pete,' Arthur Hart said. The Secretary of State shook his head sadly. 'I could wish otherwise, but that's the way it will be. *And* they'll very shortly be demanding an official explanation of why one of our scientists called one of theirs, instead of passing this important news through channels as it ought to be done.'

'That's crazy,' Peter McCleve said. 'Just plain crazy!'

'Possibly,' Secretary Hart said. 'But it's what will happen.'

'To sum up, then,' David Coffey said. 'The Soviets will shortly ask us for our official position, and they will begin mobilizing without regard to what that position is.'

Admiral Carrell nodded agreement. 'Precisely, Mr. President.'

'Then what should we do?' Hap Aylesworth asked. 'We can't let the Russians mobilize while we do nothing. The country won't stand for it.'

'I can think of senators who would be delighted,' Coffey said.

'On both sides of the aisle,' Aylesworth said. 'Doves who'll say there's never been anything to be afraid of, and will move resolutions congratulating you on your steady nerves – and hawks who'll want to impeach you for selling out the country.'

'Admiral?' David Coffey asked. Admiral Carrell was another advisor the President was in awe of. They'd known each other for more than a dozen years, since the day Vice Admiral Carrell had walked into a freshman congressman's office and explained, patiently and with brutal honesty, how the Navy was wasting money in a shipyard that happened to be one of the major employers in David's district.

Since that time, Carrell had become Deputy Director of

the National Security Agency, then Director of the CIA. David Coffey's first officially announced appointment was Dr. Arthur Hart to be Secretary of State, but he'd decided on Thorwald Carrell as National Security Advisor before his own nomination, and the announcement came the day after Hart's appointment.

'I think a partial mobilization,' Admiral Carrell said. 'We'll need a declaration of national emergency.'

'This is senseless.' Commerce Secretary Connie Fuller had a surprisingly low voice for such a small lady. 'If we believe this is really an alien ship – and I think we must – then this is the greatest day in human history! We're sitting here talking about war and mobilization when – when everything is going to be different!'

'I agree,' Arthur Hart said. 'But the Soviets will begin mobilization —'

'Let them,' Fuller said. Her brown eyes flashed. 'Let them mobilize and be damned. At least one of the superpowers will behave like – like responsible and intelligent beings! Do we want these aliens – Mr. President, think of the power they have! To have come from another star! We want to *welcome* them, not appear hostile.'

'That's what Wes Dawson thinks,' President Coffey said. 'Matter of fact, he wants to meet them in orbit. He thought that might impress them a little.'

'An excellent suggestion,' Secretary Hart said.

'Couldn't hurt,' Ted Griffin agreed.

'Except that we don't have a space station,' Admiral Carrell said.

'The Soviets do,' Connie Fuller said. 'Maybe if we asked them —'

'That's what I planned to do,' David Coffey said. 'Meanwhile, we have a decision to make. What do we do now?'

'Put the military forces on standby alert,' Admiral Carrell insisted. 'Get the A teams on duty.'

'That works,' Aylesworth said. 'We can call in the

congressional leadership before we do anything else.'

'Spread the blame,' Admiral Carrell muttered.

'Something like that,' David Coffey agreed. 'I'll call in the standby alert from the Oval Office.' He stood, and the others, after a moment, stood as well. 'Mr. Griffin, I think it would do no harm to examine our civil defense plans.'

'Yes, sir, but that's not in the Department of Defense.' Coffey frowned.

'The Federal Emergency Management Agency is an independent agency, Mr. President.'

'Well, for God's sake,' Coffey said. He turned to Jim Frantz. 'Statutory?'

'No, sir. Created by executive order.'

'Then get out an executive order putting the damned thing under the National Security Council. Ted, I want you to stay on top of this. The news will be out in an hour. God knows what people will do. I'm sure some will panic.

'You'll all want to call your offices,' Coffey said. 'There's no point in denying anything. I think the official policy is that we do in fact believe an alien spaceship is coming here, and we're trying to figure out what to do.'

'Mr. President!' Hap Aylesworth was shocked.

David smiled. 'Hap, I know you'd like the public to think I'm infallible, but it doesn't work that way. The Pentagon gives out infallibility with the third star, and the Vatican's got a way of handing it to the Pope, but it doesn't come with the job of President. I think the people know that, but if they don't, it's time they found out. We'll tell the simple truth.'

'Yes, sir.'

'Meanwhile, let's figure on getting back together in two hours.' Coffey turned to the Chief of Staff. 'Jim, I think you'd better get the crisis center activated. It looks to be a long day.'

34

CHAPTER THREE
FLINTRIDGE

Along a parabola Man's fate like a rocket flies,
Mainly in darkness, now and then on a rainbow.

— ANDREI VOZNESENSKY, 'Parabolic Ballad'

COUNTDOWN: H MINUS SIX WEEKS

The moving belt came to life. Luggage spewed out of the
bowels of Dulles International Airport.

Jenny reached for her suitcase, but before she could get
it, a fat lady in a yellow-flowered dress shouldered her
aside to grab her own. 'Excuse me,' the fat woman said.

Why should I? Jenny thought. I'm supposed to *defend*
a tub of lard like you? Why? She tried to move past the
woman, but that wasn't going to be possible.

It had been a long flight. Jenny's hair was in strings, and
she felt sticky. She drew in a breath to speak, but thought
better of it. No point, she told herself. She was resigned to
letting her bag go around the carousel when she recognized Ed Gillespie. He reached past the fat woman and
caught the suitcase before it could escape. It was big and
heavy, but he lifted it effortlessly.

'Good morning,' he said. 'Any other luggage?'

'No, sir,' Jenny said. He was wearing a dark blue blazer
and gray flannel trousers, and didn't look military at all.
She giggled. 'I don't often get a general for a porter. And
an astronaut at that . . .'

Gillespie didn't say anything, but the look on the fat

35

woman's face when she said 'astronaut' was worth a lot. 'I hadn't expected you,' Jenny said.

'I got in from California about an hour ago. Called Rhonda and found out which flight you were on. Seemed reasonable to wait for you.'

Jenny opened her big purse and fished out the clear plastic strap for the suitcase. Gillespie snapped it on and led the way out of the baggage area, up the ramp to the taxi stands. The suitcase followed like a dog on a leash, which was the way Jenny always thought of it. As far as Jenny was concerned, wheels on luggage had done more for women's liberation than most organizations.

She didn't mind letting a strong alpha male take care of her suitcase. She did have some misgivings about letting General Edmund Gillespie haul her luggage. Still, there was no point in telling her brother-in-law that she could take care of her own suitcase when they were both in civvies. If they'd been in uniform she'd have pulled her own no matter what he said.

They reached street level. Gillespie waved to a waiting taxi. His luggage was already in its trunk. The taxi was new, or nearly so. The driver was Middle Eastern, probably Pakistani, and hardly spoke English. They got into the backseat, and she sank back into the cushions. Then she took a deep breath and let it out.

'Tired?' Gillespie asked.

'Sure. Yesterday afternoon I was in Hawaii.' She looked at her watch. Seven-thirty A.M. 'A Navy jet took me to El Toro. They stuffed me in a helicopter and got me to Los Angeles just in time to catch the red-eye.'

'Get any sleep?'

'Not really.'

'Try now,' Gillespie said.

'I'm too keyed up. What's the schedule?'

'Early appointments,' Gillespie said. 'At the White House.' He saw her look of dismay and grinned. 'You'll have time to change.'

'I'd better. I'm a wreck.'

The taxi pulled out of the airport lot and onto the freeway, putting the soaring structure of the terminal building in their view.

'My favorite airport,' Jenny said.

Gillespie nodded. 'It's not too bad. I didn't used to like it, but it grows on you. Except it's so damned far out.'

'I like the building.'

'So do I, but it ruined the architect's reputation,' Ed Gillespie said. Jenny frowned.

'His name was Ero Saarinen, and he didn't build a glass box,' Gillespie said. 'So they kicked him out of the architects' lodge as a heretic.'

The taxi accelerated. A fine mist hung in the air outside, and the freeway was slick. Jenny glanced over the driver's shoulder at the speedometer. The needle hovered around seventy-five. 'I'm glad there's not much traffic,' she said. 'I didn't know you were interested in architecture.'

'Umm. Tom Wolfe wrote a book about it.'

'Oh.' He didn't need to explain further. After *The Right Stuff*, Wolfe had become required reading for the astronauts.

'How's it feel to create a sensation, Jenny?'

'I'm too tired to feel anything at all. Was it a sensation?'

Gillespie laughed. 'That's right, you've been on airplanes.' He reached down into his briefcase and took out a *Washington Post*.

The headline screamed at her. 'ALIEN SPACESHIP DISCOVERED.' Most of the front page was devoted to the story. They didn't have many facts, but there was a lot of speculation, including a background article by Roger Brooks. Jenny frowned at that, remembering the last time she'd seen Roger. She glanced at Ed. He couldn't know about Roger and Linda.

My sister's a damn fool, she thought.

There were interviews with famous scientists, and pictures of a Nobel cosmologist smiling approval. There were also pictures of Rick Owen and Mary Alice Mouton. Owen's smile was broader than the cosmologist's.

'Looks like Dr. Owen has made himself famous,' Jenny said.

'You're pretty famous too,' Edmund said. 'Your Hawaiian boyfriend took most of the credit, but he did mention your name. Every reporter in the country would like to interview you.'

'Oh, God.'

'Yeah. That's one reason I waited for you. It's a wonder the stews didn't recognize you.'

'Maybe they did,' Jenny said. 'I thought one of them was extra attentive. She didn't say anything, though.'

The taxi wove through the sparse traffic. The freeway to Dulles had few on-ramps. Originally it wasn't supposed to have any, so it would bear no traffic except airport traffic, but the politicians had managed to add a couple, probably near where they owned property. Wherever there were ramps a cluster of houses and a small industrial park had sprung up.

'What do you think they'll be like?' Jenny asked.

Gillespie shook his head. 'I don't read much science fiction anymore. I used to when I was a kid.' He stared out the window for a moment, then laughed. 'One thing's sure, it ought to give a boost to the space program! Congress is already talking about buying more shuttles, expanding the Moon Base – to listen to those bastards, you'd think they'd been big space boosters all along.'

'What about Hollingsworth?' Jenny asked.

'He doesn't seem to be giving interviews.'

'Maybe he does have some shame.' She leaned back in the seat. Senator Barton Hollingsworth, Democrat of South Dakota, had long been an enemy of the space program, and for that matter of every investment in high technology and almost anything else except dairy subsidies. Like his predecessor William Proxmire, the one thing Hollingsworth really hated was SETI, the Search for

Extra-Terrestrial Intelligence, which he claimed was a 'golden fleece' of the taxpayers. Proxmire had once spent two days trimming one hundred and twelve thousand dollars for SETI research from the NASA budget, at a time when the welfare department was spending a million dollars a minute.

Toward Washington the traffic began to thicken. They came off the Dulles access freeway into a solid wall of red taillights. The driver muttered curses in Pakistani and began to weave through traffic, ignoring angry horns. They drove past a turnoff. A long time before, the sign at the turnoff had said 'Bureau of Public Roads Research,' but now it admitted that the CIA building was invisible in the trees at the end of that road. Jenny paid it no attention. She'd been there before.

The aliens are coming, and I'm famous, Jenny thought. 'Who are we seeing at the White House?'

Gillespie shrugged. 'Probably the President.'

'Oh, dear. I don't know anything,' Jenny said. 'Nothing I didn't tell you on the telephone yesterday.'

He shrugged again. 'We'll just have to play it as it lies.'

'Yes, but – Ed, I don't even have any guesses!'

'Neither do I, but we're the experts,' Gillespie said. 'After all, we knew about it first . . .'

They crossed the Potomac and drove along the old Chesapeake and Ohio canal. The morning drizzle had stopped, and the sun was trying to break through overhead. A dozen or more joggers were out despite the chilly morning. Jenny closed her eyes.

Gillespie and the driver were in a heated argument. The driver didn't understand anything Ed was saying. He was also getting nervous, while Gillespie got angrier.

'What's the matter?' Jenny asked.

'Damn fool won't follow directions.'

'Let me. Where are we?'

'Damned if I know – that's the problem. We crossed a

bridge a minute ago. One I never saw before. Had buffaloes on it.'

'Buffaloes? Oh. We're near the Cathedral,' Jenny said. She looked around. They were in a typical Washington residential neighborhood, older houses, each with a screened porch. 'Which way is north?'

Gillespie pointed.

'Okay.' She leaned forward. In New York, they had Plexiglas partitions to seal the driver away from his passengers, but there weren't any here. 'Go ahead, then left.'

The Pakistani driver looked relieved. They drove for a couple of blocks, and Jenny nodded satisfaction. 'It's not far now. We're on the wrong side of Connecticut Avenue, that's all.'

Gillespie was still angry. 'Why the hell can't they get drivers who speak English?' he demanded. 'All the people out of work in this country. Or say they're out of work. And none of the damn airport taxi drivers at our nation's capital can speak English. The goddam politicians wouldn't know that, though, would they? They have drivers to pick up at the airport.'

Now that she'd dozed off, she wanted to sleep again, but she stayed awake to direct the driver. Finding Flintridge Manor on its hill in Rock Creek Park could be plenty tricky even if you'd been there before. 'They won't let Washington cabs pick people up at Dulles,' she said.

Which was strange, if you thought about it, since it was a federal airport, operated by the Federal Aviation Administration, and reachable only by a federally constructed throughway. Why shouldn't cabs licensed in Washington be able to pick up passengers at Dulles? But they couldn't, and nothing was going to be done about it, just as nothing would be done about a hundred thousand other bureaucratic nightmares, and why worry about it? The government had more immediate problems coming at them out of the sky.

Then again, maybe the aliens would solve it all. Those

advanced creatures could be carrying a million-year-old quantified science of government and a powerful missionary urge, and the government's problems would be over forever.

Flintridge nestled in colonial splendor atop a large hill. There weren't a dozen places like it in Washington. From its big columned porch you couldn't see another house. Most of the woods surrounding Flintridge were part of Rock Creek National Park, which was perfect because no one could build there, while the Westons didn't have to pay taxes on the park property.

Jenny directed the taxi up the gravel drive. Phoebe, the Haitian maid, came to the door, saw them, and dashed back inside. A few moments later her uncle came out.

Colonel Henry Weston had inherited most of the money; Jenny's mother's share had been useful, but hardly what anyone would call wealth. There were advantages to having a rich uncle, especially if you had to stay in Washington. Flintridge was much nicer than a hotel.

Jenny's room was on the third floor, up the back stairs; Flintridge had a grand stairway to the second floor, but there weren't enough bedrooms there. The top floor had once been a series of garrets. They'd been redesigned to be comfortable, turned into small suites with attached bathrooms, but the only stairway was the narrow twisting enclosed back stairs designed to keep servants from interfering with family.

Servants, not slaves. Flintridge wasn't that old. Eighteen seventies. Jenny set her suitcases down and collapsed on the bed. Thank heaven Aunt Rhonda wasn't up yet! She'd have gushed, admired Jenny's nonexistent tan, asked about young men – now that Allan Weston was safely married and established in a New York bank, Jenny was the only possible target for Rhonda Weston's tireless matchmaking.

Aunt Rhonda was lovable but very tiring, especially at

eight in the morning when you had an appointment at the White house at eleven!

She glanced out the window toward the large arbor and gazebo, and almost blushed. It had been a long time ago, in that gazebo after a school dance . . . She shook her head, and lay down, sinking into the thick eiderdown comforters and pillows. The bed was far too soft and luxurious.

She could easily have grown up in this house. There'd been several times when Colonel Weston, U.S. Air Force Reserve and owner of Weston International Construction, had relocated semi-permanently, leaving Flintridge vacant. Each time he'd offered the place to Jenny's father.

Linda and Jenny always hoped to move into Flintridge, but Joel MacKenzie Crichton had too much of the dour Scot in him; living in Flintridge would be living conspicuously above his station, even though Colonel Weston would have paid the taxes and most of the upkeep. It was a great place to visit, and they could keep an eye on it for the Westons, but they wouldn't live there, much to the girls' disappointment.

'What would it look like for a GS-14 to live in that house?' Jenny's father demanded. 'I'd be investigated every month!' And after he left government service and became first moderately, then quite wealthy, Joel Crichton wouldn't consider Flintridge.

He hadn't much cared for the parties Rhonda Weston had thrown for his daughters, either. 'All nonsense, this coming-out stuff,' he'd said, but he had enough sense not to try to stop them. First Linda, then Jeanette, had been presented to the eligible young men of Washington in grand balls held at Flintridge. A former President of the United States had come to Linda's party. Jenny had to settle for two senators and the Secretary of State.

The morning after Jeanette's ball, their comfortable house seemed shabby. It must have seemed that way to their father, too, because he quit his government job a

42

couple of months later to become the Washington representative of a California aerospace company. There'd even been some talk of an investigation, but it never came to anything. The Crichtons had far too many friends in Washington.

No one who knew them was at all surprised when Jenny went into Army Intelligence.

Ed Gillespie turned the Buick Riviera into the iron-gated drive at 1600 Pennsylvania Avenue. A uniformed policeman looked at Gillespie's identity cards, then at a list on his clipboard, and waved them through. When they reached the garishly ornate building once known as Old State, then the Executive Office, and now called the 'Old EOP,' a driver materialized. 'I'll park it for you, sir.'

A Marine opened the car door for Jenny, then stepped back and saluted. 'General, Captain, if you'll follow me, please . . .'

He led them across to the White House itself. From somewhere in the distance they heard the chatter of grade school children on a tour. The Marine led them through another corridor.

In all her years in Washington, Jenny had never been to the White House. Her parents and Colonel Weston had been to White House parties and even a state dinner; it seemed ridiculous for the Crichton girls to take a public guided tour. One day they'd be invited.

And this is the day, Jenny thought.

They came to another corridor. A young man in a gray suit waited there. 'Eleven o'clock,' the Marine said.

'Right. Hi, I'm Jack Clybourne. I'm supposed to check your identification.'

He smiled as he said it, but he seemed very serious. He looked very young and clean-cut, and very athletic. He inspected General Gillespie, then Jenny.

43

They took out identification cards. Clybourne glanced at them, but Jenny thought he looked at them superficially. He was much more interested in the visitors than in their papers.

Doesn't miss a detail. Joe Gland, thinks he's irresistible . . .

Finally he seemed satisfied and led them along a corridor to the Oval Office.

The interior looked very much the way it did on television, with the President seated behind the big desk. They were both in uniform, so they saluted as they approached the desk.

David Coffey seemed embarrassed. He acknowledged their salutes with a wave. 'Glad to see you.' He sounded as if he meant it. 'Captain Jeanette Crichton,' he said carefully. His brows lifted slightly in thought, and Jenny was sure that he'd remember her name from now on. 'And General Gillespie. Good to see you again.'

'Thank you, Mr. President,' Edmund said.

Ed's as nervous as I am, Jenny thought. I didn't think he would be. She glanced around the office. Behind the President, on a credenza, was a red telephone. *The* phone, Jenny thought. At SAC headquarters the general in command had two telephones, one red to communicate with his forces, and one gold. This would be the other end of the gold phone . . .

'Captain, this is Hap Aylesworth,' the President said. He indicated a seated man. Aylesworth's face seemed flushed, and his necktie was loosened. He stood to shake hands with her.

'Please be seated,' The President said. 'Now, Captain, tell me everything you know about this.'

She took the offered chair, sitting on its edge, both feet on the floor, feet together, her skirt pulled down over her knees, as she'd been taught in officer's training classes. 'I don't know much, Mr. President,' she said. 'I was at the Mauna Loa Observatory —'

'How did you happen to be there?' Aylesworth asked.

'I was invited to Hawaii to address an engineering conference. I took a couple of extra days' leave. While I was swimming I met Richard Owen, who turned out to be an astronomer, and he invited me up to see the observatory.'

'Owen,' Aylesworth said pensively.

'Come on, Hap, we have confirmation from every place we logically could get confirmation,' the President said. He smiled thinly. 'Mr. Aylesworth can't quite get over the notion that this is a put-up job. Could it have been?'

Jenny frowned in thought. 'Yes, sir, but I don't believe it. What would be the motivation?'

'There must be forty science-fiction novels with that plot,' Aylesworth said. 'Scientists get together. Convince the stupid political and military people that the aliens are coming. Unite Earth, end wars . . .'

'The Air Force Observatory reports the same thing,' Ed Gillespie said. 'Now that they know what to look for.'

The President nodded. 'As do a number of other sources. Hap, if it's a plot, there are an awful lot of plotters involved. You'd think *one* would have spilled the beans by now.'

'Yes, sir,' Aylesworth said. 'And I suppose we're *sure* this isn't something the Russians cooked up to get us off guard.'

Both Jenny and General Gillespie shook their heads. 'Not a chance,' Gillespie said.

'No, I suppose not,' Aylesworth said. 'My apologies, Captain, I'm having trouble getting used to the notion of little green men from outer space.'

'Or big black ones,' Ed Gillespie said.

The President eyed Gillespie in curiosity. 'What makes you say that? Surely you don't have any knowledge?'

'No, sir. But they're as likely to be big and black as they are to be little and green. If we had any idea of where they came from, we might be able to figure something out —'

'Saturn,' Jenny said. 'Dr. Mouton had a computer

program.' Alice Mouton had wanted to lecture, and Jenny had listened carefully. 'We don't know how fast they came, and Saturn must have moved since they left, but if you give them almost any decent velocity, they started in a patch of sky that had Saturn in it.'

'Saturn,' Aylesworth said. 'Saturnians?'

'I doubt it,' Ed Gillespie said. 'Saturn just doesn't get enough sunlight energy for a complex organism to evolve there. Much less a civilization.'

'Sure about that?' the President asked.

'No, sir.'

'Neither is the National Academy of Sciences,' the President said. 'At least those I could get hold of. But the consensus is that the ship must have gone to Saturn from somewhere else. Now all we have to do is find the somewhere else.'

'Maybe we can ask them,' Jenny said.

'Oddly enough, we thought of that,' Aylesworth said.

'With what result?' Gillespie asked.

'None,' Aylesworth shrugged. 'So far they haven't answered. Anyway. Mr. President, I'm satisfied. It's real.'

'Good,' the President said. 'In that case, if you'd ask Mr. Dawson and Admiral Carrell to come in —'

Gillespie and Jenny stood. Wes Dawson came in first. 'Hello, Ed, Jenny,' he said.

'Ah. You both know Congressman Dawson, then,' the President said.

'Yes, sir,' Ed Gillespie said.

'Of course you would,' David Coffey said. 'You told Mr. Dawson about the alien ship. Have you met Admiral Carrell?'

'Yes, sir,' Ed said. 'But I think Jenny hasn't.'

Admiral Carrell was approaching retirement age, and he looked it, with silver hair and wrinkles at the corners of his eyes. He shook hands with her, masculine fashion. His hand was firm, and so was his voice. His manner made it clear that he knew precisely who Jenny was. He waited until the President invited them to sit, then again until Jenny was seated, before he took his own seat. 'Nice work, Captain,' he said. 'Not every officer would have realized the significance of what you saw.'

Interesting, she thought. Does he take this much trouble with everyone he meets? 'Thank you, Admiral.'

Congressman Dawson had taken the chair closest to the President. 'How will Congress treat this, Wes?' the President asked. 'Will I get support for a declaration of emergency?'

'I don't know, sir,' Dawson said. 'There will certainly be opposition.'

'Damn fools,' Admiral Carrell said.

'What makes you think the aliens won't be friendly?' Wes Dawson demanded.

'The aliens may be friendly, but a Russian mobilization without reaction from us would be a disaster. It might even tempt them to something they normally wouldn't think of.'

'Really?' Dawson said. His tone made it less a question than a statement. 'Will they mobilize?' the President asked.

'We'll let Captain Crichton answer,' the Admiral said. 'Perhaps Mr. Dawson will be more likely to believe someone he knows. Captain?'

I've just been set up, Jenny thought. So that's how it's done. But I've no choice. 'Yes, sir, they will.' She hesitated. 'And if we don't react, there could be trouble.'

'Why is that?' the President prompted.

'Sir, it's part of their doctrine. If they could liberate the world from capitalism without risk to the homeland, and didn't do it, they'd be traitors to their own doctrine.'

Admiral Carrell said, 'They're jamming all our broadcasts, and they haven't told their people *anything* about an alien coming.'

47

'It's too big to keep secret,' Dawson said. 'Isn't it?'

Once again, Admiral Carrell turned to Jenny. This time he merely nodded to her.

Is this a test? she wondered. Whatever it is . . . 'Sir, the East Germans and Poles are bound to find out. Unless the Soviets want to completely disrupt their economy, they can't cut off all communication from the Eastern European satellites, so the news is bound to get to Russia. To the cities, anyway.'

The Admiral nodded behind half-closed eyes.

'Meanwhile, whatever the Russians are doing, there's an alien ship coming,' the President said. 'It may be that in a few weeks all our little squabbles will look very silly.'

'Yes, sir,' Wes Dawson said. 'Very silly.'

'There are other possibilities.' Admiral Carrell spoke in low tones, but everyone listened. Even the President.

'Such as?' Dawson demanded.

'I don't know them all,' Carrell said evenly. 'Mr. President, I want to assemble a staff of experts at Colorado Springs. One task will be to look at as many possibilities as we can.'

'Very reasonable,' the President said. 'Why Colorado Springs?'

'The hole,' Admiral Carrell said.

NORAD, Jenny thought. The North American Air Defense Command base, buried deep under the granite of Cheyenne Mountain. It was supposed to be the safest place in the United States, although there were some arguments about just how hardened it really was . . .

'Will you be going out there?' the President asked.

'Not permanently.'

'But you'll be busy. Meanwhile, I need someone to keep me informed.' The President looked thoughtful. 'We have two problems. Aliens, and the Soviets. Captain, you're a Soviet expert, and you discovered the alien ship.'

'I didn't discover it, sir —'

'Near enough,' the President said. 'You recognized its

48

importance. And you already have all the clearances you need, or you wouldn't be in military intelligence.' He touched a button on the desk. The Chief of Staff came in immediately.

'Jim,' the President said, 'I'm commander in chief. Does that mean I can promote people?'

'Yes, sir.'

'Good. Promote this young lady to major, and have her assigned to the staff. She'll work with you and the Admiral to keep me briefed on what the aliens and the Soviets are doing.' He chuckled. 'Major Crichton and General Gillespie are military. I can give them orders without going through civil service hearings. At least I assume I can?'

'Sure,' Frantz said.

Major Crichton. Just like that!

'Good,' the President was saying. 'General Gillespie, Congressman Dawson wants to go meet the aliens in space.'

Ed Gillespie nodded. 'Yes, sir.'

'You approve?'

'Yes, sir.'

Jenny smiled thinly. Ed would approve more if it was going to be him meeting the aliens. For that matter, I'd like to go.

'Help him do it,' the President said. 'I want you to work with him. Go to Houston and personally see to his training. It's possible you'll go along, too, although that's up to the Russians.' He grimaced slightly, then glanced at his watch. 'They're expecting both of you over at NASA headquarters. I wanted to see you before I made up my mind. If you hurry, you won't be too late.'

'Yes, sir.' Ed glanced at Jenny but didn't say anything.

The President stood, and everyone else stood with him. 'The Soviet Ambassador has demanded an official explanation of why news of this importance was transmitted via private telephone call, rather than through official channels,' he said. 'One of your first tasks, Major, will be to think of ways to convince them that this isn't a trick.'

'That may not be easy to do,' Admiral Carrell said.

'I realize that,' the President said. 'Others will be working on the problem.' He indicated dismissal. 'Major, they'll find you a place to work, Lord knows where, and don't be shy about asking for equipment. Mr. Frantz will see that you get what you want. I'll expect daily reports, sent through Admiral Carrell. If he's not here, you'll brief me yourself.'

Aliens are coming, and I've been assigned to the National Security Council! Personal presidential briefings in the Oval Office! All because I went for a swim and let an astronomer pick me up in Hawaii. My friend Barb believes nothing is ever a coincidence. Synchronicity. Maybe there's something to it . . .

'Now all I have to do is figure out where to put you,' the Chief of Staff was saying. 'The President will want you in this building. I guess I'll have to exile someone else to Old EOP.'

He was striding briskly down the hall. Jenny followed. They reached a desk at the end of the hall. The man who'd led her to the Oval Office was seated there.

'Jack,' the Chief of Staff said, 'meet another member of our family, Major Jeanette Crichton. The President has assigned her to his staff. NSC. She'll have regular personal access.'

'Right.' He studied her again.

'This is Jack Clybourne,' Jim Frantz said. 'Secret Service.'

'I worry about keeping the chief healthy,' Clybourne said.

'Get word to all the security people, Jack.' Frantz turned to Jenny. 'Major, I'd like you to check in this evening about four. I should have some room for you by

50

then. Meanwhile – oh. You came with General Gillespie. You've lost your ride.'

'No problem, sir.'

'Right. Thanks.' He started down the hall, stopped, and turned his head but not his body. 'Welcome aboard,' he said over his shoulder. He scurried off.

Jenny giggled, and Clybourne gave her an answering smile. 'He's a worrier, that one.'

'I gathered. What's next?'

'Fingerprints. Have to be sure you're you.'

'Oh. Who does that?'

'I can if you like.' Clybourne lifted a phone and spoke for a few moments. Presently another clean-cut young man entered and sat at the desk.

'Tom Bucks,' Clybourne said. 'Captain Jeanette Crichton. Next time you see her, she'll be wearing oak leaves. The President just promoted her. She's the newest addition to NSC. Personal access.'

'Hi,' Bucks said. He studied her, and Jenny felt he was memorizing every pore on her face.

They both act that way. Of course. Not Joe Gland, just a Secret Service agent doing his job.

Clybourne led the way downstairs and through a small staff lounge. 'I keep gear back here,' he said. He took out a large black case and put finger printing apparatus on the counter of the coffee machine.

'You really have to do this? My prints are on file.'

'Sure. What I have to be sure of is that the pretty girl I'm talking to now is the same Jeanette Crichton the Army commissioned.'

'I suppose,' she said.

He took her hand. 'Just relax, and let me do the work.'

She'd been through the routine before. Clybourne was good at it. Eventually he handed her a jar of waterless cleanser and some paper towels.

'How did you know the President had promoted me?' she asked.

'The appointment list said "Captain," and the Chief of Staff called you "Major." Jim Frantz doesn't make that kind of mistake.'

And you don't miss much, either.

She cleaned the black goo from her hands while Clybourne poured two cups of coffee from the pot on the table. He handed her one. 'Somebody said you live in Washington?'

'Grew up here,' she said. 'Which reminds me, can you call me a cab?'

'Sure. Where are you going?'

'Flintridge. It's out Connecticut, Rock Creek Park area —'

'I know where it is.' He glanced at his watch. 'If you can wait ten minutes, I can run you out.'

'I wouldn't want to put you to any trouble —'

'No trouble. I go off duty, and I'm going that way.'

'All right, then. Thank you.'

'You can wait for me at the main entrance,' Clybourne said. He took a memo pad bearing the White House seal from his pocket and scribbled on it, then took a small triangular pin from another pocket. 'Put that in your lapel, and keep this pass,' he said. 'I'll see you in ten minutes.'

He smiled again, and she found herself answering.

CHAPTER FOUR
BLIND MICE

Only one ship is seeking us, a black-
Sailed unfamiliar, towing at her back
A huge and birdless silence. In her wake
No waters breed or break.

> – PHILIP LARKIN, 'Next, Please'

COUNTDOWN: H MINUS SIX WEEKS

General Narovchatov paused at the door and waited to be invited inside even though Nadya had told him that Comrade Chairman Petrovskiy was expecting him. Petrovskiy did not like surprises.

The Chairman was writing in a small notebook. Narovchatov waited patiently.

The office was spartan in comparison to his own. Petroviskiy seemed not to notice things like rugs and tapestries and paintings. He enjoyed rare books with rich leather bindings and was fond of very old cognac; otherwise he did not often indulge himself.

There had been a time when Nikolai Nikolayevich Narovchatov was concerned that it would be dangerous to enjoy the trappings of wealth and power while the Chairman so obviously did not. He still believed that in the early days that concern had not been misplaced; but as Narovchatov rose in status, the gifts sent him by Petrovskiy had become more numerous and more valuable, until it was obvious that Petrovskiy was encouraging

53

his old associate to indulge himself, to enjoy what he did not himself care for.

Narovchatov had never discussed this with Chairman Petrovskiy. It was enough that it was so.

Chairman Petrovskiy looked up. His welcoming smile was broad. 'Come in, come in.' Then he grimaced. 'I suppose it was not a joke. They continue to come, then?' He lifted his glass of tea and peered at Narovchatov over its rim.

'Da, Anatoliy Vladimirovich.' General Narovchatov shrugged. 'According to the astronomers, at this point it would be difficult for them not to come. They move toward us very fast.'

'And they arrive, when?'

'A few weeks. I am told it is difficult to be more precise because it is a powered ship. That makes it unpredictable.'

'And you continue to believe that this is an alien ship, and not more CIA tricks?'

'I do, Anatoliy Vladimirovich.'

'So, I think, do I. But the Army does not.'

Narovchatov nodded. He had expected nothing else. And that could be a great problem for a man who had no need of more problems. The Chairman looked old and tired. Too old, Narovchatov thought. And what might happen when —

Perhaps the Chairman had read his thoughts. 'It is long past time that you were promoted, Nikolai Nikolayevich, my friend. I wish you to have the post of First Secretary. We will elevate Comrade Mayarovin to the Politburo, where he can rust in honor.'

'It is not necessary —'

'It is. Especially now. Nikolai Nikolayevich, I have long hoped to be the first leader of the Soviet Union to retire with honor. One day, perhaps, I will, but not until I can give the post to someone worthy. You are the most loyal man I know.'

'Thank you.'

'No thanks are needed. It is truth. But, my friend, I may not be with you so long. The doctors tell me this —'

'Nonsense.'

'That it is not. But before I am gone, I hope to see us accomplish something never before done. To give this land stability, to allow its best to serve without fear of their lives.'

The czars had never done that. Not the czars, and not Lenin. This was Russia. 'That requires law, Anatoliy Vladimirovich. Bourgeois lands have law. We have . . .' He shrugged expressively.

'We have had terror. It is not enough. You will remember little of Stalin's time, but I recall. Khrushchev destroyed himself in trying to destroy Stalin's memory, and we shall never make that mistake; but Khrushchev was correct, that man was a monster. Even Lenin warned against him.'

'He did what was necessary,' Narovchatov said.

'As do we. As we will. Enough of this. What shall we do about this alien spacecraft?'

Narovchatov shrugged. 'The Army has begun mobilization. The rocket forces will be brought to full strength, and we are constructing new space weapons.' He frowned. 'I do not yet know what the Americans will do.'

'Nor I,' the Chairman said. 'I suppose they will do the same.'

I hope so, Narovchatov thought. If they do not – There were always young officers who would begin the war if they thought they could win it. On both sides. 'Also, we have warned the commander of Kosmograd. I scarcely know what else to do.'

'We must do more,' the Chairman said. 'What will these aliens want? What could bring them here, across billions of miles? If they are aliens at all, and not a CIA trick.'

This again? 'Such a trick would make our space program look like children's games. It is alien, and powered. I would

55

believe a spacegoing beast with a rocket up its arse before I thought it a CIA trick. But I think it must be a ship, Anatoliy Vladimirovich.'

'I do agree,' the Chairman said. 'Only I cannot believe what I believe. It is too hard for me! What do they want? No one would travel that far merely to explore. They have reasons for coming.'

'They must. But I do not know why they have come.'

'No, nor will we, until they are ready to tell us. We know too little of this.' Petrovskiy speared Narovchatov with a peasant's crafty look. 'Your daughter has married a space scientist. An intelligent man, your son-in-law. Intelligent enough to be loyal. Intelligent enough to understand what your promotion to First Secretary will mean to him.'

'Da.'

'Someone must command the space preparations. Who?'

He means something, Narovchatov thought. Always he means things he does not say. He is clever, always clever, but sometimes he is too clever, for I do not understand him.

Who should command? The news of the alien ship had brought something like panic to the Kremlin. Everyone was upset, and the delicate balance within the Politburo was endangered. Who could command? Narovchatov shrugged. 'I had assumed Marshal Ugatov —'

'Certainly the Army will have suggestions. We will listen to them. As we do to KGB.' The Chairman continued to look thoughtful.

What is his plan? Narovchatov thought. The meeting of the Defense Council is in an hour. The heads of the Army and the KGB. The chief Party theoretician. Chairman Petrovskiy, and me because Petrovskiy has named me his associate. At that meeting everything will be settled, then comes the meeting of the entire Politburo, and after that the Central Committee to endorse what we have already decided. But what will we decide? He looked at Petrovskiy, but the Chairman was studying a paper on his desk.

What did Anatoliy Vladimirovich want? The Soviet Union was ruled by a troika – the Army, the KGB, and the Party – with the Party the weakest of the three, yet the most powerful because it controlled promotions within the other two organizations. Other schemes had been tried, and nearly brought disaster. When Stalin died, Party and Army had feared Beria, for his NKVD was so powerful that it had once eliminated nearly the entire central committee in a matter of weeks.

Party and Army together acted to eliminate the threat. Beria was dragged from a meeting of the Politburo and shot by four colonels. The top leadership of the NKVD was liquidated.

Suddenly the Party found itself facing the uncontrolled Army. It had not liked what it saw. The Army was popular. The military could command the affections of the people. If the Party's rule ever ended, it would not be the Army's leaders who would be shot as traitors. The Army could even eliminate the Party if it had full control of its strength.

That could not be allowed. The NKVD was reconstructed. It was shorn of many of its powers, divided into the civil militia and the KGB, never allowed to gain the strength it once had. Still, it had grown powerful again, as always it did. Its agents could compromise anyone, recruit anyone. It reached high into the Kremlin, into the Politburo and Party and Army. Alliances shifted once again . . .

Here, in this room, origins did not matter. Here, and in the Politburo itself, the truth was known. No one of the three power bases could be allowed to triumph. Party, Army, KGB must all be strong to maintain the balance of power. Ruling Russia consisted of that secret, and nothing more.

Petrovskiy was a master at that art. And now he was waiting. The hint he had given was plain.

'I believe Academician Bondarev might be very suitable to advise us and to direct our space forces during this emergency,' Narovchatov said. 'If you approve, Anatoliy Vladimirovich.'

'Now that you make the recommendation, I see much to commend it,' Petrovskiy said. 'I believe you should propose Academician Bondarev at the Central Committee meeting. Of course, the KGB will insist on placing their man in the operation.'

The KGB would have its man, but the Party must approve him. Another decision to be made here, before the meeting of the full Politburo.

'Grushin,' Narovchatov said. 'Dmitri Parfenovich Grushin.'

Petroviskiy raised a thick eyebrow in inquiry.

'I have watched him. He is trusted by the KGB, but a good diplomat, well regarded by the Party people he knows. And he has studied the sciences.'

'Very well.' Petrovskiy nodded in satisfaction.

'The KGB is divided,' Narovchatov said. 'Some believe this a CIA trick. Others know better. We have seen it for ourselves. Rogachev has seen it with his own eyes, in the telescopes aboard Kosmograd. The Americans could never have built that ship, Anatoliy Vladimirovich.'

Petrovskiy's peasant eyes hardened. 'Perhaps not. But the Army does not believe that. Marshal Ugatov is convinced that this is an American plot to cause him to aim his rockets at this thing in space while the Americans mobilize against us.'

'But they would not,' Narovchatov said. 'It is all very well for us to say these things for the public, but we must not delude ourselves.'

Petrovskiy frowned, and Nikolai Narovchatov was afraid for a moment. Then the Chairman smiled thinly. 'We may, however, have no choices,' he said. 'At all events, it is settled. Your daughter's husband will take charge of our space preparations. It is better that be done by a civilian. Come, let us have a cognac to celebrate the promotion of Marina's husband!'

'With much pleasure.' Narovchatov went to the cabinet and took out the bottle, crystal decanter, and glasses. 'What will the Americans really do?' he asked.

Petrovskiy shrugged. 'They will cooperate. What else can they do?'

'It is never wise to underestimate the Americans.'

'I know this. I taught it to you.'

Nikolai Nikolayevich grinned. 'I remember. But do you?'

'Yes. But they will cooperate.'

Narovchatov frowned a moment, then saw the sly grin the Chairman wore. 'Ah,' he said. 'Their President called.'

'No. I called him.'

Nikolai Narovchatov thought of the implications of that. Petrovskiy was the only man in the Soviet Union who could have called the American President without Narovchatov knowing it within moments. 'Does Trusov know this?' he asked.

'I did not tell him,' Petrovskiy said. He shrugged.

Narovchatov nodded agreement. The KGB had many resources. Who could know what its commander might find out? 'You will discuss this in the Defense Council, then?'

'Da.'

Nikolai Narovchatov poured two glasses of rare cognac and passed one across the large desk. The Chairman grinned and lifted the glass in salute. 'To the cooperation of the Americans,' he said. He laughed.

Narovchatov lifted his glass in reply, but inwardly he was afraid. This alien ship could be nothing but trouble, at a time when he had come so close to the top! But nothing was certain now. The KGB would have its own devious games, so twisted that even the KGB's masters would not understand. And the Army was reacting as armies always reacted. Missiles were made ready. Many fingers hovered over many buttons.

Nikolai Narovchatov felt much like the legendary Tatar who had saddled a whirlwind.

The shows were over, and Martin Carnell was driving home with his awards: one Best Bitch, three Best of Breed, and a Best Working Group, which he hadn't expected.

From behind him, from the crates in the back of the heavy station wagon, came restless sounds. Martin flipped off the radio to listen. None of the dogs sounded sick. Darth was just a puppy, and he wasn't used to traveling in the station wagon. His mood was affecting the others.

Martin was taking it easy. He stayed at fifty or below; he took half a minute to change lanes. You couldn't drive a station wagon like a race car, not with star-quality dogs in the back. Otherwise they'd be ready to take a judge's hand off by the day of the show.

Martin saw a lot of country this way. This had been a typical dog-show circuit. Two shows on Saturday and Sunday, sixty miles apart; five weekdays to be killed somehow, and three hundred miles to be covered; two more shows, much closer together, the following weekend; two thousand miles to be covered on the trip.

'Take it easy, guys,' Martin said, because they liked the sound of his voice. He turned on the radio again.

The music had stopped. Martin heard. 'I have spoken with the Soviet Chairman —'

It sounded like the President himself: that unmistakable trade-union accent. Martin turned up the sound.

'We are also consulting on a joint response to this alien ship.

'My fellow Americans, our scientists tell us that this could be the greatest event in the history of mankind. You now know all that we know: a large object, well over a mile in length, is approaching the Earth along a path that convinces our best scientific minds that it is under power and intelligently guided. So far there has been no communication with it.

'We have no reason to believe this is a threat —'

Martin grinned and shook his head, wishing he'd heard the beginning of the broadcast. Whoever was playing the part, he sure had the President's voice down pat. Martin laughed suddenly (and started all three dogs barking) at a divergent thought: suppose George Tate-Evans tuned in at the same moment he had? Would he bellow with the joy of vindication, or hide under the bed?

The Enclave was still going, Martin knew that much. He couldn't understand, now, how he'd got sucked into the survivalist mind-set. Spent some real money, too, before he came to his senses. The only thing that little fling had ever done for him was to turn him from miniature poodles to Dobermans. He'd bought Marienburg Sunhawk because a Doberman might be better equipped to defend his house, and found that he flat-out preferred the bigger dogs.

But the rest of the Enclave families must still be meeting on Thursday nights, all ready for the end of civilization on Earth. George and Vicki: what *would* they do? Warn the rest of the Enclave and head for the hills, of course: their natural reaction to any stimulus.

And they say dog people are crazy!

A newscaster's rich radio voice continued the theme, speaking of war and politics. It introduced a professor of physics who also wrote science fiction, and who predicted wonderful things from the coming confrontation. Martin, cruising down old U.S. 66 with a load of prima donna dogs, began to wonder if he really was listening to a remake of *War of the Worlds*. He hadn't found a plot line yet.

There was heavy traffic in the San Fernando Valley. Isadore Leiber cursed lightly, half listening to the news station, half worrying about how late he would be.

Isadore had simply forgotten. It wasn't a Thursday. His brain hadn't ticked over until four-thirty, and then: Hey, wasn't something happening tonight? Sure, Jack McCauley called an emergency meeting of the Enclave. Probably has to do with that . . . light in the sky. I'd better call Clara, remind *her*.

Clara had remembered, and wondered where he was. He fought abnormally dense rush-hour traffic straight to the Tate-Evans place, one house among many in the San Fernando Valley. Clara met him at the curb, laughing, insisting that she'd followed him right in, in her own car. He grabbed her and kissed her to shut her up. They held each other breathlessly for a moment, then by mutual consent let go and walked up on the porch.

Clara rang the bell and they waited. In those few seconds Clara stopped laughing, even stopped smiling. 'Do you think they'll be angry?'

'Yeah. My fault, and I guess I don't care that much. Relax.'

'They did tell us. Or Jack did.'

The door opened. George Tate-Evans ushered them inside. He wasn't angry, but he wasn't happy either. 'Clara, Isadore, come on in. What kept you?'

'My boss,' Isadore lied. 'What's happening?'

George ran his hand over bare scalp to long, thin blond hair. He wasn't yet forty, but he'd been half bald when Isadore first met him. 'Sign of virility,' he'd said. Now he answered, 'Jack and Harriet taped some newscasts. We're playing them now. Clara, the girls are in the kitchen cooking something.'

Girls, kitchen, cooking something. *What*? This was serious, then; or else *George* was sure this was serious. Could it be? *That* serious?

Survivalism. Specialization. Wartime rules. Isadore made his way into a darkened living room. He knew where the steps and the furniture were; he'd been there often enough. The light of the five-foot screen showed him an empty spot on the couch.

There were only men in the room. The house belonged to George and Vicki Tate-Evans, but Vicki wasn't present.

And Clara had gone to the kitchen. Clara! Ye gods, *she* thought it was real . . .

George waved him to a seat, then went to the Betamax recorder. 'Here it is again,' he said.

The set lit up to show the presidential seal, then the Oval Office. The camera panned in on President David Coffey. The President looked calm and relaxed. Almost too much so, Isadore thought. But he does look very presidential . . .

'My fellow Americans,' Coffey said. 'Last night, scientists at the University of Hawaii made an amazing discovery. Their findings have since been confirmed by astronomers at Kitt Peak and other observatories. According to the best scientific information I have been able to obtain, a very large spacecraft is approaching Earth from the general direction of the planet Saturn.'

The President looked up at the camera, ignoring his notes for a moment. He had a way of doing that, of looking into the camera so that everyone watching felt he was speaking directly to them. Coffey's ability to do that had played no small part in his election. 'I have been told that it is not possible that the ship came from Saturn, and that it must have come from somewhere much farther away. Wherever it came from, it is rapidly approaching the Earth, and will arrive here within a few weeks, probably at the end of June.'

He paused to look at the yellow sheets of paper that lay on his desk, then back at the camera again. 'So far we have received no communication from this ship. We therefore have no reason whatever to believe the ship poses any threat to us. However, the Soviet Union became aware of this ship at the same time we did. Predictably, their reaction was to mobilize their armed forces. Our observation satellites show that they have begun a partial strategic alert.

'We cannot permit the Soviets to mobilize without some answer. I have therefore ordered a partial mobilization of the United States' strategic forces. I wish to emphasize that this is a defensive mobilization only. The United States has never wanted war. We particularly do not desire war at a time when an alien spacecraft is approaching this planet.

'No American President could ignore the Soviet mobilization. I have not done so. However, I have spoken with the Soviet Chairman, and we have reached an agreement on limiting our strategic mobilization. We are also consulting on a joint response to the alien ship.

'My fellow Americans, our scientists tell us that this could be the greatest event in the history of mankind. You now know all that we know: a large object, perhaps a mile in length, is approaching the Earth along a path that convinces our best scientific minds that it is under power and intelligently guided. So far there has been no communication with it.

'We have no reason to believe this is a threat, and we have many reasons to believe this is an opportunity. With the help of God Almighty we will meet this opportunity as Americans have always met opportunities.

'Good night . . .'

The Oval Office faded, and news analysts came on. George switched off the set. 'We can skip the analysis. Those birds don't know any more than we do. But you see why I called an alert.'

They had called themselves the Enclave before there was anything more than four men meeting at George and Vicki's house.

That was at the tail end of the seventies, when the end of civilization was a serious matter. There were double-digit inflation and a rising crime rate. Iran was holding fifty-odd kidnapped ambassadors and getting away with it. OPEC's banditry regarding oil prices seemed equally safe. What nation would be next to see the obvious? The United States couldn't defend itself. The value of her money was falling to its limit: a penny and a half in 1980 money, the cost of printing a dollar bill. U.S. military forces were in shreds, and the Soviets kept building missiles long after they caught up, then passed, the United States' strategic forces.

If the economy didn't collapse, nuclear war would kill you. Either way, there were long odds against survival of the unprepared. The Enclave was born of equal parts desperation and play-acting. Which was more important depended on the morning headlines.

Things looked better after Reagan was elected. The hostages were returned minutes before the old cowboy took office . . . but the Enclave continued to meet. The dollar ceased to fall, then grew strong. The economy was turning around, the stock market was showing signs of health; but there was no money for the military, and the Soviet Union kept building rockets. The Enclave made lists of what a survivalist ought to own, and checked each other's stocks A year's worth of food, just like the Mormons. Guns. Gold coins. And they dreamed of a place to run, just in case.

The late eighties: Welfare had not increased to match inflation, and unemployment was down. There might have been a connection. Inflation had slowed too. General Motors had won its lawsuit against the unions, for damages done by a strike, and collected from the union funds; strikes ought to be less common in the future. The weapons of war had moved into a science-fictional realm, difficult for the average citizen to assess. But the Soviet space program had been moving steadily outward until they virtually owned the sky from Near Earth Orbit to beyond the Moon.

The Enclave continued to meet. They had grown older,

and generally wealthier. Four years ago they had bought a piece of land outside Bellingham, a decaying city north of Seattle that had been a port and shipyard before the silt moved in and the trade moved south. It was as far from any likely targets of war as any place that seemed able to support itself. There had once been a navy shipyard, but that was long ago.

They all made money, but they weren't rich. Their jobs kept them in Los Angeles. Over the years one or another had found wealth or peace or even both in small towns. The dropouts were replaced, and the Enclave endured, an aging group of middle-class survivalists unwilling to break away from Los Angeles and their not inconsiderable incomes.

All this time they had been meeting, every Thursday night after the dinner hour, like clockwork. Tonight was Monday; they had left work early, and Isadore was getting hungry; the dinner hour should have been just beginning. But the terrible strangeness of this night did not derive from that. Isadore Leiber sought for what it was that was bothering him, and it came, not in strangeness but in familiarity, as he reached for a cigarette.

Four years ago he'd given up smoking for the last time.

He'd given it up, but he borrowed from his friends at every opportunity. Giving up smoking became his life-style. It got to where his friends couldn't stand him: the sight of a familiar face triggered his urge to smoke; he would roll pipe tobacco in toilet paper if he had to. But he was giving up smoking, yes indeed —

And he was getting ready for the end of civilization, yes indeed. But he'd been doing it for well over a decade, and *that* had become his lifestyle. Tonight was weird. No laughter, no complaining about fools in Congress —

Tonight they meant it.

'I hate the timing,' George said. 'Corliss is about to graduate, and the rest of the kids won't like missing the tail end of the school year, and if they do, I don't.'

There were echoes of agreement. 'I can't go,' Isadore said.

The noise stopped. Jack McCauley said, 'What do you mean, *can't*?'

'I can't quit my job. I can't take leave, either. George said it, it's timing. Travel agencies get hectic with summer coming on.'

Jack made a sound of disgust. George asked, 'Sick leave?'

'Mm . . . a couple of weeks.'

'Wait till, oh, the tenth of June. Jack, this makes sense.' George jumped the gun on an automatic protest. 'We're bound to forget something. We'll keep Iz posted. Iz, you take your two weeks' sick leave just before the ETI's reach Earth. You come up then. Two weeks later you'll damn well know whether you want to go back to the city.'

'It's still costing us a pair of strong arms,' Jack groused.

Isadore decided he liked the idea. 'I'll ask Clara if she wants to take the kids up early. Maybe we'll want to keep them in school as long as we can.'

'All right, it can't be helped,' Jack said. 'But the rest of us are going, right?' He snowballed on before there could be an answer. 'Bill and Gwen are already up at the Enclave. We've got the second cistern system running, and he's got the top deck poured on the shelter. Bill says the well has to be cleaned out, but we can do that with muscle when we get there.' He pursed his lips in a familiar gesture. 'One thing, Iz. You come up a full week before the ETI's get here. Cut it any finer, and you may not make it at all. When people really *believe* in that ship, God knows what they'll do.'

'If the Soviets give us that long,' George said.

Jack frowned. 'For that matter, if there's any alien ship at all. Maybe this is something the Russians cooked up.'

They all shrugged. 'No data,' Isadore said. 'But you'd think the President would know.'

'And he'd sure tell us, right?' Jack said. 'Iz, are you *sure* you want to wait?'

'Yeah, I have to.' Christ, he's right, Isadore thought. Who the fuck knows what's happening? Aliens, Russians – a nuclear war could ruin your whole day. 'I think Clara will go up early,' he said. 'I'll have to ask her.'

The others nodded understanding.

When they'd first started the Enclave, they made a decision. One vote per adult, but all the votes of a family would be cast by one person. The theory was simple. If a family couldn't even agree on who represented it, what could they agree on?

There'd been a problem at first, because Isadore thought Clara ought to vote rather than him, but she didn't get along with Jack, or maybe Jack didn't get along with her. There'd been too many arguments. After the first year things had settled in, and only the men voted, but Isadore often went off to ask Clara's opinion before making a decision.

'Who else goes?' Jack demanded.

The inevitable question struck each of them differently. Jack was already belligerent. George looked disconcerted, then guilty. 'Well . . . us, of course,' he said. 'Our wives and children.'

'Of course. Who else? Who do we need, who do we want? John Fox?'

Isadore laughed. 'Hell, yes, we want Fox. He's a better survivor than any of us. That's why he's not coming. I talked to him. He'll be camping somewhere in Death Valley, and that's fine for him, but he didn't invite *me* along.'

'What if Martie shows?'

'Aw, hell, Jack.'

Martin Carnell had been with the Enclave for a time. He'd lasted long enough to help buy the house and land in Bellingham. Then . . . maybe he'd run into financial trouble. He'd quit. Later he'd moved further north into the Antelope Valley.

'You read me wrong, George. I just want to point out that he's got some legal rights. We're betting that won't matter much, but suppose he shows up at the gate? Before or after the ETI's get here.'

'We've turned that place into a fortress since he quit. Expensive.' Isadore grinned at them. 'What he owns is something like half his fair share. Awkward.'

'Yah. Well, I see him sometimes, and he's still single. There's just him —'

'And those damn Dobermans,' George said.

'Is that bad? We can use some guard dogs. We'll make him build his own kennels.'

'These are show dogs. They're gentle and dignified and everybody's friend. Anything else would cost Martie some prizes. They're not guard dogs.'

'Would looters know that?'

A silence fell. Jack said, 'Shall we let him in if he shows at the gate? Assuming he's got equipment and supplies. But I see no reason to phone him up and invite him.'

There were nods, and some relief showed. George said, 'Harry Reddington wants to come.'

Two heads shook slowly. Jack McCauley asked, 'Have you seen Hairy Red lately?'

George hesitated, then nodded. 'We used to be friends. I guess we still are. Hell, we took motorcycles up along the Pacific Coast Highway one time. Three hundred miles. We'd stop in a bar and Harry would sing and play that guitar and get us our drinks that way, and maybe our dinners. Hairy Red the Minstrel. I —'

'Lately?'

'Yeah, I've seen him lately.'

'He looks like he's about to have twins, and he has to use that cane. It isn't because he had those accidents.' Jack shook his head in bewildered pity. 'Rear-ended twice in two weeks, in two different cars, and neither of them had head rests! Typical of Harry. But that's not the point. The insurance company's been fast-shuffling him for two years, and his lawyer tells him he won't win if he's too healthy when he gets on the stand.' Now Jack's speech slowed and his enunciation improved, as if he were making a point for someone who didn't quite understand English. 'Harry Red has been letting his insurance company tell him to stay sick! So he doesn't exercise, and he lets his belly grow like a parasite —'

'All right, all right. Ken Dutton?'

'He had his chance.'

'Interesting mind. He collects some odd stuff, and it all seems to make sense. Maybe we're too much alike, the four of us.'

'George, you offered to let him in. He waffled. Now there's something coming, and suddenly it's not fun and games anymore. He could have got in when it was fun and games. Why didn't he? Was it the money?'

'Oh, partly. Not just the dues for the Enclave, but the gear we make each other buy. He has to pay alimony . . . Only he's got gear. It's just not like ours. And partly it's because he never really gets all the way into anything.'

'Hardly a recommendation. What has he got for weapons?'

George smiled reluctantly. 'That crossbow. It'd kill a bear, that thing, and it's advertised as 'suitable for SWAT teams.' And his liquor, he calls it 'trade goods,' and he really does keep an interesting bar —'

'A crossbow. And a rocket pistol! I've seen his little 1960s Gyrojet. How many shells has he got for it? It's for damn sure they'll never make any more. He could have been in and he didn't pay his dues, George!'

Isadore said, 'You could say the same about Jeri Wilson. We want her, don't we?'

'You're married, Iz. And I'm *very* married.'

'Martie isn't. John Fox isn't, and we'd take him. There are men we want besides us, aren't there? Do we want the men seriously outnumbering the women? I don't think we do.'

'We can't invite the whole city,' Jack said. 'We don't have the room. Izzie, who else are you going to try to drag in? You *knew* we wouldn't have Harry, and you wouldn't want him anyway —'

'It's just that a month from now . . . I can see us all being terribly apologetic.'

'The hell you say,' said Jack.

'This could be our invitation to join the Galactic Union. It could be a flock of . . . funny-looking alien grad students here to give us cheap jewelry for answering their questions —'

George made a rude noise. Jack, at least, looked more thoughtful than amused. Isadore steamed on through the interruption. ' – and who knows what they might consider cheap jewelry? Okay, so we're going off to hide. Somebody has to. Just in case. But . . . I can hear the remarks from some people I like, because we left them outside.'

Jack's look was stony. 'Remember a science-fiction story called "To Serve Man"?'

'Sure. They even made a *Twilight Zone* out of it. About an alien handbook on how to deal with the human race.'

George smiled – 'Some science-fiction fans actually published the cook-book' – and sobered. 'Yeah. Somebody has to hide till we know what they want. And just in case, we *do not* take liabilities.'

CHAPTER FIVE
SEE HOW THEY RUN

Do unto the other feller the way he'd like to do unto you
an' do it fust.

– EDWARD NOYES WESTCOTT, *David Harum* (1898)

COUNTDOWN: H MINUS SIX WEEKS

The Arco Plaza Mall was deep underground, with four-
story shafts reaching high to street level. Around the corner from the government bookstore was a B. Dalton's,
and near that was a radio station with its control room in
showcase windows. A few people with nothing better to
do sat on benches watching the radio interviewer. His
guest was a science-fiction author who'd come to plug his
latest book but couldn't resist talking about the alien ship.

The government bookstore had been crowded all day.
Ken Dutton noticed Harry shuffling in, but was too busy
to hail him.

Harry Reddington was still using a cane. Ken remembered him as a biker. He still had the massive frame, but it
had turned soft years ago. He'd shaved his beard and cut
his hair short even before the two successive whiplash
accidents. He might have lost some weight lately – he'd
claimed to when Ken saw him last – but the belly was still
his most prominent feature.

He stopped just past the doorway and looked around at
shelves upon shelves of books and pamphlets before he
sought out Ken Dutton behind the counter. 'Hi, Ken.'

'Hello, Harry. What's up?'

Harry ran his hand back through graying scarlet hair. 'I was listening to the news. Not much on the intruder. It's still coming . . . and I got to thinking how most of these books will be obsolete an hour after that thing sets down.'

'Some will.' Dutton waved toward a shelf of military books. 'Others, maybe not. History still means something. Some will go obsolete, but which books? Maybe medicine. Maybe they've got something that'll cure any disease and they're just dying to give it away.'

'Yeah.' Harry didn't smile. 'I remember there's one on how to take care of a car —'

'More than one.'

'Cars and bikes and . . . and bicycles, for that matter. Okay, maybe they've got matter transmitters. Talked to George today?'

'No. I guess I should have,' Dutton said. *Hell's bells. I should have joined that survivalist outfit when I had a chance. Now.* 'I'll call after we close.'

'Good luck,' Harry said.

'You talked to them?'

'Yeah. They're not recruiting. But they're running scared. Scared of the aliens a little, and of the Russians a lot.' Harry looked thoughtful. 'George mentioned a book on cannibal cookery. Supposed to be funny, but it was well-researched, he said —'

'We don't carry it. And, Harry, I'm not sure I want to think you've got a copy.'

'Well, you never know . . .' Harry couldn't keep it up, and laughed. 'All right, but maybe what we'll need is survival manuals. I thought I'd come in and look around.'

The shelves had been seriously depleted. Harry chose a few and came to the counter. 'There was a new book from the Public Health Service. On stretching exercises. Got it in yet?'

'Sure, but we're out. Others had the same thought you did.'

'Ken, you're actually one of the Enclave group, aren't you?'

Ken hesitated. 'They invited me in. I haven't moved yet.' *And maybe it's too late, maybe not. Jesus.*

'Are you booked for dinner?'

'I don't know. Need to make a phone call.' He went to the back room and dialed George's number. Vicki answered.

'Hi,' Ken said. 'Uh – this is Ken Dutton.'

'I know who you are.'

'Yes – uh – Vicki, is there a meeting tonight?'

'Not tonight. Call tomorrow.'

'Vicki, I know damned well there's a meeting!'

'Call tomorrow. Anything else? Bye, then.' The phone went dead.

Ken Dutton went back out to the customer area and found Harry. 'No. I don't have anything on tonight. Let's eat here in the plaza. Saves us worrying about rush hour.'

Jeri Wilson kissed her daughter, and was surprised at how easy it was to hold her smile until Melissa went up to her room. She's a good-looking ten-year-old, Jeri thought. Going to be pretty when she grows up.

Melissa had Jeri's long bones and slender frame. Her hair was a bit darker than Jeri's, and not quite so fine, but her face was well shaped, pretty rather than beautiful.

Jeri waited until she heard the toilet flush, then waited again until the light under Melissa's door vanished.

She'd sleep now. She'd be exhausted.

So am I. Jeri's smile faded. It had been such a wonderful day, the nicest for weeks, until she came home to find the mail.

She went to the living room. An expensive breakfront stood there, and she took out a red crystal decanter and a matching crystal glass. *We bought this in Venice. We couldn't really afford the trip, and the glassware was much too expensive. God, that was a beautiful summer.*

The sherry came from Fedco, but no one ever noticed the sherry. They were too enchanted with the decanter. She poured herself a glass and sat on the couch. It was impossible to stop the tears now.

Damn you, David Wilson! She took the letter from her apron pocket. It was handwritten, postmarked Cheyenne Wells, Colorado, and it wasn't signed. She thought the handwriting looked masculine, but she couldn't be sure.

'Dear Mrs. Wilson,' it said. 'If you're really serious about keeping your husband, you'd better get out here and do something right away, 'cause he's got himself a New Cookie.'

Of course he has a New Cookie, Jeri thought. He's been gone almost two years, and he filed for divorce six months ago. It was inevitable . . .

Inevitable or not, she didn't like to think about it. Pictures came to mind: David, nude, stepping out of the shower. Lying with David on the beach at Malibu, late at night long after the beach had closed, both of them buzzed with champagne. They'd been celebrating David's Ph.D., and they made love three times, and even if the third time had been more effort than consummation it was a wonderful night.

After the first time she'd turned to him and said, 'I haven't been taking my pills —'

'I know,' he said.

She liked to think Melissa was conceived that night. Certainly it happened during that wonderful week. Five months later, Jeri quit her job as a general science editor for UCLA's alumni magazine. David's education was finished, he'd found a great job with Litton Industries, and they could enjoy themselves . . .

She sipped her sherry, then, convulsively, drained the glass. It was an effort to keep from throwing it on the floor. *Who am I so damned mad at?*

At myself. I'm a damned fool. She crumpled the letter, then smoothed it out again. Then poured more sherry. No matter how often she wiped her eyes, they filled again.

She'd had three glasses when the phone rang. At first she thought she'd ignore it, but it might be about Melissa. Or it might even be David; he still called sometimes. *What if it's him, and he says he needs me?*

'Hello.'

'Jeri, this is Vicki.'

'Oh.'

'You've heard the news?' Vicki asked.

How the devil would you know about David – 'What news?'

'The alien spaceship.'

'. . . What?'

'Jeri, where have you been all day? Hibernating?'

'No, Melissa and I drove up to the Angeles Crest. We had a picnic.'

'Then you haven't seen the news. Jeri, the astronomers have discovered an alien spaceship in the solar system. It's coming to Earth.'

Aliens. Coming to Earth. She heard the words, but they didn't make any sense. 'You're not putting me on?'

'Jeri, go turn on Channel Four. I'll call back in half an hour. We have to talk.'

Saturn. They were coming from Saturn, and no one knew how long they'd been there. Jeri remembered a TV monitor at JPL. Three lines twisted into a braid, and David's grip on her arm was hard enough to hurt.

That was – that was a lot more than ten years ago! I was about twenty. I had David, and everything was wonderful.

The phone rang just as the news program was ending. Jeri lifted the receiver. 'Hello, Vicki.'

'Hi. Okay, you watched the news?'

'Yes.' Jeri giggled.

'What?'

'Aliens from Saturn, that's what! Vicki, I'll bet they were there when the Voyager probe went past. I remember all the bull sessions after that probe. John Deming and Gregory and – and David and I, trying to think how an orbiting band of particles could be twisted like that. David even said "aliens," once. But he wasn't serious.'

'Yes, well, that's what we need to talk about,' Vicki said. 'We've decided – the Enclave is going north. To Bellingham. You and Melissa are invited.'

'Oh. Why?'

'Well, for one thing, you and David were part of the group for a long time.

'That's one reason,' Jeri said. 'What are some others?'

Vicki Tate-Evans sighed. 'Because you know science – and all right, because you're pretty and unattached, and we may need to attract a single guy.'

An interesting compliment. I'm glad they think I'm pretty, at my age . . . 'I see. So I can be a playmate for Ken Dutton.'

'Jeri, he wasn't invited.'

'Good.'

'I thought you liked Ken. In fact, I thought —'

You can keep that thought to yourself, Vicki Tate-Evans.

Of course it was true. Ken Dutton had invited himself to dinner with Jeri and David after his wife left him, and when David moved to Colorado, Ken continued to come over. She wasn't interested in an affair, although it was pretty difficult sleeping alone. She missed David a lot, and in every way, and Ken wasn't unattractive, and he was very attentive. The night she learned that David had filed for divorce, Ken had been there, and held her, and listened to her, and in a blind rage she seduced him. For a few days he'd shared her bed. Then she found out what he was thinking.

'He thought I'd be convenient,' Jeri said. 'He wouldn't

have to drive far. Somehow that didn't seem a good foundation for a relationship.'

'Oh.' Vicki laughed awkwardly. 'Anyway, he's not invited. In fact I was supposed to tell you not to invite him. Well. That's good. Jeri, we'll be going up to Bellingham this week. Isadore and Clara will stay down here until a few days before the aliens come. We'd rather you came up with us, but you could wait and go up with Isadore if you want.'

'I see. Thanks, Vicki. Uh – I'll get back to you, shall I?'

'You'll have to. We need to go over your gear, find out what David left you, and what you have to take. I'll help with that.'

'Thanks. There's a lot of it here. I'll get it out. Thanks for inviting me.'

'Sure. Bye.'

Jeri put the phone down and thoughtfully pulled at her lower lip.

Aliens. Coming here, soon.

And they hid at Saturn. No sign of them, nothing that made sense, anyway. They stayed hidden for more than a dozen years. Is that a sign of friendship?

Don't be paranoid, she told herself. But it might be a good idea not to be in a big city when they came. Just in case.

She and David and Melissa had visited George and Vicki at the Enclave house in Bellingham. That had been nice, a good vacation —

It had been their last vacation together. A month later, David was transferred to Colorado.

'It's a big raise,' he'd told her. He sounded excited.

'But what about my job?'

'What about it, Jeri? You don't have to work.'

'David, I don't have to, but I want to.' When Melissa started school, Jeri needed something to do, and became

78

an editorial assistant with the West Coast branch of a big publishing house. She'd been good at the job. Her experience with the alumni paper had helped. Within a year she'd become an associate editor, and then there'd been a lucky break: she'd discovered a woman who needed a lot of help, hand-holding and reassurances, and lots of editing, but whose first book became an instant best-seller.

After that, Jeri became a senior editor. 'I'm important at Harris Wickes.'

'You're important to me. And to Melissa.'

'David —'

'Jeri, it's a big promotion.'

I was a damn fool. So was he. Why didn't he tell me they'd fire him if he didn't transfer? That a lot of eager young petroleum geologists were graduating from the schools, and the big firms would rather hire a recent graduate than a man so long out of school . . .

He didn't tell me because he was ashamed. They didn't really want him anymore, but he couldn't tell me that. And he wouldn't beg me.

Damn it, *I begged him!* But it's not really the same, and David, David, why can't I just call you and say I'm coming to you . . .

Why can't I?

———

It was a beautiful spring day in Washington. The city was surprisingly calm, despite the headlines. It took a lot to shake up Washington people.

Roger Brooks walked from NASA headquarters back toward the White House. There'd been nothing for him at the NASA press conference. It was great for Congressman Wes Dawson that he was going to go up to the Soviet Kosmograd space station to watch the aliens arrive. It might even make a story, but Jose Mavis would take care

79

of the news part, and there was plenty of time to collect background. •

For a minute he'd thought he had something. *Jeanette Crichton discovers the satellite and Wes Dawson goes to the President*. Not too many would know about the connection between Linda Crichton Gillespie and Carlotta Dawson. He was still thinking about that when the NASA press people explained it all in loving detail. *Captain Crichton calls her brother-in-law, who calls Congressman Dawson, who goes to see the President*. All out in the open for everyone to see. Nothing hidden at all. Damn.

It was a good twenty-minute walk to the Mayflower. Even so, Roger got there before his lunch appointment. The grill at the Mayflower was convenient, even if the food wasn't distinguished. Roger would have preferred one of the French cuisine places off K Street, but today he was meeting John Fox. Fox wasn't someone you ate an expensive lunch with, no matter who was paying. Brooks ordered a glass of white wine and leaned back to relax until Fox showed up.

You can't get anywhere in Washington, D.C., without a coat and tie. Sure enough, Fox was in disguise, in a gray business suit and a tie that didn't glare. It wouldn't have fooled anybody. His shirt cuffs gave him away: they were much larger than his wrists. Lean as a ferret, with bony shoulders and fat-free muscle showing even in the hands and face, John Fox looked like he'd just walked out of a desert.

Roger worked his way out of the booth to shake his hand. 'How are you, John? Have you heard the news?'

'Yeah.' They slid into the booth. 'I'm surprised you're here.'

For a fact, this wasn't the day a militant defender of deserts could get the public's attention! Roger had toyed with the idea of chasing afternews of the 'alien spacecraft.' But those who knew anything would be telling anyone who would listen, and he'd be fighting for scraps.

For a while Roger had wondered. Aliens, coming from Saturn. It didn't make sense, and Roger was sure it was some kind of trick, probably CIA. When he tried to check that out, though, he ran into a barrage of genuine bewilderment. If there were any secrets hidden inside the President's announcement, it was going to take a lot more than a few hours to find them. And John Fox had given Roger stories in the past.

So he said, 'The day I skip an appointment with a known news source, you call the police, because I've been kidnapped. Now tell me what you're doing in Washington. I know you don't like cities.'

Fox nodded. 'Have you heard what they're doing to China Lake?' When Brooks looked blank, he amplified. 'The High-Beam.'

For a moment nothing clicked. Then: of course, he meant the microwave receiving station. An orbiting solar power plant had to have a receiver. 'It's just a test facility. It's only going to cover about an acre.'

'Oh, sure. And the orbiting power plant only covers about a square mile of sky, and won't send down more than a thousand megawatts even if everything works. Roger, don't you understand about test cases? If it works, they'll do it bigger. They'll cover the whole damn sky with silver rectangles. I like the sky! I like desert, too. This thing has to be stopped now.'

'I wonder if the Soviets won't stop us before you do.'

'They haven't yet.' Fox looked thoughtful. 'All the science types say this thing isn't a weapon. I wonder if the Russians believe that?'

Roger shrugged.

'Anyway, I thought I'd better be here. Flew in on the red-eye last night. But nobody's keeping appointments. Nobody but you.' He glanced up to see the waitress hovering. 'Bacon burger. Tomato slices, no fries. Hot tea.'

'Chef's salad. Heineken.' Brooks made notes, but mostly out of habit. *Of course* no one was keeping appointments! Aliens were coming to Earth. 'They tell me it'll be clean power,' Roger said. 'Help eliminate acid rain.'

Fox shook his head. 'Never works. They get more power, they use more power. Look. They tell you an electric razor doesn't use much power, right? And it doesn't. But what about the power it took to make the damn thing? You use it a few years, maybe not that long, and out it goes.

'The more electric power we get, the more they're tempted to keep up the throwaway society. No real conservation. Nothing lasts. Doesn't have to last. Roger, no matter how clean they make it, it pollutes some. They'll never learn to do without until they have to do without.'

'Okay.' Brooks jotted more notes. 'So they'll clutter up the deserts and block the stars and give us bad habits. What else is wrong with them?'

Roger Brooks listened halfheartedly as Fox marshaled his arguments. There weren't any new ones. They weren't what Roger had come for, anyway. Fox could argue, but the real stories would come from learning what tactics Fox intended to use. He had loyal troops, loyal enough to chain themselves to the gates of nuclear power plants or clog the streets of Washington. Fox had led the fight against the Sun Desert nuclear power plant, and won, and his tips had put Roger in the right place at the right time for good stories.

Not today, though. No one was listening to Fox today. Not even his friends.

Not even me, Roger thought. This wasn't going to make any kind of news. Brooks was tempted to put away his notebook. Instead he said, 'This could be just a puff of smoke tomorrow, or later today, for that matter. Have you thought about what an interstellar spacecraft might use for power? By the time the aliens stop talking, these orbiting solar plants could look like the first fire stick, even to us.'

Fox shook his head. 'Hell, we may not even understand what these ETI's are using. Or maybe it's worse than what we've got. Anyway, nothing changes that fast. Whatever that light in the sky does for us, the High-Beam is going ahead unless I stop it. And I intend to. I had an appointment with Senator Bryant. He canceled, for today, so I'll just wait him out.'

Brooks jotted, 'John Fox is the only man in the nation's capital who doesn't care beans about an approaching interstellar spacecraft.'

'Hell, I wish I had something more for you,' Fox said. 'Thought I did.'

'It's all right.'

'No, it's not,' Fox said. 'You're like me, Brooks. A nut. Monomaniac.' He held up his hand when Roger started to protest. 'It's true. I love my deserts, and you love snooping. Well, hell, I'd help you get a Pulitzer if I could. You've always played fair with me.' He chuckled. 'But not today. Nobody's paying attention to a damn thing but that ETI comin'. Do you really believe in that thing?'

'I think so. You know that army officer who was in Hawaii when they saw it coming? I know her. I just don't think she's part of anything funny. No, it's real all right.'

'Could be.'

'There are a lot of scientists in the Sierra Club,' Roger said. 'Any of them have an opinion?'

'On High-Beam? Damn right – '

'I meant on the ETI's, John.'

Fox grinned. 'I haven't heard. I will, though, and I'll be sure to let you know.'

Jenny surveyed her office with satisfaction. The furniture was battered. Fortunately, there wasn't much of it, because if there'd been more, the office couldn't have held it all. She had a desk with nothing on it but a telephone. There were also a small typing table, three chairs, and a thick-walled filing cabinet with a heavy security lock. They said they'd get her a bookcase, but that hadn't come yet. Neither had the computer terminal.

The room was tiny and windowless, in a basement – but it was the White House basement, and that made up for everything.

The phone rang.

'Major Crichton,' she said.

'Jack Clybourne.'

'Oh. Hi.' He'd come in for coffee after he drove her home. They'd sat outside under Flintridge's arbor, and when they noticed the time, two hours had passed. That hadn't happened to her in years.

'Hi, yourself. I've only got a moment. Interested in dinner?'

Aunt Rhonda would expect her to eat at Flintridge. 'What did you have in mind?'

'Afghan place. Stuffed grape leaves and broiled lamb.'

'It sounds great. But —'

'Let me call you after you get home. No big deal, if you can't make it, I'll go to McDonald's.'

'You're threatening suicide if I don't have dinner with you?'

'I have to run. I'll call you —'

'I haven't given you the number,' she said. 'How will you call?'

'We have our ways. Bye.'

She put the phone carefully on its cradle. Holy catfish, I'm actually light-headed. Stupid. I just need lunch. But I *was* thinking about him just before he called.

———

The private phone on Wes Dawson's desk was hidden inside a leather box. It rang softly.

'Yes?' Carlotta said.

'Me.'

'How's Houston?'

'Hot and wet and windy. I'm in the Hilton Edgewater, room 2133.'

She made a note of the room number.

'I miss you already,' he said.

'Sure. You probably have a Texas girl already.'

'Two, actually.'

'Just be careful. I've seen the Speaker. We'll arrange for you to be paired whenever we can, so it'll go in the *Congressional Quarterly*.'

It was standard practice: a congressman who couldn't be present for a vote found another who intended to vote the opposite way, and formed a pair. Neither attended, and both were recorded as 'paired,' so that the outcome of the vote wasn't affected, but neither congressman was blamed for missing a roll-call vote.

'Good. Can you ask Andy to look after my committee work?'

'Already did. What kind of administrative assistant do you think I am, anyway?'

'Fair to middling.'

'Humph. Keep that up and I'll ask for a raise. I suppose Houston's full of talk about the aliens?'

'Lord, yes,' Wes said. 'And the TV shows – did you watch the *Tonight Show*? Nothing but alien jokes, some pretty clever. I think the country's taking it all right.'

'So do I, but I've got Wilbur checking things out in the district,' Carlotta said. 'So far nothing, though. Not even phone calls, except Mrs. McNulty.'

'Yeah, I expect she's in heaven.' Mrs. McNulty called her congressman every week, usually to insist on protection against flying saucers. 'Look, they've got me on a pretty rigorous schedule. Up before the devil's got his shoes on. Physical training, yet! Ugh.'

'You'll be all right. You're in good shape,' Carlotta said.

'I'll be in better in a month. You'll love it —'

'Good. Call me tomorrow.'

'I will. Thanks, Carlotta.'

She smiled as she put the phone down. Thanks, he'd said. Thanks for looking after things, for letting me go to space . . . As long as she'd known Wes, he'd been a space nut. He'd even signed up to be a lunar colonist, and was shocked when she told him she wasn't really interested in living on the Moon. His look had frightened her: he would have gone without her if he'd had the chance.

That chance never came. The U.S. Lunar Base was a tiny affair, never more than six astronauts and currently down to four. The Russians had fifteen people on the Moon – and they made it clear that a larger U.S. effort wouldn't be welcome.

What would they do if the Americans sent more people to the Moon? President Coffey hadn't wanted to find out. Maybe it wouldn't matter now.

Carlotta went back to the papers on Wes Dawson's desk. Aliens might or might not be coming, but if Wes Dawson wanted to remain in Congress, there was a lot of work to finish here in Washington.

CHAPTER SIX
PREPARATIONS

There are periods when the principles of experience need to be modified, when hope and trust and instinct claim a share with prudence in the guidance of affairs, when, in truth, *to dare*, is the highest wisdom.

          – WILLIAM ELLERY CHANNING, *The Union*

COUNTDOWN: H MINUS SIX WEEKS

Academician Pavel Bondarev sat at his massive walnut desk and flicked imaginary dust specks from its gleaming surface. The office was large, as befitted a full member of the Soviet Academy who was also Director of an Institute for Astrophysics. The walls were decorated with photographs taken by the new telescope aboard the Soviet Kosmograd space station. There were spectacular views of Jupiter, as good as those obtained by the American spacecraft; and there were color photographs of nebulae and galaxies, and the endless wonders of the sky.

There was also a portrait of Lenin. Pavel Aleksandrovich Bondarev needed no visit from the local Party officials to remind him of that. Visiting Party officials might know nothing of what the Institute did – but they would certainly notice if there was no picture of Lenin. It might be the only thing a visiting Party official was qualified to notice.

He waited impatiently. Because he was waiting, he was startled when the interphone buzzed.

'Da?'

'He has arrived at the airport,' his secretary said.

'Ah.'

'There are papers to sign —'

'Bring them,' Bondarev said brusquely.

The door opened seconds later. His secretary came in. She carried a sheaf of papers, but she made no move to show them to him.

Lorena was a small woman, with dark flashing eyes. Her ankles were thin. One wrist was encircled by a golden chain which Pavel Bondarev had given her the third time they had slept together. She had been his mistress for ten years, and he could not imagine life without her. To the best of his knowledge, she had no life beyond him. She was the perfect secretary in public, and the perfect mistress in private. It had occurred to him that she genuinely loved him, but that thought was sufficiently frightening that he did not want to deal with it.

Better to think of her as mistress and secretary. Emotional involvement was dangerous.

She came in and closed the door. 'Who is this man?' she demanded. 'Why is Moscow sending an important man who does not give his name? What have you been doing, Pavel Aleksandrovich?'

He frowned slightly. Lately she had begun speaking to him that way even at the office. Never when anyone was around, of course, but it was bad for discipline to allow her to address him in that way inside the Institute. A rebuke came to his tongue, but he swallowed it. She would accept it, yes, but he would be made to pay, tonight, tomorrow night, some evening in her apartment . . .

'It is not a difficulty,' Bondarev said. 'He was expected.'

'Then you know him —'

'No. I meant that someone from Moscow was expected.' He smiled, and she moved closer to him until she was standing beside his chair. Her hand lay on his arm. He covered it with his own. 'There is no difficulty, my lovely one. Calm yourself.'

'If you say so —'

'I do. You recall the telephone call from the Americans in Hawaii? It concerns that.'

'But you will not tell me —'

He laughed. 'I have not told my wife and children.'

She snorted.

'Well, yes. Even so, this is a state secret. It is, it is a matter of state security! Why should I deceive you?'

'What have we to do with state security? How can the state be affected by distant galaxies?' she demanded. 'What have you been doing? Pavel, you must not do this!'

'But what —'

'You wish to go to Moscow!' she said. 'It is your wife. She had never been happy here.' Her voice changed, became more shrill, accented with the bored sophistication of a Muscovite great lady, daughter of a member of the Politburo. 'Yes, the Party found it necessary to send Pavel here for a few years. The provincial people are so inefficient. I suppose we simply must make the sacrifice.'

'I wish you would not mock Marina,' he said. 'And you are wrong. This has nothing to do with a return to Moscow. Besides, when we go back, I will take you with me. All Russians want to live in Moscow.'

'I do not want to go. I want to stay here, with you. Your wife is not so careful here. In Moscow she would be concerned, lest her friends learn her husband has a mistress.'

That was true enough, but it hardly mattered. 'None of this is important,' he said. 'Not now. Things will change soon. Sooner than you know. Great changes, for all of us.'

She frowned. 'You are serious.'

'I have never been more serious.'

'Changes for the better?'

'I do not know.' He stood and took both her hands in his. 'But I promise you there will be changes beyond our power to predict, as profound as the Revolution.'

*　　*　　*

Pavel Bondarev studied the papers he had been given, but from time to time he looked past them at the man who had brought them. Dmitri Parfenovich Grushin, a Lieutenant Colonel in the KGB despite his seeming youth. Grushin wore a suit of soft wool that fit perfectly, obviously made in Paris or London. He was of average height, and slender, but his grip had been very strong, and he walked with an athletic spring to his step.

The papers told him what General Narovchatov had already said. 'I see,' Bondarev said. 'I am to go to Baikonur.'

'Yes, Comrade Academician.' Grushin spoke respectfully. It was difficult to know what the man was thinking. He seemed perfectly in control of his face and his voice.

He brought a letter from General Narovchatov, inviting Marina and the children to Moscow, and enclosing the necessary travel permits. Marina would be pleased. 'There is much unsaid here,' Bondarev said.

'Yes. I can explain,' Grushin said.

'Please.'

'General Narovchatov has become First Secretary of the Party,' Grushin said carefully. He paused long enough to allow the full weight of that to wash across Bondarev. 'This will be announced within the week. The Politburo finds this alien ship a matter of some concern. Many of the marshals of the Soviet Union do not believe in aliens.'

'Then they think —'

'That this is a CIA trick,' Grushin said.

'It cannot be.'

'I believe that. So does Chairman Petrovskiy.'

'And Comrade Trusov?'

Grushin shrugged. 'You will understand that I do not often see the Chairman of the KGB – however, I am informed that the vote of the Defense Council was unanimous, that a civilian scientist should command the preparations for receiving the aliens. You, Comrade.'

'So I was told. I confess I am not especially qualified.'

'Who is? I am trained as a diplomat. Yes – what training is there, to meet with aliens from another star? But we must do what we must do.'

'Then you have been assigned as my deputy?' That would be common enough practice, to have a KGB officer as chief of staff to a project of this importance. Certainly the KGB would insist on having its agents high within the control organization.

'No, another will do that,' Grushin said. 'My orders are to proceed to Kosmograd.'

'Ah. You are a qualified astronaut?'

'No, but I have been a pilot.' Grushin's smile was thin. 'Comrade Academician, I have been ordered by your father-in-law to trust you, to tell you everything I can. This is unusual. Stranger yet, Comrade Trusov himself instructed me to do the same.'

Strange indeed. So. The Politburo *did* take this alien craft seriously. Very seriously. And General Nikolai Narovchatov had said, 'You will trust the man sent by KGB. As much as you trust any man from KGB.' What that could mean was not obvious.

'So,' Bondarev said. 'What is there that I must know?'

'The military,' Grushin said. 'Not all will cooperate, and not all will be under your command. You will need great skills at Baikonur to learn which marshals trust you and which do not. I need not tell you that this will not be easy.'

'No.' It was safe enough to say that much. Not more.

'It is also vital that the Americans do not learn the extent of our mobilization.'

'I see.' I see a great deal. Some of the marshals are out of control. They mobilize their forces regardless of the wishes of the Kremlin. The Americans can never be allowed to know this! 'What else must I know?'

'The crew aboard Kosmograd,' Grushin said. 'Who is there now, and whom we shall invite.'

'Invite —'

'Americans. They have already requested that we allow their people aboard Kosmograd when the alien ship arrives. The Politburo wishes your advice within three days.' He paused. 'I think, though, that they will invite the Americans no matter what you say.'

'Ah. And if the Americans wish this, other nations will also.' He shrugged. 'I do not know how many Kosmograd can accommodate.'

'Nor I, but I will tell you when I arrive there. As I will advise you of the personnel aboard. Of course you will also receive reports from Commander Rogachev.'

'A good man, Rogachev,' Bondarev said.

Grushin's smile was crafty, like a peasant's, although there was little of the peasant about the KGB man. 'Certainly he has a legend about him. But he is not everywhere regarded as you regard him.'

'Why?'

'He is a troublemaker when he feels his mission is in danger. A fanatic about carrying out orders. Make no mistake, technically he is the best commander we have for Kosmograd.'

'But you doubt – doubt what? Surely not his loyalty?'

'Not his loyalty to the Soviet Union.'

'Ah.' There had been an edge to Grushin's voice. Rogachev had not always shown proper deference to the Party . . . 'In what way is he a trouble-maker?'

Grushin shrugged. 'Minor ways. An example. He has aboard Kosmograd his old sergeant, the maintenance crew chief of his helicopter during the Ethiopian conflict. This man lost both legs in the war. When it came time for his sergeant to be rotated back to Earth, Rogachev found excuses to keep him. He said that no better man was available, that it was vital to Kosmograd that this man remain.'

'Was he right?'

Grushin shrugged. 'Again, that is something I will know when I arrive there. Understand, Comrade Academician. I am to be only a Deputy Commander of Kosmograd when I board. Tutsikova will be First Deputy. But I will report directly to you. If there is need, you may remove Rogachev from command.'

Bondarev nodded comprehendingly. Inside he was frightened.

I command this space station, but there are many technical matters. I will not know which are important and which are not. I require advice – but whose advice can I trust? He smiled thinly. That would be the dilemma faced by Chairman Petrovskiy and First Secretary Narovchatov. *It is why I have been given this task.*

It will be a great opportunity, though. At last, Pavel Bondarev thought, at last I can tell them where to aim the space telescope. And be able to see the pictures instantly.

It was a bright clear spring day, with brilliant sunshine, the kind of day that made it worthwhile living through Bellingham's rainy seasons. The snow-crowned peaks of Mount Baker and the Twin Sisters stood magnificently above the foothills to the east. The view was impressive even to a native; it was enough to have Angelenos gawking. They stood near the old Bellingham city hall, a red brick castle complete with towers and Chuckanut granite, and alternately looked out across the bay to the San Juan Islands, then back to the mountains.

When Kevin Shakes saw a uniform coming toward them he wondered if something was wrong. His eyes flicked toward the truck – had he parked in the wrong place? A city kid's reaction. In a small town like Bellingham you could park nearly anywhere you liked.

The uniform was brown, short-sleeved, decorated with badges and a gun belt. The man wearing it was three or four years older than Kevin's eighteen. He was grinning and taking off his hat, showing fine blond hair in a ragged cut. 'Hello, Miranda,' he called. 'Is this the whole clan?'

'All but Dad and Mom.' Miranda was smiling, too. 'Leigh, meet Kevin and Carl and Owen. We were just doing some shopping.'

Carl and Owen – thirteen and eleven, respectively, with identical straight brown hair but a foot's difference in height between them – were looking mistrustfully at the uniformed man, who seemed mainly interested in Miranda. He said, 'Looks like you bought out the store.'

Kevin said, 'Well, maybe Miranda told you, we don't own the ranch all by ourselves. There are three other families, and they each own a fifth, and they're all coming up for a vacation.'

'Won't that be crowded?'

Kevin shrugged. Miranda lost a little of the smile. 'Yeah. We've never done this before. The idea was to take turns, one week out of five, a vacation spot, you know? But it never seems to work out that way. We've lucked out a lot. This time, well, maybe it'll work out. The other families aren't as big as we are. But I don't know them very well.'

Miranda and the cop drifted away, and Kevin let them have their privacy. Later, when they were in the truck, he asked, 'Who is he? How did you meet him?'

'Leigh Young. He was at the club and we played some tennis. He's not very good, but he could be.'

'You like him?'

'Some.'

'I think Dad would approve of your dating a policeman. Useful.'

Miranda smiled. 'It doesn't hurt that he's got good legs, either.'

Kevin looked back to be sure his younger brothers were settled inside the truck with the mounds of groceries before he started the truck. 'Sure going to be crowded.'

'Yeah.'

'Randy, what do you think about all this? Is Dad right?'

She shrugged. 'I didn't used to think so. All our friends

laugh at George, old Super-Survivor. I think Dad used to laugh at him, too.'

'You never know with Dad,' Kevin said. Miranda was only a year older than Kevin, and they'd become good friends as well as brother and sister. They both knew about their father's half smiles.

He also kept their home computers busy analyzing the cost of everything they did. William Adolphus Shakes hadn't wasted a nickel in years.

'. . . Gee, Kevin, there really is an alien spaceship.'

'Yeah. And Mrs. Wilson says it's been hiding for a long time. Claims she was out at some lab when – when something happened. But nobody knew it was the aliens, then. Why would they hide out that long?'

'I don't know.' She opened the glove compartment. 'At least it's pretty here.' Miranda pushed a tape into the player, and the stereo crashed out with the sounds of a new group. 'Glad we have the tapes,' she shouted.

'Yeah.' There sure wasn't anything on radio up here.

William Shakes and Max Rohrs walked back toward the house, across the concrete apron Rohrs had poured last week. It felt dry and solid beneath their feet. Rohrs was a tall, broad-shouldered, muscular man. William Shakes felt like a dwarf beside him, though there wasn't *that* much difference. Rohrs said, 'Looks like we're finished. If it gives you any trouble, you know my number.'

'Yeah. Thanks. I guess I'll be seeing you.'

'I hope so. You're good for business,' Rohrs said. 'The way you've been planting pipe, I wonder if you're planning to open up a hotel.' When Shakes didn't react he said, 'Just kidding.'

'Well, I'm not laughing. It's going to feel like a hotel. We've got three more families coming up. I expect we've finally got enough septic tanks to keep everyone happy, and I know we've got enough beds.'

'That's still a lot of elbows to be taking up your elbow room.'

Shakes nodded. A secretive smile lived just underneath his blank expression. Rohrs had built the septic tank last April. He'd been told that the second septic tank on the other side of the house was too old, too small. It was neither. Rohrs had just finished pouring this concrete apron; but he had no way of knowing that there was a second concrete apron under it, covered with rock and dirt. And under that, a roomy bomb shelter that *nobody* knew about.

William Shakes' smile showed in Max Rohrs' rearview mirror as Rohrs drove away.

Jack and Harriet McCauley had invited them into the Enclave six years ago. The Shakes had known pretty well what they were getting into. Jack and Harriet, and several others, were survivalists, perpetually prepared for the end of civilization. They collected news clippings on Soviet encroachments and economic failures and the national collapse of law and church and patriotism. They were bores on the subject.

Why had they picked on Bill and Gwen Shakes? Was it only because they lived in the neighborhood or because they could afford the expense? Or because they were good listeners and never called the McCauleys fools? In fact neither Bill nor Gwen thought that any man was a fool to prepare for disaster. But disasters couldn't be predicted. The Enclave was preparing for something far too specific. Reality would fool them when it came.

So the Shakes had not jumped at the chance. They had talked around the subject . . . until Bill realized what the Enclave group had in mind.

They joined. They paid their dues, a moderately hefty fee. They bought and maintained equipment as they were told to. Guns and spare food were good to have around anyway. They stored the pamphlets and books and even read some of them, and taught the kids firearms safety. At the Thursday meetings they argued strongly for buying a place of refuge in some near-wilderness area, preferably near some small agricultural village. Ultimately they found such a place, and when the rest of the Enclave agreed, the Shakes had paid 20 percent of the costs.

Bill enjoyed such games. It wasn't as if he were cheating anyone. The Enclave was getting exactly what it had paid for. But Bill and Gwen Shakes now owned a vacation site for a fifth of what it would normally have cost them.

In dollars and cents – and Bill Shakes always thought in dollars and cents – it was more like 30 percent. The place wasn't just being repaired, it was being turned into a refuge, and that cost in time and effort and money. But Bill and Gwen both liked working with their hands, and so did the boys. When they had the leisure they would drive the truck up to Bellingham – Miranda and Kevin were old enough to spell Bill at the wheel —and make order out of chaos, and play at turning the huge, roomy old house into a fortress. It backed onto a wood, with enough grounds for a garden. There was work to do, but also plenty of time out for goofing off and sailing their twenty-five footer in the San Juan Islands, some of the greatest sailing water in the world. By all odds the end of civilization would never come, or would come in some form the Enclave could never predict. Meanwhile the Shakes used the place more often than the rest of the Enclave families put together.

But *this* vacation hadn't been planned.

When Bill got home two evenings ago, Gwen and the kids could talk about nothing but the approaching alien spacecraft. The eleven o'clock news featured fanciful sketches of what an interstellar craft might look like, reminding Bill of equally fanciful cartoons of the late forties: varying designs for a nuclear-powered airplane. *That* one had certainly come to nothing. But this . . .

When the telephone woke him at one in the morning, he had felt no surprise whatever. Gwen had said nothing, only turned on her side to listen while George Tate-Evans ordered the Shakes family to Bellingham.

I don't take orders worth a damn, Bill thought, but he didn't say it. He was already thinking, muzzily, of how his boss would react to Bill's taking a sudden week or two off. Because George was right, and this was what the Enclave was for.

It was still a game, but they were playing for points now. Bill wasn't sure how the kids were taking it. Miranda and Kevin were into the social scene; Carl and Owen were having trouble adjusting to a new school. They should never have been shifted this close to the end of the school year. But they all did their stints working in the vegetable garden and shopping for masses of groceries.

Bill tried not to resent the expense, the disruption. He couldn't take this Star Wars stuff as seriously as the kids . . . or George and Vicki for that matter. Neither did Gwen, although she wasn't so sure. 'Vicki is really worried,' Gwen had said.

'Think of it as a fire drill,' he'd answered. 'Get the bugs out of the system. If something *real* ever happens, we'll know how to do it right.'

At that level it made sense.

———

What Max Rohrs told his wife that night was, 'I think I make Shakes nervous.'

They were in bed, and Evelyn was reading. It wasn't a book that took concentration. She said, 'You said he was little?'

'Yeah.' Max Rohrs was a tall, broad-shouldered, muscular man, blond and hairy. He liked the occasional fight, and some men could see that. 'Bill doesn't quite reach my shoulder. His wife's just his height, and a little wider, and his sons tower over him. Even so, he's hiding something.'

'Bodies?'

She wasn't all that interested, she was just being polite. Max, recognizing this, laughed. 'No, not bodies – but there's too many pipes. Too much plumbing. They keep adding to the septic tanks, and it doesn't look like they'd have to. I think they're survivalists. That house' – he rolled over onto his elbow – 'it's twice as big as it looks. Any angle you see it, it looks L-shaped, but it's an X. Count on it, they've got guns and food stores and a bomb shelter, too. I bet it's under that tennis court I poured them. In some of the big cities there are bookstores just for survivalists.' He frowned. 'They've sure been frantic the past week or so.'

'I heard from Linda today,' Evelyn said.

'Linda? And why are you changing the subject?'

'Gillespie. She's back in Washington. The President sent Ed and Wes Dawson to Houston. They'll train together. Wes Dawson finally gets to space —'

Max felt a twinge of envy. 'That'll be nice.'

'Linda's at Flintridge. Her kid sister – you remember Jenny? – had something to do with discovering the alien ship.'

'Oh. Hey, that's what set Shakes off! Sure, those guys are survivalists.' He knew his wife was smarter than he was, and by a lot. It didn't bother him. What was amazing was that she was so obviously in love with him, and had been since the night they met in Washington. He'd been a sailor on liberty with no place to go, and somebody suggested a social club in a church up near the National Cathedral.

There'd been girls there, lots of them, and all pretty snooty. All except Evelyn and her friends Linda and Carlotta. They were college girls, but they weren't ashamed to be seen with a petty officer —

Maybe it would have been better if she had been snooty, Max thought. *But not for me.*

Three weeks after they met, Evelyn was pregnant. There'd never been any discussion of an abortion. They were married in the church they'd met in, with a wedding reception at Flintridge. It was a nice wedding with a lot of Evelyn's family, and Linda's and Carlotta's families too, important people who talked about Max's future, and jobs he could get. It looked like he'd lucked into a great future.

And when he got out of the Navy he had to come back to Bellingham to look after his mother. Evelyn's father helped a little, enough so that Max could open his own boiler shop, but there was never enough business.

That was almost twenty years ago. He glanced over at his wife. She was reading again. Her fancy nightgown looked a little ratty. *Jeez, I gave her that four years ago! Where does the time go?*

The kids were raising some moderate hell on the other side of the wall, not enough to bother them. Evelyn adjusted her position. The bed sagged on his side. Sometimes that would roll her toward him in the night, before she had quite made up her mind, and that was nice; but it made reading difficult.

She set the book aside and turned off her bed lamp. 'A lot of people say this is survivalist country,' she said. 'But nobody we know talks about it.'

'Yeah. Hey, I'm telling you, but that's as far as it goes. They wouldn't give me any more business if they knew I was shooting my mouth off.'

'All right, dear.'

'The shipyard's been phased out for years, and there's not much work there for steamfitters. The Shakes pay on time —' But Evelyn was asleep.

CHAPTER SEVEN
GREAT EXPECTATIONS

'Tis expectation makes a blessing dear, Heaven were not heaven if we knew what it were.

– SIR JOHN SUCKLING, 'Against Fruition'

COUNTDOWN: H MINUS TWO WEEKS

The bedroom was more than neat; it was spotless. Jack Clybourne's entire apartment was that way – except for the second bedroom, which he used as a den. That one wasn't precisely messy, but he did permit books to remain unshelved for days at a time.

The first time Jenny had visited Jack in his apartment, she'd remarked on its neatness.

He'd laughed. 'Yeah, we get that way in the Service. We have to travel a lot, and stay in hotels, and we never know when the President's schedule will change, so we stay packed. I remember once the maid saw all my stuff packed and the suitcases in the middle of the room, and the manager checked us out and rented the room to someone else.'

Despite the neatness, his bedroom wasn't sterile. There were photographs, of his mother and sister, and of the President. Pictures of the Kremlin, and The Great Wall of China, and other places he'd been. Book club selections filled a tidy shelf along one wall. The shelves were full now, so when new selections came in, old ones went to the used book stores. The residue gave some clues to Clybourne's reading habits: voracious, partial to history, but interested in spy thrillers.

Jenny got up carefully. She didn't think she'd awakened Jack, although it was hard to tell. He slept lightly, and when he woke, he didn't even open his eyes. She teased him about it once, and he laughed, and it wasn't until later that she realized that kind of sleeping habit might be an advantage in his job. The Secret Service did other things besides protect the President.

She retrieved her uniform from the closet. The first time she'd come there, her clothes ended on the floor, but Jack's apartment invited neatness . . . She took her Class As into the bathroom.

The bed was empty when she came out. She could hear the shower in the other bathroom. *He's certainly the most considerate lover I've ever had . . .*

She didn't much care for the word 'lover,' but nothing else fit. He wasn't a fiancé; there'd been no talk at all about marriage. No lieutenants should marry, but male captains could, and by the time they became majors most male officers were married; but marriage would be the end to a woman officer's career.

He was certainly something more than a boyfriend. They didn't live together, partly because both the Army and the Secret Service tended to be a little prudish even if they pretended not to be, and even more because Jenny wasn't ready for all the explanations Aunt Rhonda would demand if she moved out of Flintridge. Even so, she spent a lot of time at Jack's apartment. They both traveled a lot and worked odd hours, but it was definitely understood that when they were both in Washington and had free time, they'd spend it together.

While on trips she'd twice dated other men, but it wasn't the same. Something was missing. *Magic*, she thought, and didn't care to put another name to it. That it existed was enough, and it was wonderful.

'Ready for dinner?' His tie was perfectly knotted, but he'd left his jacket off.

'Sure. Want me to cook?'

'You don't have to —'

'Jack, I like to cook. I don't get a chance very often.'

'All right. We'll have to shop, though. There's nothing here.'

'Sure. I'll get started, and you can go get —'

She stopped because he was shaking his head. 'Let's go together. We can figure out what we want on the way.'

'Sure.' She waited while he put on his jacket. As he always did before going out, he took his revolver out of the holster concealed inside his trousers and looked into the barrel, then checked the loads.

She'd never seen Jack angry, or threaten anyone, but Jenny never worried when she went out with him. The *Post* might be full of stories about Washington street crime, but no one ever bothered Jack Clybourne. Jenny wondered if it could be telepathy.

He lived in the newly rebuilt area off New Jersey Avenue, where there were lots of apartments. It was on the other side of the White House from Flintridge.

She giggled. 'Drive me home, he said. It's on my way, he said.'

'It worked, didn't it?'

She took his hand. 'Yes, and I'm glad.'

'Me, too.'

They went toward Constitution Avenue and the Federal Triangle until they reached the wide parklike Mall between Independence and Constitution Avenues. When they were in the middle of the Mall, he stopped. 'Jenny, what in hell is going on?'

'With what?'

'This alien ship — look, being around the President, I hear a lot of things. I never talk about them. Not even with you, except it's your job too — the President's scared, Jenny. If you don't know that, you'd better.'

'Scared? Jack — Oh, hell, darling. Let's walk.' She led him along the path toward the great granite shape of the National Museum.

He wouldn't talk about this in his apartment. Out here we ought to be safe if we keep our voices down and talk directly to each other. That's silly. No one's listening to us. Still, I shouldn't talk to him about this, but he knows already – 'Jack, what do you mean, scared? I've briefed him a dozen times, and he doesn't act scared with me.'

'Not with you, not with the Admiral,' Jack said. 'But with Mrs. Coffey. He's worried because they don't answer.'

'Well, we all wonder —'

'It's no wonder; he's scared! And I think he thinks the Russians are too.'

'Yeah,' Jenny said. 'Of course we can only guess what they really think.'

'It's true, though, isn't it? Every nut with a transmitter has tried to send them messages, and they don't answer . . .'

'Not just every nut,' Jenny said. 'The National Security Agency, with our biggest transmitters. The Jet Propulsion Laboratory's Deep Space Net, with the big Goldstone antenna. The Russians are doing the same thing.'

'And nothing.' Jack shivered slightly, despite the warm June night. 'Heck, maybe I'm scared too!'

She hesitated, then laughed.

'What?'

'Just thinking. If there's anybody with a higher clearance than a man who'll put his butt between the President and a bullet, I don't know what it is.' There was no one around, but she lowered her voice anyway. 'The Admiral's getting worried too.'

'I guess the Soviets decided to mobilize.'

Jenny chuckled. 'No. That's like an Australian's first reaction to *anything* is to go on strike.'

'Wha-at?'

'Or like the Watergate trials. The lawyers asked one of them, 'Who ordered the cover-up?' And he said, 'Actually, nobody ever suggested there would *not* be a cover-up.'

Unless somebody actually says *stop*, the Soviets will mobilize.'

'Get enough of those weapons, and somebody's likely to use them —'

'Yes. But things look reasonably stable over there. Their theoreticians are saying that any race advanced enough to have star travel would *have* to be economically evolved, meaning the aliens will all be good communists.'

'I wouldn't think that follows.'

'Neither do I. We know for a fact it hasn't helped the Russians communicate with the aliens. That ship isn't talking to anyone.'

'Maybe it's a robot ship.'

She shrugged. 'We don't even have any good theories, and the Admiral wants some.'

'Who has he asked?'

'Who haven't we asked?' Jenny laughed again. 'Anybody we didn't ask has tried to tell us anyway. Out at the Air Force Academy we've got the damnedest collection of anthropologists, historians, political scientists, and other denizens of academia you ever saw. There's even a psychic. But next week we go even further. The Admiral's rounded up a collection of science-fiction writers.'

Jack didn't laugh. 'Actually that might not be such a bad idea.'

'That's what I thought. Anyway, he's done it. Most of them are at the Air Academy, but he's taking a smaller group into Cheyenne Mountain. Guess what? I'm supposed to go out next week and help get them settled in. I don't know how long I'll be.'

'Oh. Okay. But I'll miss you.'

She squeezed his hand, then glanced around. It was dark, and nobody was going to see her behaving in an undignified manner while in uniform, and if they did, the hell with them. She stood on tiptoe and kissed him. He was startled at first; then he held her close and they kissed again.

'We still haven't got dinner,' she said finally.

'No. What do you want?'

'Something we can cook fast.'

He laughed. 'Yeah. There are better things to do than eat.'

―――――

'The Church has always considered the possibility of intelligence other than human,' Cardinal Manelli said. 'Angels are one obvious example.'

'Ah. And of course C. S. Lewis played with aliens,' the Episcopalian bishop added. 'Certainly the Christian churches are interested in this alien ship, but I can't agree that the existence of the aliens refutes Christian revelation.'

Jeri Wilson looked thoughtful. She'd turned on the TV, something she almost never did on Sunday afternoons, and this program had been on. The Roman Catholic cardinal, the Episcopal bishop of California, two Protestant ministers whose faces she recognized, and a history professor from the University of California. Professor Boyd seemed to be acting as moderator, and also as a gadfly intent on irritating the others.

'Lewis points out that the existence of intelligent aliens impacts Christianity only if we assume they are in need of redemption, that redemption must come in the same manner as it was delivered to humanity, and that it has been denied them,' the Episcopal bishop continued. 'I doubt we know any of that just yet.'

'What if they've never heard of Christianity?' Professor Boyd asked. 'If they have no legends of gods, no notion of sin, no thought of redemption?'

'It wouldn't change the facts of *our* revelation,' Cardinal Manelli said. 'The Resurrection took place in our history, and no alien ship will change that. We'll know soon enough. Why speculate? If you want to ask 'what if?' then what if they have both the Old and New Testaments, or documents recognizably related to them?'

That would be interesting, Jeri thought.

'I predict that what we'll find will be ambiguous,' one of the ministers said. 'God doesn't seem to speak unequivocally.'

'Not to you,' Cardinal Manelli said. The others laughed, but Jeri thought some of the laughter was strained.

The doorbell rang. She went to answer it, a little unhappy at missing the program, which was interesting. Melissa raced down the hall and got to the door first.

The man at the door had red hair and beard fading to white. His gut spilled out over the top of his blue jeans. He'd never be able to button his denim jacket. Melissa stepped back involuntarily for a moment. Then she smiled. 'Hi, Harry!'

Jeri didn't encourage Melissa to call adults by their first names, but Harry was an exception. How could you call him Mr. Reddington? 'Hello,' Jeri said. 'What brings you here?' She stepped back to let him in and led him toward the kitchen. 'Beer?'

'Thanks, yes,' Harry said. He took the can eagerly. 'Actually, I was just over to see Ken Dutton, and thought I'd stop by.'

Melissa had gone back to her room. 'Horse crap, Harry,' Jeri said.

He shrugged. 'Okay, I have ulterior motives. Look, they're throwing me out of my apartment —'

'Great Ghu, Harry, you don't expect me to put you up!'

He looked slightly hurt. 'You don't have to be so vigorous about the way you say that.' Then he grinned. 'Naw, I just thought, well, maybe you could put in a word with the Enclave people. I could go up to Washington state any time.'

'Harry, they don't want you.' That hurt him. She could see it. Even so, it had to be said. Harry had done odd jobs for the Tate-Evanses, as well as for the Wilsons, and although he'd never been invited to join the Enclave, he knew about it because David had talked about it with him.

Harry shrugged. 'They don't want Dutton, either. But they do want you.'

'Possibly. I'm not so sure I want them.'

Harry looked puzzled

'I've been thinking of going east. To join David.' *Not yet, he said. But it wasn't no!*

Melissa came in to get a Coke from the refrigerator. 'Is that your motorcycle out there?' she asked.

'Sure,' Harry said.

'Will you take me for a ride?'

'Melissa, you shouldn't bother —'

'Sure,' Harry said.

Jeri frowned. She wasn't worried about Melissa's going with Harry, but – 'Is it safe?'

Harry grinned. 'Safe as houses.' He patted his ample gut. 'If we fall off, I'll see she lands on me.'

He just might do that, Jeri thought. 'Look, Harry, not too fast —'

'Speed limit, and no freeway,' Harry said.

Melissa was dancing around. 'I'll get my jacket,' she said. She dashed out of the kitchen.

'Oh, all right,' Jeri said. 'Harry, do be careful.'

An hour later, Melissa came in the front door.

'Have a good time?' Jeri asked.

'Yeah, until his motorcycle blew up.'

'Blew up!'

'Well, that's what he said. It just died. We were a long way off.'

'How did you get home?'

'Harry asked if you let me take the bus by myself, and when I said sure, he waited at the bus stop with me.' Melissa giggled. 'He had to borrow the bus fare from me so he could get home, too.'

Linda Gillespie drained her margarita and set the empty glass down too hard. When she spoke, her voice was too loud for the dimly lit Mayflower cocktail lounge. 'Dammit, it just isn't fair!'

Carlotta Dawson shrugged. 'Lots of things aren't. At least you had fair warning! You knew you were marrying an astronaut. I thought I'd married a nice lawyer.'

'They could let us go to Houston with them.'

'Speak for yourself,' Carlotta said. 'I've got work to do. Someone has to think about his career, and it's for sure Wes won't now that he's got a chance to go to space. If you're looking for something to do, come help me with the constituent mail.'

'Yeah, sure —'

'I mean it,' Carlotta said. 'Sure, it gives you something to distract you, but seriously, I need the help. It's hard to find intelligent people who know California and live in Washington.'

'I don't blame them.'

'So why don't you go home?'

'We were going to have the house painted anyway, and when the President ordered Ed to Washington we decided to have an extra room put on the attic. The house is a madhouse, crawling with contractors.'

'You could go see Joel.'

'No I can't. That expensive boarding school doesn't *like* having Mommy drop in. Interferes with their routine. Of course if *Ed* wants to come —'

Carlotta smiled. 'Astronauts are always welcome. You knew that when you married him.'

'Yes. And I still love him, too. But it gets damned lonesome sometimes.' Linda signaled the waitress. 'Another round, please.'

'Not me,' Carlotta said. 'Two's more than enough. Linda, be reasonable. Ed and Wes don't have any time at all, that's straight enough. They're living on the base . . .'

'I could stay in a hotel.'

'Be pretty expensive, and he still wouldn't have any time for you.'

Linda nodded. 'I know. But it's still not fair.'

Carlotta chuckled. 'The aliens are coming. Our husbands are intimately involved in making contact with them – and we're sitting here grousing because we're not seeing them in Washington instead of being ignored by them in Houston.'

'You don't like it either —'

'No. I don't. Congress recesses about the time Wes actually goes into orbit, and I'll like that even less – but there's nothing I can do about it.' She stood and fumbled in her purse until she found a five-dollar bill. She put the money on the table. 'I mean it, Linda, I could use some help. Call me at the office?'

'All right.'

'I like your enthusiasm. Well, if you do, I guarantee I'll put you to work. Bye.'

Linda watched Carlotta leave, and turned back to her drink. *I probably should go help Carlotta. It's something to do —*

'Five dollars for your thoughts.'

'Uh –' She looked up at the man standing where Carlotta had been. 'Roger!'

'Yep. Were you thinking about me?' He sat down without waiting to be asked.

'No.' *He still looks pretty good. He must be – what, fifty? That's about right. Good-looking man for fifty. Good-looking for forty, for that matter.* 'After five years? Why should I?'

He chuckled. 'Because you're alone in my town. You ought to have been thinking about me for weeks.'

'That's silly.' *I did think about you, damn you.* 'How do you know I'm not waiting for my husband?'

'Because he's in Houston, sheepdogging the Honorable Wesley Dawson. You were with Carlotta Dawson until a minute ago.' He flashed a grin. 'I passed up a chance to

110

interview her, waiting for you to be alone —'

'And if I'd left with her?'

'I'd have got my interview, of course. Or at least had a chance to talk with the wife of the U.S. Ambassador to Outer Space. Now I have to settle for the chauffeur's wife. How's Ed taking it?'

'Not well . . . I've never seen him so twitchy.'

'He projects that 'Right Stuff' image. Cool and collected, like all the astronauts.'

'That's on TV,' Linda said. 'And usually he really is like that. Now he doesn't know how to feel . . . Well, look at it. That alien ship is the biggest thing since the invention of the lung, Ed's sister-in-law discovers it even, and a congressman steals his mission.'

'You ought to be glad it's Wes. If it wasn't him, it still wouldn't be Ed,' Roger said. 'The Sovs don't want Edmund Gillespie. An American military officer, a general – he outranks Rogachev, for God's sake!'

'Yeah, he knows that, really,' Linda said. 'But it doesn't help that he knows it. Roger, what are you doing here?'

'Trying to seduce you.'

'Roger!'

He shrugged. 'It's true enough. I had a lead on a story, brought her here for a drink, spotted you, and got rid of Ms. Henrietta Crisp of the Business and Professional Women's Alliance. Surprised hell out of her, it did.'

'Well, you might as well go find her again.'

'All right.' He didn't move.

Damn you, Roger Brooks! I should get up and leave right now —

'I've missed you,' he said.

'Sure you have. Three times in fifteen years —'

'Come off it. You weren't about to get divorced, and when Ed's around you don't want to see me across a football field. What was I supposed to do?'

'Yeah.' The old feeling came back, excitement and

anticipation. *Go home now!* That wasn't going to work, though.

What is this? I'm happily married, and every five years Roger Brooks finds me, and I feel like a schoolgirl on her first heavy date. How does he do this to me? 'I guess I've missed you too. Remember that movie *Same Time, Next Year?* It's like that with us.'

'Except we don't see each other so often.' He picked at the scars on his left hand. 'But it doesn't mean I don't think about you.'

'Oh, sure, and next you'll tell me I'm the reason you never married.' *Or have you?*

Roger spread his hands in an exaggerated gesture. 'Dunno. There must be *some* reason.'

'You're too busy chasing stories. That's all you see in me – a news source.'

'Come on, now.'

'Will you promise you won't try to get information from me?'

'Of course not.'

'See? Good. I don't like it when you lie to me. So what do we do now?'

He glanced at his watch. 'A bit early for dinner. What say we take a drive through the Virginia countryside? I know a nice restaurant in Fairfax.'

'And then?'

'Up to you.' Roger stood and came around to hold her chair.

'I've got to be going.' Linda said. She started to push back her chair from Roger's kitchen table, but Roger stood behind her and blocked her way.

He put his hands under the bathrobe. She felt her nipples erect in the warmth of his palms. 'What's the hurry?'

'Stop that – no, don't stop that. Roger, what will I tell Aunt Rhonda?'

'Party at the Thai Embassy. Got late. Some senator

112

from the Appropriations Committee insisted on quizzing you about the space program.'

'But —'

'There really is a big party there, so big that you could have been there and been lost in the crowd.' He bent around her, took her nipple in his mouth.

She thought she was thoroughly satiated, but his tongue reawakened sensations all through her body. Roger had always been a tiger – they'd made love three times that afternoon after JPL, all those years ago . . . 'Are you serious?'

He straightened. 'Possibly not.'

Linda giggled suddenly.

'Certainly not, then,' Roger said. 'What is it?'

'I never did get Nat Reynolds's autograph.'

'Nat – oh. Yeah. Damn, damn, damn. That ship was there all the time we were looking at Saturn. The twisted F-ring. 'Haven't you ever seen three earthworms in love?' 'You've a wicked sense of humor, Darth Vader.' Remember? The drive flame from that thing must have roiled the whole ring system. It settled down before Voyager Two got there.'

Linda stroked his hand, then put it back on her breast. He stood very close to her. 'And even if you'd known, if you'd said anything, they'd have put you away for a nice rest.'

'Ilch. Yes. I might have gone digging. Found some astronomical photographs. *Something*. I didn't know enough science, then. I've done some studying since.'

She grinned and looked up at him without raising her head. 'I hadn't noticed.' *Actually it's not funny. Nothing you could learn, nothing will ever bring back that afternoon. I know that; why do I go on looking?* 'It was a wonderful day, Roger. All of it. All those scientists, and the writers – you've been studying science; are you going to write science fiction?'

'Hadn't intended to. Maybe I should. Most of the SF

113

writers have disappeared.' He wet one finger and traced a complex pattern on her breast.

'What?'

'Well, not all of them. The ones who make up their own science are being interviewed all over the place. The ones who stick to real science are getting hard to find. Know anything about it?'

'Not really.'

He straightened and stepped away from her. 'My God, you *do* know something! What?'

'Roger, I said —'

'Bat shit! I can tell! You know something. Linda, what is it?'

'Well, it's not important. Jenny said something about going to meet the sci-fi people. In Colorado Springs. It wasn't a secret.'

'Colorado Springs. NORAD or the Air Academy?'

'I don't know. Aunt Rhonda would know – she'd have Jenny leave her phone number in Colorado Springs. Speaking of Aunt Rhonda, Roger, I really do have to leave. Now let me get up.'

'Well, all right, if you insist. I'll call you tomorrow.'

Say no. Tell him no . . . 'Fine.'

CHAPTER EIGHT
LAUNCH

What we anticipate seldom occurs; what we least expected generally happens.

— BENJAMIN DISRAELI, *Henrietta Temple*

COUNTDOWN: H MINUS ONE WEEK

The house perched on stilts above a crag in the Los Angeles hills. For years the engineers had worried that it would slide down in a heavy rainstorm, but it never did.

Wes Dawson poked about the storage area built by enclosing the stilts. In a normal house it would have been called a basement.

'It's getting late,' Carlotta called down the stairs.

'I know.' He opened an old trunk. Junk, clutter; memories leapt up at him. Waitaminute, I used to use this a lot . . . the Valentine card she'd handed him one January morning after a fight . . . so *that's* where that went! The huge mug that would hold two full bottles of beer, but the chipped rim kept gashing his lip. A T-shirt faded almost to gray, but he recognized the print on the chest: an American flag with a whirlpool galaxy in the upper left corner. A hundred billion stars . . .

No time! He closed the lid on memories and went up the stairs. The house looked half empty, with anything valuable or breakable packed away.

'Aren't you packed?' she asked. 'I mean, what could you take?'

He grinned. 'Remember my old baseball cap?'

'Good God! Whatever did you —'

'Luck. It won my first campaign. I wore it to JPL for the Saturn encounter, remember?'

She turned away and he followed her. 'I'm sorry you can't come with me.'

'Me too.' She still didn't face him.

'You've got to be used to it. I'm not home a lot of the time —'

'Sure. But you're in Washington. Maybe you don't get home until I'm in bed, but I know you'll be there. Or I have to come here, and you're still there, but we're – Jesus, Wes, I don't *know*. But it feels wrong.' She opened the Thermos pitcher and poured coffee. 'I talked to Linda, and she feels it too, when Ed's not on the Earth. She can tell. Is that silly?'

Telepathy? That could be interesting. And if I say that, she'll blow up.

Wes tried to hide his eagerness to be gone. He couldn't. Before the aliens came, Carlotta really was the most important thing in his life, more important than Congress or anything else, but not now. Not with the Galactic Congress coming in just a few days, and he'd be there to meet them! She had him dead to rights. *You'll be nowhere on the face of the Earth, and you won't be thinking about me.*

The doorbell rang before he had to speak. Thank God, Wes thought. Whoever that is, I love you.

It was Harry Reddington.

''Lo, Harry,' he said. There was no point in asking why Harry was there. He'd find out whether he asked or not. 'Come in, but I warn you' – forefinger prodding the zipper on the lineman's vest, you had to make things *clear* to Harry – 'I've got to go, right now, and Carlotta has to drive me.'

'Sure, Congressman.' Harry used his cane to help him up the steps. 'Hi, Carlotta.'

'Hello.' Carlotta's greeting wasn't enthusiastic.

It had happened several years before. Wes Dawson, two-term Congressman, stuck on the transportation safety subcommittee, interviewing bikers. He'd been young enough and new enough then to go out looking for information, rather than summoning the interested parties to Washington to testify to a committee.

And in a San Bernardino bar, Wes Dawson had let a Hell's Angel get his goat, and took a swing at the bloated barbarian, and was about to get his head stomped in, which would have been bad, and in the newspapers, which would have been worse, when Hairy Red the Minstrel made a joke of the whole affair and hustled Wes out of the bar, and only after they were outside did Harry admit that he was so scared he'd pissed in his pants. Or said he had, which made Wes laugh too.

So I owe Harry one. And he's never really collected. Just used that to keep us polite to him. And hell, I enjoy his company sometimes —

'What brings you here now, Harry?' Carlotta asked.

She hadn't been in that bar. She'd only been told. If she'd felt the vibes in that bar, she'd be more polite to Harry.

'Heard you're going up to meet the ETI's,' Harry said.

'Yeah!'

'Everyone knows that,' Carlotta said.

'I wondered if you needed anybody to keep an eye on things,' Harry said. 'I'm sort of loose just now.'

'No,' Carlotta said firmly. 'Thanks, but *no*.'

Harry must be heavily stuck for a place to sleep. Not only that he was here, but that he was so clean, so *massively* sober . . .

Wes looked around the house. All the valuable stuff was packed and stored. Especially all the breakables. But there were electronics and keepsakes and things he hadn't had time to store away (and somewhere, his baseball cap), and he'd really hate to lose them. There hadn't been time to plan *anything*. And the breakable stuff *was* stored, and

Wes was just feeling so *damned* good. He asked, 'Harry, where are you living just now?'

Carlotta eyed him suspiciously.

'Here and there —'

'Want to stay here?' Wes asked. 'Just for a few weeks. Carlotta's going to Washington and then visiting her family in Kansas, so the place is empty except for the gardener once a week. Wouldn't hurt at all if somebody kept an eye on it.'

Carlotta looked disgusted. 'Harry —'

Harry grinned. He raised his right hand, the way he would in a courtroom. 'No visitors, no friends, no parties. I swear. The kind of people I know, I wouldn't even tell them where I'm staying.'

'That's straight, then,' Wes said. 'Your word of honour on record.'

'Sure,' Harry said.

'Good,' Congressman Dawson said. 'You know, Harry, that works pretty good. I was a little worried, going off – Jesus, except for the Apollo crews, about as far as anybody ever went from his family. I was a little worried about leaving Carlotta. It feels better with you to look after things.' That can't hurt, Wes thought. With Harry, you had to be careful what you said, because he took things too seriously sometimes. But he was pretty smart when he was sober, and dammit, he didn't lie. He'd jump off a cliff before he'd steal from friends.

'Keys,' Harry said. 'And the alarm?'

'Right.' It was getting complicated. Wes looked at Harry and the eager expression, and knew it was already too late. Might as well do it right. 'Keys, alarm system. I'll write you a letter. And there's a drawer in here where we keep a thousand bucks in small bills, for *emergencies*. Only. We'll leave it for you. Kind of tricky to find.'

Carlotta looked at him again, and Wes grinned. She didn't know Harry that well. He'd *never* touch that money if they told him about it. If he found it, rooting around, as

118

he probably would, he might think of some reason why he ought to do something with it to help the Dawsons. Harry had a real knack for rationalization, but he didn't violate direct orders.

'You'll need a letter,' Wes said. 'And maybe a phone number for your friends to call you.'

'I won't give anybody yours,' Harry said.

'*That's* all right,' Carlotta said. 'We change this top number, here, every month or two.' She indicated one of the three telephones. 'Just don't give anyone the *other* number.'

Wes typed up a letter to the police while Carlotta explained the alarm system. She wasn't happy about it. Maybe I'm not happy, Wes thought. But what the hell else could I do? Throw Harry out? Fat chance. And damn, he can be useful, and anyway —

Anyway, it was time to go. Wes looked at the TV, with its continuous stream of garble about ETI's and speculation about what was coming, and grinned. I'll know before they do. Damn straight! He got his suitcases and headed for the downstairs garage, and he'd forgotten about Hairy Red before he got to his car.

———————

'FIVE.' The unemotional voice spoke in his headset. *My God! I've made it!*

'FOUR.' Wes Dawson tried to relax, but that was impossible. The count went on. 'THREE. TWO. ONE. IGNITION. FIRST MOTION. LIFTOFF, WE HAVE LIFTOFF.'

We do indeed. Goddam elephant sitting on my chest. He was vaguely aware that his companions in the Shuttle were cheering. He tried to remember every moment of the experience, but it was no use. Things happened too fast.

'SEPARATION.' The Shuttle roar changed dramatically as the two solid boosters fell free to splash into the

Atlantic Ocean for recovery. They were just worth recovering, according to figures Dawson had seen, although he'd also seen analyses demonstrating that it would be cheaper to make new ones each time – that recovery of the boosters was mostly for public relations value, to demonstrate that NASA was thrifty . . .

His feeling of great weight continued as the Shuttle main engines continued to burn. He'd been told they developed over a hundred horsepower per pound. Wes Dawson tried to imagine that, but the image that came to mind was silly.

He noticed the roar fading, and then the weight easing from his body. Silence and falling. Black sky and the blue-white arc of planet Earth, and Wes Dawson had reached space at last.

Ed Gillespie went out first. Wes waited impatiently while Gillespie helped the Soviet crewmen rig tether lines between the Shuttle and the Soviet Kosmograd space station. The Shuttle was far too large to dock with the Soviet station; at least that was the official reason they'd been given.

Finally the work was done, and it was Dawson's turn in the airlock. Captain John Greeley, Wes's escort and aide, waited behind him to go last. Ed Gillespie would be waiting outside. *Ed must hate this a lot. Greeley and I go aboard Kosmograd. Ed takes the Shuttle home. Enough of that.*

Wes ran through the pressure-suit checklist once more. The small computer-driven display at his chest showed all green, and Wes touched the Airlock Cycle button. He heard a faint whine.

He moved very cautiously. There was nothing out there but vacuum. High school physics classes and the science fiction he'd read in his teens spoke their lessons in his memory: space is unforgiving, even to a powerful and influential congressman. He listened to the dwindling hiss as the airlock emptied; none of it was coming from his million dollars' worth of pressure suit. He'd done it right.

The hiss and whine faded to nothing. Then the airlock display blinked green over red. In the back of his throat was nausea waiting to pounce. His semicircular canals danced to strange rhythms. High school physics be damned: his body knew he was falling. Skydiving wasn't like this. Skydiving, you had the wind; if you waited a few seconds the wind stopped your acceleration, and it was as if you were being buoyed up. Here there was only the oxygen breeze in your face.

The outer door opened and the universe hit him in the face.

The Soviet station was a winged hammer that tumbled as it flew. At one end of the long, long corridor that formed the handle, three cylinders, born as fuel tanks, nestled side by side. The living quarters must have been expanded since the structure was built. There were few windows, and all were tiny. *Not much of a view from in there. Best do my sightseeing while I'm outside.*

Solar-electric panels splayed out around the other end of the corridor. Dawson guessed there was a nuclear plant too, well isolated from the crew quarters. Why else would the joining corridor be so long? Though it would help the Sovs maintain spin-gravity . . .

At the center of rotation, opposite a fourth tank that served as a free-fall laboratory, was the main airlock. A line ran from the airlock to the hovering shuttlecraft. And behind it all, a great blue ball was slowly traversing a deep black sky.

Orbit? Free-fall! He'd done it! But what a strange path he'd traveled.

There was a boy who had wanted to be an astronaut.

A young man had watched that hope dwindle as he matured. Men had landed on the Moon in July of 1969, after eight years of effort. In 1980, a NASA official had stated that 'the United States could not reach the Moon again ten years from now, no matter what the effort.' The space program had been nearly dismantled. The United States had reached the Moon . . . and come back . . . and stopped.

The Soviets, beaten in the Moon race, dropped out; but when the United States rested, the Soviet space program began anew, this time systematically developing capabilities, each new exploit a bit more difficult than the last; none of the spectaculars of the early days, but plenty of solid achievement.

An angry man had grown into politics. Partly through Wes Dawson's efforts, the U.S. space program began again, led by the Shuttle and continuing toward industries in space, but too slowly.

The cold war began again, with all its implications. Editorials in U.S. papers and on television: why challenge the Soviets in space? Nothing was there. Or, alternatively: the Soviets are so strong that they cannot be challenged. Or: why begin an arms race no one can win? A drumfire of editorials, threatening to drown the American space effort.

Then had come a speck in the night sky; and a powerful, determined politician in the best of health now looked across thirty meters of line at a Soviet space station to which he had come as visiting dignitary.

It was a way into space; but he'd have had to be crazy to plan it that way . . .

'Do you feel all right, Congressman?' The Soviet crewman waited outside, clinging to a handhold on the airlock door. He floated easily, his whole posture a statement: for Soviets this is easy. We have the experience to make it easy.

He couldn't see the expression behind the darkened glass of Ed Gillespie's helmet. Gillespie waited.

'I'm fine! Fine!' Wes stayed uncertainly in the airlock. Space was wonderful, but there was so much of it! He felt bouncy, happy; he sounded that way too.

122

'Good.' The cosmonaut pushed into Dawson's glove a device vaguely resembling pliers; the business end was already closed around the line. 'If you will move out of the airlock —'

Wes grasped the line grip and moved out of the airlock door. Ed Gillespie came up beside him. Gillespie said nothing, but Wes was grateful: someone familiar, in this strange and wonderful place . . .

The airlock cycled again, and Greeley emerged. The cosmonaut handed him a line gripper. 'Remember, there is no way to get lost. You need only jump. When you near the airlock, squeeze the handle and friction will slow you.' The Russian's accent was noticeable even through the electronics of the suit radios.

'Fine.' They'd showed him most of it in briefings, but it wasn't the same.

'You're on your own, then,' Ed Gillespie said. 'See you in Houston.' He clapped Wes on the shoulder and climbed into the airlock.

'Right. My regards to Linda.' Wes spoke automatically. He was watching the Soviet cosmonaut. Dawson took a deep breath.

The Russian jumped.

Dawson waited until the Soviet was across before he moved. It took nerve, for a man who was *already* falling. A good jump . . . maybe a bit too hard . . . airlock coming up fast . . . he wasn't slowing at all! Dawson braked too soon, left himself short of the airlock.

Greeley thumped into him from behind. Greeley was massive: an Air Force Captain who had earned his letter in football as a halfback. His cheerful voice was a bit tiny in Wes's earphones. 'No sweat. Sir, if you'll just ease up on the clamps —' Wes relaxed his grip, releasing the line, and let Greeley guide him into the airlock.

Several people waited beyond the airlock. One was a woman in her forties. A legless man floated toward Wes and deftly helped him to remove his helmet. No one spoke.

'Hi!' Wes said.

'Hello.' The woman spoke grudgingly.

The airlock opened, and the Soviet cosmonaut entered. The legless man assisted him in opening his helmet. The cosmonaut grinned. 'Welcome to Kosmograd. I am Rogachev.'

'Ah! Thank you,' Wes said. 'I hadn't expected the commander himself to assist me —'

'I enjoy going outside,' Rogachev said. 'I have all too few opportunities.'

The others seemed friendlier now.

'Allow me to introduce you, but quickly,' Rogachev said. 'When we have removed these suits, you can be more properly welcomed. This is First Deputy Commander Aliana Aleksandrovna Tutsikova. Deputy Commander Dmitri Parfenovich Grushin. Station Engineer Ustinov.'

These three were lined up, Tutsikova closest to Wes. They all looked typically Russian to Dawson's untrained eye. There were three more in the crowded corridor, including the legless man, but Rogachev made no move to introduce them.

It would be difficult to shake hands in zero gravity, and Wes didn't try. The airlock door opened again, to admit Captain Greeley. The legless cosmonaut went to help remove his helmet. Rogachev was already leading the way down the corridor, and Wes had no choice but to follow.

'In here,' Rogachev said. 'Mitya will aid you with your suit. He will then show you where we will await you.' His tone changed. 'Nikolai.'

'I come,' the legless man said, and launched himself after Rogachev.

The compartment Wes was led into was small, but larger than he had expected. It had *some* gravity; hardly enough to notice, but sufficient that objects settled to one deck, and Wes could lie on that deck to allow his suit to be removed.

Mitya did not look like the others. He was small, almost

tiny, and his face was very oriental, almost pure Tatar. He talked constantly as he assisted Dawson in getting out of the pressure suit. Wes couldn't understand a word, although Mitya seemed to understand English.

When they had the pressure suit off, Mitya produced a pair of dark blue coveralls. On the left breast was the name DAWSON, in both Roman and Cyrillic letters. There was also a patch, with the stylized hammer-shaped symbol of Kosmograd. The station's image was marked with a Red Star and the Soviet CCCP.

That's why they said I needn't bring my own clothes. The want me in their uniform. Wes grinned and reached inside his suit. There was a small pouch there. Wes took out a bright U.S. flag pin, and pinned that above the Kosmograd patch. Then he looked directly at Mitya.

The Soviet was grinning. He said something incomprehensible, then waited for Wes to put on the coveralls.

———

Sergeant Ben Mailey was accustomed to shepherding VIPs, but he'd never seen a group quite like this one. Idly he listened to the chatter behind him. They'd put five passengers in a helicopter built for many more. The trip from the Colorado Springs airfield to Cheyenne Mountain wasn't very long. Civilians were talkative anyway, but they rarely tried to compete with the roar of a helicopter motor. These were winning; though half of what they said didn't make sense.

He had his share of tall this trip. Sergeant Mailey tended to notice that. Five feet five, wide and round, he dreaded what he would look like without the Army exercises they made him take. You'd want to roll him down a bowling alley. But three of his passengers were six feet or taller, and two of those were women.

He glanced at the passenger list. That tall man playing tour guide was Curtis, of Hollywood, California. It was

125

easy enough to hear him, even over the helicopter motors. 'That's the Broadmoor Hotel. One of the world's top hotels, and not built because of the Air Force Academy or NORAD or anything else. Remember the old Penrose machine? One of the younger sons got too rough even for that crowd, and they sent him out here about the turn of the century as a remittance man. Had nothing to do, so he built the world's best hotel in the shadow of Pikes Peak.'

Which was interesting. Mailey had never heard that story before. Unfortunately, the guy knew more, and now he was revealing too many of the secrets of Cheyenne Mountain for Mailey's comfort. How the hell did he ever get Inside? Because he'd sure been there.

Not that it mattered. They were all going Inside, and maybe it wouldn't be so easy to get out again . . .

Four of them had come in pairs, but the dark-haired woman had come alone. If you'd put her in *Playboy* – she was that pretty – you'd have had to use the centerfold. She was that tall. When Curtis shut up she said, 'What I meant is, we ought to be the ones to *greet* the aliens!'

'Maybe we will. But, Sherry, Wes Dawson's up there, and he's a science-fiction fan. I mean serious. He was at the first Saturn flyby. You were there. Don't you remember him? Congressional candidate in a baseball cap.'

'No.'

'Well, he was watching the screens instead of making speeches. That any help?'

'I —'

'In the meantime, if you were a government, who would you get to tell you about aliens? Us! I'd like to know who thought of it.'

The silver-haired woman's laugh was a pleasant silvery tinkle. Her husband wasn't in uniform, but from the ID he'd shown Mailey he could have been, although it would make him the oldest lieutenant in the Navy. He had a head like a bullet and a mustache like a razor's edge. The sheet on Mailey's clipboard named them: Robert and Virginia

Anson, Santa Cruz. They looked too old to be part of – whatever was going on here. All Mailey was sure of was that there was a direct order from the President concerning this new advisory group, and Mailey had never seen anything like that before.

They were to report directly to the National Security Council. Not even to General Deighton, who commanded NORAD and had taken up residence Inside.

Anson leaned forward in his chair, and Mailey noticed that the others stopped talking and turned toward him. 'We'll see enough,' he said.

'Sure,' one of the others said. 'Bob, we trust hell out of you, but can't you tell us what we're doing here?'

'Ten minutes.' Anson looked up at Mailey. 'That's about how long it will take to get Inside?'

Mailey nodded. 'Yes, sir.' Another one who'd been in the hole. They had that distinctive way of pronouncing the word. Inside. If you'd been there, you knew.

'Anyway,' Anson said, 'we'll learn as much, and as quickly, as anyone in the United States. Admiral Carrell assured me of that.'

The grins on the others were unmistakable, although some of the wives didn't seem so happy about it.

'Sounds good,' someone said. 'And an audience that wants to be told what to do, and can do it! Who could ask for more?'

Virginia Anson laughed in silver. Robert Anson leaned forward again, and again everyone else fell silent. *I've seen generals get less respect than that*, Mailey thought.

'What have you done with Nat Reynolds?' Anson asked Curtis. 'I thought you two went everywhere together.'

'We have since his divorce,' Curtis said. 'But he's got a convention. In Kansas. Yeah, I thought of that too, but where is he safe?'

He'd be safe Inside, Mailey thought. If there's one safe place in the world, this is it.

The motors changed pitch as the helicopter descended.

Jenny watched the group climb out of the helicopter, and hid her misgivings. She got the passengers loaded into the station wagon for the short drive from the helipad to the entrance.

She'd only been Inside a few times, and it was still an awesome experience. The station wagon drove through doors the size of a house, then on into the mountain —

And on, and on. Eventually it stopped and they entered an elevator that had no difficulty holding all of them, with room for the stationwagon if they'd wanted it.

No one was talking much. People didn't, the first time.

The buildings sat on coil springs as tall as people. Except for the springs, and the granite walls overhead and everywhere, the buildings might have been standard military barracks and offices.

Jenny gave them an hour to get settled. Most of them were in the briefing room in half that time. She waited the full hour. The inside of the conference room was set up like a movie theater, with folding chairs in rows. Army men ushered them to seats, a little warily, as if they didn't quite know what to make of their guests.

The army troopers stood when she came in. So did Robert Anson, although Jenny had the impression that it wasn't the gold leaves he stood for.

They waited while she went to the blackboard.

Then one of them said, 'I suppose you're all wondering why I've asked you here,' and everyone laughed. Which made it a lot easier.

'I suppose you are wondering,' Jenny said. 'Admiral Carrell has assembled an intelligence group to advise the National Security Council. You are part of it.'

'Makes sense. Who else knows about aliens?'

She looked at her seating chart. Curtis. She nodded. 'The first thing is to explain why you are *here*, rather than at the Academy with your colleagues and the anthropology professors. You are the Threat Team. The others will assume the aliens are friendly. Our group will examine the possibility that they will be hostile.'

Everyone looked thoughtful. Then a hand was raised. Jenny consulted her chart again. 'Yes, Ms. Atkinson?'

'Do we have a choice in the assignment?'

'Not now,' Jenny said.

'Too bad.'

'I thought it valuable to have you with us, Sherry,' Anson said. 'The rest of us are paranoid. You are not. It seemed reasonable to have one intelligent but trusting person on this team.'

Sherry Atkinson melted back into her seat.

'I'm afraid things will be a bit hectic,' Jenny said. 'You will have a series of intensive briefings —'

'Is there that much to know about the aliens?'

'Actually, Dr. Curtis, there is very little to know about the aliens. However, you are to be briefed on U.S. and USSR strategic weapons systems. One of the possibilities Admiral Carrell intends to examine is that the aliens make alliance with the Soviets. Against us.'

Academician Pavel Bondarev sat at his desk. His large leather chair was swiveled toward the window, with its view of the Black Sea. The weather outside was pleasant. It was pleasant inside the office as well. His secretary sat on his lap. Slowly she unbuttoned her blouse.

This was far better than he had expected! He had more power and prestige than he had ever imagined possible. To add to his joy, Marina and his grandson had vacationed on the shores of the Black Sea and were now on an airplane to Moscow.

It couldn't last, of course. Soon the aliens would come, and things would change. He could only guess at how they would change.

I may have been the proper man for this task. I know few who could have done it, and of those, two are not reliable . . .

On his desk lay thick reports from the Soviet military leaders. The largest was the report of the Strategic Rocket Command. Bondarev had always known that the Soviet Union possessed thousands of intercontinental nuclear-tipped missiles; now he knew the location and targeting of every one of them.

He also knew their reliability, which was not high. Despite the full alert, nearly a quarter of the missile force was not in readiness, and the generals did not expect more than two thirds of those remaining to launch on the first attempt.

The reports contained information on which missiles could be retargeted and which could not. Of those, some could be aimed at objects in space, and some could be targeted only toward other points on the Earth, because their warheads could not be detonated until after reentry.

He had turned so that he wouldn't have to look at those reports. Could he not keep his mind on Lorena for these few precious moments? But his mind ran on —

He had a large force that could be used to engage the United States, and a small force that could fight an enemy in outer space if that became necessary. It was not possible to estimate what that force could do because they knew nothing of the onrushing alien spacecraft. What defenses did it have? How thick was its hull, and how close would it come to Earth?

All probably unnecessary. They will not attack. But if they do, I have forces to engage them with. Some forces. I should determine more precisely what I have available.

That would not be easy, because it was no simple task to combine the targeting information with the figures on readiness and reliability. The result would only be a probability. *It is well that I am doing this. Few military officers would know how to do the mathematics. Nor would I be able to in time except for —*

He glanced at the table next to his desk. An American IBM home computer stood there. It was an excellent machine, simple to use, and it had come with a number of probability and statistics programs that he had adapted to this purpose.

'You have no need of that machine at this moment,' Lorena said firmly. She took his hand and guided it to her breast.

He had been expecting the telephone, but it startled him anyway. Pavel Bondarev disengaged his hand from within his secretary's blouse. The ringing phone was on a secure line, permanently attached to a scrambler. He had been told that not even the KGB could listen to calls on that line. Pavel didn't believe that, but it was well to act as if he did. He lifted the receiver. 'Academician Bondarev.'

'Narovchatov. The Voice of America announces that the Americans are aboard.'

'I heard. There was no jamming.'

Narovchatov chuckled. 'So long as they do our work, why should we interfere? But it is a good sign. They are not upset by our mobilizations.'

'I trust not,' Bondarev said. 'I have done much to keep such matters under control.'

'You are now satisfied with the preparations?'

'I believe so. Grushin reports that all is well aboard the spacecraft. The Strategic Rocket Forces are alerted, the Fleet is at sea, but the Air Force remains grounded and visible to the American satellites. This was not achieved without cost. Colonel General Akhmanov proved uncooperative, and has been replaced by General Tretyak. The transfer of power was accomplished without incident, and Akhmanov has been promoted to the General Inspectorate of the Ministry of Defense.'

'Um. You are becoming accustomed to military authority. Perhaps I should have you appointed a general.'

'That could do no harm,' Bondarev said. *Generals have enormous perquisites* . . . 'Meanwhile, I receive reports

131

from both Grushin and Rogachev, and there are no contradictions. Nikolai Nikolayevich, I believe we have done everything possible.'

'All we know to do. Why, then, do I worry?'

Bondarev grinned mirthlessly. 'We have nothing to guide us here. No history and no theory.'

'Da.' There was a pause, as if Narovchatov were thinking. Then the general said, 'From tomorrow on, this line will be connected directly to the Chairman. You will use it to keep us informed.'

'Certainly.' *It would be useless to ask where you and the Chairman will be.* 'Perhaps Marina and the children could visit you?'

'That has been arranged.'

'Then no more remains to be said.' Bondarev put the telephone down and stared out the window.

'You are frightened,' Lorena said.

'Yes.'

CHAPTER NINE
ANTICIPATIONS

Space *will* be colonized – although possibly not by us. If we lose our nerve, there are plenty of other people on this planet. The construction crews may speak Chinese or Russian – Swahili or Portuguese. It does not take 'good old American know-how' to build a city in space. The laws of physics work just as well for others as they do for us.

– ROBERT A. HEINLEIN

COUNTDOWN: H MINUS TWO DAYS

The meeting was called for 0900, but they were still straggling in at a quarter past. Some had hangovers. All had stayed up too late.

Too bad, Jenny thought. *They'll have to get used to military hours*. She had a strong urge to giggle. Suppose they didn't? Maybe they'd make Cheyenne Mountain adapt to the hours science-fiction writers kept . . .

They took their places in the lecture room, but they tended to sit for a moment, then get up and gather in clumps. Most of them talked at once. Working with the science-fiction people was an educational experience. They had no reverence for anything or anyone, except possibly for Mr. Anson, and they argued with him; they just didn't call him names.

They'd spent the past days learning about U.S. and Soviet weapons. Now it was time to examine what was known about the aliens.

Not that there's anything to know. Our best photos don't show details. Just that it's damned big.

One of the men, the one with the heavy mustache, began before she could. 'Major Crichton, I assume that the government has been no more successful in communicating with the aliens than all the private attempts were?'

'Correct. We've tried every means of communication we can think of.'

'And a few no one would have thought of,' Sherry Atkinson added. They all laughed, remembering that the mayor of San Diego had persuaded the citizens of his city to blink their lights on and off while they were in the alien ship's view.

'With no result,' Jenny said. 'Our best prediction is that the alien ship will arrive day after tomorrow. *Sometime* day after tomorrow. We can't predict it closer than that, because the ship has begun random acceleration and deceleration.'

'As if it didn't want us to know the precise ETA,' Curtis said.

'ETA?' Atkinson asked.

'Estimated Time of Arrival,' Jenny said. 'And yes, we've thought of that.'

'It might be their engines aren't working properly.' Atkinson looked thoughtful. 'Or that the concepts of time and regularity don't mean much to them.'

'Bat puckey,' Curtis said. 'If they're space travelers, they *have* to have clocks.'

'Doesn't mean they use them,' someone said.

Jenny spoke through rising voices. 'Lieutenant Sherrad will review what we know.' The chatter stopped.

Sherrad was a Regular Navy man hoping for his bad foot to heal so that he could go back to sea. Jenny wasn't quite sure how he'd been assigned to Colorado Springs, but she did know the Admiral thought well of him. His father had been a classmate. The Navy seemed to have even more of that sort of thing than the Army . . .

He ran new blowups of films taken by the Mauna Kea telescopes as far back as the late 1970s. A few showed a flickering star that must have been the alien ship, although at the time no one had realized it.

Sherrad showed each film in sequence. Then again. He brought the lights up and waited, as if teasing the audience.

'Son of a bitch.'

'What, Joe?'

'It dropped something.'

Sherrad nodded. 'It does look that way.'

It took me four hours to see that, Jenny thought. Maybe there is a good reason to have these birds here —

'Our best guess is that it came from the general direction of Centaurus, dropped something heavy, rounded the sun, and went to Saturn,' Lieutenant Sherrad said. 'Decelerating all the way.'

'They knew where they were going, then.'

'Well, Dr. Curtis, it does seem so.'

Jenny nodded approval. Sherrad had memorized the doctorates.

Voices arose from one of the clumps. 'Okay, they refueled at Saturn —'

'Why not Jupiter?'

'It takes less delta-V to slow down for Saturn. Jesus, but they must have been going on the last teacup of fuel for that to matter!'

'Jupiter could have been around on the other side —'

'Could we see it again?' Anson asked.

Sherrad waited until they were quiet. 'Certainly. We also have the computer simulation.'

The room darkened again.

Black dots speckled a white field: a negative of the night sky. Astronomers generally preferred to use negatives; it was easier to see the spots that were stars. The scene jumped minutely every few seconds. The stars stayed where they were – the photographs had been superimposed – but one dot jumped too, and grew larger.

135

'These were taken from Mauna Kea Observatory. Notice the point that jumps. When we realized what we had, we made some graphs —'

The first showed a curve across the star background, not very informative.

'– and this is what it would look like from above the Sun's north pole.'

Three faintly curved lines radiated from a central point. Near that point, the sun, they were dotted lines – of course, no camera would have seen anything then – and they almost brushed the solar rim. The Navy man's light-pointer traced the incoming line. 'It came in at several hundred miles per second,' he said, 'decelerating all the way. Of course the Intruder wasn't seen near the sun, and nobody was even looking for it then. This —' The light-pointer traced a line outward. 'We have only three photos of it, and of course they could be artifacts, garbage. If they're real, then this one wasn't under power when it left the sun. It was dropped.' The third line ran nearly parallel to the second, then curved away. '*This* section was under power, and decelerating at around two gravities, with fluctuations. We've got five photos, and then it's lost, but it might well have been on its way to Saturn.'

'Not good,' said a voice in the dark.

The lights came on. The Navy man said, 'Who said that?'

'Joe Ransom.' He had a gaudy mustache and the air of self-assurance the SF writers all seemed to share. 'Look: they dropped something to save fuel. Could have been a fuel tank —'

'I'd think it was a Bussard ramjet,' someone interrupted.

Ransom waved it away. 'It almost doesn't matter. They dropped something they needed to get here. They probably planned to. Odds are they didn't take enough fuel to stop inside the solar system without dropping – well, *something* massive, something they didn't need any more, something that served its purpose once it got them from Alpha Centauri or wherever. If —'

Burnham jumped on it. 'A Bussard ramjet wouldn't be any use inside the solar system. You need a thousand kilometers per second to intercept enough fuel – or there are some alternate versions, but you still —'

Ransom rode him down. 'We *can't* figure out what it was yet and we *don't care*. They used it to cross, and then they *dropped* it. Either they figure to make someone build them another one, or they're not going home. You see the problem?'

Something icy congealed in Jenny's guts. *They don't expect to go home. Maybe a Threat Team isn't such a bad idea. I'll have to call the Admiral.*

Meanwhile, the meeting was degenerating into isolated clumps of conversation. Jenny spoke up to resume control. 'Enough!' The noise dropped by half. 'Mr. Ransom, you said Alpha Centauri. Why?'

'Just a shot in the dark. It's the three closest stars in the sky, and two of them are yellow dwarfs, stars very like ours.'

'Stars?'

'Yes. What we call Alpha Centauri, meaning the brightest star in the Centaur constellation, is really three stars: two yellow ones pretty close together, and one wretched red dwarf.'

'Our own sun's a yellow dwarf,' Curtis said.

'Interesting,' Lieutenant Sherrad said. 'Our astronomers say the object came from the Centaur region. Is Alpha Centauri really a good prospect?'

The meeting came apart again. This time Jenny let it ride for a bit. Her patience was rewarded when Curtis bellowed, 'May I have a consensus? Who likes Alpha Centauri?'

Two hands went up.

'Who hates it?'

Three hands. And three undecided.

'Sherry? Why don't you like Alpha Centauri?'

'Wade, you know how many other choices there are! There are almost a dozen yellow dwarf stars near us, and

137

we don't know they came from that kind of star anyway!'

'Bob? You like it.'

The wide white-haired man with the gaudy vest laughed and said, 'I didn't at first. It's trite. But, you know, it's trite because it got used so much, and it got used so much because it's the best choice. Why wouldn't they go looking for the closest star that's like their own? And, Sherry, there aren't many yellow stars in that direction. That clump centers around Procyon and Tau Ceti and —'

'That's what I was getting at,' Dr. Curtis said. 'It's trite. As I see it, the way to bet is that they came from Alpha Centauri, or else they came a hell of a long distance. And if they dropped half their ship – you see?'

Burnham said, 'It'd be their first trip. They won't be very good at talking to us. Chances are they'll want to watch us from high orbit.'

'Maybe it's good the Soviets can't go after them. They might run.'

'It still isn't good. We should have met them around Saturn, just to get a little more respect —'

'Could have had a hotel on Titan by now —'

'Proxmire —'

They were at it again. Out of the babble she heard Curtis say, 'One thing's sure. They came from a long way off. So the next question is, what do they want?'

———

Rogachev's office was roomy enough, by station standards. Much of its furniture looked like afterthoughts: the hot plate, the curved sofa that had replaced a standard air mattress; even the window, shuttled from Earth and welded into a hole sawn in the hull: a thick-walled box, two panes of glass sandwiching a goop that would foam and harden in near vacuum. But it let light through, so that Station Commander Arvid Pavlovich Rogachev could see the stars.

They flowed past, left to right, while Arvid mixed powdered tea with boiling water in a plastic bag. The station was equipped for free-fall, in case of emergencies. He served the tea into two cups, and passed one to his second in command.

'The station will house twelve,' Arvid said. 'Twelve are aboard. Four are foreign observers. No more important event has occurred aboard any spacecraft, and it will happen while Kosmograd is both crowded and short-handed.'

'Not quite so bad as all that,' said Aliana Aleksandrovna Tutsikova. 'Recall that there's nothing to be *done* about the alien ship. We don't have to go to meet them; we don't even have a motor.'

'Neither drive nor weapons. We could not flee either.'

'Exactly. It will come. We are privileged to watch. I suggest that we are doing fairly well.'

'Perhaps we are.' Arvid smiled. 'It helps that our guests cannot talk to each other well.'

'Their dossiers said that.'

Arvid didn't entirely trust any dossier, but Aliana knew that. He said, 'I've watched them exercising their language deficiencies.'

'Do you see a security problem?'

'From them? No. It is my habit to make threat estimates. Shall we? As a game?'

'My mother would call it gossip.'

'Let us gossip, then. Which of our guests do you find interesting?'

'The Nigerian. He's the blackest man I've ever seen. I actually have trouble looking him in the face.'

'Really? What will you do when aliens are aboard?'

'Perhaps I'll hide in your office.' She lost her smile. 'Comrade Commander, I have an irrational fear of spiders and insects.'

'Then we must hope that our approaching guests will be neither.' But they will not be shaped like men, Arvid thought; and Aliana could not even see all men as *men*.

She would be of little help to him if aliens came aboard. He had not suspected this weakness in her. It was well he'd learned it now.

She said, 'The Nigerian speaks English and three native languages . . . which must make him effectively retarded. There are forty-three languages active within the borders of Nigeria. Educated in England, then Patrice Lumumba University in Moscow, but he learned little Russian. He favors economic independence for Nigeria.'

'We won't cure that here. He spends all his time with Dmitri Parfenovich and Wes Dawson. That would be good, except that Dmitri has been trying to convert *Dawson* to his own views, whereas Dawson sometimes takes the time to try to tell Giorge what's going on. Dawson is good at explaining complex matters.'

'Could you have a word with Dmitri?'

Arvid laughed. 'Do you want me to tell our Political Commissar how to convert the heathen? Aliana, I do not seek converts.'

She laughed. Officially, Dmitri Grushin was Deputy Commander and Information Officer for the station, but he was so little qualified for either job that his KGB origins showed clearly.'We may find ourselves seeking converts among people with nightmare shapes,' Aliana said. 'If so, Dawson is the one to watch. Nigeria and France would be no threat to us.'

'His nation made a good choice there, I think. The Honorable Wes Dawson is frantic to meet aliens.'

'Wasn't it politics that —'

Rogachev shrugged. 'Certainly his dossier suggests that he forced himself aboard. Even so, although I know little of American politics, I would not think a mere congressman could force the American President too far in a direction he did not wish to go.'

Aliana grinned. 'Dawson is more qualified than Dmitri. Surely they have similar positions?'

Rogachev shrugged. 'I do not think so, but it hardly matters.'

'Dawson's dossier calls him politically liberal.'

'A lazy agent wrote that. "Politically liberal" – he copied that out of some newspaper! Dawson has invariably favored the American space program.' Rogachev's face twisted into a look he didn't show to many people: a distinctly guilty grin. 'I have closely watched the Honorable Wes Dawson. He has been sick with envy since he came aboard. He does not even care much for the design. Indeed, he knows *precisely* how he would rebuild the station if it were his. But as it is not, it is killing him!'

Aliana smiled back. 'If we had the funding, wouldn't we make improvements too? Very well. Dr. Beaumont has been a French communist for two decades. We can count her an ally. She has a kind of beauty, wouldn't you say?'

'Classic and severe, but yes.'

'Have you made advances?'

Arvid laughed. 'She would not be interested. A man can tell before he commits himself. Perhaps I have grown too fat. She speaks little English. I have taken opportunities to put her together with Dawson, to see what would happen.'

'And?'

'Oh, he shows some interest . . . but Captain Greeley and Giselle Beaumont have spent much more time together. Aliana, I find that odd.'

She nodded comprehension. 'Captain John Greeley, USAF. A good-looking man, three years younger than the French doctor . . . but fourteen years younger than, for example, me. Greeley probably considers Dawson a step in his career, which might end in public relations or political campaign management. Yet he seems to be trying to share a bed with the Frenchwoman. Dawson might find her attractive as well. Greeley is competing with a man who could help or hurt him.'

He shrugged. 'Some men have little control over their gonads.'

'What would you do? I hardly have to ask, do I, Arvid? You would help your superior seduce the woman, and thereby advance your career.'

'I no longer must resort to such tactics. Yet I would have said that Greeley does.'

'Greeley knows Dawson better than we do. Dawson may be homosexual —'

'It would be in his dossier. Even if the Americans do not know, the KGB would.'

'Then again, some married people are more thoroughly married than others.' That was a dig, but meant in friendly fashion. Arvid found Aliana's position perfectly reasonable. With a husband and a child on Earth, and a career to manage as well, her life was easily complex enough without adding a lover.

Arvid poured more tea for them from the plastic bag. (Oh, yes, he would make changes here if he had the funding. Powdered tea! A samovar wouldn't occupy *that* much room.) 'I enjoy gossiping with you, Aliana.'

'We are also discussing security, are we not?'

'Perhaps. Security isn't my department either. Decisions have already been made, and not by me. My own inclination would be to bar *any* tourists from the station during this crucial time. But the Chairman favors world opinion these days —'

'I generally find that reassuring.'

'Too often it precedes an invasion. Not this time, perhaps. Mother Russia is about to greet the first visitors from interstellar space. They will come here first; intelligent creatures would not leave potential enemies above them when they land. And that coup will make the U.S. landings on the Moon look like a child reciting for his elders.'

'Must we have visitors to watch our triumph? It could be filmed.'

'We can guess at a second purpose. When the aliens arrive we will seem to represent the world . . . It doesn't

142

matter. Security is out of my hands. I can forbid our foreign visitors to enter parts of the station. I can forbid the crew to discuss technical matters. Information may leak through anyway; it usually does. But the blame will not fall on Arvid Rogachev.'

The little truck groaned up Coldwater Canyon. Harry clutched his twelve-string guitar and shivered in the windwake behind the cab. It was cold for May in Los Angeles. Lately all the nights had been cold. Cold or not, it beat walking. It was nice of Arline to duck her old man and come pick him up. Too damn bad she had five other people with her, so he had to ride in the back.

It had been a good evening in the Sunset Bar, where he played for free drinks and customer change. Once Harry had thought he'd be a real performer, but the auto wrecks had finished that. Twice within two weeks, in his own car and then his boss's borrowed car, and neither had head rests. It went beyond bad luck. His head hurt, and his back hurt, and he cursed the two separate sets of sons of bitches who'd separately rear-ended him and left him part crippled. And the insurance compa 'es and their goddam lawyers and —

Ruby moved over to sit against him. A hundred and eighty pounds of fleshy cushion: her warmth felt good. 'Want to come to my place?' she asked.

'Love to,' Harry said. *And I don't like to sleep alone.* 'But you know, I have this place I have to watch.'

'Take me with you, then.'

'Can't do that, either,' Harry said. He didn't want to. Ruby had been a nice, soft, affectionate partner, and not just in bed, ten years ago. Naive but nice. Maybe he'd been expecting her to grow up. God, how she'd changed! She'd grown out: forty pounds, maybe more. She'd been soft, then, but she hadn't sagged! You noticed the lack of brains more now. Arline, now she'd be nice, but Jesus, she lives with her old man and he'd get sticky as hell.

For a moment Harry thought it over. Arline would come with him. She'd *love* the Dawson house. And —

And *word of honor on record*. Heckfire. The truck was passing Laurel Canyon on Mulholland. He tapped on the glass. The pickup pulled over. Harry climbed out. He waved to Arline. 'Thanks,' he called.

'Sure this is all right?' she asked.

'Fine,' Harry said. He waited until she'd driven on up the hill and around a corner, then started climbing toward the Dawson house.

It's good for me, Harry thought. It's *got* to be. And, by damn, my legs *are* tightening up. He slapped his thigh – it *did* feel more solid than it had in a long time – and shifted the guitar from his left hand to his right.

The little .25-caliber Beretta was too heavy in his shirt pocket. He knew he ought to leave it at home. It wasn't much of a gun, and even so, the cops would get soggy and hard to light if they caught him with it. But it was all the gun he had, and there were some bad people out there.

Not the only gun, he thought. He'd rooted around in the Dawson house – hell, Wes *knew* he'd do that, that's why he told him about the money in the drawer behind the big drawer in the kitchen – and he'd found the Army .45, the one Wes bought for Carlotta on Harry's advice, and damn all, she hadn't taken it with her. But it wasn't his gun, and Harry couldn't carry it. It would really hit the fan if he was caught carrying a piece registered to a congressman.

Hell, he'd never carry that weight up this hill! It was always steeper. Every fucking night it got steeper.

It's good for me. It's really good for me. Oh, my, God, I have *got* to get that motorcycle fixed.

I've got enough for a deposit. They'll fix the engine. Maybe if I sing at three places, the hell with the free drinks, get to places where the tips are good, I can scrape up enough to get it out, because I can't go on climbing this hill!

And there's groceries. Jesus, I'm down to chili and cornmeal and NutriSystems —'

For the first week it had been easy. There had been food in the refrigerator. He ate vegetable omelets, then frozen stuff, then cans. But now he was down to the NutriSystem stuff Carlotta had bought years ago.

Diet stuff! Lord God. It tastes better than it ought to, and I could lose some belly, here. But opening the cans feels like opening cat food, *looks* like opening cat-food cans, and Carlotta went off the diet two years ago! Fry it with eggs, and it looks like cat food and snot! And I'm out of eggs.

He shifted the guitar to his other hand. Nothing left but breakfast cereal! I'm going to get that engine fixed.

Tomorrow, Harry thought. He shifted the guitar again. I can take the Kawasaki apart, but the engine has to be rebuilt. I'll have to carry it in. Borrow Arline's pickup again.

If you pulled a drawer in the Dawson kitchen all the way out, there was another drawer behind it, and a thousand dollars in fifties behind that. A good burglar would find it and go away, Harry thought, and that was probably its major purpose. Burglar bait, for God's sake, and thank God he didn't need it. He had enough for the deposit.

—————

Jenny stood quickly as Admiral Carrell came into her tiny office in the White House basement.

'Sit down,' he commanded. 'I'm just old enough to feel uncomfortable when ladies stand up for me. Got any coffee?'

'Yes, sir.' She took cups from her desk drawer and poured from a Thermos pitcher.

'Pretty good. Not up to Navy standards, of course. Navy coffee will peel paint. Did we get anything out of that zoo?'

145

'Yes, sir,' Jenny said.

'You sound surprised.'

'Admiral, I was surprised. I thought the exercise was a waste of time, but once those sci-fi types got going, it was pretty good.' She opened a folder that lay atop her desk. 'This, for instance. When the alien ship came into the solar system almost fifteen years ago, a few telescopes including Mauna Kea happened to be pointed that way. No one noticed anything then, but when we really looked – ' She showed the photographs.

'Look like blobs to me.'

'Yes, sir. They looked like blobs to all of us. Maybe they are blobs. But the sci-fi people suggested that the alien ship dropped a Bussard ramjet.'

'A —'

'Bussard ramjet, Admiral.' She looked down at her notes and read. 'Vacuum isn't empty. There's hydrogen between the stars. The ramjet is a device for using the interstellar hydrogen as a means for propulsion. In theory it will take ships – *large* ships – between the stars. It uses large magnetic fields for scoops, and —'

'You may spare me the technical details.'

'Yes, sir. The important point is that they dropped something massive, something they may need if they contemplate leaving our solar system.'

'Which means they intend to stay,' Admiral Carrell said mildly.

'Yes, sir —'

'Rather presumes on our hospitality. Almost as if they didn't intend us any free choice.' He stood. 'Well, we will know soon enough.'

'Yes, sir.'

'My congratulations on your work with the advisors. Perhaps I can glean more speculations from them.'

'You're going to work with them, sir?'

'I may as well. The President has decided that someone

responsible must be inside Cheyenne Mountain when the aliens arrive. That someone, apparently, is to be me.'

'Good choice,' Jenny said.

Carrell smiled thinly. 'I suppose so.'

'Any special preparations I should make, sir?'

'Nothing that isn't in the briefing book. I've discussed this with the Strategic Air Command and the Chief of Naval Operations. They're ordering a Yellow Alert starting tomorrow afternoon.'

Yellow Alert. The A Teams on duty in the missile silos. All the missile subs at sea. Bombers on ready alert, fueled, bombs aboard, with crews in quarters by the runways. 'I do hope this is a waste of time.'

Admiral Carrell nodded agreement. 'So do I, Major. Needed or not, I leave this afternoon. Before I do, we must discuss this with the President. I give you one hour to reduce all we know to a ten-minute briefing.'

Jeri Wilson piled the last of the gear into the station wagon and slammed the tailgate. Then she leaned against it to catch her breath. It was warm out, with bright sun overhead, but the morning low haze hid the mountains ringing the San Fernando Valley. She glanced at her watch. 'Eleven, and I'm ready to go,' she announced.

Isadore Leiber eyed the aged Buick's sagging springs. 'You'll never make it,' he announced. Clara nodded agreement.

'Good roads all the way,' Jeri said. 'I've left enough time so I won't have to drive too fast. You're the ones who are cutting it close; you have farther to go.'

'Yeah,' Isadore said. 'Jeri, change your mind! Come with us.'

'No. I am going to find my husband.'

Clara looked uncomfortable. 'Jeri, he's not really —.

'He damned well is, that divorce isn't final. Anyway,

147

it's not your problem. It's mine. Thanks for worrying about me, but I can take care of myself.'

'I doubt it,' Isadore said with embarrassed brutality.

Melissa came out with a large bear named Mr. Pruett. *Thank God there weren't any animals*, Jeri thought. *Except the goldfish*. She'd taken care of that problem by flushing the fish down the toilet while Melissa was asleep.

Isadore showed her an entry in his notebook. 'That's the right address and phone number?'

She nodded.

'Caddoa, Colorado,' Isadore said. 'I never heard of the place.'

Jeri shrugged. 'Me either. David thinks they're crazy, but somebody thinks he can find oil there.'

'Sounds small.'

'I guess it is. Harry marked out a route for me —'

'Harry's all right,' Jeri said. 'Anyway, I went to the Auto Club too. They say the roads are good all the way. Isadore, Clara, it's sweet of you to worry, but you've done enough. Now get out of here before George and Vicki get mad at you.'

'Yeah,' Isadore said. 'I sure would hate it if George got mad at me . . .'

'You would, though,' Jeri said. 'Give the Enclave my best. Melissa, get in the car. We're on our way. Clara, from your look you'd think you weren't ever going to see me again!'

'Sorry.' Clara tried to laugh, but she wasn't doing a very good job of it.

'Do you know something?' Jeri demanded.

'A little,' Isadore said. He sounded reluctant to talk, but finally added, 'George caught something on short wave. All the strategic forces are on alert. Also, there's some kind of problem in Russia, he thinks. I'm not sure what.'

'George is always hearing about problems in Russia,' Jeri said.

148

'Yeah, but he's been right, too. Remember how he predicted that shakeup —'

Jeri shrugged. 'Too late to worry about it.' She got into the station wagon and started the engine. 'Thanks again,' she called as she pulled away from the curb.

The Buick was sluggish, and she wondered if she really had loaded it too heavily. It was an old car, and for the past year it had been pretty badly neglected. *I ought to have new springs put in. And have the brakes looked at, and a tune-up, and - and no! If I wait, I may never go at all.*

He didn't say no. He couldn't quite get himself to say yes, but he didn't say no. And that's enough for me! 'Melissa, buckle up. We're got a long ride ahead.'

PART TWO

Arrival

CHAPTER TEN
THE ARRIVAL

Why meet we on the bridge of Time to exchange one greeting and to part?

— THE KASIDAH OF HAJI ABDU EL-YAZDI

COUNTDOWN: H HOUR

The Army had been at work in the Oval Office. Technicians had installed TV monitors in all the corners, as well as in front of the President's desk. They showed the command center of the Soviet Kosmograd satellite. At the moment nothing was happening.

Despite its large size, the Oval Office was jammed. There was the President and Mrs. Coffey, most of the Cabinet, the White House staff, diplomats, TV crew —

Jenny sat well back, behind the TV cameras, nearly in the corner. In theory she was there as Admiral Carrell's representative, ready to advise the President, but there was no way she could have spoken to him if he'd wanted her to, not in this zoo. Everyone wandered about – everyone but the Secret Service men.

It was easy to spot them, once you knew how. They were the ones who never looked at the President. They watched the people who were watching him. Jenny caught Jack Clybourne's eye and winked. He didn't respond. He never did when he was on duty.

He didn't look happy. Jenny had overheard an argument between Jack's boss and the President. 'Mr. Dimming, I appreciate your concern, but I have told the country I would watch from the Oval Office, and by God that's where I'll be, so there's an end to it,' President Coffey had said.

Selected newspeople were invited, which meant the Secret Service people as well. They knew them all, reporters and camera crew, and Jack looked as relaxed as he ever did when on duty, but Jenny could see that he was worried. They had wanted the President in a bomb shelter.

But we're here, Jenny thought. *Here and waiting, in the most famous office in the world, but we're only spectators. It's the Soviets' show.* All the computer projections showed the alien craft arriving at Kosmograd. Only the time was uncertain.

She glanced at her watch. It was very late, well past midnight. The aliens were due and past due. Coffee service was available in the hall outside, but someone would probably take her chair if she went out. Better to wait —

The television monitors blanked momentarily, then showed the dark of space. In the far distance something flickered and flashed.

Heretofore the telescopes on Earth and in Earth orbit had seen only a long, pure blue-white light and the murky shadow at its tip. Now, as the tremendous half-seen mass approached Kosmograd, something changed. Twinkling lights flashed in a ring around the central flame, round and round, chasing their tails like light bulbs in a bar sign.

The communications lounge was crowded. Eight present, four crew busy elsewhere. Wes watched the picture being beamed from the telescope to a screen half the size of the wall. The ship was minutes away. Wes tried not to think what would happen if it came a bit too fast. It was decelerating hard. Those extra engines hadn't been needed until now. Sixty or seventy tiny engines —

Symmetrical. Sixteen to a quadrant. Wes Dawson

grinned in delight. Sixty-four engines: the aliens used base-eight arithmetic!

Or base four, or binary digits . . . engines much smaller than the main engine, and probably less efficient. Fission or fusion pulse engines, judging by the radiation they were putting out. Why hadn't the alien slowed earlier?

It still hadn't replied to any message.

It had grown gigantic in the telescope field. A blaze of light washed out the aft end: Wes saw only the long flame and the ring of twinkling jets. He made out bulges around the cylindrical midsection. He saw tiny fins and guessed at landing craft spaced out around the hull. A knob on the end of a long, jointed arm: what was that, a cluster of sensing devices? It was aimed at the station.

'We have some shielding,' Arvid said without being asked. 'We can handle this much radiation, but not for too much longer. I hope they have some way of maneuvering with chemical rockets.'

Wes nodded. He thought. *You knew the job was dangerous when you took it, Fred,* but nobody aboard would have understood the reference. He said, 'This may be a violation of the Geneva Convention.'

It sparked laughter. Arvid said, 'Use tact when you tell them. Nikolai, that's enough of the telescope. Show us a camera view from —' and interrupted to strain forward.

Wes's hands closed hard on the arms of his chair.

For the alien ship was sparkling like a fireworks display. Four of the twinkling jets expanded outward, away from the drive flame; then four more. Those pulse-jets were the main drives for smaller spacecraft! Showers of sparks flowed from the hidden bow end. Missiles? Missiles in tremendous number, then, and this was starting to look ominously like a Japanese movie. Not first contact, but space war.

The picture flickered white and disappeared.

Arvid was out of his seat and trying to reach God knows what, and Wes was checking his seat belt, when the whole station rang and shuddered. Wes yelled and clapped hands over his ears. The others were floating out of their seats – free-fall? He swept an arm out to push Giselle back into her seat, and she clutched the arms. He couldn't reach anyone else.

Free-fall? How could that be? The connecting tunnel must have come apart! Nikolai was screaming into a microphone. He stopped suddenly. He turned and looked around, stunned, ashen.

Behind Wes the wall smashed inward, then outward. The buckle on Wes's seat harness popped open. Wes grabbed instinctively, a death grip on the arm of his chair, even before the shock wave reached him. The Nigerian snatched at Wes's belt and clung tight. He was screaming. Good! So was Wes. Hold your breath and you'd rupture your lungs.

For the stars were glaring in at them through the ripped metal, and the air was roaring away, carrying anything loose. Giselle Beaumont flapped her arms as if trying to fly. Her eyes met Wes's in pure astonishment – and fly she did, out into the black sky and gone. Shit!

Vacuum! Dawson's eyes and ears felt ready to pop. Giorge's grip was growing feeble, but so was the wind; the air was almost gone. So. *What have I got, a minute before the blood boils out through my lungs? I'll never reach my million-dollar pressure suit, so where are the beach balls? I located them first thing, every compartment, the emergency pressure balloons, where the hell were they? If Americans had built this place they'd be popping out of the walls, because Ralph Nader would raise hell if they didn't.*

Nothing was popping out of the walls. Dawson's intestinal tract was spewing air at both ends. His eyes sought . . . Rogachev, there, clawing at a wall. Dawson patted the shoulder at his waist and kicked himself toward Rogachev. Giorge hung on, in good sense or simple panic.

His throat tried to cough but it couldn't get a grip.

Wes bounced against a wall, couldn't find a handhold,

bounced away. Losing control. Dying? The black man caught something, but kept one arm around Wes's waist. Rogachev looked like a puffer-fish. He was fighting to tear open a plastic wall panel. It jerked open and he bounced away.

Bulky disks, four feet across, turned out to be flattened plastic bags. Wes skimmed one at Rogachev. He pulled another open, crawled inside and pulled the black man in too. Zipper? He zipped them inside. Tight fit. Some kind of lock at the end of the zipper. With his chin on the black man's shoulder Wes reached around the man's neck and flipped the lock shut, he hoped.

Air jetted immediately.

Reverse pressure in his ears. He pulled in air, in, in, no need to exhale at all. They were going to live. They were floating loose, and nothing to be done about it, because the pressure packages were nothing but balloons with an air supply attached. Rogachev's too was bouncing about like a toy, but at least he'd gotten inside.

Wes's passenger was beginning to struggle. It was uncomfortable. Wes wanted to say something comforting, or just tell him not to rip the goddam beach ball! But now his throat had air to cough with, and he couldn't stop coughing. He sounded like he was dying. So did Giorge.

Nothing happened for a long time. Giorge discovered the blood pooling in his ears. He wailed. He fought his way around until he could look into Wes's face, and then he wailed again. His eyes showed bloody veins, as if he'd been on a week-long drunk. Wes's own eyes must look just that bad. His nose was filled with blood; a globule swelled at the tip.

He had no idea how much air there was in these things.

Something showed through the ripped wall, just for an instant: reflecting glass that might hide eyes, and a glimpse of what might be a tentacle, a real honest-to-God tentacle.

Giorge made a mewling sound and ceased struggling. Wes froze too. He hadn't believed. He'd fought like a demon to be at this event, but somewhere inside him he'd been ready for disappointment.

There had been the pulsars: precisely timed signals coming from somewhere in interstellar space. Beacons for Little Green Men? He'd been in college when the pulsars were shown to be rapidly spinning neutron stars, weird but natural. Much younger when the canals of Mars became mere illusion. The dangerously populated swamps of Venus were red hot, dry, and lifeless.

The starship too would be something else, some natural phenomenon —

The alien approached cautiously. A quick look, dodge back, maybe report to a companion. Look again, reflecting face plate swinging side to side, along with the snout of what must be a weapon.

It crawled through, being careful not to snag its pressure suit.

It was compact and bulky and three or four times the size of a man. A dull black pressure suit hid most of it, but it wasn't even vaguely man-shaped. It was four-footed. The boots were armed with . . . claws? Pincers? There was a tail like the blade of a paddle. The transparency at the front might indicate its face. Reflection hid the detail behind it. But a single rubbery-looking tentacle reached out from just below the transparent plate, and then branched, and branched again.

There was no doubting that the branched tentacle held a large bore gun. The handle was short and grotesquely broad, but the rest was easy to recognize: magazine, barrel, trigger halfway up the barrel —

Packs at the alien's sides puffed gas from fore-and-aft snouts. The alien's approach slowed, and it floated toward Wes with the gun barrel and the reflecting face-plate looking right at him.

Wes lifted his hand in greeting, for lack of a better idea; waved, then opened and closed his thumb across the palm. He said, inaudibly, with vacuum between them, 'I'm a tool user too . . . brother.' The alien didn't react.

He'd been prepared for disappointment, but not for war. Idiot. Yet he could hope. He wasn't dead yet, and a border skirmish did not constitute a war.

The tentacle swept backward, slid the gun into a holster on the creature's back. The tentacle pulled a line from a backpouch, fixed something to the end, something sticky. Yes. The alien was mooring the beach ball to a line, using adhesive tape. Wes began to believe that he would not be killed just yet.

Ambassador to the Galactic Empire . . . he could still make it. Maybe they were only paranoid, only very cautious. He would have to be cautious himself. A diplomat, was Wes Dawson, good at finding the interfaces between disparate viewpoints. Let him come to understand them: he could find the advantage in friendship between Earth and aliens .

Unless they really had come to conquer Earth. The specter of Herbert George Wells was very much with him.

Everyone in the Oval Office was shouting. Jenny stared at the screen, not quite comprehending what she'd seen.

'Major Crichton!'

The President! 'Sir!'

'Please call Admiral Carrell. You people, make room for her, please. Jack, help her get over here.'

'Yes, sir.' Jack Clybourne shouldered through the crowd, then helped her get to the President's desk. Coffey was still seated. His face was ashen. Jeanne Coffey sat beside him, her eyes staring at the blank TV screen.

'I don't think we need the newspeople here just at the moment,' the President said. 'Or the staff. Or the Cabinet, except for Dr. Hart and Mr. Griffin —'

State and Defense. Yes, we'll need them. Hap Aylesworth stayed also. Jenny almost giggled. *The political*

*advisor. Political implications of war with the aliens –
how would this affect the next election?*

There were three telephones on the stand behind the
President's desk. Jenny lifted the black one and punched
in numbers before she realized there was no dial tone.
'Dead,' she said. The President looked at her uncompre-
hendingly. 'Should I use this one?' she asked. She indicated the red telephone.

'Yes.'

There was no dial tone on that one either, but the Air
Force officer on duty in the White House basement came
on. 'Yes, sir?'

'Priority,' Jenny said. 'HQ NORAD.'

'Right. Wait one, there's something coming
in – they're calling you. Here you are.'

'Mr. President?' a familiar voice said.

'Major Crichton, Admiral. The President is here.' She
held out the telephone.

His calm is going. Mrs. Coffey looks horrible, and —

'What happened, Admiral?'

The Secret Service had managed to clear nearly everyone out of the room. Jack Clybourne stood uncertainly at
the door.

The President touched a button. Admiral Carrell's
voice filled the room.

'– little left. We have no operational satellites. Just
before we lost the last observation satellite, it reported a
number of rocket plumes in the Soviet Union.'

The President looked up and caught the eye of the
Secretary of State. 'Arthur, get down to the hot line and
find out!'

'Right.' Dr. Hart ran to the door.

Secretary of Defense Ted Griffin went pale. 'If the
crazy bastards have launched at us, we've got to get our
birds up before theirs hit!'

'We can't just shoot!' the President shouted. 'We don't
know they've attacked us. We have to talk to them —'

'I doubt that you can get through,' Admiral Carrell said. 'I took the liberty of trying. Mr. President, it appears that a large nuclear device has been detonated in the very high stratosphere, far too high to do any harm to ground installations – except for the pulse effect, which has severely damaged our communications capabilities, especially on the East Coast.'

'We must get through – Admiral, do you believe the Soviets are attacking us?'

'Sir, I don't know. Certainly the aliens have attacked our space installations – ' Admiral Carrell's voice broke off suddenly.

'Admiral!'

There was a long silence. 'Mr. President, I have reports of ground damage. Hoover Dam has been destroyed by a large explosion.'

'A nuclear weapon?'

'Sir, I don't know what else it could be. A moment . . .' There was another silence.

'God damn!' Ted Griffin shouted. 'They did it, the crazy Russian bastards did it!'

The Admiral's voice came on faintly. 'One of my advisors says it could have been what he calls a kinetic energy weapon. Not nuclear. It could not have been a Soviet rocket, they couldn't have reached here in time.' Another pause. 'I'm getting more reports. Alaska. Colorado. Mississippi —Mr. President, we are being bombarded. Some of the attacks are coming from space. May I have permission to fight back?'

David Coffey looked at his wife. She shuddered. 'Fight who?' the President demanded.

'The aliens,' Admiral Carrell said.

'Not the Soviets?'

'Not yet.'

'Ted?' David Coffey asked.

'Sir?' The Secretary of Defense looked ten years older. 'Is there any way I can authorize Carrell to fight a space

161

battle without giving him the capability to launch against the Soviet Union?'

'No.'

'I see. Jeanne, what do you think?'

'I think you're the President, David.'

Jenny held her breath.

'You don't have any choice.' Hap Aylesworth said. 'What, you'll let them attack our country without fighting back?'

'Thank you,' Coffey said quietly. 'Admiral, is Colonel Feinstein there?'

'Yes, sir. Colonel —'

Another voice came on. 'Yes, Mr. President.'

'Colonel, I authorize you to open the code container and deliver the contents to Admiral Thorwald Carrell. The authentication phrase is 'pigeons on the grass, alas.' You will receive confirmation from the Secretary of Defense and the National Security Council duty officer. Ted —'

'Yes, sir.' Ted Griffin took the phone, almost dropped it, and read from a card he'd taken from his wallet. Then he turned to Jenny. 'Major —'

'Major Crichton here,' Jenny said. 'I confirm that I personally have heard the President order the codes released to Admiral Carrell. My authentication code is Tango. X-ray. Alfa. Four. Seven. Niner. Four.' *And that's done. Lord, I never —*

'Admiral,' the President said. 'You will not launch against the Soviet Union until we have absolute confirmation that they have attacked us. I don't believe they're involved in this, and Earth has troubles enough without a nuclear war. Is this understood?'

'Yes, sir. Mr. President, I suggest you come here as quickly as you can. Major Crichton, assist the President, and stay with him as long as you're needed. I'll put Colonel Hartley on now.'

———

162

Something rang in his head.

Harry Reddington woke, and thrashed, and slapped the top of his alarm clock: the pause, to give him another ten minutes sleep. The ringing went on. The room was pitch dark, and it wasn't the clock ringing, it was the telephone. Harry picked up the receiver. His voice was musical, sarcastically so. 'Hellooo . . .'

A breathy voice said, 'Harry? Go outside and look.'

'Ruby? It's late, Ruby. I've got to get up early tomorrow.'

There was party music in the background, and a woman's voice raised in laughing protest. Ruby's voice was bathetically mournful. She must be ripped; at a late party she was bound to be. 'Harry, I went outside for a hit. You know Julia and Gwen, they don't like anyone smoking anything in there. They don't like tobacco any better than pot —'

'Ruby!'

'I went out and it's, it's . . . It looks so real, Harry! Go out and look at the sky. It's the end of the world.'

Harry hung up.

He rolled off the Dawsons' water bed and searched for his clothes.

He'd stayed up too late anyway. It would have been a good night to get drunk with friends, but *word of honor on record*. He'd come home and had a few drinks as consolation for being alone while interstellar ambassadors made first contact with humanity.

The clock said 2:10, and he'd been up past midnight watching the news. There hadn't been any; whatever the Soviets were learning, they hadn't been telling. Eventually he went to bed. Now —

His eyes felt gritty. The cane was leaning against the bedstead. He gave up on finding a jacket; he wouldn't be out long.

He unlocked the back door and stumbled out onto the Dawsons' lawn.

Ruby had been using marijuana, and spreading the word of it like any missionary, since the mid-sixties. She worked as a clerk in the head shop next to the Honda salesroom. What had Harry outside in a coolish California May night was this reflection: a doper might see things that aren't there, but she might see things that are.

The sky glowed. Harry was an Angeleno; he judged the mistiness of the night by that glow, the glow of the Los Angeles lights reflected from the undersides of clouds. The glow wasn't bright tonight, and stars showed through.

Something brighter than a star showed through, a dazzling pinpoint that developed a tail and vanished, all in a moment.

A long blue-white flame formed, and held for several seconds, while narrow lines of light speared down from one end. Other lights pulsed slowly, like beating hearts.

The sky was alive with strange lights.

Harry got back inside, fished the tiny Minolta binoculars out of a drawer, found his windbreaker on a chair, and stumbled out, all without turning on a light. He wanted his night vision. The sky seemed brighter now. He could see streaks of light rising from the west, flaring, disappearing. Narrow threads of green lanced west: down. There were phosphorescent puffs of cloud, lazily expanding.

On another night Harry might have taken it for a meteor shower. Tonight . . . He'd read a hundred versions of the aliens conquering Earth, and they all sounded more spectacular than this flaring and dying of stars and smudges of lights. Any movie would have had sound effects too. But it looked so *real*.

Still without turning on the lights he fumbled his way back into the house to find a transistor radio. He carried it outside with him and tuned to the all-news station.

'. . . have fired on the Soviet Kosmograd space station,' the newsman's voice said. 'The President has alerted all military forces. People are asked to stay in their homes. We cannot confirm that the United States Air Force has fired on the alien spacecraft. Pentagon spokesmen aren't talking. Here is Lieutenant General Arlen Gregory, a retired Air Force officer. General, do you think the United States will fight back?'

'Look at the sky, you silly buzzard,' a gravelly voice said. 'What the hell do you think all the lights are?'

Harry watched and thought as a flame curved around the western horizon, flared and died. Then two more. *No question what that was. And now what do I do?*

Stay and watch the house. Only – Jesus, Congressman Wes was in Kosmograd! And Carlotta Dawson would be in western Kansas by now, present situation unknown. If she'd taken the gun . . . if she'd been the *type* to take the .45. But she wasn't.

The radio began the peculiar *beep beep* of an incoming news bulletin.

'We have an unconfirmed report that San Diego harbor has suffered a large explosion,' the announcer said. He sounded like a man who'd like to be hysterical but who'd used up all his emotions.

Maybe I should go help Carlotta. Wes would want me to. Jesus, how?

The Kawasaki was in pieces. There hadn't been nearly enough money for everything that should have been done to it, and Harry hadn't wanted to push. He'd done most of the work himself, as much as he could. But only the Honda shop could rebuild the engine. He'd finished taking the bike apart and carried the engine in, and as far as he knew it was ready. It had better be.

There must be others watching tonight. They'd sure as hell know by morning.

Harry watched and thought and made his plans. (That long blue flame had formed again, and this time it didn't seem to be dying. Stars rising from the west seemed to be reaching for it until threads of green light touched them;

165

then they flared and vanished. The blue flame crept east, accelerating. The binoculars showed something at the tip. Harry's eyes watered trying to make out details.)

Then he went inside and washed his face.

Carlotta didn't like him. And so what? Harry opened Dawson's liquor cabinet and opened a bottle of Carlos Primera brandy. Sixty bucks a bottle, but it was all that was left. He poured a good splash, looked at it, thought of pouring some back, and drank half.

Carlotta doesn't like me. The country's at war with aliens. Wes asked me to look after things. Nothing I can do here, and if I stay here long I'll *be* here, and for good.

He went to the telephone and dialed the Kansas number Carlotta had left. It rang a long time. Then a voice, not sleepy. Male. 'Mrs. Carlotta Dawson. Please,' Harry said. He could sound official when he wanted to.

It took a moment. 'Yes?'

'Harry Reddington, Mrs. Dawson. Is there anything you want me to do?'

'Harry – Harry, they don't know what happened up there.'

'Yes, ma'am. Can I help you?'

'I don't know.'

Carlotta Dawson's voice dissolved in hisses. Another voice came on the line. 'Is this an official telephone call?' it asked through the static. Then the line went dead.

Harry emptied his glass. Now what? She didn't say. And if I stay in Los Angeles tomorrow, I'll be in Los Angeles forever . . .

He drank half an inch more brandy and closed the bottle. Firmly.

When he left he was in clean shirt and a sports jacket that was years old but had almost never been worn. He carried ID and a sleeping bag and Congressman Dawson's letter. At 3:30 A.M. he was on the front steps of the Security Pacific National Bank, spreading his sleeping bag.

Pavel Bondarev stared at the blank screen. All around him officers and aides at the command and communications consoles began to speak at once, and the babble brought him to life. 'Colonel, I wish this chatter to cease.'

'Da, Comrade Director.' Colonel Suvorov was efficient if unimaginative. He shouted, and the cacophony of voices died away.

The aliens had fired on Kosmograd. He had seen that much before all communications were lost. The aliens had fired without warning, without provocation.

An amber light blinked insistently. Pavel lifted the scrambler telephone. 'Da, Comrade Chairman.'

There was only a soft hiss, then a sudden rush of static. The officers at the command consoles burst into chatter again.

'What has happened?' Bondarev demanded.

'A high-altitude nuclear explosion. Perhaps more than one. The pulse effect has crippled our telephones,' Suvorov reported.

'I see.' And without communications – Bondarev felt rising panic. The scrambler phone was dead. 'Get me Marshal Shavyrin.'

'There is no answer,' Suvorov said.

'It is vital. Use another means. Use any means,' Bondarev ordered. He fought to keep his voice calm. *The scrambler telephone remains silent. Is the Chairman in communication with anyone else? Perhaps not. Perhaps we are safe.*

'I have Shavyrin,' Colonel Suvorov said.

'Thank you.' Pavel put on the headset. 'Comrade Marshal —'

'Da, Comrade Director?'

'Have you launched any missiles?'

'No, Comrade Director. I have received no instructions from the Defense Council.'

Bondarev discovered that he had been partially holding his breath. Now he let it out slowly. 'You understand that the aliens have fired on Kosmograd?'

'Comrade Director, I know someone has. Two of my generals believe this a Western trick —'

'Nonsense, Comrade Marshal. You have *seen* that ship. Neither we nor the United States nor both nations working together could have built that ship.'

There was a long pause. Pavel heard someone speaking to the Marshal, but he could not make out the words. 'Marshal,' Bondarev insisted, 'that ship was not built on this Earth, and *we know* the United States cannot have sufficient space facilities. If they did, they would long ago have defeated us.'

There was another long pause. Then Shavyrin said, 'Perhaps you are correct. Certainly that is true. What must we do now?'

I wish I knew. 'Immediately before the aliens destroyed Kosmograd, they launched many smaller ships. I say smaller, although they were each larger than Kosmograd. Have you had success in tracking any of those?'

'Only partially. Even with our largest radars it is difficult to see through the electronic storms in the upper atmosphere. The aliens have set off many weapons there.'

'I know —'

'Also, they have fired laser beams at three of our large radars.' Marshal Shavyrin said.

'Laser beams?'

'Da. The most powerful we have ever seen.'

'Damage?'

'The Abalakovo radar is destroyed. The Sary Shagan and Lyaki radars are damaged but survive. We have not activated the large radar near Moscow for fear that it will draw their fire.'

'I see.' *Intelligent of him.* 'We will need information, but not at *that* cost. Now tell me what you know of their smaller ships.'

168

'My information is not complete. We have lost communications with many of our radars.'

'Da, but tell me what you have learned.'

'The ships have scattered. Most are in polar orbits.'

'Track them. If they come within range of the ion beam weapons, fire at them. Be prepared to fire SS-20 missiles under ground detonation control. Meanwhile, attack the main alien ship with the entire force of SS-18 missiles based in Kamensk.'

'Comrade Director, I require authorization from the Chairman before I can do any of this.'

'Comrade Marshal, the Chairman has directed me to conduct this battle. We have no communication with Moscow. You *must* launch your forces against the aliens, particularly their large mother ship. We must cripple it before it destroys us on the ground.'

'Comrade Director, that is not possible —'

'Comrade Marshal, it must be made possible —'

'If we attack the alien ship, we will destroy Kosmograd as well. And all survivors.'

A strange sentiment for the commander of strategic rocket forces. 'Kosmograd is already destroyed. The survivors cannot be important now.'

'Comrade Director,' Colonel Suvorov shouted. 'I have the Chairman.'

'Marshal, the Chairman is calling me. Please stand by.' Bondarev took the other phone.

There was no mistaking the thick voice. 'Bondarev, what must we do?'

'Destroy the alien ship. I would prefer not to, but there is no choice.'

'Have the aliens attacked the United States?'

'Comrade Chairman, I do not know.'

'They have attacked us,' Chairman Petrovskiy said. 'Can we defeat the aliens? Can we destroy their ship?'

'I do not know. We certainly cannot capture it. We can try to destroy it.'

'Da. Try, then. Meanwhile, we will do what we can. There are reports of severe damage in the harbors. The rail center west of Moscow is in ruins. So is Brest Litovsk.'

'But . . .' Bondarev spoke in horror. 'The Germans —'

'Da. The Germans may rise in revolt. The Poles as well.' The Chairman's voice rose. 'All the Warsaw Pact nations may rise against us. Our harbors are destroyed, harbors and rail centers. We face a new civil war. If the United States remains undamaged —'

'Comrade Chairman, I do not know that they are undamaged. I do know that we must destroy that ship. You must order Marshal Shavyrin to accept my orders to launch missiles at the alien.'

There was a long pause. 'We must retain enough missiles to prevent the United States from attacking us now that we are weakened,' Petrovskiy said.

'Da. I will do that,' Bondarev said. 'But if we do not act quickly, we cannot act at all.' *I have never spoken this way to the great ones, not even to my father-in-law. But I must –* 'Comrade Chairman, there is no time to lose.'

There was another long pause. Then 'Da. I will give the orders. But —have a care, Pavel Aleksandrovich. Have a care.'

CHAPTER ELEVEN
LIGHTS IN THE SKY

Be ye therefore wise as serpents, and harmless as doves.

– MATTHEW 10:16

COUNTDOWN: H PLUS ONE HOUR

The air was foul and growing fouler; it was like being trapped inside a whale's lungs. Giorge, gasping and coughing and fighting the soft walls, had finally fainted. The beach ball's oxygen supply wasn't designed for two occupants.

It was a hell of a situation in which to try to relax, but Wes tried: he held his breathing slow and steady (punctuated with coughing); he let his eyelids droop (though he *had* to watch that great armored city in the sky coming toward him!) Half curled toward fetal position, he consciously relaxed his muscles in pairs, as if he were fighting a night of insomnia.

All this, while traveling like a tethered balloon behind their massive inhuman captors.

Naked in the glare of the stars, helpless as a babe, Wes fell toward an alien artifact bigger than the World Trade Centre. He saw detail as he neared the thing: a pod on a jointed arm, rectangles of blackness, a jet of blue flame from a cluster of cones. But the air was like soup. His nose was clogged with drying blood. Hold the breathing down, *stay awake*, there are things you have to see . . . no use. His chest heaved, a coughing fit wracked his body, and everything went out of focus.

Arvid Rogachev was finding a great deal to awe him, and not much to surprise him. A ship the size of a city: of course, if they hoped to conquer a planet! The aliens: very alien. The attack: why not? Whatever they expected from contact with humankind, it was their safest approach.

Which was not to say that he wasn't angry.

How would they treat prisoners? Human precedent showed a wide spectrum . . . but wouldn't they want to inspect the natives more closely? These attackers hadn't had time to build up a hatred for the enemy, not yet. What they found alive, they would keep alive . . . unless they were xenophobic beyond sanity, or found the human shape intrinsically disgusting . . .

Still, a corpse dead of explosive decompression was not the ideal subject for dissection. Might they prefer a healthy Soviet executive?

Arvid shrugged off that line of thought. Who still lived? Dawson, of course, and Giorge. Nikolai too had reached a survival bubble. Aliana? The other American, Greeley?

A dozen of the beasts had followed the first, the scout, through the ripped wall, paused briefly to inspect the humans, then gone off into other parts of the wrecked station. The four who remained had enlarged the rip with a series of explosive gun blasts. Now the survival bubbles were being towed toward what seemed an infinite metal wall.

He wished for a better look at the aft end, the drive; but they were approaching from the side. Dark holes showed along the flank, with doors snugged against the hull. Airlocks, or missile ports? Those oval windows: for passengers, or lasers? A sudden narrow string of twinkling points against the black sky: random dust motes reflecting a laser beam? Sure enough, a new star blazed far away, then winked off. Far below, lights flashed against Earth's night sky. Something blossomed impossibly bright, and Arvid turned his head away.

A nuclear weapon. Whose? And how close was it? He fought real panic. *How long do I have to live?* Almost he laughed. It had been a long way away, near the Earth's surface, ten thousand kilometers and more. *I have looked upon the cocatrice and survived . . .*

Other lights flared far down toward Earth. Light beams stabbed downward through space flecked with dust and debris. *Bondarev is attacking the alien ship. Perhaps the United States as well.* He had never felt more helpless.

They were close enough to the ship for him to see details. Grooves ran along the spacecraft's flank, like railroad tracks, but much farther apart. Smaller craft could have been anchored there . . . smaller, but still *big*, perhaps as big as a pocket battleship. The entire hull might function like an aircraft carrier's deck. Or –

Arvid felt hampered here. This kind of guesswork was no task for an executive, nor a soldier either. He needed a combination of mechanic and strategist: a mechanic with imagination. Had Nikolai survived, or Mitya?

The ship had become a cubistic landscape.

. . . Rectangular pock, too small to be an airlock . . . No. It was larger than he'd thought. Alien-sized, he saw, as one of his captors moved up against it. A cavity the size of an alien in a pressure suit. Alien 1 disappeared within. The door closed.

The door opened. Alien 2 pushed Arvid's survival bubble into the airlock. It brushed the sides, but it fit. The outer door closed, the survival bubble sagged, Arvid's abused ears popped. An inner door opened. Alien 1 pulled the survival bubble out into a corridor . . . a wide rectangular corridor, curved, painted in three tones of green camouflage style, with carpet along two walls. Arvid was disoriented. Would they spin the ship for gravity? Certainly he was still in free-fall . . .

The doors he saw were all closed.

Then an open door, and it was thick, massive . . . as one would expect aboard a warship.

The alien paused. Arvid saw that he was boxed between the two aliens.

They acted in concert. A long-handled bayonet sliced through the side of the survival bubble, a forked tentacle reached in and closed around him. Arvid couldn't help himself: he screamed and slammed a fist against the alien's faceplate. Only his fist was hurt. The tentacle birthed him from the collapsed bubble and hurled him into the room. *Did they breathe poison? He was breathing it already!*

He hit the far wall without the jolt he'd expected. It was padded. The room was big, and padded over walls and floor and ceiling. The air . . . the air was damp, with a smell both earthy and strange. It didn't smell like it would kill him.

A large, conspicuous glass-faced tube poked through the padding in one corner of the room. A camera.

The aliens followed him in. Arvid tried to relax as they came toward him. One still clutched the bayonet in its tentacle. *Dissection?* He wouldn't scream again.

But it was difficult not to fight. One alien held him — it felt like pythons were squeezing him to death — while the other used the bayonet to slice through his clothing: down the back and along his arms and legs. They stripped him naked and collected the ruined clothing and backed out, carefully, as if he might still be dangerous.

He was alone.

His fear edged over into black rage.

Dangerous? When you can see me as dangerous, then I am harmless. This hour or this day, this year or next year, you will lower your guard. By then I will know more.

―――――――

Wes had missed it all. His oxygen-starved mind had been fading in and out, catching fragmentary glimpses of alien wonders while his lungs strained at the dirty air . . . as if he

174

were trapped in a burning theater that was showing *Star Wars*. Half-felt forces pulled him through some kind of strangling barrier into air he could breathe. His lungs clawed at air that was damp and cool, sweet life-giving air, while something sharp ran down his torso and arms and legs, and decidedly queer hands peeled him like an orange.

He was naked. Falling. Spots danced before his eyes.

Where are the others? Is this all of us?

There were other bodies, all naked. Rogachev: white skin covered with black hair, and bright eyes watching him. Giorge: black skin, almost hairless, dull eyes that saw nothing. Another fell past him and bounced against the rubbery wall. Pale skin, joltingly inhuman shape . . . stumps for legs . . . Nikolai. There were scars on Nikolai's belly. Oh, boy, that had been some accident!

Arvid Rogachev and Nikolai talked in Russian. They sounded indecently calm.

Four. Where were the others?

Giorge was curled loosely in a ball. His mouth was slightly open. Wes took his shoulder and turned him to bring them face to face. Giorge's eyes were open, but they weren't looking at anything. 'Giorge? It's all right now. All right for the moment. We're not in any danger just now. Can you hear me, Giorge?'

Giorge said a word in his own language. Wes couldn't get him to say any more.

He's nearly catatonic. Wes could understand the temptation. It would be easy to curl into a fetal position and close his eyes. Easy but not sensible.

They attacked. Without warning, without talking. Oh, God, Carlotta saw it all! She must think I'm dead. Or have they told Earth they have prisoners?

The door opened again. Dmitri Grushin flew among them, cursing vigorously in a high, hysterical voice. Rogachev snapped orders: they *had* to be orders. Grushin blinked and quieted, and Rogachev's voice went from authoritative to fatherly. Dmitri nodded.

Now there were five. Seven missing, including both women.

Arvid Rogachev turned and spoke in English. 'You are well, Congressman?'

Wes tested his throat. 'I'd want a doctor's opinion. I'm alive, but I hurt all over. Bends, probably. How are you?'

'The same. Wes, we have seen men exposed to vacuum before. We will live. You'll see ruptured veins on your face and body —'

'Shit, there goes my career.'

Arvid laughed. 'President Reagan used makeup. So did Nixon.'

'You're such a comfort. Arvid, what's going on? I would have – I *did* bet my life that conquering another planet across interstellar space just isn't cost-effective. War of the Worlds. Does it look like that to you?'

'I like the phrase your computer programmers use. *Insufficient data*.'

'Is this all of us?'

'I do not know. Dmitri tells me that Captain Greeley is dead. He saw it, after the aliens had him in tow. An alien moved into Captain Greeley's chambers, in vacuum, mind you. The door was a bit small for the alien, and while it was in the doorway Captain Greeley fired a handgun into the alien, then continued firing through the wall. He must have been firing through his survival bubble. The aliens raked the chamber with explosive bullets.'

Wes couldn't decide how he felt about that. Too many shocks . . . 'Sounds like John.'

There was a sound, almost subsonic, as if a tremendous gong had been struck. Wes saw a wall come at him: he was falling! He struck. They were all piled against the damp padding . . . and then the thrust eased off and left them floating.

'So. We still have some defenses,' Arvid said.

'Zapsats?'

'Ground-based beam weapons, I would think. The

aliens will know all about it before we do. At least it tells us
we can still fight.'

'I wish we had a window,' Wes said.

I wish we had a suitcase fission bomb, Arvid thought.
*Do I? It would end my life too. That will come soon
enough. Patience.*

The B-1B flew just above the treetops at near sonic speed.
For a while Jenny looked out the tiny crew windows, but
there was little to see: just shapes flashing past, an occasional light. Most of the United States was dark.

There was a bright flash off to starboard. Jenny
shuddered.

'What?' Jack asked. He touched her hand, then moved
his away. She reached for him and brought his hand back
and held it in both of hers.

'Another dam,' she said.

She listened as the artificially calm voice from Colorado
Springs spoke into her earphones. 'Spring Lake Dam,
near Peoria, Illinois,' it said. 'They've hit most of the
dams from there north and west. Floodwaters are rising all
along the Mississippi and Missouri rivers. We're ordering
evacuation, but it won't be in time.'

'Isn't there anything else?' The President's voice interrupted the Air Force talker. 'Get the National Guard out
with helicopters —'

'Sir, we're trying, but we have almost no communications. Most of the reports I'm giving you come from
direct observation by Air National Guard pilots flying
wherever they see a flash.'

We could lose a lot of pilots that way.

'Is there anything more on the Russians?' Jack asked.

'No. Just a lot of damage reports,' Jenny answered.

'Then we don't even know if we're at war?'

Jenny gave a short laugh. 'We're at war all right. We
just don't know who with —'

'Could the aliens be allied with the Russians?'

'Don't know. I don't think so,' Jenny said. 'I'm sure we'd have heard if they were in communication. We'd have heard *something*. I think —'

'Yeah.' He leaned back in the bombardier's seat and closed his eyes. In seconds he was asleep.

Jenny shook her head in admiration. *Nothing for Jack Clybourne to do, so he rests up for the next assignment. I wish the President would do that. There's not enough information for him to make any decisions, not here.*

I wish I could do it.

The reports continued. Missiles launched against the smaller alien ships. The large alien ship remained invisible behind a screen of noise, charge particles, and chaff. No confirmation of any Soviet missile landing in the United States, and no confirmation of any cities destroyed.

Jenny leaned back in the electronic warfare officer's seat and tried to close her eyes, but the temptation to look out the window was too much. The thick leaded glass would shield her eyes from anything that wouldn't kill her . . .

The bomber flew on toward Colorado Springs.

The steps of the bank were cold and damp. Harry settled as near the door as he could reach, and turned on the transistor radio.

'Power failures throughout Southern California,' the announcer was saying. He sounded nearly hysterical. 'We have reports that something hit Hoover Dam. *Laser beams*, for God's sake!'

The long blue flame sank into the east. Harry settled against the bank door. He thought of what else he could do. Steal a car. Steal a motorcycle. Break into the shop and steal his own motorcycle. Any of that might work, but it might not.

I'm not as quick as I used to be.

He tried to think of someone who'd help him, but any-one who'd believe him either wouldn't be any use, or would already be doing something. After a while he closed his eyes and slept a little.

He woke again when someone moved in beside him: a small, pudgy man who puffed from his climb up the steps. He settled on the step below Harry. 'Mind?'

'No,' Harry said. 'Did you see the sky? Or the news?'

'Both. The TV's gone off, though. One of the radio people keeps saying it's all a big mistake, but I can't get through to New York.'

Sure can't. Or to Dighton, Kansas. Harry nodded. The pudgy man was shivering. Harry thought he should have worn more.

'I keep remembering *The War of the Worlds*. What *are* they, what do they *want*? They could be . . . anything.'

'Not my department,' Harry said, and he closed his eyes. As he drifted off, he felt grateful for his brief military stint. He had learned to sleep anytime.

And if everything went just right, it was going to be one miserable day.

He kept waking to watch the sky. 'There,' the pudgy man said. He pointed south. 'Like – what did they call it? The high-altitude atom bomb test. Back in the fifties.'

'Wouldn't remember,' Harry said. He frowned. Some-thing came back to him. They'd blown off a nuclear weapon in the stratosphere, and mucked up the iono-sphere and communications all over the world, and it had taken months for things to get right again. And that was one bomb.

There was nothing but static on the radio. Harry tuned across the band. Sometimes he heard stations but he couldn't really make out words. He shrugged and kept tuning.

There were a lot of faintly phosphorescent smudges, north, south, and west. East was getting pink, and he couldn't tell if explosions were there, too.

War of the Worlds? In that movie, the aliens had landed. His random sweep picked up a news station. He listened, but there wasn't much news. Official announcements, everyone to remain calm and stay home. Hysterical announcers with unconfirmed reports of anything you liked. Orphanage burned in Los Gatos. Dams broken. Trains derailed. Europe laid waste. But no one had been hurt in Los Angeles, and as far as Harry could tell, the announcer didn't *know* about anybody who'd been hurt. Just lots of rumors.

When the sky turned light a dozen were in line. Only two had thought to bring sleeping bags. One weathered-looking man brought an entire backpack, with sleeping bag, self-inflating mat, a blowup pillow, a tiny stove. He got himself settled, then made coffee and sent it up and down the line in a Sierra cup. He seemed to be having a wonderful time. So were the two Boy Scouts with him.

They talked in low voices. A thin woman's voice kept rising into hysteria, then chopping off. Harry dozed.

The voices changed. Harry rolled over and was looking up at two blue police uniforms. He exposed his hands, then carefully reached into his sports jacket and opened his wallet. 'Harry Reddington. I'm here to make a withdrawal.' He didn't bother to smile.

'Sir, why are you here?'

Harry suppressed an urge to point to the sky and giggle. 'I told you, I'm here to make a withdrawal.'

'The Federal Emergency Management Agency has issued orders for all citizens to stay home,' the older policeman said.

'Sure,' Harry said. 'We always do everything Washington says, don't we?' This time he couldn't help the grin. 'How'd they learn to deal with *this* situation? Experience?'

'Sir —'

The younger officer interrupted his companion. They

whispered for a moment. Harry used the opportunity to take out his Baggie-wrapped letter. He held it out.

'If you'll shine your light here,' Harry said.

The older policeman moved closer. His light showed the Capitol stationery clearly.

'. . . Mr. Harry Reddington, whom I have authorized to stay in my house and guard my possessions and interest . . .'

If they had read further they'd have come to the weasel words, but they didn't, and Harry swallowed his sigh of relief.

'Yes, sir?' the officer said. This time the 'sir' sounded a great deal more sincere.

Some of the crowd behind them were muttering. 'Fucking pigs,' someone said, not too loud. The voice sounded cultured, and not at all what you'd expect someone saying *that* to sound like.

Harry was tempted to take advantage of that. Instead, he spoke in a low voice. 'I'll be glad to hold a place for you,' he said. 'Or one of your family.'

The younger policeman thought that through, then nodded. 'Her name is Rosabell. She'll be here in an hour.'

————————

Interstate 40 had been completely dark for an hour. One moment she had been trying to read an illuminated sign; the next moment there was no light except her headlights. The radio had gone dead at the same instant, and now she could only get static.

High mountains loomed to either side, as the car steadily climbed into the Chuska mountains of western New Mexico.

The gas gauge read less than a quarter full.

'Mom, I'm hungry,' Melissa said from the back seat.

'There's bread and cheese,' Jeri said.

'Not any more.'

'Good God, that was supposed to last a while. You mean there's none left at all?'

'Aw, there wasn't very – what was that?'

Overhead the sky blazed in green and blue, then a long red streak that went all across the sky and downward to earth. 'I don't know,' Jeri said. She shuddered. *Aliens. They were out there all the time, waiting, fifteen years, and now they've attacked us.*

'We're gonna need gas.'

'I know. Albuquerque is ahead. We can get gasoline there.'

'I don't know, Mom,' Melissa said.

'Huh?'

'Space war, aliens – you sure we want to go into a city? Lots of people running away, I bet. Traffic jams —'

'You could be right.'

Her headlights picked up a reflective sign.

'Gas food ahead,' Melissa said. 'We could use some. Eat and run the car on the gas —'

'Very funny.' Jeri watched for the off-ramp. There it was. Everything was dark over there, but she took the ramp anyway. If a town was nearby it was invisible.

'There's the station,' Melissa said. 'Somebody's in it.'

'You're right.' Jeri pulled into the station.

'Yes, ma'am? a voice said from nowhere. The station attendant switched on his flashlight. He was a young man, certainly not more than twenty, and dark. Jeri thought he looked Indian.

This is the right part of the country for it. 'Uh – I need some gasoline. Badly.'

'The power's off,' the attendant said. 'Can't get the pumps to work.'

'Oh. But I have a long way to go, and I really need some gasoline. Isn't there anything you can do?'

He looked thoughtful. 'I have a hand pump. I suppose I could pump some out into a can. It'd be a lot of work —'

'Oh, please,' Jeri said. 'I'll be glad to pay you.'

'Not sure money's worth much now. Did you hear the news?'

'Yes – ' *If you don't want money, what do you want?*

'Guess it'll be all right, though.' He went inside the station. The flashlight flickered through the window.

He seems nice enough. So why am I scared? Is civilization that fragile?

Part of her kept saying *Yes!*

The eastern windows blazed. The television hissed and sprayed random light. The radio spoke of an explosion on Interstate 5 between Everett and Marysville.

Close. Isadore rolled to his feet and turned the TV off. The radio announcer sounded hysterical. *That's got to be the long causeway,* Isadore thought. *We got over it just in time . . .*

All of the kids were asleep. Vicki Tate-Evans had staggered away an hour ago. Her husband George was snoring on the couch with Clara's feet in his lap. They got along fine as long as they were both asleep.

Isadore felt punchy, twitchy, as if he should be *doing something. War in the sky . . . Just in time! Clara was right, push on, don't stop, something might happen. If we'd waited any longer for Jeri, it would have been too late.*

And where is she? On the road somewhere, and nothing I can do about it.

We were near enough dead getting in last night. He remembered the bright flashes on the highway behind them. *Maybe that was the causeway. We hadn't got to Sedro Wooley, so if we'd been an hour later – That's cutting things close . . .*

They'd come in ready to collapse, to find the television set running and a dead silence in the crowd that faced the set. When the TV went blank they'd all trooped outside to watch the war in the sky.

He said, as he'd said before, 'Son of a bitch.'

'Yeah,' Shakes said. He came in from the kitchen carrying a cup of coffee. 'You were right.' He looked like he would never sleep again.

'*We* were right.' Isadore laughed, and didn't like the high pitch of it. 'Seventeen years we were right before it looked even *sensible*. We should be putting the shutters over the windows. We should have bricked up the windows! Is anybody feeling ambitious?'

Nobody stood up and went out to fix the metal screens in place. Shakes said, 'I never thought it was real.'

'So what are you doing here?'

'My whole damn family gets to use this place for only about thirty percent of what it would cost us. That's a damn good deal for a vacation spot. I don't even mind admitting it now. We haven't slacked off. This place is built to keep all of us alive, and me and my family did most of it. You haven't even seen the shelter, Izzie.'

Clara suddenly sat upright. 'Food. How are the food supplies?'

'The food supplies are *fine*,' Shakes said in some irritation.

'Good. I could eat your arm off. I'm going to make breakfast,' Clara said, and she stood, staggering a little, and made her way into the kitchen, veering around Jack and Harriet McCauley, who were asleep on the rug.

———

By eight-thirty the line ran around the corner. The original police had gone, but two other pairs had come, and one team of two had stayed.

Rosabell Hruska had come at eight. She was a slender, frightened woman in her twenties. She carried a baby girl, and she didn't talk to anyone except one of the visiting police.

At ten Harry watched an old man in a guard's uniform

open the doors. The line behind him rustled impatiently, but he waited. When the doors opened, Harry held it for Rosabell. Two more elbowed past him before he could let go and get to a cashier.

The cashier looked nervous.

At least there *is* a cashier, Harry thought. He'd been worried. Would they all stay home? There were twelve windows, but only four had cashiers.

'I want to make a withdrawal,' said Harry.

'We're restricting withdrawals to five hundred dollars.' The cashier was an older woman, probably long since graduated from sitting in a cage and talking to customers, now filling in. She looked defiant and afraid at the same time.

The eastern banks had been open for three hours. Harry wondered, not whether there was a rush on the banks, but how bad it was.

Two windows down, Rosabell was shouting at the younger cashier she'd chosen. 'It's our money!' she screamed.

Too bad, Harry thought. But it was no skin off Harry's nose. He had only fifty-eight dollars in his account. He asked for it all in coins, got two twenty-dollar rolls of quarters and eighteen ones. Then he moved to the deposit boxes. His contained one Mexican gold peso and thirty silver dimes. He'd been able to keep them because of the symbolic number; if he'd spent one, he'd have spent them all.

Once there had been a lot more. He took his money and left the bank. Tap city, he thought. Tap city on my total resources.

The radio spoke of the need for calm.

CHAPTER TWELVE
MESSAGE BEARER

And the LORD said, Behold, the people is one, and they have all one language; and this they begin to do: and now nothing will be restrained from them, which they have imagined to do.

Go to, let us go down, and there confound their language, that they may not understand one another's speech.

– GENESIS 11:6-7

COUNTDOWN: H PLUS SIX HOURS

The Herdmaster's family occupied two chambers near the center of *Message Bearer*. Space was at a premium. The sleeproom was not large, though it housed two adults and three children. It was roomier now; the Herdmaster's eldest male child was aboard one of the digit ships that would presently assault the target world.

The mudroom, smaller yet, gave privacy. Some discussions the children might be permitted to hear, but not this one.

Herdmaster Pastempeh-keph lay on his side in the mud. He was far too relaxed for his mate's aplomb. 'It's a thoroughly interesting situation,' he said.

K'turfookeph blared a trumpet blast of rage. A moment later her voice was quietly intense. 'If your guards heard that they'll think we've lost our reason . . . as your Advisor has. Keph, you must dissociate yourself from him!'

'I can't. That is one of the interesting aspects. The sleepers expected to wake as masters of the ship. They are as docile as one could hope, and no more. Fathisteh-tulk was their Herdmaster. They will not permit me to remove him completely from power, not even if they know him to be insane. They would lose too much status.'

K'turfookeph sprayed warm water along her mate's back. He stirred in pleasure, and high waves marched toward the high rim of the tub. Gravity was inconveniently low, so near the ship's center. But any force from outside would destroy the ship before it penetrated so far.

She asked, 'Then what can be done?'

'Little. I must listen to him. I am not required to obey his suggestions.' The Herdmaster pondered. The War for Winterhome was finally under way, and his relaxation time was all too rare. He resented his mate's encroachment on that time. 'Turn your mind around, Mother of my Immortality —'

'Don't play word games with me! It's half a year until mating season, and we don't need soothing phrases between us, not at our age.'

He sprayed her, scalp to tail, making a thorough job of it, before he spoke again. 'Your digits grasp the handle of our problem. The mating cycles for sleeper and spaceborn are out of phase. It makes all controversy worse. The seasons on Winterhome will be out of phase for both . . . Never mind. Turn your mind far enough to see the humor. The sleepers never considered any path but to conquer a new world. We spaceborn have spent seventy years in space. We feel in our natal-memories that we can survive without a planet. We know nothing of worlds. The dissidents want to abandon Winterhome entirely.'

'They should be suppressed.'

'That can't be done, Keph,' he said, using the part of their name they shared in common – as no other would. 'It would split the spaceborn. The dissidents may be one in four of us by now – and Fathisteh-tulk is a dissident.'

'Chowpeentulk should control him better! She's pregnant; it ought to mean something to him —'

'Some females have not the skill sufficient to control their mates.'

Irony? Had she offended him? She sprayed him; he seemed pleased rather than mollified. A male as powerful as the Herdmaster didn't need to assert himself over his mate . . . She said, 'The situation cannot continue.'

'No. I fear for Fathisteh-tulk, and I don't like his clear successor. Can you speak to Chowpeentulk? Will she control him?'

She shifted uncomfortably, and muddy water surged. 'I have no idea.' A sleeper was not in her class; they didn't associate.

Tones sounded. The Herdmaster stretched and went to dry himself. It was time to return to duty.

———

The target world already bore a name in the Predecessor language.

The species had been nomads once. The Traveler Herd had become nomads again. But when mating season came, even a nomad herd must settle in one place until the children had been born.

Winterhome.

Winterhome was fighting back. Its rulers were no longer an unknown. Despite damage and loss of lives, Pastempeh-keph was relieved.

During the long years of flight from the ringed planet, the prey had not acted. The Herdmaster and his Advisor debated it: had they been seen? Electromagnetic signals of the domestic variety leaked through Winterhome's atmosphere and were monitored. Most of it was gibberish. Some was confusing, with pictures of enormous spacecraft of unrealistic design. What remained held no word of a *real* starship drawing near.

Then, suddenly, beams were falling directly on *Thuktun Flishithy*. Messages, demands for answers, words promising peace before there had been war: first a few, then more, then an incessant babble.

What was there to talk of? How could they expect to negotiate before their capabilities had been tested? But the prey had sent no missiles, no ships of war. Only messages.

The Breakers wondered if the prey might not know how to make war. This violated all the Herdmaster knew of evolution. Yet even when the attack began, the prey did little. The orbiting satellites didn't defend themselves. Half of them were gone in the first hour. Warriors braced to fight and die veered between relief and disappointment.

But the natives did have weapons. Not many, used late, but . . . a long scar, melted and refrozen, lay along *Message Bearer's* flank, crossing one wing of a big troop-carrying lander. Digit ship *Forty-one* might still operate in space, but it would never see atmosphere. Four more digit ships had been destroyed in space.

Missiles still rose from the planet's surface, and missiles and beam weapons still fired from space. A few satellites remained in orbit. *Message Bearer* surged under the impact of a plasma jet, and trembled as a missile launched away toward the jet's origin.

Oh, yes, the great ship had suffered minor damage. But this was good, in its way. The warriors would know, at least, that there was an enemy . . . and now they knew something about the alien weapons, and something about their own fighting ability. And the Herdmaster had learned that he could count on the sleepers.

He'd wondered. Would they fight, these ancient ones? But in fact they were doing well. Ancient they might be, considered from their birthdates; but frozen sleep was hard on the aged. The survivors had been eight to sixteen years past sexual maturity. They had run the ship for four years before their bodies had been frozen; they knew its rooms and corridors and storage holds as well as those who had been born aboard.

'Permission to report,' said Attackmaster Koothfektil-rusp.

'Go ahead.'

'I think we've cleared everything from orbit, Herd-master. There could be something around the other side of Winterhome, moving in our own orbit. We'll have to watch for that. We find four missiles rising from Land Mass Three. Shall I send them some bombs?'

'No. Wasteful. We've done enough here. Defense-master, take us out of here, out of their range.' Most of the native weapons would barely reach orbit – as if they were designed to attack other parts of the planet. Knowing the launch site was enough. It could be destroyed just before the troops went down to test the prey's abilities.

The digit ships could trample lesser centers before they descended: destroy dams, roads, anything that looked like communication or power sources. He hoped it would go well. His son Fookerteh's eight-cubed of warriors would be in the first assault. K'turfookeph was much concerned about him, though pride would never allow her to admit it . . .

'Follow the plan, Defensemaster. Take us behind that great gaudy satellite on a freely falling curve. Hide us. Attackmaster, I want every prey's eyes on that moon stomped blind before we begin the second phase of our acceleration.'

The Herdmaster waited for acknowledgements, then ordered, 'Get me Breaker-Two.'

———————

Breaker-Two had been a profession without an object until now. Takpusseh had been chosen young. He was only entering middle age, if one excluded the decades he had spent in frozen sleep, and the years' worth of damage that had done. He had been trained to deal with aliens

190

since before the starship ever left home; yet his training was almost entirely theoretical.

Almost. There had been another intelligent race on Takpusseh's homeworld. The Predecessors had died out before Takpusseh's race developed gripping appendages and large brains. They were the domain of Fistartehthuktun the historian-priest, not of Takpusseh.

Fistarteh-thuktun was a sleeper. Since the Awakening he had become more stiff and formal, more withdrawn, than ever. His spaceborn apprentices spoke only to him. His knowledge of the thuktunthp would be valuable here. Perhaps Breaker-One Raztupisp-minz – with the authority of a spaceborn, and a tact that was all his own – could draw him out . . .

The sleepers knew, in their hindbrains and spines and in their very cells, how to live on planets, what planets were like. The spaceborn could only guess. And yet – more was at stake than this artificial division of the Traveler Herd. The sleepers would die, one by one, eventually, and the Traveler herd would be one fithp again. The fithp needed what Fistarteh-thuktun knew: the stored knowledge of that older, now alien species.

Before they received the first pictures broadcast by the prey, the question had been debated endlessly. Would Winterhome's natives resemble the Predecessors? Or the fithp?

They did not.

Breaker-Two watched the surviving locals through a one-way transparency, while his assistant and a pair of soldiers worked with the alien artifacts. 'They look so fragile,' he said.

The ship shuddered.

'They've hit us again,' one of the soldiers said. 'Fragile they may be, but they're fighting back.'

'They do fight. Some were dead and some surrendered. Their plight was hopeless,' said the Octuple Leader. 'Yet one fired a weapon through its life support system! It killed itself to kill two of my warriors!'

'Your explanation?'

'Do you forget your place?'

'Your pardon. Shall I request that your superiors ask you? Shall I call the Herdmaster and request that he tell you to answer my questions? Wish you to continue this?'

'I don't know! It killed itself to kill two warriors! Surrender would have been easy. I – I have no explanation, Breaker. This is your own task.'

'Have you a theory, Octuple Leader?'

'Mad with battle lust . . . or sick? Dying? It happens.' His digits knotted and relaxed, knotted, relaxed. 'I should be fighting.'

It happens. Fumf! The spaceborn know only what they have read, and studied, yet they – These thoughts were useless. 'If you're needed, you'll be summoned,' Breaker-Two Takpusseh told him. 'I need you now. You were aboard the ruined space habitat. I will have questions.'

'Ask, Breaker.'

Takpusseh hadn't yet learned enough to ask intelligent questions. 'What did we take, Octuple Leader . . . Pretheeteh?'

'Pretheeteh-damb . . . sir. We took out quite a lot of stuff; there wasn't room for it all in here.'

Alien voices from the restraint room formed a muted background. Takpusseh half listened while he meandered through the loot Pretheeteh-damb's troops had moored to walls. For fifteen years he had studied the alien speech that crossed on radio waves between Winterhome and the ringed giant. Sometimes there had been pictures. Strange pictures, of a herd that could not exist. Boxes that danced with legs. Bipeds that changed shape and form. Streams of very similar paintings arriving within tiny fractions of a second. Contrasts: cities with tall buildings and machines, cities of mud huts and straw roofs.

Reception was terrible, and some of what could be

resolved was madness. Such information was suspect, contaminated, contained falsehood. Better to trust what one learned directly.

One fact stood out. Most of the broadcasts had been in one language. Takpusseh was hearing that language now, but he was hearing another too.

The prisoners were of two or more herds. For the moment that hardly mattered, but it would. It would add interest to a task that was already about as interesting as a fi' could stand.

There were big metal bins filled with smaller packages, each bearing a scrawled label: FOUND FROZEN. Piles of cloth too thin to be armor: protection from cold? Alien-looking machines with labels scrawled on them:

FROM FOOD PREPARATION AREA (?)
COMPUTER (?)
PART OF WASTE RECYCLING SYSTEM.
PROJECTILE WEAPON.

Corpses, bloated by vacuum, had been stuffed into one great pressure package, half frozen during the crossing and stuck together. Breaker-Two Takpusseh pulled the package open and, ignoring a queasy tremor in his digestive system, let his eyes rest on an alien head. This body had been ripped half apart by projectiles. Takpusseh noted sense organs clustered around a mouth filled with evil-looking teeth and a protruding flap of muscle. Two bulging, vulnerable-looking eyes. The nose was a useless knob; the paired nostrils might as well have been flat to the face. But the array was familiar, they weren't *that* peculiar. Bilateral symmetry . . . He reached to pick up a partially thawed foreleg and found five digits reinforced with bone. The aliens used those modified forefeet for making and using tools. They certainly didn't use that bump-with-holes for anything but smelling. All known from pictures – but this was different.

The weapon: it was a tiny thing, with a small, curved

handle. Could this modified foot really hold it aimed and steady?'

'This is the weapon it used?'

'Yes, Breaker-Two. That weapon killed two warriors.'

'Thank you.' Takpusseh moved the digits of an alien forefoot, thoughtfully, noting how one would cross over the flat surface behind the other four. And they all curved inward —

He was wasting time. 'First priority is to get their food separated out. They're bound to need water, they're certainly wet inside. Then autopsies. Let's get some idea what's inside them. Pretheeteh-damb, did you put these things in pressure containers *after* they had been subjected to vacuum?'

'Breaker, they were bound to suffer some damage during an assault. I suppose you could have come along to guard them.'

Takpusseh was stung. 'You suppose wrongly. The Herdmaster refused me permission.' Because he was too valuable, or because a sleeper was untrustworthy: who could know?

Again he looked through one-way glass at the prisoners. 'We've watched their ships take off. Chemicals: hydrogen and oxygen, energetic and difficult to handle, but still chemical fuels. The expense must be formidable. We must assume that these prisoners are the best they breed; else they would not be worth the cost of lifting them.'

His assistant twitched her ears in assent. 'Language first. We must make them teachers for future prisoners.'

'You say that easily, Tashayamp. It will be difficult. It may be impossible, with most of our team lost to the military mission.' Breaker-Two turned to the stacked cloth from the space station, then to cloth that had been cut from the prisoners. It was oddly curved; it had fastenings in odd places. Designed to fit an odd shape. These stiffened cups for the hind feet were thicker, padded. Takpusseh found nothing that might protect the fragile-looking foreleg digits.

194

'Pretheeteh-damb, did you search this detritus for weapons?'

'Yes. There were none, not even a bludgeon.'

'The prisoners were *all* covered with cloth, weren't they?'

'They were. So were the corpses.'

'It isn't a rank symbol and it doesn't hold personal weapons. They were in a space habitat; they'd regulate the temperature. Could they be so fragile? I think we had better give them cloth to protect their skins.' He looked back into the padded room.

Could the cloth be used for humidity regulation? If they didn't exude enough moisture to be comfortable . . . Well, that would be tested.

Hunch prodded him to add, 'And get the cloth off the corpses, Tashayamp. Start with this one.'

'The Herdmaster for you, Breaker-Two.'

Takpusseh took the call. The Herdmaster looked tired, in the fashion of those whom exhaustion turns nasty. 'Show them to me, Breaker-Two.'

Takpusseh turned the camera toward the one-way glass wall. The Herdmaster was silent for two or three breaths. Then, 'And these you must integrate into the Traveler Herd? I don't envy you, Breaker-Two. What do you know so far?'

'Their skins are fragile. They need cloth for protection.'

'Will they survive?'

'One seems near death . . . and it isn't the legless one. That one seems active enough. As for the rest, I'll have to be careful. We have their stored food, thanks to the troops, though we will have to identify it.'

'How soon can I expect —'

'When I tell you so. You have heard the sounds they make. They will never speak well. Another matter: We do not have a representative sampling here. That may be to the good; they may be more easily taught than their dirty-foot kin.' Takpusseh glanced at the smallest of the half-frozen corpses, now denuded of cloth. Eyes protruding, mouth wide open, distress frozen in its face. The protected area between the legs . . .

His guess had been right. The genitalia were oddly placed. He tried to imagine how they might mate. But this was a female; the breasts confirmed it. 'Our survivors are all adult males. Before we can understand anything about the natives we will need to study females, children, the crippled, the insane, the merely adequate —'

'Do what you can, Breaker. We won't be able to furnish you with other prisoners for some days yet. Unless you would prefer to stay behind with the digit ships?'

Takpusseh's ears flattened against his head. Had he just been named a coward? 'At your orders, Herdmaster.'

'I wasn't serious, and neither are you. You're needed here.'

'Sixty-four of us are needed here, Herdmaster! You've taken all but three of us for the digit ships, and you expect —'

'They must be near the battle to advise our warriors regarding the prey's mentality, and to learn. Do what you must.' The Herdmaster's face faded.

The prisoners were not very active now. The one who spoke a known language was prowling, exploring the restaurant room. The rest were talking in their own gibberish. They must belong to Land Mass One, the largest land block, and *not* to the herd that was so free with their radio noise . . . all but the prowler, and possibly the dark-skinned one, who might almost have been dead.

Might that be a disease, a lethal skin condition? Could the rest catch it? Leaving the Breakers without a profession again. One more thing to worry about.

He assumed, and would continue to assume, that Breaker-One Raztupispminz was listening via intercom. They would talk later. Meanwhile – 'Pretheeteh-damb, your attention.' Takpusseh pointed through the one-way transparency of the wall. 'That one. He's talking now; do you see his mouth moving?'

'I see.'

'Take your octuple and fetch him to me.'

'Breaker-Two, I would have no trouble fetching it myself, save for fear of crushing it by accident.'

'Take your octuple.' Takpusseh felt no need to justify himself. They were an unknown. Best to be wary. At worst the show of strength might impress the aliens.

They did look fragile. Fragile enough to make him queasy.

He couldn't afford to think that way. He was Breaker-Two, and these alien beings constituted the only career open to him. *We must come to know each other well. Without you I'm nothing.*

The door square, ten feet by ten feet or thereabouts, and padded. When Wes pounded on it with his fist he got a peculiar echo, not quite like metal. Foamed metal? Thick, like the door on a bank vault. *What do they think we are, The Hulk? Could they have picked up some Saturday-morning TV?* It opened inward, he remembered; but no hinges were in sight. And no handle. Maybe the Invaders had prepared this cell before they knew what humans would be like. Maybe it was built for Invader felons or mental cases.

Whatever. *We won't get out of here with just muscle.*

CLACK! The door jumped under his hand. Wes kicked himself away as it swung open.

What showed first were pale brown tentacles gripping a bayoneted rifle. The Invader entered behind the blade, slowly, its wary eyes on the cloud of drifting humans. It looked – Wes found himself grinning. He let it spread. It wouldn't know what a grin meant.

The Invader looked like a baby elephant. The tentacle was an extended nose: a trunk. It branched halfway down, with a nostril in the branch; and branched again near the tip, and again. Eight digits. Base eight!

Straps of brown leather wove a cage around it, with a flap of cloth between the legs and a pouch behind the head.

Wes struck the wall opposite the door and managed to absorb most of the recoil.

Another baby elephant with two trunks entered, similarly dressed, similarly armed. They took positions against the bulkhead to each side of the door. Their claws sank easily into the thick, dampened padding. Their weapons were aimed into the room, not at anyone, but ready. A third, unarmed, stayed in the doorway.

The cell was getting crowded. Giorge was finally showing signs of life, staring wall-eyed, making feeble pushing gestures at the air. Arvid pulled the black man behind him. The recoil drifted him into the first Invader. It skillfully turned the rifle before Rogachev could impale himself, then gently thrust him away with the butt.

The Invader in the doorway held Dawson's attention. This one wore straps dyed scarlet, and a backpouch patterned in green and gold. Its feet were clawed, not really elephant-like except for the size. The tail was paddle-shaped. The head was big; the face, impressive. Grooves of muscle along the main trunk focused attention on the eyes: black irises surrounded by gray, looking straight at Wes Dawson.

It pushed itself into the cell.

It was coming for *him*. Wes waited. He saw no point in trying to escape.

The jump was skillfully done. The Invader landed feet-first against the wall, just next to Wes; wrapped its trunk around Wes's torso (and two of the eight branches had him by the neck); jumped on the recoil, thrust him through the doorway ahead of itself (a fourth Invader had pulled aside), and barely brushed the doorway as it came through behind. It would have crushed Wes against the corridor wall if its claws hadn't closed on the doorjamb.

Wes was near strangling. He pulled at the branches

around his neck, then slapped thrice at the joint with the flat of his hand. Would it understand? Yes: the constriction eased.

Five more Invaders waited in the corridor. Three moved off to the left. Wes's captor followed, and the others followed him. *They must think we're hot stuff,* he thought. *Maybe we really are hurting them. Or maybe . . . just how many are they, that they can spare eight behemoths to collect one fragile man?*

Where are they taking me?

Dissection? But with so many around him, there was surely no point in struggling.

———

They were floating down the curved corridor. A sound like a ram's-horn blared through the ship. Dawson's guards moved quickly to one of the corridor walls. Their claws sank into the thick damp matting that lined the passageway.

What? A warning? There was nothing to hold on to. It hardly mattered. The tentacles held him tightly.

The air vibrated with a supersonic hum. What had been a wall became a floor. After a few moments the baby elephants seemed to have adjusted, and released their grip. They moved off down the corridor, surrounding him but letting him walk.

They were staring. How must it look to them? A continual toppling controlled fall?

They pushed him through a large door at the end of the corridor. One followed. The others waited outside.

A single Invader waited behind a table tilted like a draftsman's table. It stared at him.

Dawson stared back.

How long does this go on? 'I am Congressman Wesley Dawson, representing the United States of America.'

'I am Takpusseh.'

My God, they speak English! 'Why have I been treated this way?'

'I do not comprehend.'

The creature's voice was flat, full of sibilants, without emotions. A leaking balloon might have spoken that way.

'You attacked us without warning! You killed our women!' Here was a chance to protest, *finally* a target for his pain, and it was just too much. Wes leaned across the tilted table; his voice became a scream. 'There was no need! We welcomed you, we came up to meet you. There was no need.'

'I do not always understand what you say. Speak slowly and carefully.'

It felt like a blow to the face. Wes stopped, then started over, fully in control, shaping each word separately. 'We wanted to welcome you. We wanted to greet visitors from another star. We wanted to be friends.'

The alien stared at Wes. 'You will learn to speak with us.'

'Yes. Certainly.' *It will be all right now! It is a misunderstanding, it must be. When I learn to talk with them* – 'Our families will be concerned about us. Have you told Earth that we are alive?'

'I do not comprehend.'

'Do you talk to Earth? To our planet?'

'Ah. Our word for Earth is – ' a peculiar sound, short and hissing. 'We do not know how to tell your people that you live.'

'Why do you lock us up?' *He didn't get that. Maybe why is too abstract.* 'The door to our room. Leave it open.'

The alien stared at Wes, then looked toward a lens on the wall. Then it stared at Wes again. Finally it said, 'We have cloth for you. Can you want that?'

Cloth? Wes became aware that he was naked. 'Yes. We need clothing. Covering.'

'You will have that. You will have water.'

'Food,' Dawson said.

'Yes. Eat.' The alien gestured. One of the others brought in boxes from another compartment.

Clothes. Canned goods. Oxygen bottles. A spray can of deodorant. *Whose?* Soap. Twelve cans of Spam with a London label. A canned Smithfield ham. *The Russians must have brought that.*

Wes pointed to what he thought was edible. Then he took a Spam can and pantomimed opening it with his forefinger, trying to indicate that he needed a can opener.

One of the aliens drew a bayonet and opened the Smithfield ham by cutting the top off, four digits for the can, four for the bayonet. He passed the can to Wes.

Stronger than hell! Advanced metals, too . . . but you wouldn't make a starship out of cast iron. Okay, now what?

'Do you eat that?' the alien behind the draftsman's table asked. The interrogative was obvious.

'Yes.'

It was hard to interpret the alien's response. It lifted the ears. The other, the one that brought the packages, responded the same way. *Vegetarians? Are they disgusted?*

The alien spoke gibberish, and another alien came in with a large sheet of what might have been waxed paper. It took the ham from the can, wrapped it (the stuff was flexible, more like thick Saran wrap), and gave it to Wes. It left carrying the can.

'You attack   you fight us. There is no need.'

'There is need. Your people is strong,' the alien said.

A flat screen on one wall lighted, to show another alien. A voice came into the room. It babbled, in the liquid sibilants Wes had heard them use before.

'You must go back now. We turn now.'

It didn't make sense. 'If we were weak, would you fight us?'

'Go.'

'But what do you want? Where do you come from? Why are you here? Why is it important that we are strong?'

The alien stared again. 'Go.'

'I have to know! Why are you here?'

The alien spoke in sibilants.

Tentacles wrapped around his waist and encircled his throat. He was dragged from the room. As they went down the corridor, the ram's horn sound came again, and the aliens held him against the wall.

'You don't have to hold me,' Wes said.

There was no response. The alien soldier carried a warm smell, something like being in a zoo. It wouldn't have been unpleasant, but there was too much of it, this close.

How many of them speak English? He – it – said I should learn their language. They'll try to teach me. He looked down at himself, naked, wrapped in tentacles. *Think like them.* They're not crazy – assume they're not crazy! – just different. *Difference in shape, and evolution, and senses. What do I smell like to this . . . soldier, pulled right up against its nostrils like this?* It held him like a nest of snakes, and its black-and-gray eyes were unreadable.

You knew the job was dangerous . . .

CHAPTER THIRTEEN
THE MORNING AFTER

Now a' is done that men can do, And a' is done in vain.

    – ROBERT BURNS, 'It was A' for Our Rightfu' King'

COUNTDOWN: H PLUS SEVEN HOURS

Son of a bitch! Sergeant Ben Mailey shepherded his charges off the helicopter and watched them climb into the staff car. *The President! Son of a bitch!* He grinned widely, then sobered. *It took a war to get the President Inside. And I'm not going in with him.*

Jenny ushered the President into the Command Center. She had enjoyed her previous trip Inside. Maps and screens showed what was going on across the nation. You could see everything at a glance. A dozen Army and Air Force officers sat at consoles. Large screens flashed with maps of the United States. Aircraft in flight, major trains, and larger ships showed up as blobs of light on the maps.

But there weren't many lights, and many of the harbors showed dark splotches. Rail centers like Omaha had pin-point dark spots as well.

Jack Clybourne followed them into the cavernous room. He looked puzzled, and Jenny felt sorry for him. There was no real need for a presidential bodyguard, not here in the national command center. His job was done the moment they got the President into the Hole, but nobody had thought to tell him that.

And I sure won't.

Admiral Carrell stood to attention as the President entered. So did the mustached civilian who'd been seated with him. Admiral Carrell wore a dark civilian suit, but he looked very much an officer. 'Glad to see you, sir.'

'Thank you.'

He sounds a million years old, and I feel older. I look like a witch – She felt giddy, and suppressed an insane desire to giggle. *Suppose Admiral Carrell inspects my uniform, with wrinkles and unbuttoned buttons and – and I'm drunk on fatigue poisons. We all are. I wonder when the Admiral slept last?*

'The cabinet will be coming later,' Coffey said. 'That is, State and Interior will be. We're dispersing some of the others so that – I don't really know the aliens' capabilities.'

Admiral Carrell nodded. 'They may know the location of this place,' he said.

'Could they do anything if they did know?'

'Yes, sir. They hit Boulder Dam with something large and fast, no radioactive fallout. As my Threat Team keeps telling me, they're throwing rocks at us. Meteorites. They have lasers that chew through ships. Mr. President, I don't know what they could do to Cheyenne Mountain.'

They, they, they, Jenny thought. *Our enemy has no name!*

'Let's hope we don't find out, then. What is the situation? What about the Russians?'

'They've been hit badly, but they're still fighting. I don't know what forces they have left.' Admiral Carrell shook his head. 'We're having the devil of a time getting reports. We used up half our ICBM's last night, firing them straight up and detonating in orbit. The aliens got half of what was left. They seem to have targeted dams, rail centers, harbors – and anyplace that launched a missile. I presume they did the same to the Soviets, but we can't know.'

'We can't talk to them?'

'I'm able to communicate with Dr. Bondarev intermittently. But *he* doesn't know the status of his forces. Their internal communications are worse than ours, and ours are nearly gone.' Carrell paused a moment and leaned against a computer console.

He's an old man! I never really saw it before. And that's scary —

'What about casualities?' the President demanded.

'Military casualties are very light — except for F-15 pilots who launched satellite interceptors. Those were one hundred percent. We've lost a number of missile crews, too.

'Civilian casualties are a little like that. Very heavy for those living below dams or in harbor areas, and almost none outside such areas.'

'Total?'

Carrell shrugged. 'Hard to find out. I'd guess about a hundred thousand, but it could be twice that.'

A hundred thousand. Vietnam killed only fifty thousand in ten years. Nobody's taken losses like that since World War II.

'Why don't you know?' the President demanded.

'We depend heavily on satellite relays for communications,' Carrell said. 'Command, control, communications, intelligence, all depended on space, but we have no space assets left.'

'So we don't know anything?'

'Know?' Admiral Carrell shook his head again. 'No, sir, we don't know anything. I do have some guesses.

'Something seems to have driven their large ship away; at least it withdrew. The Soviets attacked it heavily. According to Bondarev they probably damaged it, but if he has any evidence for that, he hasn't told me about it.'

Jenny cleared her throat. 'Yes?' Carrell asked.

'Nothing, sir. We all know about claims. If I were a Soviet official and I'd just expended a lot of very expensive missiles, I'm sure I'd claim it was worthwhile too.'

The President nodded grimly. 'Assume it wasn't damaged.'

205

'Yes, sir,' Carrell said. 'It's very hard to track anything through the goop in the upper atmosphere – and above, for that matter. The aliens have dumped many tons of metallic chaff. That gives some very strange radar reflections.

'As far as we can tell, they've left behind a number of warships, but the big ship withdrew. We think they headed for the Moon.' Admiral Carrell's calm broke for a moment. 'God damn them, that's *our* Moon.'

'Have we heard from Moon Base?'

'Not ours, and the Soviets have lost contact with theirs. I think they're gone.'

Fifty billion dollars. Most of our space program. Damn!

The President looked older by the minute.'What do we know about their small ships?'

Carrell shrugged. 'They have several dozen of them. We say small, but the smallest is the size of the *Enterprise*. I mean the aircraft carrier! We shot some of them out of space. I *know* we got two, with a Minuteman out of Minot Air Force Base. Then they clobbered Minot. We think the Russian got a couple too.'

'None of which explains why they ran away,' the civilian said.

'Mr. President, this is Mr. Ransom, one of my Threat Team,' Admiral Carrell said. 'He and his colleagues are the only experts we have.'

'Experts?'

'Yes, sir. They're science-fiction writers.'

Who else? And the President isn't laughing . . .

'Why did they run away,then, Mr. Ransom?'

'We don't know, and we don't like it,' Ransom said, 'Back in the Red Room you can get a dozen opinions. Curtis and Anson are back there trying to get a consensus, but I don't think they'll do it. The aliens could have their mates and children aboard that main ship. They came a long way.'

'I see,' David Coffey said. He looked around the big control room. 'Is there somewhere I can sit down?'

'You'd do better to get some rest,' Admiral Carrell said.

'So should you.'

'After you, sir. Someone has to be on duty. We might get through to the Russians again.'

This time Jenny couldn't help laughing. When the President and Admiral Carrell stared at her, she giggled, then sobered quickly. 'I never thought we'd be so eager to hear from the Russians.'

Carrell's smile was forced. 'Yes. It is ironic. However —'

He broke off as red lights flashed and a siren wailed through the enormous room. The Admiral took a headset from one of the sergeants. After a moment he said, 'They haven't all left. They just hit a major highway junction.'

'Highway junctions. Railroad yards. Dams,' the President muttered.

'Yes,' Admiral Carrell agreed. 'But not cities or population centers. San Diego but not New York harbor. Cities along major rivers are flooded, some severely. Some parts of the country are undamaged but have no electricity. Others are without power, and effectively isolated. Some places have electric power and are utterly untouched. It's an odd way to fight a war.'

———

Message Bearer hummed. The vibration from the main fusion drive was far higher than any normal range of hearing; but it shook the bones, and it was always there. Sleepers and spaceborn alike had learned to ignore it during the long days of deceleration into Winterhome system. It could not be sensed until it was gone.

. . . It was gone. Thrust period was over. The floor eased from under the Herdmaster and he floated. Six eights of digit ships had been left behind to implement the invasion, while *Message Bearer* fell outward toward the Foot. The acceleration, the pulses of fusion light and gamma rays, had been blocked by the mass of Winterhome's moon. Let Winterhome's masters try to detect her, an inert speck against the universe.

The Herdmaster blew a fluttering sigh. Several hours of maneuvers had left him exhausted. It was good to be back in free-fall, even for a few minutes.

'That's over,' he said. 'Now we'll trample the natives a little and see what they do.'

'It's their terrain. We will lose some warriors.' Fathisteh-tulk's lids drooped in sleepy relaxation, and the Herdmaster spared him a glare. The Herdmaster's Advisor had himself been Herdmaster; he could have saved the Herdmaster this chore, spared him for other work . . . except that spaceborn warriors might not take his orders. He was a sleeper; his accent marked him.

So he was being unjust. But Fathisteh-tulk *enjoyed* the situation. The Herdmaster sighed again and turned to the intercom. 'Get me Breaker-Two.'

Takpusseh too spoke with the archaic sleeper accent. He stood at a desk littered with alien artifacts.

'You have spoken with the prey,' the Herdmaster asked.

'I have spoken with one of them, Herdmaster. This one is of the Land Mass Two herd that babbled to us as we approached. Some of the others speak that language, but they are not part of that herd.'

'What have you learned?'

'Herdmaster, I do not know what we learned from that interview. Certainly that herdless one did not submit.'

The Herdmaster was silent for a moment. 'It was helpless?'

'Herdmaster, I sent an armed octuple to fetch it. I left it naked, and required it to stand before my table. It demanded explanations. It was abusive!'

'Yet it lives? You show remarkable restraint.'

Takpusseh vented a fluttering snort. 'I did not understand all it said at the time. It was only after it was sent back to the restraining pen that we listened carefully to the recordings. Herdmaster, these are alien beasts. They do not obey properly. It will take time to make them a part of the Traveler Herd.'

'Perhaps, being herdless, it is insane. Were there others of its herd in the satellite?'

'Yes. It said that its mate had been killed in the attack.'

'It is insane, then. Kill it.'

'Herdmaster, there is no need for haste. It speaks this language the prey call English far better than do the others.'

'Have the others submitted?'

'Herdmaster, I believe they have.'

'The herdless one comes from the continent with the most roads and harbors and dams. Surely the most advanced herd will not *all* be insane.'

'Surely not, Herdmaster.'

'Do you have advice?'

'Herdmaster, I believe we should continue the plan. Trample the prey before we speak with them. If they are arrogant in defeat, they must be impossible before they are harmed.'

'Very well. Will you continue to speak with this one?'

'Not without new reason. I found the interview painful. I will speak with it again when we have obtained more of its herd. Perhaps it will regain its sanity. Until then, Breaker-One Raztupisp-minz will study the herdless one. He chooses not to speak with it.'

The Herdmaster twitched his digits against his forelegs. Takpusseh was being tactful. Raztupisp-minz was not fluent in the language of the prey.

'The other prisoners are in my domain, but we house them together,' Breaker-two Takpusseh finished.

'Do *any* of them submit?'

'I have had no opportunity to examine the others while *Message Bearer* maneuvers violently. Instead, we have experimented with their living conditions. We gave them cloth from the great stores they kept in the orbiting habitat. They draped themselves with it. We gave them water and watched how much they used, and analyzed their excreta. We change their environment. How do they treat their food? Which of our foods can they tolerate? Do they like more oxygen, or less? Warm air or cold? To what extent can they tolerate their own exhalations?'

'I expect they breathe the air mixture of Winterhome.'

'Of course, but where on Winterhome? Equator or poles? High altitude or low? Wet or dry? We are learning. They like pressure anywhere between sea level and half that. They can tolerate our air mix but prefer it dryer. They cover their skins with cloth even when far too hot; that deceived us for a time. They drink and wash with clean water and ignore mud. Their food is treated; they have to wet and heat it. They would not eat ours. And in the process of experiment, we gave them strong incentive to learn to speak to us.'

The Herdmaster laughed, a fluttering snort. 'Of course they would like to tell you to stop. *Can* they speak?'

'We have begun to teach them. It is easier with those who speak the language called English. I see no need to learn the others' language. The herdless one called – Dawson – can translate until they gain skill at our speech. Their mouths are not properly formed. One day I think there will be a compromise language; but they will never be taken for ordinary workers of the Traveler Herd, even in pitch dark. The smell is distinctive.'

'Are they in good condition?'

'The dark-skinned one is unresponsive and doesn't eat. I think he must be dying. He too is herdless. The other four seem ready for training.'

'The other herdless one will die as well.'

'Perhaps. He seems in health. We must watch him. Herdmaster, from what region do you intend to take prisoners?'

'You have no need to know.'

'Herdmaster, I must know if Dawson will have companions of his own herd. I must know if he is insane, or if all those of his herd act so strangely.'

'He is insane,' the Herdmaster said.

'Lead me, Herdmaster.'

'Perform your task. I gave no order.'

'Thank you. Herdmaster, it is likely that he is insane. Surely he has never been as far from his herd as he is now. But we must *know*.'

The Herdmaster considered. 'Very well. We will attempt to seize and keep a foothold in Land Mass Two, North, the source of most of the electromagnetic babble. We will take prisoners.'

'As many as possible, Herdmaster. I require females and children. It would also be well to have immature and aged, cripples, insane —'

'I have other priorities, but the warriers will be told. How shall we identify the insane?'

'Never mind. Some will go insane after capture.'

'Anything else?'

'I would like to show the prisoners some records.'

'Good. Where? The communal mudroom? My officers and their mates are clamoring to see the natives.'

'I'm not sure they're ready for . . . Lead me. We will display them, but not in the mudroom. Use the classroom. They'll have to get used to us sooner or later —'

'And my fithp must get used to them. We'll be starting spin immediately. You can put your show on afterward. Will you show them the Podo Thuktun?'

'No! They're not ready. They wouldn't know what it *means*. Fistarteh-thuktun would stomp me flat.'

The Herdmaster disconnected. Fathisteh-tulk, who had not spoken during the exchange, said, 'Takpusseh was a good choice. Many sleepers have lapsed into lethargy since the awakening. Takpusseh has kept his enthusiasm, his sense of wonder.'

'Yes. Why has he no mate? He is of the age, and his status is adequate . . . though as a sleeper he lost rank, of course —'

'His mate did not survive the death-sleep.,'

'Ah.' The Herdmaster pondered. 'Advise me. Shall I expect these prisoners to develop into cooperating workers? Can they persuade their race to surrender without undue bloodshed?'

'You know my opinion,' the Herdmaster's Advisor said. 'We don't need this world or its masters. We are not dirtyfeet. We should be colonizing space, not inhabited worlds.'

Dirtyfeet: only sleepers used that term for those who had remained comfortably behind on the homeworld. The spaceborn felt no need to insult ancestors who were forever removed in space and time.

Never mind; Fathisteh-tulk had raised another problem. 'Odd, that a spaceborn should hear this from a sleeper. You know my opinion too. We came to conquer Winterhome. Regulations require that I consult you as to methods.'

'Do you intend that our prisoners shall not learn of the Foot?'

The Herdmaster frowned. 'It is standard procedure . . .'

A fluttering snort answered him. 'Of course. A soldier should never know more than he must, for he might be captured and accepted into the enemy's herd. But how could the forces of Winterhome rescue our prisoners without taking *Message Bearer* herself? In which case all is already lost.'

'I suppose so. Very well —'

'Wait, please, Herdmaster. My advice.'

'Well?'

'Your judgment was right. Tell them what they must know. Tell them that they must submit, and show them that we can force them to obey. Then let them speak to their people. But we must not depend upon their aid.'

'Breaking them into the Traveler Herd is the task of the Breakers. Takpusseh and Raztupisp-minz are conscientious.'

'Even so. Don't let them know all . They are alien.'

The Kawasaki was an LTD 750 twin with a belt drive, an '83 model which Harry had bought at the year-end sale in '84. He had saddlebags for it and a carry rack for his guitar. Two weeks ago he had borrowed Arline Mott's pickup truck and taken the engine in.

He was driving the same pickup truck now, and he felt guilty about it.

He'd telephoned Arline at 5:00 A.M., before she'd been up or able to listen to the radio. 'I'll have it back by noon,' he'd said.

Since Arline didn't get up before noon, that wouldn't be a problem. She'd put the key outside her door and gone back to bed.

She ought to be getting the hell out of Los Angeles!

If I'd told her, Harry thought. But if I didn't call her, who would? And she'd be in bed until noon anyway. So all I have to do is get the damn truck back to her.

He pulled into a 76 station. There were three cars ahead of him. He filled the truck, then filled two gas cans Arline kept in the back. *Least I can do for her.*

Gas was still being sold at the pump prices. That couldn't last.

He drove North along Van Nuys Boulevard. The tools and all of the Kawasaki except the engine were in the back. It was still in pieces. A glance at *Road and Track Specialties*, which specialized in racing motorcycles, sent him off on a daydream. He really ought to steal one of those. It would get him there faster and more dependably, if he didn't get himself arrested, and certainly the emergency justified it

213

. . . he drove past without slowing, and on to Van Nuys Honda-Kawasaki.

His walk slowed as he passed through the salesroom. His money hadn't stretched far enough. He needed a new fender, spare brake and clutch levers, a fairing . . . Jesus, that Vetter Windjammer fairing was nice. *I could use the emergency thousand that Wes keeps* – Only that wouldn't work. That thousand belonged to Carlotta, and Harry intended to take it to her. Not all, but as much as possible.

No Vetter fairing, then. Just tie-down straps, and paper bags to put his hands in. He stepped up to the counter, next to a bulky, younger man.

'Hairy Red,' the man said. Harry almost recognized him; the name wouldn't surface. 'How they hanging?'

'This is the day *nobody* knows that,' Harry said. 'Did you see the light show?'

'Damn right. I'm getting out.'

'I'm headed east. I could use a partner.'

'North looks safer,' the half stranger said. Harry nodded; he agreed. When a clerk appeared he paid the rest of what he owed out of Wes Dawson's thousand. He paid for the engine repairs and restrained the urge to buy anything. He might need money more.

He brought truck and engine to the parking lot across the alley from the motorcycle shop. The transistor radio was telling the world that there had been a horrible mistake. The aliens had attacked certain parts of the United States and the rest of the world, but now they were going away. The delegation that had been aboard the Soviet Kosmograd had been taken aboard by the aliens. Negotiations were proceeding. Citizens should remain calm. Anyone who could go to work should do that. Conserve electricity and water. Don't waste anything. There would be inconveniences. Expect rationing soon.

That was one station. On another, the announcer was

hysterical. The Martians had landed in New Jersey.

The one thing that every station announced was that all military and police personnel were to report for duty immediately.

Harry began to work.

An hour later he had some appreciation of what he'd lost.

Harry felt the urgency (what was happening now around Carlotta Dawson? And where, in hell or heaven, was Congressman Wes?) and the certain knowledge that hurrying was a mistake. His vertebrae, dreaming that they had become solid bone, woke to grating agony as he lifted and twisted and crouched and crawled. He worked muscles that had forgotten their function. They protested and were ignored. He worked as he had to, letting details fill his mind from edge to edge. It was like the calm from being ripped on marijuana, or (he presumed) from transcendental meditation. He had read *Zen and the Art of Motorcycle Maintenance* long ago.

It was killing labor, and Harry was drenched with sweat. He was old, old. But the Kawasaki was a motorcycle again.

This would be a hellish shakedown tour for a newly mounted engine. Harry smoked while the crankcase drained onto the weeds. He refilled it with a very light oil. He started the engine and let it run for the life span of a cigarette. He drained the engine again and refilled it with a heavier oil.

Puffing, he began to pack the Kawasaki. The sleeping bag went on the rack. It would normally carry his guitar, but not this trip! He'd already turned that over to Lucy Mott for safekeeping. He ran his spare cables alongside the working cables, ready to be attached in an instant. He reached into the fuel tank's wide-mouthed fill – was there anyone to see? – to attach the gold peso and the dimes. Carlotta Dawson's .45 auto went under the seat, with two clips. The .25 Beretta was in his jacket pocket. A one-quart botta bag was more convenient than a canteen for drinking while riding; he'd want to fill it before he left.

What had he forgotten? He had spare belts, high-speed belts built for industry, which fit the cycle and cost a quarter as much as store-bought. He checked everything: spare oil, ratchet set, screwdriver set, four wrenches, electrical tape, spare fuses, a can of hydraulic oil for the brakes. Tubing cut to fit. Spare clothing in a plastic garbage bag. The binoculars.

Finally he buckled on the wide kidney belt. It reduced his stomach by inches, and made him feel ten years younger.

He went to the head shop next door for cigarettes. There was only one clerk, and Harry was surprised to see her.

'Ruby?'

'Yeah, man. How's it, Harry?'

'I thought you'd be in the mountains by now,' Harry said.

She looked puzzled.

'Aliens? Space war? Lights in the sky?'

She laughed. 'What you need, Harry?'

'Two cartons of Pall Mall. No filter. Ruby, you told *me* about it.'

She got out the cigarettes. Harry handed her money, and she gave him back change. No premium price. 'Told you about what?'

'What I said. Space War.'

She laughed again. 'I thought I remembered calling somebody; was that you?' She laughed some more. 'Wow, that Colombian stuff is *strong*, Harry. I really thought it was real!'

He was still shaking his head when he got outside. It was tough loading the Kawasaki into the truck, but he got help from the guys in the shop.

Got to return the truck, he told himself. Got to.

Fifteen hundred miles, near enough. Wish I didn't have

to take the truck back. Ought to get started . . . Hell, it's only five miles to Arline's place. Damn near on the way. Let's get it done.

If he'd been in a car, he'd never have made it.

All the highways out of Los Angeles were jammed. Cars all over the road. Cars stalled on the wrong side of the road, people driving on the left side, anything to get out. And then the first wrecks, and the endless fields of cars behind them.

Many were piled high with clutter. Baby cribs. Footlockers. A typewriter. Blankets, toys, any damned thing you could think of, lashed on top of the cars. One king-size mattress on top of a car full of kids.

There weren't many police, and where there were any, they were turning people back. Harry had to take out Dawson's letter a dozen times, until he was good with the spiel.

'I'm Congressman Wes Dawson's assistant,' Harry would say. 'He's aboard the alien ship. I have to look after his wife.'

One of the National Guardsmen even said 'sir' to Harry after he'd seen the letter.

'Heard much, Sergeant?'

'No, sir. They hit Hoover Dam. We know that much. Seem to have hit a lot of dams and power plants and railroad yards. Nobody knows why. Now they've gone.'

Harry nodded sagely. 'Thanks.' Then he couldn't resist. 'Carry on, Sergeant,' he said, and roared off.

By mid-afternoon he was through the Cajon Pass, headed east across the Mojave Desert. His back had begun to hurt.

CHAPTER FOURTEEN
THE DAM

Better one's own duty, though imperfect,
Than another's duty well performed.

– THE BHAGAVAD GITA

COUNTDOWN: H PLUS 36 HOURS

Jeri Wilson woke with a start. The sun was in the west, sinking toward one of the snowcapped peaks that surrounded the twisting mountain road. Melissa sat quietly in the backseat.

'It's after noon,' Jeri said accusingly. 'Why did you let me sleep so long?'

'You looked like you needed it.'

Jeri yawned. 'I guess I did, punkin.' She glanced at the seat beside her, then looked down at the floor. 'Where's the map?'

'I have it,' Melissa said. 'I was trying to figure out where we are, but I can't.' She handed over the Auto Club map.

Jeri traced a yellow line along the map. 'I'm not exactly sure myself,' she admitted. 'I thought about what you said and decided we didn't want to go through Albuquerque. Hairy Red marked a route up into Colorado. He'd have loved it, lots of twists and turns. Good thing you slept through it; you'd have got carsick.'

'So how far is it now?'

'About three hundred miles in a straight line, but I don't know how far on the road.'

'Is – does Daddy really know we're coming?'

'Well – sort of.'

'Does he want us to come?'

'I think so,' Jeri said. *He didn't say no!* 'Pour me some coffee from the Thermos. We've got to cross the Continental Divide this afternoon. Best we get started.'

Jeri coasted down the twisting Rocky Mountain roads in low gear, with the motor turned off, scared as stiff as the unpowered power steering. The highway was nearly deserted. Twice she pulled off for huge trucks, then used the motor to get back on the road. Once a Corvette shot into her rearview mirror, fishtailed as the driver saw her, and was still wobbling as it went past. Melissa, stretched out on the backseat, didn't wake up.

The highway began to straighten out as it reached the bottom. The Great Plains stretched infinitely ahead. Jeri took the car out of gear, started the motor to get her brakes and steering back, and reached the Great Plains doing sixty in neutral. She waited until she'd lost some speed before going into gear.

It was mid-afternoon of a cloudless day. Behind her the Rockies, receding, seemed to grow even larger as the scale came into focus: a wall across the west of the world. She held her speed at fifty-five.

She jumped when she realized Melissa was peering over her shoulder. Melissa said, 'When the gas needle says Empty, how much gas is left?'

'I don't know. Could be anywhere from none to . . . five?'

They'd be out of gas soon. All she could think of was to get as far as she could. Maybe there would be gasoline at the next station, wherever that might be . . .

Jeri's rearview mirror flared like a spotlight in her eyes. She slapped the mirror aside and screamed, 'Don't look, Melissa! Get down on the floor!' Hoping Melissa would obey; wishing she could do the same. Braking carefully,

219

edging toward the right lane. Melissa said, 'What —'

WHAM! Ears popped, the car lurched, the rear window crazed and went opaque. She'd expected it to shatter, to lace her head and neck with broken glass. The news had spoken of bombs falling on hydroelectric dams, railroads, major highways. George and Vicki Tate-Evans had told her (speaking in relay, impossible to interrupt) how to recognize a thermonuclear bomb flash, and how to survive.

She pulled off the road and waited. *When you see the whole world turn bright, don't look. Drop to the ground. Grip your legs, put your head between your knees. Now kiss your ass good-bye.* Behind her, a Peterbilt ten-wheeler that had been charging up on her tail wobbled and tipped over and kept coming, on its side, leaving a trail of fire as it slid past and finally came to a stop ahead of her.

'Atomic bomb,' Melissa said, awed.

'Stay down!'

'I *am*.'

A man crawled out of the truck shaking his head. That really wasn't much of a fire: just a streak leading to the truck, a few flames under it. Maybe the truck was out of gas too.

She waited for the softer WHAM!, the second shock wave as air rushed back to fill the vacuum beneath the rising fireball. When the station wagon stopped shuddering she pulled around the burning truck and kept going. A flaming toadstool lit her way. She kept glancing back, watching it die.

She made another six miles before the motor died. She hoped they were far enough from the radioactive cloud. She hoped it wouldn't rain.

The old one-lung Harley had begun sputtering ten miles back. Now it died. Gynge let it coast and thought of his alternatives.

He could probably make it run another couple of hundred miles, but the damned thing had been nearly dead last year. It wasn't getting younger.

He could walk.

There had to be something better. Up ahead was a rest area. Gynge let the Harley's last momentum take it off the edge of the highway and into the picnic area.

The highways were deserted. At first the cops and National Guards were stopping everything. Gynge had detoured three times around them. Damn good thing he knew the country. After he got into the mountains he left the main roads. There weren't any cops at all.

A semi roared past. There was a little traffic. Food trucks. Come to that, in normal times one out of every three trucks carried food. People had to eat. But there wasn't a hell of a lot except trucks.

The rest area was empty. Almost empty. Not quite. He heard sounds at the far end, and went to investigate.

What Gynge saw was a tired old man on a picnic table with his pants off and a girdle stretched out beside him. Bikers called it a 'kidney belt,' but it did the same thing any girdle did: it held in a sagging gut. The old man's gut was a good-sized beer belly. He was trying to hug one knee against his chest, but his gut blocked the way.

The man sat up, blowing. His frame was large; Gynge saw that he must have been formidable in his time. He didn't look formidable now. His red beard had gone mostly gray, and the hair of his head was following. He sat up, consulted the book beside him. Then he stretched his right leg out in front of him, bent forward as far as he could manage, threw a hand towel around the arch of his foot, and pulled on both ends.

If the man had brought friends, they had had plenty of time to appear. Gynge watched a little longer. The red-and-gray-haired man switched legs, groaning.

One full day on a motorcycle had done him in.

Harry lay on the picnic table and groaned. Two whiplash accidents within two weeks would leave their mark for the rest of his life. His spine felt like a crystal snake dropped on flagstones! He knew well enough that he was overweight. That was what the kidney belt was for, but it hadn't been enough, and his guts were about to fall out all over the picnic table.

He'd bought a book of stretching exercises. Some of those were supposed to help a bad back. It was worth a try . . . but it felt like he was breaking his back rather than mending it.

He had switched legs before the stranger stepped into view. A biker, probably. He strolled up to Harry's bike, in no apparent hurry; ran his eyes over it; then stepped up to Harry. Looming. He was all muscles and hair and dirt, no prettier than Harry felt, though younger and in better condition.

He asked, 'Why a towel?'

Harry flopped on his back, panting. He said, 'A towel is the most massively useful thing a traveler can have. And that was a stretching exercise, because my back is giving me hell. See —'

'Skip it. Give me the key to the Kawasaki.'

'Help me up.'

The bandit did, by the slack of Harry's jacket. He looked down at the feeling of something hard over his heart. Harry's jacket trailed from his hand, and the .25 Beretta was in the jacket pocket.

'I hold the key to a door you don't want to open,' Harry said.

Anyone with a grain of sense would have at least stopped to think it over. The bandit reacted instantly: he batted at the threatening hand and swung a fist at Harry's jaw.

Harry fired at once. The fist exploded against his jaw and knocked him dizzy. His gun hand was knocked aside too. Harry brought it back and fired twice more, walking the pistol up the man's torso.

He shook his head and looked around fast. The gun wasn't very loud. It wasn't big either, and Harry didn't entirely trust a .25 bullet. Any sign of a companion? No. The bandit was still on his feet, looking startled. Harry fired twice more, reserving one bullet for mistakes.

Now the bandit toppled.

Harry had spent some time finding the campground, but it wouldn't be possible to stay. He rolled off the table, pulled his pants on, then his kidney belt. He paused to catch his breath and to listen.

The bandit was still breathing, almost snoring. Harry looked down at him. 'I'll do you the best favor I can,' he said. 'I won't check to make sure you're dead.'

The wounded man said nothing. Ah, well.

Harry walked his bike to the bandit's motorcycle. There was nearly a gallon of gasoline in it. Whistling. Harry disconnected the fuel line and drained the gas into a pickle jar he fished out of the trash. When he'd put the last drop into the Kawasaki, he went through the bandit's possessions. There wasn't much.

Then he mounted the Kawasaki and rode away, groaning. Harry was a firm believer in natural selection.

Jeri woke at dawn. Melissa was awake, but huddled in her sleeping bag. 'I never knew deserts could be cold,' she said.

'I told you,' Jeri said. 'Now watch.' The sleeping bags were head to head, with the Sierra stove between. Jeri made two cups of cocoa without poking more than her head and shoulders out of her bag. In the half-hour they spent drinking cocoa and eating oatmeal, the world warmed. Jeri put her hat on and made Melissa don hers. They left their sleeping bags and rolled them with one eye each on the highway below.

They had moved uphill, away from the car, into a clump

of bushes at the crest. With heads above the bushes, using binoculars, they could see clearly for miles. The highway ran straight as a bullet's flight, broken by a dish-shaped crater nine miles to the west. The precision of that crater grew scarier the more Jeri thought about it. It sat precisely on the intersection of two highways.

They watched for traffic. Jeri's hand kept brushing the hard lump in her purse, the .380 Walther automatic. If she saw a safe-looking ride, she and Melissa could get down to the highway in time to stick out their thumbs. She hadn't seen much yet. Traffic was nearly nonexistent. A clump of four motorcycles had passed, slowed to examine the stalled car, argue, then move on west. She stayed hidden.

'What will we do?' Melissa asked.

'We'll think of something,' Jeri told her. *I may have to pay for a lift. Hopefully with money*. She prayed for a policeman, but there weren't any. *Someone ought to come look at the crater. Is it radioactive? And why here? what could aliens possibly care about, this far from anywhere?*

From the west came a motorcycle. It slowed as it approached the crater. Jeri wondered if it would turn back. It moved out into the desert and circled the lip of the crater. Big cycle, big rider. He had some trouble lifting it back onto the road. He rested afterward, smoking, then started up again. They watched him come.

Ten minutes later Melissa lowered the binoculars and said, 'It's Harry.'

Jeri snorted.

'It's Hairy Red, Mom. Let's go down.'

'Unlikely,' Jeri said wearily, but she took the glasses. The lone biker's head was a wind-whipped froth of red hair and beard; that was true enough. He kept the bike slow. He couldn't be a young man, not with the trouble he'd had lifting the bike. The bike: it sure looked like Harry's bike. Hell's bells, that was Harry Reddington!

'Go,' Jeri said, 'run!' She sprinted downhill. Melissa surged past her, laughing. They reached the bottom well ahead of the biker. Jeri puffed and got her wind back and screamed, 'Harry! Harreee!'

It didn't look like he would stop.

Harry saw the four bikers coming from a long way off. They were on the wrong side, his side, of the dirt divider. He was seeing trouble as he neared them . . . but they veered across the divider and, laughing, doffed their helmets to him as he passed. Harry would have liked to return the gesture, but he had one hand on the handlebars and one on the gun Carlotta hadn't taken . . . because Hairy Red sure wasn't in shape to defend himself with his fists. His belly band was tightened to the last notch, and Harry felt like he was leaking out from under it.

Beyond the bikers was a station wagon, presumed DOA. Beyond the wagon, two figures running downhill. Harry made out a woman and a little girl.

He didn't have time for emergencies or room for passengers.

They reached the road. They were yelling at him. The adult was a good-looking woman, and it was with some regret that he twisted the accelerator.

—'Harreee!'

Oh, *shit*. Harry's hands clamped the brakes. Jeri and Melissa Wilson, standing in the road. Just what he needed.

Your word of honor on record, he thought. Dead or captured by God knows what, Wes Dawson had left his life on Earth's surface in Harry Reddington's care. Carlotta Dawson wasn't the type to survive without help. Stuck out here with a dead station wagon, what were the chances that Jeri Wilson and her daughter would ever tell anyone that Hairy Red had driven past them? He twisted harder, and stopped precisely alongside Melissa, and smiled at the little girl. *Shit.*

*   *   *

Harry Reddington climbed from the bike as if afraid he'd break, and straightened up slowly. 'Jeri. Melissa. Why aren't you at the Enclave?'

'I have to find my husband. Oh, Harry, thank God! Where are you going?'

Harry answered slowly; he seemed to be doing everything slowly. 'I was staying at Congressman Dawson's house. Now his wife is in Dighton, Kansas, and *he* sure can't do anything to take care of her, so it's up to me.'

'Well. Want some cocoa?'

'Sure, but – You've got a Sierra stove?'

'Up the hill.'

'What's wrong with the car?'

'Out of gas.'

'Let's get that cocoa.' Harry accepted Jeri's hospitality knowing full well what it implied, knowing that it was too late. Three passengers on a motorcycle was going to *kill* his shock absorbers. 'Those bushes at the top? I'd better ride the bike up. I'd hate to lose it.'

Harry let the bike coast to a stop. It was hot as soon as they stopped moving. Harry poured a little water onto his bandana and mopped his face. *Getting sunburn to go with the windburn. Bloody hell.*

'We're almost there,' Jeri said. 'Why are you stopping?'

'Got to,' Harry said. 'Everybody off.'

Melissa leaped off from her perch on the gas tank in front of Harry. Jeri climbed off the back. Every muscle complaining, Harry slowly got off and set the stand. Then he tried to bend over.

'Back-rub time?' Jeri asked.

'Can't hurt,' Harry said. He pointed to a stream that ran beside the road. 'Melissa, how about you go fill the canteens.'

'Doesn't look very clean —'

'Clean enough,' Harry said.

'Pour all the water we have into one canteen and just fill the other from the stream,' Jeri said. 'Harry, you look like a letter S. Here, bend over the bike and I'll work on that.'

Harry waited until Melissa was gone. 'I don't quite know how to say this. I hate to be the one to do it, but somebody's got to. We're almost there. Another ten, twelve miles —'

'Yes. Thank you. I know it was out of your way, and it can't be comfortable, riding three on a bike —'

'It's not, but that isn't the problem,' Harry said. 'You got across the Colorado River the day before the aliens came, didn't you?'

'Yes —'

'And all you've seen since is a few towns, and that crater.'

'Harry, what are you trying to say?'

'I looked on the map. That town you're headed for – there's a dam just above it.' He didn't say anything for a moment, to let that sink in. 'Jeri, I goddam near didn't get across the Colorado River. There's nothing left of the town of Needles. Or Bullhead City. Or *anything* along the Colorado. They hit Hoover Dam with something big. When Lake Mead let go, it scoured out everything for two hundred miles. I mean everything. Dams, bridges, houses, boats – all gone. I had to get a National Guard helicopter to take me and the motorcycle across.'

'Oh.'

'Yeah. So I don't know what we're going to find up ahead. You got any idea of where Dave lived in that town?'

'No,' Jeri said. 'He never told me anything about it. Harry – Harry, it's got to be all right.'

'Sure,' Harry said. He couldn't even try to sound sincere.

One more rise. Over the top of that little ridge —

Jeri sat uncomfortably among the gear tied to the bike. She couldn't stop crying. Wind-whipped, the tears ran tickling across her temples and into her hair. *Damn it, I don't know anything yet, why am I crying? At least Melissa can't see.*

What should I tell her? Warn her? But . . .

The bike lumbered over the top of the ridge.

A sea of mud lay below. The reservoir had been ten miles long and over a mile wide; now there was only a thick sluggish ripple at its center, a tiny stream with obscenely swollen banks. A thick stench rose from the mud. They rode slowly, feeling that hot wind in their faces, smelling ancient lake bed mud.

There was no need to tell Melissa anything. She could see the dead lake, and must be able to guess what was ahead. *It used to be we could protect children, spare them from horrible sights. They always do that in the old novels.*

They rode along the mud banks toward the ruins of the dam at the far end. Long before they reached the dam there were new smells mingled with the smell of decayed mud and the hot summer. Everywhere lay the smell of death.

The town below the dam was gone. In the center the destruction was complete, as if a bulldozer had come through and removed all the buildings, then another came along to spread mud over the foundations. Farther away from the stream bed was a thin line of partially destroyed houses and debris. One house had been torn neatly in half, leaving three-walled rooms to stare out over the wreckage below.

Above the debris line nothing was touched. People moved among the debris, but few ventured down into the muddy bottom area.

They've given up looking for survivors. She could feel Harry's chest and back tighten as they got closer to the ruined town.

A sheriff's car stood beside a National Guard jeep to

block the road. Harry let the bike coast to a stop. He had his letter ready to show, but it wasn't needed.

'I am Mrs. David Wilson,' Jeri said. 'My husband lives here, at 2467 Spring Valley Lane —'

The young man in sheriff's uniform looked away. So did the Guard officer.

She knew before the sergeant spoke.

'You can see where Spring Valley Lane was, just down there, about a mile,' the sergeant said. He pointed at the center of the mud flat.

'Maybe he wasn't home,' Melissa said. 'Maybe —'

'It happened about two in the morning,' the sergeant said. 'Maybe five minutes after they blasted the Russian space station.'

'Warning didn't help anyway,' the deputy sheriff said. 'They did something that knocked out the phone system at the same time. The only way we could warn anybody downstream was to try to drive faster than the water. That wasn't good enough.'

'How bad was it?' Harry asked.

'Bad,' the Guard officer said. 'The whole Great Plains reservoir system, everything along the Arkansas River, is gone. There's flooding all the way to Little Rock and beyond.' He drew Harry aside, but Jeri could make out what he was saying.

'There's a temporary morgue in the schoolhouse three miles east of here,' the officer was telling Harry. 'Some bodies still there. The best-looking ones. We've had to bury a couple of hundred. Maybe more. They've got a list of all they could identify.'

'Thanks. I guess we better go there. Any place I can get some gas?'

The officer laughed.

———

The wallet held two pictures of Jeri and one of Melissa. Jeri stared at her own face distorted by the tears that kept welling in her eyes.

My pictures. I think he would have been glad to see me. The driver's license was soaked, but the name was readable. 'That's his,' Jeri said.

The thinly bearded young man in dirty whites made notes on a clipboard. 'David J. Wilson, of Reseda, California,' he said. 'Next of kin, Mrs. Geraldine Wilson —'

He went on interminably. He took David's wallet and went through that, noting down everything inside it. Finally he handed her a shoe box. It contained the wallet, a wristwatch, and a wedding ring. 'Sign here, please.'

She carried the box out into the bright Colorado sunshine. *My God, what am I going to do now?* There was no sign of Harry or Melissa. She sat down on a bench by the school.

What do they want? Why are they doing this? Why?

'Mom —'

Jeri didn't want to look at her daughter.

'Harry told me, Mom.' Melissa sat beside her on the bench. After a moment Jeri opened her arms, and they held each other.

'We have to go,' Melissa said.

'Go?'

'With Harry.'

'Are we – where are we going with Harry?'

'Dighton, Kansas,' Harry said from behind her. 'And we got to be starting right now, Miz W. We're on the wrong side of the river, and there aren't any bridges downstream at least as far as Dodge City. We have to go upstream and cross above where the reservoir was. It's maybe two hundred miles the way we've got to go. We need to get started.'

Jeri shook her head. 'What – I don't know anyone in Kansas.'

'No, ma'am, and I don't either, except Mrs. Dawson.'

230

Harry snorted. It was easy to tell what he was thinking. Harry Red had no woman of his own, just other people's widows . . .

'Harry, you don't want us on your bike.'

'I sure don't,' he said. 'What's that got to do with anything?'

Melissa stood and pulled her by the hand. 'Come on, Mom, we don't want to stay *here*.'

I might meet David's friends. Find out how he spent his last months —

That's morbid, and you'll more likely meet his New Cookie. Or was she with him? Did the Earth move for you, sweetheart? 'All right, let's go, then. Harry, I thought you were out of gas.'

'He used his letter,' Melissa said. 'Talked the highway patrolman into a full tank for the motorcycle.'

'Should get us there,' Harry said. He led the way around the corner. The bike stood there. It didn't look in very good shape. It looked overloaded even with no one on it.

'Even loaded down with three?'

'Should.' Harry climbed aboard, groaning slightly. He looked a little better; the monstrous belly was tighter, and his back wasn't quite so thoroughly bent. 'Anyplace you want to go first?' he asked.

Jeri shook her head. 'They . . .' – she took Melissa's hand – 'they buried over a hundred in a common grave. I don't want to see that —'

'Me, neither, Mom.' Melissa hopped onto the bike in front of Harry.

The young are so damned – resilient. I guess they have to be. Especially now. Jeri crammed the shoe box into the saddlebag and climbed on behind Harry. 'All right. I'm ready.'

She didn't look back as they drove out of the town.

CHAPTER FIFTEEN
THE WHEAT FIELDS

When even lovers find their peace at last,
And Earth is but a star, that once had shone.

– JAMES ELROY FLECKER, Prologue to *The Golden Journey to Samarkand*

COUNTDOWN: H PLUS 60 HOURS

They were through the last of the foothills and into the rolling prairies of Kansas, a land of straight roads and small towns. Wheat and cornfields made the landscape monotonous. Whenever they stopped, the hot winds and bright sunshine drove them back into motion again.

Conversation was impossible over the noise of the motorcycle. The radio had nothing to say. Harry drove mindlessly, trying not to think of his back and the cramps in his legs. Fantasies came easily.

Jeri's a right pretty woman, and she's all alone. Don't know what she'll do in Kansas. Maybe there wouldn't be enough rooms. They'd have to share a room and a bed, and the first night he could just hold her, and —

Part of his mind knew better, but the thoughts were more pleasant than his back pains.

Dighton, Kansas, was forty miles ahead. The engine sputtered, and Harry switched to the reserve tank. They'd just make it, with a dozen miles to spare. Good enough, thought Harry. Good enough. There was a smaller city four miles away. Logan, Kansas. Nothing to stop there for —

There was a bright flash ahead and to the left. 'Holy Shit!' Harry shouted. He clamped the brakes, skidding the bike to a halt. 'Off! Off and down!' He'd heard George and Vicki's lectures too.

Jeri and Melissa threw themselves into the ditch alongside the road. Harry laid the motorcycle down. He found he'd been counting. It was nearly a minute before thunder rolled over them. There wasn't any shock wave.

'Ten, twelve miles,' Harry said.

'We were closer to the other one,' Melissa said. She was trying to look brave and calm, but she was having trouble forgetting that she was a ten-year-old girl who'd been protected all her life.

There were more rumblings, a series of sonic booms, and the sky was full of sound.

'What in hell is worth bombing here?' Harry asked.

Jeri sat up. She shook her head. 'I don't – Harry!' She pointed up. Something dart-shaped crossed the sky, high up, glowing orange at the nose and leaving a wavery vapor trail. 'What is that?'

Harry shook his head. The fading vapor trail curled and twisted. Winds did that in the high stratosphere. 'Russian? Not like any American plane I ever saw.' They looked at each other in wonder. 'Naw,' Harry said. 'It couldn't be.'

The craft was already too small to see . . . until it began blinking, pulsing in harsh blue pinpoints of light, like the lights Harry had seen that first night.

Dust motes were drifting out of the vapor trail.

Another ship crossed the bright sky, and another, on skewed paths. Dust sifted from the vapor trails. The motes left by the first ship were growing larger, becoming distinct dots. Harry watched with his knees in ditch water. A fourth ship . . . and the first two were pulsing now, pulling away.

They must be much larger than they seemed. Thirty miles up or more: they *had* to be that high, given what they were doing. They were streaking through the high atmosphere at near-orbital speed, dropping clouds of . . . dots, then accelerating free of Earth. So. Dots?

The fourth ship wasn't pulsing. It was turning, banking in a wide arc.

The dots had become falling soap bubbles, and the lowest of them were breaking open. Hatching. Hatching winged things —

'Paratroopers,' Melissa said. Her voice held wonder. 'Mom, they're *invading!*'

————

At nearly sixty-four makasrupkithp of altitude* the troposphere tore at the hull, blasting the digit ship with flame. Its mass seemed no more protection than the transparent bag around Octuple Leader Chintithpit-mang. The planet was all of his environment, vast beyond imagination, and dreadfully close.

He was one in eight rows of sixty-four bubbles each, and each flaccid bubble held a fi', his face hidden by an oxygen mask. He was first in his line, with the transparent door just a srupk from his face.

They were holding up well. Why not? The lowest ranks were all sleepers. A planet was nothing new to a sleeper. This must be like homecoming to them. As for the spaceborn, the Octuple Leaders and higher ranks, how could they let the sleepers see their fear? And yet —

Aft is raw chaos, a roiling white fog of vapor trail. But look down, where greens and blues and browns sweep beneath. Here the patterns are equally random, for worlds

* Thirty to thirty-five miles (A standard trunklength or srupk = 5.8 feet = 176.78 cm = 1.77 meters. 512 srupkithp = 1 makasrupk = 905.13 meters.)

happen by accident, and there is no sign of mind imposing order. Layers of curdled water vapor *almost* make patterns. They seem more real, more solid, than the land. The snaky curve of yonder river holds more water than is stored in all of *Message Bearer*. Any one in that line of mountains they'd crossed a few 64-breaths ago would outmass the Foot itself —

'Octuples, you disembark now.'

Octuple Leader Chintithpit-mang's breathing became shallow, fast.

He had been born in the year that *Thuktun Flishithy* rounded this world's primary star. The Year Zero Herd had all been born within a couple of eight-days of each other - naturally - and that age group was closer than most. One and all, males and females, they were dissidents. They had no use for worlds.

Chintithpit-mang fiercely resented the Herdmaster's splitting of the Year Zero Herd. He did not want to be here.

The aft door cracked. Air hissed away. The bubbles grew taut. The door folded outward while the chamber filled with a thin singing: troposphere ripping at the digit ship. A line of bubbles streamed out, sixty-four fithp falling above the fluffy cloudscape. Another stream of bubbles followed them. Then —

The Octuple Leader was first in line, of course.

Falling meant nothing to Chintithpit-mang. It was the buffeting that held him in terror. The survival bubbles dropped through the troposphere, slowing. The digit ship shrank to a dot . . . and presently began pulsing, accelerating, pushing itself back to orbit.

The buffeting increased. Thicker air. The shape of the land was taking on detail. There, the crater that was both landmark and first strike; beyond, the village that was their target. Chintithpit-mang watched the numbers dropping on his altimeter.

Now. He opened the zipper. Air puffed away. He

crawled out of the fabric and let it fall away into the wind. The land was yellow and brown, crossed by a white line of road, and now was a good time to learn if his flexwing would open.

It popped out by itself, and dragged at the air, unfolding as pressurized gas filled the struts. His senses spun as blood tried to settle into his feet. The landing shoe on a hind foot had been jerked almost loose. He bent his head and stretched to adjust it; his digits would just reach that far.

The shoes prisoned his toes: big, clumsy platforms of foamed material that would flatten on impact so that the bones of his feet would not likewise flatten.

He looked for other flexwings. The colors of his Octuple were rose and black and green. He found six others and steered toward them. One missing. Where?

The land drifted. He steered above the road that the crater had broken, then along the road toward the city. Six flexwings moved into line behind him. Still one missing. And no way to avoid the ground now. The planet was all there was.

Details expanded. Three dots scrambled from a tiny vehicle to lie by the side of the road. He steered toward them. They grew larger, LARGER! Chintithpit-mang bellowed and pulled back in his harness to catch more air in his flexwing, increasing lift, striving desperately to avoid contact with the planet.

The planet slammed against his feet. They stung. His landing shoes were smashed flat. He stripped them off, dropped his flexwing and looked about him.

Big. Planets were big.

———

A line of insect-sized flyers converged toward the town ahead. Those weren't parachutes. 'Delta wings,' Harry Red murmured. 'Hang gliders.' The shapes hanging under the delta wings were not human.

236

Harry ran to the bike and lifted the seat. The .45 Government Model felt comfortable in his hand, and the slide worked with a satisfying click, but the secure feeling the big pistol usually gave him was entirely lacking.

A group of hang gliders broke away from the formation and came toward them. They split into two groups, one on either side of them.

Melissa peered through the binoculars. 'Elephants,' she said. 'Baby elephants.'

Jeri grabbed the glasses. Then she began to laugh. She handed the glasses to Harry.

He said, 'That funny, eh?' and looked.

Baby elephants with two trunks drifted out of the sky beneath paper airplanes. Harry chortled. They were wearing tall, conspicuous elevator shoes. He laughed outright. Rifles with bayonets were slung over their backs. Harry stopped laughing.

Two lines of delta-wing gliders swept along a hundred yards to either side of them. They were sinking fast into the wheat fields. A much larger group had drifted over Logan.

'Let's get the hell out of here!' Harry shouted. He raised the bike.

It wouldn't start. Laying it on its side in the dirt hadn't been a good idea. The smell of gas was strong.

The electric starter whirred again. The engine caught. Harry turned the bike —

A delta-wing craft glided onto the road half a mile behind them. The Invader came down hard. It freed its weapon, then stepped out of the elevator shoes. Other gliders settled to each side. A much larger vehicle swept overhead: a flat oval with upward-pointing fins. It glided along the road, settling slowly, until it landed more than a mile away.

'We're surrounded.' Jeri sounded tired, already defeated.

'Let's go,' Harry ordered. 'Out in the fields. Get out there and lay low. Go on, now.'

Jeri took Melissa's hand and dragged her off into the

wheat fields. They left an obvious trail behind them. The wheat stalks were thickly planted, and you couldn't move through without knocking some of them down.

We can't hide. Maybe they don't want us. Harry took a fresh grip on the pistol and followed.

———————

Eight-cubed Leader Harpanet kept only the vaguest memories of his fall.

Bubbles had streamed from digit ship *Number Twenty-six* into a dark blue sky and were instantly lost in immensity. Far, far below, a vast rippling white landscape waited for him. Voices chattered through a background of static; voices called his name. He didn't answer.

He might have spoken anytime during the years of preparation. He'd heard lectures on planetary weather: the variations in temperature, 'wind chill factor,' and the coriolis forces that cause air to whirl with force sufficient to tear dwellings apart: *A vast worldwide storm, accidentally formed, beyond the control of fithp. The Predecessors' messages tried to tell us. Random death in the life support system!*

Harpanet had been in the Breaker group, trying to learn of the prey. They'd watched broadcasts that leaked through the target world's atmosphere. *I can't make sense of these pictures. They don't mean anything.* The more he knew, the more alien they seemed. Breaker Takpusseh could live with his ignorance and wait to learn more. To Harpanet, *these are not fithp at all. They build tools, and they kill, and we will never know more.*

Others of the spaceborn had had private interviews with Fistarteh-thuktun, and later been taken from the lists of Winterhome-bound soldiers. What they told the priest must have resembled his own thoughts: *I can't stand it. The things who will try to kill me are the least of it. I fear the air and I fear the land, and I can't tolerate the thought*

238

of an ocean! They were shunned thereafter. Their mothers never mentioned them again.

Harpanet could have joined the dissidents. He had kept his silence.

He kept it now. He couldn't move, he couldn't make a sound save for a thin keening like the keening of the air through which he fell. The thin skin of the bubble rippled under the atmosphere's buffeting. The sky grew more inaccessible every second.

He was late to open his bubble. The flexwing popped and the struts began to expand before it was clear. Harpanet shrieked. He was falling toward a rippling white landscape, vast in extent, and his collapsed bubble was still tangled around his flexwing. He clawed his way up the suspension harness and forced his digits under the fabric against the resistance of the inflated struts, and *pulled*. The planet's white face came up to smash him.

It was nothing. He fell through it without resistance. He was still clawing at the bubble fabric, and suddenly it was floating loose above him. He had to nerve himself to let go of the flexwing; and only then did it begin to drag at the air until he was flying.

It was some time before he recovered enough to look for other flexwings.

He found a swarm of midges far away. *Away from the sun. It is late in the day. The planet turns away from the star. My warriors are spinward.*

The octuples under his command had steered toward their place on the rim of the great circle on the Herdmaster's map. The circle would converge. Defenses would be erected. Digit ships would presently pick them up and return them to the darkness, the immensity, the security of space.

A rise of land blocked his view of the other wings. Undulations of yellow fur streamed beneath him, terribly fast, and Harpanet had seconds in which to learn to fly. Through his terror came a single memory, that lifting the fore edge of the flexwing would cause him to slow and rise. He slid back in the harness. The wing rose, and slowed . . . and hovered, and dropped, and picked up speed, and hurled him against the dirt. He rolled. The harness rolled with him; the flexwing wrapped around him; one of the struts hissed in his face as his bayonet punctured it. When he finally managed to disentangle himself, his radio was dead. One knee was twisted, so that he could walk on three legs only. Gravity pulled at him.

It was an experience he would never want to remember. But he was sixty-fours of makasrupkithp to antispinward from his assigned landing point.

Jenny woke with a start. A duty sergeant was standing over her. He chattered excitedly. 'Right now, Major. The Admiral wants you in the war room now; it's an emergency. There's an invasion.'

Invasion? She sat up. 'All right, Sergeant. I'm coming.'

'*Now*, Major —'

'I heard you. Thank you.'

'Yes, ma'am.'

She dressed quickly, putting on combat fatigues. He hadn't said anything about sidearms. We're at war, but surely they weren't invading Colorado Springs!

When she reached the war room she wasn't so sure. Admiral Carrell, still in civilian clothes, was in one of the balcony offices overlooking the control room. Jenny stood outside the door, wondering what to do.

'Come in, Major.' Carrell pointed to the big screens below. They showed Kansas and southern Nebraska dotted with red flashes and hand-drawn gray squares. Jenny stared for a moment, trying to understand.

'We don't have symbols for a parachute invasion of Kansas,' Admiral Carrell said. 'So we had to draw them in. Not that it means much, since we don't know all the places they're landing.'

'Are all those red marks nuclear strikes?' Jenny asked.

'Probably none of them,' Carrell said. 'So far they haven't used nukes. They haven't had to.'

'No, sir.' *Kinetic energy weapons. Throw big rocks.*

An Army lieutenant general bustled in. He wore combat fatigues and he'd buckled on his pistol.

'You've met General Toland,' Carrell said. 'No? General, Major Crichton is my assistant. What's the score, Harvey?'

'Damned if I know. Thor, this doesn't make *sense.* They can't possibly be invading Kansas. I don't care how goddam big that ship is; it can't hold that many troops.'

'Then what are they doing?'

General Toland shook his head.

Carrell said, 'Jenny, I want you to get those sci-fi gentry together and get them *working.* You can use the big briefing room. Get TV monitors set up, get maps, get coffee, get whiskey, hell, get them prostitutes if that's what they want, but get me some *explanations*!'

Harry lay in the wheat field and sweated. There was a hot wind and bright sun, but he'd have sweated in a blizzard.

He couldn't see the road, but he heard a vehicle on it. The motor didn't sound like anything Harry had ever heard before.

Now there were sounds in the wheat. Someone – *something* – was coming.

The wheat was too thick to see through. His world had shrunk to five yards or less. He could just see Melissa's bright head scarf. *Should have told her to take it off. Too late now. Not that we can hide anyway.*

The sounds came closer. They were all around him.

What the fuck do I do? The pistol held no comfort for him. He wasn't a good shot. He remembered a merc who'd served in Africa telling him about elephants. They were hard to stop, harder to kill. You had to hit them just right. A .45 probably wouldn't even bother one, not unless he hit a vital spot —

They aren't elephants. Maybe they're not as tough. And maybe I don't know where the vital spots are.

He heard Jeri scream, and then two shots from her Walther. Melissa's scarf bounced up, then something happened and she disappeared into the wheat. There was nothing to shoot at. Harry leaped to his feet and ran toward the sound.

As he did, he heard something behind him. He turned —

An elephant was charging him. Another closed in from the side. *They were wearing hooded coats!* Harry held out the pistol and fired. The elephant kept coming. A flurry of whips lashed his arm and side, spinning him around, tearing the pistol from his hand.

The other elephant came toward him. The trunk was built like a cat-o'-nine-tails: it held a bayoneted rifle. The bayonet was pointed at his throat.

'Melissa! Run!' Jeri screamed.

Harry turned to go to her.

Something lashed around his ankles and whipped them away from him. He fell heavily into the wheat field. The elephant stood over him, bayonet pointed at him. The other came and stood with it.

'Psh-thish-ftpph.'

Harry glared up.

The elephants repeated their phrase, only louder.

'Okay, goddamm it, you got me!' He stayed where he was, rolled half onto his knees. Give him half a chance and he'd —

Once more the aliens shouted. Then suddenly the trunk swept down and rolled Harry onto his back. One Invader pulled Harry's hands out over his head. The other reared above him.

My God, they're going to trample me! Harry writhed to

get away. The foot came down on his chest. It settled almost gently. Harry struggled: he yanked one hand free and scraped at the foot with his nails, tried to push it upward, tried to roll. The pressure increased. There were claws under his jaw, and a mass that was crushing his chest. The air sighed out of him in a despairing hiss. He blacked out.

Fog in his mind; memory of a nightmare. He was breathing like a bellows. Harry rolled over in . . . wheat? Inhuman screaming and bellowing reached his ears, sounds like a fire in a zoo.

Oh, God. *Jeri!* Harry tried to stand up and made it to one knee.

The baby elephants were converging on the road. Harry glimpsed Melissa on an Invader's back, held firmly by a branching trunk. Jeri was walking, stumbling, with Invaders around her.

A vehicle waited on the road, the size of a large truck, but it had no wheels. It looked like a huge sled. The motor wasn't running.

They loaded Melissa into the vehicle, then pushed Jeri in behind her. Others jumped onto the broad platform. The vehicle lifted on a cloud of dust: an air cushion. It sped away.

They seemed to have forgotten Harry entirely.

He crawled away slowly, disturbing the wheat as little as possible. What else could he do? They'd taken the big gun, but they might have left the motorcycle, and Carlotta still waited. Unless they'd landed there too.

———

By vehicle and on foot, the prey fled the village. Humans on foot were allowed to surrender. They had to be taught: in many cases they must be knocked down and rolled into position. Then, if they could stand, they were allowed to

243

pass. But vehicles were considered to be weapons and were treated as such.

The village had suffered more damage than was needed. It grieved Chintithpit-mang: locals dead, or torn and still screaming, buildings smashed, the smell of explosives and of burning, the flattened crater where the rock came down . . . *We're dealing with unknowns. Better to err on the side of excessive strength.*

By asking those he passed, Chintithpit-mang found the leader of his eight-cubed in a large red building with pillars in front.

Siplisteph was surrounded by squarish bundles of printed sheets, bound at one edge and gaudily decorated. He was leafing through a bundle of print with drawings in it. The youthful sleeper seemed relaxed, very much at home. He looked up dreamily and said, 'It's so good to see a *sky* again.' His eyes focused on Chintithpit-mang. 'You come late.'

Chintithpit-mang said, 'One never reported. Otherwise we have no casualties.'

Siplisteph lifted his digits in response. 'We have lost warriors. You are promoted. In addition to your octuple, you will be deputy leader to your eight-squared.'

'Were there heavy losses, eight-cubed Leader?'

'Many within the leadership. We have lost an eight-cubed leader.'

'The leadership. They are all spaceborn —'

'It would be well not to finish that thought, Chintithpit-mang.'

Sleeper! Winterhome is home to you, but how can we find ourselves within this infinite horizon, beneath this tremendous sky? He could say none of that. 'Lead me.'

'Continue your report.'

'I obey. Eight-cubed Leader, I took two females. One was mated to a big male, the other their child. I took the male's surrender and left him.'

Siplisteph's ears snapped alert. 'The male surrendered?'

'He had to be shown.' But the episode had left a bad taste, and Chintithpit-mang went on talking. 'Eight-cubed Leader, I knocked him down and put my foot on him, lightly. He struggled, he fought. I pushed harder until he stopped struggling. But when I took my foot away he did not move. I wonder if I simply killed him.'

'This is the Breakers' problem, not ours.' Siplisteph's eyes returned to the pictures.

'Lead me,' said Chintithpit-mang, and he went to rejoin his octuple. But it bothered him. By now the taking of Winterhome, in falling rocks and disrupted supply chains, must have killed close to eight to the sixth of the poor misshapen rogues. Well, that was what war was about. But a fi' did not kill needlessly, did not kill when he could take surrender. If the beast was so fragile, why did it continue to fight?

Chintithpit-mang remembered its rib cage sagging under his foot. It thrashed and clawed and finally stopped moving . . . it didn't know how to surrender. They didn't know how to surrender. *Bad*.

CHAPTER SIXTEEN
SUBMISSION

A human being in a prison camp, in the hands of his enemies, is flesh, and shudderingly vulnerable.

The disciplines that hold men together in the face of fear, hunger, and danger are not natural. Stresses equal to, and beyond, the stress of fear and panic must be laid on men. Some of these stresses are called civilization. And even the highest of civilizations demands leadership.

– T. R. FEHRENBACH, *This Kind of War*

COUNTDOWN: H PLUS 80 HOURS

The hullside wall was down and level; the door was in the ceiling. Wes judged that things were likely to remain so for some time.

There had been an hour or so of acceleration, then half an hour of free-fall; then the ship had begun to spin. Some days had passed without further change. Odds were it would take an hour or more to remove the spin.

Spin would hamper the mother ship in a battle. Earth must be far aft and out of reach.

Nikolai and Dmitri talked quietly: Nikolai sullen, Dmitri doing most of the talking. Wes understood a few words, and sympathized. Nikolai was once again a cripple.

The aliens had wasted no time. They were already teaching their language to the humans. Wes found this reassuring. However, the Soviets were educated separately, and they had expressed disinterest in sharing their lessons with Wes. He went over them alone, whispering alien sounds as he remembered them.

Srupk: Wes had memorized the term as *strunk,* 'standard trunklength.' It was just about six feet. A *makasrupk* was five hundred and twelve strunks, just about a kilometer.

Wes had sought a word for the trunk. There wasn't one. A sharp snort, *snnfp,* named the nostrils, or the upper trunk. *Pa'* was one branch, one finger of a trunk; *pathp,* the plural, could mean the entire cluster.

Chaytrif meant *foot.*

Sfaftiss was Takpusseh's title; it meant *teacher.* The other *sfaftiss* didn't speak, and his name was harder: Raztupisp-minz. The two *sfatissthp* looked aged, but as if they had weathered in different patterns. Were there two races of Invader? But they called themselves by the same words:

Chtapt meant move. *Chtaptisk*: moving. *Chtaptisk fithp* meant themselves, everyone who had left their home planet. The Traveler People?

Fi' was the word for an alien. A syllable chopped short by a kind of hiccup, it sounded like a piece of a word. And *fithp* was the entire species. As if an individual was not a whole, complete thing, just as a *pa'* was only one branch of the *pathp*, the trunk. Herdbeasts? Takpusseh said *tribe*, not *herd*; but men didn't say *herd* to mean thinking beings.

Tashayamp was Takpusseh's assistant. Dawson thought of her as female; the leather or plastic patch on her harness covered a different area, further back on her torso. He knew he might have the sexes reversed; he was not prepared to ask —

The door opened upward, a trapdoor. The prisoners looked up, waiting.

Takpusseh: Wes had learned to recognize their teacher or trainer by the loose look of his thick skin, and by his eyes, which behaved as if the lights were always too bright.

Takpusseh watched while alien soldiers attached a platform at the level of the trapdoor. The platform descended smoothly along grooves in the padding of the starboard wall. The platform might have held one alien; it held Wes and Arvid with room to spare. Wes had expected a ladder, but a ladder would be useless to these aliens.

Takpusseh and Tashayamp and eight armed soldiers waited in the corridor. The platform descended again for Dmitri and Nikolai. They had left Giorge behind.

————

Arvid had been hoping for a window. There were none. The soldiers moved four ahead, four behind. Takpusseh and Tashayamp moved forward to join the prisoners. They had found a wheeled cart for Nikolai. Arvid took charge of pushing it. Wes was trying to tell Tashayamp that they needed heat to prepare their food. Arvid ignored that. He was trying to get some idea of the mother ship's layout.

The rug was spongy and squishy-wet; the prisoners had not been given shoes. Doors in the floor opened upward against the corridor wall.

'I believe,' Arvid said in Russian, 'that any aperture big enough for one of the aliens would pass two or three of us at once. Perhaps they will not think to guard small openings that will pass a man.'

Dmitri nodded.

'They are surely not built for climbing. A wall that could be scaled by a man would be impossible for one of them.'

Dmitri nodded again.

'Have you seen anything I might have missed?'

Dmitri spoke. 'You waited until we were in a corridor, and moving, before you said any of this. I approve, but are you certain that our trainers do not speak Russian?'

'They speak English and do not hide the fact. Why

would they hide a knowledge of Russian? In any case, we must speak sometime.'

'Perhaps. Do you think we could use their rifles?'

Grooves for the branched trunk were far forward on the barrel, and so was the trigger. The bore was huge. The butt was short and very broad. 'It would not fit against a man's shoulder, and it would probably kick him senseless, unless . . . you'd have to brace it against something, a floor, a wall, a piece of furniture. Difficult to aim.'

'Don't do anything at all without word from me. What of Dawson? Will he try something foolish?'

'I —' Arvid cut it off. They had reached their destination.

The wide doorway would be used when the mother ship was under acceleration. The permanently fixed platform elevator next to it would be for use under spin gravity. The room below was big, and more than a dozen aliens were already present.

The prisoners descended; the soldiers remained above.

The aliens stared up. Most of them had their trunks folded up against the top of the heads: evidently a resting position. The eyelids drooped mournfully. The eyes had black pupils fading to smoky-gray whites. They were set wide, but not too wide to prohibit binocular vision. The thick muscle structure at the base of the trunk formed grooves; with the trunk up, the eyes focused along the grooves . . . like gunsights. Their stare was unnerving.

Nikolai was wire-tense, staring his captors down. Arvid murmured, 'Docile, Nikolai. We docile servants of the new regime await instructions.'

Nikolai nodded. His eyes dropped. He sounded calm enough. 'I saw no air vents. The air may be filtered through the carpeting. And the rug was wet. They like wet feet.'

The room would have held three or four times as many. Takpusseh spoke rapidly to the assembled aliens, then more slowly to the humans. Arvid tried to file the introductions:

Pastempeh-keph. K'turfookeph. Fathisteh-tulk. Chowpeentulk. Fistarteh-thuktun. Koolpooleh. Paykurtank. Two smaller aliens were not introduced. They stared at the humans and huddled close against larger aliens. Children, then.

He'd have trouble remembering the names. It was the array that was important. The aliens came in clusters; he'd be a long time learning their body language, but that much was obvious.

Pastempeh-keph (male) and K'turfookeph (female), with their child (male), were the top of the ladder, the Chairman or President or Admiral. The similarity in the last syllable meant they were mated; he'd learned that much already. One would hold title. Arvid would not lightly assume that it was the male. Similarly, Fathisteh-tulk and Chowpeentulk were mated, and they stood with the Admiral. Advisors? The male was doing all the talking. So.

Fistarteh-thuktun (male), Koolpooleh (male), and Paykurtank (female) also formed a cluster. The extra syllables would mean that Fistarteh-thuktun had a mate. He was an old one, with wrinkled skin and pained-looking eyes . . . like the teacher, Takpusseh. He wore elaborate harness, like tapestry made with silver wire. He studied the humans like a judge. The pair with him were younger: clear eyes, smoother skin, quick movements.

Nikolai said, 'I thought the top ranks would wear uniforms. They all wear those harnesses with the backpacks. The colors and patterns, could those —'

'Yes, insignia of rank. Dawson believes that we will not see clothing on any alien. With those bulky bodies they will have trouble shedding heat.'

'I would not have thought of that.'

The room darkened. One wall seemed to disappear, and Arvid realized that he was in a motion picture theater.

Rogachev recognized the huge Invader spacecraft, a cylinder about as wide as it was tall. The aft rim was spiky with smaller craft, and some had not been moored in place yet. An arc of worldscape, blue and white, might have been the Earth, though Arvid could not pick out any detail of landscape. A polished sphere nearby . . . a moon? No, it was drifting slowly.

Takpusseh was talking. Arvid caught a word here and there, and translated freely to 'Watch, don't move. You see . . . trip (chtapt) to (Earth?). Build . . . *Thuktun Flishithy*.' Arvid smiled. He had thought that was their name for the mother ship, and sure enough, that was what they were putting together onscreen.

He watched and didn't move. The aliens around him were silent, motionless.

The last of the smaller craft were moved into place in seconds. This was time-lapse photography. A length of stovepipe, a little wider than *Thuktun Flishithy*, drifted in from the edge of the screen and was moored in place behind the ring of smaller craft.

The shiny sphere was moved into place at the fore end of the mother ship. It was bigger than all of the rest of the ship combined. A pod, perhaps a cluster of sensing instruments, reached out on a snakelike arm to peer around it.

Something fell inward from the edge of the picture: bright flames of chemical rockets around . . . something rectangular. It dwindled to a dot, headed straight for the ship. 'Put Podo Thuktun in *Thuktun Flishithy*,' Takpusseh said.

That word: *thuktun*. He had thought it meant *skill* or *knowledge*, but — Fistarteh-thuktun? A mate for that one had not been named. Was that particular fi' married to the *ship*?

All in good time. Arvid glanced at Dawson; Dawson's eyes were riveted to the screen. That left Arvid free to covertly observe the aliens.

Five of the fithp showed signs of a lingering illness: an illness that left loose skin and wounded-looking eyes. It didn't seem to be a matter of age. Pastempeh-keph and

K'turfookeph (Admiral and mate) were not youths, but they hadn't had the sickness either. The sick ones tended to cluster. They looked to be about the same age; the rest varied enormously.

The Admiral's advisor and his mate were among the sick ones. Another sick one was trying to talk to them, while a female rather unsubtly tried to prevent it.

A division among the aliens might be useful.

———

Wes Dawson was watching a planet recede . . . a world colored like Earth, blue with clotted white frosting. He spent no more than a few seconds trying to make out the shapes of continents. None were familiar. Of course not.

The Invader ship had been on camera for only a minute or so. The camera that filmed that would have remained behind. But *Thuktun Flishithy* was more than the cylindrical warship that had reached Earth. A sphere rode the nose, a tremendous fragile-looking bubble in contrast to the warship's spiky, armored look. Fuel supply, of course, And the ring —

He was looking aft along *Thuktun Flishithy*'s flank, past a massive ring like a broad wedding band, watching a sun grow smaller. A second sun moved in from offscreen. Both shrank to bright stars: white stars, the light not too different from Earth's own sun. He'd anticipated that from the color of the lights in his cell.

The cameras showed a steady white light behind the ring. Wes saw — and wasn't sure he saw – the drive flame go dim, and a faint violet tinge emerge from the black background.

Wes Dawson wouldn't have noticed a bomb going off in the theater. With a fraction of his attention he tried to track what the instructor was saying. '*Thuktun Flishithy* must move very fast before we use the (long word). Saves – ' something. 'Halfway to Earth-star' – Earth's sun? – 'we begin to slow down. This is difficult.'

But the pictures made more sense than the words.

Time onscreen speeded up. The drive flame brightened, then died – and the background violet glow he thought he'd seen wasn't there. Tiny machines and mote-sized aliens emerged to dislodge the bubble at the nose; the stars wheeled one hundred and eighty degrees around; the drive flamed again, and dimmed, and the stars forward were embedded in violet-black —so he hadn't imagined it – and *Thuktun Flishithy* surged past the abandoned fuel tank and onward.

The way the film jumped, a good deal of it must have been missing. Perhaps it would have shown too much interior detail. Wes took it for granted that prisoners would not learn much of the interior detail of *Thuktun Flishithy*. The next scene was a time-lapse view of an ordinary star becoming a bright star, and brighter, until it virtually exploded in Dawson's face. He cursed and covered his eyes, and immediately opened them again.

They must have dived within the orbit of Mercury. Somewhere in there, the white glow of the drive had brightened . . . and the ship's wedding band had vanished. Dawson hadn't noticed just when it disappeared. Now he grunted as if he'd been kicked in the stomach.

Takpusseh stopping talking, and his eyes flicked Dawson with the impact of a glare. Nobody else noticed.

The camera looked along the mother ship's nose while Earth's sun shrank. There were long-distance telescopic photos of Mars and Jupiter, then Saturn growing huge. The great ship moved among the moons, neared the rings, still decelerating. Wes picked out the three classic bands of the ring, separating into hundreds of bands as the ship neared. The F-ring roiled and twisted as the ship's fusion exhaust washed across it.

Ships departed *Thuktun Flishithy*, launched aft along rails. The cameras didn't follow. A telescope picked out

253

something butterfly fragile but not as pretty. Freeze-frame. Takpusseh pointed and made noises of interrogation.

'Voyager,' Dawson said. He tried a few words of the Invader language. '*We made it. My fithp.* United States of America!'

'Did it come to —' garble. The instructor tried again. 'To look on us? Did you know of us?'

The word must be *spy*. 'No.'

'Then why?'

'To see Saturn.' An anger was building in Wes Dawson, and he didn't understand it. They had come in war and killed without warning, but he'd known *that* for days. What new grievance —

They had used Saturn! Deep in his heart Dawson felt that Saturn belonged to Earth – to mankind – to the United States that had explored Saturn system, to the science establishment and science-fiction fandom. Goddammit, Saturn is ours!

He kept his silence. The film started again, and jumped. They'd skipped something: they'd skipped most of what they were doing in Saturn system. Two crescents, Earth and Moon, were growing near. Wedge-shaped markers pointed out the United States and Soviet moon bases, artifacts in orbit, weather satellites, Soviet devices of unknown purpose, the space station . . .

'Question, time you know we come,' Takpusseh said. Then louder: 'Time you know we come!'

'One sixth part of a year,' Arvid said in English. 'A year is —' His hands moved, a forefinger circling a fist, while he spoke alien words: 'Circle Earth around Earth-star.'

'You slow to fight. You know we come. Why slow?'

Why had Earth's defenders responded so slowly? Wes said, 'Earth fithp, chtaptisk fithp maybe not fight.'

'You fight, you not fight, two is one. Earth fithp is chtaptisk fithp. Sooner if Earth fithp not fight.'

The last time Wes Dawson had felt like this, he had put

his fist into a Hell's Angel's mouth just as far as it would go. 'You came to make war? Only to make war?'

'Make war, yes,' Takpusseh said, as if relieved to be understood.

Wes barely felt a large hand closing on his arm, above the elbow. 'What can you take, move to fithp world?' What could they possibly hope to steal? They'd dropped too much of their craft; they'd be lucky to return home themselves!

'Earth is world for chtaptisk fithp,' Takpusseh said.

———

Warriors had come at Takpusseh's bellow. The humans were gone now. Fathisteh-tulk helped Takpusseh to his feet. 'Are you injured?'

'My pride hurts worse than my eye – and snnfp. Dawson surprised me entirely. They look so fragile!'

'They don't know when to fight and they don't know how to surrender,' the Herdmaster's Advisor said. 'One would think that would be good news for the invasion, but I wonder.'

'Dawson is mad,' Breaker-One Raztupisp-minz said. 'His behavior tells us nothing. Must we keep him?'

'He is a puzzle that needs cracking. He speaks English as his native language, and we will need that too until the others know the speech of the fithp a srupk or two better.'

'They must surrender, at once, formally,' Raztupisp-minz stated. 'We should have taught them how, and much earlier, so that they can teach future prisoners.'

The memory flashed in Takpusseh's mind; it hurt worse than his eye. Takpusseh realized why he had delayed this crucial step. 'Of course you're right, Breaker-One. I want to visit the medical section. I'll meet you afterward, above the restraining cell.'

———

It hurt to breathe, but he had to breathe. Hands were on him, probing a stabbing agony in his ribs. Wes gasped and fought to open his eyes. Red mist . . . gradually clearing . . . the shapes around him resolved into human faces . . .

'What happened?'

'You attacked the teacher, Takpusseh. I tried to stop you,' Dmitri said. 'Do you remember?'

Seeing red . . . but his mind must have been working well on some level. He hadn't just swung a fist. He'd lunged forward and reached between the branches of Takpusseh's trunk, closed his fingers hard in Takpusseh's nostril, and pulled back savagely to keep himself moving. The teacher screamed; his digits had whipped around Wes's rib cage. With his ribs collapsing and the air sighing out of him, Wes Dawson reached along the trunk and slid his thumb under Takpusseh's thick right eyelid – was he flying? – and did his damnedest to twist it off. He didn't remember any more.

'Why did you do it?'

'They never had the least intention of negotiating anything,' he said. 'They came to take the Earth away from us.'

Dmitri Grushin took Dawson's chin in his hand and twisted it to put them eye to eye. 'Do not attack them again. You would kill us all for nothing. For nothing.'

They were quiet for some time. Then Arvid and Dmitri began to talk. Wes, with too little Russian, quickly lost track. He was more interested in the pictures in his own mind.

Presently he asked, 'Did you notice? They threw away half their ship.'

'Yes,' Arvid said. 'The external fuel tank, and the massive-looking ring.'

'I think it was a modified Bussard ramjet.'

'Explain.'

'It's a way of reaching the stars. Fusion drive, but you get your fuel by scooping up interstellar hydrogen.'

Arvid dismissed that. 'Certainly nobody has ever built a Bussard ramjet. How would you recognize one?'

'After they got going they changed something. It made a violet glow behind the ship. Arvid, the point is that they threw it away when they got here. It was used to cross interstellar space, and they *dropped* it. They let it fall back toward the stars. They're serious. They've got no plans to go home.'

'I was more interested in watching our captors. So. They dropped it to save weight, of course, but . . . well. As if your ancestors had burned the *Mayflower*. Yes, they came to stay.' Arvid's eyes went to the trapdoor in the ceiling, which once again was closed against them. 'Did you notice anything else worthy of comment?'

Wes pounded a fist on his knee, twice. 'They were at Saturn when the Voyagers went by. They spent *years* there. We might have noticed something if Saturn wasn't so weird. We'd have had fifteen years warning!'

'It is difficult to put the mushroom cloud back into the steel casing.'

'At least we know this *is* the mother ship. This is all they've got.'

'They did not exceed lightspeed?'

'They didn't even come very close.' Wes had been watching for the effect of relativity: stars blue-shifted ahead and reddened aft. It hadn't happened.

'Good. They cannot expect help. But they must be desperate. Where can they go if we defeat them?'

'They'll have to land sometime. They must expect to beat us on the ground. They're crazy.'

Arvid saw no reason to answer. Dawson was not of his nation. But any cosmonaut knew that from a military standpoint the command of space was priceless. The Soviet Union, which had always expected to rule the world, had held that position until three days ago.

'Yeah. Well. They didn't show much of the inside of the ship. They showed only the last leg of their approach to

Earth. They showed the mother ship being refueled, but they didn't show where the fuel came from. So maybe they scooped methane snow off a moon and refined deuterium and tritium out of it. But why didn't they show that? They're hiding something.'

'Of course.'

'Something specific.'

'Of course.'

The trapdoor swung open.

The platform descended into a wary silence. Takpusseh was quite alone. His right eye was covered with soft white cloth. Another patch covered his nostril. He carried his branched trunk at an odd angle. A second fi' followed him down. The soldiers remained above.

The Breakers faced the humans alone.

The captives looked harmless enough. They were clustered in a corner, frightened, wary. The black one was on his back and trying to roll over. He seemed to be just becoming aware of the aliens.

Raztupisp-minz told them, 'Move away from the dark one.'

The humans discussed it. Instant obedience would have been reassuring, but in fact they seemed to be interpreting for each other. Then they moved away. The black one protested and tried to move in the same direction. Then his eyes fixed on Raztupisp-minz. He breathed as if the chamber had lost its air, his eyes and mouth opened improbably wide, as Raztupisp-minz walked toward him.

Raztupisp-minz set his foot solidly on the black man's chest.

He lifted it and backed away. 'You,' he said, and his digits indicated the crippled one. 'Come.'

The humans discussed it heatedly. Then Nikolai pulled himself across the floor on his hands.

Dawson had moved, without permission. He knelt by the black man with his bony digits on the man's throat. he spoke to the others, in English. 'Dead.'

Takpusseh let it pass rather than interrupt the ceremony.

'Roll,' Raztupisp-minz said, and he rotated his digits in a circle. Nikolai didn't appear to understand. Raztupisp-minz forcibly rolled the man onto his back, set his foot on the man's chest, and stepped away. He pointed to another. 'You.'

One by one the Soviets submitted to the foot on the chest until only Dawson was left. Then, as they had discussed, Raztupisp-minz stepped aside and Takpusseh came forward.

The man stood balanced, forelegs slightly bent, hands open, palms outward. It came to Takpusseh that Dawson expected to die.

It wouldn't bother Takpusseh that much if he did. He swung his digits with nearly his full strength. Dawson ducked under it, fast, and lunged forward. Takpusseh caught him on the backswing and flung him spinning across the cell and against a wall. As the man started to topple, Takpusseh was there, catching him and rolling him on his back. The man blinked, opened his eyes and mouth wide. Frozen in fear? Takpusseh raised his foot over Dawson's chest.

I was almost the last to be thawed awake. Some of the sleepers were brain-damaged. They fought, or they didn't respond at all. Most accepted the change.

It was Breaker-One Raztupisp-minz who accepted their formal surrender. My grandson, though older than I, discounting the eights of years I slept. This was nothing new to him.

His task it was to break me too. Nonetheless he was uncomfortable, because we are related, or because afterward I must teach him his profession. 'Your position won't change, Grandfather. Who but you has the training to break alien forms of life to the Traveler Herd? But the Traveler Herd has changed, and you must join it again.'

I rolled over on the floor, feet in the air, trunk splayed, vulnerable. Others watch. My spaceborn grandson's foot on my chest. 'There, that's over. Now you must begin to train me,' his voice dropping, for my ears alone, 'to break me. I must know something of what we must do.'

I feel it now, the foot lightly crushing my chest. Takpusseh lowered his foot. A mere tap would not do; this was no token surrender. He felt the man's ribs sag before he lifted his foot.

Dawson waited for more, but there was no more. He rolled aside, convulsively, groaning with the pain of damaged ribs.

'Now you belong to the Traveler Herd,' Takpusseh said in his own speech. He saw Dawson take it in and relax somewhat. Dawson moved to join the other prisoners. 'Is the black one dead?' Takpusseh asked. 'What killed him?'

The one called Dmitri answered in the fithp speech. 'Fear you. Fear foot make dead. Take him out?'

Takpusseh summoned the warriors. Two came down and moved the black man onto the platform. It rose. It descended to take the fithp up one by one. Takpusseh went last.

CHAPTER SEVENTEEN
FARMHOUSES

Generally in war the best policy is to take a state intact; to ruin it is inferior to this. To win one hundred victories in one hundred battles is not the acme of skill. To subdue the enemy without fighting is the acme of skill.

– SUN-TZU, *The Art of War*

COUNTDOWN: H PLUS 100 HOURS

The house had belonged to Carlotta's grandmother. Trujillo had married Castro had married de Alvarez, families whose names were respected when the Lowells and Cabots were field hands. Carlotta's sister Juana had inherited the house. She married a man with the unlikely name of David Morgan.

Of course Dawson wasn't exactly in our conquistador heritage either. Carlotta lay in the exact center of the big four-poster and tried to count the spots on the ceiling. Thoughts came unbidden.

Her superb imagination showed her a torn puffball of a corpse, dry and brittle, falling through vacuum and the savage sunlight of space. A dissection table with monstrous shapes around it. A carved corpse, the parts arrayed on a silver platter, surrounded by cooked plants of unearthly shape; voices chittering or booming as the banquet began.

No! She leaped from the bed. The floor creaked as she scurried across the room to the door. The house was old, begun as a ranch house before the Civil War, added to as family required and money enabled. It had been built in clumps, and not all the additions fitted well together, although Carlotta rather liked the general effect. Now it had only four inhabitants, Carlotta, David, Juana, and an ancient housekeeper from Xuahaca who called herself Lucy. Juana's children had long moved away.

And Sharon is in Peterborough, New Hampshire. Will I ever see her again? Thank God the telephones worked long enough for me to tell her to stay there. How could she travel?

Bright sunlight flooded the hall outside her bedroom, and when she reached the kitchen the windup clock said it was mid-afternoon. Lucy had put away the gin bottle. *Or did I finish it to get to sleep? There should be some left in it.* She went to the cabinet, but she felt Lucy's disapproving stare.

'Desayuno, señora?'

'Gracias, no. Por favor, solamente café.' *And damned right I'm going to sit on the patio in my housecoat. Who's going to see me, or care if they do?*

The patio was too large. When Carlotta had visited as a child, the gardens were famous through the state. Pumpkins, melons, vegetables —all won prizes at county and state fairs. Now there was a big flagstone patio where the melon patch had been, and a field of sweet peas where celery and chard had grown. *No gardeners. Plenty of people unemployed, but no one wants to raise vegetables for a retired professor and his wife. But it does make a nice patio*. She sat at the big wrought-iron table. Lucy was setting the coffee down when the thunder began.

Thunder from a clear sky was not unheard of in Kansas, but this didn't come in claps and die away. It rolled in and stayed, renewed itself, grew louder and faded and grew louder still.

Then brilliant points were drawing straight white lines across the sky, sowing clouds of dots that drifted away to west and south. Lucy whimpered in terror, and the need to reassure the older woman kept Carlotta calm. *Invasion. Parachutes. What came for Wes has come for me.* But nothing showed directly overhead. *Not here. Not yet, anyway.*

'Carla,' a voice spoke from behind her.

'Yes, Juana?'

'What is happening?' The noise had brought her sister outside. Juana Morgan held a small transistor radio that poured out static as she frantically turned the tuning knob this way and that.

For once you will not look disapprovingly at me in my housecoat in mid-afternoon. 'Vapor trails, I think. Perhaps the professor will know.'

'He went to town to buy newspapers.' Juana paused. 'And more gin.'

'Ah.' Carlotta shrugged, and glanced significantly at Lucy. 'They're not coming here,' she said. 'Miles away. Not to Dighton, either.'

'Are you sure?' Juana demanded.

'Yes.' *How the hell can I be sure? And what could we do about it if they were coming here, or to Dighton? It's ten miles to Dighton, and David has the only damned car —*

'David didn't think they'd come, either,' Juana said. 'But his National Guard colonel wanted to mobilize. Maybe that's where David is! With the Guard.'

'Could be.' *What good is that? Bunch of old men with worn-out equipment . . . Wes always voted for bigger appropriations for the Guard, but nobody was really pushing it.*

'Lucy, perhaps it would be well to get out the candles and the storm lanterns,' Juana said.

'Sí.' Lucy shuffled away, still glancing up at the sky and looking away in fear.

'Give her something to do and she bears up well,' Carlotta said. She stared at the open work of the tabletop. 'I wish I had something to do.'

'So do I.'

263

Carlotta nodded. 'Yeah. I wouldn't approve of me as a houseguest either.'

'It's as much your house as mine,' Juana said. 'I haven't forgotten how much you and Wes loaned us.' She sat across from Carlotta. 'Hell, get smashed every night if that's what it takes. You really loved the guy, didn't you?'

'Yes. Still do.'

'Sorry —'

'You don't know he's dead.'

'No.' There was another peal of thunder. Juana shuddered. 'I wish it had happened to me.'

Carlotta frowned.

'I mean, that it had been David up there. Instead of Wes. Damn. That sounds horrible. I mean – well, you're really in love with Wes. It's breaking you up. I'd miss David; we're very comfortable together, but – well, I wouldn't be like you. I hate to see you like this, Carla. You were always the strong one —'

'Yeah. I sure look it, don't I. Oh damn, Juana, damn, damn, damn, what am I going to *do*?'

Juana looked up at the dot-filled skies and shuddered.

The motorcycle was intact. Harry looked around furtively. No sign of the enemy. He lifted the motorcycle and stood it on its stand.

The saddlebags with his gear had vanished. They'd taken them along with Jeri and Melissa —

God damn the bastards! Harry cursed steadily until he had control of himself. Then he felt ashamed. Cursing wouldn't change the situation. He'd lost two women he was supposed to protect. The fact that he couldn't have done anything about it didn't help much.

He felt a lump in his pocket. The little .25 Beretta was still there. They hadn't bothered to search him. He thought about that for a moment, then began to search the wheat field. Sure enough, a blue-gray object was just visible in the wheat. The .45 automatic, with dirt in the barrel. One of the invaders must have flung it aside.

Why the saddlebags, then? *Clothes? Jeri's and Melissa's clothing. Which means they'll be keeping the girls. Why take them and not me?* But there was no answer to that.

The motorcycle started easily enough. It hadn't been damaged at all. He heard noises ahead. The Invaders were still in Logan. Harry cleaned out the barrel while he felt something stir in his guts, but then he shook his head. It would be pointless. The Invaders wore body armor. His pistol hadn't done him any good at all when there were only a few of them. Charging into Logan to rescue Jeri wouldn't do Jeri any good. She might not even be there any longer.

He tried to remember the map. That part of Kansas was laid out in a grid, roads at section and range boundaries, other roads parallel to them. Few diagonal roads. Farmhouses at regular intervals. Dirt tracks crossed the wheat fields. Those tended to parallel the main roads, too, but they led to farmhouses, not towns.

Logan was several miles ahead. Harry gambled that there'd be a farm access road leading north before he came into sight of the Invaders. He put the pistol into his kidney belt where he could reach it easily, and started off east.

He saw the smoke long before he reached the ruined farmhouse. He came up slowly, ready to leap off the motorcycle and run into the wheat. He stopped several times to listen, but there was nothing to hear. The dirt road led through the wheat fields to the farmhouse. He could go back the way he'd come, or go on. He went on.

The house itself was a wreck, roof sagging, doors torn from their hinges, but it hadn't burned. The barn was burned to ashes. The bodies of a man and two dogs lay in the dusty yard between the house and the barn. A shotgun lay across the man's chest.

Another dog whimpered from under the wreckage of the farmhouse.

'Ho! Anyone home?' Harry shouted. There was no answer except the whimpering of the dog. He stopped the motorcycle and got off. Large tracks were visible in the dust. They didn't really look like the tracks of elephants, because they left claw marks. Nothing on Earth left tracks like that.

He stalked cautiously around the yard, and after a while he went inside the house. There were women's clothes in the closet with the farmer's clothes. Another room had been occupied by a boy. Harry guessed he'd been about Melissa's age, ten or eleven. A model of the starship *Enterprise* hung from the ceiling and toy guns stood in the corner. Clothing for a small boy was flung onto the floor. Two dresser drawers were empty.

Prisoners? They're taking women and children, but not men? That doesn't make sense.

There were letters scattered across the front room floor. John Thomas Kensington, RFD#3 . . . Harry went back outside. Kensington lay on his back, his eyes staring upward to the sky. He'd been torn in two halves by one shot. The bore on those alien guns was as big as a fist. Twenty yards from his body the ground had been torn up by something large thrashing in the dust, and there were dark stains. John Thomas Kensington had sold his farm dearly. Harry saluted and went back into the collapsing house.

They take their dead with them. Dead or wounded. A shotgun ought to do some damage at that range. Wonder what he was using?

The refrigerator had been wrecked, but the food inside wasn't spoiled. Harry rooted around until he found bread and cheese and lunch meat and made a sandwich. While he was looking for bread he found a box of shells for the shotgun. It was number six bird shot, suitable for doves and quail. *Not much of a load for elephants.* He waited until he'd eaten before he went to take the gun from the man's lifeless fingers.

The dog under the porch continued to whimper.

Bury the dead? Shoot the dog before it turns feral or starves?

Harry had always believed himself tough, but he'd never thought he'd be faced with decisions like this. Dead bodies were matters for the police and the coroner's office and the undertakers.

There won't be a coroner. Harry went looking for a shovel.

He made another dozen miles before the sonic boom tore at his ears. Harry braked the motorcycle and looked up. Three contrails led from the west, passing nearly overhead. Harry cheered. 'Go get the bastards!' he shouted.

As he watched, one of the contrails broke into a ball of black smoke. Something bright seemed to stab upward from the east, and the second contrail died. The third traced a complex curve; then it, too, ended in a ball of black smoke.

'Damn. Damn and hell.' Harry started the bike again.

———

The big situation map in the war room changed every few minutes, but no one was sure how current its information was. A vast area of Kansas, stretching northward into Nebraska, was covered with bright red symbols. Someone had finally got stylized parachutes to show where alien units had landed. They covered an area that looked much like an amoeba, with its nucleus at Great Bend. Pseudopods reached east and west.

The Situation Room was the center of the underground North American Air Defense complex. It was located under nearly a mile of granite, separated from the outside world by sealed corridors, water barriers, guard rooms, and more granite. A row of offices overlooked the Situation Room. Jack Clybourne stood outside one of the office doors.

Jenny came up to him and winked. He didn't respond. 'I'm supposed to report to Admiral Carrell,' Jenny said. Her voice held slight irritation.

'Sure.' Jack shook his head. 'Sorry, hon. I'm about as useful as a fifth leg here. Where's the President safer? But I'm the only Presidential Protective Unit agent here, and I have to act like it.'

'Yeah. Look, there's no such thing as off duty down here, but we have to eat sometimes. Sleep, too . . . Dinner tonight?'

'I'd love that —'

'I'll be around.' She grinned. 'If they leave the door open, be sure to watch the screens.'

'You've got pictures of the aliens?'

'We think so.' Jenny tapped at the door. It wasn't closed properly, and the door swung open. One wall of the office was glass. It overlooked the big screen displays and control consoles on the floor below. There was one desk. President David Coffey sat there staring at the maps. Admiral Carrell stood next to him. General Toland stood grimly on the other side of the desk from Carrell, his lips a tight line.

'Roughly a circle,' Admiral Carrell said.

'But what do they want?' the President asked.

'This is obviously a reconnaissance in force,' Carrell said. He shook his head. 'As to what their ultimate aims might be, I don't know, sir.' He looked up to see Jenny at the door. 'Come in, Major. Have your intelligence people got the displays ready?'

'Yes, sir. We have reports from refugees, and some pictures one brought out. The pictures should be up from the lab any minute.'

'Have you seen them?'

'No, sir, they're color, and you don't look at color while it's being developed.'

'But you have descriptions?'

'Yes, sir.'

'Well, tell us!' the President demanded.

'Mr. President – sir, it will only be another minute until the pictures are ready. I'd – sir, I'd rather you saw for yourself.'

'Refugee reports,' General Toland said. 'They're letting people out, then?'

'Yes, sir, if they're walking. No vehicles allowed out. Anyone who goes out is required to undergo a sort of ceremony.'

'Ceremony?'

'Yes, sir. They – the science-fiction people say it's reasonable, given the way the aliens look, but —'

'Major, your air of mystery is rapidly becoming tiresome,' Admiral Carrell said.

The phone chirped. *Saved.*

The Admiral lifted the phone. 'Carrell . . . Yes, put the photographs up on the big screens. Let everyone see what we're up against.'

There were five screens. One by one they filled with pictures of baby elephants. Some hung from paper airplanes and wore elevator shoes. Others were on foot. All carried weirdly shaped rifles.

Laughter sounded on the floor below, but it soon died away as the screen showed photographs of ruined buildings and wrecked cars, with alien shapes in the foreground. Bodies lay in the background of most of the pictures.

Jenny studied the photographs. They were quite good; the photographer who'd taken them said she'd sold to *Sports Illustrated* and other major magazines. *That's the enemy.*

'They do look like elephants,' Admiral Carrell said.

'Yes, sir,' Jenny said. 'But they're not really elephants.'

'No. They're invaders,' General Toland said.

The President studied the screens carefully, then turned to Jenny. 'This ceremony. What was it?'

'Before they'll let anyone leave the area they control, they make you lie down on your back, arms stretched out overhead. Then one of the – aliens – puts his foot on you. After that you're free to go.'

'And your sci-fi people think that's reasonable?' the President asked.

'Yes, sir. The way the aliens are built, they must think in terms of trampling their enemies beneath their feet. They may be the biggest animals on their planet. Most Earth species have a surrender ritual. This is theirs.'

The President nodded slowly.

God, he looks awful. I wonder if he got any sleep at all?

'Do your experts have any theories on what the invaders *want?*' the President demanded.

'The Earth,' Jenny said.

General Toland was adamant. 'Kick their butts, don't piss on them,' he said. 'Mr. President, we cannot commit our forces piecemeal! You've got to let me gather my strength before we go in there.'

'American citizens are being killed there. Property destroyed. God damn it, they've invaded the United States.' David Coffey's voice was cold with anger. His hands gripped the arms of his chair. 'We have to do something! What's the Army for if it can't defend the nation?'

Toland fought visibly to control himself.

'That is hardly fair, Mr. President,' Admiral Carrell said. 'The Army is not generally deployed to fight enemies within the nation.'

'If they'd let us call up some reservists before that goddamn ship got here,' General Toland muttered. 'Mr. President, I'm doing all I can. Our best units are in Europe and Central America and Lebanon, and there's no chance we can get those troops home. Not while the enemy dominates space. They can see everything we do!'

See it and kill it, Jenny thought. *Lasers for the airplanes, kinetic energy weapons for ships . . .*

270

'So when will we be able to do something for our people, General Toland?' the President demanded.

'Two more days, sir. I hope. Mr. President, we can't mass our forces! The commander at Fort Knox loaded tanks onto a train to send west. They hit the train. Their air defenses are superb. Anything we sent into that area either gets zapped from space or hit by a ground-launched missile.'

'Or worse,' Jenny said.

They all looked at her.

'They're setting up ground-based laser defense systems. The reports are just coming in. I'll have them on the screens in a few minutes.'

'Lasers,' the President said.

'Yes, sir. Much better than ours.'

'So what the hell are they doing with them?' General Toland demanded.

Jenny shook her head. 'We don't *know*, sir. It appears they're setting up a strong perimeter defense inside the area they control – but we don't know, because we can't get inside there to find out.'

'So they have it all their way.' The President's voice was low and tired, as if he'd already been defeated.

It frightened Jenny. 'Not all their way, sir,' she said. 'Some reports get out. Mostly ham radio. They don't get to broadcast long before something smashes them. Also, there's bound to be resistance. National Guardsmen. Farmers with deer rifles.'

'Sure, they'll fight,' Toland said. 'Even without orders.'

Jenny nodded. 'But they'll be disorganized. We can't communicate!'

'And there's nothing else we can do?' the President asked. There was despair in his voice. 'With all our power, all our nuclear arsenal – can't we use nukes on them?'

'They're all mixed in with our people,' Admiral Carrell said.

'General, do something. Hurt them,' the President said. 'Hit them hard. Isn't there any place where there are a lot of them, and none of our people?'

'None, no. Not many, yes,' Toland said.

The President stared grimly at the screens. 'Hurt them. Now. It will help American morale.'

'But, sir —'

'That was an order, General.'

Toland snapped to attention. 'Yes, sir. I take it you don't want a general bombardment.'

'No. But they can't have it all their way. We have to hurt them. How else will we drive them out of America?'

Why are we so sure we can do it? Jenny almost blurted it out.

'We may not be able to drive them out,' Admiral Carrell said. 'We may simply have to kill them all.'

'It may come to that,' General Toland said. 'It comes under the heading of destroying the country in order to save it. What we need is neutron weapons.'

'What would they do?'

'They kill without destroying the cities.' General Toland drummed his fingers against the glass wall of the office. 'If our people are inside, behind stone walls, in basements – don't most Kansans have root cellars? Places underground?'

'Many do,' the President said.

'A few feet of dirt would protect our people,' Toland said. 'If the elephants are out in the open, we could zap them without destroying Kansas. Only trouble is, we don't have the bombs.'

'Why not?'

'The few we have are in Europe,' Admiral Carrell said carefully. 'Because of public protest, we were never allowed to manufacture any large number of neutron weapons. I have asked the laboratories at Sandia and Los Alamos to try to assemble makeshift enhanced radiation weapons, but they cannot give us a schedule for their delivery.'

'But this is insane,' the President said. 'A few thousand elephants —how many are there, anyway?'

'We don't know,' Jenny admitted. 'Certainly fewer than fifty thousand.'

'Even so, it must be a significant part of their ground combat strength,' General Toland said. 'More troops than they can afford to lose. If we kill them all, they may have to leave us alone in future.'

'They still control space,' Admiral Carrell said. 'Major Crichton, you look like a lady who wants to say something.'

'Yes, sir,' Jenny answered. 'You asked me to get the science-fiction people to work. It wasn't hard. They've got a number of ideas about the war.'

'Well?' the President demanded.

'Sir, I think it would be better if you heard for yourself.'

David Coffey frowned. Then suddenly he grinned. 'Sure, why not? As you say, they're the only experts we have.'

When night came, David Morgan still wasn't home. *No gin, either,* Carlotta thought. *Only two inches in his bottle.* She'd found blackberry wine in the root cellar. It would have to do.

They sat by candlelight in the living room. There were distant sounds of thunder, and far to the east and south were flashes of light.

The skies were clear overhead. Juana sat next to a kerosene lamp with a Jane Austen novel.

'Aren't you worried?' Carlotta asked.

'Sure, but what good does that do? David's got a good car and a rifle. He can't phone. What should I do?'

'I don't know. What about —' She paused, and after a moment there were more distant sounds. 'About that?'

'Nothing we can do. Should we run away? Where would we go? It's miles to the nearest house, and Lucy can't walk that far.'

'Don't you have another car?'

'Not one that works. Even if we did, where would you rather be?'

'I don't know. Want some wine?'

'No.'

And you don't think I should, either. To hell with you. Carlotta drank the blackberry wine. It was much too sweet.

Morning came, bright and clear and cloudless, a glorious Kansas day except for ominous black clouds rising far away in the east. There was still no sign of Professor Morgan. Carlotta and Juana sat outside on the patio with coffee. The night sounds were gone. An hour passed, then part of another; then there were noises, and dust to the west.

'Cars. Trucks. Lots of them,' Juana said. She listened again. 'Sound strange. *Now* maybe is a good time to run.'

'What's the difference?' Carlotta asked. *Maybe they'll know something about Wes!*

Juana peered down the road. 'It's the army!' she shouted. 'Our army!'

Carlotta was almost disappointed.

She counted a dozen tanks, and five truckloads of soldiers. They came up the drive and circled on both sides of the house, going right on past and out toward the abandoned barn. One vehicle that looked like a tank, but had wheels, drove up to the house and stopped. An elderly officer with a graying mustache got out.

'Joe!' Juana called.

He saluted. 'Lieutenant Colonel Halverson, Kansas Militia, ma'am.' He tried to grin. 'Come to see if you need help.'

'Have you seen David?' Juana demanded.

'Yes, ma'am, Major Morgan will be along in a bit. He helped us round up troops. Thought he ought to come home last night and tell you, but he said you'd understand,

274

and we sure did need him, him and that four-wheel of his.'

'What do you intend, Colonel?' Carlotta asked. She remembered she was dressed in a wrinkled housecoat, and was ashamed.

'This is my sister,' Juana said.

'Mrs. Dawson?' Halverson asked. 'Pleased to meet you, ma'am.' He climbed down off the armored car. 'As to what we intend, well, first I'm waiting for my helicopters. Takes time to get them spruced up. Meantime, we came out to see if you needed help. When the choppers get here, we're going south and east until we see what the hell has invaded us.'

Carlotta nodded. *A dozen tanks, two of those armored car things, trucks. And helicopters. Weekend warriors. Most of them are pretty old, but –* 'You look formidable enough. Fast work.'

'Started mobilizing the Guard the night they started shooting,' Halverson said. There was pride in his voice. 'Been rounding up troops from all over the county. Would have called Major Morgan, but the phones were out. Lucky we ran into him in town.'

'But what is happening?'

Halverson shrugged. 'Juana, we haven't been in touch with any government above the county seat since those – aliens started shooting. Phones don't work, nothing but static on the radios. Most of our communications stuff was designed to work with satellites, and we sure as hell don't have any of *those* left. Even so – ' His back straightened. 'I don't figure Washington wants me to just sit back and wait for orders, not while they're dropping out of the skies! Soon as my choppers get here, we're going to show 'em what it means to mess around with Americans. Especially Kansas Jayhawks!'

CHAPTER EIGHTEEN
THE JAYHAWK WAR

A general never knows anything with certainty, never sees his enemy plainly, nor knows positively where he is. The most experienced eye cannot be certain whether it sees the whole of the enemy's army, or only three-fourths of it. It is by the eyes of the mind, by the combination of all reasoning, by a sort of inspiration, that the general sees, commands and judges.

– NAPOLEON BONAPARTE, *Memoirs*

COUNTDOWN: H PLUS 120 HOURS

Harry spent the night in a wheat field, using wheat straw for bedding and more of it piled on top to stay warm. He didn't dare risk a fire. There were flashes and thunder all around him. By counting time between flash and sound, he estimated some were as close as three miles, far too close.

Morning came, and he missed Jeri's camp stove and cocoa. *Can't think about that. Got to get moving. But goddammit, I should have done something; I should have saved her. Hell, I should have left her by her car – she'd have been safer! Come with me. I'll take care of you, shit —*

The motorcycle ran fine. He estimated that he had another twenty miles to go, and fuel for thirty.

Harry turned up the lane toward the big house and shook his head in disbelief. *Made it, by God!* At least it certainly looked like the place Wes had once described, and it was on the right road, ten miles west of Dighton, and there was no other house within a mile.

It was nearly noon. The skies were blue and clear, and there were only occasional thunderclaps and flashes of colored light.

He frowned. An army Light Armored Vehicle stood in front of the house. There were deep tread marks on both sides of the drive, leading out behind the house. Half a mile out through the fields were at least six tanks, a couple of obsolete M-1 Abrams tanks and at least two Bradley Infantry Fighting Vehicles.

A big blue GM Jimmy four-wheel-drive truck stood in the driveway beside the LAV. Harry nodded at it approvingly. He let the motorcycle coast up to the front porch. Two soldiers older than Harry sat on top of the armored car. One waved at Harry.

'Hi,' Harry called.

'Hi,' one of the soldiers answered.

Something moved behind the glass-paneled front window.

'Is Mrs. Dawson at home?' Harry asked. No point in asking why the army had surrounded the house.

'Think so,' a sergeant said. 'Hey, Juana, visitor for your sister.'

The front door opened. Carlotta Dawson, in blue jeans, her hair bundled into a kerchief, rushed down the steps. She didn't say anything. She just grabbed Harry and pulled herself against him, burying her face in his beard.

She stood that way for a moment, then looked up at the soldiers on the LAV. 'He came all the way from L.A.,' she said. 'To help me.'

'Tough going?' the sergeant asked.

'Some,' Harry said.

'Heard it was bad out west.'

'Hoover Dam's gone,' Harry said. 'They took out all

the cities along the Colorado River. Same things happened with all the dams along the Platte. They seem to like hitting dams.'

An officer came out of the house. 'Colonel Halverson, this is Harry Reddington,' Carlotta said. 'A friend of – of Wes and me. He's come from L.A. Harry, you must be starved.'

'Yeah, but, Miz Dawson, we've got to *move*. The damned elephants —'

'Elephants?' Colonel Halverson demanded. 'Elephants?'

'Yes, sir,' Harry said. 'The Invaders —'

'Why do you say elephants?'

'They look like baby elephants with two trunks.'

'You've seen them, then?'

'Yes, sir, I sure have.' Harry winced. This wasn't going to be easy. *Why tell it at all?* 'Shot one, too, but they wear armor, so I doubt if I hurt it.'

'Armor?'

'Yeah. Body armor, and they have rifles. They kill people. They kidnapped – they took some people prisoner from a farmhouse. Killed the farmer.'

'Just how close did you get to them?'

Harry shuddered. 'Too damn close! Close as you and me!' *One stood on my chest* – He wouldn't say that. It shamed him.

Halverson looked skeptical. 'How'd you get away from them?'

'They let me go. Look, you guys do what you want, but Mrs. Dawson and me have to get *out* of here. They're all around, it's damned lucky they didn't get here yet.'

'Tell me more,' Colonel Halverson said. 'Tell me everything.'

'There's just not that much,' Harry said. *They wore elevator shoes and they came down on paper airplanes. If I say that –* 'They came down on hang gliders. Then bigger stuff landed.'

'How big? Where?'

'Near Logan. They had flying things about as big as a jetliner only not so wide in the wings. And a floating thing about as big as a diesel semi. That's what I saw. There may have been bigger.'

'Tanks? Field guns?'

'None I saw.'

'And they let you go?'

'Yeah, sort of.'

'They let others go?'

'Yes —'

'From Logan. Southwest of here.' Halverson pounded his right fist into his left hand. 'But we know they're east of us, and *nobody's* come out of there. They would, too, if the – if those things would let them. Maybe there's something they want to hide. Son, you better tell me everything you know.'

Gradually Halverson dragged the story out of Harry. Finally it was done. 'So I found the gun,' Harry said. 'I thought about going after Mrs. Wilson, but I came here, instead.'

Halverson looked thoughtful. 'Hell, what else could you do? You're no army. The next time they'd just shoot you. But I sure wish I knew what they're hiding out to the east —'

'Colonel?' The sergeant seated on top of the armored car jumped off. He looked older than Halverson.

'Yeah, Luke?'

'Colonel, I heard a funny story last night. Over in Collinston.'

'Collinston? That's fifty miles from here! What were you doing in Collinston?'

'Took some of the boys over for a drink. You didn't need us. We weren't going anywhere.'

'Next time you leave camp, you tell me.' He chuckled. 'Okay, so you found a bar open in Collinston. Guess it takes more than war and a parachute invasion to close the bars in that town.'

'Sure does. Anyway, there was a guy in the bar. He'd been drinking a lot, so nobody paid much attention. He said he'd seen an elephant. A little one. In a willow patch outside of town. Thought it escaped from some circus, because it was a trained elephant.'

'Trained? Trained how?' Halverson demanded.

'Don't know.'

'Harry.' Carlotta's voice was low and urgent. 'Harry, that's an Invader. We have to go capture it. We have to get it alive. Maybe it knows about Wes. Harry, we have to!'

Harry gulped hard. 'Sure, but I need gas —'

'I'll get it out of David's car.'

'Hey, hold on,' Colonel Halverson said. 'I can't let you do that —'

'Why not?' Carlotta demanded. 'You're going east. You'll see lots of Invaders. You don't need this one.'

'But – look, those things are armed —'

'It didn't hurt that man in the bar,' Carlotta said. 'Why would he think it was trained? Maybe – maybe it lay down and rolled over!'

'Holy shit!' Harry said. 'Hey, she might be right.'

'Yeah, but —'

'Colonel, my husband was a personal friend of the President. President Coffey himself sent Wes up to meet the aliens. It's my right to find out what happened to him. You give Harry some gasoline, and then go fight your war. Harry and I will do the rest.'

Yeah, Harry thought. *Sure.*

———

'I say we go in after them.' Evan Lewis sounded very sure. 'Hell, Joe, we have to! We can't let those – things run all over Kansas.'

'Wasn't me arguing with you, Captain,' Lieutenant Colonel Halverson said. He looked at the others seated at Juana Morgan's dining room table. Evan Lewis, who ran a tractor sales and repair agency, and commanded the tanks. George Mason, lawyer, who commanded the six helicopter gunships. The fourth man at the table was David Morgan, retired professor of business administration. Halverson's adjutant and chief of staff. Morgan was the smallest one at the table, and he spoke with a clipped eastern accent that irritated hell out of Joe Halverson, but he was certainly the smartest man in the battalion.

'And I still don't like it,' George Mason said. 'Colonel, we don't know what we're up against, and we don't know what the Army has in mind.'

'So what do you suggest we do?' Halverson asked.

'Wait for orders.'

'How heroic,' Captain Lewis said.

'Enough.' David Morgan spoke quietly, but they all heard him. 'We don't need bickering.'

'So which side are you on, Professor?' Evan Lewis had never liked Professor Morgan. On the other hand, it was David Morgan's house, and they all felt like guests, military uniforms or not.

'I agree with Colonel Halverson's reasoning,' Morgan said. 'The invaders are hiding something to the east. We're a cavalry outfit. It's our duty to explore – but carefully. In particular, we have to be certain that any information we get will be useful. That won't be easy. They're jamming all communications and the phones don't work.'

Joe Halverson nodded thoughtfully. 'Suggestions, Major?'

'We'll have to string things out. Use the Bradley vehicles as communications links.' He sketched rapidly on the table cloth. 'Corporal Lewis' – Morgan nodded to Evan Lewis; everyone knew that Evan's son Jimmy was an electronic genius – 'Jimmy rigged up those shield things that let the tanks talk to each other, as long as the antennas are aimed straight at each other. Fine. We send the choppers forward as scouts and flankers, making sure they stay in line of sight to the tanks. Tanks in the middle, concentrated enough to have some firepower, spread out enough to not make such a good target. Then string the Bradleys and the LAVs out behind as connecting links.'

'What do they connect to?' Mason asked.

'We leave two troopers here with my wife and a radio. Juana writes down everything. If we don't come back, she gets the hell out.'

'No much chance she'd have to do that,' Halverson said. 'Hell, we're not an army, but we've got a fair amount of strength here.' He looked out the window at his command. Six helicopters, with missiles. A dozen tanks, with guns and missiles. The communications weren't any good because the Invaders were broadcasting static from space. But even without communciations a troop of armored cavalry was nothing to laugh at.

'Sounds all right to me,' Lewis said. 'At least we'll be doing something.'

'I'd rather wait for orders,' George Mason said. 'But what the hell, I'm ready if you are.'

Joe Halverson stood. 'Right. Let's go.'

———

'I'm Jimmy Lewis,' the corporal said. He climbed through the attic window to join Harry on the roof of the big frame house.

Harry nodded greeting. 'Hi. They tell me you invented this.' He hefted the handi-talkie radio whose antenna was wrapped in a tinfoil cone stiffened with coat-hanger wire.

'Yeah,' Jimmy Lewis said. His tone was serious. 'It's the only way I've figured to keep communications. You have to point it pretty tight, though, or you'll lose the signal.'

Harry regarded the device, then the similar but larger tinfoil monstrosity on one of the Bradley Fighting Vehicles in the yard down below. 'Yeah. So I point this at the Bradley, and maybe I can hear. What then?'

'Use this,' Jimmy Lewis said. He handed Harry a Sony tape recorder. 'There's three hours of tape on there. More than enough. Just plug it into the radio, here, like that, and turn it on when we move out. Listen in the earphones, and you'll hear a tone if you're pointed *close* to the tanks, and nothing at all when you're dead on, except when they're talking; then you'll hear them talk, of course. It sounds hard, but it's pretty easy, really.'

'Sure.'

Major Morgan was in the front yard. Harry couldn't hear what he was saying, but Juana Morgan didn't like it. Their housekeeper sat in the front seat of the four-wheel-drive Jimmy, but Juana Morgan didn't want to drive it.

Finally, though, she got in, and the blue Jimmy drove off. *And now it's just Carlotta and me.* David Morgan stood very straight as he went to his tank and climbed in.

Colonel Halverson came over to stand below them. ''Bout time, Jimmy,' he shouted up at them.

'Yes, sir.' Corporal Lewis waved to Harry and crawled back inside through the window.

'Thanks, Mr. Reddington,' Halverson shouted. 'I need all my troopers. Good of you to fill in. I doubt you'll be needed, but —'

'Yeah. No problem, Colonel.' *Of course Carlotta's goin' nuts, wanting to go get that elephant. Maybe it's safer up here!*

'Thanks, then,' Halverson said. He walked briskly up the line to the lead tank and climbed in. He stood in the turret for a moment, then waved dramatically. 'Wagons – hoooo!' he shouted.

The helicopters rose in a cloud of dust and swept forward and off to each side in groups of three. The tanks fanned out and moved ahead, leaving the Bradleys behind.

'Watcher, this is Jayhawk One. Do you read?'

Harry keyed the mike. 'Roger, Jayhawk One, this is Watcher.'

'Course is 100 degrees, moving forward at 1220 hours,'

the tanker's voice said in Harry's ear. Harry started guilt-ily and switched on the tape recorder.

When the Bradley began to move eastward, it was much harder to keep the radio aimed properly. Harry braced it against the chimney. The rooftop was steep and it wasn't easy to keep his footing.

The helicopters wove in complex patterns ahead of the tanks. 'Moving ahead at twenty klicks,' the voice said.

About ten miles an hour, Harry thought. He could still remember kilometer signs on highways, although he hadn't seen one in years.

A half-hour went by. The helicopters and lead tanks were nearly invisible. The others were strung out behind them. Harry's radio contact was a good five miles ahead, and it took all his attention to keep the antenna aimed properly. He was about to key the mike to tell them that.

'Light overhead,' the tanker's voice shouted.

Harry could see it. A bright green flash, more visible high up than near the ground.

'It's moving in a circle – Number Three Helicopter reports the beam is moving around them in a circle, it's tightening in on them —' There was a pause. 'No contact with the choppers. Colonel Halverson reports they've all been attacked by some kind of beam —'

Jesus.

'So far nothing's shot at us —'

There was a roar and the sharp snap of multiple sonic booms. Harry looked up. Dozens of parallel white lines crossed the sky from the south-west. They dropped like the lines in *Missile Command*, downward toward where Colonel Halverson's force was centered. There were bright flashes at the horizon and along the line where the connecting vehicles had been strung out. After a long pause, there was the sound of thunder.

'Jayhawks, this is Watcher,' Harry said. 'And Jayhawk, this is Watcher. Come in —'

*   *   *

Harry poured the last of the gas into the motorcycle.

'What was it?' Carlotta asked.

'I don't know. It looked like a video game. It was unreal.' Harry went on checking the motorcycle. Making a motorcycle work was a good test of sanity, and one he could win. Death from the sky – *We owned the sky once. Then the Soviets took it away. Now we've got to take it back from baby elephants.*

'Motor's in good shape. We'll make it fine. You'll have to hold the rifle.' He handed Carlotta the 30-06 Winchester that David Morgan had loaned him.

'Not an elephant gun, but it'll give them pause to think,' Morgan had said.

Not a loan anymore. They were dead, all of them. He'd waited an hour. 'Maybe I ought to go look?'

'No.' Carlotta was positive. 'You'll get yourself killed. It's more important that we capture that stray —'

'Mrs. Dawson, you don't *know* that's a stray.'

'What else could it be?'

Harry shrugged. *All I know is I'm gettin' damned tired of ridin' this motorcycle, and I wish I had another tube of Preparation H. But my back isn't as bad as it was.* 'All aboard.'

He patted his pocket to be sure the tape was in it. Somebody would want that tape.

'I will never go metric —' Harry sang.

A clump of cars and people was clustered around a big semi ahead. 'We're just about to Collinston,' Harry shouted. 'That looks like trouble.'

He slowed, and drove the motorcycle up to the semi. A highway patrol cruiser was parked nearby, and a lieutenant of the highway patrol stood facing a knot of angry farmers and truckers. Most of them held rifles or shotguns.

'Oh, *shit*,' Harry muttered.

The lieutenant eyed Harry and Carlotta. Red beard,

dirty clothes; middle-aged woman in designer jeans. He watched Carlotta dismount. 'Yes, madam?'

'I am Carlotta Dawson. Yes, *Dawson*. My husband was aboard the Soviet Kosmograd. Lieutenant, I gather there is an alien here?'

'Damn straight,' one of the truck drivers shouted. 'Goddam snout blew George Mathers in half!' He brandished a military rifle. 'Now it's our turn!'

'We have to take it alive,' Carlotta stated.

'Bullshit!' This one was a farmer. 'I come out of Logan, lady. The goddam snouts killed my sister! They're all over the fucking place.'

'How'd you get out? Foot on your chest?' Harry asked.

The driver looked sheepish.

'Thought so,' Harry said. 'Look, give us a chance. The military wants to question that thing. We'll go in after it.' He pointed to the willow trees a hundred yards from the highway. 'Over there, right?'

'Over there and go to hell,' someone yelled.

'Let's go,' Harry said. He gestured to Carlotta. She climbed on behind. 'In there.'

'There' was a dirt path leading to the clump of willow trees. As Harry started the motorcycle, he heard one of the truck drivers. 'We can blow it away when he gets out.'

There were mutters of approval.

When he stopped at the swamp's edge, he could hear something big in the creek.

For Harpanet, things had become very odd. He had gone through terror and out the other side. He was bemused. Perhaps he was mad. Without his herd about him for comparison, how was a fi' to tell?

Try to surrender: fling the gun to the dirt, roll over, belly in the air. The man gapes, turns and lurches away. Chase him down: he screams and gathers speed, falls and runs again, toward lights. Harpanet will seem to be attacking. Cease! Hide and wait.

A human climbs from the cab of a vehicle. Try again? The man scampers into the cab, emerges with something that flames and roars. Harpanet rolls in time to take the cloud of tiny projectiles in his flank instead of his belly. The man fires again.

He has refused surrender. Harpanet trumpets: rage, woe, betrayal. He sweeps up his own weapon and fires back. The enemy's forelimbs and head explode outward from a mist of blood.

In Harpanet's mind his past fades, his future is unreal. His digits stroke his side, feeling for the deathwound.

No deathwound; no hole big enough for a digit to find. What did the human intend? Torture? Harpanet's whole right side is a burning itch covered with a sheen of blood. An eight to the eighth of black dots form a buzzing storm around him. He lurches through the infinite land, away from roads, downhill where he can, within the buzzing storm and the maddening itch. The jaws of his mind close fast on a memory, vivid in all his senses, more real than his surroundings. He moves through an infinite fantasy of planet, seeking the mudroom aboard *Message Bearer*.

Green . . . tall green plants with leaves like knife blades, but they brush away the hungry swarming dots . . . water? Mud!

He rolls through mud and greenery, over and over, freezing from time to time to look, smell, listen.

Harpanet's past fades against the strange and terrible reality. If he has a future, it is beyond imagining, a mist-gray wall. There is only *now*, a moment of alien plants and fiery itch and cool mud, and *here*, mudroom and garden mushed together, nightmarishly changed. He rolls to wash the wounds; he plucks gobs of mud to spread across his tattered flank.

Afraid to leave, afraid to stay. What might taste his blood in the water, and seek its source? The predators of the Homeworld were pictures on a thuktun, ghosts on an old recording tape, but fearsome enough for all their distance. What lurks in these alien waters? But he hears the distant sound of machines passing, and knows that they are not fithp machines.

A machine comes near, louder, louder. Harpanet's ears and eyes project above the water.

The machine balances crazily on two wheels, like men. It slows, wobbles, stops.

Humans approach on foot.

Harpanet's muscles know what to do when he is hurt, exhausted, friendless, desperate, alone. Harpanet's mind finds no other answer. But he sees no future —

He lurches from the water. Alien weapons come to bear. He casts his gun into the weeds. He rolls on his back and splays his limbs and waits.

The man comes at a toppling run. No adult fi' would try to balance so. The man sets a hind foot on Harpanet's chest, with such force that Harpanet can feel it. He swallows the urge to laugh, but such a weight could hardly bend a rib. Nonetheless he lies with limbs splayed, giving his surrender. The man looks down at his captive, breathing as if he has won a race . . .

————————

'We got him!' Harry shouted. 'Now what?' He waved uphill, where a score of armed men, hidden, waited with weapons ready.

'I can talk to them —' Carlotta sounded doubtful.

'They won't listen.' *And dammit, this is my snout, they can't kill it now.* Harry thought furiously. A guilty grin came, and he lifted the seat of the motorcycle, where he kept his essential tools.

'You've thought of something?'

'Maybe.' He dug into the tool roll and found a hank of parachute cord. It was thin, strong enough to hold a man but not much use against one of *those*. He gestured to the captive, using both hands to make 'get up' motions.

The alien stood. It looked at them passively.

'Gives me the creeps,' Harry said. He clutched his rifle. *One 30-06 in the eye, and we don't have a problem.* 'See if it'll carry you,' Harry said.

'Carry me?'

'Sheena, Queen of the Jungle. I know they're strong enough.'

A dozen truckers and farmers stood with ready weapons.

Harry walked ahead of the invader, leading it on a length of cord. Carlotta rode its back, sidesaddle. She beamed at them. 'Hi!' she called.

None of the watchers spoke. Perhaps they were afraid of saying something foolish.

'It surrendered,' Carlotta shouted. 'We'll take it to the government.'

There was a loud click as a safety was taken off.

Harry whistled: *Wheep, wheep, wheep!* 'Here, Shep! Hey, it's all right, guys. Shep big gray peanut-loving doggie!'

There were sounds of disgust.

CHAPTER NINETEEN
THE SCHOLARS

Deign on the passing world to turn thine eyes,
And pause a while from learning to be wise.
There mark what ills the scholar's life assail —
Toil, envy, want, the patron, and the jail.

    – DR. SAMUEL JOHNSON, *Vanity of Human Wishes*

COUNTDOWN: H PLUS 150 HOURS

Pavel Aleksandrovich Bondarev fingered the priceless tapestry covering the bare concrete wall. 'It doesn't really look like a bomb shelter,' he said.

Lorena rolled lazily in the big bed. 'They are very nice rooms,' she said.

Her own room was just down the corridor, close enough that only a few of Bondarev's staff knew just how late she stayed. They wouldn't talk. As secretary to the acting commander of the Soviet space defense forces, Lorena was one of the most powerful women in the Soviet Union. *As long as my wife is not offended. She must know, but so long as I am discreet . . .*

Lorena rolled off the bed and walked to the closet, where his uniforms hung. She fingered the shoulder straps on one of them. 'I had never thought to see you a general,' she said. 'And now there is talk of making you a Marshal of the Soviet Union —'

'Hah.'

'You do not wish promotion?'

'Of course not. I never wanted to be part of the military

at all. I would rather talk with the aliens than fight them! They were in space for decades, out between the stars where there is no interference, no radio noise – think of what they must have learned!'

'They have destroyed half of Russia, and you wish to *talk* to them!'

He sighed. 'I know it is impossible. Perhaps, though, when we defeat them, I will learn what they know of stars.' *Only it is not so certain that we can defeat them. Whenever we launch a missile, they destroy the missile base.*

'They have landed in America. Perhaps the Americans have captured aliens.'

'Perhaps.'

'And perhaps not. It is late.' She moved provocatively. He didn't react. 'So. You are satisfied for the moment,' she teased. 'Perhaps later   '

'I have other things to concern me,' Bondarev said.

Lorena laughed. 'They do not always keep your attention —'

A chirp sounded from the other room. Bondarev put on a robe. He could not cut short a conversation with whoever called on *that* phone. 'Bondarev here,' he said.

'Narovchatov.'

'Da, Comrade Narovchatov?'

'I am told that the Americans have called you.'

'Only to test the telephone line. I did not myself speak to them.'

'Who did?'

'My secretary.'

'What was said?'

'Nothing, Nikolai Nikolayevich. Comrade Polinova spoke to an American technician. She was told that the Americans wished to speak with me, but then the connection failed.' Bondarev spoke nervously. *Should I have reported this? But there was nothing to report.*

'It is a matter of great concern,' Narovchatov said. 'We have been unable to make contact with the Americans.

The Chairman wishes to speak with the American President. Are your technicians working on reestablishing this connection?'

'The failure was not here, Comrade Narovchatov. I understand that the cable crosses the Atlantic, then passes under the Mediterranean, and comes through Istanbul. I believe the break was in Marrakech.'

'Where there is chaos,' Narovchatov muttered.

'Da.' Bondarev had sporadic communications with a large Soviet armored force in Africa, but that group was far to the south and east of Marrakech.

Lorena came in with a glass of hot tea and set it beside him. Bondarev nodded his thanks.

'Perhaps the KGB has agents in Marrakech,' Bondarev said. 'Perhaps they could facilitate the repair of the cable.'

'A splendid suggestion. I will send the orders. The matter is urgent, Pavel Aleksandrovich. There is unrest in Germany and Poland. We have reason to believe the West Germans may attempt something. The Americans must restrain them.'

If they can. And if they will. 'Da. I understand.'

'Have you anything to report?'

'Only rumors. Our station in Tehran confirms that the Invaders have landed in the central United States, and there is land warfare. The Americans in Tehran know little else, but they pretend high confidence.'

'You will call if you learn more, or if you make contact with the Americans.'

'At once.'

'Your wife sends her regards,' Narovchatov said. 'She is well and your children are well.'

'Thank you.'

The connection broke. Bondarev sipped his tea. 'My family is well,' he said musingly.

'But they did not say where.'

'No. With the Chairman and the Politburo. Somewhere near Moscow, I would presume.'

She sat on the couch and leaned against his shoulder. 'I am glad they are safe. I am also glad your wife is not here.'

'The Chairman wishes to speak with the Americans. It is urgent.'

She sat up quickly. 'Why?'

'There is unrest, in Poland and Germany.'

She cursed. 'They dare!'

'Da. They dare.' *Now that we cannot send the army. Now that the army is needed in the Turkic republics, and Latvia, and Estonia.*

'I hate them,' Lorena said.

————————

They were under the house, inspecting the support pillars. Carlotta was more frightened than Wes. He tried to reassure her – not hearing what he was saying, but knowing he was lying badly. The quake was coming. Soon. These pillars had to be reinforced before the San Andreas fault tore loose and sent everything rolling downhill in a spray of debris.

A sound like a brass trumpet ripped through the world; and then the world tilted and everything started to roll.

Wes Dawson woke to the blare of the acceleration warning, and Russian curses, and the deep hum of *Thuktun Flishithy*'s drive. The floor was tilted, not toward a wall but toward one corner . . . the outer-aft-antispinward corner. The fithp must be accelerating *and* decreasing spin, simultaneously.

The fithp would have no time for prisoners during maneuvers. Wes did what the others were doing. He spread out on his belly like a starfish and curled his fingers and toes in the padding – dry here, though damp throughout the rest of the ship – and dozed.

The tilt grew more pronounced as *Thuktun Flishithy*'s spin decreased. After several hours everyone shifted to the aft wall. They were awake and talking, but not to Wes

Dawson. Once he heard 'amusement park' in English, and Nikolai made roller-coaster motions with his hands while the rest laughed.

Another several hours and the aft wall had become a flat floor. *Thuktun Flishithy*'s drive was pushing at one Earth gravity or close to it.

The door opened.

It *was* a door now, and four fithp warriors rolled through without pause. They herded the humans into the corridor, where four more warriors waited with the teacher's female assistant, Tashayamp. Dmitri bowed to her. 'Greetings,' he said (the pattern of sound that they had learned for a greeting; it had the word *time* in it). 'Question, destination selves?'

'Destination Podo Thuktun,' Tashayamp said. 'Ready your minds.'

With no superior present, she seemed surer of herself. Now, what gave him that impression? Wes watched her. She walked like an unstoppable mass, a behemoth. She wasn't adjusting her gait! He had seen her veer from contact with warriors and humans alike. Now the warriors were presumably *her* guardians, and her human charges had demonstrated both the agility and the motivation to dodge her ton-plus of mass.

Never mind; there was something he wanted from her. 'Question, destination *Thuktun Flishithy?*'

'In two mealtime-gaps this status will end. There will be almost no pull. You will live floating for a long time. You must learn to live so,' she said.

She hadn't answered his question; but then, they often didn't.

The corridor branched. The new corridor dipped, then curved to the right. Now, why the curve? This ought to be a radial corridor. Wes remembered that the streets of Beverly Hills had been laid in curves just to make them prettier. Was that it? Under spin the corridor would rise at twenty or twenty-five degrees . . .

But under spin, a radial corridor would be vertical. Fithp couldn't climb ladders. The routes inward had to be spirals. Look for fast elevators too?

As the Soviets had stopped talking to Wes, so Wes had stopped talking to them. He had fallen into a kind of game. Observe. Deduce. Who will learn faster, you or me?

Tashayamp says we'll be living in nearly free-fall in a day or so. What makes *nearly* free-fall, and why not spin the ship to avoid it? The fithp liked low gravity, but not *that* low. What could prevent them from spinning the ship?

Ah. An asteroid, of course. They've got an asteroid base, a small one, and we're going to be moored to it. I wish to hell they'd let us near a window.

And now we're to see the Podo Thuktun. They showed that in the picture show. Installing the Podo Thuktun was a big deal, so important that they recorded it and showed it to us. As important as the fuel. So what was it?

Thuktun means message or lesson or a body of knowledge; I've heard them use it all three ways. *Thuktun* is part of the mother ship's name. Fistarteh-thuktun, the sleeper with the tapestry harness, is mated to *thuktun* and doesn't seem to have a normal mate. What, then, are we about to see?

The curved corridor ended in a massive rectangular door. Unlike most, this door didn't seem to have automatic controls, and it took two warriors to shoulder it aside.

The troop marched in.

A spiral ramp ran up the sides of the cylindrical chamber. The cylinder was nearly empty; conspicuous waste in a starship. In the center was a vertical pillar no thicker than Wes's wrist. He looked up to where it expanded into a flower-shaped cradle for . . .

For the Podo Thuktun, of course. It was a relic of sorts: a granite block twenty-five or thirty feet long by the same distance wide by half that in height. Its corners and edges were unevenly rounded, as if it had weathered thousands of years of dust-laden winds.

There was writing on it. *In* it: Wes could see overhead light glinting through the lines. Something like a thread-thin laser had written script and diagrams all the way through the block.

He was being left behind. Tashayamp and half the warriors were escorting the Soviets up the spiral ramp; the other warriors were coming for Wes. He hurried to join them. Platforms led off the ramp at varying heights, and on one of these three fithp were at work. They ignored the intruders.

Fistarteh-thuktun and his spaceborn acolytes looked down for a long moment of meditation before beginning their work. It was a ritual, and necessary. One could become too used to the Podo Thuktun; could take it for granted. That must never happen.

At one time bloody wars had been fought over the diagram in the central face of the Podo Thuktun. Was that diagram in fact a picture of a Predecessor? Half the world had been conquered by the herd that thought it was. Many generations had passed, and heretics had been raped for their status with dismaying regularity, before the fithp realized the truth.

Message Bearer's interstellar ramjet had been made from that diagram.

The priest and his acolytes turned to the library screen. Paykurtank tapped at a tab the size of a human's fist. The screen responded by showing a succession of photographs. One after another, granite half-cubes appeared in close-up against varying half-seen backgrounds.

'Skip a few,' Koolpooleh suggested.

'I countermand that,' Fistarteh-thuktun said instantly. 'We'll at least glance at them all. We're seeking *any* relevant information left by the Predecessors regarding aliens, or Winterhome, or its natives.'

The thuktunthp were arrayed in order of their discovery, and roughly in order of simplicity of the lesson delivered. The history of the fithp could be read in the order of discovery of the thuktunthp. Uses of fire, mining and refining of metals, uses of the wheel: the Predecessors had made these easily available to their successors. Later discoveries had been found in caves or mountaintops or lifeless deserts.

'Pause that. Koolpooleh, is this *nothing* but mathematics?'

'I have no trouble reading the Line Thuktun, Fistarteh-thuktun. Simple plane geometry, a list of axioms.'

'Go to the next one.'

'The Breaker has arrived with trainees.'

'Ignore them. Pause that!'

Koolpooleh and Paykurtank were watching the humans, furtively, with one eye each. Fistarteh-thuktun pretended not to notice. Perhaps they could learn from watching the aliens. Perhaps not. The fithp warriors were even now aground and dealing with the prey.

Fistarteh-thuktun remembered what it was like to run, to take prey from a rushing stream, to see nothing but mountains in the distance and clouds overhead . . .

These creatures must first be defeated. Surely the knowledge was here! All knowledge was contained in the thuktunthp.

The Life-Thuktun was surely interesting enough. The script and diagrams dealt with biology, and Fistarteh-thuktun had studied it before. Hierarchies of plant life to the left, animal life to the right. Tiny, ancient single-nucleated life at the bottom, scaling toward complex warm-blooded air breathers at the top. Simple sketches at every level. The sketch that was third from the top resembled a stunted fi'. It was bulky, flat-skulled, with but one branch to its trunk. The feet were clubs, each with a tiny afterthought of a claw.

The creatures sketched above the proto-fi' were extinct, though skeletons had been found preserved in soft sedimentary rock. Other pictured life forms had disappeared too, but . . . shouldn't that top sketch be the lineaments of a Predecessor? Wouldn't they have considered themselves the top of the ladder of life? Wars had been fought over that question, too.

It was not easy to ignore Tashayamp, half an octuple of soldiers, and four of Winterhome's small, flat-faced natives, including one in a wheeled cage. Fistarteh-thuktun could hardly fail to hear Takpusseh lecturing them in baby talk. He let himself glance at the humans. They didn't resemble that top sketch in any way. Fistarteh-thuktun felt a relief he would not let himself admit.

Since his revival from the death-sleep, the priest's position had never been stronger. The average fi' aboard *Message Bearer* had no grasp of what the Predecessors were all about, or how much Fistarteh-thuktun didn't know.

But he had a task. He must advise the officers. He must seek *any* relevant information kept by the Predecessors.

He had Koolpooleh's attention again. 'Go on,' he said.

The next thuktun explained the making of aluminium.

'Not known, the shapes of the – ' Others? Predecessors? 'No pictures of selves. Shape of Predecessors minds, half known.' Tashayamp was speaking slowly, and Wes was catching most of the meaning, he thought. He had to concentrate.

'There were eights of eight-cubed of thuktunthp scattered about the world. The Predecessors' – Tashayamp glanced toward the priest, busy at his huge display screen, and her breathy trumpet of a voice dropped a little — 'did not know everything. They did not know that what they did with their machines would ruin the world for them.

298

Maybe they did not know where life would be in the world, after the world healed. They left the thuktunthp everywhere.

'Not told, things about fithp, things about Predecessors. Perhaps thuktunthp were thuktun' – meaning *message* here – 'to Predecessor children's children. But Predecessor children were not made.'

Arvid asked, 'What happened?'

'Fistarteh-thuktun knows. I talk to him. Wait.' Tashayamp turned away. She stood behind the priest and did nothing, waiting.

Wes looked down.

From below, the cradle had blocked some of the script. From above, it didn't. The sculptors had left a meter or more of margin around the writing; it had worn away unevenly, leaving bulges the cradle arms could grip.

The script was lost to him. Wes studied the diagrams.

The patterns in the Podo Thuktun: here a spray of dots in which Wes could recognize the Summer Triangle: a star pattern. There a pattern of curves that might be the magnetic fields in a Bussard ramjet . . . *Podo* could mean *starflight* or stars or just *sky*. Certain words and phrases became clear. He was sure that *Thuktun Flishithy* meant *Thuktun Carrier* or *Message Bearer*. Fistarteh-thuktun was a priest; it might be that he worshiped the Podo Thuktun. He seemed to function as a librarian too. *Loremaster.*

Fistarteh-thuktun had turned from the screen and was talking with Tashayamp, too fast to be understood.

'Not known what happened to end Predecessor children,' Tashayamp said. 'Perhaps they do not want children because they have destroyed the world. Perhaps they cannot have children.' She spread her digits in the pattern Dawson had come to call a shrug: a futile clawing at the air. It meant, 'I do not know and do not believe it can be known.'

She turned back to Fistarteh-thuktun. Wes studied the

star patterns again. *The constellations are nearly the same as Earth's. Nearly, but not identical. They must be from somewhere near –* He shuddered. *Can more be coming? No, only one ship was in the films they showed us. 'Nearby' is meaningless when we're talking about stars!*

Fistarteh-thuktun was speaking again. Wes moved closer to listen to Tashayamp translate into fithp baby-talk.

Their quarters had become tolerable as the fithp learned what they liked. The padding over the six walls was no longer wet. Dawson was almost comfortable.

Dmitri was speaking English. Dawson was ashamed at how glad that made him. *I am not a communist. Nobody ever called me that except the goddam Birchers. But I can't live alone!*

'They were dying. Wes, did it sound as if they destroyed their environment themselves?'

'I thought that's what Fistarteh-thuktun said.'

'But they must have thought some of them would live. Changed. Could it be true?'

'Do you mean, could the Predecessors be their ancestors? No. There was a *thuktun* onscreen with a column of biology sketches till Fistarteh-thuktun shifted to something else. Didn't you notice the sketches? That misshapen fi' was third from the top. If you were making a hierarchy of life on Earth, would you put humanity third from the top?'

'No,' Dmitri said in some irritation, 'but I might leave humanity off entirely if I were Christian or some such! Then I might put apes third from the top, if I seriously liked dolphins and whales!'

'That's too many ifs.'

'Or a Christian or Muslim might put fanciful angels above him —'

300

'For the moment, we might as well believe as Tashayamp believes,' Arvid said soothingly. 'The fithp have studied the subject for much longer than the hour we have been granted. So. A race died of overpollution. The world was changed. In the changed world something new grew up – perhaps a pet or a work animal, an evolved dog or horse. They do seem to worship the Predecessors.'

'Why wouldn't they?' Wes wondered. 'Consider what would happen to tribes who didn't study the thuktunthp. There were . . . eight to the fourth power is around four thousand thuktunthp, and a lot of them were duplicates. For every one of those, the first tribe – herd? – to use the information would be the first to rule. It must have happened hundreds of times. Of course they worship the Predecessors!'

Arvid shrugged. 'I like to think of them as a tamed elephant. Then the world came apart. Dwarfing is caused by ages of famine. Flash floods winnowed those who could not grow claws to grip a passing rock.' He smiled. 'There is no proof. Choose the picture you like.'

' – Shape wars,' Dmitri said. 'Is it your belief that these were religious wars based on interpretation of the thuktunthp?'

'Yes,' Dawson said. 'Wars over the shape of the Predecessors.' He shook his head. 'Very strange.'

Dmitri laughed. 'Why strange? Human history is full of such. The Byzantine Church was divided, and civil wars resulted, from what icons were permitted to be shown in churches. The Christian god has no shape, yet one of the prophets was permitted to see his hindquarters. Not his front, you understand. Only his hindquarters. I do not know if that resulted in wars among the Jews, but it easily might.'

'You'd think there would be some pictures of the Predecessors,' Dawson said.

'Perhaps there were,' Dmitri mused. 'Only – suppose there were descendents of the Predecessors, and the fithp killed them. It would not be an easy thing to face, that you had killed the sons of your gods.'

One hell of a guilt trip. 'Or maybe there *were* pictures of the Predecessors,' Wes said. 'Maybe they were destroyed as blasphemous, in the period when they thought the Bussard ramjet diagram was the shape of a Predecessor.'

'Perhaps,' Arvid said.

'And then – excuse me,' Dmitri said. He spoke rapidly in Russian. After a while the Russians moved away to their own corner, leaving Wes Dawson alone again.

They don't trust me. I might do something to warn the aliens. At least I have a few answers. I need answers!

————

Nat Reynolds could remember exactly when he got into trouble. It started the second morning after the aliens blew up Kosmograd, ending the science-fiction convention where he was guest of honor, and stranding him in Kansas City. He was sitting in Dolly Jordan's breakfast room, with good coffee and eggs sunny-side up, trying to think of what to do now that all the stories about alien invaders were turning bloodily obsolete.

Why couldn't it have been Wells' Martians? We'd have had 'em in zoos inside of twenty-four hours.

'There's somebody here to see you,' Dolly Jordan had said. She set another plate and a coffee cup at the table.

Nat looked up with irritation. Someone he'd met at the OZcon? But the man Dolly led into her breakfast room didn't have the look. He was too old (although there were older science-fiction fans) and too well dressed (although some fans dressed well), and what *was* it? He just didn't have that sensitive fannish face.

'I've looked all over for you,' the man said. 'Hah. You don't remember me, do you? I'm Roger Brooks. *Washington Post.*'

You'd think the press would know by now: no science-fiction writer can be expected to function before noon. Nat shook his head. 'I have a lousy memory.'

'It's all right. Mind if I sit down?'

'Dolly already set a place for you.'

Brooks sat. Dolly appeared with a coffeepot. She was plump and cheerful, and smart enough not to chatter in the morning. After she filled Brooks's cup, she went back to the kitchen, leaving them alone.

'Why were you looking for me?' Reynolds asked.

'Because you probably know where the government is.'

Reynolds shook his head in confusion.

'Just before the aliens arrived, all the science-fiction writers vanished,' Brooks explained. 'At least all the hard science-fiction writers did.'

'Oho!'

'You do know something.' Brooks leaned forward eagerly. 'What?'

'Nothing real,' Nat said. 'A month or so ago, Wade Curtis called. Asked where I'd be when the aliens arrived. When I told him I'd be Guest of Honor at OZcon, he changed the subject.'

'And that's all?'

'Yeah. Wade wouldn't ask me to violate that kind of promise. What's this about the government?'

'The President left Washington two hours after the aliens blew up Kosmograd,' Brooks said. 'By yesterday morning, the Cabinet and most of the Pentagon brass were gone.' Brooks shrugged. 'No stories left in Washington. Nobody there knows what's happening.'

'So you came looking for me?'

'Yeah. The writers vanished a couple of weeks ago. Then just before the aliens arrived, the President sent an important intelligence officer to Colorado to talk to them. I figure that's where the government went, to Cheyenne Mountain. Kansas City's on the way.' Roger sipped his coffee. 'When the hotel said you'd left with the whole SF convention, I took a chance and came to the chairman's house.'

'Sorry you went to so much trouble for nothing —'

'Maybe not for nothing,' Brook said. 'Look, the writers are in Cheyenne Mountain. I'm sure of it. You were invited. You have the invitation, I have a press pass and a VW Rabbit diesel with more than enough fuel to get there. Want to pool our resources?'

I don't have any invitation to Cheyenne Mountain. I was booked at the OZcon, so I wasn't invited. All I had to do was say so!

And I always sign too many book contracts. I have trouble saying no. If I were a woman I'd be pregnant all the time.

Reynolds stood at a second-story window at Collins Street. The apartment building was separated from the street by a wide grassy strip. The buildings were old brick, with a new McDonald's just down the block.

They were in Lauren, Kansas, somewhere near Topeka. He'd never been in the town before, and didn't want to be here now, but there wasn't much choice, because while they were driving across Kansas the sky erupted with paper airplanes carrying baby elephants.

He'd met Carol North at the convention, and his address book showed she lived in Lauren, Kansas. They'd gone to her apartment. *We could have kept on driving. There can't be that many aliens. They can't be everywhere . . .*

Instead they'd parked in an underground lot and waited.

The invaders came.

A ceremony, Reynolds thought. *It even makes sense. Humiliating, but it makes sense. And once they've put you through that, they leave you alone.*

What do they want?

Reynolds turned back to the window. In the street outside, three men hid among the trash cans behind the McDonald's. They'd laid dinner plates on the street surface. From somewhere nearby came the roar of large motors.

304

'You had to tell them,' Reynolds said.

'It was a story I'd heard from the Hungarian uprising. How did I know they'd try it?'

'Bat turds, Roger! George Bergson was itching to kill an alien, so you told him now! You *knew* he'd try it if it killed him. It will, and we're too close. What if they bomb this building?'

Roger Brooks shrugged. 'George promised they wouldn't do anything to call attention to this place.'

'He's going to get himself killed,' Reynolds said. 'And probably us with him.'

'Stop saying that,' Carol North said. 'Please stop saying that.'

'Okay.' *But it doesn't change anything. Your friend is doomed, lady.* A thought came unbidden. She'd come to his room at the convention. Her relationship with George Bergson was clearly an open one. Would she be faithful to his memory once he got killed? That could be inconvenient.

The roaring grew louder. 'They're coming,' Roger said. 'The snouts are coming . . .' He stayed well back in the room and aimed his camera out toward the dinner plates in the road.

Two large armored vehicles came into view. They floated a foot or more off the road surface. Their crews were invisible inside.

It'll be okay. George will kill some invaders and live through it, and we'll all learn levitation and fly to safety, Right? But Nat's belly and guts were knotted in fear. He heard Roger say, 'It worked in Budapest . . .'

The first ground effect vehicle approached the line of dinner plates and stopped. Something protruded from the forward deck and extended toward the plates.

George Bergson and his friends stood and threw their bottles at the armored vehicles. Two of the bottles hit the lead tank, and burst into flames. Flame spread across the vehicle, and rivers of fire ran off its sides and were dispersed by the ground effect fan. There was a high-pitched whine and grinding noises, and the vehicle fell heavily to the roadway.

Two more gasoline bombs arced out.

The second vehicle began rapid fire. Holes the size of baseballs appeared in the buildings behind Bergson and his crew. The men dashed behind the McDonald's building.

The gunfire continued. The McDonald's building was chopped nearly in half. The upper part of the building fell into the lower part.

From somewhere far above a beam of greenish light speared the McDonald's building. The wreckage exploded in flame. The green light-pencil drew an expanding spiral around the pillar of flame, first tightly, then in ever-spreading arcs that grew and grew . . .

Reynolds dived away from the window.

There was the sound of crashing glass. The tank outside continued to fire, and two large holes appeared in the wall in front of him. Carol and Roger Brooks dove into the hallway. Carol lay next to Reynolds. 'Jesus,' she whispered. 'Jesus Christ. They're killing everybody – you *knew!*'

Reynolds shook his head. 'I didn't *know*, but it was a good guess. Look at them! Herd beasts. No speed, and all their defenses in front, and have you ever seen less than six together? I bet their ancestors stood in a ring to fight. It was a reasonable guess that if someone does something they don't like, they go after the offender's whole herd, not just the individual!'

The gunfire continued to pound.

'Smoke!' Carol shouted. 'The building's on fire.'

Trapped!

'Out the back way,' Roger Brooks said. 'Quick!' He crouched low and ran down the hallway to the stairs. 'Stay low. Stay away from windows!'

Nat Reynolds ran down the hall. He heard Carol behind him.

Roger sat in the biggest Cadillac in the lowest level of the underground parking structure. It was noon. They'd been here almost twenty hours.

There were sounds from inside another Caddy two cars away. *Jeez, what does she see in him?* Roger wondered. *They were at it not six hours after her live-in boyfriend bought it.*

And you're jealous, because you had nothing to distract you from the thought that they'd tumble the building down on your head. Or from them —

There hadn't been any sounds from outside for hours. Roger couldn't stand it any longer. He crept toward the exit. Another small group – a man, two women, and four small children – huddled in one corner of the garage. They stared at Roger as he went past, but they didn't say anything.

The ramp was blocked by debris, but the stairs were intact. Roger climbed up, pausing at each landing.

'Ho.'

He jumped, startled. The voice had been feminine and definitely human. 'Hello.'

'It's quiet out there,' she said.

Roger climbed up to the landing.

She was older than he'd thought from her voice. Roger guessed she was almost forty. She wore jeans and a wool shirt and a bandana, and her face was covered with soot and grime. Her nose had once been broken, and wasn't quite straight. *Not quite ugly, but she could work on it.* 'What's happening?'

'I think they've gone. I'm Rosalee Pinelli, by the way.'

'Roger Brooks. Where did they go?'

She shrugged. 'All I know is they were out there all night. I could hear them. But they never came in here.'

'Did you go look?'

She shook her head vigorously. 'Not me. We didn't hear anything for a couple of hours, so about dawn the five guys who were in here with me went out to look.' She indicated a hole in the concrete structure. 'You can see 'em through here.'

Roger looked. There was a pile of bodies in the street. 'That's more than five.'

'They made a pile,' Rosalee said. 'They left people alone until some guys blew one of their tanks.' She shook her head. 'Goddam, it was beautiful! They used dinner plates to look like mines, and when one of the snouts stopped they hit it with Molotov cocktails! Beautiful!'

'Until the snouts blew up the town,' Roger said under his breath. 'Yeah. I saw it.'

'After that, the snouts started that pile of bodies out there,' she said. 'I haven't seen or heard anything since about nine this morning, but I've been afraid to go out.'

'I'll look around.'

'Be careful – here, I'll come with you.'

'They're gone,' Brooks said. 'Let's get the hell out of here.'

'How?' Nat Reynolds asked.

'There's some junk on the ramp,' Brooks said. 'But with a little work we can get it clear and drive out.'

'Aren't there cars up above?'

'Not like this one,' Brooks said. He patted the VW diesel Rabbit. 'I can get two thousand miles on the fuel in this. More, now that we drained that truck.'

'Come on, Nat. I'll help,' Carol said. She took his hand.

Possessive as hell. 'Yeah, let's get at it,' Roger said.

Rosalee was already tossing away light debris. In an hour they had a pathway he could drive through. The four of them piled into the Rabbit.

I don't remember asking either of the women. Not that it matters. Reynolds isn't going to leave that one behind, and there's room for Rosalee. I might as well get her story.

'Where to?' Reynolds asked.

'Colorado Springs. The government's got to be there.'

'East!' Rosalee shouted. 'Away from the snouts!'

'I'm for that,' Reynolds agreed.

They drove up the ramp.

'You sure they're gone?' Carol asked.

'Yeah,' Roger said. 'I looked.' They came out of the structure.

Lauren, Kansas, looked like Berlin after World War II. Buildings were gutted. Bodies lay in the streets, not just the pile the snouts had created, but others as well.

'Godalmighty damn,' Roger muttered. He threaded his way through the debris. 'All that in revenge for one tank —'

'Traitors,' Reynolds said. 'They were killing traitors, or rogues, or crazies.'

'What the hell do you mean by that?' Rosalee demanded.

'We surrendered,' Reynolds said. 'As far as they're concerned, we surrendered, and then we attacked them.'

'That doesn't make sense,' Carol protested.

I wonder. Roger drove past another ruined building. 'How do you *know*, Nat?'

Reynolds laughed. 'I don't. I'm guessing. But look, gang, I'm not a scientist and I'm not a newsman. When I guess wrong, nothing happens. Maybe I even sell the story —'

'If you guess wrong here you'll get us all killed!' Rosalee snarled.

'Shall I stop guessing? We could die that way too, because I'm the only expert you've got.'

When they reached the end of the debris, he turned south despite the others' protests. There was no sign of an enemy.

CHAPTER TWENTY
SCHEMES

No battle plan ever survives contact with the enemy.

– Ancient military maxim

COUNTDOWN: H PLUS 180 HOURS

The engineers who built *Message Bearer* must have considered the communal mudroom expendable. They had located it just inside the hull. This had its advantages.

Under spin, a srupk's depth of mud formed a shell inside the hull; it would shield the ship from an unexpected attack. Mud boiling from a rent would freeze in place, a plug to hold air.

The mudroom was under full spin gravity. Winterhome's mass and surface gravity had been established by telescopic studies, a year before the ship reached the ringed giant. For sixteen years, since birth in many cases, the communal mudroom had taught fithp to move under Winterhome gravity. Warriors bound for the surface would have at least that advantage.

It was the biggest room aboard *Message Bearer*, covering an eighth of the hull surface of the life support region. From the middle it curved out of sight in both directions. The mud was good sticky-wet Homeworld dirt below, with nearly clear water floating on top. Fathisteh-tulk remembered the ceiling as oppressively close, and bare. It was still close, but not oppressively so. Generations of spaceborn had decorated it with painted friezes.

Above his head was a full-sized representation of a thuktun: a weathered granite rectangle covered with script and with a centered representation of a thuktun, which was covered with script and a representation of a thuktun, which . . . Fathisteh-tulk wondered if the priest Fistarteh-thuktun had ever seen this part of the ceiling. Such a thuktun would be a legendary thing. The thuktunthp spoke of every subject a fi' could imagine, but none spoke of the thuktunthp themselves, nor of their makers.

Fathisteh-tulk was the only sleeper in a crowd of spaceborn.

'It's not that we don't trust planets,' the gangling warrior said. 'We trust one planet, the Homeworld, the world on which you were born, sir. We trust other worlds to obey other rules.'

'Mating seasons,' Fathisteh-tulk said, half listening.

He filled his mouth and sprayed water at a spaceborn female, barely mature, who had been avoiding him. This social barrier between spaceborn and sleepers had to be broken, even if done one fi' at a time. There was power in Fathisteh-tulk's lungs. She preened in the spray, then (belatedly, but as protocol required) sprayed him back. She was just able to reach him.

The gangling warrior – Rashinggith? something like that – was still talking. 'Exactly! The target world orbits in about seven eighths of a Homeworld year. After three generations in space, we still follow a mating season of one year; and the sleepers, because they were wakened at the wrong time —'

'I know. During your mating season we feel a discomfort, an itch we can't wet.'

'It's the same with us. So. Will both mating seasons be skewed on the target planet?' The spaceborn dissidents did not obey the custom established by the Herdmaster. They would not call the target world Winterhome. 'Suppose some of us adjust and some do not? A few generations on the target world and we could all be mildly in heat all the time. Pfoo!'

311

'Two mating seasons a year might be fun. If it comes, it will come whether we land or not.'

'And that's only one possible problem. There are bound to be parasites we never adjusted to —'

A voice bellowed through the room. '*Tulk!*'

'I am summoned,' Fathisteh-tulk said, and he moved toward the voice of his mate, answering with a cheerful '*Tulk!*'

Moving among sleepers now, spraying muddy water to greet friends, he passed beneath an older frieze. The time was mating season, by the state of the foreground plants and the activities of half-seen fithp among the trees. He had worked on this bas-relief himself. He was pleased to see that it had been kept up, repainted.

But these next ones were recent. Here a swath of jet black powdered with white points, and a small pattern of concentric rings; the Winterhome sun, repeatedly outlined as it grew larger over the decades. There the ringed storm-ball with its company of moons, and the raggedly curved horizon of the Foot, with a mining party around a digit ship tanker —

'Tulk!'

He stopped his dawdling.

She waited impatiently at the exit. Smaller than the average female, Chowpeentulk was turning massive with the increase in her unborn child. She said, 'Come. We must discuss.'

The platform elevator lifted them into a corridor. Fathisteh-tuk said, 'We are halfway between Winterhome and the Foot. What can be urgent?'

'You were among dissidents!'

'So I was. Dissidence isn't forbidden.'

'Tulk, I think it will be, soon. The dissident claim that the War for Winterhome is unnecessary. I remind you that we are fighting that war now. Will you persuade warriors not to fight, even as they struggle with the prey? Need I remind you that Fookerteh is even now on the ground of

312

Winterhome, and that he is the favorite of K'turfookeph?'

'I've said little. Mostly I listen. What I hear makes sense. We reached the ringed gasball with the ship depleted of virtually every necessity. Within three years *Message Bearer* was resupplied. We could have left then if we had not needed the Foot, or we could have stayed as long as we liked.'

Fathisteh-tulk had not bred her when mating season followed the Awakening. This was common enough, even expected, among males who had lost status. Chowpeentulk remembered that she had been almost relieved. Her next child would not be of fighting age during the War for Winterhome.

The Traveler herd had reached the ringed gasball and were at work on the Foot when her season came again. Again her mate was impotent. Perhaps she had treated him badly then. She remembered her own irritability well enough.

The next season he had recovered; and the season after that had borne fruit. Her mate's status as the Herdmaster's Advisor had been enough; he had recovered his self-respect. She had been slow to recognize the other change in him.

Fathisteh-tulk was still talking. 'Space holds most of the resources we need, and no prey to be robbed. We —'

'Tulk! Have you forgotten what it is like to wallow in natural mud beneath an open sky? To take natural prey? The difference between a shower and rain?'

He hesitated. 'No.'

'Then what is this nonsense?'

'I've talked to spaceborn. They don't remember. They don't miss it. Tulk, we've started the war, and that is well. But if we have to back off, *we know the natives can't follow us*. We should be prepared for this. A generation hence we may be trading with them, nitrogen for refined metals —'

313

'*Trading?* With fragile, misshapen things that look like they would fall over any moment?'

'Isn't that better than enslaving them into the Traveler Herd? We would then be living with them. Can you picture them as our equals, generations from now? That is the fate of successful slaves.'

He laughed as she flinched from that picture. 'It won't hurt to keep those now in power a little unbalanced. I want to keep their minds working. The dissidents are doing something worthwhile.'

That dangerous, destructive humor. She simply hadn't noticed in time.

Fathisteh-tulk was not mad, exactly. Not suicidal. He would never hurt the Traveler Tribe or his family or their cause. But political interactions just didn't mean anything to him anymore. Nor did his mate's authority in matters of family. In the twelve years that passed between her first and second pregnancies, he had lost his sense of these nuances too.

'We are at war,' she said. 'When a herd moves it must not scatter to the winds.'

'It may be a needless war. Certainly these think so.'

'Let them do their work without your support. You're damaging the position of all sleepers. The first step is docility.'

'We have not joined a new tribe. Our tribe was captured from within. Tulk, it may be that I am wrong. I intend to find out.'

'How?'

But that he would not tell her.

———

Jenny led the way inside. The large conference room was filled with sound, although there weren't more than a couple of dozen people in the room. Knots of people, mixed groups of science-fiction writers, uniformed officers, and

314

civilian defense analysts stood at blackboards, others around tables. Viewscreens had been set up to show what was displayed on the big situation-room screens. It reminded Jenny of the newsroom at JPL during the Saturn encounter.

There's Ed. One of the officers was her brother-in-law, Ed Gillespie. She'd heard about his arrival, but she'd been too busy to see him. There'd been nothing useful in his report on the mission to deliver Congressman Dawson to Kosmograd, and Jenny had no time for social visits.

Jack Clybourne came in after Jenny. He looked nervously at the crowd in the room. 'Seems all right,' he said.

But he watches everyone just the same. Jenny advanced into the room. 'Ladies and gentlemen, the President of the United States.'

She got a reaction to that. All the military people jumped to attention. The science-fiction writers stared curiously; then those sitting down remembered their manners and stood. The babble quieted, although there was an undertone of whispered conversation.

The President came in with Admiral Carrell and General Toland. He looked blankly at the large room with its disorderly crowd.

'Carry on,' Admiral Carrell said. 'Well, Major? It's your show.'

'Yes, sir.' Jenny led the way to the blackboard where Ed Gillespie stood with the group of writers who'd been chosen as spokespeople. *Anson, of course. He doesn't look very strong. Dr. Curtis. Joe Ransom. I guess Sherry Atkinson was too shy –*

By the time the President arrived the writers were talking to each other, but they fell silent when he reached them.

The President nodded to Ed Gillespie. 'Glad to see you, General.' He turned to let Jenny introduce him to the writers.

'Mr. President, this is Robert Anson. He's the senior man among the writers.'

315

'Mr. President,' Anson said formally. He introduced the others.

'David Coffey,' the President said. 'Major Crichton says you've got something for me.'

'Yes, sir,' Anson said. 'Thank you for coming. I'll not waste more time in pleasantries. First. It now seems clear that their objective is conquest, either of the Earth or of a substantial part of it. The evidence says they want it all.'

'What evidence is that?' the President asked. He sounded curious, rather than demanding.

'They chose to attack the United States,' Anson said. 'Clearly the strongest nation on Earth.'

'But —'

Anson fell silent at the interruption, but when the President didn't say anything else, he continued. 'Clearly the strongest nation, at least as seen from space. Roads, dams, cities, cultivated lands, harbors, electronic emissions – all would indicated that the United States is the dominant nation.' Anson looked around as if for contradictions, but no one said anything. 'Yet they chose to land here, and according to all the intelligence reports we have, they're setting up a perimeter defense. As if they intend to stay.'

'We'll see about that,' General Toland muttered.

Anson raised an eyebrow.

Toland looked around nervously. 'We're planning a big attack,' he said. 'In about two hours.'

'With what?' Dr. Curtis demanded.

Toland looked at the writer with disapproval.

'It will be a large assault,' the President said. 'Mr. Anson, I agree that they intend to stay. Do they have a choice? I don't see how they can expect to launch enough ships to get their people off the Earth.'

'Lasers,' Curtis said.

They all looked at him. He shrugged and pointed to Anson. 'Sorry, it's Bob's turn.'

'We'll let Dr. Curtis explain in a moment,' Anson said. 'We agree then that they've come to stay. Despite their

316

early successes, I would be greatly surprised if they expected this first effort to succeed. Eventually we'll win, throw them out of Kansas. Surely they expect that. Therefore, they plan other attempts. One supposes they will make certain preparations for those attempts.'

'What might they do?' the President asked.

Anson turned to Joe Ransom. 'Mr. Ransom will address that.'

'They've already used kinetic energy weapons,' Ransom said. 'It's clear that any ship capable of crossing interstellar space will have a very powerful engine. Mr. President, I think they'll drop a Dinosaur Killer.'

The President looked puzzled, but Joe Ransom was only hitting his stride. 'An asteroid some nine kilometers across very probably killed the dinosaurs and wiped out most of the life on Earth at the time. There's a layer of dead clay that corresponds to that era, and we find asteroidal material in it, all over the world – but skip the evidence; it almost doesn't matter. What matters is that the aliens have already thrown rocks, and they've got the power to move a small asteroid. We've got the mathematics to work out the results. The effects will be global, and very bad.'

There's an understatement, Jenny thought. *Jack's scared too. Well, we ought to be.*

'Depending on how large, and where it strikes, an asteroid could do just about anything,' Anson said. 'Tidal waves may destroy many coastal cities. Cloud over: we could get weeks or months of endless night and endless rain. It could trigger a new ice age.'

'You can't be sure they'll hit us with an asteroid,' the President said.

'It's the way to bet. I wish we could guess how big it will be.'

'Mr. President,' Anson said. 'They obviously have the ability to do it. They've been out in space for fifteen years. Surely they've thought of it.'

'I see.' Coffey nodded seriously.

317

'Is there anything we can do about it?' Admiral Carrell demanded. 'Could we deflect it?'

'How? They shoot down anything we send up,' Curtis said.

'So what do we do?' Admiral Carrell asked.

Anson turned to the other writer. 'Dr. Curtis has given that some thought. Wade —'

'We'll never beat them while they own space,' Curtis said. 'As long as they control space, they can find junk to hit us with. One Dinosaur Killer after another.'

Blunt son of a bitch, Jenny thought.

'We can't stop them from bombarding us with asteroids until we can take control of space again, and we'll never get space away from them while they have that mother ship,' Curtis continued.

'Perfect naval doctrine,' Admiral Carrell said. 'But a navy needs ships, Dr. Curtis!'

'Orion,' Curtis said. 'Old bang-bang.'

The President looked puzzled, and Jenny thought Curtis looked pleased as he turned to the blackboard. *Not too often a writer gets to lecture to the President of the United States.*

'Take a big metal plate,' Curtis said. 'Big and thick. Make it a hemisphere, but it could even be flat. Put a large ship, say the size of a battleship, on top of it. You want a really good shock absorber system between the plate and the ship.

'Now put an atom bomb underneath and light it off. I guarantee you that sucker will *move.*' He sketched as he talked. 'You keep throwing atom bombs underneath the ship. It puts several million pounds into orbit. In fact, the more mass you've got, the smoother the ride.'

Admiral Carrell looked thoughtful. 'And once in space —'

'The tactics are simple,' Curtis said. 'Get into space, find the mother ship, and go for it. Throw everything we have at it. Ram if we have to.'

318

'Hard on the crew,' the President said.

'You'll have plenty of volunteers, sir,' Ed Gillespie said. 'The whole astronaut corps for starters.'

True enough. Most of them had friends at Moon Base. Odd, they did use nuclear weapons there, but nowhere on Earth. . . .

'Is this – Orion – feasible?' Admiral Carrell asked.

Curtis nodded. 'Yes. The concept was studied back in the sixties. Chemical explosive test models were flown. It was abandoned after the Treaty of Moscow banned atmospheric nuclear detonations. As far as I know, though, Michael is the only quick and dirty way we have to get a battleship into space.'

'Michael?' the President asked.

'Sorry, sir. We've already given it a code name. The Archangel Michael cast Satan out of Heaven.'

'Appropriate enough name. However, our immediate problem is to get them out of Kansas . . .'

'That does no good,' Curtis said. 'As long as they own space, they can land whenever and wherever they want, and there's damned little we can do about it. Mr. President, we have to get to work on Michael *now*.'

The President looked thoughtful. 'Perhaps I agree.' He turned to Ed Gillespie. 'General, we're pretty shorthanded here. I believe you're presently without an assignment?'

'Yes, sir.'

'Good. I want you to head up the team for Project Archangel. Look into feasibility, armament, who you need for a design team, where you'd build it, how long it would take. Report to Admiral Carrell when you know something. Perhaps these gentlemen can help you.' He looked to the writers.

'Sure,' Curtis said. 'One thing, though —'

'Yes?'

'We could use my partner. Nat Reynolds. Last I heard, he was in Kansas City.'

'Combat area,' General Toland said.

319

'Nat's pretty agile, though. He may have got away. And he's just the right kind of crazy,' Curtis said earnestly.

'Major Crichton can see to that,' the President said. 'Now, to return to something you said earlier. Lasers?'

'Yes, sir,' Curtis said. 'I believe they'll use lasers to launch their ships from the ground.'

'Why?'

'Why wouldn't they? They've got good lasers, much better than we have, and it's certainly simple enough if you've got lasers and power.'

'I asked the wrong question,' Coffey said. '*How?*'

Curtis looked smug again. He sketched. 'If you fire a laser up the back end of a rocket – a standard rocket-motor bell shape, but *thick* – you get much the same effect as if you carried rocket fuel aboard, but there's a lot more payload, because you can leave your power source on the ground. Your working mass, your exhaust, is air and vaporized rocket motor, hotter than hell, with a terrific exhaust velocity. It uses a lot of power, but it'll sure work. Pity we never built one.'

'Where would they get the power?' the President asked. 'They've blown up all our dams. They can't just plug into a wall socket.'

Curtis pointed to a photograph pinned to his blackboard. It showed a strange, winged object, fuzzily seen against the background of space.

'Ransom found that picture, among a lot of them Major Crichton's people gave us to look at,' he said. 'Joe —'

Ransom shrugged. 'An amateur astronomer brought that in to the intelligence people. I don't know how he talked the guards into getting it inside, but I ended up with it. It looks like they're deploying big solar grids, way up in geosynchronous orbit.'

'We looked into building those,' the President said.

'Sure,' Curtis said dryly. 'But Space Power Satellites were rejected. Too costly, and too vulnerable to attack.'

'They're vulnerable?'

'Not to anything we have *now*,' Curtis said. 'To attack something in space you've got to be able to *get at* space.'

Coffey looked around for support. Admiral Carrell shrugged. 'It's true enough,' he said. 'They'll shoot down anything we send up long before it can get that high.'

'So what can we do?'

'Archangel,' Ed Gillespie said. 'When we send something up, it needs to be big and powerful and well armed. I'll get on it.'

'And meanwhile, they're throwing asteroids at us,' the President said. 'General, I think you'd better work fast.' He turned to go.

'One more thing, Mr. President,' Curtis said insistently.

'Yes?'

'Today's attack, I suppose you'll be sending in lots of armor.'

The President looked puzzled.

'We'll do it right, Doctor,' General Toland said. He turned to leave. 'And I'd like to get at it.'

'Thor,' Curtis said.

Toland stopped. 'What's that? It sounds like something I've heard of —'

'Project Thor was recommended by a strategy analysis group back in the eighties,' Curtis said. 'Flying crowbars.' He sketched rapidly. 'You take a big iron bar. Give it a rudimentary sensor, and a steerable vane for guidance. Put bundles of them in orbit. To use it, call it down from orbit, aimed at the area you're working on. It has a simple brain, just smart enough to recognize what a tank looks like from overhead. When it sees a tank silhouette, it steers toward it. Drop ten or twenty thousand of those over an armored division, and what happens?'

'Holy shit,' Toland said.

'Are these feasible?' Admiral Carrell asked.

'Yes, sir,' Anson said. 'They can seek out ships as well as tanks —'

'But we never built them,' Curtis said. 'We were too cheap.'

'We would not have them now in any case,' Carrell said. 'General, perhaps you should give some thought to camouflage for your tanks —'

'Or call off the attack until there's heavy cloud cover,' Curtis said. 'I'm not sure how well camouflage works. Another thing, look out for laser illumination. Thor could be built to home in that way.'

'Yes. We use that method now,' Toland said. His tone indicated triumph. These guys didn't know *everything*.

'Maybe we should delay the attack,' the President said.

General Toland glanced at his watch. 'Too late. With our unreliable communications, some units would get the word and some wouldn't. The ones that didn't would go in alone and they'd *sure* be slaughtered. On that score, we've got to get back to Operations.'

'Thank you, gentlemen,' the President said.

As they left, Jenny heard Curtis muttering. 'What do they do if it doesn't work? They'll have to call the Russians for help.'

————

The sign read ELVIRA. It couldn't have been a large town to begin with. Now it was deserted, except for some military vehicles.

There were soldiers in camouflage uniforms at the entrance to the Elvira Little League playing field. Brooks stopped the car.

'What?' In the backseat, Reynolds struggled to wakefulness. 'Where are we?'

'Not far from Humboldt,' Brooks said. He got out. Rosalee, half awake now, got out on the passenger side. Nat eased himself out from under Carol's head and arm and wiggled out past the driver's seat. Carol stretched out in the backseat without waking.

Roger had seen people sleep like that after some disaster. In the dark of Carol North's mind, kinks were straightening out . . . or not. She would wake sane, or not.

'You can't park that here,' one of the soldiers shouted. He was a very young soldier and he looked afraid. There'd been an edge of panic in his voice, too.

Out beyond him the Little League field was covered with troops. They huddled around small fires. *Plenty of soldiers. No tanks. No vehicles at all. Why?* Further down the road and on the other side, in what had been a park, was a big tent with a bright red cross on it. Other tents had been put up next to it. There were stretchers outside the tents.

'A MASH unit,' Nat Reynolds said. He kept his voice low. 'Full up, from the stretchers outside. Roger, Rosalee, I think we better get out of here.'

'Not yet.' Brooks went up to the soldiers at the gate. he showed them his press card. 'What happened, soldier?'

'Nothin'.'

Roger pointed to the MASH. 'Something did.'

'Maybe. Look, you can't park that thing here. They shoot at vehicles. Maybe at cars! Move it, damn it, move it! Then think about going on foot!'

'In a second. Can you call an officer?'

The soldier thought about that for a moment. 'Yeah.' He shouted back into the camp. 'Sarge, there's a guy here from the *Washington Post* wants to talk to Lieutenant.'

They went from the Lieutenant to the Colonel in one step. By then Rosalee was back in the car, but Nat wasn't. He found that odd, but he trailed along.

'We don't have facilities for the press,' Colonel Jamison was saying. 'In fact, Mr. Brooks, we don't have accommodations for civilians at all, and I don't see any reason why I should talk to you.'

Brooks looked around the tent. It held two tables and a

desk, a field telephone, and a canteen hanging from the center pole. 'Colonel, I'm the only national press reporter here.'

Jamison laughed. 'And where are you going to publish?'

Roger gave him an answering chuckle. 'Okay. I don't even know if my paper exists anymore! But surely the people have a right to some news coverage of this —'

Jamison spoke slowly, from exhaustion. 'I've never been sure of that. Whatever happened to *Loose lips sink ships?* Okay, Mr. Brooks. I'm going to tell you what happened, but not for the reason you think.'

'Then why?'

Jamison pointed to Nat Reynolds. 'Your friend there.'

Nat Reynolds looked up from the map he'd been studying. 'What?'

'You're an important man, Mr. Reynolds,' Colonel Jamison said. 'We have a total of no fewer than forty messages from Colorado Springs, and one of them asks us to watch out for you. That's why Lieutenant Carper brought you to me. We're supposed to cooperate with you, and send you back to Cheyenne Mountain first chance we get. Now why is that?'

Reynolds thought it over, and smiled. 'Wade.'

The colonel waited.

'Dr. Wade Curtis. My partner. He must be working with the government. It follows that he's alive . . .' Reynolds looked back down at the map. 'We're still a long way from Colorado if we can't go through Kansas.'

'We can't,' Jamison said. 'God knows we can't.'

'So what did happen?' Brooks asked.

Jamison sighed. 'Nothing to brag about. This morning we were supposed to make a big push. Throw the goddam snouts all the way back to Emporia. Went pretty good at first. And then —'

'Then what?'

'Then they stamped us flat.'

'A whole armored division?'

'Three divisions.' Jamison shook his head as if to ward off the memory. 'The tanks went in. Everything was fine. We saw some of those floating tanks they use, and we shot the shit out of them! Then these streaks fell out of the sky. Lines of fire, hundreds of them – parallel, slanting, like rain in a wind, they pointed at our tanks and the tanks exploded.'

'Thor,' Reynolds said, as if he were talking to himself. He looked up from the map. 'That's what it was.'

'You *know* what did that to us?'

'Yah. It wasn't just science fiction,' Reynolds said wonderingly.

'Reynolds! *What did they do to my men?*'

'It's an orbital weapon system. They dropped meteors on you, Colonel. There wasn't anything you could do. Shall I explain?'

'Sure, but not just to me,' Jamison said. 'Marty! Marty, get on the line and see what's keeping Mr. Reynolds's transportation! They need him back at the Springs!'

The helicopter came an hour later.

Rosalee was over by the car, pacing, but Carol was awake and frightened. 'What will happen to me? Nat, you can't leave me here —'

'No, of course not.' Reynolds looked around helplessly for someone in charge. He shouted toward the chopper, and a uniformed woman came out, a major.

By God! 'Jenny!' Roger Brooks called. 'Jenny, it's me, Roger! Can you take me to the Springs?'

'Roger? Hi! No, there's not room.'

'You have to make room,' Reynolds shouted. 'For Carol!'

Jenny shook her head. 'Mr. Reynolds, we have several hundred miles to go. The fuel situation is critical. We can't carry extra weight.'

Picture of a torn man, Brooks thought. *So what will he do?*

'Carol's not heavy,' Reynolds said. 'I'll leave my suitcase.'

'No.' Major Crichton was firm. 'Mr. Reynolds, you'll endanger all of us if you insist. Believe me, your friend is safer here.'

'Then why am *I* getting into that thing?' Reynolds demanded.

'Because the President of the United States told me to bring you,' Jenny said. 'Sergeant, help Mr. Reynolds aboard.'

Reynolds spread his arms, broadcasting helplessness. 'If they want me that bad – Sorry, Carol.'

He let the Army sergeant assist him into the helicopter, Major Crichton climbed in after him. She turned in the doorway to wave; then the door closed and the engine revved up.

And now I've got five hundred miles to go, fuel for six hundred, and two women to worry about. 'Come on, ladies,' Roger said. 'We'll just have to take the low road.'

CHAPTER TWENTY-ONE
WAR PLANS

The rules of conduct, the maxims of action, and the tactical instincts that serve to gain small victories may always be expanded into the winning of great ones with suitable opportunity; because in human affairs the sources of success are ever to be found in the fountains of quick resolve and swift stroke; and it seems to be a law inflexible and inexorable that he who will not risk cannot win.

– JOHN PAUL JONES

COUNTDOWN: H PLUS TWO WEEKS

Jenny laid the printed copies of the agenda on top of the yellow tablets, and stepped back to admire her work. Then she grinned wryly. It didn't look much like the Cabinet Room in the White House. Instead of a big wood conference table, there were two Formica-topped folding tables set together. Most of the chairs were Army issue folding chairs, although they had managed to get one big wooden armchair for the center of the table.

A slide projector was set up at one end of the room. Jenny inspected it, turning the light on and off. In addition to the places at the table, another score of chairs faced the President's seat in the center.

The U.S. and presidential flags stood behind the chair. They looked out of place against a bare wall.

'It'll have to do.'

'What's that?' Jack Clybourne came in.

'The conference room,' Jenny said.

Jack nodded. 'Made you a secretary, did they?'

'Somebody's got to do it,' Jenny protested. 'We don't have a full staff, and —'

'Gotcha.'

'Yep.'

'Heck, they have me typing his appointment list,' Jack said. 'Not that I mind. Gives me something to do.'

She grinned. 'Not going to search for bombs in the flag stands?'

'Phooey. Watcha doing after dinner?'

'I don't know – why?'

'My roommate's going Outside,' Jack said. He grinned. 'Of course I *could* clean up my room —'

'You can do that tomorrow. See you about midnight. Now I've got to go get my science-fiction writers.'

Three aides sat at chairs near the wall. No one else was in the room. It would fill according to rank, with the most junior coming in to wait for the more senior.

Jack Clybourne studied the names on his list. Joe Dayton from Georgia, the Speaker of the House of Representatives. He'd be the highest-ranking man after the President. Senator Alexander Haswell of Oregon, the President Pro Tem of the Senate. Senator Raymond Carr from Kansas. Admiral Carrell. Hap Aylesworth, with no title listed after his name. Mrs. Connie Fuller, Secretary of Commerce. Jim Frantz, Chief of Staff. General Toland. Arnold Biggs, Secretary of Agriculture. They'd all have seats at the table.

Jenny came in with the science-fiction people. Robert Anson. He seemed older than the last time Jack had seen him. Dr. Curtis. And a new one.

'This is Nathaniel Reynolds,' Jenny said. 'Mr. Reynolds, Jack Clybourne is in charge of security for the President.'

'Hi,' Reynolds said.

He looks confused. Not that I blame him.

Jenny conducted the writers to chairs near the wall. Then she went out again. After a few minutes she returned with an older woman.

Attractive, if a bit used. Important. And not on my list at all —

'This is Mrs. Carlotta Dawson,' Jenny said.

Aha. 'Thank you.' Jack waited to see where Jenny would seat her. At the table, but at one end, facing the President but with her back to the writers and staff.

Jenny went out again. A few minutes later, the rush began.

'Ladies and gentlemen, the President of the United States,' Jack Clybourne announced formally.

He does that well, Jenny thought. *And it's needed, a formality to remind us that what we're doing is important, that this is the real thing.*

President Coffey took his place at the table. He noticed the flags and acknowledged Jenny with a nod. Then he nodded to the Chief of Staff. 'Jim —'

'Yes, sir.' Frantz indicated the Xeroxed agenda sheets. 'As you can see, we have a lot to cover.

'Item One. Appointments. The President has appointed Admiral Thorwald Carrell as Secretary of Defense. Mr. Griffin, who formerly held that post, will become Under Secretary, and remain with the Vice President. Admiral Carrell will also retain the post of National Security Advisor. Lieutenant General Harvey Toland is promoted to General of the Army, and has been designated Commanding General of the United States Armed Forces.

'The Vice President, the rest of the Cabinet, and a number of congressional leaders will remain in the alternate command post,' Frantz continued. 'For the moment, the

Congress is represented by the Speaker and the President Pro Tem of the Senate. Mr. Speaker.'

Joe Dayton stood. 'Mr. President, this is Mrs. Carlotta Dawson. Being that Congressman Dawson is missing, we've asked Mrs. Dawson to take his place. Sort of represent him. It's not strictly constitutional, but nothing's very normal just now.'

The President nodded wearily. 'Thank you, Mr. Speaker. Mrs. Dawson, welcome aboard. We all pray for your husband's safe return.'

'Thank you, Mr. President.'

'There's another reason for Mrs. Dawson to be here,' Speaker Dayton said. 'She's brought in our first by God captive Invader!'

And that got a reaction! Jenny almost laughed, but she managed to control her face. *What if I'd brought Harry Redd to this Cabinet meeting!*

'Thank you, Mr. Speaker,' Jim Frantz said. 'To return to the agenda. Our first item of business. The Secretary of Defense.'

Admiral Carrell didn't stand. 'There's little to say. Early this morning we launched a non-nuclear attack employing three Regular Army armored divisions, supported by a number of National Guard units and all the military aircraft we could muster. As you all know, they are utterly defeated.'

There were murmurs, but no one said anything.

'The enemy used a variety of advanced weapons,' Carrell continued. 'The most important were lasers, ground-based and orbital, and space-based kinetic energy weapons. Flying spears, if you prefer to think of them that way. They seek out and destroy armored vehicles.

'The lasers intercept our missiles. They also backtrack and home in on missile launch sites and artillery. The ground-based laser weapons are radar directed and sufficiently powerful to punch their way through cloud cover. The result was not merely the defeat of our forces but their near annihilation. Major Crichton has recently visited the headquarters of Third Army. Major, how would you describe what you saw?'

'Sir, it was a disaster area,' Jenny said. 'I found only one General Officer. The rest were killed or missing. The MASH was overfilled, and the only vehicles were commandeered civilian machines, or the very few that hadn't been committed to the attack.'

'Thank you,' Carrell said evenly. 'Was it your opinion that the attacking forces gave it their best?'

'God, yes, Admiral. We could give out a hundred posthumous Silver Stars without even trying.'

'You agree, General Toland?' Carell asked.

'Yes, sir. We took our best shot.'

'That concludes my report, Mr. President.'

There was stunned silence.

'Jesus,' the Speaker said. 'Admiral, General Toland, what did we do to the enemy?'

'Mr. Speaker, I don't know,' Admiral Carrell said. 'To the best of my knowledge, very little.'

'They whupped us,' Dayton said in his careful drawl.

'Yes, sir. They whupped us.'

'So what do we do now?' the Speaker demanded.

'Use nukes,' General Toland said.

'That's what we're here to decide,' the President said.

'You can't nuke Kansas!' Senator Carr was adamant. 'No way!'

'We don't have any choice,' General Toland said.

'Choice be damned!' Carr shouted.

'Gentlemen,' Jim Frantz said.

'Senator, I agree it's an extreme measure,' the President said. 'But what else can we do? The aliens must be driven off this planet!'

'At the expense of my people —'

'Senator, we aren't saving the people of Kansas by doing nothing. The invaders are slaughtering them. Major Crichton, you were there. Describe what you saw.'

331

'Yes, sir. Sergeant —'

Sergeant Mailey turned on the slide projector. Photographs of a pile of bodies, at least fifty, covered one wall of the room. There were gasps.

'We took these pictures in Lauren, Kansas. Much of the slaughter was witnessed by Mr. Nat Reynolds, a member of our special advisory staff. Mr. Reynolds will answer questions later.

'Mr. President, our attacking forces found a number of such scenes during the brief period of their advance. Refugees report that wholesale slaughter of hostages is their general response to any act of resistance. Next slide, Sergeant.'

She showed another dozen pictures before mercifully turning the lights back on. *Senator Carr looks sick. Well he might. I don't feel very good myself.*

'Mr. Reynolds,' the Speaker said. 'You saw this happen?'

Nat Reynolds stood. 'Yes, sir. More or less —'

'Why did they do that?' the President demanded.

Reynolds explained the attack.

'As soon as the one tank was destroyed, the other started shooting, and they called in the lasers. After they'd shot up enough buildings, they went hunting individual people, and when they found anyone, they killed him and added him to the pile.'

'Jesus.' Senator Carr crossed himself.

'They thought they were killing traitors,' Reynolds said.

'What does that mean?' the President asked.

'They're herd beasts. I doubt they do very much on their own initiative. As far as they were concerned, the whole town had surrendered, and when they were attacked, the whole town was in rebellion. It's the way their minds work.'

'Major Crichton,' the President said. 'You've been interrogating the captured alien?'

'Yes, sir.'

'Do you agree with their assessment?'

'We haven't learned much from the prisoner except his name, sir.'

'Name, rank, and serial number, eh?'

'No, sir. He seems totally cooperative. It's just that he's confused.'

'He's insane.' Curtis muttered. 'Or certainly will be.'

'Why do you say that, Dr. Curtis?' Admiral Carrell asked.

'Herd beast,' Curtis said. 'What Nat said – they don't do things on their own initiative. Like elephants. Like zebras. Isolate one of them, and what happens?' He shrugged. 'So we're trying to bring this one into our herd. It might work, too.'

President Coffey looked interested. 'How do you do that?'

'Never leave him alone,' Curtis said.

'Talk to him,' Reynolds said. 'Surround him with people —'

'Until he believes he's human,' Curtis finished.

'Have you learned anything useful?' the President demanded.

'No, sir,' Jenny said.

'We know they took prisoners from Kosmograd,' Carlotta Dawson said.

'Ah. That's good news,' President Coffey said. Then he frowned. 'I suppose it's good news. At all events, we must decide what to do now.'

During the fifty years since its first construction, the underground complex east of Moscow had been decorated, air conditioned, carpeted, and enlarged. There were swimming pools, barbershops, and fine restaurants; the reinforced concrete walls were covered by tapestries and paintings; and everything had been done to disguise the fact that it was, at bottom, a bomb shelter.

Party First Secretary Narovchatov strode on parquet wooden floors to the Chairman's office, and remembered another time long ago, when Stalin had reviewed a Guards division during the Great Patriotic War against Hitler. The Germans were so close that the Guards had marched across Red Square and walked directly to the front to take part in an attack.

From review to engagement with the enemy, he thought. *That will not happen now. The enemy is not so close, but there are enough enemies.*

Tartars, Hungarians, Poles, Latvians, Czechs, were in open revolt, and many others, even the Ukrainians, were restless.

Narovchatov strode past the Chairman's secretary.

'Halt, Comrade Narovchatov.'

Narovchatov looked up in surprise. A Guards Division colonel stood with three armed soldiers.

'I regret, Comrade Narovchatov, that we must search you —'

There was a roar of laughter from inside the office. Chairman Petrovskiy appeared in the doorway. He chuckled again. 'It is well that you are alert, Comrade Colonel,' Petrovskiy said. 'But I think you need not be so diligent with the First Secretary, who is, after all, my oldest friend. Come in, Nikolai Nikolayevich. My thanks, Comrade Colonel. Return to your duties.'

Nikolai Narovchatov closed the massive door behind him and stood against it. He had not had time to react. Now he thought of the situation outside and frowned.

'Da,' Chairman Petrovskiy said. 'It can be that serious. Come and sit, I have much to tell you. Will you have vodka? Or whiskey?'

'I will join you in a cognac.' Narovchatov took the drink and sat in front of the massive desk.

'To humanity,' Petrovskiy said. 'No idle toast.' They drank. 'Not an idle toast at all,' the Chairman said. 'I had a call today. From the American President.'

'Ah!'

'A very strange call,' Petrovskiy continued. 'The Americans want our help.'

'As we need theirs,' Narovchatov said.

'Exactly.'

'Did you tell them this?'

'In part. I told them that unless they undertook to restrain the Germans, we would not be interested in talking with them.' Petrovskiy paused dramatically. 'They agreed instantly. I heard the President give the orders.'

'But —'

'Of course I could not be certain,' Petrovskiy continued. 'But I believe they were sincere. Nikolai Nikolayevich, they are truly desperate. The alien invasion is succeeding.'

Narovchatov shook his head in disbelief, as he had when he first heard that an alien army – of small elephants! – had landed in the American heartland.

'Succeeding?'

'Da. The enemy holds their breadbasket, the source of their grain – and the Americans have been unable to dislodge them. They have lost some of their best military units.'

For a moment Narovchatov felt triumph. Then his grin faded. 'But Anatoliy Vladimirovich, if they cannot drive the aliens from the planet —'

'If they cannot, we certainly could not,' the Chairman said grimly. 'Nikolai Nikolayevich, no matter who wins, we have lost. It will be many years before we regain our strength. Do you agree?'

'Da, Anatoliy Vladimirovich. Even if there were no military difficulties, even if we regained control of the provinces and the Warsaw Pact nations without further difficulty, it will take years merely to replace the dams and bridges.'

'I believe we must help the Americans,' Petrovskiy said slowly.

'How?'

335

'In every way we can. They have a plan. A coordinated attack, on the enemy ships in space and on the alien forces in Kansas. We will both use our remaining strategic rockets.'

'We have few enough left,' Narovchatov said.

'I know.' The Chairman paused. 'The Americans also want us to use submarine forces.'

'For what?'

'Some to fire at enemy ships in space, some to fire at Kansas.'

'At Kansas!'

'They also wish us to fire long-range strategic rockets at Kansas.'

'To bomb Kansas,' Narovchatov said wonderingly. 'Anatoliy – Comrade Chairman, this is madness!'

'Da. The KGB believes that too.'

'They know of this?'

Petrovskiy nodded. 'My call was recorded. I had not known that Trusov could do that – but within minutes after the President called, he was here.'

'He admitted listening! To you!'

'Da. He professed loyalty, but regarded conversations with the Americans as a matter of state security.'

Narovchatov thought furiously. 'Thus the colonel and his guards outside your office?'

'And elsewhere. I have sent them to your quarters. And to protect your daughter and grandchilden.'

'Are things that serious, then?'

Petrovskiy shrugged. 'Chairman Trusov was nearly hysterical. He could not believe that I might seriously consider this proposition. "Let the aliens destroy the United States," he said. "The enemy of my enemy is my friend, and the Americans are the enemies of communism everywhere. The aliens are herd beasts, they will respect communism. That is why they have invaded the United States. The Americans have lost only one state. They have fifty. Let the aliens weaken them more." That is what he said.'

'Could he be right?'

'Do you believe so?'

Narovchatov shook his head slowly. 'No. These aliens, these – elephants! – are the real enemy. They will enslave us all.'

The Chairman's face clouded. 'And that we will not permit,' he said. His frown deepened, and he pounded his fist against the desk. 'No one shall rule us! Russia shall always remain independent. The worst of the czars knew that much! Russia shall obey orders from no outsider! We must not allow that.'

Narovchatov sighed. 'You are correct, as always, Anatoliy Vladimirovich. But I am afraid. The KGB is everywhere, and if they resist – What shall we do?'

'We will call your son-in-law, and order him to work with Marshal Shavyrin. Together they will develop a plan.'

Narovchatov nodded agreement. 'Pavel Aleksandrovich will be loyal,' he said.

'I have known Shavyrin almost as long as I have known you,' Petrovskiy said. 'I can trust him. Within hours he can be with Bondarev at Baikonur. But he must be warned. When he joins Bondarev, he must take with him his loyal troops, his headquarters guards and his personal staff.'

It has come to this. 'Da.' Narovchatov stood. 'I will see to it.' He moved to the door, then turned. 'When, Anatoliy? Will Russia ever have a government without fear?'

He did not wait for an answer.

An octuple of warriors came for them.

Gravity was next to nothing. The humans moved in a chaotic cloud, bounding from the corridor walls, Nikolai as agile as the rest. Warriors moved four ahead and four aft, keeping orderly pace, using slippers with surfaces like Velcro that interacted with the damp rugs.

Takpusseh and Tashayamp waited where a section of rug-covered wall had been pulled up, leaving a black hole.

'Greeting,' Takpusseh said cheerfully. 'We must find a task for you until *Number Six* digit ship arrives. You will clean the air circulation system. Climbing is one thing you may do better than fithp. You will find it easy now that Thuktun Flishithy-chaytrif.'

'What?' Wes remembered that *chaytrif* meant *foot*. Now that the mother ship is mated to a foot?

Never mind. Tashayamp was distributing equipment. To each human was given a sponge, a bag like a plastic garbage bag, a smaller bag filled with soapy water, and a flashlight. All had handles, big metal loops suitable for a fi's digits. They were strung on a loop of cord.

'The outer ducts need you most,' Takpusseh said. 'Empty the collectors into the bag. Wipe the sides. For this day's mission, circle this way, spinward.' His trunk described a clockwise arc. 'Go as far as you can, prove your endurance, then come out at any grill. Summon the first warrior you see. Any warrior will escort you to your cells.'

Would the fithp *really* allow prisoners to explore their air duct system? Arvid and Dmitri seemed as bemused as Wes, but they were obeying, looping the line loosely around themselves.

Best to assume that he'd be watched. Even so, Wes would enjoy the chance to spy a little. Certainly the Soviets would . . . Nikolai was being urged into the hole. Arvid and Dmitri followed.

They'll assume that we'll want to stay together, but I don't think we'll have to. Wes moved toward the opening.

A branch of living hose looped around his ankle. 'Pause a moment,' Takpusseh said. 'Dawson, you are to be separated from the others. From this moment Raztupisp-minz is your teacher. When you see a warrior, tell him, "Raztupisp-minz".'

Wes shrugged. The Soviets hadn't been good company lately. 'The cause, I attack you?'

'The cause, we decide this. Go.'

He moved through the air ducts, cleaning as he went. The work was not difficult. *Do what they want for now. Dmitri wants us docile. He may be right, for now.*

He worked until he was too tired to go on: five or six hours, he thought.

There were wing nuts on the outsides of the grills. Fingers had to reach through the grills to turn them. That was easy enough: the wings were five inches across, suited to fi' digits. Wes was talking to himself before he realized that the screws turned the wrong way. Takpusseh must have wondered if the humans would be reduced to screaming for help through the grills.

He called to two passing warriors. 'Take me to Raztupispminz.'

One stopped. 'Wes-Dawson? You are to go to a restraint room.'

Wes paused to refasten the grill, then moved away between the warriors.

Lorena brought the teapot. 'More tea, Comrade Marshal?' she asked.

'Thank you, no,' Marshal Shavyrin said. He glanced at the clock on the wall, then at Lorena.

Pavel Bondarev saw, and made a tiny gesture of dismissal. Lorena left the room. Bondarev thought she closed the door heavily, but if so, Marshal Shavyrin did not notice it.

'It is fantastic,' Shavyrin said. A hastily assembled report with bright red covers lay on Bondarev's desk next to Bondarev's ancient brass telescope. Shavyrin lifted the report and idly thumbed through the pages. 'Fantastic,' he repeated.

'I agree,' Bondarev said. 'Yet we must believe —'

The telephone chirped. Bondarev touched a button to put the telephone on amplifier. 'Bondarev.'

'Petrovskiy.'

'Da, Comrade Chairman!' Bondarev said. 'We have prepared the report you ordered. Marshal Shavyrin is here . . .'

'Good. You are well, Leonid Edmundovich?'

'Da, Comrade Chairman.'

'Very well. General Bondarev, you have spoken with the American generals?'

'Da. What they ask is barely possible, Comrade Chairman.'

'Will it succeed?'

Bondarev looked helplessly at Shavyrin. The Marshal was silent for a moment, then said, 'Comrade Chairman, who can know? Yet it may be the only possible plan. The timing, however, is very critical.'

'And your recommendation? Do we do this?'

Shavyrin was silent.

'Well?' the Chairman demanded.

'It is very critical,' Shavyrin said finally. 'Part of their plan depends on their Pershing missiles. They are to fire them from Germany, to attack the alien spacecraft. Many of those missiles will come toward the Soviet Union. There will be no way to know their real targets – which might be Moscow or Kiev or our remaining missile bases.

'There is more,' Shavyrin continued. 'Whenever we have launched missiles, the aliens have bombarded the base from which they came. They will attack our remaining bases. Few strategic rocket forces will remain after this battle. If the Americans do not use their missiles, we will be disarmed and nearly helpless, and they will retain their strategic striking power. Suppose they do not launch their Pershing missiles, but keep them. They could destroy us within minutes, whenever they wanted, and we would be unable to retaliate.'

Narovchatov's voice came onto the line. 'Is it your recommendation that we do not cooperate with the Americans?'

'No, Comrade First Secretary,' Shavyrin said. 'But it is my duty to make you and the Chairman aware of all the implications.'

'We have very little time,' Chairman Petrovskiy said. 'The American President is waiting for my answer. He says the situation is desperate. I am inclined to agree. I must give him our decision now.'

'All depends on the Pershing missiles,' Shavyrin said. 'If the Americans do not launch them – for any reason – then it is unlikely that our missiles will get through the enemy defenses. If the Americans are successful, then some of our missiles will reach their targets.'

'Bondarev?' the Chairman demanded.

'I believe this may be our last chance. If we do not aid the Americans now, then the Americans will be defeated, and how long will it be before Russia falls to the aliens?'

'Your recommendation?'

This is recorded. Not only the Chairman. The KGB will listen. If we fail — 'Comrade Chairman, I recommend that we aid the Americans, provided that they use their Pershing missiles, all of their Pershing missiles, in both England and Germany, to assist our penetration.'

'You agree, Marshal Shavyrin?'

'Da, with those conditions, Comrade Chairman.'

There was a long silence. Then the Chairman said, 'Very well. I will inform the American President, and we will soon tell you the time for this attack.' There was another pause, then the Chairman's voice came on again. 'Academician and General of the Army Pavel Aleksandrovich Bondarev, and Marshal Leonid Edmundovich Shavyrin, I instruct you to take command of all strategic forces of the Soviet Union, including the submarine forces,

341

and to employ them in aid of the battle plan code-named
WHIRLWIND. If you jointly agree, you are authorized
to use all of the forces in your command in aid of the
American effort to drive the aliens from the planet. Is this
understood?'

'Da, Comrade Chairman,' Shavyrin said.

Pavel Bondarev gulped hard. 'Da.'

CHAPTER TWENTY-TWO
SOMETHING IN THE AIR

The enemy of my enemy is my friend.

– ARAB PROVERB

COUNTDOWN: H PLUS THREE WEEKS

Pavel Bondarev looked up at the big clock on his wall. 'Ten minutes,' he said.

Marshal Shavyrin grinned. 'Da. You are nervous, Comrade!'

'Of course,' Bondarev said with irritation. 'We are about to make the most important decision in Russian history. Should I not be nervous?'

'Certainly, but you will permit that I do not openly join you? I have known for five years that I might be faced with this moment.'

'True,' Bondarev said. He looked at the twin electronics consoles installed against one wall of his underground office. Lights winked in complex patterns. In the lower right corner of each console was a switch. Bondarev patted his throat, to feel the key on its silver chain. 'Does it make it easier?'

'The peasants say you can become accustomed to anything, even hanging, if you hang enough – what was that?'

There were sharp sounds from outside. Bondarev went to the door.

'No! Do not open that door!' Shavyrin commanded.

He lifted his telephone. 'Colonel! What is the situation?' He listened for a few moments. 'They must not enter,' he snapped. 'The cost does not matter. Our orders come from Chairman Petrovskiy himself! Do what you can. What you must,' he said. He put down the phone.

Bondarev looked the question at him.

'KGB,' Shavyrin said. 'They have sent soldiers as well as their agents. My security forces are resisting them.'

'But —' Pavel lifted the telephone. 'Get me Chairman Petrovskiy —'

Shavyrin shook his head. 'Colonel Polivanov has already reported that the KGB has cut the telephone lines. We no longer have communications with Moscow.'

Bondarev looked up in horror. 'But —'

Before he could speak, the door opened. Lorena came in.

'What are you doing here?' Bondarev demanded.

She hesitated for a moment, then showed what was in her hand. She held a small automatic pistol. 'You are both under arrest, in the name of State Security,' she said.

'No!' Bondarev shouted. 'Not you!'

'The KGB is everywhere,' Shavyrin said. He reached for the telephone.

'Stop that!' Lorena shouted. Hysteria tinged her voice.

'Comrade, I must speak to the rocket forces,' Shavyrin said.

'To order them to aid the Americans,' she said. 'Never! The aliens will destroy the Soviet Union —'

'Then they will do it anyway,' Shavyrin said. 'Understand this. The Americans are to launch' – he glanced at the clock on the wall – 'even now are launching their Pershing missiles. Those missiles will come toward us. They are supposed to provide a diversion to allow our missiles to penetrate, but there is always the chance that the Americans will use this as an opportunity to attack us. With that in mind I have given orders that if the rocket forces do not hear from us, they will attack the United

States. Not attack Kansas, but all of the United States!'

'I know nothing of this,' she shouted. 'You will move there, to that wall, away from the desk, away from the telephones!'

'Lorena,' Bondarev said. 'Lorena, you cannot do this.' He moved toward her. She backed away.

'Stop! I will shoot! I will!'

Bondarev advanced.

The little gun spat at him. He felt a sharp pain in his chest. 'Lorena!' he shouted. He swayed against the wall.

She looked in horror. 'Pavel, Pavel —'

As she spoke, Marshal Shavyrin moved. He lifted the brass telescope from Bondarev's desk and swung it, bringing it down on Lorena's head, striking so hard that the telescope bent over her head and a lens fell onto the floor.

She collapsed instantly. Shavyrin dropped the telescope and moved to close the door. Then he hurried to Bondarev. 'Comrade,' he said. 'Pavel —'

Pavel heard him as from a distance. He tried to take a deep breath, but pain prevented him, and he heard blood burbling in his lungs. More shots sounded from outside in the corridors. They seemed much closer.

'I – am alive,' Bondarev said. Each word was an effort. He looked at the clock. 'It is time! We must know, did the Americans fire the Pershing missiles?'

Shavyrin lifted the telephone. 'Polivanov. Shavyrin here. Colonel, did the Americans fire their Pershings?' There was a long pause. 'I see,' Shavyrin said. 'Do we have communications with the strategic forces? I see. Thank you.' He put the telephone down. 'The KGB has cut us off from all reports from the West,' he said carefully. 'Their *spetsnaz* troops came in such force that we could not hold all of this headquarters. My troops chose instead to defend the command circuits, which remain intact.' He pointed at the winking lights. 'The keys will work, Comrade Academician. What do we do?'

Pavel breathed in short gasps. It hurt terribly. He collapsed in a chair in front of his console. 'The Pershings —'

'We will never know about the Pershings,' Shavyrin said. 'And from the sounds in the corridors, we do not have much more time.' As he spoke he unbuttoned the breast pocket of his uniform and took out a key. He looked at it for a moment, then inserted the key into his console and turned it.

'You know more of these things than I, Pavel. I have armed my panel. It is your decision now.' Shavyrin drew his pistol and turned toward the door. 'But I think you must decide quickly.'

It felt as if his head was padded with cotton wool. Each breath hurt, and Shavyrin's voice seemed to fade and return. *What must I do? We cannot know, we cannot know. Have the Americans tricked us? Could the KGB be right?*

Lorena lay on his Persian carpet. The broken brass telescope lay over her left arm, partly covering the expensive bracelet that Pavel had bought her. He could not see whether she was breathing.

The gunfire in the corridors outside was very close.

Quickly! Pavel fumbled with his shirt buttons. It seemed to take forever to open the links of the chain, and when he tried to jerk it off it wouldn't break. *Patience* – He opened the catch at last, and for a moment stared at the brass key; then quickly and decisively he thrust it into the key switch and turned it.

One by one the lights on the board blinked from green to red.

'It is done,' Bondarev said.

'Da,' Shavyrin said. There was a loud click as he released the safety catch of his pistol.

————

There was something in the air. It affected all fithp differently. Spaceborn females only felt a nervousness, a wrongness; they tended to snap back if approached wrongly.

Sleepers were easily distracted; they had to be held to their duties. Even spaceborn males felt a belligerent optimism, as if their bodies wanted to dance or fight.

Defensemaster Tantarent-fid had the air circulation running on high. The only effect was a breeze. Something in the air: even the human fithp might have known the difference among all the alien scents. The sleeper mating season had begun.

The skewed mating seasons had come twice a year for fifteen years. The Herdmaster knew the feeling well, but he couldn't help it: he felt good all over. The war was going well. Minor reversals had occurred on Winterhome, but the base was still in place. *We learn. And this gathering will produce results.*

Pastempeh-keph didn't use the display room much, though his predecessor had. It was too large for comfort. He hadn't seen it since the history lesson, since the day Dawson attacked his own Breaker. He felt he needed it now. *Message Bearer* could run itself for a few hours, and screens wouldn't do. It must be a full gathering. He wanted to watch their body language.

Seven fithp rested on their bellies in a circle: the Herdmaster, his Advisor, both Breakers, the Attackmaster, the Defensemaster, and Fistartch-thuktun. The Herdmaster looked around at the fithp he had summoned. He said, 'We are going to learn why the humans behave as they do. We will learn *now*.'

Even Fathisteh-tulk looked uneasy; and that was somehow gratifying.

'Priorities first. Defensemaster, what is our status?'

Tantarent-fid was the youngest present. He was a smallish male, spaceborn, mated, father of two male children well below fighting age. He was not known to have dissident leanings. His predecessor, who did, had been retired while the Foot was departing the ringed giant.

The Defensemaster's business was the survival of the Traveler Herd. His domain included air systems, food sources, hull integrity, the main drive, course determinations, the mounted digit ships, and the lasers that would defend the ship from meteors or alien weapons. He shared these last three domains with the Attackmaster.

He answered readily enough. '*Message Bearer* is fully able to defend itself, and well beyond attack range in any case. Main drive running well. We've used more than half our fuel, of course, and that will have to be replaced sometime. Sixteen digit ships moored for boost, and more returning from Winterhome. We're on schedule. We'll match with the Foot in two days. In twenty-two days we'll have set the Foot on course, as you and Attackmaster Koothfektil-rusp may decide. We'll disengage and leave Winterhome on a fast parabola.'

'You have prey in the air ducts.'

'Yes, the Breakers have had some success in training the human fithp. They show a gratifying agility. For two days now we've had them cleaning and re-impregnating the filters. We had hoped that would take the mating scent out of the corridors, but – ' Tantarent-fid clawed the air, perfunctorily. 'We'll reserve the humans as backup to the automatic systems. The Breakers can best tell you whether they would react well during a real emergency.'

'Good enough. Attackmaster Koothfektil-rusp, how's the texture of the mud?'

The Attackmaster's business was war. 'I believe we can hold the base on Land Mass Two,' he said. 'Digit ships are in transit with prisoners and loot. If things continue to go well, we will not need the Foot; but we must make that decision *soon*.' He paused, then, 'We've lost Digit ship *Twenty* —'

'How did you lose *this* digit ship?'

Koothfektil-rusp reared up on his forelegs. 'Digit Ship *Twenty* was rising on a launch laser during heavy weather. We believe that the beam itself precipitated a funnel storm. The beam was blocked by clouds and debris. The ship rose too slowly; the pilot tried to land. During that vulnerable period an aircraft fired a missile.'

Some losses had to be expected, of course. Spaceborn had little grasp of planetary weather. Choose another topic – 'Attackmaster, I have the impression that the prey continually repudiate their surrender.'

'They do.'

'Your response?'

The Attackmaster looked uncomfortable. 'Which thuktun shall we read? Fithp do not do such things. My warriors trample all humans within sixty-four srupkithp of where prey break their bond to the Traveler Herd. If a prey hides well enough to survive our wrath, we take him to be sane and harmless. But this is hard on my fithp, Herdmaster. It is hard to crush those who have surrendered!'

'I have my problems too. Breaker-One, is the Attackmaster's approach correct?'

'I don't – It won't teach them surrender, Herdmaster. Attackmaster Koothfektil-rusp has told us this; they attack after surrender, singly and in octuples and in still larger groups. This goes beyond an epidemic of rogues. It grows likely that the typical human resembles Dawson, and not the Soviets. They make their own decisions: each an entire fithp wobbling on two legs. Killing those who were not involved in a breach of faith . . . may accomplish nothing at all, or give them reason to question *our* sanity.'

'Dawson. Fumf.' The Herdmaster considered. He *must* have answers. Was he even asking the right questions? 'To call such behavior insane is futile. If all are insane – Advisor, you have been uncommonly silent.'

'Lead me Herdmaster. Breaker-One, there is the matter of predictability. If all are insane, are they all insane in the same fashion?'

'Not even that . I have no complaints of the Soviets.'

But Takpusseh stirred, and Fathisteh-tulk caught it. 'Breaker-Two?'

'They keep secrets. The Soviets speak their own language, though they practice the thuktun-speech too. They know more of the air ducts than we have asked them to learn. Ask us again after Digit Ship *Six* gives us more prisoners.'

Fathisteh-tulk turned to another source. 'Keeper of the thuktun, what have you learned? The prey are described as insane. I remember the pflit of the Homeworld —'

Speaking of the Homeworld to a fellow sleeper, Fistarteh-thuktun waxed loquacious. 'Of course, the pflit reproduced at a furious rate. They were little mottled gray beasts the same colors as the Sunward Forest they lived in, and the way they clustered made fithp look roguish. An individual life meant nothing in the survival strategy of the pflit, so they evolved no defense against predators, and they migrated in swarms, even if the path led off a cliff . . . What insight are you seeking? The prey throw their lives away, but they don't breed faster than we do.'

'Probably true,' Takpusseh said.

'You miss my point,' the Advisor said. 'Is it not true that nature shapes life to fit its style of life?'

We're wasting time, Pastempeh-keph thought, but he wasn't sure and he didn't speak. A Herdmaster must trumpet softly, lest a suggestion be taken for an order.

'The Life Thuktun tells us so,' Fistarteh-thuktun said slowly. 'The Thuktun of the Long Path shows how new forms arise from old. Evolution goes by groups, by herds; but ripper fthuggl live alone, attacking their prey one on one: all rogues. They need room to find prey; they meet only to mate. Fithp surrender in herds, or accept surrender into the victor herd. What style of life has shaped our prey? The prey – they don't surrender to superior force. Perhaps they die to guard genes related to theirs. Or —'

'Think of a hunting carnivore,' Takpusseh said in sudden excitement. 'Food is scarce, so they scatter. Siblings might be hundreds of miles away. More dangerous predators come. Might a prey die to kill them, because the marauders might reach its genotypes?'

'But humans are omnivores,' Raztupisp-minz reminded them. 'Still, the sky of Winterhome seethed with aircraft before our attack. I think you have it. *They do not remain in families*. Like ripper fthuggl, individuals go to make their own territory. To kill something dangerous is for the good of all. For surviving heroes it may even mean mating privileges, to judge by our studies of their broadcasts. We believe that they have no specific mating season. Indeed, they do not always remain with one mate!'

The Herdmaster called them back to specifics. 'What does this do for us, if true?'

Into the uneasy silence Fathisteh-tulk said, 'It makes us aware of the awesome magnitude of our problem. We take surrender in herds, do we? Our prey doesn't come in herds! A family might be scattered across half the planet!'

'Surely —'

Whatever the Attackmaster was about to say would never be heard. His digits flipped back to cover his skull – the classic reflexive response to threat – as he listened to the shell-shaped phone under his earflap.

It is not good news. The Herdmaster waited. If there were danger to the ship, both he and the Defensemaster would know instantly. What could be important enough to interrupt *this* meeting —

He knew soon enough.

The Attackmaster took a microphone from his harness. 'Flee. Save what we can.' He returned the microphone. 'Herdmaster, we no longer have a base in Kansas.'

'How is this?'

'The prey have used thermonuclear bombs. Bombs rise among the orbiting digit ships —'.

'But these can be stopped.'

'Stopped, of course. But more bombs fall on our base, and our ships are too busy to stop them. Bombs are rising from both land masses and from the sea.'

'From *both* land masses?' The Advisor looked thoughtful. 'You are certain?'

'I am certain of nothing, Advisor. They sow radioactive fire on their own croplands! Herdmaster, I must —'

'Certainly.' The Herdmaster stood, releasing his fithp to their duties. They scattered.

'What now?' he demanded. 'What do you make of this?'

Advisor Fathisteh-tulk struck at invisible flies. 'I would not tread on the Breakers' ground —'

'Your advice, drown you!'

'Soviets and Dawson's tribe cooperate. When they must. As we hear of our losses, we must not forget this. Go fight your war.' He spoke to the Herdmaster's back.

———

Roger Brooks drove south, then angled west. For two days there had been cornfields and no sign of war.

Rosalee was stretched out, taking advantage of the now roomy backseat of the Rabbit. Road conditions had been mixed, good roads alternating with stretches where the highways and intersections were utterly destroyed. *It's still a long way to Colorado Springs. There's nothing on the radio, and I'm half asleep.*

Roger asked, 'Carol, are you slept out?'

She hadn't spoken in hours. Her eyes were wide, doing a continual slow swivel. She jumped when he spoke and said, 'Yeah. I must say, that's the damnedest convention I ever half saw.'

'I believe it.'

'Though I heard about one in St. Louis that was canceled, and nobody told the Guest of Honor.'

'Why do you go?'

'Oh . . . mostly we go to meet each other, I guess. And the people who write the books we read.' Flicker of a smile. 'There were three men for every two women, and the ratio used to be even better. And fun things tend to happen, like the masquerades and listening to the dirty filksongs —'

'Filksongs?'

'And half a dozen writers going off to dinner, with an editor to pay, and Nat taking me along. And the room parties, and the elevator parties, and smoffing . . . damn.' She was crying. 'I guess I'm in mourning.'

'I'm sorry about George. But he did get a tank. I don't think anyone could have stopped him.' Did she blame Roger?

Apparently not. 'George. I thought that was stupid, I told him so . . . George.' Her head was turned away, watching the passing cornfields. She broke a long silence in a sudden rush of words. 'It'll never happen again. It's *all* dead! The publishing industry is probably dead, half of science fiction is obsolete, we're all going to be scrabbling for something to eat for years to come, and how can you hold a convention with no airlines?'

She misses science fiction. If the best troops in the Army can't drive the aliens out, the whole damn planet is doomed, and she misses science fiction. It came to him, suddenly and frighteningly, that the war might already be lost.

'That first night Nat had a three-pound Lobster Savannah, and he started talking to it. "Hospital Station thinks they can cure you." "The Federation doesn't think your people can defend themselves alone." "Now will you speak of your troop movements, wretched crustacean?" By dessert we were calling him *Speaker to Seafood* – ' Her voice changed. 'Oh my *God!*'

The corner of Roger's eye had caught light brighter than sunlight. He braked without looking. 'What is it?'

'They're hitting us again!'

He eased the Rabbit over to the dirt rim of the highway before he dared look. One glance was enough. 'Don't look.' He opened the door and slid out, low. 'Follow me. Rosalee, wake up and get out on my side! Stay low!'

The blast came, not as bad as he had expected, followed by a wind, followed by another blast and more wind. The Rabbit's windows rattled. By then all three were crouched on the highway side of the car. There were more bright lights high overhead, and another to the north. When the light died a little, Roger peeked over the hood.

Fiery mushrooms bloomed amidst the Kansas wheat fields.

'Mushrooms. I think this is the real thing,' he said. 'Not meteors. Atomic bombs, and that's occupied territory. 'Those are ours.'

'Bombing *Kansas*?'

Roger laughed, and meant it. 'If you've got a better idea, you should have been in the helicopter. At least we're fighting back!' He peeked again. There were four fire-mushrooms in view, all a good distance north.

A thread of actinic green light rose from hundreds of miles away . . . something was blocking it at the skyward end, something rising . . . another fireball winked near the base of the beam. Roger ducked fast, waited, looked again. Fireball rising. No laser beam. An orange point high up, drifting down. What was that all about?

Whatever. Lasers were aliens, atomic bombs were men, and the bomb had interrupted something. 'Come on, guys,' Roger gloated. 'Ruin their whole morning!'

PART THREE

Footfall

CHAPTER TWENTY-THREE
CLEANUP

The destiny of mankind is not decided by material computation. When great causes are on the move, we learn that we are spirits, not animals, and that something is going on in space and time, and beyond space and time, which, whether we like it or not, spells duty.

    – WINSTON CHURCHILL, Rochester, New York, 1941

COUNTDOWN: H PLUS FOUR WEEKS

Western Kansas was a black, dimpled land.

The army pilot gave the craters a wide berth, flying carefully upwind. A stutter tried to surface when he spoke, and he spoke seldom. His motions were jerky. He couldn't have seen films of death-beams spiraling in on other helicopters, but rumors must have spread. Jenny guessed that he was waiting to be speared by green light.

Sitting beside her, Jack Clybourne was as calm as an oyster.

Jenny saw reports from the observatories as they came in, and she kept no secrets from Jack. Earth's most recent moons still included more than a score of destroyer-sized spacecraft; but the mother ship had disappeared into interplanetary space with half its retinue, and the remaining ships seemed to be doing nothing. Waiting? If the pilot had known what Jenny knew, he might be calmer. But the vivid green death was still possible. Jenny wasn't as calm as she looked. Jack Clybourne was Jenny's own true love, but he was not about to out-macho her.

From time to time, at Jenny's orders, the pilot skimmed low over burned cornfields and along broken roads. The roads were strewn with hundreds of what might have been gigantic tablecloths in neon-bright colors, and thousands of dinner-plate-sized pieces of flattened foam plastic. The hang-glider fabric would become clothing, come winter, for refugees who would be glad to have it. But the alien landing shoes would be indestructible litter. A hundred years from now farmers would still be digging them up in the cornfields. Would those farmers have hands, or bifurcated trunks?

There were black skeletons of automobiles, and corpses: enough half-burned human and alien corpses to satisfy anybody.

The helicopter circled a village, and Jenny couldn't find a single unburned structure. The inhabitants had fled ahead of the aliens, and the aliens had fled from fission bombs, and nobody remained to fight the fires.

Rarely, bands of refugees looked up to watch the helicopter pass. Few tried to wave it down.

Jenny's eyes kept straying to the alien ship.

It had been in sight for nearly an hour. Less than ten miles away now, it dominated the flat black landscape. It had fallen several miles. It was foreshortened, its hull split, like a Navy battleship dropped on its nose. It must have loomed large in the refugees' eyes.

Like a coyote on a freeway, a fi' corpse lay in the road, flattened to a pancake silhouette and rotted almost to its crushed bones. Its hang glider hadn't opened. She'd seen dead snouts here and there. They stripped their dead, but often left them where they lay. Cremation would have been easy enough: stack the bodies, and one blast of a fithp laser would do it.

The helicopter settled near the stern. Jenny and Jack got out.

They walked alongside the ruined hull. Only the warship's tail, an outsize rocket-nozzle-shape with jet scoops facing forward, had survived the crash intact. The hull had split halfway along its length. Jack chinned himself on the edge of the rip. 'Nothing. A fuel tank.'

Forward of the tank wall, the hull had wrinkled and torn again. From the bent nose a glassless window winked, the opening squeezed almost shut. Where ripped metal gaped conveniently wide, they climbed inside, Jack leading the way.

They came out faster than they went in. Jenny took off the gas mask and waited. Jack Clybourne ran into the cornfield. After a few moments she heard sounds of gagging. She tried not to notice.

'Sorry,' he said when he came back.

'Sure. I almost lost my lunch too.'

'First assignment I get Outside —'

'You haven't done any harm,' Jenny said. 'We're not likely to do any good here, either. The ship's a mess, it's a job for experts.'

'Experts.' He looked at the wreckage. 'You'd send your dreamers-for-hire into *that?*'

'It's their job.'

Jack shook his head. He said, 'Well, it's for sure there weren't any survivors.'

'Yes. Too bad.'

'Damn straight. Jeez, you'd think they'd have left *some* of their troops behind.'

'They must have been ready to evacuate. Just in case,' Jenny said.

'Maybe they planned it that way. Maybe they did just what they came for. Kansas is *gone*. This place is a wound, a cemetery. We've got no dams, no highways, no railroads, and we're afraid to fly. And we've got one prisoner. How many of our people did they get?'

Jenny shook her head. 'I don't know. A lot, from the missing persons reports. But we can't rely on those.' *We're stalling*, she thought. 'Look, I've got to go back in. Alone. No need for both of us to get sick.'

'No. I wanted to come. I wasn't doing any good inside the Hole.' Clybourne put on the gas mask. 'Rrready.' His voice sounded hollow from inside the mask.

They reentered the rip in the life support system.

The interior was twisted and bent. Crumpled walls showed crumpled machinery and torn wiring buried inside. Alien bodies lay in the corridors. They stank. Too many days had passed since the combined U.S. and Soviet bombardment had driven the aliens back to space. Alien bodies had bloated and/or ruptured. Jenny tried to ignore them; they were someone else's job. She hoped the biologists would come soon to remove them.

Not that I know what I'm looking for. She went deeper into the ship. Her flashlight picked out the remains of equipment; wherever she pointed, Jack took photographs. The whine of the recharger for his electronic flash sounded loud in the dead ship.

Nothing was intact. *There can't be anything here, or they'd have melted it from space. Wouldn't they? How do they regard their dead? I'll have to ask Harpanet. Get Reynolds to ask him,* she corrected herself. The science-fiction writers seemed to spend all their time with the captured alien; and Jenny couldn't face one, not after this.

A large steel door lay ahead. It had been locked, but sprung partially open in the crash. Jenny pulled and it moved slightly. She wasn't strong enough to move it farther. Jack slung the camera over his shoulder and took a grip on the door. When they pulled together it opened just far enough to let them squeeze by.

The room was tremendous, with a low ceiling and a padded floor that was now a wall. It was filled with death.

For a moment she didn't recognize what she saw. Then her flashlight played across a human face, a child's face, sweetly smiling – she was relieved to see that it was a doll. There was a white bloated thing wrapped in bright colored tartan under the doll. Jenny moved closer until her light showed what the doll rested on.

Like a find-the-face puzzle: now her eyes found human shapes, a knee, the back of a head, a man folded in two around a snapped spine; but all piled together like melting clay. They must have been jammed in like cattle. Here a shape that made no sense at all, with human and snout features, until it snapped into focus. An alien guard must have struck like a bomb when the ship came down, and at least three prisoners had been under him.

She gagged, and bile filled her mouth, splashed against the gas mask. Reflexively she lifted the mask. The smells of death filled her lungs. She turned and ran from the ship.

———

The bridge hummed with soft voices.

Behind *Message Bearer* a glow was fading, dying. Its death was carefully monitored. One couldn't turn the main drive on and off like a light switch, lest showers of lethal particles burst from the magnetic bottle and spray through the ship.

Puffballs of flame streamed from sixteen digit ships mounted along the aft rim, fine-tuning *Message Bearer*'s velocity. Bridge personnel watched the view from a sensor pod that reached out from the hull like a big-headed metal snake. Pastempeh-keph watched the screens, letting it happen. His fithp could manage this without his help.

Thrust shifted him against the web that held him to his couch. He watched a black-and-gray mass approach his ship.

The Foot was woefully changed.

Within the outer fringe of the gas giant's ring they had found a rough-surfaced white egg, two makasrupkithp along the long axis, against a backdrop of terrible beauty. It had been like something out of the Shape Wars, a heretical representation of the Predecessors: a featureless head, lacking digits and body, lacking everything but brain.

361

The mining team had chosen it for its size and composition, out of an eight-cubed of similar moonlets. Over the next ten Homeworld years its icy strata had hatched water and air and fuel; its rock-and-metal core gave up steel alloys, and soil additives for the garden section.

It was no longer an egg. Six-eighths of its mass was gone. The ice was gone, leaving ridges and gouges and runnels and pits in a makasrupk-long nugget of black slag. A faceless alien head had become an asymmetrical alien skull. It drifted closer now, an ugly omen.

'I hoped that we could shunt it aside,' Pastempeh-keph said.

'We gave ourselves the option,' said his Advisor. 'If the prey had proved tractable, our present foray might have become a base of operations. We might have taken Winterhome without the Foot.'

Pastempeh-keph trumpeted in sudden rage. *'Why do they always wait to attack?'*

'It's not a serious question, Herdmaster.' Fathisteh-tulk was placed as always. 'We organized our foray over the past several years. Why would they not take a few eights of days to gather their forces? So. Now they have used fission bombs on their own Garden regions, and I must admit that that seems excessive —'

'Mad.'

'Mad, then. If they are truly mad, our problem is worse yet. Give thanks that it is the Breakers' problem, not ours, not yet.'

'It will be soon.'

'Yes. But Digit Ship *Six* approaches with new prisoners and a considerable mass of loot. The Breakers should learn a great deal when it arrives.'

The Herdmaster trumpeted satisfaction. That, at least, was as expected. *Nothing else is.* 'Why have the natives not sent messages?'

'Before there was anything to say, they wanted to talk,' Fathisteh-tulk said. 'Now that we have some estimation of our relative strengths, they say nothing. No demands, no offers. Twelve digit ships are destroyed, and vast stretches of cropland, and the prey's herdmasters have nothing to say to us. Perhaps the Breakers will learn why.' Again, that overly placid, languid, irritating voice. *There is nothing to be done,* the Herdmaster told himself. *He is Advisor. What would I do, in his place?*

Message Bearer surged backward, and shuddered. A fi' turned and said, 'Herdmaster, we are mated to the Foot. Soon we may begin acceleration. Have we a course?'

This was the moment. Long ago the Predecessors had destroyed a planet. Now – 'Continue the Plan. Guide the Foot to center its impact on Winterhome. The Breakers' group will find us a more specific target.' He stiffened suddenly. In a lowered voice he said, 'Fathisteh-tulk, I believe I forgot to do anything about the mudroom!'

'Phoo. Defensemaster —'

'I saw to it that the mudroom was fully frozen before we stomped our spin,' Tantarent-fid said complacently. 'I evacuated your private mudroom too, Herdmaster.'

'Good. Well served.' Pastempeh-keph shuddered at a mental picture: globules of mud filling the air, fithp in pressure suits trying to sweep it away —

Lack of a communal mudroom would cause its own problems. Henceforth every fi' would be vaguely unhappy – as if the skewed mating seasons were not enough. He lifted his snffp high. *I drown in a flood of troubles.*

Fathisteh-tulk made sympathetic gestures.

Not sympathy. Answers. 'Defensemaster, bring the Breakers, the Attackmaster, and the priest to the conference pit. We must make decisions regarding the prey and the Foot.'

'Attackmaster?'

'We have discontinued the base in Kansas,' Koothfektil-rusp said. 'Digit ships are in transit with prisoners and loot. We lost Digit Ship *Thirteen*, which carried the bulk of what we had gathered, but we saved several prisoners and some material on other ships.'

'How was this one lost?'

Koothfektil-rusp's digits snapped back to cover his head. Did he feel threatened? 'We did not anticipate that the American Herd would bomb their own major food-bearing domain! We did not anticipate that the Soviet Herd would cooperate with them; and that they surely did! Our beams stopped many of their suborbital bombs, but many got through, and the launch devices had moved before we could fire on them.'

'The ship?'

'*Thirteen* was rising on a launch beam when a thermonuclear missile from a submarine vehicle destroyed the laser facility.'

'The bombs: were they all from the Soviet Herd?'

'From desert territories on the Soviet continent, and from offshore of the American continent, from submarine vehicles that were shielded by water when our lasers fell. None of the thermonuclear devices came from the United States itself.'

The Herdmaster pondered that. 'Breaker-One, must we assume that the United States Herd has surrendered to the other? Or has the Soviet Herd attacked our foothold in Kansas, risking their wrath?'

Raztupisp-minz glanced at Takpusseh before speaking. 'You must also consider that two human herds may cooperate when neither has surrendered to the other.'

The Herdmaster had feared this. Too many answers were no answer.

'And yet we may prosper,' Attackmaster Koothfektil-rusp said soothingly. 'There is little industry, little transportation in our chosen target area. We may find genotypes clustered when we land following Footfall.'

'Footfall, yes.' Keep to specifics. 'Must the Foot fall? Breaker-One?'

Raztupisp-minz said, 'They must be made to know that they are hurt.' Takpusseh stirred but kept silent.

'Hurt? In America they will starve! They have seared their crops with radioactive fire!' The Herdmaster took firm hold of his emotions. The air was heady with pheromones, and seven spaceborn males were ready to butt heads! 'Attackmaster? The Foot?'

Koothfektil-rusp's answer was predictable. 'Stomp them. Show our might. We have chosen the location, Herdmaster. This time we attack a weaker herd. We must secure a foothold on Winterhome, and expand from there. Weather following Footfall will make retaliation difficult. Fate gifts us with a side effect: the weather worldwide will be wetter and more to our liking.'

'Show me.'

Koothfektil-rusp lit the wall screen. Under his direction a globe of Winterhome rolled, and stopped. The Attackmaster's digit indicated the body of water that Rogachev called the Indian Ocean. 'Here, in the center. Look how the waves expand from the impact point. East, they roll many makasrupkithp to the island nations. North, even further. Westward, they cover the lowlands where we see city lights; the highlands are left free. Northwest, fuel sources that serve worldwide industry are drowned. These herds that cooperated against us may still not cooperate with the savage herds of the Southern Hemisphere, and wild air masses make transport impossible to them, and where would they send their forces? We might land east or west or north; the rolling sea subdues the prey in all directions. My sleeper aides tell me that the Foot has the mass and velocity to do the work we want.'

They would drown, by eight to the eighths. The Herdmaster mourned in advance. 'Have you chosen our foothold?'

'Here, I think. We would find not only mines but

365

possible allies. One problem, Herdmaster: launching facilities will be a problem, here or anywhere. We must build in continual rain. Perhaps we must launch through rain, requiring more laser power, making a launch more conspicuous . . .'

The Herdmaster felt himself relaxing. He knew military strategy. This was easier than talking about the craziness of the prey, which made his mind hurt.

Advisor Fathisteh-tulk vented a fluttering snort. 'Possible allies?' His digits swiped at thin air: *We can't know that*.

The Attackmaster snapped back. 'They have little transportation! We will find true herds. When they surrender —'

The Herdmaster was tired. 'Enough. Do it your way, Attackmaster. I've heard no better suggestion. Breakers, keep me aware. We must understand the prey; we must teach them our way. To your duties.'

He waited while the rest scattered. Then, 'Fathisteh-tulk, you know planet dwellers better than we.' *Have we erred? Could we win without the Foot?* A Herdmaster could not ask.

The Advisor repeated what Breaker-One had said. 'They must know that they have been hurt. Whether that will be enough . . . Herdmaster, can you spare me now?'

'Go, Fathisteh-tulk. Your mate nears her term.'

―――――――

The Soviets moved in a series of horizontal leaps, launching themselves down the corridor in long trajectories. The gravity was very weak, so weak that it took many seconds to fall from the center of a corridor to its wall. Nikolai found the conditions perfect. He had no trouble keeping up with the others even though they used their legs for propulsion and he had to launch himself with arms alone.

Sometimes he turned flips as he traveled through the corridor.

'They keep Dawson in his cell,' Dmitri said. 'For five days they have done this. Why?'

Arvid shrugged. 'It did not seem to me that he caused them any special trouble. Perhaps Takpusseh bears a grudge.'

'I think not.' Dmitri cursed fluently. 'Dawson is a fool, and may get us all killed.'

'We could strangle him,' Arvid said.

Dmitri looked thoughtful for a moment. 'No. We do not know how our captors will react. Docile, Comrade. We will continue to be cooperative. If they wish more geography lessons, you will give them. They learn nothing they have not obtained from children's books from the United States. They wish us to join their herd. We will do so.'

They reached the entry point. Nikolai removed the grill and climbed into the air duct. Dmitri and Arvid followed.

When they had first been given the assignment, Arvid was sure that the ducts would be too small for fithp. In an emergency a young fi' might be sent in to make repairs; but there were not even handholds for such a case. Yet, would prisoners be let loose where they could not even be monitored? Surely there would be cameras.

He had thought the cameras would be hard to identify, but they were not. Nikolai located a brush-rimmed ring of just the right size to fill a duct. It was in a recess, not moving. There were glass eyes at opposite points, and a metal tentacle coiled around the inner surface.

A cleaning robot. During the next few days they looked for others. Occasionally one would be seen far down a tube. It was comforting to know that they were watched – and *how*.

'Show your stamina,' Takpusseh had said. Dawson wouldn't have the wit to hide his capabilities if they permitted him out of his cell. They had not seen him for days. Dmitri and Arvid and Nikolai stopped when they were

367

tired, but before they were exhausted, four days in a row.

Today was the fifth day, and it was time to move.

A ring-shaped duct cleaner was far behind them, rolling on ball bearings in the outer rim. Arvid and Dmitri moved side by side, close together. They had become good at that. Nikolai was ahead of them. Perhaps the cameras would not see him. Perhaps he would be seen but not observed: in the waving of alien limbs, three humans might well seem to be two. If another duct cleaner appeared ahead, Dmitri would say, casually, 'Another time.'

None did.

Nikolai spotted a side duct ahead. He speeded up. Taking his cue, Arvid and Dmitri speeded up too. The curve of the corridor had left the duct cleaner behind when Nikolai disappeared, axis-bound.

Arvid stopped to clean out a dust-catch. The robot had him in view when he caught up to Dmitri.

———————

The Rabbit topped a final rise. Pikes Peak had been visible ahead for hours; now they could see its base. The city of Colorado Springs lay spread out in the valley below them.

'We're here,' Roger said.

'Now what?' Carol asked. 'Are you sure Nat is here? Will he want to see me?'

'Yes, and I don't know,' Roger said.

'What will we do?' Rosalee asked.

With a possessive tone. Why is it that women get that tone when they've been sleeping with you? And that men respond to it? But I'm glad I met her. 'There are bound to be newspapers. The *Washington Post* still exists. It might even have a Colorado Springs headquarters. I'll be welcome there. So will you, if I bring you in.'

'I can type,' Rosalee said. 'And maybe I can help in other ways.'

*She probably can. Librarians read a lot. She's smart.
Not very pretty, but there's something about her –* 'Sure.
We'll work together. Reporters need research assistants.'

'Where will Nat Reynolds be?' Carol asked. 'I want to
see him.'

*He'll be Inside, and I've told you that a dozen times, so
why the hell are you asking me again?* 'We'll see.' He
started the car down toward the city center.

'It's all so damned – different,' Carol said.

'Yeah. That's for sure,' Rosalee agreed. 'Maybe it will
always be different.'

CHAPTER TWENTY-FOUR
MEETINGS

Who travels alone, without lover or friend,
But hurries from nothing, to naught at the end.

– ELLA WHEELER WILCOX

COUNTDOWN: H PLUS FIVE WEEKS

Digit Ship *Six* was moored in place at *Message Bearer*'s stern. While fuel flowed into the digit ship, Chintithpit-mang's eight-squared, now reduced to forty-one, moved through the airlock and forward along the mating tube.

The prisoners had suffered on the trip out. Hours after takeoff, warriors checking their cell had found the air stinking with the smell of half-digested food. They must have been breathing the stuff until the air flow pulled it out. In free-fall they were like fish out of water. They acted like they were dying. Chintithpit-mang's warriors had to tow them like baggage. They towed other baggage: food stocks, maps, books full of pictures, tape cassettes, and projection machines.

Chintithpit-mang himself moved clumsily. One leg was braced straight, and it interfered with his every motion. A thermonuclear device had exploded near the ship just before takeoff. Chintithpit-mang and six prisoners had slammed against a wall. The prisoners, with their negligible mass, were barely bruised, but Chintithpit-mang's right hind leg had snapped under him.

Two octuples of warrior met them at the end of a makasrupk of tunnel. They all looked irritatingly clean and healthy. Chintithpit-mang was glad to turn his prisoners over to them. If any died, he preferred that another have them in charge.

He took the shortest route toward Shreshleemang. His mate would be waiting.

Humans in a corridor startled him. He was reaching for his gun before he realized that they must be prisoners. They seemed to want something . . . He glared at them and kept moving. The next corner brought him face to face with Fathisteh-tulk.

Had the Herdmaster's Advisor noticed? 'May your time stretch long. Advisor,' he said, and would have passed.

'Stay,' said Fathisteh-tulk. 'I need you.'

Chintithpit-mang suppressed a fluttering snort of displeasure, but the Advisor sensed it anyway. 'This is of massive importance, and none other will do,' he persisted. 'You are of the Year Zero Fithp, and a dissident. So is your mate. She will assume that your duties kept you at the ship until you can explain to her. Come.'

———————

Dmitri and Arvid climbed wearily from the air duct.

Two female fithp looked at the Soviets and passed on. A passing fi' warrior trumpeted anger at them; they flinched back. Dmitri frowned. 'Why did he do that? I thought they had their instructions —'

'He may have had other instructions,' Arvid said.

'No. He was injured. A ship must have arrived from Earth – that series of *thuds* this morning —'

'Da. Injured warriors will not like humans.'

The next fi' warrior seemed friendly enough. Perhaps he was glad of a touch of strange in his life. He made conversation, and the Soviets answered in kind. He dawdled for the benefit of the tired duct-cleaners, who moved a little more slowly than necessary. *Hide your strength!*

The Herdmaster looked up from his viewscreen and snorted angrily. His digits pounded a baseball-sized button. 'Communications, get me Fathisteh-tulk. Find out why he isn't on duty.'

'Will you talk to him yourself?'

'No. Send him here. Has Digit Ship *Six* arrived?'

'It arrived while you slept, Herdmaster.'

'After you have the Advisor, get me Breaker-One.'

'The Advisor doesn't answer, Herdmaster.'

'What? Never mind. Get me Breaker-One.'

The screen showed Raztupisp-minz looking as if his youth had returned. Power could do that for an aging fi'. He had had power while breaking the sleepers to their new role. Now his human charges had given him his authority back.

'We will put the new prisoners to distributing the dietary supplements,' he said, 'and let them talk with the Soviets, with Tashayamp present. First, however, I intend to house them with Dawson. Dawson has been alone for several days now. We hoped that, like a newborn meatflyer, he would fixate on me if he had no other companionship.'

'Did it work?'

'It is too soon to tell, but I think not. Dawson is not newborn. He talks to me, but not as a new slave talks to one who has taken his surrender. There is anger if not impudence. Herdmaster, I wonder if there is a surrender symbol among humans that we have not discovered.'

'He surrendered. He must be made to know the implications.'

'At your orders —'

'Drown you, your task is not within my thuktun! I advise only. You will do what you can, in whatever way you feel is good, and you will accept full responsibility for failure!'

'Lead me, Herdmaster. Companions from Dawson's herd may give him back his rationality.'

'Your scarlet-tufted female was considered a curable rogue. Will her presence in Dawson's cell affect Dawson's sense of reality?'

'Alice accepted surrender. She obeys orders. Eight-cubed leader Siplisteph says she seems saner than most.'

'Keep me informed. Are the air ducts clean?'

Raztupisp-minz bridled at his sarcastic tone. 'The prisoners have covered perhaps six sixty-fourths of the network. They're doing well. Herdmaster, you are aware that a battle might destroy the duct sweepers or rip the ducts open. The humans are gaining practice against real need.'

'Your meaning wets my mind. I take it that they are indeed being broken to the Traveler Herd.'

Breaker-One hesitated. Then, 'They do not interpret orders rigorously. One has explored regions to which he was not assigned. This may demonstrate the curiosity native to a climbing species, or they may hope to gain knowledge that will make them of more benefit to us —'

'Still they do not obey. Carry on.' The Herdmaster broke contact. 'Get me Chowpeentulk.' If he knew Chowpeentulk, she would know where her mate was under almost any circumstances.

Communications tracked her to the infirmary, where Chowpeentulk was in the act of delivering an infant. Even a Herdmaster had to wait sometimes.

The cell door was ajar; it opened to Wes Dawson's touch. He pushed it shut with his feet, and heard the lock click. Thoughts and memories boiled in his head. He pushed them deep into his mind, concentrating on the pain in his leg, and on not appearing injured. *The fithp are not telepathic,* he thought. *But why take chances?*

The cell was large and lonely. He had lived there for five

373

days now. He liked the elbow room and he hadn't liked dealing with the Soviets. Nonetheless – *They're punishing me. But for what? It must be punishment. To a herd beast, being left in solitary must be agony.*

They want to break me. I won't let them. Think of something. What? There's nothing to read . . .

Thuktun Flishithy's main drive was a universal subliminal hum in Dawson's mind. Its source was a gnawing ache.

It must be pushing against an enormous mass, for the acceleration to be so low. The fithp must have a hell of a big reserve of deuterium-tritium mix. That's an ominous thought. It's a big ship, and it can fight.

It has to be D-T mix. Any other assumption is worse. A fusion motor using simple hydrogen would have to be far more sophisticated, halfway from science fiction to fantasy. Wes Dawson preferred a more optimistic assumption.

Endlessly he waged the Fithp-Human War in his mind.

The door opened.

The intruder wailed as she entered. She had bright red hair and a pale face that would have been pretty if she hadn't looked so sick. She was slender as a pipe cleaner, fragile-looking. Free-fall was making her terribly unhappy.

Wes caught her arm. The newcomer wailed at him without seeing him.

Others came into the cell. A blond girl, no more than ten years old, floated gracefully to remove his hand from the slender woman's arm. 'It's all right, Alice,' the girl said.

'Makes me sick, oh God, I'm faaalllinggg . . .'

New prisoners. Not astronauts. My God, they've invaded Earth! The thin-faced redhead screamed again, and the blond girl said something soothing. Wes pushed woman and girl toward a wall, recoiled from the opposite wall, and was with them before they could bounce away. He pushed the woman's hands into the rug surface until she got the idea: her fists closed tight and she clung. The blond girl stayed with her.

Now he could look at the others.

There were four more. One was a boy of nine or so, black-haired, darkly tanned. Two were in their fifties, weathered like farm people, unmistakably man and wife from the way they clung to each other.

The final one was probably the blond girl's mother. She had the same shade of blond hair and the same finely chiseled nose. She floated at arm's length, like an acrobat.

The blond woman looked at him hard. 'Wes Dawson? Senator?'

Did she expect him to recognize her? He didn't. He smiled at her. 'Congressman. Which way did you vote?'

'Jeri Wilson. We met at JPL, fifteen years ago, when the Voyager was passing Saturn. . . . Uh, Republican.'

A long time ago. She couldn't have been more than twenty then. Maybe not that old. And he'd met a lot of people since. 'Right. The Saturn encounter seems almost prehistoric now. How did you get here?'

'We were captured —'

'Sure, but where?'

'You don't know?' Jeri asked. 'Oh, I guess you wouldn't. We were captured in Kansas. The aliens invaded.'

'Kansas – where in Kansas?'

'Not far from your wife's home,' Jeri said. 'About forty miles from there —'

'How the devil do you know where my wife is staying?' Dawson demanded.

'We were on our way there,' Jeri said. 'Do you believe in synchronicity? I don't, not really, but – well, actually it's not too big a surprise. Nothing is, now.'

Wes shook his head in confusion. Aliens in Kansas. 'Why were you going to find Carlotta?'

'It's a long story,' Jeri said. 'Look, we were going west, getting out of Los Angeles, when we ran out of gas. I was

375

afraid to stop anyone until I saw Harry Reddington —'

'Hairy Red? You know him?'

'Yes. He tried to help us, and when – when that didn't do any good, he was trying to go help your wife, and he took us with him, only the aliens landed —'

'All right,' Wes said. 'I can get the details later. Is Carlotta all right?'

'I don't know. Something happened in Kansas. Something bad for the snouts, because first they were happy, and then all of a sudden our guards turned mean.'

'Snouts?'

'That's what everyone calls them now.'

'Good name.'

He turned to the others. 'Didn't mean to ignore you. You must have a lot of questions?'

'Some,' the man said.

'Reckon the Lord will tell us what we have to know,' the woman added. She put a protective arm around the boy.

'John and Carrie Woodward,' Jeri Wilson said. 'From Kansas, but they didn't see any more of the war than I did. And Gary Capehart. They left his parents behind. We don't know why. And that's my daughter, Melissa, and her friend there is Alice. What's going to happen to us?'

'Good question. I wish I knew. What's wrong with Alice?'

The redhead's face was pressed tight into the wall padding, and her back was stiff. Jeri said, 'She wouldn't tell us her last name. She said a bomb hit Menninger's and they all ran. You know Menninger's? She must have been a patient.'

Carrie Woodward sniffed, loudly.

The voice came muffled. 'Free wing.'

Wes said, 'I beg your pardon?'

The small face turned halfway. 'I was on the free wing. No locked doors. You know what that means? I wasn't one of the really sick ones, okay?'

Wes said, 'Pleased to meet you all. I was getting lonely.'

He didn't try to shake hands. None could have spared a hand; they were all clinging to the dubious security of the wall rug. 'Aren't there others?'

'We thought so,' Jeri said. 'But we haven't seen any. Are – you the only one alive from Kosmograd?'

'No, there are some Russians. The fithp – that's what they call themselves, and you'll have to learn their language – the fithp sometimes keep us together and sometimes separate us. There are a pair of them in charge of teaching us.'

'Teachin' what?' Carrie Woodward asked. Her voice was filled with suspicion.

'Language. Customs. People, they will expect you to surrender. Formally. Sooner or later Takpusseh or Raztupisp-minz – one of our fi' teachers will come here and expect you to roll over on your back, and he'll put his foot on your chest. Don't fight. He won't crush you.'

'They already did that,' Melissa said.

Jeri laughed. 'We were scared silly. But really, why would they wait till now? We'd just float away.'

'Once that's done, they expect you to *cooperate*. Not just passively.'

'You mean they think we're one of them now?' Melissa asked.

'Something like that,' Dawson agreed. He pointed casually to the large camera in one corner of the room. 'They have no sense of privacy,' he said. 'They watch us when they please.'

Jeri Wilson frowned.

John Woodward looked at the camera, then seemed to hunch into himself.

He doesn't look good. Like Giorge did. . . .

'It isn't right,' Woodward said. His wife nodded agreement.

'Maybe, but that's how it is,' Dawson said.

'Okay,' Jeri said. 'So we learn to act like snouts —'

'And learn their language. Are you hungry?'

Melissa shook her head. Jeri said, 'Hah! No.'

Alice said, 'Oh,' and reached into her blouse and pulled out a big vitamin bottle. The pills were big too, and the label was a book's worth of tiny print, listing thirty-odd vital nutrients and their sources: bee pollen, comfrey, dandelion, fennel, hawthorne berry, ginger, garlic . . . Fo-Ti, Dong Quai . . . Siberian ginseng, rose hips . . .

'You raided a health food store?'

Alice said, 'Yeah. They took me through a grocery and a health food store and made me point at things I thought we'd need. Any objections?'

'Not bloody likely.' He swallowed a fat pill with greenish flecks in it, dry. 'There's some food from the Soviet station, and the fithp grow some things we can eat if you close your eyes first, but I've been worrying about vitamins.'

'What was it like?' Jeri Wilson asked. 'You were on the space station —'

He told it long. It didn't look like anything would interrupt them for a while.

'Your turn,' Dawson said.

Alice wasn't eager to talk until she got started. 'We were in the basement, along the walls. It was just like a tornado scare. They crowd all the patients in, in any order, mixed in with the orderlies. It's the only time you see the ones on the locked wing. . . . Anyway, there was a terrific noise and some of the walls fell in. Anyone who could still stand up ran away screaming, even some of the orderlies. I just ran. I got into the zoo next door and hid in the mammal house, but there wasn't any place to hide, really. James came in and I told him to go away, but he wouldn't. When the horrors came in I thought some of the zoo animals had got loose.'

The aliens had moved through Topeka, through shattered buildings and corpses beginning to decay. They took books and magazines from libraries and drugstores: anything with pictures. They led the prisoners through a supermarket and various small stores. Jeri and Melissa and the Woodwards had refused to cooperate, but Alice tried to assemble a collection of fresh and canned food, vitamins and mineral supplements —

'Did you have a chance to get coffee?'

'Hell, no, I didn't get cigarettes either. Bad for you. I got some herb teas, though.' And when Dawson laughed she looked furious.

The images on the video screen faded. Raztupisp-minz continued to stare at it, as if that would bring meaning to what he had seen. Finally he turned. 'What do you believe this means?' he asked.

Takpussch's digits flared.

'The Herdmaster will not be amused,' Raztupisp-minz hissed. He glanced at the camera in one corner. 'Perhaps he has seen already.'

'His annoyance will be as nothing when Fistarteh-thuktun sees these recordings,' Takpusseh said. He flared his digits again. 'We know they have curious courtship and mating habits. Apparently the females are continuously in estrus, and do not care what male satisfies their urges.'

'Then how do the females control them?' Raztupisp-minz demanded. 'It cannot be possible —'

'Much is possible,' Takpusseh sighed. 'Forgive me, grandson, but you have seen only life aboard ship. You have never lived on a world rich with life.'

'They eat their own kind! And sing as they do! I do not care to live on such a world.'

'If that is what we saw,' Takpusseh said. 'We must ask the prisoners.'

'Does Dawson speak well enough?'

'No. Nor do I know their speech so well. But Tashayamp does. She has been studying.' Takpusseh took a deep breath. Then another.

Raztupisp-minz did likewise. Pheromones filled his lungs. A sweet flavor.

'Grandson, you are my only relative,' Takpusseh said. 'Leader of my family, I wish to speak with you.'

Raztupisp-minz backed away slowly, then settled to a crouch. He waited until Takpusseh was similarly postured. 'Speak.'

'I wish you to carry winter flowers with me.'

'Ah. I have seen you grow stronger with new domains. I am glad, Takpusseh – but have you not waited overlong? The Time is upon the Sleeper Herd, and you are hardly able to be rational.'

'I know of no unmated Sleeper who would have me to mate. I speak of Tashayamp.'

'Ah. Of acceptable lineage, and competent in her work. Yes.' He let his voice trail to nothing, without a stop.

'But,' Takpusseh said. 'Yes. She is not comely. Indeed, some would say she is misshapen. Yet I find her attractive enough, and as you say, she is diligent at her work.'

'It happens seldom that spaceborn mates to sleeper. Do you know that you are acceptable?'

'How should I? I have no one to speak for me. None save you —'

'Yamp,' Raztupisp-minz mused. 'Her grandfather is Persantip-yamp. He is said to be irascible. A warrior in his day.' *And say no more; there was no war, but had there been, it could only have been against the sleepers.* 'You wish me to speak with him.'

'I ask that, my leader.'

'Tashayamp.' Raztupisp-minz snorted wry mirth. 'I have little experience in this, I should ask *you* what to say! Our roles are indeed reversed, in all ways. Let me see if I recall the words I am to say —'

'I know them,' Takpusseh admitted. 'But let the customs be kept.' He listened as Raztupisp-minz stumbled through the traditional lecture: that the fithp mate for life, that mating is an alliance forever, not to be entered through passions.

'Are you certain it is *not* passion? It is Time for your herd —'

'Not mere passion,' Takpusseh said. 'Recall, I am – somewhat – older than you. I was mated to your grandmother. I know something of passion, and of reason as well.'

'Yes. Politically, it is a good match. The yamp clan holds a wide domain; and you have taken your own.' *And you are male, acting with a spaceborn female. It is not as if it were the other way, spaceborn male to submit* – 'I will speak with Persantip-yamp, and if he will consent, I will come with you to present the winter flowers.' Raztupispminz rose to his feet. 'And my congratulations!'

381

CHAPTER TWENTY-FIVE
THE GARDEN

The opinion of the strongest is always the best.

– JEAN DE LA FONTAINE

COUNTDOWN: H PLUS FIVE WEEKS

They had floated forward, then inward along half a mile of spiral corridor, not quite in free-fall, but with so little gravity that motion was difficult for the newcomers. Wes tried to help where he could.

Two alien warriors carried large boxes. Tashayamp led the way.

A huge door opened for them: a cargo door, much bigger than would be needed to pass a fi'. They entered.

This huge chamber must be along the axis of the ship, forward of the chamber of the Podo Thuktun. A line of yellow-white light ran down the middle, too bright to look at directly. Elsewhere there was green, everywhere green, with splashes of carmine and yellow. Alien plants grew in cages, rooted in thick wet pads fixed along the walls. Green banners flapped in the breeze from the air conditioning. A field of yellow flowers turned as if to look at the intruders.

Here was a roughly rectangular block of loose dirt. Vines wrapped it loosely, and it was riddled with seven-inch holes. A head popped from a hole and was gone before Wes could react. A streamlined head, it had been, like a ferret's, with red beads for eyes.

It was, finally, like being on another world.

Wes stole a glance at the others. Jeri Wilson was keeping her calm. Carrie Woodward expected to be killed at any moment. The prospect didn't seem to frighten her much. Before she allowed herself to be escorted from the cell, she had led the others in prayer, and stared disapprovingly at Wes Dawson when he didn't join in.

Melissa and Gary were gaping: not frightened, but delighted. Plants, birds, animals – and distant objects, after confinement in cells and corridors. Melissa pointed at something above them. It was gone before Wes could see it, but they all stopped to look.

Takpusseh looked back impatiently. 'Come!' They followed hastily. Otherwise the warrior fithp would use their gun butts as prods, not brutally but playfully, as if they were herding children.

A tree grew along the ship's axis, thirty feet tall. One continuous green leaf ran round it in a spiral. Guy wires along its trunk braced it against lateral acceleration.

Something dived at Wes's head. He ducked as the warrior behind him casually brushed the thing aside with his trunk. The thing flapped off shrilling a musical curse. A bird. They were everywhere: long-necked birds with large, colorful aft wings that turned up sharply at the tips, and small canards set to either side of the long neck. Wes gaped in wonder. 'Is this your food source?' he asked.

'Ours and yours.' Takpusseh waved his trunk at a plot of bare dirt. It must have been recently cleared: dust and plant detritus floated in the air around it. The teacher said, 'Now you have plants from your own world to grow here. Space has been set aside.'

John Woodward came forward to the boxes of soil. Gingerly he took a handful and rubbed it in his fingers. 'Good Kansas soil,' he said. 'Maybe we'll live long enough for something to grow.'

'You will live,' Takpusseh said. He peered at the

farmer. 'Do you suffer for your distance from your home? One day you will land with us.'

Woodward didn't answer. His eyes glittered.

'For now you will grow your own food,' Tashayamp said. 'On the level trays, and in those.' She pointed to cages filled with earth. 'Climbing is one thing you may do better than fithp. There is a flower. This.' She held out a flower, bright, shaped like a long, thin trumpet. It was as large as a sunflower, with wild colors. Strange shapes lurked deep within the blossom.

She's learned English fast, Wes thought. *But her posture is – strange. Why? I wish I could reach their body language.*

'We have seeds,' she said. 'You will grow this in soil from your world.'

'What if it won't grow?' John Woodward demanded.

'It will grow. If need, we will mix soil from other world. It will grow.'

'And that's important?' Wes asked.

'It may be,' she said. She glanced at Takpusseh. 'You will begin now.'

'You will also grow to feed you.' Takpusseh took a seed packet from one of the boxes. It was tiny in his ropy digits. He peered at it, tore it open. Some of the seeds spilled. A warrior was prepared: he swept a fine-mesh net through the cloud. Takpusseh himself ignored the incident. 'Farming is different when you float. Seed must be pushed in, so, with small tool . . . no, your digits are small enough. Water comes from below, from wall. Against forward wall, find special tools. Sticks to hold plants against thrust. Tools to stir dirt.'

John and Carrie Woodward were examining the dirt plot. They began taking seeds out of the boxes. John said, 'Plants should grow taller here,' with a question in his voice.

The children moved warily away, their eyes wide with wonder. Something like a bird whizzed past.

'Not there,' Tashayamp called. She motioned the children back to the group. 'You wait here. Do not disturb those —'

Aft, from the grove of spiral-wound trees, came the wind-instrument murmur of fithp voices.

———————

The Herdmaster had climbed a huge pillar plant. Like the humans themselves, in the minuscule gravity he had become a brachiator. He found the viewpoint odd, amusing. He watched.

In a forward corner of the Garden the human prisoners worked. The Herdmaster admired their agility, newly trained dirtyfeet that they were. They seemed docile enough as they planted alien seeds in alien soil. Yet the Breakers' disturbing reports could not be ignored much longer. It was more than enough to make his head ache.

Yet here were smells to ease his mind: plants in bloom, and a melancholy whiff of funereal scent. The end of life for the Traveler Fithp was the funeral pit, and then the Garden. Twelve fithp warriors, wounded on Winterhome, had gone to the funeral pit after Digit Ship *Six* returned them to *Message Bearer*.

The Garden was in perpetual bloom. Seasons mixed here, created by differing intensities of light, warmth, moisture. The alien growths might require alterations in weather. He hoped otherwise. Winterhome would be hospitable to Garden life, if the humans actually persuaded anything to grow here.

The Herdmaster would have preferred to loll in warm mud, but *Message Bearer*'s mudrooms had been drained while her drive guided the Foot toward its fiery fate. He had sought rest in the Garden; and it was here that the Year Zero Fithp confronted him. In the riot of scents he had not smelled their presence. Suddenly faces were looking at

385

him over the edges of leaf-spiral, below him on the trunk of the pillar plant.

He looked back silently, letting them know that they had disturbed his time of quiet.

Born within a few eight-days of each other in an orgy of reproduction that had not been matched before or since, the Year Zero Fithp all looked much alike: smooth of skin, long-limbed and lean. Why not? But age clusters didn't always think so much alike. These were the inner herd that led the larger herd of dissidents.

One was different. He looked older than the rest. His skin was darkened and roughened, one leg was immobilized with braces, and there was a *look*. This one had seen horrors.

With the Advisor's consent, the Herdmaster had chosen to divide the Year Zero Fithp. Half the males had gone down to Winterhome. They were dead, or alive and circling Winterhome after the natives' counterattack. That injured one must be fresh from the wars.

The Herdmaster's claws gripped the trunk as he faced nine fithp below him. For a moment he thought to summon warriors; then a sense of amusement came over him. Dissidents they might be, but these were not rebels. So. They sought to awe the Herdmaster, did they?

And they had brought a hero fresh from the wars. No, these were no rogues. They wanted only to increase their influence . . .

'You have found me,' he said mildly. 'Speak.'

Still they were silent. Two of the smaller humans wandered toward the group, but were retrieved by Tashayamp. Now the humans worked more slowly. They watched, no doubt, though they must be out of earshot. What passed here might affect all the herds of Winterhome. Still it was an imposition, and the Herdmaster would have asked Tashayamp to remove them if he could have spared the attention.

Finally one spoke. 'Advisor Fathisteh-tulk had said that

he would gather with us. He said that he had something to tell us. He did not come. We are told that he has not been seen on the bridge in two days.'

'He has neglected his duties,' Pastempeh-keph said mildly. 'He has avoided the bridge, and his mate, nor does he answer calls. I have alerted my senior officers, but no others. Is it your will that I should ask for his arrest?'

They looked at each other, undecided. One said firmly, 'No, Herdmaster.' He was a massive young fi', posed a bit ahead of the others: Rashinggith, the Defensemaster's son.

'So you do not know where he is either?'

'We had hoped to find him through you, Herdmaster.'

'Ha. I have asked his mate. She has not seen him, yet she has a newborn to show.' The Herdmaster became serious. 'There are matters to decide, and we have no Advisor. What must I do?'

They looked at each other again. 'The teqthuktun —'

'Precisely.' Pastempeh-keph breathed more easily. They still worried about the Law and their religion. Not rogues, not yet. 'I can take no counsel nor make any decisions without advice from the sleepers. It is the teqthuktun, the pact we made with them, and Fistarteh-thuktun insists upon it. Now I have no Advisor, and there are matters to decide. Speak. What must I do?'

'You must find another Advisor,' the wounded one said.

'Indeed.' This hardly required discussion. The Traveler fithp might continue on their predetermined path, but no new decisions could be made without an Advisor.

Fathisteh-tulk might be dead, or too badly injured to perform his duties. He might have shirked his duty, crippling the herd at a critical moment. He might have been kidnapped . . . and if some herd within the Traveler Herd had been pushed to such an act, it would be stripped of its status. But the Advisor would still lose his post, for arousing such anger, for being so careless, for being *gone*.

387

The Herdmaster had already decided on his successor. Still, he must be found. 'You, the injured one —'

'Herdmaster. I am Eight-Squared Leader Chintithpit-mang.'

He had heard that name; but where? Later. 'You must come fresh from the digit ship. Do you know anything of this? Or are you only here to add numbers?'

'I know nothing of the Advisor. What I do know —'

'Later. You, Rashinggith. If you knew where the Advisor might be, you would go there.'

His digits knotted and flexed. 'I assuredly would, Herdmaster.'

'But you might not tell me. Is there a place known only to dissidents? A place where he might commune with other dissidents, or only with himself?'

'No. Herdmaster, we fear for him.'

There must be such a place, but the dissidents themselves would have searched it by now. 'I too fear for Fathisteh-tulk,' the Herdmaster admitted. 'I went so far as to examine records of use of the airlocks, following which I summoned a list of fithp in charge of *guarding* the airlocks —'

'I chance to know that no dissidents guard the airlocks,' Rashinggith said.

An interesting admission. 'I was looking for more than dissidents. Did it strike any of you that what Fathisteh-tulk was doing was dangerous? Consider the position of the sleepers. In herd rank the Advisor is the only sleeper of any real authority. The sleepers could not ask his removal. Yet he consistently opposed the War for Winterhome. How many sleepers are dissidents? I know only of one: Fathisteh-tulk.'

They looked at each other, and the Herdmaster knew at once that other sleepers held dissident views. *Later.* 'There are sleepers in charge of guarding the airlocks. The drive is more powerful than the pull of the Foot's mass. A corpse would drop behind, but would not disintegrate. The drive flame is hot but not dense. Our telescopes have searched for traces of a corpse in our wake.' Pause. 'There is none.'

'Shall we consider murder, then? By dissidents seeking a martyr, or conservative sleepers avoiding future embarrassment? Or did Fathisteh-tulk learn something that some fi' wanted hidden? Or is he alive, hiding somewhere for his own purposes? Rashinggith, what did Fathisteh-tulk plan to tell you?' The Herdmaster looked about him. 'Do any of you know? Did he leave hints? Did he even have interesting questions when last you saw him?'

'We don't *know* he's dead,' Rashinggith said uneasily.

'Enough,' the Herdmaster said. 'We will find him. I hope to ask him where he has been.' That was a half-truth. Fathisteh-tulk would cause minimal embarrassment by being dead. On to other matters. The Herdmaster had remembered a name.

'Chintithpit-mang, you had something to say?'

Nervous but dogged, the injured warrior got his mouth working. 'The prey, the humans, they don't know how to surrender.'

'They can be taught.'

'There was a – a burly one, bigger than most. I whipped his toy weapon from his hand and knocked him down and put my foot on his chest and he clawed at me with his bony digits until I pushed harder. I think I crushed him. Of the prisoners we brought back, only the scarlet-headed exotic would help us select human food! Even after we take their surrender they do not cooperate. Must we teach them to surrender, four billion of them, one at a time? We must abandon the target world. If we kill them all, the stink will make Winterhome like one vast funeral pit!'

Chintithpit-mang was one of six officers under Siplisteph.

Siplisteph was a sleeper; his mate had not survived frozen sleep, and he had not mated since. He had reached Winterhome as eight-cubed leader of the intelligence group. It was an important post, and Siplisteph had risen higher still due to deaths among his superiors. The Herdmaster intended to ask him to become his Advisor, subject to the approval of the females of the sleeper herd – and Fistarteh-thuktun, as keeper of the teqthuktun.

Chintithpit-mang was among those who might have Siplisteph's post.

'Why did you seek me?' the Herdmaster demanded.

The response was unexpected: first one, then others, began a keening wail. The rest joined.

It was the sound made by lost children.

Frightening. Why do I feel the urge to join my voice to theirs?

'We no longer know who we are, Herdmaster,' Chintithpit-mang blurted. 'Why are we here?'

'We bear the thuktunthp.'

'The creatures do not seek the thuktunthp. They have their own way,' Chintithpit-mang insisted.

'If they do not know the thuktunthp, how can they know they do not seek them?' Could this one be worthy of promotion? Are *any?* Shall I ask him to remain? No. Now is not the time to judge him, fresh from battle and still twitching, injured, and plunged suddenly into the scents of blooming Winter Flower and sleeper females in heat. 'Chintithpit-mang, you need time and rest to recover from your experience. Go now. All of you, go.'

For one moment they stood. Then they filed away.

The Herdmaster remained in the Garden, trying to savor its peace.

Chintithpit-mang did not now seem a candidate for high office. Another dissident! yet he had fought well on Winterhome; his record was exemplary. Give him a few days. Meanwhile, interview his mate. Then see if she could pull him together. He didn't remember Shreshleemang well . . . though the mang family was a good line. At a Shipmaster's rank the female *must* be suitable and competent.

Where was Fathisteh-tulk? Murdered or kidnapped. He

had suspected the Year Zero Fithp, but that now seemed unlikely. They were nervous, disturbed, as well they should be; but not nervous enough. They could not have hidden that from him. Who, then, had caused the Herdmaster's Advisor to vanish? How many? Of what leaning? He might face a herd too large to fear the justice of the Traveler Herd; though the secrecy with which they had acted argued against it.

There were herds within herds within the Traveler Herd. It must have been like this on the Homeworld too, though in greater, deeper, more fantastical variety. Even here: sleepers, spaceborn, dissidents; Fistarteh-thuktun's core of tradition-minded historians, the Breakers' group driving themselves mad while trying to think like alien beings: the Herdmaster must balance them like a pyramid of smooth rocks in varying thrust.

'He is late,' Dmitri whispered. 'We must go.'

'Not yet. We will wait for him,' Arvid Rogachev said.

'But —'

'We will wait.'

Dmitri shrugged.

He obeys me because he has no choice, yet he considers himself my superior. Perhaps he is. He is a better strategist.

There was a rustle behind them, and Nikolai's legless form appeared from a lateral shaft. He fell to the corridor between them, catching himself with his arms just before he struck the deck. Once more Arvid marveled at how agile a legless man could be in low gravity.

'Where have you been?' Dmitri demanded.

Nikolai ignored him and turned to Arvid. 'Comrade Commander, I have success,' he said.

'Come.' Arvid led the way out of the air shaft. They took their time about attaching the grill covers. Arvid worked in silence. Although he didn't feel especially tired, he thought of how exhausted he was, and presently he felt it. *Be wary. Do not let them know our true strength. Dmitri says this. I am beginning to think like KGB now. Is this good?*

'I have seen women,' Nikolai said in an undertone.

'Ah,' Dmitri said.

Arvid felt a twinge. *Women! I have been long in space* – 'Where?'

'In the center of the ship, in a garden area, Comrade Commander. They were with the American, Dawson.'

Dawson! How has he deserved this —

'The newly arrived warriors,' Dmitri said. 'They came with those. New prisoners from Earth. Were they Russian?'

'No, Comrade Colonel. They were by their dress American. There were children also. Three women, two children, a man, and Dawson. I could not know what they were saying.'

Nikolai lifted the heavy grill. *Crippled*, Arvid thought. *He has more strength in his arms than I have in my legs.*

'Tell us,' Dmitri said.

'As you ordered, I explored farther than ever before. At first I took each turn that presented itself. There are grills everywhere. There are radial ducts. Some ducts are too small even for me, but' – Nikolai stretched his arms above his head, exhaled completely, and grinned – 'I can make myself narrow.'

'The fore end of *Thuktun Flishithy* is too far. We expect to find the bridge there, but I made no try to reach it. I saw a big room full of sleeping fithp, all females, sleeping with all four feet gripping the wall rugs, like gigantic fleas. I saw a slaughterhouse or a kitchen. Fithp were cutting up plants and animal parts and – and arranging them, but there was nothing like a stove.

'I tired of this and went inward along radial ducts. I found the room of the Podo Thuktun, and the priest all alone at the television screen. He muttered to himself; too

392

low to understand. I found the greenhouse region. It is lighted. It was there that I saw Dawson and the newcomers. They were all at work planting things. The garden is at the center of the ship. There were many fithp.

'I saw no need to watch Dawson longer, and I had little time, so I continued aft. I found what may be a bridge aft of the greenhouse. No ducts run aft of that point. It may be an engine room, serving the main drive, but it is also an emergency bridge.'

'Da,' Dmitri said. 'At the axis it would be quite safe, like the Podo Thuktun. So?'

'The room is circled by television screens, square and thick, with the same proportions as the Podo Thuktun. I saw our prison, empty, of course. I saw Dawson and one of the newcomers, a red-haired woman, working in the garden. They worked together, but they ignored each other. I saw you, Comrade Rogachev. Heh-heh-heh. Very industrious you looked.'

'Go on,' Arvid said.

'There was much on those screens. One showed three of the fithp watching a viewscreen. On the screen they were watching, were scenes of a man and a woman – Comrades, the man had an enormous pecker, and she *swallowed* it, all of it.'

'What is this?' Dmitri asked sharply.

'I have told you what I saw,' Nikolai said. 'On one viewscreen were three fithp who watched a viewscreen. On that viewscreen was that scene, and others like it.'

'What else did the woman do?' Arvid asked.

'Nonsense,' Dmitri hissed. 'What did the fithp do when they saw this?'

'Comrade Colonel, they must have found it interesting, because they rewound the tape and watched it again. Then they spoke among themselves, and spoke into communications equipment.'

'So,' Dmitri said to himself.

'What?' Arvid demanded.

'I do not know why, but I find it disturbing,' Dmitri said. 'Did you see who they spoke with?'

'No. Soon that screen was blank. I waited, but there was no more. Then when I was ready to leave, I saw two views of the main control room, and there is a window, so it must be at the fore end. I knew there must be other screens, so I circled through the ducts for another view.' Nikolai's voice had dropped until he was nearly whispering. Dmitri and Arvid crowded close. They pretended to have difficulty replacing the fastenings for the grill.

'I saw outside. Four screens in a row. Three look at the stars, and the views move back and forth. So does the fourth, but it looks out on black rock. At one end of its swing the screen looks along the hull of *Thuktun Flishithy*. The fore end is right up against the rock.

'Do you remember the films they showed us? *Thuktun Flishithy* leaving that other star? The nose was up against a kind of ball, pushing it. Now it is against black rock that has been carved like the kind of sculpture the Americans in New York are so fond of, twisted shapes that tell nothing.'

Arvid said, 'So they have an asteroid base.'

'But they are pushing it,' Dmitri said. 'Can't you feel it?'

The hum of the drive: he had learned to ignore it, but it was there. 'Pushing it, yes. Where? I cannot think we will like the answer. So, Nikolai, you saw along the hull. Was it smooth, or was there detail?'

'I was lucky. One of the star-views turned to look sideways at an oval hatch. It opened while I watched, and a big metal snake uncoiled. Then the view shifted, and it was a view from the head of the snake, looking at another metal snake as it coiled itself into its own hatch. Then it turned and looked back along the hull. I saw quite a lot before it turned again and looked at nothing but stars. Aft of the ship is a violet-white haze. Ships are mounted along the rim, big ships, but there were many empty mountings.'

'Empty. Good,' Dmitri said. 'Perhaps ships we have destroyed.'

'And perhaps ships that remain to attack our world,' Arvid said. 'You have done well, Nikolai.'

Women! It has been long. . . .

CHAPTER TWENTY-SIX
CONFRONTATION

For we know that the law is spiritual: but I am carnal, sold under sin.

For that which I do I allow not: for what I would, that do I not; but what I hate, that do I.

If then I do that which I would not, I consent unto the law that *it* is good. . . .

For the good that I would I do not: but the evil that I would not, that I do.

– ST. PAUL, EPISTLE TO THE ROMANS 7:14–19

COUNTDOWN: H PLUS SIX WEEKS

The Herdmaster paused at the door. More problems awaited him inside. *At least I will no longer have the strange views of Fathisteh-tulk to confound me.* One of the guards moved to open the door.

Where can he be? He must be dead. A secret corpse, and a key to more terrible secrets. 'Thiparteth-fuft!'

'Lead me, Herdmaster.'

'Have the funeral pits searched. I am certain that the Advisor is dead, and I wish to know how he died.'

'At once.'

Dead or not, I had no choice. Pastempeh-keph trampled conflicting feelings deep into the muddy substrate of his mind. *The Traveler Herd must continue, and without an Advisor no decisions are possible. A replacement was needed. I have found one. Why am I so disturbed?*

Siplisteph is a good choice. He has been to Winterhome. He commanded spaceborn, and they accepted his leadership. The sleeper females acclaimed him even though he is not mated. Now he must mate – Pastempeh-keph thought of eligible females. *There are so few. Would the sleepers accept a spaceborn mate for the Advisor? That would go far toward uniting the Traveler Herd.*

The door opened. Pastempeh-keph moved decisively into the theater. He need not have bothered to compose himself. Siplisteph, Raztupisp-minz, and Fistarteh-thuktun were shoulder to shoulder before the projection wall. They did not look up.

Thiparteth-fuft lifted his snnfp to bellow for attention, but the Herdmaster laid his digits across the guard officer's forehead. 'There is no need. Come, let us see what so fascinates them.'

The equipment had come from Winterhome; the only fithp equipment was a makeshift transformer to mate the human recording machines to *Message Bearer*'s current.

The Herdmaster stood behind them. The forward and inward walls were a smooth white curve, a screen that would serve under thrust or spin. Advisor, breaker, and priest were in agitated argument. Their waving digits made shadows on the forward wall, where two humans similarly waved their arms and bellowed, trumpeted, a sound no fi' could have matched. To fithp ears it seemed a song of rage and distress. Their clothes were thick, layered, a padding against cold. The male waved something small and sharp that glittered.

' "At last my digits are whole again," ' Raztupisp-minz translated.

'Meaning?' the Herdmaster asked.

The three fithp turned quickly. 'Your pardon,' the Breaker said. 'I did not hear you enter.'

'No matter. I ask again, what was the meaning of what the human said?'

'None. He was not crippled.' Raztupisp-minz turned back to the screen.

The Herdmaster waited. The humans on the screen huddled, conspired, all in that ear-splitting keening voice. 'Have you ever heard them speak like that?' the Herdmaster demanded.

'Once. Nikolai, the legless one, spoke like that at length once, but far more softly. They call it "singing." '

'What are they building?'

Breaker-One Raztupisp-minz only folded his digits across his scalp.

'The other recordings,' Raztupisp-minz demanded. 'Siplisteph, you have brought others.'

Siplisteph only needed a moment to change tapes.

The four humans looked soft and vulnerable without their clothing. Two patches of fur apiece only pointed up their nakedness. Alien music played eerily across fithp nerves. 'Mating,' said Breaker-One. 'Odd. I had the idea they sought privacy when they did that. Herdmaster, that isn't the female's genital area at all!'

'But that is the male's.'

'Oh, yes. I've never seen it in that state . . . but of course they usually cover themselves. Does it seem to you that she might harm him accidentally?'

The priest spoke. 'Why would they record this? Advisor, where was this found?'

'All tapes came from two sources, a building that displayed 83 of such, and one room of a dwelling. They're marked. Ah, this came from the dwelling.'

The scene had shifted. Here was the same female and a different male, both covered. Not for long. Raztupisp-minz said, 'I don't see how children could be born of this. yet they seem to *think* they're mating . . . Ah, that seems more likely. Could we be viewing an instruction tape? Might humans need instruction on how to mate?'

'A ridiculous suggestion,' the priest scoffed. 'What animal does not know how to mate?'

'Entertainment,' Siplisteph said. 'So I was told by one who surrendered.'

'You are certain?' Breaker-one asked.

'No. I know too little of their language.'

Fistarteh-thuktun continued to stare at the screen. 'I . . . I think there can be no good reason for such an entertainment.'

The Herdmaster moved forward to join Siplisteph. It was irritating that his Advisor must here perform two functions at once. 'You have been to Winterhome. You have seen thousands of humans, more than any of us. Have you formed opinions?'

'None. Nowhere in these tapes do humans act as I have seen them act. I wonder if they act the part of something other than humans. Not Predecessors, but . . . there are words, *god* and *archetype*.'

'They could hardly *pretend* to be ready to mate. Show me the first one again,' the Herdmaster said. And presently he asked, 'Did we just witness a killing? Show that segment again.'

Siplisteph did. An arm swung; the man in the strange chair mimed agony; the chair tilted and the man fell backward through the floor. 'They never die so calmly,' the new Advisor said. 'They fight until they cannot.'

'The neck is very vulnerable,' Raztupisp-minz objected. 'A nerve trunk could be cut – but the fat one would then be a rogue. Why does the female associate with him? Could a pair of rogues form their own herd?'

'You are quiet, Fistarteh-thuktun. What do you believe of this?'

The priest splayed his digits wide. 'Herdmaster, I learn. Later I will speak.'

'You do not seem pleased.'

There was no answer.

'A place of puzzles,' Pastempeh-keph said. 'They surrender and have not surrendered. Their tapes show rogues acting in collusion. They live neither in herds nor alone. What are they?'

'What do they believe themselves to be?' Fistarteh-thuktun asked. 'Perhaps that is more important.'

'An interesting question,' Raztupisp-minz said quietly.

Pastempeh-keph bellowed, 'I want answers! I have enough interesting questions to keep me busy, thank you very much. Raztupisp-minz, bring them all. All humans, here, now.'

'Herdmaster, is this wise? Bring just one. I want to keep them separate as we study —'

'Bring them!'

'At your orders, Herdmaster.'

Raztupisp-minz waited. *This is the moment, if there is to be any challenge.*

There was none. Raztupisp-minz turned to the communications speaker on one wall.

———

Gary and Melissa were bounding around the cell in an elaborate game of tag. The rules weren't apparent, but it was obvious that the game couldn't have been played in normal gravity.

Jeri Wilson lay against the 'down' wall and hugged her knees. She was wishing that the children would stop, and glad that they didn't. They were all right. Prisoners of monsters, far from home, falling endlessly: they were taking it well.

Stop feeling so damned sorry for yourself! Hell, if Gary can take it, you sure can. Next you'll be whimpering. Jeri turned her head within her arms. *No. We don't want Melissa to hear that.*

John Woodward lay near by. *He's trying, but it's like he's fading out. Carrie's all that keeps him going.*

It's the toilets. I could stand anything, if they'd just give us a decent toilet. We're not built to use a stupid pool of water, with everyone watching.

She heard the low-pitched hum that signaled the door was opening. By the time it was open, the tag game was over; by tacit agreement they were all together opposite the doorway.

Jeri recognized Tashayamp. Behind her was a full octuple of warriors, all armed. *They don't bring guards unless they're taking us somewhere,* Jeri thought. *But they don't always bring them then, either. We've gone places with no one but Tashayamp or one of the other teachers. So why do they sometimes have armed guards? It's like Melissa's tag game. There are rules. I just don't know them.*

'All come,' Tashayamp directed in the fithp tongue.

'Where?' Wes Dawson demanded.

'Come.' Tashayamp turned to lead the way out.

'Right,' Jeri said. She uncurled, and dove across the pen. 'Come on, Melissa.'

The others followed, with Dawson bringing up the rear. Tashayamp led them through corridors toward the center of the ship.

They entered a large, nearly rectangular room, with huge steps around three sides. Machinery had been set up near the fourth wall. Four fithp watched them without comment.

Tashayamp followed them in. The eight fithp soldiers stayed in the corridor. Dawson moved up beside Jeri and said, 'Theater. We've been here.'

'No seats,' Jeri said, then laughed at a mental picture of a fi' collapsing a beach chair. 'Of course, no seats. What's . . . ah. That videotape machine must have come from Kansas.'

'The one in the fancy harness, he's a priest or librarian or both. The one at the top of the stairs is the big boss. They call him the Herdmaster, something like that.' Dawson imitated the fithp sound. 'The other two are teachers. At least I call them that, they're supposed to teach us, but they don't always, so I'm not sure. Every time I think I understand them, something else happens, and —'

The door opened again, to let in three men in coveralls. One had no legs, but it didn't seem to bother him.

Russians. That stocky one was on TV before the snouts came. I thought he was handsome —

'Arvid Rogachev, Dmitri something or another, and the one with no legs is Nikolai. I never heard them call him anything else,' Dawson said.

Rogachev. He looks even better in person. Wes Dawson is a bit of a wimp compared to him.

And what does that mean? Am I looking for a big strong man to take care of me?

Would that be such a bad idea?

'You will watch,' Tashayamp said. She bellowed something in fithp.

The screen lit up. Jeri caught a glimpse of the lead-in.

DEEP THROAT

'What is this?' Jeri asked.

Carrie Woodward had a puzzled look. 'John, didn't we hear something about that movie?'

The Russian Dawson had called Dmitri frowned. The other one seemed amused. 'For this they have taken casualties?'

The screen raced past the titles to the sex scenes. Then it slowed to show Linda Lovelace doing her stuff in living color.

Carrie Woodward watched just long enough to be sure of what she was seeing. 'Gary! Melissa! Come here. You're not to watch this. Come —'

Gary Capehart went to her at once. Melissa looked doubtful.

'You come here, young lady. Now.' Carrie was insistent. Melissa looked to her mother for guidance.

O Lord. Now what? 'Melissa, do as she says.'

'Aw, Mom —'

'Now.'

Carrie gathered the children to her ample bosom. 'How

dare you?' she shouted. 'Don't you critters have any sense of decency at all? No shame?'

The Herdmaster trumpeted something. Tashayamp replied.

Now what kind of trouble has she got us into?

'What is your difficulty?' Tashayamp demanded. 'Why have you done this?'

'You know perfectly well it's not decent to show pictures like that.'

'Mrs. Woodward,' Dawson said. 'They don't think the way we do —'

'And of course you've seen worse,' Carrie said. She faced away from the screens, away from the Herdmaster. That left her facing the Russians. 'I leave it to you, is this decent for children?' she demanded of them.

'Not at all,' Arvid agreed. Dmitri said something harsh in Russian.

'Bad – worse,' Tashayamp said. 'What does it mean, 'bad'? Why is this bad?'

'I think they really don't know, Mother,' John Woodward said. His voice held wonder. 'They really don't.'

'I was trying to tell you,' Dawson said.

'You keep out of it. You don't know either,' John Woodward said. 'Your kind never did.'

All of the snouts were talking at once until the Herdmaster trumpeted. They fell silent instantly.

'I keep telling you they don't see things as we do,' Dawson said. His voice rang loudly in the silence. 'John, *they didn't make these movies.* They found them in Kansas. Remember that.' John Woodward interrupted him, then Carrie started to say something —

One of the teachers trumpeted.

'Raztupisp-minz commands that you speak one at a time,' Tashayamp said.

'There are many meanings of good and bad,' Dawson began. The teacher said something else.

'Not to begin with you,' Tashayamp said. She pointed to the Russians. 'What is bad about this?'

'Filth. Typical capitalist garbage for the mind,' Dmitri said. 'Why does this surprise anyone? The capitalist system caters to anyone with money, and inevitably produces decadence.'

'It's freedom of speech!' Dawson shouted. 'I don't like it, but I don't have to. If we start shutting people's mouths, where —'

'Not *we*,' Carrie Woodward said. 'We'd lock up the people that peddle that filth if it wasn't for you federal people. We had a nice, decent town until your judges and your laws came.'

The two teachers were both speaking at once until the Herdmaster intervened. Tashayamp spoke at length, obviously translating since she used several human words. *What can they make of this? What do I make of it?* Jeri wondered.

'You believe this bad,' Tashayamp said. 'You, all show digits extended if you believe bad.'

The Woodwards showed palms up held at arm's length. Then the Russians. Jeri held her hand out. *What do I believe? I don't really want Melissa watching this stuff. She might get the wrong idea about what men and women are supposed to do. Women aren't toys. Free speech and all that, but, yes, I guess I'd be happier if they still had laws against pornography. Less ammunition for perverts . . .*

Dawson was the only holdout. Finally he raised his own hand.

'You agree this is bad?' Tashayamp asked.

'I do, for children,' Dawson said. 'I just don't think we have the right to stop it.'

'Why bad for children?'

'It's filth,' Carrie Woodward protested. 'Not fit for anyone.'

'You do not – do these things?' Tashayamp asked.

Jeri smothered a laugh. Carrie Woodward's face turned

404

beet red. 'My Lord, no, we don't do that, no one really does that.'

Well, in your world, maybe. My turn to blush . . .

'This is true? No one does these things?'

'Some do,' John Woodward admitted. 'Decent people don't. They sure don't put it on film!'

'The word. Decent. Means what?' Tashayamp demanded.

'Means right-thinking people,' Carrie Woodward said. 'People who think and act like they're supposed to, not like some people I know.'

Tashayamp translated. There was more discussion among the fithp.

'We've got to be careful,' Wes Dawson said. 'Lord knows what ideas they're getting —'

'None they shouldn't have, Congressman,' Carrie Woodward said firmly.

'They *don't* think like us. You've seen the toilets, haven't you? Look, we all have to give them the same story,' Dawson insisted.

'Say little,' Dmitri said in Russian. Jeri was surprised that she could still understand. *It has been a long time . . .*

Evidently Dawson had understood that, too. 'Right. Best they don't find out too much.'

Find out what? That we don't act the way we want to? That's the very definition of human —

'You explain this,' Tashayamp demanded. 'How many humans do bad things?'

'All of them,' Jeri blurted.

'Capitalists,' Dmitri said.

'Commies,' Woodward retorted.

'All humans do bad things?' Tashayamp demanded. 'All do what they know they must not do? Tell me this.'

They all began speaking at once.

Jeri sat against the wall with Melissa. She wasn't really part of the discussion Wes Dawson was having with the Russians, but she was too close to ignore it.

'Perhaps we have told them too much,' Dmitri said.

Dawson said, 'It's better if they understand us —'

'What you call understanding a military man would call intelligence information,' Arvid Rogachev said.

'What can it hurt? Arvid, you've been helping them with their maps!'

'They show me maps and globes. I nod my head, and tell them names for places. This is not your concern.'

'It's my concern if you side with the fithp. Look, Arvid, you've seen what they've done. Destruction and murder —'

'I understand war. I —'

'But do you understand what they could have done? They came here with a mucking great asteroid, and we're still moored to it. Suppose they'd come with the same size asteroid, but a metal one. Hundreds of billions of dollars worth of metals. Now they negotiate. Trade metals for land, for concessions, for information, anything they want. They could *buy* themselves a country. If we won't play, even if we buy the metals and don't pay their bills, they've still got their mucking great asteroid to drop!'

Dmitri Grushin was nodding, grinning. 'What a pity. They don't understand money. They are not capitalists. That's your complaint, Dawson.'

And who cares? They're going to smash the Earth. At least they decided they wouldn't make the children watch Deep Throat *and those other tapes.* Jeri recalled going to a theatre to see *Deep Throat.* Stupid. But they've put us all together, and now there are three more men to watch me use the toilet.

John and Carrie Woodward stayed near Jeri, as far from the Russians as possible, but it wasn't far enough. They could still hear. They kept Gary with them.

They've got a problem. But we're going to have to get along with the Russkis — Jeri said, 'Carrie, did you notice that you and John sounded a lot like the Russians?'

406

'Yeah,' John Woodward said. 'I noticed. They're for decency. Not like Dawson. He'd excuse anything —'

'No, he wouldn't.'

'There are things people can do and things they can't do,' Carrie Woodward said. 'Isn't that what insanity means? Can't tell right from wrong?'

'No.' Alice was across the room, far enough away that they'd nearly forgotten her. 'It wasn't why I was in Menninger's.'

'Why were you there?'

'None of your business. I was afraid all the time.'

'Of what?' Carrie Woodward asked.

Alice looked away.

Dawson looked over at them. The Woodwards wouldn't meet his eyes. Carrie continued to talk to Jeri as if Dawson were not there.

'Don't tell me you never wanted to be better than you are,' Carrie Woodward said. 'Everyone wants to be better than they are. It's what it means to be human.'

'Maybe you're right,' Jeri said. 'We don't do the things we think we should, and we do things we're ashamed of - what was it, in the *Book of Common Prayer?* "We have done those things we ought not to have done, and we have left undone those things we ought to have done, and there is no health in us." People have wanted to do the right thing for most of history.'

'But nobody really knows what right and wrong are,' Dawson protested.

'Sure they do,' Jeri said. 'C. S. Lewis saw that well enough. Most of us know what's the right thing, at least most of the time. The problem is we don't do it. That's how we're different from rocks. They don't have any choice about obeying the laws. They do what they have to do. We do what we want. We sound like an undergraduate bull session.'

'Perhaps this is true,' Arvid said. 'But we would not say laws, but —'

'Moral principle,' Dmitri said firmly. 'Established by Marxist science.'

'Commies don't have morals,' Carrie Woodward protested.

'This is unfair. It is also not true,' Arvid said. 'Come, we do not so much disagree, you and I. It is your leader, your congressman who protests.'

Carrie looked to her husband. They didn't say anything.

———————

An hour later they were summoned to the theater again. This time the fithp stood in formal arrays. Herdmaster and mate at the top, others on steps below him, most with mates. Tashayamp stood near him. She trumpeted for silence.

The Herdmaster spoke at length.

Finally Tashayamp translated. 'You are a race of rogues. You say you wish to live by your laws, but you do not do it. You say you have always wanted to live by your rules and you do not. Now you will. You will become part of Traveler Herd, live as fithp live, but under your rules. This we will give you. This we promise.

'You will teach us your laws. Then you will live by them.

'You go now.'

CHAPTER TWENTY-SEVEN
THE PHONY WAR

'Let us remember,' Lord Tweedsmuir had told a wartime audience in a ringing phrase, 'that in this fight we are God's chivalry.'

The British people, far from remembering they were God's chivalry, began to show such a detachment from what was variously called the Bore or the Phoney War that the government became seriously worried.

– LAURENCE THOMSON, *1940*

COUNTDOWN: ONE WEEK TO FOOTFALL THREE WEEKS AFTER THE JAYHAWK WARS

High fleecy clouds hung over the San Fernando Valley. The temperature stretched toward a hundred degrees, with a hot wind sweeping down to shrivel any vegetation not protected from it.

Ken Dutton carefully closed the door to his greenhouse. Once inside he dipped water from a bucket and threw it around, wetting down the lush growth. Then he hastened outside to turn the handle on the makeshift fan, drawing fresh hot dry air through the greenhouse.

When that was done, he went inside. The house had thick walls and cooled rapidly at night, so that it was tolerable in the daytime. Dutton lifted the phone and listened.

There was a dial tone. There often was. He took a list from the telephone drawer and began to make his calls.

* * *

'I'm still the chef,' he told Cora Donaldson, 'but I can use some help. Can you get here around noon? Bring whatever you can find in the way of food, and tell me what I can count on *now*'

'Rice.'

'Rice.' He made a note. 'How much rice?'

'Lots. I mean really a lot.' She giggled. 'Only good thing about this war, I'm losing weight, because I'm getting sick of rice – hey, I look good. You'll like the new me.'

'Great. Okay, then. Bye.' He inspected his list and dialed again.

There was no beef in the land, Sarge Harris complained. 'Cattle cars are too big. Snouts blast 'em, think they've got tanks or weapons in them.'

Probably not. The major says they're not doing that just now. But no point in arguing. 'Yeah. Chicken costs an arm and a leg, too.'

'Maybe that's how chicken farmers get red meat,' Sarge said.

'Heh-heh. Sure. Look, what can you bring?'

'Eggs. Traded some carpentry work for them.'

'Good. Bring 'em.' Ken hit the cutoff button and dialed another number.

Pasty Clevenger admitted to being one of the lucky ones. An occasional backpacker, she'd stored considerable freeze-dried food in sealed bags; but the steady diet was driving her nuts. She jumped at his offer. Sure, she could bring a freeze-dried dessert, and flavored coffee mix, and pick up Anthony Graves, who was seventy and couldn't drive anymore. Ken shifted the receiver to his other ear.

The Copeleys lived at the northern end of the San Fernando Valley. They could get fresh corn and tomatoes, and almonds, and oranges. Could they bring a pair of relatives? Because the relatives had gas. Hell, yes!

He tried Marty Carnell, just on the off chance. The

410

meteor-chewed highways had probably stranded him somewhere on a dog-show circuit —

But Marty answered.

'I've done this once before, and it worked out,' Ken told him. 'It isn't that everyone's starving. Things haven't got *that* bad. But anyone's likely to have a ton of something and none of everything else, and the way to make it work is to get all the food together and make a feast.'

'Sounds good.'

'Okay. Get here around noon —'

'For *dinner*?'

'Stone soup takes time, and I want sunlight for the mirror. I'd guess we'll be eating all day and night. Come hungry. Have you got meat?'

'I found a meat source early on. I can keep the dogs fed till I run out of money, but it's horsemeat, Ken. I've been eating it myself —'

'Bring it. Can you bring five pounds? Four will do it, and you won't recognize it when I get through, Marty. I've got a great chili recipe. Lots of vegetables.'

The Offutts would have to come by bicycle. Chad Offutt sounded hungry. With no transportation, how the hell were they to get food? How about some bottles of liquor in the saddlebags? Ken agreed, for charity's sake. Damn near anyone had liquor; what was needed was food.

Ken hung up.

He caught himself humming while he lugged huge pots out into the backyard and set them up around the solar mirror. It seemed almost indecent to be enjoying himself when civilization was falling about his ears. But it did feel good to finally find a use for his hobbies!

The Copeleys had brought everything they'd promised, and yellow chilis too. The pair of guests were a cousin's daughter and her husband – Halliday and Wilson; she'd kept her maiden name – both much younger than the others, and a little uncomfortable. They seemed eager to

411

help. Ken put them to cutting up the Copeleys' vegetables.

'Save all seeds.'

'Right.'

The lost weight looked nice on Cora Donaldson. She chatted while she helped him carry dishes. Things were bad throughout the Los Angeles Basin . . . yeah, Ken had to agree. Cora had tried to get to Phoenix, but her mother kept putting her off, she wouldn't have room until her brother moved out . . . and then it was too late, the roads had been chewed by the snouts' meteors. Yeah, Ken had tried to get out too.

He should have asked someone to bring dishwashing soap! Someone must have an excess of that.

Marty was cutting horsemeat into strips. 'Could be a lot worse,' he said. 'We could be dodging meteors. I can't figure out what the snouts think they're *doing*.'

'They think they're conquering the Earth,' Ken said. 'It's their methods that're funny. They're thorough enough. I haven't heard of a dam still standing. Have you?'

'No big ones. No big bridges either.'

'But they don't touch cities.' Could be worse. He might have fled with no destination in mind. Still, it was hard times. Food got in, but not a lot, and not a balanced diet. There would have been no fruit source here without the Copeleys' oranges and the lemon tree in Graves' backyard.

Reflected sunlight blazed underneath Ken's largest pot. The water was beginning to boil. He ladled a measured amount into the chili pot, then moved it into the focus.

He'd built the solar mirror while he was still married, and after the first month he'd almost never used it. They'd gone vegetarian for a few months too, and his wife hadn't taken the cookbooks with her. He had the recipes, he had the skills to build a balanced meal, and the phones worked sometimes. If the snouts shot those down, he might try to form a commune. His next-door neighbor had fled to the mountains, leaving the keys behind. More important, he'd left a full swimming pool. Covered, to prevent evaporation, the water would last until the fall rains, and the goldfish would keep the mosquitoes down.

Then there was the golf course across the street. The President asked everyone to grow food, especially to put up greenhouses. There wasn't any water for the golf course, but there were flat areas, good places for tents if the commune got big enough.

When the aliens had blasted Kosmograd, everything had turned serious. So had Kenneth Dutton. Two years before he'd *studied* greenhouses; but in one two-day spree he'd *built* one, from plastic and glass and wood and hard work, and goddam had he been proud of himelf. It worked! Things grew! You could eat them! He'd built two more before he'd even started the Stone Soup Parties, just because he *could*.

Past two o'clock, and the Offutts weren't here yet. Not surprising, if they were on bicycles, especially if malnutrition was getting to them. Sarge Harris hadn't arrived either. Lateness was less a discourtesy than a cause for worry: had dish-shaped craters begun to sprout in city roads? The snouts had been gone for three weeks, but when might they return? And with what?

Patsy Clevenger arrived with Anthony Graves. Graves was short and round and in fair health for a man pushing seventy. He had been a scriptwriter for television. He brought treasure: lemons from his backyard and a canned ham. They settled him in a beach chair from which he could watch the proceedings like a benevolent uncle.

Ken pulled the kettle to the side, where sunlight spilling from the mirror would keep the chili simmering. 'An hour,' he announced to nobody in particular. He dumped rice into another pot, added water, and set it in the focus. Fistfuls of vegetables went into the water pot. Cook them next. Chop up vegetables, boil or steam them, add mayonnaise and a chopped apple if you had it. Leave out a few vegetables, fiddle with the proportions, forget some of the

413

spices, as long as you didn't put in broccoli it was still Russian salad if you could get mayonnaise. *Where* was Sarge Harris?

Sarge didn't arrive until four. 'I got a late start, and then there was a godawful line for gas, and then I tried three markets for potatoes, but there weren't any.' At least he had the eggs. Ken set Cora to making them into mayonnaise.

The sun was getting too low for cooking. Mayonnaise didn't need heat. Coffee did. Better start water warming now. Sometimes there was no gas. Patsy's flavored coffee could be drunk 'iced': room temperature, given the lack of ice.

The chili was gone, and a vegetable curry was disappearing, and the Copeleys' young relatives were just keeping up with the demand for lemonade. There was breathing space for Ken to find conversations; but he tended to drift when his guests started talking about how terrible things were. By and large, they seemed cheerful enough. It felt like Cora might stay the night, and that would be nice, since it felt like Patsy would not.

Tarzana didn't have electricity. Ken Dutton and his guests stayed outdoors. Light came from the bellies of the clouds, reflected from wherever the Los Angeles and San Fernando Valleys still had electricity. Occasionally a guest would go inside, feeling his way through the darkness toward the flickering light from the bathroom. At the next Stone Soup Party there would probably be no candles at all.

He'd boiled a few eggs to decorate the Russian salad. That looked like it would hold up until the party was over.

Some of the guests were cleaning out the pots. It had been settled without much discussion: better to get most of the cleaning done before Ken served coffee. The suspicion existed that anyone who conspicuously shirked cleanup

414

duties might not be invited back. For some it was true.

Sarge poured a torrent of dirty water into a patio drain. 'At least we kicked them out of Kansas,' he said.

Graves, who had seemed half asleep in his beach chair, said, 'Did we? I'm told they spent much of their efforts raiding libraries and collecting . . . well, memorabilia, items that might tell them something of our nature.'

'Sure. Wouldn't you?'

'It was a reconnoitering expedition. In a way, it reminds me of the Phony War.'

'The what?'

The old man laughed. 'I don't blame you. Nineteen thirty-nine to summer of 1940. Germany and France were officially at war, you see. But nothing was happening. They stared at each other across the Maginot Line, between two lines of trenches, and did nothing. The papers called it the Phony War. I expect they didn't like not having a story. For the rest of us, it was a calm and nervous time.'

'Like now. Nothing happening.'

'Precisely. Then the Nazis came rolling across and took France, and nobody said Phony War any more.'

Patsy followed through. 'Suddenly they'll bomb all the cities at once?'

'They might give us a chance to surrender first. The trouble is, they've never answered any of our broadcasts. This may *be* that chance, by their lights, and we're obliged to work out how to surrender. Well, how?'

'If we spend all our time thinking about how to surrender, then they've got us beaten,' Patsy said heatedly. 'I'd rather be trying to flatten them. Even if we lose a few cities.'

Ken nodded, though the thought brought a chill. Los Angeles? Behind him Marty said, 'Ken, could I have a word with you?'

They stepped inside, found chairs by feel. It was too dark to read expressions. Faint sounds from somewhere in the house might indicate that a couple had felt their way to a couch or a bedroom. Life goes on.

Marty asked, 'Were you serious about getting out?'

'Sure, Marty, but there are problems. I don't own a piece of the Enclave.'

'Yeah. Well, I do, as long as the law holds up. Heh. After the law stops mattering is when a man *needs* something like the Enclave, and I'm short in my dues.'

'Well, they might —'

'No, what I was thinking was John Fox. He's in – this isn't to get around – he's in Shoshone, just outside of Death Valley, camping out till this is all over. He knows what he's doing, Ken.'

'I never knew you were much of a camper.'

'No. But Fox is, and he might be glad to see us if we showed up with food. Would you like to go with me?'

Ken glanced through the picture window, automatically, before he answered. No fights going, nobody looked particularly unhappy; the Russian salad hadn't disappeared yet, though Bess Church's wheel of Cheddar cheese had gone like snow in a furnace. The host wasn't needed: good. He said, 'Food and camp gear, sure. I don't have camp gear, and I bet it's in short supply. Anyway, suppose John *isn't* glad to see us? No way we could phone ahead.'

'Shoshone's still a good bet! Why in God's name would even snouts bomb Shoshone? And John doesn't own those caves. We camp out nearby —'

'No.'

'Then *where*?'

'I mean no, I'm not leaving.' Ken Dutton had made his decision before he understood the reasons. Now they were coming to him, in the sight and sounds of his crowded and happy territory. 'Maybe I'm crazy. I'm going to stick it out here.'

'Yup, you're crazy. Thanks for dinner.'

Marty'd go, Ken realized. He hadn't done any of the cleaning up. He wasn't planning to come back.

416

Jenny woke to a tingling in her left arm, the one that had been under Jack. When she opened her eyes, she saw his.

'Hello, sailor. New in town?'

He grinned. 'I like watching you.'

She extracted her arm to look at her watch. 'Time we got to work.'

'We still have an hour.' He moved closer to her. 'Not that I can —'

'It's all right. But I can't sleep.'

'So?'

She sat up. 'Let's watch the weirdos. We've got pickups in the Snout Room.'

'Sounds good.'

He stayed in bed, with the sheet over him. *Fastidious.* Likes to see me nekkid, but not to be seen: I'd say it was cowardice, but how can you say that about a guy who'll put his ass in front of a bullet for the President? Maybe his scars are classified . . .

'Is this legal?' Jack asked.

'Sure. I'm Intelligence. I can do anything!'

'Yeh, as long as they don't replace the Supreme Court. Jenny, we've got to obey the rules, because we can get away with *not* obeying them.'

'It's all right. The writers know they're being watched. And Harpanet's a prisoner. No rights. Satisfied?'

'Yeah —'

'And there's nothing else to watch on my TV, I guarantee you that.' She switched on the set.

The picture swam into focus. An empty box of a room: no rugs, no furniture, no occupants; nothing but a movie screen and projector, and a broad doorway with edges of freshly cut concrete. 'Wrong room,' she said, and fiddled again. 'We've already assigned three rooms in the complex, and God knows what they'll think they need next. Here.'

The alien lolled at his ease in a sea of steaming mud. The humans around him were in beach chairs and swimsuits. Mud had splashed Sherry and Joe and Nat, who were crowded close to the edge. Wade Curtis stayed farther back, wearing an African safari bush jacket and seated in a fold-up chair with a beer can in his hand. Just above him was a huge globe of the Earth. A bar on wheels showed in one corner.

'See? They took our swimming pool! We move the furniture out when nobody's using it. The alien likes his floor room,' Jenny said. 'How about a swim?'

Jack eyed the mud with distaste. 'No, thanks. Have you got all the rooms bugged?'

'No. Hell, no! Half these hard-SF people are ex-military, and they'd spot that, and the other half are liberals! We've got pickups in the mudroom and the Snout Room and the refuge, that's the room they use to write up their notes and talk and get drunk, but it's right next to the Snout Room. The mud's new. He seems to like it, doesn't he?'

'Can you get us sound too?'

'Sure.' Jenny turned a dial.

Wade Curtis' unmistakable voice boomed from the speaker. 'We've pretty well driven the Traveler Fithp out of Kansas. We're picking through the debris now. We'd like to know where the fithp will attack next.'

'I wasn't told,' Harpanet said. His pronunciation was good, yet something blurred the words: loose air escaped through the nose and lips, and there was an echo-chamber effect, perhaps due to his huge lung capacity.

Jack said, 'He learns fast. I've talked to French diplomats with thicker accents.' But Jenny was repressing a shudder. The carnage in the smashed digit ship was still with her, and she had trouble facing the snout.

Curtis was saying, 'Your officers don't seem to tell you much of what you're doing.'

'No. A fi' learns little because he might be taken into the

enemy herd. That has happened with me. I have told you this.' The alien might have been affronted.

'It is a new way of thinking, and hard for us,' Sherry Atkinson said. 'We must learn what we can.' She slipped into the mud, quite unselfconsciously, and rubbed behind the alien's ear with both hands. She was already the muddiest of the lot, Jenny noted.

Curtis asked, 'Did your superiors show interest in any area besides Kansas?'

'Kansas?'

'The region you invaded, *this* area.' Wade pointed. The erstwhile snout-held territory in Kansas was already circled on the great globe, with a black Magic Marker.

'No such interest was shown in my presence.'

'What we're afraid of is a massive meteorite impact, something of asteroid size.'

The alien was silent for a time. Reynolds busied himself at the bar. Suddenly the alien said, '*Thuktun Flishithy – Message Bearer?* – was docked to a moonlet of the ringed planet for many years. This many.' The alien's trunk emerged from the mud, and he flexed a clump of four digits, three times. 'Pushing. We were not told why. I once heard officers call the mass *chaytrif*.'

'What does it mean?'

'It means this part of a fi'.' The alien rolled (and Sherry shied from a wave of mud). One broad clawed foot emerged.

The sci-fi types all seemed to freeze in place; but Jenny didn't need their interpretation. Her hand closed painfully on Jack's arm. 'My God. It's real. Of course, the *Foot*, they're planning to *stomp* us —'

'They're talking too damn much.'

'Huh? The alien's talking a lot more than they are.'

The blurry voice from the TV set was saying, 'It was not so large as many of the – asteroids – at the ringed planet. I think 8 to the 12th standard masses —'

'Standard mass is your mass? About eight hundred

pounds . . .' Curtis took a pocket calculator out of his bush jacket. 'Jesus! Twenty-seven billion tons!'

Nat Reynolds said, 'At . . . ten to twenty miles per second, that could – Harpanet, where are they going to drop it?'

'I was never told that it would be impacted against Earth. If so, the Herdmaster may have sought more data, perhaps in Kansas.'

'Jesus, Jenny,' Jack said, 'they're telling too much. We have to see them. Now.'

———

When a pretty girl enters a swimming pool, the natural thing to do is follow. Nat didn't follow at once. The pool was filled with thick mud, but he was already muddy, and there were showers . . . he set his glass down, jumped in, and waded forward.

Harpanet turned and sprayed Sherry with a jet of dark mud.

Nat saw her startled and appalled before she threw up her arms and turned her back. Hell, Sherry was from *Oklahoma*; this was hardly fair! A California boy knows how to water-fight. Nat half cupped his hands and sent water jetting at the invader.

The alien preened. He liked it. Sherry was laughing, and three others had leaped to her aid and were jetting mud over the alien's back. Curtis' tall wife showed impressive ambidextrous firepower. The alien sprayed them back impartially, with the capacity of a small fire truck, his digits splayed from around the nostril.

Jack Clybourne and Jenny walked into a mist of mud and a roar of echoing laughter, and a water fight raging at the center. They stopped in the doorway and waited.

None of the Threat Team noticed them. The water fight stopped, and two muddy writers were now fondling the alien's trunk. Reynolds asked, 'Can you bend it in any direction?'

'No.'

Sherry began *braiding* the bifurcations, the 'digits.' 'Does this hurt?'

'No. Discomfort.' The trunk lifted and writhed and was no longer braided.

'I wonder just how mobile your tail is,' Curtis said from behind the alien.

The short, somewhat flattened tail flapped up, down, left, right. 'Control the speed of a floating car with tail. Accelerate and stop.'

'Mmm. We couldn't drive your cars, then, even if we could capture one.'

'Not one. Two human could drive. Or I drive for you.'

Nat Reynolds noticed the visitors. He moved to the doorway without disturbing the rest. 'Major Jenny, did you notice that he's telling us how to steal fithp cars?'

'I wondered how much you were telling *him*,' Jack said.

Nat looked at Jack. He grinned and said, 'Anything. Everything. Harpanet is part of the Threat Team.'

'You needn't be so damned flippant. He *acts* like he's switched sides, snout to human. I take it he's got you convinced —'

'We're still watching, Clybourne, but it's a little more than that. He expects *us* to act like he's switched sides. He's not putting any sweat into convincing us. Sherry thinks it's herdbeast behavior.'

'I still don't think you should be telling that alien exactly what we're afraid of at all times!'

'Why? What is he going to do, disguise himself as a general and walk out? Change clothes with one of us? Come on! Or wait for rescue? Clybourne, if the snouts can get him out of Cheyenne Mountain, we've bloody well lost!

'But never mind that. Think about this. Somewhere in the sky, aboard their mother ship, they've got human prisoners. They got some from Kansas, they may have saved some from the Soviet space station. They're probably treating their human prisoners as if they had changed sides. If nobody's shot his mouth off too much, it'll be just like *Hogan's Heroes*, with the fithp totally gullible and the prisoners running rings around them!'

Jack's eyes changed. He said, 'Mr. Reynolds, do you really believe that? Or are you spinning daydreams?'

'Oh . . . some of both. But it *could* be true. For a while. Before the aliens catch on, our people might actually do some damage.'

'And then? One human does some damage, they'll kill them all, won't they? I saw those piles of bodies in Topeka.'

Nat nodded soberly. 'I'd have liked to meet Wes Dawson again. The snouts are ruining what used to be a fun thing. Anyway, you can see we're learning things.'

'Yeah.'

'The asteroid strike will be an ocean strike. They like things wet. Vaporizing a billion tons of seawater won't bother them at all. I guess it's time to talk to the President again.'

————

Shoshone was a short strip of civilization in the midst of alien wilderness: a market, a gas station, a primitive-looking motel, a diner. The population must once have been about twenty. Now, at first glance, there were none.

He drove up the dirt track behind the motel. The track led through a field of immature tumbleweeds, still growing, not yet nomadic. They were well distributed, as if cultivated, or as if the plants had made agreements between them: this three square feet is mine, you get the same, intrude at your peril. But the plants looked dead and dried, the kind of plant that ought to grow in Hell.

Martin Carnell drove on through, slowly. Fox had

described Shoshone to him once. Where were those caves?

He spotted Fox's truck.

He parked beside the truck and went wandering on foot. There was a timeless feel here, as if nobody could possibly be in a hurry.

Martin turned the dogs loose into the desert. They dashed about, enjoying their freedom, running back to make contact and dashing away over the small knolls. He missed Sunhawk. At fifteen years Sunhawk had gotten too old. Marty had had to put him to sleep, just before Ken's Stone Soup Party.

Marty wandered up and down the low rock hills. Presently he found the rooms.

Five of them, dynamite-blasted into the rock. They were roughly rectangular, with shelves and, in one instance, a door. All the comforts of home, he thought. Miners? Miners would think in terms of dynamite. What were they after, bauxite? Had there been real caves to be shaped?

Marty crossed the low ridge, puffing. On the other side were more caves, and John Fox dressed in khaki shorts and a digger hat, looking up at him.

Fox didn't seem surprised to see him. 'Hello, Marty. I heard you clumping around. The rock carries sound.'

'Hello, John. I'm carrying some perishables. You're invited to dinner.'

'Is it just you?'

'Me and the dogs. That's Darth, he's just a puppy' – Darth had come running up to sniff at Fox before rejoining his master – 'and I've got Lucretia and Chaka and – here, this's Othello.' The dogs were behaving, more or less.

'How are things in Los Angeles?'

'Not good. Short of food, no electricity in spots . . . but mainly there's a feel. I think the snouts are going to start bombing cities any minute now.'

'Why?'

'No reason. Anyway, I got out.'

'What are your plans?'

'Stay here, if you don't mind a neighbor. I have fresh artichokes. And avocados and bay shrimp. Also fresh.'

Fox looked doubtful.

'A case of wine, too.'

Fox stood up. 'Okay.'

CHAPTER TWENTY-EIGHT
THE PRISONERS

Thus in the highest position there is the least freedom of action.

– SALLUST, *The War with Catiline*

COUNTDOWN: ONE WEEK TO FOOTFALL

It was exhausting work. Jeri hated it. *Machines can do this. They have machines to do it. Why us?* The why didn't matter. She didn't know what the fithp would do if she refused to work, but she didn't want to find out.

Raztupisp-minz sent them out in groups, but no one objected if they separated. Jeri didn't think the fithp would ever understand the human need for privacy, simply to be *alone* some of the time, but they were beginning to accept it. *They can watch us. Better work.* Wearily she took up the cleaning materials and began.

'You are diligent.'

The voice from behind startled her. 'Oh. Hello, Commander Rogachev —'

'Arvid. We have no rank here.' He laughed cynically. 'We have achieved an equality that Marx would have admired, although perhaps not in quite the way he envisioned.'

'I thought you were a good communist.'

He shrugged. 'I am a good Russian. You work too hard. Take a short rest.'

'But they —'

He lowered his voice. 'Dmitri says, and I agree, that we must not show them our true strength. If you work hard, they will expect hard work always. You harm the others if you do too much work.'

'Sounds like a good excuse – all right. Lord knows I'm tired.' She stretched out in midair, letting the weak gravity slowly take her to the air-shaft walls. 'Feels good to relax. I would kill for a cigarette.'

Arvid snorted. 'There is nothing to kill. There is nothing to smoke, either.'

It wasn't that funny, but she wanted to laugh, and she did.

Playing up to the nearest hero?

Shut up.

'So. You are here with your daughter. Where is your husband?'

'Drowned.'

'I am sorry.'

'So am I. We hadn't lived together for a year, but – I was going to meet him, and the snouts blew up a dam, the first night, I guess the same time they captured you. His house was below it.'

Arvid pointedly looked away.

He's nice. Or trying to be. 'Are you married?'

'I do not know. I was. Like you, we had not lived together for some months, but that was not estrangement. I was in space. Now – so many have died. My wife was Russian; the base was in the Ukraine. John Woodward tells me he heard tales of revolt in the Soviet Union. The Moslem republics would see this invasion as the punishment of Allah. The Ukraine was never satisfied to be part of Russia either. Perhaps – ' He shrugged. 'So many have died.'

'Doesn't it upset you? Not knowing?'

'Of course. We Russians are great sentimentalists. What should I do, mourn? To her I am dead, even if she lives. I am not likely to see her again in any case.'

Jeri gasped. 'I – I guess I never thought about it that way. We're none of us going to get back alive, are we?'

Arvid shrugged again. 'The only way we will be taken to Earth is as part of their herd. That implies victory for them. I do not believe Russia will surrender easily. Or the United States. Americans are stubborn.'

'Stubborn. Maybe that's it. We like to say we love freedom.'

'Did you hear much of Russia?' Arvid asked seriously.

'No. There was a little on the radio, about how Russia was being attacked just like we were. I didn't see much of what they did to us. The dam, I saw that. And Harry told me about other dams and bridges. And they made a big crater on a main highway, right where two highways crossed. But I didn't see much until they landed.'

'And that was the first attack,' Arvid said. 'The next time will be more serious.'

'What will they do?'

'The ship is "mated to a foot." I do not think it will be long mated. Nikolai has seen it.' He told her of Nikolai's report.

'So you think they'll throw the asteroid at Earth?'

'Why should they not?' Arvid asked seriously.

'No, of course it makes sense.' She shuddered. 'And we thought it was bad when they attacked the bridges and dams! Now's when it gets really bad.'

'Yes. I must say it is pleasant not having to explain these things to you.'

She made an irritated gesture. 'Women aren't stupid, you know.'

He shrugged. 'Some are, some are not. As with men. Perhaps it is time to begin work again. Come, we can stay together. If you do not mind?'

'It's all right.'

———

Fog lay across the Bellingham harbor, and rain drizzled from the skies. From the harbor area distant sounds of work drifted up to the Enclave: hammers, trucks, barge motors . . . something that buzzed . . .

'They're sure building a hell of a greenhouse,' Isadore said. He laughed.

George Tate-Evans looked at their own efforts and joined the laughter. 'Well, I guess it's more than we did.' They went back into the house.

Kevin Shakes watched them go, then went back to work. 'I thought we'd done pretty well,' he said.

'Sure,' Miranda answered. 'Enough to send Mom up the walls.'

In fact they had done a lot. Where picture windows had surrounded the X-shaped house, now there were steel shutters. Where the tennis court had been, above the hidden bomb shelter, there stood the skeleton of a greenhouse. Kevin was nailing glass plates into place with exquisite care. He'd finished the bottom two rows. Now he must work on the ladder, with Miranda to hand him tools and panes and move the ladder on its wheeled base.

George Tate-Evans and Isadore Leiber came out carrying half a dozen sheets of glass, laughing as they came. Kevin heard: ' – still isn't talking to you?'

'Vicki is ominously silent. Iz, I thought it was over once we got the shutters up. You know, "The house feels like a prison! I never thought we'd be living in a *prison* – " And then she settled down. And then there was the President saying everyone should build greenhouses, and two days later you and Jack were saying that for once the fuzzy-headed liberal son of a bitch was probably right – Kevin, Miranda, how're you doing?'

'So far so good,' Kevin said. 'Maybe another two days. You could start planting now.'

'Let's look it over, Iz.'

The older men set the glass on a pair of sawhorses. Isadore followed George around the corner and into the greenhouse. They walked the imaginary aisles, avoiding the white chalk markings put down to show where the plants would go. There was no glass to diminish their voices.

George was saying, 'Iz, by the time we got serious about the greenhouse, all the glass in Bellingham and most of the plastic was bought up. Where else were we going to get glass?'

'You can see their point, though.'

'Clara too?'

'Damn straight.'

'All right, so it's ugly. Why do we have to have *all* the women on our backs?'

'It's not just ugly. We took out the windows. That means we'll have these damn shutters till we can take down the greenhouse. If ever. Maybe we can put the windows back after the government job gets going.'

From above their heads Kevin said, 'What?'

Isadore looked up in surprise. George didn't bother. 'Iz, you're nuts. Depend on the *government* for *food?* God knows what the government's going to do with the stuff it grows, but you can be sure we don't get any of it.'

'Sure,' Kevin said. 'Why else would they build greenhouses at the *harbor* unless they were going to ship it all out? We'll never get any.'

'What make you so sure it *is* a greenhouse?' George asked.

'Oh, come on, it's been all over the radio,' Isadore said. 'Anyway, what else could it be? They say they're setting up a whole regional grain belt. They'll renovate the harbor and dredge it because they need it to ship the grain out. Isn't that great? After all the trouble we spent finding ourselves a sleepy little backwater town.'

'Yeah, I suppose,' George said.

Isadore nodded. 'Another thing. Prices'll go up. That'll *kill* your dad, Kevin, but we can stand it. Rohrs should like it.'

'Things'll get crowded. Tourists. Traffic jams.'

'Kevin?' Miranda called.

'Yeah?'

'Let's take a break.'

'But – ' When his sister had that edge in her voice, there was something to it. Even their father knew that. 'Be right with you.' He slid down the ladder.

'What?' he asked when they got to the water bucket.

'I was out with Leigh last night . . .'

'Yeah, you sure were. You were out late enough to have Dad pacing the floor. Mother wasn't too happy, either. She kept saying you had to be safe, you were out with a policeman, but she didn't mean it. Something happen – something we need to tell them?' *Did he propose? Are you pregnant?*

'Well, maybe but not *that*.' She giggled. 'No, Leigh told me something. He's seen an astronaut.'

'Astronaut?'

'Gillespie. The one who commanded the last Shuttle, the flight that took that poor congressman up to the Russian space station. Gillespie's in charge of this big government project – and they're setting up all kinds of guard stations, fences, everything.'

'For a greenhouse?'

'That's what I wondered. Leigh says they told him it's to protect the food —'

'That makes sense. Look at all the trouble Dad went to to protect ours!'

'Sure, maybe, but an astronaut? Why, Kevin?'

'I don't know, Randy.'

'I don't either, and I think we should tell Dad.'

Bill Shakes was toting up accounts with the help of his pocket computer. Kevin and Miranda waited until they saw him pause. Then Kevin said, 'We've got an astronaut in Bellingham.'

Shakes looked up. 'So?'

'Major General Edmund Gillespie. He went up to Kosmograd with Dawson. Now he's here. Miranda found out about it yesterday.' He was careful not to say *last night*.

Miranda took up the tale. 'Leigh spent day before yesterday and part of yesterday taking him all over Bellingham. I asked him where he was, and he told me all about it.'

'What's he want? I mean Gillespie.'

'I don't know. Leigh says he looked over *everything*. He looked at the harbor, he looked at the railroad, he toured the whole town. All that, for a government greenhouse?'

Shakes scowled. 'So we've got a real live astronaut scouting Bellingham. We're getting too damn conspicuous. The thing about being a survivalist is you keep your head down.'

'We have to,' Miranda said. 'There's no gasoline, and Leigh says they're going to close off the highway except for essential traffic, to save maintenance.'

'Hmm.' It was easy to see what Bill Shakes was thinking. Bellingham lay between mountains and the Straits of Juan de Fuca. Restricting highway use was the same as not letting them leave town. 'Not that there's anyplace better for us to go to,' Shakes said carefully. 'We've invested a lot here, and we can't take it with us.'

'Well, we thought you should know,' Kevin said.

'Yeah. Yeah . . . why an astronaut? I s'pose he doesn't have much of anything better, with the snouts shooting spaceships out of the sky. Still . . . it doesn't fit.' Shakes frowned. 'You like the deputy sheriff, don't you?'

'Yes —'

'Good. See more of him.'

Kevin suppressed an urge to giggle.

Jack Clybourne stood in the doorway, blocking the President's path. 'No, sir,' he said firmly.

'Mr. Clybourne,' Admiral Carrell said mildly.

'No,' Jack said firmly. 'Before the President goes in there, you get that alien out, or you give me a hell of a lot more gun than this pistol, and that's final.'

Admiral Carrell sighed.

'Jack – ' Jenny stepped forward. *How do I get him out of this?* 'Jack, will you agree if I bring in Sergeant Bonner and two MPs with military rifles?'

'You can't do that,' Sherry Atkinson protested. 'We can't make Harpanet feel that we don't trust him!'

'Damn it all, Mr. President!' Wade Curtis said.

'Yes, Mr. Curtis?' the President asked. He sounded as if he was suppressing a chuckle.

'Their top brass travel with armed guards.. Harpanet won't see anything unusual in having the President escorted by soldiers.'

'Do you think I will need them, Mr. Curtis?'

'No. But I see Jack's point. If Harpanet decided to take out the President, he'd be damned hard to stop. Incidentally, if you're going to do this, do it right. None of those dinky little Mattel toy rifles. Get a couple of thirty-nought-sixes.'

'And where will we find those?' Jenny asked.

'There's one in my room. Ransom's got another,' Curtis said.

'That's why, Mr. President.' Joe Ransom finished his presentation. The room, filled with writers and engineers and soldiers, stood in silence, so that the only sound was the heavy breathing of the alien captive.

'Impressive,' President Coffey said. He looked bewilderedly around the room until his eyes met those of the alien. Harpanet stood thirty feet away, as far as Clybourne could put him, with four armed combat veterans between the alien and the President.

And still too close, Jenny thought.

432

'What do you call him? Has he a title?' the President asked.

'Just Harpanet, Mr. President,' Robert Anson said. 'Any title he might have had from his own people was lost when he surrendered, and we have not yet given him one.'

'Harpanet,' the President said quietly.

'Lead me.'

'Have you understood what was said here?'

'Yes.'

'Is it true? They will drop a large asteroid on the Earth?'

The alien spread his digits.

'He says he can't know,' Sherry interpreted.

'But your ship was to be – mated with a foot?'

'Yes.' The *s* sound fluttered.

'Is there anyone here who disagrees?' the President demanded.

There was only silence.

President Coffey began to pace. 'We'll have to warn as many people as possible. Worldwide. God, I wish they hadn't made such hash of our communications. Yes, Admiral?'

'I think we don't dare.'

'Dare what? Warn the world? We'd be condemning millions! Tidal waves, storms, earthquakes, volcanoes, it'll be like a week-long disaster movie festival!'

'And if we do issue a warning, we will *certainly* condemn thousands. Tens of thousands,' Admiral Carrell said. 'They will flee from the coasts. All the coasts.'

'But it's better than doing nothing —'

'Mr. President.' Robert Anson seemed to have aged ten years in months, but his voice was firm and insistent.

'Yes, Mr. Anson?'

'If you issue a warning, people will flee the coastal towns. Bellingham is a coast town.'

'But —'

'You dare not have people flee from every town except Bellingham,' Anson said.

'He is certainly correct,' Admiral Carrell said. 'If you issue a warning, you will disrupt Project Archangel. Perhaps permanently.'

'And Archangel is the only goddam chance we have,' Curtis said.

The President sat heavily. His fingers drummed against the desk. After a few moments he looked up. 'Thor, would you send Mrs. Coffey in, please? I'll speak with the rest of you later. Thank you for your advice.'

Mrs. Carmichael had told Alice a story once. Later Alice had asked around, and everyone had heard it. The psychiatrists probably thought it did their patients good. Maybe it did.

A motorist finds himself with a flat tire on a back road, late at night. There's a fence. Someone is peering through it, not doing anything, just watching. The motorist sees a sign in the headlights. He's parked next to a mental institution.

He takes the flat tire off, putting the five nuts in the hubcap. The stranger watches. He pulls the spare tire out of the trunk. The stranger watches. Motorist is getting nervous. What's a maniac doing out so late at night? Why is he staring like that? Motorist rolls the tire around from the back and steps on the rim of the hubcap, which flips all of the nuts into tall weeds. Motorist goes after them. He finds one nut.

The mental patient speaks. 'Take a nut off each of the other tires. Put them on the fourth wheel. Four nuts each. It'll get you to a gas station.'

Motorist says. 'That'll work.' Then. 'Hey, that's brilliant! What the hell are you doing *here?*'

Patient says, 'I'm here for being crazy. Not stupid.'

The air pipes were a little more than a yard across. There

434

were no handholds. At first Alice had floundered, lost and nauseated and fighting the fear of falling. It was better now. Jeri and Melissa actually *enjoyed* the low gravity, and they'd shown Alice how.

Alice had always been thin. Pale face, fiery hair, slender body: vividly pretty, for whatever that was worth. Now she was gaunt. She tried to eat, but there was no appetite, and the horrors tried to foist nauseating alien plants and meat on her. The others accepted such treatment. They ate canned food and alien food, they ate the vitamins and protein powder and brewer's yeast *she* had supplied, and they thrived.

Living wasn't worth the effort under these circumstances. Alice had slashed her wrists once, long ago, for reasons that seemed trivial now. Something sharp would presently come her way. Yet she was half sure she wouldn't use it.

After all, who would care?

The little girl, Melissa, treated her with something between fear and contempt. Jeri was nice, but she spent a lot of time with the Russians. *I think she likes the big one. He does things for her. Brings her things. Got the blanket to put around the toilet pool, that was nice.*

Nobody does things for me. They resent me —

With Wes Dawson it went far beyond resentment. He gave orders. He lectured. He taught the language of the horrors and expected the women to use it. He was persuasive and smooth and condescending, like that first psychiatrist they had given her, the one who thought using Q-tips was a form of masturbation. She'd gotten along all right with the second one. Mrs. Carmichael had looked a little like Jeri Wilson. A little plumper, and not as scared, Alice thought.

The horrors were worse than Dawson. Anything short of instant obedience puzzled them. They solved the problem by prodding with their trunks or the butts of the twisted-looking guns. They wouldn't listen to anything she had to say. They treated her like a *thing*. If Alice McLennon slashed her wrists, it would be one less damn thing for the horrors to worry about.

This cleaning of air pipes: it was make-work, a way of keeping the prisoners busy, like picking tomatoes at Menninger's. Alice wasn't fooled. *I'm here for being crazy, not stupid*. The horrors were too big to fit in the pipes. What had they done before people turned up? Maybe they had Roto-Rooters, or maybe the pipes just never needed cleaning, or – She'd glimpsed something like a steel doughnut just the size of the pipe, with a glittering eye that watched her from a distance. Robots?

And like the make-work at Menninger's, it served its purpose.

They'd pushed her into the ducts when she balked. Those rubbery split trunks were irresistibly strong. She floundered in there, disoriented and nauseated, and took the great wad of cloth and the plastic bag that were shoved in after her. Then she hadn't done anything for a while. Then . . . she started to clean the pipes.

Well, there was dust and rust, and it came off. There were wads of goop and soil and feathers in the filters. And, moving around in the pipes, she began to learn a kind of skill. There were no handholds; of course not, the horrors had never expected that living things would need them in here. She learned to move in a zigzag jumping style, swiping at the sides with the cloth. It *worked*.

It worked, and she was getting better at it, but it was make-work, and she couldn't wait to get back to the garden, with its open spaces.

––––––

Some of the plants were sprouting. Alice was afraid to touch them. Mrs. Woodward chuckled. 'Rice. I might have known it would be rice. Rice likes it wet.'

'What do we do now?'

'Nothing. There ain't any bugs here. If it ain't broke, don't fix it. Maybe we want to block off the water pipes that feeds some of the other stuff.'

Alice nodded. She pushed herself back to look at the vegetable plot. Was that another tuft of green, where they'd planted corn and runner beans together? Alice belatedly realized that she was too far from a handhold.

It didn't bother her much. She was used to free-fall. She floated, waiting for *Thuktun Flishithy*'s minuscule thrust to pull her someplace useful.

Something wrapped around her ankle. She jumped as if she'd been electrocuted, and looked down at a cluster of tentacles – a broad brown head, wrinkled with age, and recessed eyes – 'Raztupisp-minz?'

'You have learned to recognize me? Good. How is your health, Alice?'

'I'm fine.'

'Your plants are sprouting. I am pleased. I think our plants will grow in your world.'

Alice held her face expressionless. Dawson had suggested that if the plants grew well, Earth would become more desirable to the horrors – and she hadn't believed him. Should the plants die? Easy enough – but she'd have to go on eating what they fed her now.

'I want to explain something,' the teacher said. 'You may have noticed that some of the fithp are acting strangely. The mating season has started for one class of us, the sleepers, and it affects their behavior. They are not turning rogue, but do not irritate them.'

'You're not a sleeper, are you? And Takpusseh is.'

'Mating season goes with the females, the sleeper females. I am space-born, and so is Tashayamp. For most of the year, for many days to come, you may see me as neuter.'

She studied him, but there was nothing to be read in his alien face. Yet this was a teacher and a manipulator. 'Can you hear thought?'

'Hear thought?' He snorted. 'No! But I can see. You talk only with females. You shy from males when you can. You are thin in the hips, your breasts are flat. Sometimes there are fithp who are shaped like females but never come into season —'

Alice leapt away, back to the seed plot, back to the company of the other prisoners. Nobody had ever suggested such a thing to her! They thought she was strange, yes, but a neuter? A *freemartin*? If she didn't like men, it was because men were – were —

She feared the teacher would follow, but in fact he was now speaking to another fi' – to the other teacher, Takpusseh.

She remembered, now, that men *had* tried to tell her that she was strange, to put her on the defensive. *Fuck me to prove you're a woman.*

The thought of being raped by Raztupisp-minz was ludicrous and horrible . . . mostly ludicrous, she decided. No man had ever started by telling her to think of him as a neuter.

Tashayamp took her back to the cell, with Mr. and Mrs. Woodward and Wes Dawson. They were there long enough to eat and use the toilet. The only thing that could have made that tolerable to Alice was watching how it bothered the others.

An hour's rest, then fithp came to escort them to the ducts. None of the humans had noticed that she wasn't talking. Maybe they were glad.

Alice broke away from the others as soon as she could, and let the wind carry her away, farther than she'd ever gone before. She wasn't feeling sociable. Presently she braked herself and began desultorily to clean the walls.

The wind had grown cold. It matched her mood; she hardly noticed at first. But the wall was even colder, on one side. Here was a curve to mark a side channel in the duct, but it was blocked by a hatch. She passed it. Soon the wall warmed.

Alice went back.

She didn't like taking orders, and she didn't like knowing that things were hidden from her. The goddam psychiatrists *always* had something they weren't telling her.

There was a slot to house the hatch. Alice got her fingers into a crack and pushed, and the door moved back against springs, enough to let her through.

The air was terribly cold and still. She followed a short duct and found a grill.

Ten yards beyond was a peculiar surface, black and nearly smooth, but with undulations in it, like very dirty ice. With her face pressed to the grill Alice could see the curve of it, like the inner wall of a cylinder.

She studied it for a time. There was a bulge in the surface . . . like an unfinished raised relief painting . . . a frieze of one of the horrors. Dirty ice? Dawson had said . . . what? The horrors liked mud. It puzzled them that humans bathed in clean water. But *frozen* mud?

The grill was loose in her hands.

She pushed it aside and floated in.

It was frozen mud on one side, a ceiling of painted friezes on the other. The artwork was weird, alien, sometimes beautiful. Horrors – fithp – half hidden among weird trees; she recognized some from the Garden area. Here a good representation of one of the horrors faced a block covered with alien script. And sculpted into the oppposing mudbank was a similar shape . . .

She'd freeze here. Alice backed into the duct, pulled the grill after her, and set it in place.

Alice didn't like secrecy. She would have to learn more. She found an exit from the air shaft.

This part of the ship was strange, and she didn't know how to get home. It was hard, stopping one of the horrors in the corridor. She said, 'Raztupisp-minz,' and followed it after it gave up trying to talk to her.

She was tired and she ached. The horrors on Earth had stopped her before she got around to collecting conveniences like cosmetics and liniment. Cleaning out air ducts was so much like flying! She hadn't noticed how hard she was working. She wanted Ben Gay. She wanted to curl up and wait for the pain to go away.

'Alice wants to tell you something,' Melissa said.

Jeri stirred wearily. 'How do you know?'

'She keeps looking at you. But she wants to see you alone. I know, Mom. I can tell. Alice is —'

'Yeah.' *Interesting. Can you read her mind? Or are you guessing? Or what?* Jeri floated lazily over to grip the wall beside Alice. 'How'd it go?'

Words bubbled out quickly. 'Jeri, I found a peculiar place. Cold enough to freeze your ass off. Locked off. Black ice everywhere, or something like it. A long way from here.'

'Storage room? Anything stored there?'

'No, just ice, all along the one wall, the hull wall. Dawson said they like mud. Maybe it's their idea of a big spa. Why would they freeze their spa?'

'Let's ask Arvid.'

Alice looked afraid again.

'He won't – he's a good man, Alice.'

'Oh, all right —'

Rogachev frowned deeply. 'Frozen solid?'

'I didn't touch it. It must have been. It was *cold*.'

'No gravity. No spin, because we are mated to the foot. They cannot bathe in mud under those conditions, but from the pictures they showed us we know they enjoy that. They will have a place for mud, and they must keep it when there is no gravity. Da. So they froze it in place.'

'That makes sense,' Jeri said.

'Yeah,' Alice agreed. 'All right, explain this one. There was a shape in the mud, like a frieze – like one of those horrors under a blanket.'

'How? As if it were lying on its side?'

'Yeah. Now, what was that?'

Wes Dawson was close enough to hear. 'You're sure of this?'

'Yes.'

'A frieze of a fi'?'

'I didn't say it was a frieze! I said it was like that,' Alice said.

'Certainly.' Dawson made his voice soothing. He made no move to come closer to her. 'Arvid, what do you think?'

'I do not know.'

'I think we should tell Raztupisp-minz.'

'We will consider that,' Arvid said. He turned to Dmitri. 'You have heard?'

'Da.'

They spoke rapidly, in Russian.

Jeri took Arvid's arm. 'They learn languages quickly,' she said. 'They *say* they don't know any Russian.'

Arvid smiled. 'If they have learned rapidly enough to comprehend the accented dialect we are now speaking, nothing will defeat them.' He turned back to the others. The liquid syllables continued. Finally Dmitri nodded. Arvid turned to the others. 'Da. We will do it, then. Alice, you must tell your story to our masters.'

The mudroom was warm enough for comfort, and the mud was thawing, by the time Pretheeteh-damb arrived.

Raztupisp-minz had told him that the red-haired human was certified rogue. She could be hallucinating . . . The comfort that gave Pretheeteh-damb vanished as he entered. There in the ceiling was a frieze of Thowbinther-thuktun, a half-legendary priest of two eight-cubeds of years ago. Opposite Thowbinther-thuktun was an entirely similiar bulge.

Some fi' must have an odd sense of humor. He must

441

have entered the mudroom after acceleration stopped; had shaped the mud into a ribald parody of the ancient discoverer of the Podo Thuktun. But Preetheeteh-damb was beginning to shiver, and it confronted him that his octuple were all spaceborn. 'Remove that mud,' he told one of his fithp, 'carefully. But waste no time. We resume acceleration shortly.'

This couldn't have happened at a worse time. Within hours they would release the Foot. Then there would be violent maneuvers as they placed *Thuktun Flishithy* in position to send down the digit ships.

The Invasion of Winterhome was about to begin, and now this!

The warrior scraped away softened mud with the back of his bayonet, and Fathisteh-tulk began to take shape.

The Herdmaster waited impatiently for the call. Then Pretheeteh-damb came onto the screen. There was activity behind him.

'Report.'

'It is indeed Fathisteh-tulk, Herdmaster. He was drowned. We find no breaks in the skin.' By now the corpse was free from the ice, visible in the screen. It rotated slowly for inspection by the octuple's physician. 'There's a deep groove in Fathisteh-tulk's trunk, above the nostril. It might have been made by a cord pulled very tight, but it wouldn't have killed him. Mud caked in the poor fi's mouth. It looks like a ritual execution. He was drowned.'

'Thank you.' Pastempeh-keph broke the connection. *The tulk clan must be informed. The women will not be pleased. Murder!* Murder was rare among the fithp. It was almost always the beginning of rebellion.

'We approach the final moments, Herdmaster,' the Attackmaster said. 'What shall we do?'

Run away. Drop the Foot to slow the humans. Confine

442

*them to their planet while we take the rest of their solar
system, which is more valuable than the planet anyway.*

*Fathisteh-tulk would have given that advice. Gladly.
Advisor Siplisteph will not. The sleeper women will never
consent to that. Nor will Fistarteh-thuktun.*

'Attackmaster.'

'Lead me.'

'Continue with the battle plan. You are in charge of
Thuktun Flishithy.'

CHAPTER TWENTY-NINE
FOOTFALL

I dreamt the past was never past redeeming: But whether this was false or honest dreaming I beg death's pardon now. And mourn the dead.

– RICHARD PURDY WILBUR, 'The Pardon'

COUNTDOWN: FOOTFALL

The funeral pit was a cylinder of soil, garbage, bones, and what remained of the honored dead, all being gradually churned into an indistinguishable matrix. Instruments sampled the blend for acidity, bacterial population, temperature. The atmosphere within was unbreathable. Workers in pressure suits maintained a cavity in the matrix, open at the fore end. They had removed several tons of it into the Garden to make room for this day's funeral proceedings.

The cold had preserved Fathisteh-tulk. His eyes looked off at different angles. As lines lowered him to join the Silent Fithp, his digit-cluster bent strangely above the nostril. One eye met Pastempeh-keph's. *My breath was closed with rope, and then with mud. Why both? What might I have said that I did not say while alive I who never hesitated to speak? Who closed my mouth with mud?*

The Herdmaster shook his head. *I will learn.* He had already spoken his formal farewell to today's half-dozen dead, recognizing posthumous accomplishments, sometimes authorizing upgrades in harness colors before a corpse was stripped for burial.

Elaborate funeral practices had evolved among the spaceborn during three generations of interstellar flight. Inevitably they were geared to a life in spin gravity. The funeral pit was on the ship's axis. Ceremonies were held in the leavetaking chamber, a partial ring along the lip of the funeral pit, where spin gravity was almost nil. Today's ceremony obeyed tradition. The main drive was running at high thrust; the hum of it was everywhere; yet there was almost no acceleration.

Pastempeh-keph sensed the immense mass against which *Message Beurer* was pushing. *Message Bearer* was even now imparting its final direction to the nickel-and-iron residue of an icy moonlet. She must break loose within a 512-breath, or ride the Foot down to Winterhome. Had a lesser personage led these rites, they might have been postponed until after the maneuvers; but after they separated from the Foot, there would never again be time. Fathisteh-tulk deserved all honors. *And even if he did not, I could not seem niggardly in granting honor to a former Herdmaster!*

Chowpeentulk watched through glass as Fathisteh-tulk came to rest in the moving earth. Her digits wrapped the child and held it to her throat to suckle. He was male, eight days old. Under normal thrust he would already have walked. In nearly free-fall he drifted with waving legs. He seemed to enjoy it.

'My mate was murdered,' Chowpeentulk said. 'Who?'

'I face too many answers,' Pastempeh-keph said. 'Your mate was never careful of whom he might offend.'

She trumpeted wildly. The child, startled, flung its stubby digits across its head and tried to burrow between Chowpeentulk's legs. In the minuscule thrust its efforts lifted her from the floor. It was strong for a newborn.

The loss of dignity slowed her not at all. 'This crime was committed against the whole of the Traveler Fithp!' she bellowed. 'Sleepers and spaceborn, how can we hold together unless the murderers face judgement?'

The Herdmaster let silence follow, letting Chowpeentulk see how the others, the fithp and the little clump of humans, stared at her. Then, 'We will solve this. You know that I like puzzles. Do you also know that I must fight a war?' He looked into the funeral pit. 'Farewell, Fathisteh-tulk. You have too much company.'

He joined Takpusseh as they were leaving. 'Fathisteh-tulk had always the virtue of asking interesting questions,' he said. 'Now I must find my own.'

'You will have an Advisor,' said Takpusseh.

'Bah. Siplisteph will have to be trained. Breaker-Two, did Fathisteh-tulk ask you interesting questions?'

Takpusseh snorted. 'I did not find them so. He wanted to interview the humans in privacy.'

'Why?'

'He would not say. The humans are not his thuktun. I told him that I myself would translate, and that I would inform you of all that transpired. He declined. He said that he would simply wait for me to do my job.'

'Very proper,' said Pastempeh-keph. 'Did he propose questions for you to ask?'

'He did not.'

A pity. 'Will you be on the bridge during Footfall?'

'No. To think of humans as enemy or prey would ruin my empathy with them . . . such as it is.'

Tashayamp left them at the cell door. 'You will stay in place. Be prepared to cling to the walls. First that wall, but change walls when you are warned. The direction of pull will change often. Before each change you will hear this.' She trumpeted, then spoke in a breathy-trombone chant. 'You understand? Good.'

They went to the bulkhead. Jeri dug her nails into the rug.

'It is indelicate,' Arvid said. 'But they gave no indication of time. It would be well to use the facilities while we are able.'

'Good thinking,' Dawson said. 'Ladies first.'

Nobody else wanted to be first, so Jeri went. It wasn't so bad now that Arvid and Nikolai had rigged a blanket to enclose the shallow pool.

Jeri went back to the wall. 'Melissa, I want you here —'

'If you do not object, I will stay with you also,' Arvid said.

'Thank you.'

'What did you think of their funeral rites?' Arvid asked.

'My anthropology teacher said funeral rites were the most important clues to a tribal culture,' Jeri said. 'But I think that was because she was an archaeologist, and graves are about the only things they can find with anything important in them.'

'The Predecessors must like bad smells,' Melissa said. 'Because that place stank.'

Gary giggled agreement. Jeri said. 'There, *that's* what I meant. There's nothing arbitrary aboard a spaceship. They don't have to put up with that smell. They *want* it. It must be part of the funeral, the sense that the dear departed is turning into fertilizer, then plants, then —'

Arvid said, 'You understood more of his speech than I.'

'I got some of it too,' Wes Dawson said. 'The long speech by the priest. He talked about Fathisteh-tulk 'coming back to the Traveler Fithp.' I wondered if he meant in person.'

'Do you think they believe in that?' Jeri asked.

'Dunno,' Dawson said. 'The body recirculates. Maybe they think the soul does too.'

'I think not,' Arvid said. 'Else why would they make such mention of the newborn one?'

' "The Predecessors are always with us," he said. How could that other species join the Traveler Fithp? Their bodies recirculate, and there are the thuktunthp, but —'

'Of course they do not believe bourgeois myths of gods and immortality,' Dmitri said. 'There is much to admire in these fithp. They work together, and if need be they give their lives for the herd.'

John Woodward sniffed loudly and turned away.

'That one didn't,' Alice said. 'The widow said he was murdered, and the Bull Elephant wasn't happy about it, either.'

'An interesting mystery,' Arvid said. 'Who might have killed him?'

'We'll never know,' Dawson said.

'Why do you say that?' Dmitri demanded. 'The Leader told the widow that he would find the murderer. He has great resources. Why would he fail?'

'Why would he tell us? If he did, would we know the name? Hey, I read mysteries too, but I expect to know the names of the suspects!'

'The Bull isn't a detective,' Jeri said. 'He has too much else to do. And — people, I'm kind of scared. All this violent maneuvering, they're going to do something special, but what?'

'I am very much afraid we all know,' Arvid Rogachev said.

Jeri took a fresh grip on the wall carpeting.

'Major! Major, wake up!'

Jenny sat bolt upright. 'Yes, Sergeant?'

'Message from Australia, ma'am. They've seen it!'

Oh my God. She strained to open her eyes and peered through sleep at her watch. Five A.M.

'Comin' fast, about an hour to impact,' Sergeant Ferguson said.

'The Admiral —'

'Mailey already woke him up. 'Scuse me, ma'am, I got to get the others.'

448

The Threat Team had split into two groups around the coffeepot and the large globe. Ransom and Curtis already had coffee, and were tracing paths on the globe.

'Water. I was sure of it,' Ransom said.

'Sure,' Curtis muttered. 'Why at bloody dawn?'

'Why water?' a naval officer asked.

Ransom didn't look up from the globe. 'Lieutenant, a meteorite that size actually does more damage if it hits water. It'll rip through the water and the ocean floor into the magma. The energies don't go back to space; the water absorbs them, and you get even more heat from the exposed magma. It all goes into boiling the ocean. We think a quarter of a billion tons of seawater may vaporize. Salt rains all over the world —'

Jenny shuddered. 'How many people will it kill?'

'Lots,' Curtis said. 'Look.' He traced a path northward from the Indian Ocean. 'Bays. They funnel the tsunamis, let them build even higher before they break. Calcutta, Bombay, the Rann of Kutch – all gone. Persian Gulf, same thing. East Africa —'

'We have to warn them —'

'I'm sure the Aussies have done that,' Ransom said.

'It does not matter.' Admiral Carrell's voice was even.

Jenny reflexively straightened to attention. 'Sir?'

'We have no reliable communications with East Africa. I believe that Mr. Ransom is correct and that the Australians have sent a warning, but if not —'

'They'll know soon enough,' Curtis said. 'What about ships? Subs? We still have communications with the submarine fleet, don't we?'

'In fact, yes,' Carrell said. 'Our long-wave devices still function. I have already given the appropriate orders.'

Reynolds came over with coffee. Curtis pointed to a spot on the globe. Reynolds bent to examine it.

'Tsunamis. Hurricanes. I wish we knew *exactly* where it'll hit,' Curtis said. 'Maybe we could tell just how much weather slop will get into the Northern Hemisphere.'

'Lots,' Ransom said. 'It's too near the equator.'

'Mess up *both* hemispheres,' Reynolds said. 'Neat.'

'Fear, fire, foes,' Curties muttered. 'Tsunamis, hurricanes, rainstorms . . .' He stood with a satisfied look. 'One thing, it won't hurt Bellingham.'

'That's a comfort,' someone said.

'Goddam right it is,' Curtis said. 'About the only one we've got.'

'As strategy it's hard to beat,' Joe Ransom said. 'Look where the tidal waves —'

'Shut up,' a young naval officer shouted. 'Later, man, but for now just shut up.'

Jenny bent over to listen as Curtis and Ransom continued to talk.

To the east: the island of Madagascar would shadow Mozambique and South Africa, a little. The waves would wash Tanzania, Kenya, the Somali Democratic Republic, wash them clean of life. Northeast, it would wash the Saudi Arabian peninsula. The Arabian Sea would focus the wave; a mountain range of water would march into Iran and Pakistan. *That's the end of OPEC*, Jenny thought with a flash of vindictive triumph. *The end of the oil too.* . . India would be covered north to the mountains. The Bay of Bengal would focus the wave again: it might cross Burma as far as China. The islands of the Java Sea would be inundated. The wave would wash across western Australia . . .

'My God,' the naval officer said in sudden realization. 'They'll try to land afterward, of course, but where?'

'That's why it's such a —'

'Marvelous strategy, yes, Mr. Ransom,' Admiral Carrell said. 'Where would we send our fleets? India? Saudi Arabia? Australia? Africa?'

'South Africa,' Curtis said. 'Look here. Most of the industry and white population are down at sea level. Tsunamis will wreck all that. Beyond the coast is the Drakensberg escarpment, up to the high plateau country, and that'll survive just fine. So they land at Johannesburg and Pretoria and they have themselves an isolated industrial foothold.'

Admiral Carrell bent over to examine the globe. 'Perhaps —'

A horn warbled through the room. 'Now hear this. Ten minutes to estimated time of impact.'

The room fell silent.

———————

Herdmaster Pastempeh-keph felt the tiny thrust decrease further as he made his way to the bridge.

Matters there ran over smooth trails. Koothfektil-rusp turned to say, 'The Foot is on target. The Defensemaster may break us loose at any time.'

'Do it,' said Pastempeh-keph. 'Defensemaster, you lead now.' He settled himself on his pad and set his claws on the recessed foothold bars.

A recording bellowed for attention throughout the huge ship. 'Take footholds! Take footholds! Thrust in eight breaths.'

The Herdmaster's claws tightened on the bars. *What can go wrong? The drive won't fail us; we've been running it steadily for many eight-days. The prey can't possibly stop the Foot now. If they could harm* Message Bearer, *they would have acted earlier —*

Message Bearer surged steadily, smoothly backward, swinging round to face outward from Winterhome.

As the pitted and gouged mass of nickel and iron moved away, a magnificent blue-and-white crescent moved into view. Thrust built up, and the Herdmaster felt himself sagging into the pad. His muscles, grown slack in low gravity, protested. He welcomed it.

At a thrust higher than Homeworld gravity, acceleration peaked. Then the motors on the digit ships began to fire, and thrust rose again. The crescent was dead aft, growing

451

tremendous. *Message Bearer* was accelerating outward and backward from Winterhome.

The Foot would strike ahead of *Message Bearer*. The impact point would still be in view.

The Herdmaster summoned a view of the humans' quarters. They'd reached the restraint cell safely; they were on their bellies on the padding. It looked uncomfortable.

Thrust dropped in increments as pairs of digit ships left their moorings around the aft rim. The Herdmaster watched their pulsing drive flames curve away. They must decelerate more drastically to take up orbit about Winterhome. The last four merely took up station alongside the mother ship. If something deadly rose from Winterhome, they might be of help.

But nothing broke the curdled clouds. The terminator swung round until half the disk was lighted, and the Foot was invisible against the night side.

There, just inside the shadow, a red pinpoint flare —

The pinpoint glowed orange, then white, then blinding white, all within the fraction of a breath. Herdmaster Pastempeh-keph contracted his pupils. It wasn't enough. He turned away. The lurid light on the walls of the control complex flared, and held, and dimmed. He turned back.

A white flare was dimming, expanding, reddening. Rings of cloud formed and vanished around an expanding hemisphere of flame. Clouds spread outward through the stratosphere, hiding what was beneath.

Fistarteh-thuktun spoke formally. 'Our footprint is on their sea bed.'

'Attackmaster, it's right in the middle of that stretch of water. Is that where you wanted it?'

'Exactly on target,' said Koothfektil-rusp.

'Well done.'

Message Bearer was passing Winterhome at sixty makasrupkithp per breath; but Winterhome's rotation kept the Footprint in sight. A fireball stood above the planet's envelope of air. It clung to the mass of the planet like a flaming leech.

Light reflected orange from a solid stretch of cloud over. The fireball stood in a ring of clear air. A ring-shaped ripple picked up distortions as it traveled.

'The shock wave through the ocean distorts the cloud cover,' Koothfektil-rusp said. 'Like bulges moving beneath a fallen tent. Our experts will be able to pick out the contours of the continents and ocean floor by the way they retard the wave.'

It was mysterious and horrible. It only suggested the millions of prey who would drown beneath the clouds and the seawater.

'Thus we achieve equality with the Predecessors,' said Fistarteh-thuktun.

The Herdmaster was jolted. 'Are you serious?'

'I don't know. What horror lies beneath that fortunate shroud of water droplets? How many of the prey will we drown? How much terrain do we bar to the use of any living thing? What was our own world like when the Predecessors were dying and our fithp were brainless beasts?'

The layer of cloud was now flowing backward, into the fireball. Another layer formed above, high in the stratosphere, beginning to spread. Waves of blue light formed and dispersed. Pretty pictures, abstracts, but on an awesome scale . . .

One may hope that we have not invented a new art form. Awe and horror: the Herdmaster trampled them deep into the bottom of his mind. 'We came to take Winterhome. Do the thuktunthp hold knowledge to help us understand this?'

'Perhaps. We accept, do we not, that the Predecessors altered the natural state of a world? Their world, our world. Now Winterhome is our world. *Look* how we distort its natural state. What did their meddling cost the Predecessors? Have we done better?'

Have we done better? We must speak again, you and I.

453

But this path was chosen long ago, and we must follow it.
'Attackmaster. You may assume command of the digit ships. Begin your landings.'

———

Commander Anton Villars stared through the periscope and tried to look calm. It wasn't easy.

An hour before the message had come to *USS Ethan Allen*. The longwave transmitters were reliable but slow. The message came in dots and dashes, code tapped out and taken down to be put through the code machines —

It couldn't be orders to attack the Soviet Union. There was no Soviet Union. Villars had been prepared to launch his Poseidon missiles against an unseen enemy in space. Instead:

LARGE OBJECT RPT LARGE OBJECT WILL IMPACT 22.5 S LATITUDE 64.2 E LONGITUDE 1455 HOURS ZULU OBSERVE IF SAFE STOP IMPACT ENERGIES ESTIMATED AT 4000 MEGATONS RPT 4000 MEGATONS STOP ANY INFORMATION VALUABLE STOP GODSPEED CARRELL.

Safe? From four thousand megatons? There wasn't any safety. Villars' urge was to submerge and flee at flank speed.

Off to starboard, the island of Rodriguez blazed with the colors of life. Jungle had long since given way to croplands. In the center bare rock reared sharply, a peak a third of a mile high. Waves broke over a surrounding coral reef. That reef would provide more cover when the tsunami came, but it was a danger too.

Fishing boats were straggling in through the reef. Probably doomed. There was nothing Villars could do for them.

It was just dusk. Clouds covered the sky. It would be difficult to see anything coming. *Four thousand megatons. Bigger than any bomb we ever dreamed of, much less built.*

454

The crew waited tensely. John Antony, the Exec, stood close by.

'About time,' Antony said.

'If their estimate was on.'

'If their time was off, so were their coordinates.'

I know that. I had the same instructor at Annapolis as you did.

Somebody laughed and choked it off. The news had filtered through the ship, as news like that always did.

The cameras were working. Villars wondered how many would survive. He peered through the darkest filter available. *Four thousand megatons . . .*

Suddenly the clouds were blazing like the sun. 'First flash at 1854 hours 20 seconds,' he called. 'Log that.' *Where? Where would it fall?*

All in an instant, a hole formed in the clouds to the northeast, the glare became God's own flashbulb, and the cameras were gone. 'Get those other cameras up,' Villars bellowed at men who were already doing that. His right eye saw nothing but afterimage. He put his left to the periscope.

He saw light. He squinted and saw light glaring out of a hole in the ocean. A widening hole in the ocean, with smoothly curved edges; wisps of mist streaming outward, and a conical floodlight beam pointing straight up. The beam grew wider: the pit was expanding. Clouds formed and vanished around a smoothly curved wall of water sweeping smoothly toward the sub.

The rim of a sun peeped over the edge.

'I make it about forty miles east northeast of present position. Okay, that's it.' Villars straightened. 'Bring in the cameras. Down periscope. Take us to ninety feet.' *How deep? The further down, the less likely we'll get munched by surface phenomena, but if those tsunamis are really big they might pile enough water on top of* Ethan Allen *to crush us.* 'Flank speed. Your course is 135 degrees.' *That leaves us in deep water and puts Rodriguez between us and that thing, for whatever good it'll do.'*

So we've seen it. A sight nobody ever saw – well, nobody who wrote it down, anyway. Now all I have to do is save the ship.

Ethan Allen was about to fight the biggest tsunami in human history — and just now he was broad on to it. He glanced at his watch. Tsunamis traveled at speeds from two hundred to four hundred miles an hour. Call this one four. Six minutes . . .

'Left standard rudder. Bring her to 85 degrees.'

'Bring her to 85, aye, aye,' the quartermaster answered.

'Warn 'em,' Villars said.

'Now hear this. Now hear this. Damage control stations. Stand by for depth charges.'

Might as well be depth charges. . .

The ship turned.

It surged backward. Villars felt the blood rushing into his face. Somewhere aft, a shrill scream was instantly cut off, and the Captain heard a thud.

Minutes later: 'There's a current. Captain, we're being pulled northeast.'

'Steady as she goes.' *Goddam. We lived through it!*

The news came on at nine A.M. when you could get it. Marty always listened. Fox didn't always bother.

No matter how early he got up, Marty always found Fox was awake with a pot of coffee. It was no use persuading Fox to go easy on the coffee.

'When we run out, we do without. Until then, we have coffee,' was his only answer to Marty's pleas to conserve.

'You know your trouble, Marty?'

Marty looked up from the radio he was trying to tune. 'Eh?'

'You're still connected to that world you left. As long as you let civilization worry you, it's one more way the desert

456

can kill you. Relax. Go with the punches. There's nothing they can do to us. We've already given up everything they control. Now it's us.'

'Yeah, sure.' Marty tuned the set carefully. 'You think you've quit, huh?' He'd thrown a wire for an antenna across the top of the tall pole somebody had set up as a flagpole years ago. It worked pretty well.

Four hours after dawn Shoshone would normally have been a furnace. This morning some strange clouds, wispy and very high, had begun to form quite early. They weren't thick enough to block off the sun, but they must have had some effect. It was still hot enough to bring sweat.

Fox said, 'I'm just taking a break. I'll save the world when it wants saving again.'

'Okay, so nobody's worried about the snail darter when the sky is full of bug-eyed monsters. But I've listened to you, John, and you'd still like to make Washington —'

'Not Washington anymore.'

'Yeah. Atom bombs in Kansas don't ruffle your feathers? . . . I think I got it tuned.'

'Ruffled feathers be damned.' Fox had his self-inflating mattress stretched out on a flat rock. He didn't seem to notice the heat. Sprawled out with his coffee mug sitting on a flat stone, he looked indecently comfortable. 'The question is, who's going to *listen* —'

'Shh.'

'Ladies and gentlemen, the President of the United States.'

'Hey, John, we got the President on.'

'Yeah?' But Fox moved his mattress closer.

'My fellow Americans, this morning the alien invaders struck at Earth with a large artificial meteor, which landed in the Southern Hemisphere, in the Indian Ocean. The effect was that of a tremendous bomb. My advisors inform me that we can expect some severe weather effects.'

'Meteor,' Fox muttered. He looked up, and Marty did too. There were more clouds now . . . and they were swirling, changing, growing dense and dark, streaming east like foam on a breaking wave. Marty remembered how fast clouds moved in a Kansas tornado. These were moving faster.

'. . . Global weather will definitely be affected. This makes Project Greenhouse even more important. I call upon every one of you to raise food. In small pots, indoors, outdoors, wherever you can. If you can build greenhouses, do so. County agents and other Department of Agriculture experts will show you how.

'America must feed herself.'

Marty thought. *Not here, we won't.* But the grin wouldn't come.

'Global weather,' Fox said again. 'Christ, have they thrown us a dinosaur killer? Indian Ocean. How long will that take? Marty?'

'I wouldn't know.'

'How much gas do we have?'

'About five gallons.'

'Better gas up the truck. I think I want to use it.'

———

By noon the clouds covered the sky. The sun that had blazed like a deadly enemy since Marty's arrival two days ago was hidden now. Marty watched Fox with some concern; for Fox watched the sky as if he feared a corrosive rain.

The rain started at one. The first huge drops drummed on the truck cab, and Marty lifted his face to taste it. It was only plain water . . . not plain, not at all, and Marty felt a thrill of fear when he tasted silt and salt. Fox shouted, 'Let's go.'

'Go where?'

'Come on, damn it!'

Marty jumped in after him. He had just time to whistle up the dogs and let them jump into the truck bed. He was a little worried about Darth, who was young enough to try jumping out when the truck was moving.

'Damn dogs, can't even stay and watch the camp —'

'Sure they can, if that's what you want,' Marty said. 'Are we coming back?'

'Huh? Yeah, we're coming back.'

'Then stop long enough for me to tell them what to do!'

'Oh. Yeah, sure.'

Fox stopped the truck. Marty posted the dogs, except for the pup, who'd have to come with them. 'Guard.'

Chaka looked up mournfully, but obeyed.

The rain was falling hard now. *Rain in July? In Shoshone above Death Valley? Sea-bed silt, when the meteor struck in the Indian Ocean? I don't believe this.*

'Where are we going?'

'Place I know. Come on.' Fox drove down the dirt track to the main road.

A big gasoline tanker was parked at the diner. Marty felt a twinge. That tanker held enough gas to get them both to the Enclave in Bellingham a hundred times over. *I wonder where he's taking it?*

They drove up the paved road, then turned left onto a gravel road. Fox drove as he always did, faster than Marty would, but carefully. He ground his lean jaw as he drove.

What's got to him?

They rounded a peak and drove onto a wide ledge.

Fox got out slowly. Marty followed. Darth came with him, huddling against his leg.

Death Valley was spread out below them, barren as the Moon. More like Mercury, Marty thought, remembering the terrible heat. But he could see very little. Rain obscured the view, and a fog was rising too. The rain would evaporate as it struck.

Fox gestured, like Satan offering Christ the world. 'This is what trapped them, the first ones here. Look how

459

gently it slopes down. It's just barely steep enough to stop a horse-drawn wagon from getting back up —'

'I've been here.'

'And you've seen the Devil's Golf Course and Scotty's Castle, I don't doubt, and the dunes. But have you seen the life?' The rain was loud, but John Fox was louder. He wasn't shouting; he was letting his voice project, as if he had an audience of thousands. 'It's like another planet here. Plants and animals have evolved that couldn't survive anywhere else. If conditions —'

For a moment the roar of wind and rain drowned out even John Fox. It was as if a bathtub of salt water had been poured on Marty's head. He screamed, 'John, John, what's happening?'

'The damned aliens, they're terraforming Earth to their own needs! They've thrown an asteroid in the Indian Ocean! And I was trying to stop atomic plants. I should have been screaming for atomic plants to power laser rockets! I tried to stop the Space Shuttle, damn me for a fool. They've smashed every environment on Earth! Damn you,' he shouted into the sky. 'Pour fire on the Earth, pile bodies in pyramids! We can live anywhere! We'll hide in the deserts and mountain peaks and the Arctic ice cap, and one day we'll come forth to kill you all!'

Death Valley was a bowl of steam. There was nothing to see, yet John Fox peered into it, seeing nightmares. 'An old sea bed,' he said in an almost normal voice. 'A salt sea. They'll all die.'

The rain fell.

PART FOUR

The Climbing Fithp

CHAPTER THIRTY
FOOTPRINTS

Hear now this, O foolish people, and without understanding; which have eyes, and see not; which have ears; and hear not.

– JEREMIAH 5:21

The contorted moonlet dropped away, dwindled, vanished. Earth grew huge. A flashbulb popped above the Indian Ocean, and was replaced at once by a swelling, darkening fireball. Ring-shaped shadows formed and faded in and around it. Far from the central explosion, new lights blinked confusingly in points and radial streaks.

The Earth's face streamed past, terrifyingly close but receding now. A wave in the cloud cover above the Indian Ocean raced outward, losing its circular shape as it traveled. Northward, it took on a triangular indentation, as if the edge of a blanket had snagged on a nail.

'India,' Dawson said. 'How fast are you running this tape?'

'Thirty-two times normal,' Tashayamp answered.

'What is – that?' Alice asked.

'Land masses. The tsunami distorts the clouds,' Arvid said.

'So does the ocean floor,' Dawson amplified, 'but not as much. That's India going under. Those flashes would have been secondary meteors, debris, even water from the explosion thrown out to space and reentering the atmosphere.'

That's India going under. Good-bye, Krishna, and Vishnu the elephant god. Jeri shuddered. 'Dave took me to India once. So many people. Half a billion.'

Arvid stood near. She felt his warmth and wanted to be closer to him.

Tashayamp said, 'Number?'

Arvid said, 'Eight to the eighth times eight times three.'

'Human fithp in India? Where the wave goes now?'

'Yes.'

Dmitri spoke rapidly in Russian.

'Stalin thought that way,' Arvid snapped.

Dmitri shrugged expressively.

What was that about? Jeri wondered. *Arvid didn't like it at all. Stalin? He would have been pleased to have a simple answer to the India 'problem.' It's easier to deal with 'problems' than people.*

The distortion in the clouds swept against Africa, then south. Here was clear air, and a ripple barely visible in the ocean . . . but the outline of the continent was changing, bowing inward.

'Cape of Good Hope,' Jeri muttered. She watched the waves spread into the Atlantic. Recorded hours must be passing. She found herself gasping and suspected she had been holding her breath. The waves were marching across the Atlantic, moving on Argentina and Brazil with deceptive slowness and a terrible inevitability.

Cloud cover followed, boiling across the oceans, reaching toward the land masses

'My God,' Jeri said. 'How could you do this?'

'It is not our choice,' Raztupisp-misz said. 'We would gladly have sent the Foot safely beyond your atmosphere, but your fithp would not have it so.'

' "Look what you made me do," ' Alice said in a thick, self-pitying whine. Her voice became a lash. 'All the sickies say that – the *rogues* say that when they've done something they're ashamed of. It was somebody else's fault.'

'They can say all they like,' Carrie Woodward said. 'We

464

know. They came all the way from the stars to ruin the land.'

'You should not say such things,' said Takpusseh. 'You do not want this to happen again. You will help us.'

'Help? How?' Dawson demanded.

'You, Wes Dawson, you tell them. More come.'

Dmitri spoke again in Russian. Arvid shuddered.

The screen changed again. Clouds moved so unnaturally fast that Jeri thought they were still watching a tape until Takpusseh said. 'That is now. Winterhome.'

Earth was white. The cloud cover was unbroken.

'Rain. Everywhere,' Nikolai said. 'The dams are gone. There will be floods.'

The Earth was distant now, and no longer turning beneath them. 'Synchronous orbit,' Nikolai said. 'Above Africa. Look!'

White streaks blazed across Earth's night. That was Africa, and the digit ships were going down.

'Go now. Tashayamp, take them,' the Bull Elephant said. 'Dawson, Raztupisp-minz, stay.'

The Herdmaster waited until the rest had left the theater. Then, before he could speak, Dawson said, 'I will not tell my fithp to surrender.'

If Dawson made to grip his eyelid, the Herdmaster would simply slap him across the room. He said, 'You will, Raztupisp-minz, tell him details, but later. Wes Dawson, did you speak with Fathisteh-tulk?'

'Name not known.' Dawson's eyes flicked sideways, at Raztupisp-minz.

'Wait. Second in leader status? Advisor?'

'Yes.'

'He came to me.'

'Raztupisp-minz, you permitted this?'

Breaker-One Raztupisp-minz hesitated, then gestured

affirmation. 'The Advisor thought he might find an unusual angle of approach. I thought it worth a try.'

Takpusseh's thuktun at the time had been the Soviets. Raztupisp-minz had been studying Dawson alone. Balked by Takpusseh, Fathisteh-tulk would have had to go to Raztupisp-minz. 'Dawson, what was said?'

The human still lacked skill in the speech of the thuktunthp. Questioning him took more time than the Herdmaster liked, but he persisted.

According to Dawson's tale, when he reached his room after his first foray into the ducts, there was a piece of cloth over his night lights, and a fi' was waiting for him. A pressure suit helmet and glove covered its face and digits.

'Then how can you know you spoke to Fathisteh-tulk?' the Herdmaster demanded.

'I make him take it off'.

'Did you. How?'

'Reason he was in my room, he will not tell. He asked questions. "We take Winterhome. Query: is this wrong? We use moons and circling rocks, not want planets. Query: is it true? Tell why. Tell if humans took wealth from space." '

The rogue human shrugged. 'I tell fi', Wes Dawson. Congressman. 514-55-3316.'

'I don't understand,' said the Herdmaster.

'Warrior under foot of enemy give his name, standing, and number, and not else.'

'Wrong. Tell more.'

'He said, "Dawson, you gave your surrender." I said, "I not surrendered to you. Who are you? If I talk to you, who is enraged?" '

The arrogant creature actually had a point. 'Very proper.'

'He take his helmet off. I take the cloth off the light. He said, "I am the Herdmaster's Advisor. Query: war with Earth is wrong? We want space, not Earth?" '

'I said, "Yes." '

'Of course you did. Go on.'

'What is' – *Dawson tried to wrap his mouth around an unfamiliar fithp word* – 'fufisthengalss?'

Dissident. 'You have no need to know. Speak further.'

'He said he is fufisthengalss. Fufisthengalss are many. Fufisthengalss want to go away from Winterhome. I say, 'It sound pretty to me. Query: I can help?'

'He said, "Give me reasons if *Thuktun Flishithy* leave Winterhome." '

'I tell him about loot of Moon and Mars and asteroids. Metals. Oxygen bound in rocks and dust. Things to make in free-fall, cannot do under thrust. Power from sunlight, not thinned by Winterhome air, not blocked by Winterhome storms and Winterhome night. We only begin to take the loot of space when you come to take the loot of Winterhome. Let us alone and we move all dirty industry to space, turn Winterhome into . . . into Garden.'

'Fathisteh-tulk would have enjoyed hearing that.'

'He enjoy. He is hurrying. He leave before I finish. I not see him after.'

Dawson's digits flicked toward the screen that showed Fathisteh-tulk's corpse. 'Some fithp disagree with fufisthengalssthp?'

'Did you have more to tell?'

'Yes. One time we have foolish entertainment given by television. Imaginary fithp from another star come to Winterhome, rob oceans of water for their own planet. No sense. Why not go to Saturn – to ringed gas giant for water, where it is already frozen to be moved with ease, where are no human fithp to shoot back?'

'The tale sounds foolish enough, but —'

'Traveler Fithp are no smarter. *Message Bearer* is fithp home for eight-squared years or more. Supplied again at Saturn. Could last forever. Why you need to smash Winterhome?'

'That is in my thuktun, not yours. Do you know or guess who killed my Advisor?'

'Many fithp, not one. No fi' does things alone.'

This insight was hardly worth the mentioning, save for one thing. The Herdmaster had asked around. Dissidents, warriors returned from Winterhome, mated and unmated females, juveniles: nobody knew anything. It seemed impossible . . . and even Dawson thought so. 'You speak well. More?'

The human's shoulders moved. 'Not fufisthengalssthp, for Fathisteh-tulk must have been of that – fithp. Not human, for he wanted to leave Winterhome unhurt. Did he offend Fistarteh-thuktun? Do fithp kill for what they believe?'

'We do. Why do you suspect Fistarteh-thuktun?'

'I do not. The warmakers, they killed the Herdmaster's Advisor. Are they many? Can you choose one who is nearest to becoming rogue? Smashing Winterhome is a rogue's act. You must have many possible rogues.'

The Herdmaster bristled. His urge was to kill the creature on the spot . . . yet he had never even considered the priest. 'You have thought this through in detail. Why?'

'We love puzzles like this.' Dawson reverted to English. *'Detective stories.* I have read many. Tell me all you know of the Advisor's death. It may be I can help.'

'Another time. Raztupisp-minz, you should not have concealed the Advisor's activities. Did it never strike you that they might have caused his death?'

'No, Herdmaster. How could they?'

Pastempeh-keph splayed his digits. 'I can't know that yet. Tell Dawson what to say to his fithp on Winterhome. Afterward I will send you to Winterhome. The African fithp must have one who understands human behavior, and the Breaker fithp must learn more.'

Raztupisp-minz gasped, covered his scalp, and said nothing. The Herdmaster turned away. He would never have sent the leader of the Breaker team into action except as punishment, and the Breaker knew it. Yet he was probably the best choice . . .

In a few 64-breaths there would be spin. The Herdmaster's family mudroom would be available again.

———————

Jenny had never seen the President look so tired. He wore a faded flowered robe, and his feet were thrust into slippers without socks. He took the cup of coffee Jack Clybourne brought without thanking him, and listened impassively as Jenny and Admiral Carrell delivered their report.

'In South Africa,' the President said. 'Dr. Curtis was right, then. How do we know?'

'The cable through Dakar is still working,' Admiral Carrell said. 'We have reports from their government in Pretoria. I wouldn't count on that lasting. Understand, Mr. President, we *know* very little.'

'Is there anything we can do?' the President asked.

Carrell nodded to Jenny.

'We can't think of anything, sir. We could try to send ships, but —'

'But they still have lasers and flying crowbars,' President Coffey said. 'Tell me, Major, is there anything to oppose them?'

'South African Commandos,' Jenny said. 'Their National Guard.'

'Don't they have a regular army?'

'Yes, sir. They've always had the largest army on the continent. Most of it was on the seacoast.'

David Coffey ran both hands through his thinning hair, then carefully smoothed it down. 'We can assume they destroyed the rest from orbit. What else?'

'Sir, there is – or at least there was, when we still had communications – a Soviet army about three thousand miles north of their landing zone, but we don't know if they've heard about the invasion.'

And when we call Moscow, nobody answers. We can't

count on the Russians. The President nodded wearily. 'They'll *see* something weird happening in the sky. Can you get a message to them?'

'I don't know. Or if they'd believe anything we said.'

'Try, Admiral. So. There's nothing we have that can drive them out?'

Admiral Carrell shrugged. 'Nothing I know of. We have a few missile subs. We could order them to attack – except that we do not know the precise areas to strike, and we can be certain they have placed their laser battle stations to protect their troops.'

'It took everything we had – everything we and the *Russians* had – to burn them out of Kansas,' the President said. 'I guess it's obvious. We won't throw them out of South Africa.'

Jesus. Is he giving up?

'So long as they control space they can do as they will,' Admiral Carrell said. 'Suppose we throw them out of Africa. There are millions of asteroids in the solar system. Perhaps they will drop the next one on Colorado Springs. Or perhaps they'll bring in a series of smaller ones to land in San Francisco Bay, Lake Michigan, Chesapeake Bay . . .'

'Admiral, must we surrender?'

Carrell snorted. 'You're in command, Mr. President. I'm from Annapolis. For two years my table was just under the banner. "Don't give up the ship." Certainly I won't.'

'But —'

'Archangel,' Admiral Carrell said.

Coffey snorted. 'Do you really believe in a spacecraft powered by *atomic bombs*?'

'It has to work,' Carrell said.

'You're saying that's our only hope.'

'I know of no other.'

'I see.' The President looked thoughtful. 'So everything depends on keeping secrets. If they learn, if they so much

470

as get a hint that —' He frowned. 'I've forgotten. Bellingham?'

'Yes.'

'They blast Bellingham, and we're finished. All right. If that's our best hope, let's protect it. I want a personal progress report. Jenny —'

'Sir?'

'Send Jenny, Admiral. Promote her and send her up there.' He looked around the room and saw Jack Clybourne.

'Jack —'

'Yes, sir?'

'You must feel useless here.'

'Yes, sir. Hell, most of the time the only person who's armed who can get within a mile of you is me.'

'You know security procedures. Go with Colonel Crichton and look into what they've set up at Bellingham.' The President ruined his hair again. 'I should put on a swimsuit and go talk to the Dreamer Fithp.'

Jenny thought, *What?*

He grinned at her fleetingly. 'The sci-fi writers, they cheer me up. They don't tell me horrible things aren't happening, I don't mean that. But it doesn't seem to bother them. They think bigger than that. Like an interstellar war is a great way to build up to the *real* story. And that tame snout of theirs – It helps to know that they *will* surrender if we can just hit them with something hard!'

Dawson appeared in the cell something more than an hour after the rest arrived. He was shaking. He looked about at several sets of more or less questioning eyes, and he said, 'They want me to tell the Earth to surrender.'

The Russians' eyes met. Arvid grinned and Dmitri shrugged and Nikolai's expression went quite blank.

'I won't do it,' Wes Dawson said. 'Vidkun Quisling,

Pierre Laval, Benedict Arnold, I'd be remembered longer than any of them!'

Dmitri asked, 'Why would you consider it?'

Wes flopped on his back on the padded aft wall. Looking at the featureless ceiling, he said, 'There's a symbol. It looks like a fi' on its back. It means "Don't bomb me." People can paint it on greenhouses and hospitals and trucks carrying food . . . like a Red Cross. But if they use it wrong, it'll be rocks from the sky again.'

'If you do not speak, you cannot make food shipments safe?' Dmitri demanded.

'Yeah. There was some other stuff. Threats, mostly. Another Foot.' Wes shuddered. 'I won't tell them that.'

'We have no evidence that they have other asteroids ready to drop,' Arvid said.

'They don't need them. There are plenty more where they got that one,' Jeri said. 'Or in the asteroid belt. It might take a few years, but they've got years. They've already spent, what —'

'Fifteen years just since they reached the solar system. Sure, they can bring another and another. But it's worse than that.'

Alice demanded, 'What could be worse than another Foot?'

'They'll go to the Moon,' Wes said. 'They don't need to go to Saturn or the asteroids! They've wiped us off the Moon. The gravity's low, and they can get as much Moon rock as they want.'

No. *God, why?* Jeri wanted to curl into a tiny ball. 'Wes, what will you do?'

'You tell me. I need help.'

And all the time they're listening, watching, while we talk about it . . .

'Perhaps,' Arvid said, 'just perhaps it would be better if you make this speech. It would have to be carefully done. We could help you prepare.'

He looked significantly at Wes.

'They want me to talk the human race into surrendering! They'll tell me what to say. If I say something else, they'll cut me off. What's the good of that?'

Arvid glanced casually at the watching camera. 'One may paraphrase.' A long moment passed. Then Wes mused, 'Of course, the fithp will need help with their phrasing. Their English isn't that good . . .'

'But yours is.'

The rest were asleep. Alice curled in a protective ball, one arm thrown across her face, the other reaching to clutch the wall rug. They had never been given blankets; they slept in the clothes they wore. *Thuktun Flishithy* had gone over to spin gravity, and Alice could feel an eccentricity, a wobble. Dmitri snored with a sound like complaint.

Alice uncurled. The hell with it.

Congressman Dawson slept a few feet from the rest, on his side, with his head pillowed on one arm. Alice watched him. Sleeping, he looked quite harmless. Yet he frowned in his sleep. 'Foot,' he muttered. 'Feet. Giant mee . . . meteoroid imp . . .'

Everybody in Menninger's had nightmares. It wasn't rare for Alice to wake in the middle of the night. Then she would watch and listen . . . and the others weren't any better off than she was. She used to wonder about that. If she'd spent any amount of time in a dorm, she thought, she would have known she wasn't unusual.

And if she hadn't been sent to a girls' high school, she might have grown used to . . . persons of the male persuasion. She'd have known how to handle them, like other women did. If her parents —

'Dinosaurs. Oh, God, like the dinosaurs . . .' Dawson said in a breathy moan. Alice had never seen a man whimper.

Poor bastard. He could tell the world how to safeguard

their food and hospitals, but what would they remember? Wes Dawson urging them to surrender to the horrors. Wes Dawson, traitor.

Unfair! Learning what the horrors had planned, Wes Dawson had tried to tear the nose and eyelid off Teacher Takpusseh. He'd told Mrs. Woodward about it in Alice's hearing. Alice tried to picture that. It must have been a short fight.

So safe, so harmless, asleep; but he was the only one who had fought back.

Greatly daring, Alice reached out and touched Wes Dawson's wrist. Too little pressure would tickle him, too much would wake him.

He stopped breathing, and so did Alice. Then, 'I'll kill them. They can die,' Wes said. His face relaxed; his lips parted slightly and he was deep asleep.

After a moment Alice curled up beside him.

CHAPTER THIRTY-ONE
MAXIMUM SECURITY

Those who will give up essential liberty to secure a little temporary safety deserve neither liberty nor safety.

– BENJAMIN FRANKLIN

The helicopter settled onto the parking lot behind an odd old building, granite base, brick towers at each corner. An elderly man waited with two others, all in tan uniforms. They held umbrellas against the drizzling rain. Jenny and Jack followed them inside.

'I'm Ben Lafferty. Sheriff. This is Deputy Young and Deputy Hargman. Anything you want, just ask them.'

'Actually, we'd expected to see the military intelligence people,' Jenny said.

Lafferty screwed his face into an exaggerated squint and eyed Jenny's bright new silver oak leaf. 'Well, *Lieutenant* Colonel, I'm a colonel in military intelligence myself. Matter of fact, I'm the senior one here.' His grin faded, and his face lost all traces of joviality. 'This is my town, lady. The state of Washington never had much need for Washington, D.C., and Bellingham never got much out of the state. We had a nice little university town here until you federal people came.'

Jack Clybourne reached into his pocket. Jenny laid her hand on his arm. 'I can sympathize, Sheriff,' she said. 'We're just doing our job.'

'And what's that? What the hell are you people building down in that harbor? And don't give me crap about

475

greenhouses. Greenhouses don't need big iron things brought in hung under barges —'

'There is a war,' Jack Clybourne said.

'So they tell us.'

'Tell you! If you'd seen that crashed ship —' In a moment Jack Clybourne had calmed himself, but the sheriff had backed away a step. 'I brought some films and I can get more. I believe I can persuade you that there's a war. We're losing it. We need all the cooperation we can get.'

'Yeah, sure you do.' The sheriff glanced at his watch. 'Okay. Hargman and Young will take care of you. I got to go.' He left the office without looking back.

'What was that all about?' Jack Clybourne asked.

Deputy Young looked thoughtful, then lowered his voice. 'He has a point. We got along fine until all of a sudden they announced this big greenhouse project. Only it isn't a greenhouse, is it? I never heard of a greenhouse needing an astronaut general to run it.'

'Air Force,' Jenny said. 'He happens to be my brother-in-law.'

'That so? You still didn't tell me why we need the Air Force to raise groceries. Or why all the security stuff.'

'There is a reason.'

Deputy Hargman snorted. 'Sure there is. One good enough to get this town and everybody in it killed by a meteor.'

'Not if they think it's a greenhouse,' Jenny said. 'They've never bombed a food storage place.'

'How will they know that's what this is?' ·

'Maybe you take your chances,' Jack said. 'Just like the rest of the world. Look, one hint gets to the snouts that Bellingham has a secret, and —' He spread his hands.

'No more Bellingham,' Young said. 'How would they find out?'

'TV. More likely radio. Police radio. Even CB'.

'Jeez,' Hargman said. 'Look, just what is this secret we're protecting?'

'What do you care?' Jack demanded.

Jenny remembered the gray face of the President. 'Hey, look, we're all on the same side, remember? What's important is not to let them get the idea there is any secret about Bellingham. Let's work on that.'

'Round up the CBs,' Hargman muttered. 'Won't be easy – hey, won't that make the snouts suspicious? No CB chatter here at all —'

Jack's chin bobbed up and down. 'We'll set up fakes. Lots of chatter, but it will be our people doing it. Thanks.'

'Sure,' Deputy Young said. 'But – dammit, I don't like not knowing what I'm protecting.'

'You don't want to know,' Jenny said.

General Edmund Gillespie closed the door, and the sound of hammers and riveting guns died away. Jenny could still hear them, but they no longer tore at her eardrums. The office was cluttered. Plans and blueprints covered every desk and table, and more hung on the walls.

Jack Clybourne removed his ear protectors with a look of relief.

'Max,' General Gillespie said, 'you remember my wife's kid sister. They promoted her. Lieutenant Colonel.'

A wide grin split Max Rohrs' face. 'Hey, Jenny. Good to see you. That's great.'

'And this is Jack Clybourne,' Gillespie said, 'Max is the chief construction foreman on this job. Max, Jenny and Jack are here as – let me put it right – as personal representatives of the President. They'll go back and report to him.'

'Okay,' Rohrs said. 'I knew we were important —'

'Max, you're all we have,' Jenny blurted.

'Yeah, I knew that.'

Gillespie waved them to chairs. 'Drinks? We have a good local beer. I recommend it.' He opened a refrigerator and produced several bottles. They had no labels, and the bottles were not all alike.

'Sure,' Jenny said.

Jack frowned but accepted a bottle.

'So how *are* we doing?' Jenny asked.

'Not bad,' Max Rohrs said. 'Matter of fact, we're way ahead of schedule.'

'Why's that?'

'Well, we got that nuclear sub hid out in the harbor. Plenty of electricity. And we've got every computer design system on the West Coast. That all helps. Mostly, though, it's just there's no paperwork,' Max said. 'No telephone lines to Washington. The engineers plan something, the computer people check it out, Ed and I agree, and it goes in, no conferences and change-approval meetings. We just do it.'

'It helps that everybody busts ass,' Gillespie said.

'That's for sure. We're here to get this done, not make money and take coffee breaks.'

It shows, too, Jenny thought. *Max doesn't look as if he's had a night's sleep in a month, and Ed looks worse.* 'So, when can I report she'll fly?'

Max looked thoughtful. 'Supposed to take a year more, but I'll be surprised if we can't launch in nine months. Maybe sooner.' He unrolled a sheath of drawings. 'Look, the heavy work is the base plate. The barges bring that in pieces, and we have to put it together. Heavy work, but it's still just welding and riveting. Then there's the gun that puts the bombs behind the butt plate. If that fouls . . . well, we're putting in two separate TBGs.'

'What?'

'Thrust bomb guns.'

'Oh. But there's all the electronics, and life support, and – don't I remember they needed nine months just to change toilets on the Shuttle?'

'Sure, NASA style,' Gillespie said, 'We just install the damn thing. Of course it helps that we're not shaving off ounces. We've got plenty of lifting power —'

You sure do. 'Is everything coming in on schedule?'

'No, but we're dealing with it,' Gillespie said. 'Maybe you've noticed, there aren't many of my Air Police here, just enough to guard the inner fences. I sent the rest over with Colonel Taylor to the Bremerton Navy Yard to put the fear of God into those bastards . . .'

'Which sped up deliveries something wonderful,' Rohrs said. 'Here, let's have another round.' He fished out more beer bottles.

'We've learned a lot of security tricks,' Gillespie said. 'From Vietnamese, mostly.'

'Refugees?' Jenny asked.

'Some refugees, but mostly former Viet Cong. They know a lot. Ways to hide convoys. Hollow out logs to transport steel. Tunneling. All the things they did to us.'

'Maybe you should have kept your security troops here,' Jack Clybourne said. 'I don't think your local sheriff is enthusiastic about your project.'

'Yeah, I know,' Gillespie said. 'I thought of telling him what we're doing. Maybe that would get him working.'

'Why not?' Jenny asked.

'No. No telling *what* those people will do if they know what's going to power this beast.' Gillespie shook his head. 'The only safe place for miles around will be *in the ship*. Everything else will go. Somebody may think it's better that the snouts drop a rock on the harbor than have fifty atom bombs go off here.'

'It's hard to believe anyone would deliberately inform,' Jenny said. 'But it's better to be safe. All right. What we need, then, is cover stories. What are you building if it's not greenhouses?'

'We thought about that a lot,' Gillespie said. 'How do you like a prison?'

'Prison?'

'Secret, for political prisoners. Explains why there are so many soldiers. If anybody gets too suspicious, we let them think we've got political prisoners from Kansas. Collaborators we couldn't keep in Kansas because they'd be torn apart by mobs. Deserters.'

'It might work,' Jack said. 'And if they don't believe that? What do you fall back on?'

'That's as far as we've —'

'Nested cover stories. Like an onion.' Jack began drawing concentric circles on a notepad. 'Penetrate one and you come to the next, and you still don't have the real secret. So what's the next one?'

'Bathyscaphe?' Gillespie asked. 'Underwater research facility under construction?'

'No. Why keep *that* a secret? . . . Hell, we'll come up with something. Let's keep talking.'

Jenny leaned over to look. Outside the circles Jack had printed GREENHOUSE. Inside the first, COLLABORATORS.

They drank.

'Snouts,' Jenny said.

'Eh?'

'Captives. A big research facility, to study captive snouts. The aliens wouldn't bomb that, but we'd have good reason to keep it secret from *our* people.'

'That'll work —'

'In fact, that's why we house the collaborators here, to talk to the snouts!'

Clybourne smiled. 'So. Who do we have who can design prisons?'

'Eh?'

'We have the skeleton of a good story. Now we put flesh on it. What would you import? Whatever it is, we have to bring it in and show it. We're supposed to be growing food. Ships would take food out. We'll bring them in full and send them out empty.' Next to GREENHOUSE he wrote FOOD and an inward-pointing arrow. Next to COLLABORATORS he wrote JAIL, JAILERS. Within the second circle, SNOUTS. GET SNOUTS. 'We've got snout prisoners, but they're crazy. They go where they're pushed. They don't

480

talk even to each other. But we can show them to people.'

Jenny grinned. *It's the first time I've seen Jack get really turned on about something. Other than me —*

'Circles,' Jack said. 'Layers. The security system is in rings, just like the cover stories. They look like they're set up to keep you out, and they will if you're too determined, but the real purpose is to keep you *in* if you do manage to penetrate – heck, we'll *have* a prison, not too large, maybe, but big enough to take care of anyone who learns too much.'

'It all sounds wonderful, but aren't you forgetting something?' Rohrs asked. 'Sheriff Lafferty isn't going to help you do any of this.'

'We do it ourselves.'

'Yeah.' Rohrs scratched his head. 'But, Mr. Clybourne —'

'Jack.'

'Jack, I don't have anybody to spare.'

Jack chuckled. 'Now, how did I guess that? It's okay. First thing, we get some Army troops in here.'

'Intelligence types,' Rohrs said. 'Sure.'

'MPs, too. Construction engineers to build prisons. And combat troops, just in case,' Jack said. 'The next time we talk to Sheriff Lafferty, I want him to *know* he's talking uphill.'

'Did I just hear something tear?' General Gillespie asked. 'It sounded like the Constitution.'

Jenny caught the look on Max's face. Interesting. He looked disgusted. *A liberal general? We're fighting snouts here!*

'No.' Jack Clybourne was positive. 'What you hear is the sound of Bellingham being put outside the boundaries of the United States.' He opened his briefcase and removed a document. 'I hold here a presidential order suspending the rules of habeas corpus in the Bellingham area. It's quite constitutional. I play by the rules, General.'

'Yeah, but when word of *that* gets out —'

'It won't. The first thing we do when the troops get here is seal off Bellingham. No one leaves.'

'What about people from the highway?'

'There isn't much traffic now,' Rohrs said.

'You can't see the harbor area from the highway,' Jack said. 'The big hill with the university on it is in the way. So we leave service stations alongside the highway, and all's well for people who go to them, but anybody who goes further into town, to the other side of the hill – they don't leave, that's all.'

'But what about —'

There was a knock at the door. Rohrs shouted, but no one heard. He went to the door. A flood of sound washed into the room. The workman at the door shouted. 'Max, turn on the radio, there's something important —'

'Okay, Thanks!' Rohrs closed the door and the hammers and rivet guns become tolerable again.

'What station?' Clybourne asked.

'There's only one.' Rohrs went to the radio that perched above a file cabinet.

A voice boomed out. It sounded familiar, like a professional orator. ' – They will take the surrender of all humans, and they will incorporate them into their herd. Those of their race who surrender become the property of the herd. Eventually they or their descendants may find status therein.'

'Son of a bitch!' General Gillespie said. 'That's Wes Dawson!'

———

They all stood when the President came in. He gestured impatiently for them to be seated. Reynolds stood with the rest of them. With its haphazard furniture and refreshments the room looked like the Green Room at an underfunded science-fiction convention, but it felt weirdly like the White House. Most of the Dreamer Fithp were present. Harpanet was not.

'Commander, I understand that you have a tape?'

The naval officer looked young for his rank. 'Yes, Mr. President. It's just as we received it. We've put it through filters to clean out the noise, but nothing else.'

'Play it, then.'

'Yes, sir.' The navy commander gestured.

There was a short hissing sound, and then a voice from outer space.

'My fellow Americans, I'm Wesley Dawson, formerly a congressman from California. I'm now a member of the Chtaptisk Fithp – which is to say the Traveler Herd. I am alive and well, and I send my regards to my family. We have been well treated by their standards.'

By their standards. The words stood out; Dawson must have intended them to.

'The human fithp aboard *Message Bearer* have been brought together. There are three Russians. Commander Rogachev, Lieutenant Colonel Dmitri Grushin, and Commander Rogachev's sergeant. There are six Americans in addition to me. Mrs. Geraldine Wilson and her daughter Melissa. Gary Capchart, aged nine. John and Carrie Woodward of Lawton, Kansas; and Alice McLennon, who was formerly resident in Topeka. We're all alive, in reasonable health, due largely to Alice's forethought in bringing us dietary supplements.

'The fithp complain that their warriors have not been well treated, and that many were killed as they attempted to surrender. The fithp regard this as barbaric.' Dawson's voice registered bitter amusement.

'The surrender gesture is easily seen. They lie on their backs, rendering themselves helpless. This gesture is deeply embedded into their psychology. One might say it is deep within their very souls. They do not surrender lightly, and when they do, the submission is total. You may believe this. It is true.

'Their leader or Admiral – the word translates to herdmaster as closely as anything else – has asked me to speak to you in order to save slaughter. He says that he can delivery many asteroids, and drop them precisely where he wishes. They do not need to go to the asteroid belt. They can use lunar rocks. Their command of space is complete and they have begun construction of a lunar base.

'When they first approached Earth we all wondered what they wanted. We know now. They intend to live on the Earth. They intend that all humans submit. They have come to stay. They mean to be the dominant but not the only intelligent species on Earth. They have assured me – and I believe them – that they will take the surrender of all humans, and they will incorporate them into their herd.

'Those of their race who surrender become the property of the herd. Eventually they or their descendants may find status therein. For biological reasons humans will never be able to integrate as fithp have traditionally done, but our descendants will be their partners. The human herd will be allowed to live under man-made rules. They will study us to know what those rules shall be.

'We will be allowed to choose our own rules so long as they do not conflict with fithp dominance, but they insist that we must live by the rules we choose. They do not tolerate rogues. We will achieve mankind's oldest dream, to be one people, with one philosophy, one set of rules for all of us. They do nothing alone. An individual's acts are taken to be the responsibility of his group. In particular, the fithp mating practices are entirely instinctual, going by mating seasons, and they mate for life.'

Good-bye to individualism. Reynolds shuddered. A moment later, *Hello, monogamy. Interesting.*

Dawson went on. 'They intend to do what they must to rule the Earth. They regret the great loss of life from the Foot, but this will not stop them from sending another, and another, until humans understand the great power of the fithp.

484

'Until you do understand, they have no wish to kill noncombatants. There is a symbol —'

Dawson was describing a fi' on its back. Oh? *We use a red cross* —

'– urge you not to misuse the symbol. They will be watching. Using the 'harmless' symbol for military equipment or installations will result in bombardment of all the places so marked. They see more than you believe they can see. Their radars and lasers are efficient and powerful.'

They would be.

'Do understand,' Dawson's recorded voice said. 'The Chtaptisk Fithp mean what they say. They have crossed light-years of space to come here. They will not go home. They will be here for centauries.

'They are a collective people who live by strict rules in herds. Evolution has eliminated all the rogues from the fithp. They will give humans good treatment by their standards. They would prefer to take the Earth in good condition, but take it they must. Their large spacecraft is their world until they do.'

'Very good,' Wade Curtis said. His voice was loud in the quiet room. Thoughts boiled in Nat's head. *We should wait for the President to say something. Fuck him, he's staring at the walls.* 'Centauries, Alpha Centauris.'

Joe Ransom said, 'They let him get away with a lot. You caught that, at the end? There's no backup. What they've got, we've seen. And they can't go home, I was right there.'

'– Uses his tone of voice like a fine working tool. "By their standards." Sherry mused, 'I wonder if they'll want us to follow their mating seasons? And of course the fithp won't catch any of that.'

The President and the Navy men watched in evident surprise. The Dreamer Fithp were all over that speech like dogs on a stag.

'Monogamy, anyway, Sherry. He made quite a point of it. I wonder if they saw some X-rated movie.'

'Whatever,' Curtis said, 'Dawson is one smart son of a bitch. Can we hear that again?'

———————

The air-duct pipes narrowed. Alice felt trapped, and for a moment she thought of turning back. Then she set her jaw, hard, and went on.

She rounded a turn. He was there.

Wes Dawson was curled into a small ball. *Fetal position. The really sick ones do that. In the movies they always go violent. The therapists would love it if they could get that much action on the closed wards.*

Dawson didn't move as she came closer to him.

'Wes?'

He didn't answer.

'Wes, it's Alice —'

'I ate shit for the sake of that Don't-Bomb-Me symbol.'

She said nothing. *Didn't I used to do that? Try to blow the therapist's mind by using dirty words? And Mrs. Fitzpatrick caught me at it.*

'Well, I'm going to be famous.'

'You were wonderful! You told them all about the horrors – God, the way you used your voice! And the snouts didn't even suspect —'

He started to uncoil. Alice moved away slightly.

'But *you* already *know* what I was trying to do,' Wes said. Half uncoiled, he still wouldn't look at her. 'They won't. Wes Dawson. Now they can forget Quisling.'

'We all agreed,' Alice said. 'We all thought you should do it.'

'Yeah. Just like fithp. Everybody does everything together. Look, it's all right, Alice, I'll be all right.' He faced her at last. 'Thanks for finding me. I'll be okay.' He smiled, and damn, it looked real, but she'd seen so many phony smiles. 'See? I'm fine.'

486

Maybe he is. He didn't look helpless now. Alice took a deep breath. I am not a freemartin! She moved closer to Dawson.

Abruptly he launched himself at her. She couldn't move fast enough to get away, and he wrapped his arms around her and drew her against him. She felt panic. *If I fight him now, he'll never get over this.* She felt him draw her closer still. She felt smothered, and wanted to flee. She tucked her head down, nose below his armpit, to breathe. She didn't struggle.

He curled against her and was still, except for his jerky breathing. He held her, but he wasn't moving. Slowly she relaxed the tension in her muscles as she'd been taught, beginning with her toes, ankles, then calves . . .

His tears soaked through her hair and wet her scalp. Almost without volition her arms went around him, and she held him. 'It's all right,' she said. 'It's all right.'

'I needed a hug. My God, I needed to be hugged. Alice, thanks.'

'It's all right.'

CHAPTER THIRTY-TWO
MUDBATH

We shall not fail or flag. We shall go on to the end. We shall fight in France, we shall fight on the seas and oceans . . . we shall fight on the beaches, we shall fight on the landing grounds, we shall fight in the fields and in the streets, we shall fight in the hills; we shall never surrender.

– SIR WINSTON CHURCHILL, after Dunkirk

FOOTFALL PLUS SIX WEEKS

Nat was measuring ingredients into a blender. He moved briskly. Lime juice, sugar, rum, scoop out half a Crenshaw melon, add ice. Low setting. The blades tended to break on the ice at higher settings. In defense against the godawful noise he moved up alongside Harpanet's head and raised his voice.

'You're used to long wars.'

'There are records from the homeworld. The Shape Wars lasted five generations. There were others.' Harpanet paused for thought, then: 'I cannot comment from the loser's point of view. I never wondered until you taught me. For the winning fithp, wars are long. Losers cease to be a fithp. The Traveler Fithp did not taste war until now.'

'Was the taste to your liking?' Nat hit the button that ended the howl of the blender.

Digits swiped at thin air: *How can I know?* 'I fell from the sky, I lost my fithp, I tried to surrender. No human knew how to take my surrender. You have warriors from Kansas, isn't it? Ask them.'

'They're not sane.' Curtis joined the group. 'Left alone too long maybe.'

Harpanet let his digits and lower eyelids droop in the gesture they'd learned to interpret as sadness.

Ransom held his glass out for Reynolds to fill. 'I sure feel sorry for Dawson.'

Curtis nodded. 'Yeah. Poor bastard risks his ass to give us some information, and a lot of nerds think he's turned traitor. What worries me are the ones who think he meant it and want to take his advice.'

'Maybe we should,' Sherry said. 'But it wouldn't work. There are too many like you and Ransom.'

'You ought to be glad of that.'

'Hey.' Reynolds moved between them. 'Have a drink.' He poured.

'Sherry, you don't want to surrender.'

'No, but I don't want to fight, either!'

'Wasn't *you* we asked to fight,' Curtis said.

'Enough,' Ransom said. 'The question is, what will the President do?'

'He sure didn't take it very well. Maybe he'd want to quit.'

'Nah,' Curtis said. 'He's not my favourite choice, but he's got more guts than that.'

'Sure?'

'He damned well better have.'

Harpanet spoke insistently. 'What are you leading me to?'

'Eh?'

'You speak of challenging your herdmaster.'

'Naw —'

Sherry laid her hand across Harpanet's brow. 'It's not what it sounds like,' she said.

'But they said —'

'We are the Dreamer Fithp,' Reynolds said. 'We say

489

anything. But we're not going to challenge the President. Wade wasn't even thinking that way.'

He put an edge to his voice. 'Were you, Wade?'

'No, of course not,' Curtis grinned wolfishly, 'Besides, it wouldn't work.'

Nat filled a sizable mug with what remained in the blender: about half. 'Swim?'

'Ssshure.'

'Yeah,' Ransom said. 'Only I want a real drink, not that slop. Wade? Sherry?'

'Thank you, yes,' Curtis said. After a moment Sherry Atkinson nodded and followed them out.

Reynolds and Harpanet walked into the mudroom, and into the mudfilled pool, without interrupting their conversation. It faltered when they noticed the near stranger. The President of the United States floated in the warm mud with his eyes closed.

Harpanet dipped his nostril. Nat said, 'Not in the face. He looks too tired to play.'

'I heard that,' the President said. 'I am.'

Harpanet shimmied. The wall of his flank sent warm, muddy water sloshing gently across President Coffey. The President smiled. 'Heating just one end of the pool,' he asked, 'who thought that up?'

'Human fithp need it too warm. Too much surface for volume. Shed heat too fast.'

Nat said, 'The guy who thought of that was the curator of the San Diego Zoo, George Pournelle. He had some very rare rhinos, and he didn't know what kind of temperature they liked. So he put a temperature gradient across the cage and let them make their own decisions.'

The President nodded. He was in the hottest part of the pool. He looked very relaxed. He opened one eye and fixed it on Harpanet. 'You've hit us hard.'

Harpanet asked, 'Was it the Foot?'

'It was. You've killed a great many people.'

490

'Not I. I am of the Dreamer Fithp now. Can I help?' It was a rebuke.

The President stirred. 'Reynolds, have you seen the tapes?'

'Yeah. This is a melon daiquiri. Have some. I don't have any mouth diseases.'

'Neither do I, and thanks for not asking. Jesus, you make them big. Were you going to drink all of this?'

'Yeah. I told you, I've seen the tapes.'

The President drank. He said, 'Nice. Are we going to live through this?'

'The species is. Hell, they can't conquer us. Some of us will live. We could get down to "The Men in the Walls" —'

'What's that?'

'William Tenn. Humans living like parasites in the aliens' environment, and we still win, because we're small enough to hide in places they can't get to. But it won't come to that. This is our planet, and we own every corner. Siberia, the Sahara, Greenland, they can't come after us there.'

'They don't have to,' David Coffey said. 'They just keep pounding away, killing more and more people, until we can't stand it any longer. If we have to give up anyway, why prolong it? Let the survivor types go to Siberia. The rest surrender.'

'It is sensible,' Harpanet said.

'No.' Reynolds wanted his drink, but he was too polite to reach for it.

'In the first place it wouldn't work. Too many would stay behind. Pretend to surrender, but they'd hide weapons and kill snouts whenever they got a chance. You can't surrender for everybody —'

'I agree.'

'Well, the fithp think you can. They'll hold us all responsible. What the fithp call surrender, we don't know how to do that.'

Coffey said, 'But we have to do something.'

491

'Maybe the fithp lasers only come in a couple of frequencies. We can make reflective paint for those frequencies. Paint them on the bombers.'

'That'll take a while, won't it?'

'Sure. Set up a research station.'

Harpanet said, 'The lasers can be – changed. The color can be made different.'

Reynolds shrugged. 'So maybe that doesn't work.'

The President let himself sag into the mud. He still had Reynolds' mug of melon daiquiri. 'What else should we be doing?'

'Study our friend Harpanet. Find out how to keep him happy.'

'I'm for that,' Harpanet said.

'Why isn't anyone studying me?' the President asked plaintively.

'Harpanet's bound to need things. Maybe it's dietary supplements, things that don't get into our foods. Settlers in Brazil had a terrible time with vitamin deficiencies. The soil is peculiar. Well, there's *bound* to be something missing from African soil. Not for us, we evolved there, but the Traveler Fithp didn't! What's missing? How can we stop the fithp from getting to it? Maybe they can't sleep in total darkness. Keep knocking out their power sources and in a few days they'll fall over —'

'No,' said Harpanet.

'Okay, *no*, but you see what I'm getting at. We tried playing baseball with Harpanet. There's no way to put a glove on him, of course, so we tried tossing a softball around, maybe he could catch it bare-handed. He can't. He can't throw it either.'

'This skill was not prized among the Traveler Fithp,' Harpanet said placidly.

'We could probably rig up a glove for him,' Nat said earnestly. 'It would look like an umbrella, but he could catch. He still couldn't throw. He's hopeless with a football. I thought he would be; but it's – we've got films, and

492

we've been showing them to your soldiers, and it gets them rolling around on the floor. Harpanet spreads his trunk like a great fan, and the ball either goes through it or ricochets away. We want to try basketball or volleyball. We think the ball is big enough that he won't lose it —'

The President was laughing so hard that it looked like he was going to lose the mug, so Nat took it. 'This is *research*?'

'Mr. President, the delicate point I'm trying to pound home is that Harpanet is at his limit. He —'

'Mug.'

Nat drank, then handed across the mug. 'He's at his limit, that's all. He gets just so good and no better. We still play, of course. We all need exercise, him most of all.

'Sherry's sure we're anthropomorphizing. Maybe the fithp have games we'd be awful at. But I think she's assuming symmetry where there just isn't any need for it.

'The fithp have bad hands. They're just bloody clumsy, and no wonder, with no bones in their grasping digits! I think they're a young race. God knows humanity never finished evolving in *any* direction, but I think the fithp are even younger than that. They're too young to have space travel. They didn't even discover it for themselves! What got them here was those great granite messages left by an extinct species. They shouldn't be here at all.'

'They're doing well, considering their handicaps.'

'We need to *know* their handicaps. Set up a research station. You have other prisoners now. Study them. They've got a mating season – Dawson said so too, and emphasized it – and their mating practice is more reflexive than ours. Can we duplicate their pheromones and drive them nuts?'

The President was still laughing. 'Somebody told me once that I'm not fit to mold the future because I'm only allowed to think up to the next election. Who is it that plans for the future of the human race?'

'Speaking.' Nat took the mug, drank deeply, passed it back.

'Then why am I in charge?'

493

'Somebody told you it was your turn in the barrel, and made you believe it.'

Coffey laughed. 'That's one way to look at it. My God, when I think of what I had to do to get this job! Mr. —'

'Reynolds. Nat Reynolds.'

'Nat, I ought to come down here more often, only I don't suppose I can.'

'Why?'

'Mr. Clybourne. I've sent him off on an errand, but he'll be back.'

'So you ignore him,' Reynolds said.

'I can't do that. He's doing his job, the best he can – and maybe one day I really will need him.'

You might at that, Reynolds thought. 'If you're done warming that mug —'

Things got a little hazy thereafter. Nat remembered making another batch of daiquiris. Harpanet cut the melon, but he was fairly clumsy at it. He did none of the drinking. The fithp didn't use alcohol.

'There's plenty we can do. Elephant guns. We should be producing them as fast as we can. Who makes elephant guns?'

'There are people I can ask,' said the President. 'The British? They made a big double-barreled rifle, a "Nitro Express" —'

'Round up all you can find,' Reynolds said, 'Send 'em to Africa. Somebody there can use them.' He laughed. 'It worries me to excess, there may be a young Zulu warrior somewhere who doesn't have an elephant gun.'

'Are your stories that bloody too? Ah, I've got something. Harpanet, are you willing to speak to your ship?'

'I am. They will take it that I am speaking for your fithp.'

'I know, but you can at least tell them that you were allowed to surrender. They may be afraid to try by now.'

'Good,' said Nat. 'Now, Dawson's sign of the friendly fithp . . . the "Don't Bomb Me" —'

'Yeah,' said the President. 'Is it possible they want that

sign so they'll know where our food sources are? So they can bomb them?'

Harpanet reared; displaced mud made a godawful sucking sound. 'They would not. Bomb the local-surrender sign? They would not!'

'All right,' Coffey said mildly.

'By the same token, we use it only where appropriate.' Reynolds thought. *If it isn't on the Bellingham greenhouse, they'll notice. If the sign is too big, they'll notice. I can't say any of that where Harpanet can hear.* At that moment the President winked at him.

Reynolds looked at the foaming glass and shuddered. 'What's that?'

'One of the last Alka-Seltzer in existence, you ungrateful bastard,' Joe Ransom said. 'And Wade found you a vitamin B1. Here.'

'Bless you.' Reynolds washed the tablet down. 'I think it was worth it. Even at worst, he needed to get drunk. Did I save civilization? I can't quite remember.'

'Yeah. We watched you from the TV in the lounge. You got him thinking about the long run. We think you put some iron in his spine.'

'I hope so.' Nat moved gingerly down the hall toward his room. Then he stopped. 'It shook up Harpanet a bit. He told me he'd never had a conversation with his herdmaster. Much less an argument.'

'He'll get over it. Now he thinks you're more important than he thought.' Ransom glanced at his watch. 'My turn, I guess. You know something? I hate mud. Why couldn't they like swimming in something sensible, like lime Jell-O?'

CHAPTER THIRTY-THREE
ARCHANGEL

We are done with Hope and Honor,
  we are lost to Love and Truth,
We are dropping down the ladder rung by rung;
And the measure of our torment is the measure of our
  youth.
God help us, for we knew the worst too young!

  – RUDYARD KIPLING, 'Gentleman Rankers'

'Did you have a good flight?' The President didn't wait for an answer. 'What did you learn?'

'They're in good shape, sir,' Jenny said. 'The scheduled launch date was late next year, but General Gillespie thinks he'll be ready months before that.'

'Good.' David Coffey rubbed his hands briskly together. 'The sooner the better. Jack, how's the security situation?'

'Better now that I was there,' Clybourne said. 'There was a bit of a problem with the local sheriff, but we fixed that. He'll cooperate now.'

He sure will, Jenny thought.

'We've laid it all out,' Jack said. 'Like an onion. Highway patrolmen, only they're Marines. No CB radios except ours, with Army intelligence people simulating CB chatter.'

'I expect you had your work cut out, rounding up all the CBs,' the President said.

'Yes, sir,' Jack said. 'There was one place full of survivalists, mostly from Los Angeles of all places —'

'Los Angeles is in pretty good shape,' the President said.

'Yes, sir, but they can't get back there. Anyway, they had a dozen radios. We got them all. They sure didn't like giving them up.'

'Sure you got them all?'

'Yes, sir.'

'General Gillespie has put together a weapons team,' Jenny said. 'Boeing engineers. Some Navy people. Even a retired science-fiction writer —'

'Good choice. They've been useful here.'

'Yes, sir. Anyway, they've invented a lot of weapons. Stovepipes. They take one of the main guns off a Navy ship. Wrap a spaceship around it. Not a lot of ship, just enough to steer it. Add an automatic loader and nuclear weapons for shells. Steer it with TV.'

'Jeez. Who'd fly that?'

'They've got volunteers.'

The President smiled broadly. 'Good. Damn good. What else?'

'Sir, you won't believe all the stuff they're putting on that ship. Torpedoes with H-bombs. Cannon. Bundles of gamma-ray lasers that go off when the burst from the drive bomb hits them. Anything that can hurt the alien ship. One of the engineers was trying to get them to truck the old X-15 from the museum at Edwards. "It maneuvers in space, doesn't it?" But I don't think they'll do that. It's easier to add another stovepipe.'

'And people really will fly that,' the President said. 'Damn all, we'll beat them yet! All we have to do is hang on until it's finished.' He glanced at his watch. 'Cabinet meeting in an hour. You two have been Outside. I'll want you there to answer questions. One thing, though, nothing about why you went north or even where you went. Most of the Cabinet doesn't know about *Michael.*' The President

497

paused. 'I'm thinking about making it a total restriction. Anywho knows about *Michael* stays Inside. What do you think?'

Jack shrugged. 'If you say so, sir —'

'I didn't necessarily mean you two. I may have to send you up there again. But everybody else, eveybody who won't be going up north – why should they know? There were all these stories about UFOs kidnapping people —'

'That wasn't the fithp,' Jenny said. 'Sir —'

He laughed. 'I know that. They're not that smooth. They shouldn't even be in space at all!' He sobered. 'They evolved too fast. They're clumsy, they're bad at tool-making. There are gaps in their knowledge, and we can exploit those. We'll win, Colonel. You know, I could even begin to feel sorry for them.'

What's got into him? Pictures flashed through Jenny's head. A doll resting on a gingham skirt – *I don't feel sorry for them. But I'd rather see the President like this than ready to give up . . .*

———————

Jenny fidgeted uncomfortably. Cabinet meetings were important, but most of the Cabinet didn't know the crucial secret. *It must be tough trying to run the country without knowing how we plan to win.*

'Item Two. The Secretary of Commerce,' Jim Frantz said.

Connie Fuller pushed her chair back as if she were going to stand, but decided against it. 'I too will be brief,' she said. 'And, I'm afraid my report is almost as gloomy as Admiral Carrell's was.

'First the good news. A *lot* of greenhouses are going up. Crops are being planted in backyards, on school play-grounds, golf courses, lawns of public buildings – nearly everywhere. Given any luck at all, we won't have people starving.

'I wish I had more good news, but I don't. Most of our dams are destroyed. So are most bridges. Some were fired on, others were washed out in the floods that followed the dams. The earthquakes got more. Mr. President, the United States is chopped up into a series of isolated regions, and there's not much we can do about it.

'The interstate highway system is destroyed. There are secondary roads and old highways, but travel on them has not been safe. Sometimes they let big trucks alone, not always. No train is safe. Ships are often fired on.'

'Even now?' the President asked. 'After using Mr. Dawson's symbol?'

They all looked at Carlotta Dawson. For a moment she meet their gaze with a smile, then she looked down at the table.

She doesn't know about Archangel. Shouldn't they tell her? She deserves that much —

'I was just coming to that,' Mrs. Fuller said. 'So far we have no confirmed report of a vehicle or installation marked with the "harmless" symbol being fired on. We've been somewhat careful about where we use it —'

'Good,' the President said. 'That's vital. We *must not* abuse the symbol. Mr. Speaker?'

'Yes, Mr. President?'

'We need new legislation, making it an act of treason to misuse the snout 'harmless' symbol. I would appreciate it if you would get that done immediately.'

The Speaker nodded slowly. 'If you think that's wise —'

'It's vital, Mr. Speaker. If you insist on knowing why, I'll tell you at another time —'

'Thank you, no.'

'I want strict enforcement,' President Coffey said. 'Any law enforcement agency is authorized to stop attempted abuse of that symbol by any means required, including destruction of the offending installation. That's important.'

The Chief of Staff wrote in his book. 'Yes, sir. I'll get the executive order right away.'

'I can understand the need,' General Toland said. 'But the troops sure won't like taking casualties.'

'Tell them to shut up and soldier,' Admiral Carrell said.

We've put the fithp symbol on the Archangel dome. And on the ships coming into there. No bigger than anywhere else. We had to. Otherwise we might as well paint Bomb Me *on them. But if somebody paints that on an ammunition truck . . .*

Connie Fuller shuffled her notes on the plastic tabletop. 'We don't have much eléctricity. Gas pipelines are working, and some oil lines. They haven't bothered nuclear power plants. There's no reliable way to move coal, so we don't have much electricity.

'We're able to ship some staple foods, but we can't move enough foodstuffs.

'In short, Mr. President, there is no national economy.'

There was a long silence. The Speaker cleared his throat.

'Yes, Mr. Dayton.'

'They don't hit nuclear plants. Seems to me there were a bunch of those stalled by red tape. All across the country. Could we get cracking and complete them?'

'A good question,' the President said. 'Jim, look into that, will you?'

'No problem.'

There's a switch! Of course we can get them completed, if all the anti-nuke idiots stay out of the way. Including you —

'We'll need that electricity,' Mrs. Fuller said. 'If we have electric power, we have a civilization. If we don't —'

There wasn't any point in finishing that statement.

Message Bearer was under spin. The fithp seemed to prefer their gravity low, and Alice was near the axis anyway. The ducts curved more tightly here. She moved in low-angle leaps, against the wind, hurrying. Dust puppies tended to clump where the pipes turned, and she stopped occasionally to clean them away.

She heard something ahead. She called, 'Wes?'

'Yeah. How are you doing? I don't think the ducts were this clean when they were new.'

She rounded the curve. 'It's make-work,' she said.

'Yeah, but it lets us explore. Sooner or later we'll use what we know.'

'Want to make love?'

He banged his elbow. He turned around clutching it, staring open-mouthed. She started to laugh.

He said, 'Sure I want to make love. I've been chaste for months. Are you aware that I'm a married person?'

'How far away is your wife?'

'Carlotta's twenty-two thousand three hundred miles away. Wait a minute. That's geosynchronous orbit, measured from the center of the Earth, and we're over Africa, so . . . another two, three thousand miles.'

He was treating this as all too amusing. Alice said, 'So she's not likely to come barging in on us.'

'No. Why me, Alice?'

'I think you killed the Bull's Advisor.'

Good, the amusement had gone out of him. 'Again, why me?'

'Who else would have the guts?'

'Any cluster of eight or more fithp who didn't like his politics.'

Alice grinned. She'd been scared to death when she made this decision, but – 'Play your games, Congressman, but you wouldn't be hesitating if you weren't guilty.'

'Oh, I . . . don't . . . It wasn't like you think.'

He did it! 'How was it then?'

'I didn't sneak up on the poor fi' and strangle him in his sleep. I – ' The violence she knew was buried in Wes Dawson surfaced in his face. For a moment she regretted her decision. *You can always find an excuse.* If the horrors were listening there'd never be another chance. She moved closer to him.

Rage was in his eyes, and they looked through her. 'I thought I had it all fixed! The Herdmaster's Advisor wanted to leave Earth. What he wanted from me was arguments to use. I by God was willing to give them. He ran out of time, the first time we met, so we set something else up.

'After five days we were still cleaning out the ducts near the hull,' Dawson said. 'The Bull probably thinks he's training us to make repairs in that area. I'd seen the mudroom, I knew how to reach it. Fathisteh-tulk was supposed to be waiting in the mudroom.

'The duct was warmer this time. You saw the door, with a knob the size of a soup bowl? I turned the knob and the door went back on springs. I squeezed through. I left my gear in the duct, just behind me.

'There were warm and cold currents mixing. Grill at the end. I looked through and saw a lot of black mud. The air currents set up ripples in it, but there wasn't enough thrust to move it. We were still pushing on the Foot then.

'Nobody was there.'

She could feel the disappointment. 'Nobody? Nothing?'

'Not then. I was very very nervous. I keep wondering what he really wanted. Military information? It was a silly way to get it – '

'They're not that tricky.'

'Yeah. I didn't know that then. If he tried something I didn't like, I was going to back down the duct, scream for the warriors, and lay a charge of mutiny on him. But maybe he just wanted me on record, encouraging mutiny myself. I thought I'd better see if there were witnesses.

'So I took the wing nuts off and worked the grill loose. I was going to go in, but I heard something, so I pulled the grill back in place. Fathisteh-tulk came in, walking along the wall on those Velcro shoes they wear.

'He got right to the point, like we'd never ended the last

conversation. He told me about the dissidents, the fulfisthengalss, mostly spaceborn, who don't think conquering Earth is worth the bother. It sounded ideal. I was actually wishing I had Dmitri Grushin with me. He said there are a lot of dissidents, and they want to make peace, but they, um, they're diffident. They don't want to make waves, they don't want to be rogues. Stick with the herd. Like voters in the natural state. They need jazzing up, something to get them moving.'

His eyes shone, and he waved his hands excitedly. *I can see why they vote for him. Especially women.* She felt a tingling in her loins. It was a feeling she'd long since known was dangerous, and for a moment the old fears came back. *He won't like me –* He left her no time for more thought.

'I said it would be easy to make peace. I tried to tell Fathisteh-tulk how often yesterday's enemies become today's allies. I think that confused him. For the fithp, yesterday's enemies are today's slaves are tomorrow's citizens. I think he believed me, though.'

He would. I would. 'I told him. If the fithp would mine the asteroids, we could trade their metals for our fertilizer and soil and nitrogen. We'd all get rich! I told him we'd grow fithp plants and animals for them. There's bound to be somewhere on Earth where *any* damn thing will grow that grows in water and air. I really don't think I lied to him at any point.

'Alice, I can't *blame* myself. I was being as persuasive as I knew how —'

'They're different. They're crazy.' *It's a great story. But get through with it!* She'd never felt that way, not since a certain high school dance. The anticipation had been there, but things had gone too far too fast and she panicked and ran from the car . . . and the next morning everyone knew the tale. For a moment the dread rose in her again —

503

But this was very different. She hadn't expected to find herself playing therapist. Should she resent it?

'Oh, but I had Fathisteh-tulk all figured out,' he said. 'I talked about how to *use* space. I'm good at that too, I was doing the research in my *teens*. Solar power collectors. Free-fall chemistry. Alloys that won't mix in gravity. Single-crystal fibers stronger than anything you can make in a gravity field. They'd missed a lot of that!'

'Why?'

'It's not in their granite cubes. Alice, they're powerful, but they're *stupid*!'

'Not stupid. Crazy, maybe.'

'Or something in between. They don't think for themselves. Maybe they never had to. But I told him. I told him about mass drivers. It's easy to put stuff in orbit from the Moon. O'Leary's plan to mine the asteroids, do you know that one? You land a fully equipped mine on a metal asteroid. Put a big bag around the asteroid. You refine the metal, but you keep the slag – that's what the bag is for. You make hemispherical mirrors from the metal and use them for solar power. More metal becomes a linear accelerator. It gets longer and longer. Before you quit, the accelerator's so long that the asteroid looks like the head of a sperm. Now you run slag down the linear accelerator. You get a rocket with arbitrarily high exhaust velocity! You put the rest of the asteroid into orbit around Earth and —'

'You told him all that in fithp?'

Wes Dawson stared, then laughed. 'I stuttered a lot and used simple words and waved my hands through the air. I must have got it across. It killed him.'

'How?'

'I told him too much the fithp don't know. He said, "You must be of our fithp when we take the riches of the worlds! You must be swallowed into the Traveler Herd."

Wes's chest was heaving. 'I think – if I hadn't *known* it was *my* mistake —I wouldn't have been so mad. I said we

504

could tell them anything they wanted to know. He said, 'I hear more than you say, Dawson. You want this wealth for your fithp. If we do not fight you for your own planet, we will presently fight you for the others.'

'I threw the grill at him and jumped behind it. The grill bounced off his head. Must have startled him. I was still in the air when I realized I was committing suicide. He turned his head away – he must have remembered how I attacked Takpusseh – and I kicked against his shoulder and was headed back into the duct, just trying to get away, thinking, Damn! I've blown it.

'I made the duct and wiggled in, quick like an eel. Something wrapped around my knee. I looked back and the grill aperture was full of a fi's face, and the other digits were reaching for me.'

Nightmare! Alice found herself gripping his arm, and her nails – She eased off, but didn't let go.

And he hadn't noticed. 'I must have been crazy. Maybe I couldn't have pulled loose. I didn't even try. I snatched my gear and swarmed back down the duct at him. Felt like I was attacking an octopus. I squirted that bag of soapy water in his eyes, *pfoosh!* He backed away a little, and I jammed my feet into the duct walls and shook the line loose and knotted it around his trunk, above the nostril, and pulled it tight. Then I heaved backward.

'You know, he didn't have any leverage. I pulled back and he came with me. He had all eight digits around me. It felt like he was tearing my leg off, but he couldn't get a digit around my neck because I kept my chin tucked down. I pulled that line just as tight as I could and hung on, and after a bit the grip slacked off. I guess the digits weren't getting any blood. I pulled him farther into the duct, and I clawed that door-on-springs open and hooked the line over the knob.'

Wes looked at her suddenly. 'From there on it was murder.'

'So you're an inhuman murderer. Go on.'

'What? . . . Yeah. But this inhuman would have blown the dissident movement apart. It was easy. It wasn't as if I was fighting a fi' any more. I was fighting a fi's head. His torso was out there in the mudroom, useless as tits on a boar. I had a tourniquet above his nostril. I crawled down toward his mouth. He said, "Dawson, you gave your surrender."

'I said, "I was raped." '

Alice burst out laughing. Wes said, 'English, of course. I wish I could have said it in fithp . . . hell, they don't *have* rape. I crawled down until I could get my knees braced under his jaw, and I jammed his mouth closed. His digits were patting at me, and I could hear him thrashing outside. After a while all of that stopped. I held on for . . . God, I don't know how long. His eyes weren't looking at anything and he wasn't moving.

'I kicked him out into the mudroom. I pulled the grill into place, and then I couldn't find the goddam wing nuts. It looked like it'd stay, so I just left.

'He'd wrenched my knee and hip. They were hurting when I got out of the ducts. I hailed a soldier, and he didn't notice. Couldn't read a man's face, maybe, or a politician's. By the time I reached my cell, my knee was the size of a football. In gravity I couldn't have moved. But I had four days to heal before *Thuktun Flishithy* disconnected from the Foot.'

'You didn't push him into the mud?'

'Nope. I don't know who did that. There are some funny politics going on aboard this ship.'

Alice smiled slowly. 'That's frustrating. Well, Congressman? I'm still here.'

'Yeah.' He studied her for a moment. He was a little afraid of her, she saw. As if she were dangerously fragile? 'You've had some time to think. Maybe what you need is just a hug? God knows I owe you.'

What was he waiting for? She hadn't intended to say – 'Do I look to you like a freemartin?'

'A what?'

506

'Raztupisp-minz thought I might be a —'

'That's ridiculous. You get a freemartin when a female calf has a twin brother. It gets too much of the male hormones. Humans can't be freemartin.'

'Good,' she said, and launched herself at him.

———————

'Down periscope. Surface.' Captain Anton Villars deliberately kept his voice flat and dull. *They can't watch the whole ocean. It's just too damned big. Isn't it?*

Ethan Allen rose silently to the surface. The lookouts swarmed up into the conning tower. After a moment Villars felt moist cool night air.

'All clear, sir.'

Villars climbed the steel ladder into the moonless overcast night. Topside was a steady westerly wind. He estimated it at nine knots. The sea rolled with large stately swells, some topped by whitecaps. A light rain pattered down onto the submarine's deck.

The African coast lay dead ahead. Villars studied it with his night glasses. He didn't dare risk a radar sweep.

'Quiet as the dead,' his exec said.

'Not the most cheerful image,' Villars muttered.

'Sorry, Captain.'

'Bring 'em up,' Villars said at last.

There were twenty-six of them. Fourteen had painted their faces black. The others, including Colonel Carter, their commander, hadn't needed to.

Carter looked at the sea and grimaced. 'More weather than I like.'

'Not much choice,' Villars said.

'Yeah. Okay, Carruthers, get the boats inflated.'

The troopers climbed gingerly to *Ethan Allen's* pitching deck. Some of the waves broke just high enough to send spray flying across it. They inflated their boats. 'Ready, Colonel,' one called softly.

'Right. Captain, if you can send up our supplies —'

Villars nodded to his exec. The crew passed up a number of boxes, each wrapped in waterproofing materials. They laid them into the boats and helped the soldiers lash them into place.

'You've got a long walk,' Villars said. 'Sorry I couldn't get you any closer.'

'It's okay,' Carter said.

'I didn't want to ask before,' Villars said. 'But I will. How'd you get this assignment?'

Carter grinned wolfishly. 'My grandmother always said we were Zulu. Made me study the language. I hated it. I never really believed her, but what the hell, it made a good story. So when the President wanted to send elephant guns to the Zulu nation, who better to send?'

He was still grinning as he climbed into the boat.

———

The warning bell bonged. Miranda Shakes put down her book and went to the window to see who had opened the gate. 'Kevin!'

'Yeah?'

'Get Dad.'

Kevin came in from the kitchen. 'Why?'

'Look.'

'Oh, crap. Carnell. Look at all those dogs! Who's that with him?'

'I don't know. We've seen him before. Look, they're coming here. Get Dad.'

William Shakes wasn't happy. 'Look, you never paid your share. You sure as hell haven't done your share of the work.'

'Relax, Bill. Nobody's pointing a gun at your head, but I do own a piece of the place, and you *invited* Fox —'

'I didn't. George did.'

508

'Hell, if I'm too much trouble,' Fox said, 'I can always find a place —'

'Not now,' Miranda said. 'Nobody gets out of Bellingham now.'

'Yeah,' Kevin agreed. 'You won't even get close to the highway.'

'We didn't have any trouble getting in,' Carnell said dubiously.

'Getting in isn't the problem.' William Shakes said. 'It's getting out. And what will you *do* there?'

'Hell, there's got to be work,' Fox said.

'That's what we thought,' Kevin said. 'All those Army people, Navy too. Trucks. Ships. But it's like it's in another country, a long way off. The only jobs are down in the harbor.'

'Doing what?'

'Nobody's telling,' Kevin said.

'So we go to the harbor —'

'I thought of getting a job down there. Miranda's friend warned me. It's like the whole town. People go in, but they never come out.'

'Military stuff,' Fox said. 'I don't suppose they need me. It rains all the time. Who needs a desert rat? Anywhere . . . What do they say they're doing down there?'

'They say greenhouses,' Kevin said.

'I know greenhouses —'

'But that's not it.'

'Something important,' Miranda said. 'Important enough that the whole town doesn't exist anymore. You never hear about it on the radio.'

'Something big,' Fox mused. 'Something to hurt snouts?'

'Bound to be.' Miranda shook her head wistfully. 'That's the only reason Jeananne would do that —'

'Jeananne?'

'Jeananne was a friend of mine. Some big shot from Washington came here and talked to her. Whatever he told her really got to her, because she told the Army about our radios. A whole bunch of soldiers came up to take them, the CBs, ham gear, everything. Not just here. Everywhere in Bellingham. But Jeananne, she brought them here!'

'Some friend,' Kevin said.

'What the hell could he have told her?' Fox demanded. 'It must have been important.'

'I never got a chance to ask,' Miranda said. 'After they searched the Enclave and took all our radios, they took her with them. I've never seen her since. Not that I want to.'

'Yeah, but if it hurts snouts —'

George Tate-Evans came in from the kitchen. He'd obviously been listening. 'Okay, Fox, I give up,' George said. 'What's got you so pissed off at snouts?'

Fox's eyes had a haunted look. 'No matter what they did, people never hurt the Earth the way the snouts did. They don't *care*. It's not their planet. I could always get to people's consciences. How do I get to the snouts?'

'None of which solves our present problem,' William Shakes said. 'You can't stay here. There's barely enough for us to eat.'

'What do they do with people who come in and don't have a place to go?' Fox asked.

'I don't know —'

'I don't think I want to find out.' Fox looked out across the Enclave.

'What's in the greenhouses?'

'Squash. Tomatoes —'

'Know a lot about hydroponics?'

'We have books,' George Tate-Evans said.

'Sure you do. I wrote some of them.'

'I guess you did at that —'

'Let me see your compost heap.'

'Our what?'

'You must have a compost heap,' Fox said. 'I taught you that much.'

'Yeah – ' Shakes led the way outside.

Fox kicked at the layer of sodden dead grass that lay atop the mound. 'You don't turn it often enough. Not enough dirt mixed in, and you ought to be taking finished compost out from the bottom layer. You'll have other stuff wrong, too. Like I thought, you guys need me. Marty owns part of this place. He'll work with me. We'll earn our keep.'

CHAPTER THIRTY-FOUR
THE MINSTRELS

Is war a biological necessity? As regards the earliest cultures the answer is emphatically negative. The blow of the poisonous dart from behind a bush, to murder a woman or a child in their sleep, is not pugnacity. Nor is head-hunting, body snatching, or killing for food instinctive or natural.

– BRONISLAW MALINOWSKI, Phi Beta Kappa Address, Harvard University

FOOTFALL PLUS TWELVE WEEKS

Roger Brooks drank the last of his coffee. It tasted of burnt bread crumbs. *They made coffee with bread crumbs in the British navy. Or at least the Hornblower novels said they did. Could Mrs. Tinbergen be doing that? She surely could!*

Outside his boardinghouse window was pouring rain. It had been that way almost every day in the months since Footfall.

Rain, and everyone too busy to talk to me.

He repressed other memories: of Army guards ordering him away from the gate into Cheyenne Mountain, and one sergeant getting so impatient that he'd drawn his automatic; of the three weeks before he'd found a representative of the *Post* and got a new credit card so he didn't have to fish in garbage cans for food . . .

That memory got too near the surface, and he growled.

'Trouble?' Rosalee asked.

'Nothing much —'

'Like hell.' She came around the table and put her hands on his shoulders.

'I know you too well.'

Yeah. Actually it was strange: Rosalee was very nearly the perfect companion. He'd even considered marrying her.

'Can I distract you? I met this Army girl. About nineteen. She said Mrs. Dawson is inside the Hole —'

'I guess that figures —'

'Shut up. Inside the Hole. Came in just before Footfall with a strange character. And a captured snout.'

'A what?'

'Yeah.' Rosalee looked smug. 'Still love me?'

'Jesus, Rosalee —'

'This character she came to the Springs with sings every night in a bar across town. Interested?'

The name and the sign outside were new. The sign in particular was a good painting of a fi' on it back, an oversized man standing with his foot on its torso.

'I like that,' Roger said. They both got off the bicycle.

Rosalee shrugged. 'I'll come get you at dinnertime.' She pedaled off.

To where? She gets money – no, dammit, I don't want to know.

It was still early afternoon. The *Friendly Snout* was cool inside, with a smell of old wood and leather and tobacco smoke. The customers were few, and some wore Army uniforms. At the bandstand a small toughlooking Army man was teaching a ballad to a civilian. The big redheaded man was jotting down what he heard, repeating each verse by guitar and voice.

That's him. Roger took a table against the wall. The waitress wasn't more than sixteen. *Owner's daughter? For damn sure nobody cares any more. Interesting how disasters make people mind their own goddam business instead of other people's* . . . 'Rum sour.'

'No rum. Whiskey.'

'Whiskey sour.'

'Lemons cost four times as much as whiskey. Still want it?'

Roger produced his gold American Express card. 'Sure.'

'Yes, sir.'

As he'd expected, the drink was corn whiskey, probably not more than a week old. It *needed* the lemon juice. *And so do I. Vitamin C, and the* Post *can afford it* . . .

The music and words were sung not quite loud enough to hear, and distracting. *Hell, if they'd just sing it straight through and get it over with* . . . The red-bearded man seemed intent on his lesson. Roger decided to wait him out. He took out his notebook and idly flipped through the pages. There was a column due at the end of the week. *Somewhere in here is the story I need* . . .'

COLORADO SPRINGS: Military intelligence outfit. Interviewing National Guardsmen from the Jayhawk War area. (Goddam, those Kansans think they're tougher than Texans!) Two turned loose two days before. Didn't want to talk to me. Security? Probably. That bottle of I.W. Harper Rosalee found took care of that . . .

RAFAEL ARMANZETTI: Didn't look like a Kansan. *'I was aiming for the head, of course. It was standing broadside to me, and it shot at something and the recoil jerked it back and I thought I'd missed. It whipped around and I was looking right into that huge barrel while it pulled the trigger a dozen times in two seconds. I must have shot out the firing mechanism.*

'It must have known I was going to shoot it.' Armanzetti had laughed. *'It did the damnedest*

514

thing. It fell over and rolled, just like I'd already
shot it. Belly up, legs in the air, just like a dog that's
been trained to play dead.'

'You shot it?'

'Sure. But, my God! How stupid do they think we
are?'

JACK CODY: 'When that beam started spiraling in
on us, Greg Bannerman just pulled the chopper hard
left and started us dropping. 'Jump out,' he said. No
special emphasis, but loud. Me, I jumped. I hit water
and there was bubbles all around me. Then the lake
lit up with this weird blue-green color. I could see the
whole lake even through the bubbles. Fish. Weeds.
A car on its back. Bubbles like sapphires.

'Something big splashed in, and then stuff started
pattering down, metal, globs of melted helicopter –
I've got one here, I caught it while it was sinking.

'The light went out and I came up for air – there
was a layer of hot water – and then I looked for the
big chunk, and it was Chuck, waving his arms,
drowning. I pulled him out. When I saw his back I
thought he was a deader. Charred from his heels to
his head. I started pushing on his back and he
coughed out a lot of water and started breathing. I
wasn't sure I'd done right. But the char was just his
clothes. It peeled off him and left him, like, naked
and sunburned, except his hands. Black Crisp. He
must have put his hands over his neck.

But we'd be dead like the rest if we didn't just
damn well trust Greg Bannerman. Here's to Greg.'

LAS ANIMAS, COLORADO: prosperous man,
middle-aged, in good shape. Gymnasium-and-
massage look. Good shoes, good clothes, all worn
out.

He needed a lift. I didn't want to stop, but Rosalee made me do it. Said he looked like somebody I ought to know. Damn, that woman has a good head for a story. Good head —

HARLEY JACKSON GORDON. '*I kept passing dead cars. Then burning cars. I tried to pick up some of the people on foot, but they just shook their heads. It was spooky. Finally I just got out and left my Mercedes sitting in the road. I walked away, and then I went back and put my keys in it. Maybe someone can use it, after this is all over, and I couldn't stand the thought of that Mercedes just rusting in the road. But it felt like bad luck. So I walked. And yes, the snouts came, and yes, I rolled over on my back, but I don't much like talking about that part, if you don't mind.*'

COLORADO SPRINGS: GENEVIEVE MARSH. Tall, slender, not skinny. Handsome. Solid bones. No money. Nervous. Sick of talking with military people. Wanted a change. Dinner and candles –

Rosalee left me the money to buy her dinner and bugged out. Goddam. She'd make a hell of a reporter if she could write.

'*They had us for two days. We thought they were getting ready to leave, and I guess they were, and they were going to take us with them. We all felt it. But on the last day some of them brought in a steer and some chickens and a duck, or maybe it was a goose. The aliens took us out of the pen, and they looked us over. Then they pulled me out, and I was hanging on to Gwen and Beatrice so tight I'm afraid I hurt them. And that crazy man from Menninger's who spent all his time curled up with his head in his*

516

arms, they pulled on one arm and he had to follow. He never stopped swearing. No sense in it, just a stream of dirty words. They aimed us at the road and one of them s-swatted me on the ass with its – trunk? and I started walking, pulling Gwen along, Beatrice in my arms, and then we ran. Beatrice was like lead. We didn't wait for the crazy man. When the space-ship took off we were far enough away that we only got a hot wind, and that glare. But they took the rest with them, and the animals took our place.' (Laughter). *'Maybe they think the steer will breed!'*

NEAR LOGAN. Whole bunch, all types, digging around in a wrecked Howard Johnson's.

Nobody's too proud to root for garbage now. Shit.

GINO PIETSCH. *'I knew there'd be a tornado shelter. Every building in Kansas has something, even if it's a brick closet in a motel room. I broke in, and I found the tornado closet, and I hid. The snouts never even came looking. I guess they didn't care much, if you were the type to hide. Every so often I came out just long enough to get water. And I was in the closet when the bombs came, and getting pretty hungry, but not hungry enough to come out. How much radiation did I get? Am I going to die?'*

LAUREN, KANSAS:

That page was nearly blank. Roger stared at it. *I have to write it down someday. Damn. Damnation.*
Not just yet . . .

ROGER BROOKS, NATHANIEL REYNOLDS, ROSALEE PINELLI, CAROL NORTH. The snouts were all over the city. George Bergson came up with the notion of using Molotov cocktails to wreck a snout tank . . .

The guitarists put away their instruments at last. Roger got up unsteadily. Three corn-whiskey sours had hit him harder than he'd expected. He moved over to the man with the fading red beard.

'Mr. Reddington?'

'Hairy Red, that's me. And you?'

'Roger Brooks. *Washington Post. Capital Post* now.'

'Yeah?'

Gotcha! Heroes need publicity. 'I hear you have some good stories to tell. I'm collecting war stories. Drink?'

'Sure, but I gotta run. My ride leaves in five minutes.' Reddington turned to the bar. 'Watney's, Millie.'

'Money, Harry.'

'On me,' Roger called. 'Things are tough, eh?'

'Toward the end of the month,' Harry admitted. 'The Army gives me a little something, but I had a bad run at poker —'

'Sure —'

'I got gasoline, too,' Harry said. 'But I can't sell that. Use it or lose it.'

Roger let Harry lead him to a table. They sat, and Roger studied Harry while opening his notebook. *Beard and hair trimmed. Competently but not artistically. Clothes are clean and almost new and don't quite fit . Supplied by the Army?* 'Harry, we have a lot to talk about. I'd like to buy you dinner.'

He took out the gold Amex card and handed it to the barmaid.

Reddington hesitated a bare instant. 'May I bring a friend?'

'Sure. What time do you like?'

'Call it seven-thirty.'

*   *   *

The *Friendly Snout* was more crowded now, with citizens and Army and Navy Personnel.

The civilians had dinner. The service people drank.

'I like it,' Rosalee said. 'But where do they get the food?'

'Mess sergeants making a bit on the side,' Roger said. 'That's why the service types won't eat here.'

'You know that for sure?'

'Don't have to.'

She drew away from him in mock horror. 'But Roger, it's *news*, and you're not digging it out —'

'Now just a damn minute —'

'Gotcha!'

'Yeah, okay. Look, Rosalee, it would only be a *little* story. No prizes. And I'd get the Army on my case, and I don't *need* —'

'Roger, I'm the one who keeps telling you to relax!'

There were no menus. Prices were listed on a blackboard, mostly too high.

'The drinks are dependable,' Roger said.

'Dependable?'

'You can depend on them to take the lining out of your throat. Harry was drinking a brand-name beer, but I noticed there was yeast in the bottom of the bottle . . . Anyway, they take plastic.'

'Oh, goody. Is that him?' She glanced toward the doorway. 'Hairy and red. But he's with three people.'

'Hardly surprising – Carlotta!' Roger bounded across the room.

Carlotta Dawson grinned widely and came to meet him. 'I thought it had to be you from what Harry told me. I saw your column —'

'You knew I was out here and you didn't come find me?'

'We're busy in there, Roger.' She lowered her voice so no one else could hear. 'They have me sitting in for Wes. Roger, that's off the record. *Really* off the record.'

Shit. 'Carlotta, I'm glad to see you. Hell, I've lost track of everybody. All my girls —'

'Everyone's all right. I just heard from Linda. She says Evelyn's fine.'

'Great.' *Say what? But Evelyn lives in . . . later.* 'Harry, you sure know some famous people.'

'Didn't know you knew her . . .'

'Roger and I are old friends,' Carlotta said.

'Carlotta, have you heard anything about Wes?'

'Not since his speech. Roger, what are they saying about him? Do they call him a traitor?'

Roger gestured helplessly. 'Not around me —'

'Or me,' Harry said.

'But they do.'

'Some do. Not the doctors. Not the farmers and grocers. Just damn fools.'

'There are always damn fools,' Harry said.

And then there are the ones who say Dawson was insufficiently persuasive, because we ought to give up before they kill us all. 'Lots of fools,' Roger said.

'Harpanet - the alien Harry captured - says that Wes told the truth, they do treat captives well —'

Roger let thick sarcasm creep into his voice. ' "By their standards." Wes did that well, Carlotta. Anybody who knew him would know that.'

'I guess I worry too much.' Her mood changed. 'Harry, thanks for inviting me out. I've been Inside far too long. Time to have a little fun. Roger, it's really good to see you again.'

'This is Rosalee. I picked her up in Lauren - ah, hell, that sounds wrong. We've been together since —'

'Never heard you run out of words.' Carlotta laughed. 'Hi, Rosalee.'

Good. She doesn't know she told me something. 'Let's sit down. Harry's promised us a song.' Roger led the way to the table. Millie had already pulled up another table to accommodate the extra guests, and brought out a new pitcher of beer.

'What did you get?' Rosalee whispered.

'Mind your own business.'

'You expected that woman.'

'Shhh. I hoped. You told me Harry knew her. Now just listen.' They sat. 'Rosalee, I've known Carlotta since she was in high school.'

'Pleased to meet you, Rosalee.' Hairy Red bowed as he took her hand.

'This is Tim Lewis . . . Lucille Battaglia.' Lewis was the man who had been teaching Harry to sing. Lucille was small and dark and pretty, and in uniform.

Spec. 4. Adjutant General corps. Personnel. Probably shuffles papers, when she isn't mooning over every word Reddington says.

'When does it stop raining?' Roger asked.

'The Colonel says in about six months,' Lucille said. 'If we're lucky.'

'Colonel?'

'Lieutenant Colonel Crichton. I work for her —'

'Jenny?' Roger demanded.

'Right.' Carlotta smiled. 'That's why I brought Lucille. Jenny couldn't come.'

'Hey. Lieutenant Colonel. She must have done something important . . .'

Carlotta smiled but she didn't say anything.

'Yeah. Rosalee, Jenny is – well, it's pretty complicated. I've known her family a long time. Six *more* months of rain?'

'If we're lucky,' Carlotta said. 'Actually, nobody really knows. It might be more than that.'

'What do you do Inside, Mrs. Dawson?' Rosalee asked.

'Well, I work for the government.'

'Everybody wonders what it's like, though,' Roger insisted. 'Families. I've heard the senior staff have their families with them —'

'Some do,' Carlotta said. 'Roger, I hear you were part of a raid on the Invaders —'

Roger laughed. 'Okay, I give up. Look, I only witnessed that raid. Mostly it was George's idea. Who'd you hear it from?'

'Carol.'

Oh, shit. Carol had gone Inside, on the insistence of Nat Reynolds. *The goddam sci-fi people can get their groupies Inside, and I can't even get past the outside gate.*

'Actually, it was George's idea. I was along to watch.' *How much did that woman tell? Reynolds was no more a hero than I was.* 'Hell, I'm not blowing a month's expense money to talk about me! Harry, tell your story . . .'

'Wow,' Lucille said. 'That's really something. I've never seen a snout except Harpanet. The one you captured, Harry.'

'Well, it was sufficiently hairy,' Harry said. 'If the snout didn't kill us, the farmers would. We took the motorcycle downhill till we could smell the swamp, and then we walked . . .'

Lucille found Hairy Red awesome. Roger found that amusing. But —

Carlotta laughed, something between a snort and a giggle. ' "See if it'll carry you," the man says. "Sheena, Queen of the Jungle." A snout armed with an assault rifle! I don't think it ever crossed Harry's mind that I might chicken out. So I couldn't. Harry's just the right kind of crazy. You know what he said when we got to those farmers?'

But Carlotta's backing him up! He must be a real hero. Aw, come on —

Roger moved his now-clean dinner plate so he could take notes. (All of the plates had been cleaned. People didn't waste food these days.)

'I never saw action,' Lucille said. 'But I've seen Harpanet – nuts. Classified.'

'Are there any stories you can tell?'

'I haven't been told so. Harry has all the good stories.'

Harry has the stories, but Carlotta knows what's happening. Bellingham! Evelyn got pregnant and married that guy, what was his name? Max. Max Rohrs. Has a sick mother in Bellingham. Had to live there, and Evelyn went with him. She'll still be there. What in hell is Linda Gillespie doing in Bellingham?

He watched Corporal Lucille from the corner of his eye when he said, 'We didn't see any sign of snouts after the bombs went off. Now they tell me those were Soviet bombs.' She didn't react. 'I wonder how the sub commanders felt. They finally got to bomb us.'

'I never saw a snout,' Tim Lewis said. 'I talked to plenty of guys who did. Dave Pfeiffer and I made a song about what happened to him. He joined the Army after we got here. I don't know where he is now, but I'd guess he's chasing down refugee snouts.'

'Let's sing that song.' said Hairy Red.

'Dessert's coming,' Tim Lewis protested. ' – Oh, hell. Sure.' They moved to the bandstand and opened guitar cases. Customers started to look around.

Bellingham. Linda's not there to meet a lover. I'm the only lover she's got. If she's there, Ed Gillespie is there. Air Force general. On the President's personal staff. In Bellingham. Why?

'Penny for your thoughts,' Rosalee said.

'Shh. They're going to sing.'

THE BATTLE OF GARFIELD
by David Pfeiffer and Tim Lewis

It was just five days after the battle in orbit.

Like snowflakes they came drifting down from the sky:

Monster-things dangling from bright frail gliders.

We watched and we talked, and we all wondered
why.

To northward and east of us they made their landing.
    Set up a strong point out near Great Bend,
But some had been scattered by wind while they
drifted,
    And four landed near us to settle with men.

Bob and Les Forward and Bill 'Top Kick' Tuning,
    Old Amvets, came by on the sixth morning bright.
They had fifteen men with them, combat vets mostly.
    They called 'Saddle up' for a hell of a fight.

Tom Kinney had seen them and told us about them,
    Right down toward Kinsley and headed our way.
'Elephant dwarves with their two trunks a-swinging
    And rifles to shoot with' is what he did say.

*Ed Gillespie. Air Force general. Fighter pilot, but with
administrative and science experience. Can't fly now.
There's nothing to fly. No airport worth mentioning there
anyway.*

*Evelyn told us about Bellingham. Seaport town. Old.
Decayed. University. Pacific Northwest, where it rained
all the time even before Footfall . . .*

So Mike tried to track them, and we kept our distance.
    We set up an ambush and bid our time.
As they came in closer, I picked out the last one
    And sighted my 'H.K.' to make his life mine.

Charley cut loose with AK-47,
    An old souvenir from that old Asian war.
The rest of us fired on time from position.
    These snouts wouldn't push us around anymore.

The snouts fired back, as was to be expected,
    But two tumbled over and thrashed in the wheat.
Grenades came a-flying and I picked up shrapnel
    That peppered my right hand and both of my feet.

Pacific Northwest. Rains all the time. Cloud cover.
Railroad goes there. Old seaport. Goddam, it's perfect.
They're building something there, something they want
hidden under cloud cover. It flies, why else have an astro-
naut general there? Something that flies into space.

I rolled to a culvert just under the roadway,
    I was lucky I did as we fired last round;
'Cause they called on their buddies that waited in orbit,
    Called for support and laid hell on the ground.

Green fire came humming and cracking and burning,
    Scorched out our positions and killed every one,
Left me in the culvert, a-wounded and bleeding,
    And one living snout that had started to run.

It came to my refuge and looked up the pipe there,
    Then reached in and grabbed me and pulled me out-
side.
Its trunk gripped my rifle as it pulled me from safety,
    But I put a .45 slug through its eye.

Now out from Garfield, police came a-riding
    On horses to look around after the fight.
They found me and patched me and gave me some
bourbon.
    And took me towards home in the quiet twi-light.

So raise your glass slowly to memories around us,
    And drink to those boys who have gone on their way,
They died fighting bravely for freedom and Kansas
    Against enemies of the US of A.

Something they want to hide, too big to hide in a factory building, something BIG that flies into space. God damn!

Carlotta had listened politely. 'Harry's a hero, not a bard.'

'Yeah,' Roger said. 'He's better than the writer, though. It could be improved with an axe . . . How's Linda?'

'I haven't seen her in months.'

'You said —'

'Harry! That was great.' Carlotta stood. 'But it's getting pretty late.'

'Max and Evelyn moved to Bellingham.' *I'm pushing it. Maybe too hard. But I have to know . . .* 'Is Linda with them?'

'Roger, it's really late. Tim, it's time – Lucille, you have work to do tomorrow morning.'

'Yes, ma'am – can't I stay?'

'No. Come along.'

'Yes, ma'am.'

Roger watched Carlotta lead Tim and Lucille out of the restaurant.

'Hasn't changed a bit. Still gives the orders.'

'Except to Wes,' Harry said.

'Yeah, guess so. Harry, you look like a man who could use another drink.'

'Reckon I could.'

'Dessert?'

'Roger, there's only apple pie, and I have had enough of that to last me.'

'Good pie?'

'Not bad, if you don't eat it every night for a month.'

'Getting tired of the Springs, Harry?'

'Not really – well, maybe.'

'You have gasoline. For what?'

'Motorcycle —'

'Harry, how would you like to be a reporter for the *Capital Post*?'

*　　*　　*

526

'Take you where?' Harry demanded.

'Can't tell you. Long way,' Roger said. His head reeled. They'd had far too much corn whiskey.

Harry moved unsteadily to the men's room.

'Where are you going?' Rosalee whispered fiercely. 'I'm coming with you!'

'Not on a motorcycle.'

'But —'

'I'll be back,' Roger said. 'Rosie, this is a big one. I can feel it. Big. Maybe the biggest thing I ever got wind of.'

'What are you talking about – that Dawson woman! She told you something.'

'Rosie, do you love me?'

'Why ask?'

'I love you. But — '

'But you smell a story.'

Roger nodded helplessly.

She took his hands in both of hers. 'I can't come?'

'It's a long way, Rosie. I might get there on a motorcycle. No way in a car. Three on a motorcycle won't work, even if Harry would try it, which he won't —'

'What makes you think he'll take you?'

'Come on. The role of retired hero isn't a very attractive one. He's getting fat again, and he hates it, and he doesn't know what else to do. Too old for the Army . . .'

'Why him?'

'He probably knows the way. He has a gas ration card. Know anyone else who does?'

'But – Oh, God damn it, Roger. Come back? Please?'

'I will. I promise.'

———

Sarge Harris pulled out a big bandana and wiped his face. 'That's the last of it.'

'Good,' Ken Dutton said. He went over to the pool edge

to inspect. Sarge and his crew had shoveled the last of the mud out. 'Let's hope the new wall holds.'

Sarge laughed. 'It will.'

'But —'

'Come on! It's a good wall. So was the old one. It just wasn't designed to live through a giant meteoroid impact.'

Patsy Clevenger looked up from the pool bottom where she'd been scooping the last of the mud into a bucket. 'The dinosaurs weren't either. Ken, we're lucky the *house* didn't slide down the hill.'

'You're right there.'

Footfall had triggered earthquakes. Houses fell, freeway overpasses collapsed. Power lines went down. Ken Dutton had heard it was much worse in San Francisco and through Northern California. In Los Angeles the quakes had merely been annoying, compared to the mudslides three months of hard rain had produced. Now, maybe, the worst was over, with three swimming pools cleared of mud and ready to fill.

The encampment across the street was growing. Part of the golf course was covered with aluminium-framed plastic greenhouses filled with young tomatoes and beans. Chickens clucked in the pens he'd built in what had been his neighbor's cabana.

Patsy climbed out of the pool where she'd been working. 'Lord of all you survey,' she said.

'Something like that,' Ken admitted.

'You love it,' she accused.

'That's not fair —'

'I don't mind,' Patsy said. 'I didn't used to like you very much. You tried everything and weren't very good at anything. Now – now it's like you found what you do best. I'm glad *somebody* can cope.'

'Thanks, but I'm hardly the only one. I hear about people all over the valley. Greenhouses, cornfields – one chap came by the other day hoping to borrow an olive press. I never thought of that one. There are lots of olive trees in Los Angeles.' Ken looked up at the sky. It was partly overcast, but there were patches of blue. Los Angeles was supposed to be a desert. One day it might be again. Nobody really knew. 'Anyway, we have another place to store water. Come on in, I'll spring for coffee.'

'Real coffee?' Sarge asked.

'Why not?'

'Damn, I'm for that!'

The sink worked fine, now that Sarge had rigged up pipes. They'd have running water as long as the rains filled the swimming pool up on top of the hill above them. The house that stood there had been one of the first to go. Fortunately it had gone down the other side of the hill . . .

Ken watched Cora carefully measure out water into the kettle.

'Coffee,' Sarge Harris said wistfully. 'I think I miss not having morning coffee more'n anything. Sure wish we could have another Stone Soup Party —'

'I already put out the invitations,' Ken said. 'The next time there's enough sunshine. Or if the gas comes back on.'

Cora carefully lit the bottled gas stove. 'Which it won't. I keep hoping we can save up, get a bottle or two ahead, but we can't, not with all those kids to cook for.'

'It works out,' Sarge said. 'Or has so far.'

'Just barely,' Ken said. Cora was watching the kettle, ready to turn it off the second it was hot enough. She didn't look up. Ken felt relieved. Cora was the only one who knew how well he'd done by taking in city orphans. It hadn't been as much trouble as he'd thought, with Sarge and his wife to help. They put the kids into two empty neighboring houses, and Sarge got them organized like a military outfit with their own leaders and everything. Ken hardly saw them.

And it had paid off nicely. Not only were there enough ration coupons and gas bottles to trade for a few luxuries,

529

but everybody knew about the kids and his increased ration tickets, so the local ration wardens didn't come searching his place. Hoarders weren't highly regarded . . .

Ken had known food would be scarce. *But who'd have thought that heat to cook it with would be the hardest thing to come by? No sun!*

Cora was just beginning to bulge. *I suppose I'll have to marry her. Maybe not. Either way, she's going to make me send Patsy away. Unless I can get somebody to marry Patsy? Somebody hungry who'll act jealous?*

They took the coffee into the front room. Anthony Graves was in his usual place by the big front windows. They faced southeast, and got just enough sun to grow tomatoes in pots if somebody would spend enough time taking care of them. Graves was glad to do it. There wasn't a lot else for somebody his age.

Randy Conant was there, too.

Sarge gave Anthony Graves a quarter cup of his coffee. He liked Graves. He carefully ignored Randy Conant. 'Get much written, sir?'

'Some,' Graves said. He grinned. 'I never expected to write my magnum opus long after I retired.'

'I think it's great,' Sarge said.

Randy Conant mumbled something.

'What?' Cora asked.

'I said it was shit.'

'Enough, Sarge,' Ken said. Sarge Harris hadn't moved, but his face told it all. 'Randy, why don't you go turn over the compost heap?'

'Fuck all, let somebody else do some of the work!'

'Sarge, I said that'll do! Randy, we all work. Now get going before I forget you're my sister's kid —'

'Don't do me any favors, *Uncle Ken*.'

'Maybe I'll take that advice.'

'Whew,' Patsy said. 'It gets thick —'

'Hey, I'm sorry,' Randy said. 'I get upset, that's all. All this work, and what for?'

'What *for*?' Sarge demanded.

'Yeah, what for? We're gonna lose anyway. Just like that Dawson guy said, they can keep dropping rocks on us until we have to give up. Why don't we do it while we've got something left?'

' "Peace in our time." Thank you, Neville Chamberlain,' Graves chuckled.

'You're gonna fight the snouts with quotes?'

'Sure. Have another. "Some folks win by winning, some folks win by losing." I think you get off on looking stupid, Randy.'

'There's a lot of people think like I do!'

'Bullshit!'

'Sarge, you won't hear it,' Patsy said. 'But he's right. I hear them down at the market. Nice people. They just want things the way they were before the war started.'

'That's what they won't get,' Graves said. 'Whatever else, they won't have that. Look what happened after World War II. Everything changes after a war. Win or lose.'

'It'll be worse if we lose,' Sarge insisted.

'Sure. People don't tame very well.'

'I don't want us to surrender,' Cora said. 'But – well, would it be so awful? That congressman, Dawson, he said they'll let us live under our own laws, live the way we always said we want to —'

Monogamously. You'd like that, Ken thought.

'That's what the commies always said!' Sarge shouted.

'True enough,' Graves said.

'I'd rather have them than snouts,' Patsy said.

'What difference does it make, what you'd rather have?' Randy demanded. 'Nothing we do makes any difference! They're up there and we can't hurt them!'

'The Army's doing something.' Sarge was positive.

'What? Just what can they do?'

'I don't know, but they're doing something. You heard the President! He sounded good, confident —'

'And you really believe in politicians. I mean, you really trust them! Hell, you *hate* President Coffey!'

'A lot of people hated Roosevelt,' Graves said. 'A lot more than you'd think. But he won the war.'

'It's different now,' Randy said. 'Don't you see, it's different. If there was something we could do, some way we could fight, but there's nothing, we just sit here and let them drop rocks on us, nothing we can do, and they'll get bigger and bigger. They'll kill us all and we can't do anything about it.' He laughed. 'Shit, *we* sure can't do anything. We can't even surrender.'

'We can hang on,' Graves said. 'Stay alive and be ready to put things back together.'

CHAPTER THIRTY-FIVE
THE WASHING OF THE SPEARS

An assegai has been thrust into the belly of the nation. There are not enough tears to mourn the dead.

– CETSHWAYO, King of the Zulu, after the battle of Rorke's Drift

'We are winning.' Attackmaster Koothfektil-rusp's image blurred slightly, and his voice hissed.

African night lay below *Message Bearer*. The dark cloud cover flared with chains of wild power surges. The Herdmaster's nerves screamed at the sight, but he couldn't look away. *Repair the broken lines, lest the ship die!* He waited for the atmospheric electrical discharges to end. They came less frequently now. When the fithp had landed in the first weeks after the Foot, they had been nearly constant.

The image solidified. 'We have captured wonderful machines, which make electrical power, and transportation devices, machines that make other machines. We have slaves. The land is wide, and it is ours. We eat the native food —'

'We must learn if poisons are present or nutrients are missing. Ship samples to *Message Bearer* for chemical analysis.'

'We will, on the next launch. Herdmaster, Chintithpit-mang wishes to return for the mating season. We will miss him sorely, but he has surely earned the privilege.'

'Yes, I remember your reports.' *Yet Chintithpit-mang*

is a dissident, of the Year Zero Fithp! What have they found, that they look so far? 'Can you truly spare your best warriors? You continue to lose fithp.'

'Yes, Herdmaster. We will always lose warriors until we have culled out the rogues from among these humans. Fistarteh-thuktun was correct. This is a race of rogues, rogues everywhere, there may be more rogues than normals. The acolytes are studying this, to see how it could have come about. Herdmaster, we may have come just in time to save these humans. As if it were meant to be. Herdmaster, we gain a new domain, a wide domain. We stand on high places and we cannot see the bounds of our territory!'

'Your domain grows large and the fithp grow fewer. The warriors sicken of slaughter.'

'It will not always be so. The true humans learn. We kill rogues only. It is the task of warriors to kill rogues.'

The Herdmaster suppressed an urge to trumpet. 'How are you sure there are what you call true humans?'

'I will show you.' The Attackmaster gestured and stepped aside. Two stepped into camera view: Breaker-One Raztupisp-minz, and a dark human male covered with drab cloth, as the important ones always covered themselves. He stood half out of camera view, for fear of standing too close to the Breaker.

'This one is called *Botha*. He held high rank in the Afrikaans tribe. He knows little of our speech, but I will give you his words. He is eager to end this war.'

The human spoke at length. His voice went up and down, now a mumble, now a whine. Pastempeh-keph heard it as a plea.

'He speaks strangely,' Tashayamp said.

Pastempeh-keph turned to her. 'Is it not English?'

'Yes, Herdmaster, but not as I have learned it.'

The Breaker spoke. 'He says that the war destroys, and both humans and fithp lose. He says that he would do what he could to end the fighting and let humans and fithp live together. This he calls *peace*. He says that now he can do nothing. We took his surrender in a ceremony broadcast to all the humans here, and because they have seen my foot on his chest, many will no longer obey him.'

The Herdmaster trumpeted in rage. 'Then why seek leaders at all? Must we take surrender from each? We have not enough feet for every human!'

'No, Herdmaster. We allow them to gather. They have gatherings, much as we do, where the eldest speak for all. Their decisions are binding. These humans do nothing without meeting and talking. We will allow these eldest to meet and take their surrender. They will name this Botha as leader. He will then command the human warriors to keep order and enforce our domain.'

Something had changed in the African fithp – it was visible even in the monitor screens – and the Herdmaster began to see why. 'Was this peculiar approach your own idea, Breaker?'

'Herdmaster, the human fithp *always* want to discuss terms before they surrender. From curiosity I began to discuss "conditional surrender" with small human fithp —'

'Over my objection,' Attackmaster Koothfektil-rusp put in. 'I was mistaken. When a human fithp surrenders under agreed terms, the members tend to honor their surrender.'

'Not all, surely.'

'Some fight on, Herdmaster, but those are rogues, known to all to be rogues, in defiance of their own leaders. We kill the rogues. The humans will aid us in this. Then we will have one herd again.'

———

Colonel Julius Carter tried once more. 'I've got three wounded men. One of them will die if we move him. Man, I'm only asking for shelter!' *The Afrikaners turned us away. I hadn't expected it, but they did. But this one is English!*

The farmer spread his hands helplessly. 'I can't.'

'He – he's a white soldier. Blanqui! Not black like me.'

Brant Chisholm laughed bitterly. 'Do you think that matters now? Great God, man, don't you think I *want* to help?'

Carter let his voice grow cold with menace. 'If you don't help us, we'll kill you and burn your place.'

The farmer nodded wearily. 'I expected that. Will you kill my wife and children too? And my neighbors, and their women, and all their children?'

'We're Americans, not monsters!'

'If the jumbos find you here, they'll kill us all. Do your worst, Colonel. You're not as bad as them.'

'Ah, shit,' Carter said. 'You know damned well I can't just shoot you.'

'If you're going to stay here, it would be better if you did. Shoot me and put my body where the jumbos will find it,' Chisholm said, dropping his voice conspiratorially. 'Maybe then they'll blame you and not everyone here.'

'Shit.' Carter couldn't keep it up. 'We won't hurt you. But man, we need help. We worked our way up from the coast —'

'Bad down there?'

'It's bad. It's worse than you can think. Buzzards everywhere.' *Buzzards and bugs and everything dead and smashed. Rotting corpses left by the waves. New corpses too. We brought the guns as far as we could. Now we have to find somebody willing to go get them and use them, and there's nobody left with guts.* 'All right, we'll move out. Can I leave Corporal Allington with you?'

'Yes. Take all his equipment. Take his uniform too. What's wrong with him?'

'We shot up a snout patrol, and they called in their lasers. He's burned over almost half his body.'

'Okay. We'll take care of him as best we can. If they

ask, I'll say he was burned in a motor accident. They probably won't. As long as we bring in the crops they pretty well leave us alone.'

'I guess it's pretty rough for you, too,' Carter said.

'Rough? Yes, you could say that. I'd head for the bush, but what would happen to the wife and kids? Let me tell you, Yank, a man with four small children doesn't have a lot of choices.'

'Sure.' *What would I do?*

'Brant! *Magtig*, commandos —' A tall blond woman rushed into the room. She stopped when she saw Carter. '*Magtig!* Here, in our house!'

Chisholm spoke briefly in Afrikaans. Despite the lessons he'd taken while aboard *Ethan Allen*, Carter didn't understand any of it.

'My wife, Katje,' Chisholm said. 'Colonel Carter of the United States Army.'

'I see that he is. Colonel, do you understand the danger you cause here?'

'Yes, ma'am. I didn't have a choice. One of my soldiers is hurt —'

'Where is he?'

Carter waved toward the barn.

'And what do you wish to do?'

'Leave him with you, I guess,' Carter said. 'Then we'll go back in the bush.'

'And what will you do there?'

'Whatever we can to hurt the snouts.'

'Och, I could wish to go with you. That is impossible. Let us bring your soldier into the house, and get your commando away into the bush. Three miles north from here you will find a deep ravine, filled with brush. Go into it and wait. I will send Mvubi. You must speak with him.'

'Mvubi?'

'Our Zulu headman. He will help you. Go now. Go and hurt them. But in the name of God, go far from here.'

*   *   *

Mvubi was old, and darker than an American ever gets. Carter guessed him to be sixty. He squatted to make drawings in the dirt. 'Here. Kambula. White soldiers. They do not speak English or Afrikaans. Jantji says they are Russian. They hide. They wish to fight. They ask Zulu to help them. Some go to join them.'

Russians. They must have come south, through Mozambique. Hell of a long way to come. 'Do you know any Zulu who want to fight?'

'Yes.'

'Take me to them.'

Mvubi rocked back and forth on his heels. Finally he stood. 'I will.'

————

The airlock door swung ponderously outward, and the smell of Winterhome hit him in the snnfp. Fookerteh flinched, then sniffed. Mustiness. Alien plants, quite different from the life of Kansas. A tastelessness: the buildup of biochemical residues in *Message Bearer* was missing here. Over all, the smell of the funeral pit.

Lesser ranks waited behind him, but Fookerteh paused at the top of ramp to examine the spaceport. It was large, with hard, paved strips set within other strips of close-cropped green vegetation.

Strange winged craft, man-built and large enough to hold eight-squared fithp, were parked at one end of the field. Humans were loading them. Other machines guided by humans moved across the field to the digit ship, and a human crew began loading boxes and baggage from the digit ship onto their vehicles.

Orderly and proper. Koothfektil-rusp has not stretched his domain with words. The humans work for us.

There were tall thin columns in the distance. Smoke trailed from their tops. Wind blew much harder than comfort demanded. Water fell in fat drops. The sky was a textured, uneasily shifting gray, vast and far.

And everywhere was the faint but unmistakable smell of the funeral pit.

Fookerteh went down the ramp to where Birithart-yamp waited. They clasped digits. 'Your presence wets my back.'

'Welcome to my domain, companion of my youth,' Birithart-yamp said formally. Then he lifted his digits. 'I am truly glad to see you. When they told me you would come down, I arranged to greet you myself. Come, I will take you to the mudrooms.'

'I thank you.' They walked across the hard surface. Gravity pulled at Fookerteh. The sky was so *big*, stretching distances he had not seen since he left the war in Kansas. 'Can you not – is there no way to bury the dead?'

Birithart-yamp sniffed. 'I had nearly forgotten. You will not notice the smell after a few days. Perhaps at night, or when you come from the clean air of the mudrooms. Fookerteh, we have buried the dead within our domain. Beyond —' He swept his digits in a wide arc toward that endlessly distant sky. 'The waves drowned numbers you cannot hold in your head. When the wind blows from that way or that, it is strongest. Today the smells are faint.'

Fookerteh shuddered.

'It will pass. In a season, in two seasons.' They had left the hard-surfaced spaceport. Soft loam sank under their feet, and a new smell was in the air. Spiral plants stood as tall as their knees. Winterflowers were just visible as loops of vine above the soil. In a year they would be blooming.

'See, death makes the land fertile. The flying scavengers – they are called *aasvogel* in the dominant language, *vultures* in English. They do their work, as do the running creatures, and the worms and insects. They do their work, that the Garden will be green. Is it not always so?'

'You sound like a priest,' Fookerteh said.

Birithart-yamp flailed digits across his friend's shoulder. 'Mocker! Here is the mudroom. My officers await us inside, all but one who will join us presently. You know him. Chintithpit-mang.'

'Yes.' Chintithpit-mang was a dissident; Fookerteh had avoided him.

'Before we go in – why are you here?' Birithart-yamp asked urgently.

'It is as you suspect. My mother's mate wishes to smell through my nostrils and feel through my digits. He trusts Koothfektil-rusp, but he wishes another view. I was sent.'

'Good. It is as I hoped. The Herdmaster will sniff your thoughts and believe. We are winning, Fookerteh. The path is long and twisted, but we can follow it – and the domain is endless!'

The mudroom had a random, primitive look. Of course it lacked the curve of spin gravity; but it was shapeless, a mere hole dug in the dirt, filled with water, churned and heated. It was twice the size of *Message Bearer*'s communal mudroom. On the far side was an endless cascade of water plummeting into a separate pool.

This was the way a mudroom should be! Fookerteh sagged in the warmth, resting muscles strained by Winter-home gravity, eyes half-closed, his snnfp just above the surface. He was glad to be out of the stinking wind. 'We were told of an animal. Large, resembling the fithp —'

'They call it *elephant*,' Birithart-yamp said. 'Imagine a tremendous fi' with only a single digit. These creatures are truly enormous. I will show you one that masses more than eight times your weight.'

Fookerteh snorted incredulity.

'I agree, but it is true.'

'And these are not the dominant species of this planet?'

'They are not. Many humans believe them to be the most intelligent of all species living on the Earth, save for themselves.'

'Of course. Even a single digit may manipulate tools.'

'Yes, but badly. Their digit is primitive compared to ours, and our digits are —'

'Yes?'

'It is not important. They are large and powerful, but the human called Botha said that unless these *elephants* were protected, they would all be killed.'

'Killed? By what?'

'By the lesser humans, for food. By those we fight in the wild areas. Fookerteh, we win, but you do not yet know the valor of their warriors, and ours.'

Fookerteh let warm mud flow along his sides. A creature that massive should be unstoppable . . . yet humans killed them. Technology?

He sensed a mass above him, and reached up to clasp digits with Chintithpit-mang.

'Well met, companion of my youth.' There was a strangeness, a distance in Chintithpit-mang's voice. The fi' bore new scars. He was armed, and wore the harness of an eight-cubed leader. Infrared night-seeing goggles, and other equipment Fookerteh did not recognize, hung from his harness. He stood like a wall in the gravity that had Fookerteh sagging. His look made Fookerteh uneasy.

'Well met.' Fookerteh responded. 'Will you not join us?'

Birithart-yamp said, 'Chintithpit-mang is one of the elite jungle warriors. Most of them are sleepers. You've seen reports —'

'I have. Chintithpit-mang, have you seen these *elephants?*'

'I have. They are large.'

'And fearsome?'

'Not so fearsome as the humans, who kill *elephants* and fithp alike.'

Machines speak with as much warmth as you. 'The reports say that we have lost many fithp in the jungles. Many more simply refuse to fight there. Why?'

'Death and madness wait in the jungle,' Chintithpit-

541

mang said. 'Winterhome is strange enough to fithp who know only the closed spaces of *Message Bearer*.'

Two young warriors came to take their leader's weapons, and aid him in removing his harness. Fookerteh recognized members of the Year Zero fithp. They looked like each other, but not like the Year Zero dissidents that Fookerteh had just left on *Thuktun Flishithy*.

Chintithpit-mang might not have seen his subordinates. His eyes looked past the walls of the mudroom. 'We are warriors, and our enemies find us all too conspicuous in the open. The jungles – you haven't seen them, Fookerteh, but you've seen the spiral plant in the Garden. Picture that as average size, and eight to the eighths of them growing, and smaller plants swarm at their feet —'

It sounded strange and terrible. But Chintithpit-mang was saying, 'At first the jungle felt safe. We couldn't see that terrible infinity of sky and landscape. We could hide from human rogue snipers among these huge plants.' He snorted, a sound like a gun going off. 'In the jungles the humans move where we stand fast, tangled, trapped. There is a strangling creature like a length of rope. The plants hide human snipers far more easily than they hide us. They use arrays of pointed sticks planted butt down, angled, and smeared with poisonous substances. Throw yourself out of the path of a spray of missiles, and you will find yourself impaled on pungi sticks hidden in the low vegetation.

'We learned. There came revolts among warriors who refused to enter a jungle. We ended with the elite jungle-warrior fithp . . . But most spaceborn simply cannot find the right mind-set. Fookerteh, you may inform your father that sleepers will eventually hold the highest ranks among the African warriors.'

'But you adjusted.'

'I did. Do you notice anything strange about me, Fookerteh?'

'You have surely changed.' Fookerteh had been

avoiding the thought. Now he could not: Chintithpit-mang behaved like an incipient rogue.

'Some warriors hunt alone. We move through the jungles and on the plains, seeking human rogues. When we find them we call down laser fire from the digit ships. An octuple would find no rogues. The best hunters are those who go alone or in pairs. Without those we must needs cede the jungles to the humans, yet I fear what it does to our minds. Fithp minds are not geared for such wholesale killing. We don't speak of the numbers of the dead, not among ourselves and not to the lesser warriors. Yet rumor spreads, and there is always the stink. We are always aware of what our foothold here has cost both humans and ourselves.

'The wholesale killing of human tribes due to the rogue behavior of one or two members has been forbidden by your father and the Attackmaster both. It continues nonetheless, for it is effective. Day by day the humans become more submissive. Many now cooperate with us.'

'And so we are winning,' Fookerteh mused.

'We win. There are costs. Many deaths were caused by difficulties in perception. Our lives aboard *Message Bearer* haven't prepared us to recognize what we see. Fithp have wandered off cliffs, or broken their legs in holes, or shied from something harmless into real danger. The human enemy finds the simplest of hiding places indecently effective. In spotted green clothing they seem to vanish. Many have guns, yet even without guns they kill us. Pointed sticks fly from the greenery – ' Chintithpit-mang's voice trailed off, and his eyes focused on Fookerteh, as if seeing the mudroom for the first time.

'Fookerteh, I have applied to return to *Message Bearer* for mating season.'

Well you might. 'You shall. I was told.'

'Good.' Chintithpit-mang walked into the mud, bringing a bow wave with him. He sank, eyes half-closed, and it seemed he would not speak again. Then, 'I fear the paths my mind would walk if I missed mating season. I have already walked too far from the life I knew.'

'I came to learn such things.' The Attackmaster had never spoken of such. 'Can you tell me how Pheegorun died? I'm told you were there.'

'I was there.' Chintithpit-mang was deep in the mud, eyes fully closed now, only his head protruding. 'We were not even in danger. I cannot think we behaved stupidly. Nonetheless we did not understand Africa as we do now.

'You must see the jungle. I will show you. We had tamed it when I arrived, though the cost was high. When I stepped off the float-fort I found Pheegorun examining what might have been a primitive digging tool . . .'

Chintithpit-mang spoke without body language. His voice was almost a monotone. It was as if the emotions raised by his terrible tale had long since been burned away, by time or by worse to come.

———

Pheegorun said, 'Here, Eight-cubed Leader, you can see that there's a blade moored to one end. The native throws the stick and hopes the blade-end hits one of us hard enough to penetrate skin.'

Were Pheegorun a friend, Chintithpit-mang would have swatted him across the shoulders. *Mocker!* But this was a subordinate, a sleeper, a stranger – 'Are you in fact joking?'

'No. They make it work. They kill us with these. Why doesn't it turn end for end? How can they throw it so hard?'

Chintithpit-mang considered. A long, thin mass would have the proper moment of inertia if it could be thrown straight. But how? 'Perhaps if you hold it properly? At the end, perhaps?'

'Lead me.'

Chintithpit-mang picked up the long shaft with just the

544

tips of his digits. He raised it into place, above and behind his head, point foremost, and threw it. It traveled some four srupkithp and landed sideways.

Pheegorun tactfully said nothing. Chintithpit-mang said, 'Pause. Maybe if I – ' He retrieved the spear. This time he carefully wrapped all eight segments of his trunk the same way round. 'Now when I let go, it should spin, right?'

'Lead me, Eight-cubed Leader.'

The spear traveled four srupkithp and landed sideways.

'Take it,' said Chintithpit-mang. 'Give it to a prisoner and let him demonstrate.'

Chintithpit-mang, who had been seeing nothing at all, was abruptly staring Fookerteh in the eye. 'Of course Pheegorun must have tried this already. He had seen the spear kill, and he had studied it longer than I. He must have perceived me as a talkative novice, an interloping fool. He was a good fi', a good officer. He might have been one of the elite.'

'What happened?'

'He followed my orders.'

The man was very black and tall and nearly naked of clothing and hair. The hair of his head formed a huge puffball. There was paint on his face and patterns and ridges in his skin, carefully applied scars. Of the prisoners he was the only one unwounded. He had stood up from the bush with a spear in his hand, too close to the column. A soldier in the rear had knocked him flat with a swipe of a gun butt, rolled him over, and taken his surrender.

He wore strange harness. Ancient fur pieces encircled his ankles and wrists. Once splendid but now bedraggled feathers hung about his neck. His head was circled by a green furred band. All of his harness was old and brittle, stained with earth and sweat.

They had seen many dressed that way.

545

The man listened to his orders. He looked about at his audience of a hundred fithp warriors. Then, without answering nor so much as nodding, he strode to the spear and picked it up, holding it in the middle.

Chintithpit-mang felt he would never get used to the sight. It made his belly uneasy, as while a spacecraft was involved in a finicky docking. Why didn't the man fall over? He was tall and narrow even by the standards of men, and if he fell he ought to break his neck. But he didn't fall. He stood almost motionless, weaving slightly, as Pheegorun pointed to the target.

'Put it as close to the dot as possible,' he called. He was standing a safe eight srupkithp away. Would this work as he expected? Pheegorun must know how closely his Eight-cubed Leader was watching.

The man raised the spear, level with the ground, aimed at the target. He raised himself on his toes, and *still* didn't fall. He slapped the spear haft with his free hand; the spear turned ninety degrees, and so did the man, and Pheegorun was looking straight down the haft.

Pheegorun turned to run. Eight srupkithp distant or not, he turned to run, and half his soldiers were raising their weapons. The spear flew.

It thudded deep into Pheegorun's side. Pheegorun froze. Chintithpit-mang glimpsed the black man standing calmly, arms at his sides, in the instant before the guns tore him apart.

Pheegorun took his surrender. They don't think like us . . . never mind. It flew straight. I saw it.

The medic studied Pheegorun without touching him. 'I want him to lie down,' he said. 'Some of you help. First, brace him while I pull the stick-blade out.'

Two soldiers held him with their mass while the doctor pulled. Pheegorun screamed at the pain. It was deep inside him, tearing its way out – it was out, held bleeding before his face. Chintithpit-mang, watching horrified, felt the tearing inside when Pheegorun tried to breathe.

'Good. Now brace him. Pheegorun, can you hear me? Lean to the left. You should be lying down.'

Pheegorun couldn't make himself move. The doctor pushed, and he leaned away, and was lowered to his left side. His own weight was forcing his lungs shut. Exhaling was a matter of letting it happen, despite the agony, but inhaling was like lifting a mountain. The doctor said, 'This will end the pain. I believe the stick-blade punctured a lung. I must cut him open and sew up the wound.'

'Save him if you can,' said Chintithpit-mang.

Pheegorun was dying. He must have known it. He had to speak now or die silent. His eyes found and locked on Chintithpit-mang. 'Did you see? The danger – ' and he was reduced to gasping. His eyes filmed over. The doctor's knife was cutting into him. He tried to make his mouth work.

Not loud enough. Chintithpit-mang bent his ear next to Pheegorun's mouth. Pheegorun gathered his will, forced his rib cage to move, gathered breath like a thousand daggers, and spoke.

'*Thumbs*,' he said, and died.

'His village.' Chintithpit-mang screamed the demand. 'Coordinates!'

Someone answered. Chintithpit-mang shouted into the communications box.

Five eights of makasrupkithp away, green lines laced down in tight spirals. When they were done, Chintithpit-mang turned to the prisoners.

'Who from his tribe?'

They all were. When the work was finished, Chintithpit-mang sent two captives away to tell others.

'I can guess what he was thinking. Their thumbs are more dexterous than our digits. We were the supreme tool users until we came here. We were ready for the wrong things. We guessed some of the prey's advantages: his greater numbers, his knowledge of his own territory, his grasp of

547

an inferior technology that he had at least built himself, with no thuktunthp for guidance.

'Pheegorun was dying, and he thought to warn me. I have heard such talk from others since. But it is wrong! What if their thumbs let them make their machines smaller? We have the thuktunthp to give us more powerful tools, and they have only themselves.'

'You violated orders,' Fookerteh remarked. 'You destroyed an entire fithp —'

'I did. I did it in rage, and I did it to correct my own mistake. Shape your own lessons. We have lost only two more fithp in that region,' Chintithpit-mang said. 'The others bring us cattle and milk.'

'Have you done it since?'

'No. Not yet, But it changes me, this war. I need the wisdom of the females. I need my mate.'

CHAPTER THIRTY-SIX
TREASON

Treason doth never prosper: what's the reason? For if it prosper, none dare call it treason.

– SIR JOHN HARINGTON

A light drizzling rain kept them zippered and sweating in their waterproofs. Today wasn't bad. They had huddled through days of rain-laden gales that would have blown Harry's motorcycle off the road.

The sign read BELLINGHAM CITY LIMITS. The freeway off-ramp led to what had once been a main road. Now it hardly looked used. They drove past closed service stations, closed motels, a closed Black Angus restaurant. One gas station was open, but there was a sign: NO GAS. NO SERVICES. I DON'T KNOW WHY I'M OPEN EITHER. WANT TEA?

Most of the houses were boarded up.

'Bellingham has an unfriendly look,' Roger shouted in his ear. It seemed to make him happy.

Where the hell was that turnoff? The map showed the main road forked, with one fork going off west around Western Washington University and down to the harbor – there it was. Harry took the other branch. It curved east and went under the freeway, past a shopping center that didn't look completely closed. After that there were only houses.

The Enclave wasn't easy to find. It lay at the end of a winding road, and it didn't look much like the place that had once been described to Harry. It seemed too small, and the tennis court had become a greenhouse. There was a heavy fence, and a gate, with a big J. Arthur Rank kind of gong set up so he'd have to get off the bike and go past a concrete barrier to ring it. 'They sure don't encourage casual visitors. Which figures . . .' Harry drove slowly past, unsure. There was a small wood at the end of the lane. From there they had a view of the area in front of the garage.

'John Fox! He's there!' Roger shouted.

'Fox? Oh, yeah, I remember him. Never met him,' Harry said. 'How do you know?'

'How many pickup trucks have a California personalized license plate that reads ECOFREAK?'

'Oh. That one.' Harry turned the motorcycle around. 'So now what?'

'We go in. Before, I just wanted a shower. Now I *know* I want to meet your friends.'

'Okay.' Harry stopped at the gate. The gong wasn't as loud as he'd thought it would be.

Jack McCauley's round face had picked up angles and a close-clipped black beard. Men wore beards these days, all across the country. His shoulders and arms had gained muscle mass; they strained his old shirt. 'I'm telling you up front, we've got no room,' he said, 'but drive on in. George'll be glad to see you, Harry. But what in hell is a newsman doing here?'

Roger smiled lightly. 'We're planning a feature on lifestyles. There's a lot of interest in Colorado Springs on how the rest of the country is doing.'

McCauley eyed Roger closely. 'Yeah. Sure. Well, come on in, but there's no story here.'

The house and grounds looked like a construction site, Harry thought. They put the bike next to Fox's truck. Roger looked at it and nodded in satisfaction.

They found George Tate-Evans working on the greenhouse. Harry wasn't surprised to see that George was clean-shaven. He would be. George drove in a nail, straightened, stared at Harry, and whistled. 'It's really Hairy Red.' He smiled warmly. 'Damn all, Harry, you're not as clean as you used to be, but somehow you look a lot better. How's the back?'

'Wonderful. I haven't had to see a lawyer in months. Meet Roger Brooks, with the *Washington Post*. We've both come out of Kansas.'

'Kansas. Harry, I expect everybody would like to hear some stories about Kansas. You've come all the way from Washington?'

'Naw, from Colorado Springs,' Harry said.

'Colorado Springs,' George said carefully. 'Yes, Harry, I guess you better come to dinner, as long as you understand the situation. There's no room here, Harry. No spare beds.'

'We have tents —'

'Look around you. The only place you could put a tent would be in the driveway.'

'We'll think of something,' Harry said. He grinned. 'Look, George, I'm used to telling tales for my supper. Tonight, though – think you could throw in a shower?'

———

It didn't surprise Roger Brooks that there was plenty of water, because there was water everywhere, too damned much water.

This was different. He showered in *warm* water; not as much as Roger wanted, because the pipes in the rooftop heat collector didn't hold that much, but more than Roger had enjoyed for a long time.

I better enjoy it. I'll pay for it. It had been a long trip. *I chose the right guide. We got here. But now Harry will tell his war stories again* . . .

* * *

The dining room was large, with a long table in the center. At one end was a lectern. The whole place reminded Roger of the refectory in the Christian Brothers monastery they'd stopped in on the way up from Colorado Springs. The Brothers had taken in travelers the way monasteries did in medieval times. They'd also put all the local indolents to work in gardens and vineyards.

The room grew crowded. John Fox seemed genuinely glad to see Roger. Roger's memory held the names as they came: a useful skill for a newsman. Fox's friend Marty Carnell, George and Vicki Tate-Evans. Harry had called George 'super survivor'; his wife was quiet, and it became clear that visitors made her uncomfortable. Isadore and Clara: Roger didn't get their last names. Clara wanted to know what was happening in the capital. Others: the man at the gate, Jack McCauley. His wife was Harriet, and she was listening a lot while making up her mind about something.

Bill and Gwen Shakes occupied the head of the table. There were a lot of Shakes kids – a lot of kids, for that matter, and Roger let their names slip through his head unclaimed.

Shakes was concerned about Roger's story. 'We don't need any publicity. Don't need any, don't want any. I'd tell you how tough things are if I thought you'd believe me.'

'I won't be writing much about Bellingham,' Roger said. 'Or any other specific place. Anyway, if you're worried about getting lots of new company, forget it. Harry and I could have been stopped cold half a dozen times, and that's on a motorcycle, with press credentials and a gas ration card! Nobody's coming to Bellingham.' *And nobody's printing anything about Bellingham, either. Before we left the Springs I went through all the files I could find. Nothing, nothing at all, since long before the snouts dropped their Dinosaur Killer. I can taste it, a secret a year old, hidden from snouts and citizens alike —*

'A lot of people *have* come to Bellingham,' Harriet McCauley said.

'Yes. It's getting crowded,' Clara added. 'The markets are crowded. Lines, long lines for almost anything except staples and dairy products.'

'Hah. Most places there are lines for those, too,' Harry said. 'Maybe you have it better than you think.'

Dinner was spaghetti. There wasn't any meat in the sauce, but there was cheese, and fresh stewed tomatoes from the greenhouse. Conversation became local while they ate.

'It's wet everywhere, isn't it?' Fox asked.

'Pretty much so,' Roger told him. 'We were never able to dry out except for a couple of days in Utah. You must get more sun here than I'd have thought.'

Fox snorted. 'Heck, Bellingham wasn't noted for its sunshine before that snout asteroid hit. Not like Death Valley,' and sudden fury surged into his face before he could hide it. 'What makes you think we get sunlight now?'

'Hot water,' Roger said. 'That was heated in those roof-top collectors, wasn't it?'

'Sure, but it was warm, not hot,' Fox said.

'It collects diffuse sunlight,' Miranda Shakes said. 'We get hot water when there's real sunshine. Three days so far this year. I'd *kill* for a hot bath.'

When dinner ended, almost everyone left.

'Chores,' Fox said. 'Nice to have seen you again, Roger.'

Bill Shakes and George Tate-Evans helped carry dinner dishes out, then came back. 'We'll offer you brandy, but it's getting dark out,' Bill Shakes said. 'Maybe you'd rather go make camp while there's light?'

'It's no problem for us,' Roger said.

'We've made camp in the dark before,' Harry added.

'Okay. The best place will be up the lane. It runs into the woods. Go up about half a mile, cross the creek, and there's a clearing. Be careful how much wood you burn, and don't cut any.'

553

'Okay.'

Isadore brought in two bottles of California brandy. 'Two more cases,' he said to nobody in particular. He took thin glass snifters from a cabinet and brought them around. George Tate-Evans went to help, but poured his own glass half full first. The doses that Isadore poured for guests were considerably smaller.

Bill Shakes waited until they were all seated with their glasses. 'Harry, you said you have a gasoline ration card.'

'Yep.' Harry grinned. 'Hero's reward, you know. I captured a snout.'

George Tate-Evans started to say something, but Shakes' quiet voice was insistent. 'We've located some fertilizer. A dairy farmer about thirty miles from here will sell us some, but we have to go get it. We've got trucks but no gas. What are the chances of buying some gasoline from you?'

'Zero,' Harry said. 'The card's personal.' He took a plastic-encased card from an inner pocket. 'See, my driving license on one side, gas card on the other, picture on both. Nobody can use it. Unless you want to grow a beard and dye it to look like me.'

'Most amusing,' Shakes said without a smile. His head might have come level to Harry's shoulder.

'Maybe we can exchange favors,' Roger said. 'We go get your fertilizer. You let us use a truck for a couple of days.'

Harry frowned at him. 'Why do we need a truck? Especially need one that bad?'

'I'd like to look around, and my tail-bone is tired,' Roger said.

'I'll buy that one. Okay, Bill. We'll haul your cow shit.'

'Thank you.'

Harry lifted his glass. 'You've done pretty well.'

'Not too bad.' It was hard to read Shakes' smile. 'Do you know anything about Los Angeles?'

'They're coping,' Harry said.

'You didn't go through there?' George asked. He brought over a bottle of California brandy and poured a generous second drink.

'No,' Harry said. 'But they're coping.'

'Eh?'

'Just about everywhere,' Harry said. 'Things are tough. Tougher than here, mostly. But people are managing, one way or another. Greenhouses. Vegetable gardens. Chicken coops on rooftops.'

'Surprising,' Bill Shakes said.

'Yes, considering there's not much the government can do,' Roger said. 'Colorado Springs can't even find out what people are doing, much less help them.'

'That's why things are working,' George said. He knocked back his brandy and poured more. 'Get the goddam government out of the way and people can cope. You watch, if things get a little better, good enough for the government to get active, everything will get worse again. Look at us! We've got government. Boy, do we have government! Government people out the ass!'

George was wrong, of course. Roger had seen it: what made it all work was just enough government. Government wasn't powerful enough to meddle any more, but it could tell those who would listen how to help themselves: how to build greenhouses, keep the plumbing working, deal with untrustworthy water supplies, eat *all* of a steer carcass: the things once printed in the survival manuals. George Tate-Evans must have expected his survivalists to *be* the government by now. Instead of decently dying away, the government had taken over his territory!

If Roger could say that just right, he'd get himself and Harry kicked back into the street. Instead he said, 'Clara said there are lots of new people here. Why?'

Bill Shakes looked edgily at George, but George didn't notice. 'Big government project in the harbor,' George said. 'New people coming in. Navy people. Computer programmers. Shipfitters. Plumbers – we have to do all our own plumbing now. Every plumber for a hundred miles seems to work down there at the harbor.'

'They don't moonlight?' Harry asked.

'They don't even come out for a visit.'

'Hoo-hah.' Harry was on his second brandy. 'And you guys came up here to get away from the crowds!' Harry chortled and poured himself another drink without asking.

'There is an amusing aspect to it.' Bill Shakes still wore his enigmatic smile. 'I remember a story. There was a guy who *knew* the Second World War was coming. The news said it all. So he looked around for a quiet spot to sit it out, and he moved his whole life there. He picked an island out in the middle of the Pacific, way the hell away from everything. Called Iwo Jima.'

'We haven't done that bad,' George said.

'No, but it isn't the quiet little backwater with the silted-up harbor any more,' Isadore said. 'The roads are crowded, the prices have gone up, there are MPs minding everybody's business —'

'Screw them,' George muttered.

'But what are they *doing* down there?' Roger asked.

'Who knows?' Isadore said. 'They *say* they've built greenhouses and they're growing wheat. You can believe as much of that as you want to.'

'And if I believe none of it?'

'Miranda's Deputy Sheriff heard rumors that it's a prison,' Isadore said. 'Political prisoners from Kansas. Collaborators. They've built greenhouses, all right, but they're working them with prisoners. Slave camp.'

'Serve the snoutlovers right,' Harry said.

'They may not have had much choice,' Roger said.

'They could fight —'

'You captured one, Harry,' Roger said carefully. 'But he was alone. I saw what happened to people who tried to fight them all. It wasn't pretty.'

Bill Shakes leaned forward. 'You were in alien occupied country? Tell us about it.'

Roger's digital watch said 3:00 A.M. Both brandy bottles were empty, and they were better than halfway through a third.

Somewhere during the evening Miranda had brought down Kevin's guitar for Harry to play, and nearly everybody came to listen while Harry sang his songs, but then the others had gone away, leaving George and Isadore and Bill.

Kevin Shakes was working on the government project – and hadn't come home since he went down to the harbor. They got letters from him, and word through Miranda's boyfriend.

Roger felt the tightness in his guts. *I shouldn't have had so much brandy. It's hard to stay in control.*

Something big in the harbor. Big.

George knows something he hasn't said. What?

'About time to turn in,' Bill Shakes said.

He's not drunk. I wonder just how much he really drank?

'Let me finish this drink,' Roger said unsteadily. He knew he was rapidly wearing out his welcome. *But I may not get a better shot.* He went over to George and lifted his glass. 'Death to tyrants! Down with the state!'

'Right on!' George grinned and clinked glasses.

'Secrets,' Roger said. 'They always have secrets. Like in Vietnam, when they kept it a secret they were bombing in Cambodia. Who was it secret from? The Cambodians knew. The Viet Cong had to know. I bet they even told the Russians. So who didn't know?'

'Right,' George said. 'Right.'

'So now they've got more secrets —'

'George,' Bill Shakes said quietly.

George didn't listen.

'What the hell could they be hiding?' Roger shook his head. 'Probably something silly —'

George dropped his voice to a conspiratorial mumble. 'Snouts. They've got snouts down there.'

Roger woke on the living room floor. His head pounded.

Snouts. No big secret. Nothing but a hideout for captured snouts —

That's ridiculous! Bellingham vanished from the news before anyone captured a snout! And they wouldn't put General Gillespie in charge of a snout prison camp.

But Bill Shakes believes it. He didn't want me to find out. If Shakes doesn't know what's really going on in the harbor, nobody out here does. We'll have to go inside.

He heard Harry's voice from the other room. 'Like Sheena, Queen of the Jungle. Miz D. hopped on, and out we came. Hey, real coffee! Great!' There were other voices, children, and giggles.

Coffee! But to get any, he'd have to listen to Harry's story yet again . . .

———————

So. We achieve escape velocity, Pastempeh-keph thought. *From here we coast. We'll hold the African continent forever, and if new resistance rises, we'll trample it from space. Ultimately the dissidents may rule* Message Bearer *while my descendants trade them metals for food.*

The door to the mudroom opened. Pastempeh-keph waved happily from the mud. His fithp's mating season had come round at last —

'I have a guest,' said K'turfookeph.

You what? Pastempeh-keph didn't say that. He said, 'Enter. Soak your tired selves.' *This had better be urgent!*

K'turfookeph entered with Chowpeentulk. The females eased into the mud, carefully, under the low spin gravity. A few moments of quiet were allowed to pass, during which none of the tension left Chowpeentulk. Then she said, 'My mate was murdered, Herdmaster. What have you done to find the rogue?'

He had thought he could postpone this. There was a war on, and a sufficiency of dead fithp. Some fi' had removed a problem. The Herdmaster had taken steps to learn who, for he might act again, but there had been yet more urgent problems.

He said, 'Tell me first, what would you have done?'

Chowpeentulk considered. 'A rogue *shows*. He does not speak to his fithp, he abandons his mate, he does not trouble to hide who he is.'

'We have rogues enough,' the Herdmaster conceded. 'Warriors on Winterhome face strange and terrible pressures. But here? So you must have noticed him. Is there a herdless one aboard? A member of the Tráveler Herd whom none will associate with? No? Then who could have come and gone so unnoticed?'

Chowpeentulk shook her head. She was terribly tense. Why not? She had invaded the Herdmaster's private mudroom!

He said, 'Not a rogue. Then he did not act alone, and if he did, he must have shared the secret with someone. What would you do now?'

'I would ask! No fi' can lie to the Herdmaster.'

'That statement is too sweeping, but it has some truth. I have interviewed the heads of every fithp aboard *Message Bearer*. The sleepers do not ask that I seek a killer; they demanded only that I choose an Advisor from among them at once. This seemed promising. I set my attention on them. When that failed me, I questioned randomly chosen fithp: Fistarteh-thuktun's apprentices, Tashayamp, weapons officers aboard, warriors newly come from Winterhome, mothers, newly mated females, unmated females, humans.

'Some spoke of roguish behavior in others. I challenged the alleged rogues; every accusation was unwarranted. None know how Fathisteh-tulk died. Few even know what his interests were, where he might have overturned a secret worth concealing —'

'*Few?* What have you learned?'

'I learned what you must have *known*, Chowpeentulk. Your mate was interested in the human prisoners. He questioned one, Dawson, while Dawson was isolated.'

'So.' She said, 'In the communal mudbath, days before he disappeared . . . he wouldn't tell me what he intended, but he thought to learn something. It had to do with whether Winterhome was worth the taking.'

'It would. And where does that leave me? Did he question the Soviet prisoners? Did he learn anything? Humans may lie even to the Herdmaster, for I cannot read their body language. The Breakers were no help. It doesn't matter. Even if we consider that a surrendered human might murder a ranking fi', another fi' must be involved. No frail human could have pushed him into a vertical wall of mud under minuscule thrust. A fi' must have chilled the mudroom again after Fathisteh-tulk was dead.

'Meanwhile a fithpless killer walks *Message Bearer*. He killed among the highest rank, yet nothing shows in his stance. He knows that he has played the Herdmaster for a fool.'

'We feared you had forgotten,' K'turfookeph said, with a trace of apology in her tone.

'Losing my fithp to thermonuclear bombs and wooden sticks and madness, why should I ignore yet another death? But I have no more footholds here! What should I seek? Some fi' appeared and killed and went, unnoticed, speaking to none.'

Chowpeentulk sprayed him. The Herdmaster didn't react at all. 'A rogue who came and went. So simple. Chowpeentulk, I will produce your mate's killer within eight days. Leave us.'

Chowpeentulk knew enough to keep silent. She surged from the mud and left, dripping. Pastempeh-keph said, 'Was there not another place where you and that other female could confront me?'

'Keph, she persuaded me. There are others who wonder too —'

'Don't do that again. Now forget it, mother of my immortality. The mating season flows always too fast.'

The column made slow progress across the veldt. Movement was impossible at night. The snouts had excellent IR detection equipment. On a good day the commando could travel thirty kilometers on foot.

They had learned that, and more.

Julius Carter wanted time to understand what he had learned: of the strange relationships between the Afrikaner tribe – they could only be thought of as a tribe – and the various black tribes.

Van der Stel, the thin Afrikaner who spoke of 'Kaffirs' and expected blacks to call him 'Baas' – but who also had genuine respect for the Zulu scouts, and always listened to their advice.

Mvubi, who seemed servile to van der Stel and treated Carter as an equal – but took his orders from Carter.

And the Russians, who understood none of this. Of the dozen who'd joined forces with Carter, only two spoke English, and none spoke any other language relevant to South Africa.

A strange country. It had been strange before the invaders came. Now —

Now the whole Earth is strange.

Despite the chill wind, Carter sweated under his heavy pack load. They moved in small groups, slowly and carefully, taking advantage of every patch of cover, every depression in the ground. Up ahead Mvubi and his Zulu scouts were nearly invisible. A steady hiss sounded in Carter's left ear, showing that his radio receiver was on. Mvubi wouldn't activate the transmitter except in an emergency. A short, low-power transmission probably couldn't be heard by the snouts, but why take chances?

'It is not far now,' van der Stel said. 'When we reach those trees, you will see their spaceport. The missile can be fired from there.'

'Thank God,' Sergeant Harrison muttered.

Lieutenant Ivan Semeyusov looked disapproval at Harrison. Russian non-coms did not speak to their officers until invited, and good communists would hardly invoke deity. Colonel Carter hid his grin. 'Give 'em a ten-minute break, Sarge.'

'Yes sir.' Harrison whistled long and low, knowing that Mvubi's people would hear. Then he crawled back down the column to pass the word to the Americans and Russians.

Carter hunched in the lee of the best shelter he could find and wished he could smoke his pipe. *How good is their sense of smell?* The wind blew continuously. He looked cautiously around the weird landscape. After all these months, there was still the odor of death in the air. *What is a black boy from Pruett-Igoe doing away down here?* 'At least the rain has stopped,' he said.

'It is cold for November,' van der Stel said. 'Summer will be late.'

If there's a summer at all, Carter thought. November in South Africa should have roughly the same weather as May in Southern California, warm and dry, not this blustery cold. The Russian officer produced a package of cigarettes. 'No,' Carter said.

The Russian officer put the pack away.

'This is a mad scheme,' van der Stel said.

'So? And why are you here? Lt. Semeyusov asked. His mouth twisted into a deliberate grin.

Learning some manners, anyway, Carter thought.

'It is known that I am mad now,' van der Stel said. 'The English found that all Afrikaners have the capability. Now we must show the olifants. Tell me, Lieutenant, what brings you so far from home to aid me in my madness?'

Semeyusov wasn't going to touch that one. 'You are certain they will launch a large craft today?' the Russian demanded.

'Certain? How can I be certain of anything? Our friends at the spaceport, those who load the craft, say they believe it will be launched today or tonight or tomorrow. I have told you this. Do you think I deceive you?'

'Naw,' Lieutenant Carruthers said. 'None of us think that, mynheer. Ivan's nervous. We all are.'

With good reason. Carter glanced at the sun. 'Since we don't know when they'll launch, the sooner we're in position, the better. Let's get moving.'

'Looks like they're about to button her up,' Carruthers reported. He handed the binoculars back to Carter. 'Last-minute loading?'

Julius Carter lay in the grass and turned his binoculars on what had been an airport, eight kilometers away.

The Sunday comics had taught him to call them 'rocket ships.' This was the first rocket ship he had ever seen. Shuttles didn't look like this. Its belly was flat. It was the size of a building; it made the nearby C-47 cargo transport look like a toy. Take that massive cone off the back and it would look more like an airplane, but not very. Too short, too wide, too little in the way of fins. The only windows were on a canopy the size of a 727 fuselage, and that was *underneath* the nose. The point of the nose glittered like a lens, but it wouldn't provide a view. A laser cannon?

Van der Stel had been right, as usual; this was an excellent place to observe the spaceport, high enough to give them a good view, but not conspicuously high.

Carruthers might have been reading too much into what he could see. On the other hand, he might not. In the past hour the snouts had certainly closed two cargo hatches on the big ship. They'd removed the two loading cranes that went with those ports. Most of the other baggage carts had been removed to the other side of the field. 'It sure looks like they're doing *something*. How're the Russkis coming?'

'We are coming quite well, *Colonel*,' a voice said from behind him.

Ooops! 'Thank you, Lieutenant. You've got your missile set up?'

'Presently.'

'Good. Looks like we have about half an hour.'

'I will encourage the crew to hurry.'

Carter sat in the tall grass and took out his pipe.

'Nice thing about a pipe,' Carruthers said. 'Don't need to light it. Colonel —'

'Spit it out.'

'Will it work? Sir? I mean, they had to carry it a long way, and —'

'Got a better plan?'

'No, sir.'

'It's worth a try, Lieutenant.'

'Yes, sir.'

And no, I didn't answer your question, son. How could I? He grinned, but to himself, as he remembered a story from one of the innumerable Arab-Israeli wars. An Arab president had cabled to Moscow: 'Stop sending surface to air missiles. Send surface to aircraft missiles.'

So far it hasn't cost us anything but some sweat. So far. When they launched that Russian missile that would all change. They'd have to run for it, scatter, and hope they all made it to the rendezvous points. Carter glanced at his watch, then back to the low railed structure the Soviet troops had bolted together. 'Okay, Sergeant. Spread 'em out.'

'Sir.'

There was definite activity at the spaceport. All the auxiliary vehicles had been withdrawn. Now the great hulk of the alien spacecraft sat alone.

An enormous concrete structure opened nearby.

564

'The laser,' Carter said. 'Hit that, and we splatter that ship all over the landscape.' He handed his binoculars to Lieutenant Carruthers and turned to the Soviet officer. 'All set?'

'Da.' Semeyusov's eyes glittered expectantly. 'It is a good missile. A *good* missile.'

'I sure hope so.'

'Colonel!'

'Yeah, Carruthers?'

'They've opened a hangar. Something coming out – coming this way. Shit!'

Carter grabbed the binoculars.

More than a dozen of the fast-moving light ground effect vehicles Carter had come to call 'skimmers' moved across the spaceport. When they reached the fence they rose over it, then spread out across the veldt. One was coming directly toward their hill.

Behind the skimmers came eight tanks.

Lieutenant Semeyusov's voice was emotionless. 'Your orders, Comrade Colonel?'

'Wait. Maybe they won't see us.'

The skimmer came on, past the area where Mvubi's scouts were hidden.

'Still coming,' Carruthers said. 'Colonel, if they didn't see his people, they won't see us.'

'And if they go straight past us, they'll see the damn missile,' Carter said. *They'll be here in a second. Once past us, they're sure to see the missile.* He thumbed the channel control on his helmet radio. 'Sergeant Harrison. If that skimmer comes within fifty meters, take it out.'

'Sir.' Harrison was invisible somewhere off to the left.

Lieutenant Carruthers unlimbered a light antitank tube. 'Custer's last stand.'

'Something like that,' Carter said. 'Maybe they won't come.'

'Yeah, sure.'

Semeyusov spoke quickly into his phone. 'They are ready —'

The first skimmer reached the bottom of the hill. Another converged toward it.

Carter lifted the transmitter. 'Mvubi. Suthu!'

'Tchaka!' A moment later automatic weapons chattered from the veldt between Carter and the spaceport. The trailing skimmer wobbled, then fell.

'Launch your bloody missile,' Carter ordered. 'It's too late to get the spaceship. Try for the laser anyway.'

'With respect, Colonel, perhaps they will launch their ship anyway. It is a better target.'

'Why in hell would they launch during an ambush?'

For answer, Semeyusov pointed. Thick white smoke rose from the base platform around the alien spacecraft.

'Son of a bitch! Okay!'

'Only now we got to stop those tanks,' Carruthers said carefully. 'I don't think Mvubi's people will hold them long.'

'We'll do the best we can —'

The alien ship rose suddenly. The rocket platform that boosted it fell back, as a brilliant blue-green beam stabbed up from the concrete structure at the center of the spaceport.

'Any time now!' Carter shouted. Lieutenant Semeyusov spoke rapidly.

The leading skimmer was climbing the hill toward them. There was a sharp flash from the bush to their right. A dark shadow moved toward the alien hovercraft, rushed at it, touched it —

The skimmer exploded in fire.

'Two down! Hoo hah!' Carruthers shouted. 'Bring on the mother-fucking tanks!'

Tanks hell, where's that damn missile —

Thunder rolled toward them. The spacecraft rose on its beam of green fire.

Three smaller beams stabbed downward. They moved in an odd pattern —

There was a flash of fire, and the Russian missile tumbled in smoke. It fell into the veldt.

566

The smaller beams moved up the hill toward Carter, moved past him, curved back toward him.

He was encased in a wide spiral of green. The spiral tightened.

The alien spacecraft vanished in the clouds.

CHAPTER THIRTY-SEVEN
THE IRON CRAB

One minute with him is all I ask; one minute alone with him, while you're runnin' for th' priest an' th' doctor.

— SEAN O'CASEY, *The Plow and the Stars*

The truck was an older Ford Club Cab with a roomy area behind the backseat. The space back there gave Roger ideas. He brooded.

The truck rattled and stank of manure, but the seats were padded and softer than a motorcycle saddle, a difference Roger sorely appreciated.

'Snouts,' Roger said. 'Harry, *why* would they hide snouts all the way up here in Bellingham?'

'Beats me —'

'Me too, but there's a story in it. One the people are entitled to know.'

'Well, maybe —'

'Maybe a Pulitzer Prize,' Roger mused.

'Robert Redford and Dustin Hoffman,' Harry said. 'Both with beards. *Yeah*. Look, though, they've got guards on all the gates. There's no way in.'

'Maybe I can think of something.' *I see the fine hand of Colorado Springs here. In's no problem. Out's something different.* 'Want to give it a try?'

'I guess so. Sure. Why not? But how do we get in?'

'Harry Reddington. I have a letter from Mrs. Carlotta Dawson for Mrs. Linda Gillespie. In case you haven't heard, Mrs. Dawson and I captured a snout in the Kansas war.'

'That doesn't add up to a pass.'

'Nobody in Colorado Springs knows dick about passes,' Harry said. 'Dawson. Did you catch the name? Dawson, as in the poor schmuck up there on the snout ship.'

'I heard the speech,' the guard said. 'Whose side does he think he's on?'

'Ours, by God, and he's the only spy we've got, too!' From the sound of that indignant scream, Harry was about to deck the schmuck! But his next words were almost calm. 'And here's my ID. Gas ration card, even. Presidential commendation. Look, here's the letter. For Linda Gillespie,' Harry said. 'Mrs. General Edmund Gillespie.'

'I heard of her.'

Roger's heart pounded. If they reached the truck . . .

If Harry knew how serious this was, he'd never carry it off. Snout prisoners, in Washington State? Bullshit. Not a bad story, because the snouts on the mother ship wouldn't drop a meteor on their own people. And it would have to be concealed, because the good citizens might rise to violence against snout prisoners. But *why confiscate the CBs?*

Something was happening here that would bring meteors if the snouts ever learned of it. The CBs had to disappear, Bellingham had to vanish from the news . . . and what if they found Roger Brooks of the *Capital Post* hidden in the back of a pickup truck?

There was a long silence, with things happening but no way for Roger to know what they were. Finally he heard the guard again.

'Okay, Mrs. Gillespie says to send you on down with your letter. Her house is downhill from the Officers' Club. That's the old university student union building. I've marked it on this map. Just before you get to the Officers'

Club, you'll come to another guarded gate. They'll be expecting you. Go straight there. Nowhere else. When you've gone through that gate, go directly to Mrs. Gillespie's house. Nowhere else. Here. Take this pass. You'll need it to get out. Come back through the same way you went in, and end up back here. Nowhere else. Got all that?'

'Yeah – you sure make it complicated.'

'Wasn't us wanted you in here.'

'Right. Thanks, Sergeant.'

'Sure. Any time.'

The truck started up. After a while it stopped again. 'Okay, you can come out for a minute,' Harry said.

They were on a hillside. Off to the left was the harbor. Mist obscured water from water's edge. There were outlines of ships, like ghosts. Closer in there were *big* structures, domes, some on land, some apparently floating on water. Further out in the harbor was the dim outline of a *really* big dome. A rounded metallic shape lay in the dock area —

'Look like greenhouses to me,' Harry said.

'Too much activity,' Roger said. 'Look. Listen.' Vehicles moved among the domes. Industrial sounds – rivet guns, pounding hammers, the whine of electrical drills – drifted up to them.

A thing like the shell of a huge metal crab covered several of the docks. It was a slice of a sphere – curved, with curved edges – like a section of a nuclear plant containment, before the sections were welded together. Curved and wedged-shaped and two yards thick! If they were building a power plant here, it would be the biggest ever.

He said aloud, 'There's lots of work happening, but it's *inside*. They're not building those domes. They're *built*. So what are they hiding inside the domes? That piece of steel shell, what does *that* have to do with anything?'

'Not snouts?'

'Well, sure, snouts. But what do they have them working on? Slave labor? We better get moving.' Roger ducked back behind the seats.

It wasn't much of a house for a general to live in. There was moss growing on the roof, and it hadn't been painted in years.

'What the hell do I do if they catch me?' Harry demanded.

'Catch you what?' Roger asked. 'Walking the streets? Harry, there's a whole *city* here. Look out there, a lot of uniforms, but a lot of civvies too. Act natural. Nobody'll know you don't belong here.' He glanced at his watch. 'Meet you here in an hour.'

'Well, all right.'

Roger waited until Harry was out of sight down the street. Then he went up the steep stairway to the dilapidated wooden porch and knocked.

The door opened. 'Yes – Roger! What in the world?'

'Special delivery from Carlotta. She sends her best,' Roger said. 'Aren't you going to invite me in?'

Automatically she stepped aside. Roger closed the door behind him. 'Is Ed here?'

'Working. He works all the time. Roger, what *are* you doing here?'

'Carrying Carlotta's mail —'

'Roger, that's silly!'

'Well, we're touring the country, getting stories on how people are living. It's not all just news, I'm reporting back to Colorado Springs. When I told Carlotta I was coming to the Northwest, she said I should look you up.' Roger had never felt less horny in his life, but he did his best to leer at her. 'You don't look glad to see me —'

'Ed isn't in orbit this time, Roger! And security – Roger, I don't *know* how hard they watch the housing,

571

but – Ed effectively owns this place. Roger, you'd be better off doing espionage for the snouts!'

———————

At four o'clock there were crowds streaming out of the harbor area. Men, women, mostly dressed for work. They spread outward through the gloomy afternoon drizzle. They must live close, Harry thought. They didn't seem to be making for parking lots.

These weren't guards for snouts. There were far too many. The men were big, loud, dressed for durability even in their civvies, and many still wore hard hats and overalls. Heavy construction work types. What in hell is going on?

Half a dozen men, a dozen, more, streamed toward a smallish building. It wasn't labeled, but Harry suddenly knew. A club, a tavern, a bar.

He contrived to emerge from between two buildings. He strolled toward the bar, trying to look thirsty as opposed to nervous. The noise level was high. A machine-shriek could be heard through a hundred boisterous conversations. That, and a sound like an elephant's scream, but elaborated, like a maniac's babbling too. Somewhere there was a snout. Harry ignored it for the moment.

Nobody stopped him at the door.

The bar was too deep in customers and getting deeper. Harry eased into the crowd. His hand came out of his pocket with money in a clip. *Think priorities. Drink first, talk second, or I'll look funny.*

The hard hats were being stacked in piles near the door, no problem that Harry didn't have one. He was dressed rough enough otherwise. At the tables they were already chugging beer. From the corner of his eye Harry watched a big guy finish a pitcher, order another, drink a glass of that, while the big round table was filling up around him. *That* one would be loose enough already.

Harry ordered a pitcher. The bartender looked curiously

at Harry's money. 'New in town, huh?' he said.

'Yeah.'

The change he gave back said 'Federal Reserve Note: Northwestern Grain Project.' It was colored dull blue.

Harry took the pitcher to the big table. 'Mind if I sit here?'

'All the same with me.' The big man had nearly white blond hair cut very short. He was bigger than Harry, with huge hands that had been through the wars.

The voice was accented. *Lots of them are. Southern, southwestern. Not from up here. Why?* Harry sat down next to him. He pocketed his clip of Colorado Springs notes, but not before the big man had seen it. *He'll know I'm new here.*

'Whitey Lowenstein,' the burly man said. 'You?'

'They call me Hairy Red.'

Lowenstein chuckled. 'Reckon they might. What crew you with?'

'Well —'

'Yeah.' Lowenstein's grin was knowing. 'You'll get over that after a while. The security system's ridiculous. Me, I'm a welder.' He studied Harry carefully. 'Bet you a pitcher I can figure out your job.'

'You're on.' Harry remembered to drink.

Lowenstein reached out suddenly to pat Harry's breast pocket. 'Hmm. No film badge. Maybe you pocketed it, though. Clean clothes. Big guy. You an educated man?'

Harry laughed. 'School of hard knocks —'

'Sure. I got a feeling about you, though. All newcomers get the security lecture, but you didn't say *nothing*. You're an atomjack, Harry.'

Atomjack? In a snout prison? 'I'll buy the next pitcher, and let's leave it at that.' *And what in hell is an atomjack?*

An hour later he knew. It wasn't difficult. Everyone in the bar knew.

Somewhere in Bellingham – nobody seemed to know or care exactly where – there were more than a thousand atom bombs. The atomjacks tended them. *A thousand fucking atom bombs. What am I doing here?*

'You've got to get out of here, Roger.'

'I never thought I'd see the day when you started checking papers! Linda, what is going on here?'

'Believe me, Roger, you don't want to know.'

She's colder than a witch's tits. Jeez — 'Linda, you're actually scaring me!'

'I hope so.'

He'd never heard her speak in that tone of voice. 'What do you think I'll do, reveal the dark secret of the captured Invaders? Don't you think I've figured it out?'

She looked beautiful. 'I never thought you were stupid, Roger.'

'Look, Linda, for God's sake, maybe I should just wait for Ed to come home —'

'You won't be here that late.'

'Linda, I give up. What do you want me to do?'

'I want you to go away and not come back.'

'You sure made that plain enough!'

'If it's plain, why haven't you left?'

'Linda, damn all, I came thousands of miles to see you —'

'Uninvited.'

'Uninvited, but I haven't always been unwelcome. I know you don't love me, but you can at least be friendly —'

'That's all over, Roger.'

'It isn't what I meant by friendly, either.' Roger sighed. It was coming home to him with an impact he hadn't expected: *It's over*.

But there's something else here – 'Look, I wanted to see you again. But I've got a girl back in Colorado Springs. I think I'm going to marry her. I don't know why I wanted to see you first, but I did. Does that make sense?' *That got her!*

'I – who is she?'

'Her name is Rosalee. Linda, you won't believe it, I picked her up in a parking structure in Kansas.'

She laughed. 'No, I don't think I do believe that.'

'It's true, though, and she's wonderful.' *Goddam, she really is.* Roger told her about Kansas. *She's listening, just like the Enclave people listen. Not much news gets to Bellingham.* Roger told it long, but paced the story so Linda wouldn't get bored. 'So that's Rosalee, and I guess I'm in love.'

'Does she see through you, Roger?'

'Better than you do.'

'I think you really should marry the girl,' Linda said. 'Now. The problem is to get you out of here. I'll call the gate.'

Roger fingered his beard. With Linda's call, he could pass for Reddington, seated in a truck, in the dark, with a new shift of guards. No. Best wait for Harry. Maybe Harry would be outside already? He glanced at his watch. No. Not time enough. Have to stall.

'Tell them Reddington.'

'What?'

'Couldn't give my right name. And share a drink with me, for old times' sake?'

'Maybe I'm a little ashamed of our old times, Roger.'

'Maybe I am, too. Some of them. But not the real old times, Linda. You didn't know Ed then. Goddam, I wish I'd married you. Would you, if I'd asked?'

'Yes.'

'You say that quickly.'

'I thought about it a lot.'

'Are you sorry I didn't?'

'Let me get you a drink, Roger.'

* * *

'Good night, Linda.'

'Good-bye, Roger.'

'This is final, isn't it?'

'It *is* final. Don't come back, Roger. Next time I'll call the guards.'

'Speaking of that —'

'Sure. I'll see they let you out. Reddington.'

'One kiss. Old times.'

'I didn't give you that much whiskey. Even if I did, I didn't have that much myself. Good-bye, Roger.'

Roger went down the wooden stairs to the truck.

'She sure was glad to see you.'

'Harry. I was hoping you'd be back.'

'Yeah. Let's get out of here.'

'Sure. Learn anything?' *His voice sounds thick. Can he drive?*

'Naw.'

Damn! He did get something. What? 'Too bad. I hoped you'd be smart enough to pick up a clue. I struck out. She *wasn't* glad to see me.'

'Yeah. I saw. Here, you pile in back behind the seat and we'll get going. Did she call the guards to get us out?'

'Yes. Damn. We're both too stupid to get anything.'

'Well, maybe I got something,' Harry said. 'For one thing, this is no prison.'

'Really?'

'Nope. No guards. Lots of welders, plumbers, construction people, but no guards. You know what most of those guys are doing? Welding up a big hemispheric steel plate. I mean *big*. That was a piece of it we saw on the docks. Know something else? There's a thousand atom bombs in this town.'

'Bullshit.'

'No shit, Roger. A thousand motherfucking atom bombs, all identical. They got special crews to work with them. Call them atomjacks.'

A thousand atom bombs. Why? Atom bombs, welders, big steel plate —

Atom bombs. Big hemispheric *steel plate*. Long-buried memories surfaced. Freeman Dyson and Ted Taylor. Lectures at a meeting of the L-5 Society, that bunch of fanatics who wanted to put colonies into space. Steel plates and atom bombs and a whole colony comes down in one piece. Don't worry about the landing spot because it'll be flat when you get down . . . 'Christ on a crutch.'

'What?' Harry took the keys from his pocket and climbed into the driver's seat.

'Nothing.' *They let people in, but if they search on the way out . . .*

Roger waited until Harry's attention was fully on the truck. Then he took the big jack handle from the floor of the cab and rose silently.

'Reddington,' the guard said. Roger sighed in relief. As he'd thought, this was a new one, not the one who'd passed Harry into Bellingham. The guard shined his flashlight onto Roger's face. Roger clenched his eyes against the light . . . distorting his face.

'Sorry. Mind moving that blanket?'

'Sure.' Roger turned from the light, twisting to lift the blanket from over the space behind the seat. *I'd have been just there . .*

The guard was thorough. He looked behind the seats and under the truck. He inspected the pass. He looked at his clipboard notes and compared times.

But he was polite enough not to shine the light in Roger's eyes again.

———

Harry woke in a bare-walled office. He was lying on a cot. Two Air Police sat at a desk across the room. When Harry groaned and opened his eyes, one of the APs went out the door.

'What the hell?' Harry demanded.

He got no answer at all. The AP didn't smile or get up or do anything at all.

Presently the door opened. The first AP came in with a man in U.S. Air Force coveralls. Four stars gleamed from the shoulders.

'Thank you, Airman,' the general said. He turned his attention to Harry. 'All right, Mr. Reddington, would you care to tell me what's going on here?'

'Sure – hey! You're General Gillespie.' Harry had watched TV coverage of the last Shuttle launch, a lifetime ago. Gillespie looked many years older.

He said, 'That's obvious enough. Now who are you?'

'You said my name —'

'Mister, you have about twenty seconds to start explaining.'

Oh, shit! 'General, could you make that a minute? I'm just getting used to the idea that Roger whacked me on the head.'

'Roger?'

'Roger Brooks, sir.'

'Roger Brooks.'

Shit fire, that name registered.

'I take it that the man who left this post using your credentials was Roger Brooks, then?'

'Yes, sir.'

'And you and Brooks came to see Mrs. Gillespie. I take it that was Roger's idea.'

'Sure. Didn't do him any good, though.'

'What do you mean by that?'

'She threw him out.'

'I see.'

Shit, what have I got into?

'Your minute is up, Reddington.'

'Yes, sir. Look, it started in Colorado Springs. Actually,

it started earlier.' *Talk fast!* Harry babbled, how Congressman Wes left Harry in charge of his house, how Harry and Carlotta Dawson had captured a snout and Harry got a presidential citation and a gas ration card —

'Later,' Gillespie interrupted.

'Dammit, General, I'm telling you the truth!'

'Oddly enough, I believe you. For now, though, I have a different question. Where has Roger Brooks gone?'

————

The Enclave looked normal, no one near the gate but Miranda Shakes. Roger drove up carefully.

He was tempted to drive on past, take the logging trail and fire roads that led to the Nooksack Valley, and continue east past Mount Baker. *Great idea. One problem. Harry knows about those fire roads. He'll tell.*

Even if Harry wouldn't tell about the route east, the truck would never get to Colorado Springs. The motorcycle would.

Emotions chased their way through Roger's mind. *I've got a secret, a big secret, the biggest ever. Wow! No wonder they made Bellingham vanish. Orion!*

If they catch me, they'll lock me up until the war's over. I need insurance. There's only one kind of insurance that can work. I have to tell an editor now, quick, so the Post *will keep looking for me if they try to hide me somewhere.*

Great plan. One problem. No telephones. No radios. Not even a CB. How am I going to tell the Post?

If I can't tell the Post *who can I tell?*

'Hello, Roger,' Miranda Shakes said. 'Where's Harry?'

'Trying to pick up some supplies. I'll take the bike down to meet him and then we'll move on. Here's the truck key.'

'Where to?'

'Back to Colorado Springs.' *I have to get moving. Harry can wake up any minute.*

'Is something wrong, Roger?'

'Huh? No, it's just a long ride back. I'm not looking forward to it. Their packs stood next to the motorcycle. It took only a moment to lift them onto the rack and lash them in place. *And now what? If they catch me – they could do anything.*

What will I do if I get away? Damn, it's a big story, the biggest, too big? Like finding out about the atom bomb before they dropped it on Japan. Can't print it, can't let the snouts find out, but —

But people have to know, have to know there's hope. So many have given up, think there's no chance. They have to know there is a chance.

How? How to tell people but not snouts? There has to be a way. It won't happen if they catch me. They'll lock me up, secrets, security, they've made this whole town a prison. There's too good a chance they'll catch me and just make me vanish, an unperson. I need insurance. Maybe I need something else, too. Maybe I need help getting out of Bellingham. 'Is Fox around?'

'In the greenhouse.'

John Fox. If there's anybody who can get out of Bellingham and back to the Springs, it's Fox. He has friends everywhere. Just telling him can be good insurance.

There was something reassuring in the smell of the greenhouse. It smelled like life. A green and brown smell, plants and rich dirt, growth and decay.

John Fox didn't turn as Roger came up behind him. He was even thinner than Roger remembered. The chamois shirt and lederhosen hung from bones and long, hard muscles. He was pulling smaller sprouts from a tray, leaving the largest. 'Have to transfer these in a few days,' he said.

'John?'

'Wha – Roger? What's news?' And he chuckled.

'The Navy's got a thousand atom bombs in the harbor complex.'

Fox turned, stared into Roger's face. 'You went in?'

580

'Yeah. A thousand atom bombs all exactly alike, and they're making an enormous steel hemisphere. Ed Gillespie is running it all. Thousands of workmen, and they're all welders or atomjacks. What does that mean to you?'

'Orion.' A smile flickered, then died. 'They're building an Orion.'

'Yeah. And *launching* an Orion, John. A thousand bombs going off one by one under that plate. I seem to remember you like preserving the environment. Can you imagine what that'll do to Bellingham?'

Fox nodded. His eyes seemed curiously unfocused. 'You're going to publish?'

'Publish? I'm telling *you*. At least the Enclave can get their heads down when it happens. But what about Bellingham? Shouldn't they know?'

Fox was still nodding. 'And who else?'

That was the sticking point. 'John, I'm not totally sure. Maybe there's no way to tell the people and keep it from the snouts. The Navy's right about that; the snouts can't learn. They can't take their CBs away from the whole country! At the same time —'

'You'll think of something.' Fox lashed out.

Roger was doubled over. Something huge and heavy had tried to drive itself through his solar plexus and the spine behind it. Through a haze of pain he tried to sense, to orient . . . Fox had hit him. His bony elbow was crooked around Roger's neck, squeezing. Roger could barely breathe. They were walking . . .

The pressure constricted his voice to a whisper. 'I only wanted. To tell you. You. I hadn't decided. Anything else. John, let —'

Fox released a hand to push a door open. Roger thrashed. The elbow tightened. Oh, God, Fox was *strong*. 'I know you,' Fox said. 'You want that Pulitzer Prize. You'd publish. You'd tell the aliens yourself if that was the only way to get it out.'

They were bending over, Fox's weight pushing him down, face down into water. Roger got his hands on a cool, hard surface and pushed up. The porcelain rim of a toilet. He was drowning in a toilet . . . and he couldn't get his face high enough . . . and the strength was leaking out of him while the urge to breathe grew to agony. *I hadn't decided! I hadn't decided!*

CHAPTER THIRTY-EIGHT
PRAYERS

Hear now this, O foolish people, and without understanding; which have eyes, and see not; which have ears, and hear not.

– JEREMIAH 5:21

Digit Ship *Forty-nine* carried vitamins for the human fithp, stocks of plants and frozen meat for analysis, seeds and small animals and an infant elephant, and three spaceborn warriors returning for the mating season. Chintithpit-mang arrived to find himself summoned to the funeral pit.

Who had died? The airlock guard who gave him his orders hadn't known. He had aborted his time with Shreshleemang, he had gone down to the War of Winterhome ahead of mating season, he had been out of contact . . . and the scent of mating was in the air, but Chintithpit-mang felt only fear. Who had died while he was gone?

A small delay could hardly matter. Chintithpit-mang passed through the Garden on his way to the funeral pit.

It was not as he had expected.

The Garden was small. Cramped. The single thriving pillar plant seemed a pitiful reminder that once the Traveler Fithp had known jungles. Chintithpit-mang had fought in jungles bigger than *Message Bearer*! His own reactions shocked him. He hastened through the Garden and into the leave-taking room that half circled the funeral pit. It smelled of Winterhome . . .

A crowd was waiting; or so it seemed; and one of the crowd was Shreshleemang. He said, 'Mang . . .'

His mate did not respond. There were eyes on him: Herdmaster Pastempeh-keph, K'turfookeph, Fookerteh, a female he didn't know, Breaker Raztupisp-minz, and a human Chintithpit-mang recognized. He asked, 'Who is dead?'

'Fathisteh-tulk,' said the Herdmaster. 'I have taken the task of learning how he died. Chintithpit-mang, you returned from the first battle on Winterhome with Digit Ship *Six*.'

'I did.'

'What did you do then?'

'I turned my cargo and prisoners over to another octuple. Then I went to see my mate.'

'Shreshleemang, when did your mate reach you?'

'Two-eighths of a day after Digit Ship *Six* coupled aft,' said Shreshleemang. Above the smell of the funeral pit he found her special scent – she was in season – but her voice was cold as winter.

The Herdmaster asked, 'What delayed you, Chintithpit-mang?'

'I was interrupted.'

'In what fashion?'

Chintithpit-mang was afraid to speak. The Herdmaster blew softly, vexed. 'On your way to see your mate for the first time in eight-squareds of days, what could have interrupted you? A fi' high in status? Or with an urgent mission? Or allied with your own dissident movement? You were intercepted by Advisor Fathisteh-tulk!'

This was going to be very bad. Chintithpit-mang saw nothing for it but to tell us much of the truth as he must. 'We met in the corridors. He demanded that I go with him.'

'Where? Why?'

'Why, he did not say. We went to the mudroom. It had been thawed. He said, "Cold, it would be uncomfortable

584

for us. It might freeze my guest. Chintithpit-mang, I insisted that my contact come alone, and he demanded that I do the same, though he is a slave.''

'I said, "What is he then, a rogue?" And then I knew. He was to meet a human.

'He said, "I want to question him. I think he has much to tell me about the uses of space. He surely has motive to be convincing. When I speak of this meeting to the Year Zero Fithp I don't want to depend on my unsupported word. You must witness, unseen.''

'I stayed near the far end of the mudroom, hidden from the grill by the curve of the ceiling. The human was behind the grill. I listened. Herdmaster, I hate and fear humans, but this one said things I have always believed. He knew more of the wealth of the spaces between worlds than we have guessed! He spoke of marvelous dreams, of asteroid mines, of towers to take loot from a world to beyond orbit —'

'He told the Advisor that the dissidents were right. I am not amazed,' said the Herdmaster.

'Suddenly the grill came flying out and struck Fathisteh-tulk a stunning blow. The human came after it, kicked at Fathisteh-tulk, and leaped back into the duct.'

'What did the Advisor say?'

'He said nothing. He leapt after the human, to punish —'

'Pause. What upset the human? It had what it wanted. You were there to witness. Exactly what did the Advisor say that so enraged a surrendered human?'

Trapped. After what he had done, lying to the Herdmaster would be a trivial crime; but what did the Herdmaster already know?

The Herdmaster's accusation rolled forth. 'You confronted me in the Garden to tell me that humans are a terrible enemy, that we should turn our backs on them. After one day aboard *Message Bearer* you volunteered to return to Winterhome. You fought well. Chintithpit-mang, what was here that you feared more than the war? What were you afraid that a fi' might ask? *What did Fathisteh-tulk say to the human?*'

It was impossible. 'Fathisteh-tulk said that descendants of the human prisoners would serve the Traveler Herd in space, with their smaller food requirements and dexterous digits and their greater knowledge of the worlds of Winterhome-light.'

'Was this what enraged the human?'

'It was.'

'Would you recognize this human again?'

'It was him! That one!'

The Herdmaster turned. 'Wes Dawson, did you speak to my Advisor a second time?'

The man said, 'Wesley Dawson. Congressman. 514–55–2316.'

'Chintithpit-mang saw you. Did you see him?' The man was silent. 'The line you were given for cleaning the ducts, we found its mark deep in Fathisteh-tulk's snnfp.' Still he was silent. The Herdmaster said, 'You must speak.'

'I don't think so.'

'Chintithpit-mang, why didn't you help the Advisor?'

'I was stunned.'

'Did it cross your thoughts that the Advisor would say things you didn't want heard?'

'No! My mind had not moved at all. I knew so little of humans then. A surrendered prisoner attacked a fi' of the herd!'

'Stunned. Speak further.'

'Fathisteh-tulk went after him. I thought he was reaching for the human, to scoop him out and kill him. But it went on too long, and I tried to think what to do, and then Fathisteh-tulk was pushed out into the mudroom. He was dead.'

'And you?'

'I looked into the duct. I pulled the grill out and looked again. There wasn't anything. I . . . put the grill back . . .

I couldn't find the twist fasteners . . . I . . . took the line off Fathisteh-tulk's snnfp and pushed him into the mud until he was completely covered. Then I left. I went to the emergency control room and set the mudroom to freeze again.'

'Why?'

'What the human said, he might say again if we caught him.'

'Pfoo. You were stunned. From the way the Advisor reacted, don't you think even a human might learn a lesson? You've been on Winterhome, you know they're bright. Next time he would say, we've certainly wondered if there might be things in space worth having, the meteors lead us to think that there are all-metal asteroids and ice strata and air bound loosely in rock, but we have not looked. Well?'

'I didn't think of it.'

'I think you have lied. You shall be isolated. None shall speak to you henceforth. If you have more to tell me, tell a guard.'

The females' eyes were fixed on Chintithpit-mang, and he cringed. He tried, 'Mang . . .?' and then Shreshleemang turned away.

The Herdmaster had already forgotten him. 'Dawson. We kill rogues.'

The rogue human said, 'We kill murderers ourselves, or else we imprison them.'

'When a fithp conspires to murder, we may kill them all, or not. It depends on their grievance. Did you act alone in this?'

'Alone? Of course I was alone. You had kept me isolated for a week.'

'And did you tell others afterward?'

'Wesley Dawson. Congressman. 514–55–2316.'

'You shall be imprisoned alone. None shall speak to you. If you have more to say, tell a guard.'

* * *

The Herdmaster watched them being led away. He had toyed with the notion of imprisoning them together – but Chintithpit-mang would surely kill the man. Pastempeh-keph wanted more than that. *Why* had Dawson done what he did? Was there no strategy that would hold a human's surrender?

To exterminate an intelligent race really would make the Traveler Fithp equal to the Predecessors. Godlike criminals. For all of history the priests had taught the fithp children the words of the Squuff Thuktun. It told the tale of the Homeworld's ruin. 'Our mistakes are mapped here, that you may walk around them . . .'

Isolation would break Dawson soon enough. It would take longer with humans. No matter. There was time . . . and he must be studied. Let him be only a rogue, a rarity! Otherwise . . .

Chowpeentulk stood proud, victorious; but the victory here was Pastempeh-keph's. Her mate had died because he rejected the dissident cause. She would talk. The dissidents were broken now. They would never again stand between Winterhome and the Traveler Fithp.

————

Something had changed in Tashayamp. She visited the humans' cell less and less frequently. She rarely talked to them. The morning after John Woodward died, she appeared in the spin hatch, and looked down without curiosity, and was already backing out when Jeri called up to her.

'Tashayamp! John Woodward is dead; he died in the night. Tashayamp?'

The teacher's mate peered down at the little group clustered around Carrie Woodward, and John's body all alone. 'I thought he sleeps. He looks like he sleeps. Wait.' Tashayamp disappeared.

Tashayamp was quite wrong. John's face was slack; his

eyes were open; he wasn't breathing. How could anyone have missed the presence of death?

Fithp soldiers descended via the lift platform. Carrie was huddled with her face between her knees. The children hung back; they didn't know how to help. When the warriors wrapped digits around John's shoulder and ankles, Carrie surged to her feet . . . and stood, rigid, while they put him on the platform and sent him up.

The warriors rose after him. Tashayamp looked down. 'How did he die?'

There was venom in Carrie's answer. 'Slowly. Weeks, now, he's been getting sicker and sicker. He couldn't handle the gravity changes. He couldn't sleep right. You weren't giving him the right vitamins. We don't have a doctor. Being penned like an animal, knowing you're smashing our world, he couldn't take it. Now he's dead.'

'You come,' Tashayamp said. 'All.'

Tashayamp led them toward the axis via spiral ramps.

By the time they reached the funeral room they were nearly weightless. Above their heads, beyond a glass ceiling, a dark slush was in queasy churning motion. The stink of it permeated the air.

Two fithp awaited them: the Bull and the Priest.

The Russians were quiet; they appeared resigned. Jeri knew that was how they wanted to appear. *But what else can we do anyway? We will not escape without outside help, and no one is going to help us.*

Here were all of humanity for twenty thousand miles around, save for Wes Dawson. Alice was edgy; her eyes kept straying to the entrances, as if she expected him to appear.

Wes had disappeared over a week ago. None of the fithp would speak of him to the humans. Seeing him absent, Jeri at last believed that he was dead.

She moved to rest a hand on Carrie's shoulder. 'How're you holding up?'

'I'll manage.' Carrie laughed: a cracked, joyless sound. 'None of us dares go crazy. They'd leave us all together, wouldn't they? We'd all go off our heads one by one. Don't look at me like that, Alice. I'm all right.'

Fistarteh-thuktun said something to the Herdmaster, too fast to catch. The Herdmaster nodded at Tashayamp, who said, 'Query: does Fistarteh-thuktun speak last words for John Woodward? Query: does one of you speak?'

'There's no preacher,' Melissa said. 'Mom —'

'I don't know – ' Jeri began.

Carrie stepped forward jerkily. 'I'll do it. I've been to enough funerals to know the words. He was my husband.'

Jeri was close enough to catch the Herdmaster's words to Tashayamp. 'Do not translate, but remember.'

Through the glass she watched two fithp emerge on the lip of the funeral pit, carrying John Woodward like a sack of grain between them.

' "I am the resurrection and the life,' saith the Lord. "He that believeth in me, though he were dead, yet shall he live: and whosoever liveth and believeth in me shall never die."

' "I know that my redeemer liveth, and that he shall stand at the latter day upon the earth, and though after my skin worms destroy this body, yet in my flesh shall I see God; whom I shall see for myself, and mine eyes shall behold, and not another." '

The fithp soldiers launched Woodward toward the center of the vortex of brown muck. He moved slowly, tumbling, stiff with rigor mortis. Carrie stopped. The look on her face was dreadful.

'Remember this good man, Lord. Remember him and bring him to Your peace. Bring him to rest in Your arms. Let him fly to Jesus.'

An empty-eyed skull showed through the slowly churning compost heap. It was almost conical, an animal's skull, with knobs where the tendons of the trunk had been anchored. Jeri ground her teeth with the need to get *out* of here before John Woodward brushed against the glass! Carrie must be hanging on to her sanity by her teeth —

Yet she looked and sounded as calm as any early Christian about to face Nero's lions.

' "The Lord is my shepherd; I shall not want. He maketh me to lie down in green pastures: he leadeth me beside the still waters."

' "He restoreth my soul: he leadeth me in the paths of righteousness for his name's sake."

' "Yea, though I walk through the valley of the shadow of death, I will fear no evil, for thou art with me; thy rod and thy staff, they comfort me."

' "Thou preparest a table before me in the presence of mine enemies: thou anointest my head with oil; my cup runneth over."

' "Surely goodness and mercy shall follow me all the days of my life: and I will dwell in the house of the Lord for ever." '

She turned toward the fithp, aging but ageless, a woman of farms and fields. 'You can't hurt him now. He's in the arms of Jesus.' She raised her hands high. 'Deliver me from mine enemies, O God. Defend me from them that rise up against me. Deliver me from the wicked doers. Stand up, arise, awake O Holy One of Israel, and be not merciful unto them that offend these little ones!

'I say it were better that a millstone were tied about their necks, and they were cast into the sea! Thou, Lord, shall have them in scorn. Consume them in thy wrath, consume them that they may perish, and know that it is God that ruleth unto the ends of the world!'

She fell silent.

What will they do? They can't be afraid of curses. God, my God, have you forsaken all of us? Are you there? Are you listening? Can you listen?

Tashayamp waited.

God, let us out of here!

'Return to your place,' Tashayamp told them. 'Follow the guards.' She herself departed with the Bull and the Priest.

'Eat them. Rage and eat them, that they will die and know that God leads everywhere. That's as near as I can translate,' Tashayamp finished.

'You see!' Fistarteh-thuktun trumpeted. 'Of course we might have learned something by dissecting the creature, but *this* we would have lost! We have never before witnessed such a ceremony.'

'And what do you think you have learned?'

'I was wrong,' said the priest. 'Despite their shape, they are not totally alien. We can lead them. Herdmaster, do you see it? They have no Predecessors. None lead them, they must lead themselves. They have made for themselves the fiction of a Predecessor!'

Pastempeh-keph signaled assent. 'It must be a fiction. This God would hardly have tolerated our incursions. I wonder how they see him? Does their God have thumbs? And they give him male gender —'

'I cannot make myself care. They seek a leader greater than themselves! Tashayamp, did you render that phrase accurately? '*Fear* God?'

'I think so. We have a book of words from Kansas. I will examine *fear*.'

They had reached the bridge. The warrior on duty covered his head. 'Herdmaster, a message. Chintithpit-mang wishes to speak to you.'

'I hear.'

'We shall be their Predecessors,' Fistarteh-thuktun said. 'I must learn more. I wish I could go down to Africa —'

'You may not. We need you here. Get your data from Takpusseh-yamp. Tashayamp, is your mate —'

'Easily distracted, but at your service,' Tashayamp said, and the mating scent thickened in the air.

The Herdmaster left them there. The bridge was busy; some site in Africa was about to get a consignment of meteors. The Herdmaster settled onto his pad and tapped at the console.

Chintithpit-mang was a brown ball in the center of his cell. The Herdmaster watched him for a bit. Huddled in his misery, he might have been asleep but for his nostrils and digits, which moved restlessly, as if they had independent life.

Eight days! Give him credit, that's a tough-minded fi'. The Herdmaster said softly, 'Chintithpit-mang, speak to me.'

The fi' started convulsively. He looked toward the camera. 'Herdmaster I will speak to the dissidents.'

'You have done so. I recorded our last conversation, and broadcast it. What would you tell them?'

'Fathisteh-tulk said that human help would be beyond price in the conquest of space, with their ambitious plans and their smaller food intake and dexterous digits. Winterhome must be conquered and the humans broken into the Traveler Herd.'

'This is what you said an eight-day past. What have you to add? You should have helped Fathisteh-tulk.'

'Herdmaster, I would have joined the argument against the Advisor. The human attacked first.'

'You let him die.'

'He would have destroyed the dissident cause.'

'He has. You have no other to speak for you. Why did you hide the corpse?'

Chintithpit-mang's digits were tight across his skull, as if welded. 'I was in shock! The Advisor betrayed us! If the human were caught, he might repeat Fathisteh-tulk's words!'

'Dawson holds his peace better than you have. You weren't trying to protect Dawson. Must I return you to the silence of your cell?'

593

'I heard a snoring sound.'

'When?'

'A 64-breaths or so after the human left the Advisor for dead. I still didn't know what to do, so I did nothing. I heard a snoring sound. I turned and his chest was heaving.'

'Speak further.'

'I knew what he'd say. The dissidents – we would have – I pushed his face in the mud. I pushed mud in his mouth. The snoring stopped. I pushed him the rest of the way.'

It was what the Herdmaster had expected to hear; yet he had hoped. 'What shall I do with you now, Chintithpit-mang? I cannot have you loose in *Message Bearer*.'

'Kill me. Gather the herd as tradition requires.'

'We are roguish enough these days. I cannot order my fithp to trample you and expect them to stop short of riot! Besides, too many owe you their lives, or their mates' lives. The Attackmaster regrets your absence. Chintithpit-mang, will you return to Africa to fight?'

'Yes, if I am allowed.'

'You are *sent*, not allowed. Forever, Chintithpit-mang. I can grasp the pressures that made you rogue, but if such happens again, you will be trampled.' The Herdmaster tapped at keys.

And that is well done. Chintithpit-mang will serve us well. I will send down others of the Year Zero Fithp. Let them make amends in Africa. He tapped more keys. The picture changed.

Wes Dawson was . . . running nowhere? Pastempeh-keph watched for a bit. Dawson ran, legs pumping, making no progress; forelimbs pumping in rhythm, though they never touched the ground. Was he already mad? Did he dream that he chased a fleeing meat animal, or that something chased him?

'Wes Dawson.'

Dawson turned as he ran, to face the camera. He said

nothing. The desperate longing to hear another's voice
. . . might have been present, but the Herdmaster saw no
trace of it.

He said, 'Chintithpit-mang tells me that he killed the
Advisor. Fathisteh-tulk was still alive when you released
him.'

Dawson's mouth twitched upward at the corners. In
fair fithp he said, 'I do it better next time.'

Pastempeh-keph turned off the screen. Just whose
mind was being broken by this treatment?

————————

Spinward around the curve of the mudroom there were
the sounds of splashing and soft-trumpeted gossip.
Shreshleemang ignored it. Her status had become uncertain when her mate's confession was broadcast. This was
an embarrassment to her friends. These days they avoided
her. Shreshleemang understood this, and resented it
nonetheless. She could do nothing about it. She lolled in
the mud with eyes half closed.

She grew aware of others gathering around her. They
rested in the mud, quiet, but she could feel their eyes.
When it became clear that they would not go away, she
said, 'I remember a time when the mudroom was a refuge
from the day's cares —'

'There was never such a time,' said Chowpeentulk. 'The
mudroom has forever been a pond of politics.'

Shreshleemang looked up. Chowpeentulk and K'turfookeph seemed to be cooly studying her. K'turfookeph
said, 'Your mate is not be trampled. He will be returned to
Africa.'

'He told me himself. He has already departed.'

'Shreshleemang, you should join him.'

Shreshleemang surged from the mud. With the greatest
effort she managed to curb her bellow. 'The Herdmaster

may send me where he wills. Have you come as his emissary?'

'No. You are a mated female of the Traveler Herd, with no stain on your character. Will you listen?'

She sank back. 'I will.'

'He needs you. Males go rogue far more easily without a mate to steady them. Chintithpit-mang lives close against that barrier.'

'Yes, for he has crossed it.'

'Africa is being conquered, but there remain many human rogues in the pacified territory. Effective warriors are needed. Chintithpit-mang is one of the best, but the jungle hunters live under terrible strain. Often they hunt alone, as if already rogue. Unmated, Chintithpit-mang will be rogue within a 64-days. Mated, he can be an effective leader.'

'Yes, he needs me. He has destroyed the dissident cause, he has humiliated me personally. Do I need him?'

Chowpeentulk said, 'Unmated females go rogue too.'

'Nonsense.'

'We show it differently. We do not go on killing sprees. But we often develop a distaste for males and for children. We play dominance games instead of cooperating with our fithp.'

'What are you doing here, Chowpeentulk? What is your interest? Did you want my mate trampled?'

'No . . . I am widowed. At my age it is certain that I will never mate again. The war kills males, particularly unmated males. My interest now lies with my children and the Traveler Fithp. The Traveler Fithp needs your mate, sane.'

'If you knew how I feel about him, you might send me down in order to punish your mate's murderer.'

'You were dissident too.'

'I was and am. The Traveler Fithp owned the stars and planets before ever we saw the shape of the prey. We don't need them.'

596

K'turfookeph spoke softly. 'There is no dissident fithp. The matter has been decided, consented by the new Advisor, accepted by Fistarteh-thuktun. Winterhome will be ours. The danger of leaving it for the humans is too great. Fathisteh-tulk found a true path.'

'Nothing tried to kill us when we circled the gas giant.'

K'turfookeph stood silent. Chowpeentulk spoke in a voice like falling water. 'Shreshleemang, did you advise your mate to exercise proper restraint in his efforts for the dissident cause?'

'Proper restraint? We – ' She stopped.

'Restraint is the thuktun of females. Males don't understand restraint. Chintithpit-mang would do *anything* to advance the dissidents. He proved that. Males need their mates to protect them from such folly.'

'He was fighting in Kansas, tens of thousands of makasrupkithp from me!'

'My mate made a mistake there,' K'turfookeph acknowledged. 'The Year Zero Herd were a working fithp. Separating them drove some toward rogue status just when they were facing a madly alien environment. But do you not share blame?'

'You will not drive me from the ship,' said Shreshleemang. Females don't normally fight, but she was ready.

'We would not drive you,' K'turfookeph said.

'I will not go! To live on Winterhome, forever – what would I do there?'

'There is much to do. We have a world to hold, a new species to bring into the Traveler fithp. Your mate is there. Many of the Year Zero will be sent there.'

Another spoke from behind K'turfookeph. 'Once the mang fithp was great. Now there are few. If you die childless, there will be fewer still.'

Shreshleemang had not noticed Flarishmang's approach. Her own great-aunt. Shreshleemang's anger rose at being reproved by a childless sleeper – but they

597

weren't giving her time to answer. The females were gathering round her like a wet brown wall.

Chowpeentulk said, 'Your mate will go rogue again. It will be remembered that he committed murder while you were present to advise him. You will be blamed. No male will risk your company. You will remain unmated and childless. Your friends will gather to comfort you, of course . . . won't they? Perhaps not. And you will grow old, held within the womb of *Message Bearer*, while others carve our future across the face of Winterhome!'

Chowpeentulk's voice had risen to a bellow. 'Do you really think I seek vengeance? Against whom? If your mate went mad, who failed to pull him back? It was known that Digit Ship *Six* was arriving. Why did you not meet him at the airlock?'

'I will go.'

'*Where were you?*'

'I was busy. Cease! I will join my mate in Africa. We will conquer the human fithp and bind them to us. History may judge the result.'

CHAPTER THIRTY-NINE
THE SILVER-TONGUED DEVILS

And how can man die better
Than facing fearful odds
For the ashes of his fathers,
And the temples of his gods?

     – THOMAS BABINGTON, Lord Macaulay, 'Horatius'

COUNTDOWN: TEN MONTHS AFTER FOOTFALL

The eye-searing light died. Harry tipped back the welder's mask. 'Good work.' He ran his hand along the gridwork. 'Now they can put the electrical stuff in.'

His companion grunted. 'What the hell *is* this? Narrow rails ran straight down to an opening in the cylinder within which they worked, and ended above the floor.

'Launching rails,' Harry said. 'Look, they got these things they call spurt bombs. I don't know how they work, but when an atom bomb goes off near one of them, the thing sort of curls up and dies, and when it dies it shoots off a really strong gamma-ray laser beam. What we have here is a gizmo to throw the spurt bombs out where they can soak up some of the energy from the bombs that move this ship.'

'How do they aim them?'

'Black magic. Hell, I don't know. All I know is they have to be thrown out, and we're building the gizmo that does that.'

'Okay.' The welder gestured toward the tangle of wires

and pipes surrounding them. 'Christ, this whole ship is one big kludge.'

'Yeah —'

'More all the time, too.'

'I guess. Anyway, all we have to do now is get out of here.'

Harry led the way into the empty bay. The spurt bombs were big; the nests for them were ten feet tall and a foot across. Harry climbed a ladder, slid sideways through spurt bomb nests, and emerged through an unwelded hatch onto the hemispherical slope of the Shell.

The shock absorbers rose above them, holding nothing. The Brick, the section that would house men and spacecraft, hadn't been mounted yet. There were four spurt bomb bays. The pair of drive bomb bays were far larger. Conveyors and a pair of cannon already in place would lead the propulsion bombs under the rim of the Shell and fire them into the focus. It was all welded to the Shell itself, six towers rising around a steel forest of shock absorbers; and it was all as massive as any freighter. Nothing delicate about *Michael*!

A catwalk took them down the Shell to the concrete floor.

'Beats me how you find your way around.' Whitey Lowenstein took off the welder's mask and cap. 'Ten minutes to quitting time. Beer?'

'I'll join you if I can.'

The Chuckanut was crowded, but Whitey had saved a corner booth. He had two girls with him. Harry sank into the booth gratefully and waved for a pitcher.

'We'd about given you up,' Lowenstein said. 'You remember Pat.' He took Pat's hand and held it. 'And that's Janet. What kept you?'

'Rohrs wanted to go over some stuff. Hi, Pat. Nice to meet you, Janet. What do you do for the project?'

'Pat's a clerk,' Janet said. 'I'm a welder, like Whitey.'

'Tough job.' She didn't look big enough, either.

'I can handle it,' Janet said.

Whitey watched Harry chug a large glass, refill it, and chug again. 'Okay, Harry, I give up. I've seen you carrying General Gillespie's briefcase. I've heard your stories about Kansas, and I even believe them, but then I've seen you sweeping floors. I watched you connect up electrical lines. Today you show me where to weld that rail thing, and then you're in a conference with Rohrs for an hour after quitting time.

'Harry, just what in hell are you?'

Harry laughed. 'You'd never guess in a million years. Whitey, I'm a trusty.'

'A what?'

Pat giggled.

'Remember when we met?'

'Yeah, I thought you were an atomjack.'

'Remember there was a big security flap that day?'

'No —'

'You remember the big flap, right? Trust me, it was the day you met me. I caused it. I helped smuggle a newspaper reporter into here, right into General Gillespie's house.'

'Harry, goddammit, I never know when you're bull-shitting me.'

'Not this time. The guy's name was Roger Brooks. I don't know how he found out there was a story here, but he hired me to bring him here from Colorado Springs. Turns out he'd known Mrs. Gillespie a long time.'

'Jeez, and you brought him in here?' Janet didn't sound very friendly.

'Yeah, well, I'd been told you weren't hiding anything but snouts. And I'd captured a snout —'

'You what?' Janet demanded.

'Captured a snout.'

'He did, too,' Whitey said. 'He'll tell you about it if you ask. Or if you don't ask.'

'Aw – Anyway, bringing Roger in seemed like a good

601

idea at the time. But Roger figured out what Archangel was before I did, and he clipped me and stole the truck. Next thing I know I wake up in General Gillespie's front yard with about a zillion Marines and Air Police. Every one of them's pointing a gun at me, and here comes the General himself. He didn't look too friendly.'

'I don't reckon he would have,' Whitey said. 'What did you do?'

'Do? I pleaded for mercy.'

'Must have worked —'

'Yeah. I had one thing going for me. I used to work for Congressman Dawson —'

'Right. You told me. The guy the snouts have making speeches for them. It was his wife you had ride the snout.'

Janet laughed. 'Harry, you sound like a good man to know.'

'Oh, I am, I am. Anyway, since I knew his friends, it made the General a little more ready to listen. After a while he decided I wasn't really a bad guy, so he made me an offer. I could go to work as a gofer, or they'd send me off to Port Angeles.'

'Better than Walla Walla,' Whitey said. 'Port Angeles is where they send you if you quit.'

'Yeah,' Pat said. 'But it's a drag. I must know ten, twelve guys who went over there and decided they'd rather be back here. It's not a bad place, but there's nothing to do except grow vegetables, and they still censor any letters you want to send out.'

'That's what the General told me,' Harry said. 'I thought about it for maybe fifteen seconds. Christ, I was beginning to rust in Colorado Springs. I'd have gone nuts in Port Angeles.

'So they made me a gofer. I do what the General wants. They pay me pretty good, and – I'm *in* it, I'm where it's happening. I've been all *over* that ship, I bet I know my way around inside the Brick as good as anybody except maybe Max Rohrs. I've worked on the steam lines for the attitude controls, and I helped the Navy guys install those big guns off the *New Jersey*, Jesus those are *big*, and the Army guys with their missile launchers.' Harry grinned wolfishly. 'Shee-it, if we can get this thing up there, those snouts'll think Mount Whitney is coming after them next!'

Whitey lifted his glass. 'Bigger and better surprises.'

'Right. A willing foe and sea room!'

'What's that?'

'Nelson. A British admiral —'

'Hell, I know who Nelson was.'

'Okay. It was his toast. And that's the story.'

'Pretty good story. You fall in the shit and come up smelling like a rose.'

'I thought so. Now I don't know! These twelve-hour workdays are killing me.'

Whitey nodded agreement. 'Won't last much longer, though.'

'No, I guess not. We still have to mount the Brick on the Shell and the Shuttles on the Brick. I wish there was more than just one way to test those shock absorbers.'

'How are they —'

'Launch. What else is *big* enough for them? Christ, the ship's just *full* of kludged-up stuff, it's all we can do to get all the kludges put down on the drawings. I sure feel sorry for anybody who has to *fix* this sucker.'

'You, maybe.'

Harry laughed sardonically. 'Not me.' He broke into song. 'You can call out your mother, your sister or your brother, but for Christ's sakes don't call me!'

'They won't call your sister,' Janet said. 'No women on the flight crew at all.'

'Yeah, I know,' Harry said. 'Matter of fact, I know most of the crew. Nice clean-cut young men —'

'*Men*'s right,' Janet said. 'And it's not fair.'

'Oh, come on,' Pat said. 'Janet, you have to be crazy, why would anybody want to go up with *that*?'

'Well, they could ask!'

'It's Gillespie,' Harry said. 'He says women aren't strong enough.'

'Stupid,' Janet said.

'It doessn't have to be the truth. Look, those idealistic young men are supposed to be fixing what the snouts shoot. Gillespie may not want them rescuing idealistic young women instead, if you follow me. Anyway, they don't want you. They don't want me, either. What would either one of us do? I learned to do a lot of things when I hung around with the bikers. Little welding, electrical stuff, this and that. So that's what I do. This and that. Whitey, you owe me a pitcher.'

The Dreamers' Workroom was a chaos of tables, black-boards, maps, papers, and personal computers. One of the tables had been cleared of all such junk. A cloth was thrown over it, and an impressive array of bottles, glasses, mixers, and ice stood there.

Jack Clybourne had the bourbon. Jenny held out her glass for a refill.

'It was the ancient Persians. It's in H-Herodotus.' Sherry Atkinson wanted to talk faster than her memory would serve her, and it caused a stutter. 'There have been plenty of cultures that wouldn't implement a decision they'd taken when drunk until they'd discussed it sober. Only the Persians wouldn't do anything they'd decided sober until they'd discussed it drunk.' She poured herself another large glass of white wine, and drank half of it.

Her colleagues nodded in sage agreement. 'Interesting philosophy,' Reynolds said.

Carol laughed. She was enjoying her role as the only fan in an endless science-fiction convention.

'We can discuss it all to death. The problem is, we don't have any decisions,' Curtis muttered. 'Not a goddam thing we can do but wait.' He was working on his fourth tall drink. His wife had long since gone to bed in disgust.

'Volunteer for Africa if you're so eager to fight,' Sherry said.

Curtis laughed and poured another drink. 'Hah.' He jerked his thumb toward Jenny. 'The Colonel there is the only one they let out of here.'

'They don't let me anywhere near Africa.' Jenny was about to say something else, but the door opened. Admiral Carrell came in. It took Jenny a moment for that to register through the bourbon. Then she jumped to her feet. After a moment Jack Clybourne stood as well.

Curtis looked at Carrell, then pointedly looked at his watch. 'Off duty, Admiral, but we could sober up in a hurry. Something we're needed for, I hope?'

'Not really. This is a social visit. May I come in?'

Curtis looked up and down the table. 'I see no objections. Come in. This is Liberty Hall. You can spit on the mat and call the cat a bastard. What'll you drink?'

'Scotch, thank you. And don't drown it.' Carrell sat heavily at the table, then raised his glass. 'Cheers.'

The others responded.

'Hope there's something to be cheerful about,' Curtis said.

'Very little, I'm afraid. Angola just surrendered, and we're pretty sure Zaire will when their eight-day ultimatum is up.'

Joe Ransom took a globe from another table and set it on theirs. Idly he spun it. 'South Africa, Botswana, Lesotho, Mozambique, Zimbabwe, Angola – when Zaire goes they'll have just about everything to the equator.'

'There was a sizable Cuban mercenary army in Angola,' Curtis mused.

'Yes. They'll work for the Invaders now,' Admiral Carrell said.

'Divide and rule,' Sherry said.

'Surrender with conditions,' Ransom said. 'They do learn.'

605

'Learn too damn fast,' Curtis agreed.

'I don't know.' Reynolds poured another drink. 'What did you think of the message they sent last week?'

'Not a lot,' Curtis said.

'Wade, if you knew just how alien the whole idea of surrender terms is to them,' Sherry said.

Carol laughed. 'Alien,' she chuckled.

'Sure. It shocked Harpanet,' Curtis said. 'So they've got themselves a Ruth Benedict.'

'Eh?' Clybourne asked.

'Ruth Fulton Benedict,' Sherry explained. 'Anthropologist. She tried to explain Japanese culture to the U.S. War Department in World War II.'

'How'd she do?' Jack asked.

'Pretty good.'

'Trouble was, there wasn't much anybody could do with the information,' Curtis added.

'They've done something with theirs,' Sherry said. 'Governments surrender, and now they've got human diplomats talking to other governments, and some of their tame politicians broadcasting to the rest of the world —'

'Like Lord Haw Haw,' Ransom said.

'What gets me is some of the bastards buy it,' Curtis said.

'Sticks and carrots,' Jenny blurted. Three large bourbons had left her light-headed. 'They've taken to promising electricity from space. Industrialization powered from space satellites. All you have to do is surrender.'

'A big deal for the undeveloped countries,' Reynolds said.

'It could be a big deal for *us* one of these days,' Ransom said. 'How far are we from being an undeveloped country?'

'And getting closer all the time,' Reynolds agreed.

There had been no more big rocks since the Foot, but innumerable smaller ones still fell. Their targets were carefully chosen, although there was a random element to the bombardment.

Transportation, factories, crossroads, big ocean vessels:

you never knew what would be hit or when. America was slowly becoming a loose-knit chain of semi-independent feudalities, and there was nothing you could do about it.

'They hit another one today,' Jenny said. 'In Chicago. An eighteen-wheeler truck carrying military uniforms. Moving. About a block from a hospital, two blocks from a big grain elevator. The center of the crater was fifteen feet from the truck. Shredded it, of course.'

'Show-offs,' Reynolds said.

'Impressive, though,' Ransom said.

'Perhaps what we need is another pep talk,' Admiral Carrell said. 'The President too. What's depressing is the stories we get out of Africa. There are people in their puppet governments who *like* the way things are.'

'Quislings,' Curtis said. 'Vidkun Quisling was an ideological convert to the Nazis.'

'Yeah, but what's attractive about the snouts? Why would anybody want them in charge?' Clybourne demanded.

'Africa's so divided you can find a group to cooperate with *anything* if it will put them on top,' Ransom said.

'Unity,' Sherry said. 'They'll unite us —'

'– even if it kills us,' Reynolds finished.

'Here's to Unity!' Sherry lifted her glass in a toast.

Curtis raised a clenched fist and sang off-key. 'And the Inter-nation-ale unites the hu-man race.'

Reynolds leaped on it. 'More than the human race. All the sapient races. Thinkers of the galaxy, unite! You have nothing to lose but your chains.'

'Down with arboreal chauvinism!' Sherry shouted.

'And you want these guys to cheer up the President?' Jack Clybourne's voice was dull and serious in the general laughter. 'They don't care who wins!'

'Hey –' Ransom protested.

'You didn't see it,' Clybourne said. 'I did. A huge cargo bay stuffed full of people. Just ordinary people from Kansas. Men, women, kids. Dogs. Dolls. All mashed into jelly. If you'd seen it, you wouldn't talk like this!'

'We've seen it,' Joe Ransom said.

'Uh?'

'They've seen your ship,' Carol said. 'Your ship, and the bodies in Kansas, they've all of them seen all of that.'

'Films? If you'd been there, if you'd *smelled* it, you'd hate the snouts with your minds and guts!'

'Come off it,' Curtis said.

'Hey, we're all on the same side,' Carol said. 'Come on. Have a drink.'

'Maybe we've all had too much,' Sherry said.

'You don't really think we'll surrender?' Ransom asked.

'I won't,' Clybourne said.

'Well, we won't either. Our problem is that we're in here. Outside we might have something to do, some way to help rebuild the country. In here we're useless.'

'They also serve,' Curtis muttered, 'who only stand and wait. That's our problem, Jack. We're supposed to plan for failure. What can we do if Archangel doesn't work? And every damn one of us knows that Archangel is *it*! Damn right all our eggs are in the basket. There isn't another basket and there won't be more eggs. So here we sit, waiting —'

'And the longer we wait,' Ransom said, 'the longer it takes to finish Archangel, the better the chances the snouts will find out about it. Or drop a rock on Bellingham for the pure hell of it.' He raised his glass. 'Here's to you, Mr. Clybourne. I just hope you got *all* the CBs.'

'There's another problem,' Admiral Carrell said.

'Yeah?'

'That message inviting us to discuss surrender terms. It was received here fine.'

'So?' Ransom prompted.

Jenny felt the beginnings of a chill at the base of her spine.

'It wasn't heard ten miles away,' Admiral Carrell said.

'Tightbeam!' Reynolds said.

'Tightbeam, direct to here,' Curtis added. 'It took you a week to find out?'

'Direct to here?' Clybourne looked puzzled. 'A message for the President sent here —'

'And nowhere else,' Ransom said.

'We've got to get the President out of here!' Clybourne shouted.

'In due time,' Admiral Carrell said. 'However they got their information —'

'Quislings,' Curtis muttered.

'Perhaps. However they learned, they have had a week and more to act on their knowledge. They have not done so.'

'But we're safe here,' Carol protested. 'Aren't we?'

'Against what?' Curtis demanded. 'Nothing's safe from another Foot.'

'They won't do that,' Sherry protested.

'How do you know?' Clybourne demanded.

'Harpanet. They don't attack the top leadership of a herd. If humans surrender —'

'Which we won't,' Ransom said. He raised his glass. Curtis clinked glasses with him.

'If we did,' Sherry continued. 'The President would probably become a high official, an advisor to their herdmaster. It's the way they work. They won't kill the President if they can help it. It would be like starting a court trial by shooting the other fellow's lawyer. They just don't do things that way.'

'They don't offer conditional surrender terms, either,' Curtis said. 'They're learning.'

This was the heart of *Michael*. The bridge looked like an unfinished *Star Trek* movie set. Around the walls were large viewscreens and control consoles, with acceleration couches made of webbing at each station, and two large command chairs in the center. Scattered through it all were wooden desks, tables, and drafting tables, nearly all covered with blueprints.

Some of the wall screens were split, blueprint at the bottom and camera view of that area at the top. As Harry watched, one of the screens flashed, and a new drawing appeared at its bottom.

'Done, by God!' Max Rohrs stood. 'Harry, break out the champagne!'

'Right on!'

General Gillespie rose from his seat at one of the wooden desks. 'Are we really done, Max?'

'Well – Ed, we both know this ship won't *ever* be finished, we'll be making changes right up to launch time, but yeah, we're done. You can tell the President that as of tomorrow noon we can launch on twenty-four hours' notice.'

Harry retrieved champagne from a small portable refrigerator. It would have to go, along with the desks and tables and file cabinets. It was good champagne, Mumm's. There were a dozen crystal glasses in the refrigerator too. 'How many glasses, General?' Harry asked.

'Three just now,' Gillespie said.

Harry worried the cork out and let it fly to the ceiling. He poured and handed glasses out, then lifted one. 'A willing foe, and sea room.'

Gillespie made a face. 'I'd as soon the snouts weren't willing at all. I just want to win.'

Max Rohrs said, 'Ed, we've just worked a miracle.' He went over to the calendar and drew a ring around the date. 'A real live one hundred percent miracle.' He lifted his glass. 'So God bless us, there's none like us. You too, Harry. You were a damn big help.'

'Thanks.'

Gillespie poured Harry's glass full again. 'Lot to do yet,' Gillespie said. 'First, we have to bring in the ferryboats. Tomorrow morning we'll send all the dependents, and everybody but the launch and flight crews, over to Port Angeles.'

Harry dropped into one of the command chairs, dodging TV screens. 'What about the rest of Bellingham?'

'We wait on that one.'

'Yeah, if the snouts see there's nobody here – going to be tough, though. What do we do?'

'We don't do anything,' Gillespie said. 'We'll give the sheriff as much notice as we can. You don't need to worry, Harry. We've got speedboats for the last-minute crew.'

'Sure – how far away would you have to be?'

'A couple of miles if you have shelter. At Hiroshima the damage at five miles wasn't too bad. Of course we're setting off a lot more than one bomb.' Gillespie drained his glass.

'Of course the safest place is in the ship,' Max Rohrs said.

'That'll be all military people —'

'Well, but some will be more military than others,' Rohrs said, 'I'm going.'

'You?' Harry almost laughed.

Max didn't laugh. 'Yes. Chief Warrant Officer Maximilian Rohrs, Damage Control Officer, at your service. Who else knows as much about the way this ship is put together?'

'Well, Harry does,' Ed Gillespie said.

'Hey, wait a minute —'

'He does, doesn't he?' Rohrs came over and clapped Harry on the shoulder. 'Don't I remember you doing some entertaining in the Chuckanut? Something about it wasn't your regular line of work, your regular work was hero?'

'Something like that,' Gillespie agreed. 'So. Want to take up your regular occupation again?'

Harry tried to stand up, but Rohrs' heavy hand was on his shoulder. 'Now hear this. I am not an astronaut.'

'Neither am I,' Max Rohrs said.

'I didn't tell you to go! And, Max, you and the General *designed* this ship. If —'

'Have some more champagne, Harry.'

'A pleasure. Look, I've met most of the crew. You're not really filling it out at the last second, are you?'

'No. I thought this over fairly carefully,' General Gillespie said. 'What is it that those kids *don't* know? That stuff shouldn't be allowed to get warm, Harry.'

Harry drank. Gillespie said, 'They know the ship. They know what's most likely to happen to it. They're dedicated. They know how to be tired and hurting and still keep going, because we taught them that, pretty much the same way I was taught. But, Harry, it was *us* making them hurt, and they knew we could make it *stop*.

'Harry, you had a back problem. You got yourself a book of back exercises, and you used it while you crossed the country on a motorcycle, and got beat up on by the fithp, and lost two women, and you still kept going, and all to keep a promise. And you hadn't even promised to do that! I want my dedicated astronauts and I want you too. I don't know who'll fall apart up there.'

'And what is it I want?' Harry inquired politely.

The General half closed his eyes. He seemed in no hurry to answer. Rohrs finished his glass and poured again. He was watching the screens.

The screens hadn't changed in several minutes. One, from a camera on the dome wall, showed *Michael* in full. Two great towers stood on the curve of the hemispherical shell, with cannon showing beneath the lip, aimed inward. Four smaller towers flanked them. A brick-shaped structure rose above them. The Brick was much less massive than the Shell, but its sides were covered with spacecraft: tiny gunships, and four Shuttles with tanks but no boosters. The Brick's massive roof ran beyond the flanks to shield the Shuttles and gunships.

Rohrs said, 'The biggest spaceship ever built by Man. Done, by God.'

'And I'm done too,' Harry said.

Gillespie said, 'If we win this. If. We'll kill a lot of snouts and the rest will surrender. Thousands of snouts, all trying to join what our Threat Team has started calling the Climbing Fithp. Thousands of snouts – sane snouts, mostly – all learning to be human. Who will want to learn the name of the man who first captured a snout?'

'Pour me some more of that,' said Harry.

CHAPTER FORTY
THY DASTARDLY DOINGS ARE PAST

Neither their silver nor their gold shall be able to deliver them in the day of the LORD's wrath . . .

– ZEPHANIAH 1:18

A fire devoureth before them; and behind them a flame burneth . . .

– JOEL 2:3

COUNTDOWN: M HOUR

Jenny winked at Jack, then went into the balcony office. The Situation Room down below was crowded. Every console held a group, all the regular duty crew plus most of the Threat Team, and anyone else who could think of a good reason to be there.

'Come in, Colonel,' Admiral Carrell said. 'Your station is here.' He indicated a table facing the big screens beyond the glass wall. The table held a small switchboard and computer terminal. Jenny put on the headset with its microphone and single headphone, and pushed buttons.

'Operations, Colonel Walters.'

'Control here, communications test.'

'Roger. I read you five by five.'

Another button.

'Dreamer Fithp here,' a voice said.

'Control here. Communications test.'

'Fine.'

She pushed other buttons. Finally she nodded to Admiral Carrell. 'Communications checked out, sir. The link with Michael has a lot of static.'

'It will probably get worse. All right.' Carrell went to the door. 'Mr. Clybourne, please tell the President that everything is ready, and he can join us whenever he likes. Colonel, begin Operation Moby Dick.'

'Yes, *sir*.' Jenny touched another button. On the floor below a siren wailed and red lights flashed. 'Harpoons, this is Gimlet. Let Fly!'

They could hear the cheers through the glass wall. Then the Situation Room fell silent. Crews hunched over consoles.

One of the situation screens showed the locations of the Invader Mother Ship and all the digit ships they could locate. The mother ship and sixteen digit ships were in geosync over Africa. They posed no danger yet. The moon was just setting; snout installations there would see nothing. Africa was wrapped in night. For whatever it was worth, the Invaders would start from their sleep to find themselves attacked.

Eight digit ships were in twelve-hour orbits, evenly distributed around the Earth, and three of these passed to east, center, and west of the United States every twelve hours. One would be passing over the South Pole when *Michael* launched. The others would have to be distracted.

Another screen showed all the effective missiles remaining under U.S. control. Lights blinked and colored lines flowed across the screens as the main battle computer matched missiles with Invader targets.

General Toland came in. 'All ready at my end,' he said. *Not that the Army has much to do – unless the snouts start dropping rocks at random!*

'Good.' Carrell stood at the balcony window, his eyes fastened on the screens below. After a moment, General Toland sat at one of the desks.

One screen faded, then was replaced by a map of the

615

South Atlantic. A bright red line rose from the ocean and arced toward Johannesburg.

'God, what if it really hits?' Toland said to no one.

'It won't,' Carrell said.

Other lines arced upward from the South Atlantic. One rose straight up: the EMP bomb. Then a bright blue ring sprang up to surround that area.

'We've lost communications with *Ethan Allen*,' Jenny reported. 'The *Nathaniel Greene* is launching now.' The EMP bomb bloomed into a red patch, wide of Earth's arc. More lines sprang up, this time from farther south, almost directly below the Cape of Good Hope. After a few moments a blue circle appeared there, too.

'No communications with *Nathaniel Greene*,' Jenny said. 'Or anywhere else for the next few hours. We got our electromagnetic pulse.' The room seethed with static.

The office door opened. Jack Clybourne ushered the President in. General Toland stood. Jenny saw him, but remained seated.

'Good afternoon,' President Coffey said. 'Continue with your duties.' He sat at the large desk in the middle of the room.

'Actually, we have very little to do,' Admiral Carrell said. 'The tough work was planning this. Now it either works or it doesn't.'

Reassuring bullshit, Jenny thought. *No battle plan ever works. Seventeen digit ships destroyed in the war. We can't find three. Assume one destroyed, unreported, and two on the ground in Africa, where they can't rise in time. Can we get that lucky?*

Another of the battle screens flashed to show Georgia and South Carolina. A network of red lines leaped upward toward the digit ships patrolling in low orbit.

Ten minutes went past. The red lines began rapidly to wink out. Red blotches appeared south of Atlanta.

'They're damned fast.' Toland muttered.

'Yes. Too fast,' Admiral Carrell agreed. He turned to

the President. 'We'd hoped to keep them distracted for half an hour or more.'

'When does *Michael* go up?' the President asked.

'In eighty minutes,' Admiral Carrell said.

'God help the people in Bellingham,' President Coffey muttered.

God help us all.

'God, Miranda, we can't keep this up. I'm supposed to be on duty!'

'So you are.' She made a point of buttoning her blouse as she moved away from him to the passenger door of the squad car, and pretended to be interested in the sparse scenery of the Lummi Indian Reservation. 'All right, you'll just have to take me home —'

'Well, but not just –' He rolled over in the seat, prepared to follow.

'All units, all units, proceed with Big Tango, proceed with Big Tango,' the radio blared.

Leigh sagged back, stunned.

'What is it?' Miranda demanded. His look frightened her.

'I don't even know where to start!'

'Start what, damn you?'

He was buttoning buttons, fumbling it. 'It's – we're supposed to evacuate the city. Everybody within five miles of the harbor.'

'Five miles?'

'Your place isn't in the zone,' Deputy Young said. 'You're almost six miles out. But the Rez is.' He leaned forward and started the cruiser. 'And I guess you're riding with me. Miranda, how the hell do I get a bunch of Indians to leave their homes?'

'Tell them why. Tell *me* why, Leigh!'

'I don't know! They told me that when Big Tango

started we'd have one hour, one frigging hour to get everybody out of their houses and away.' He put the car in gear. 'So here we go, not that it will do any good.'

It didn't look like an Indian reservation. It looked more like a rural slum punctuated by occasional suburban houses. There was only one paved road. Leigh drove along it and spoke at intervals through the loud speaker mounted on top of the police car.

'Hi! This is Leigh Young. I have bad news. The aliens are going to bomb Bellingham. You have about half an hour to get the hell out of here. Drive, ride bikes, run, walk, do anything you can, but get the hell away from Bellingham Harbor.' He drove around the paved loop.

There was a numbness in Miranda's brain. *John Fox expected something, something he wouldn't talk about. What can I do? Give Leigh half an hour to get the Indians moving, but then he'll damned well take me home so I can tell Dad!*

They were at the end of the loop. There were speedboats in the harbor, all racing southwest and away. Headed for Port Angeles? Escaping. Escaping what?

Leigh was driving back into the loop. 'Run for the hills,' his amplified voice blared. 'Get out any way you can, foot, horse, car, don't take anything you don't value more than life. Don't look back because the glare will burn your eyes out —'

Already there were cars moving the other way. 'Some of them listened,' Miranda said. 'Leigh, we have to go warn Dad if the snouts are going to bomb us —'

'They're not going to bomb us.'

'Huh?'

'I made that up,' Leigh said.

'Then why are we doing this?'

'Damfino.'

'Ask the Sheriff.'

'Miranda, I already asked him, and he wouldn't tell us.'

'Ask now! He has to tell us now!'

'Well —'

Miranda took the microphone from its hook and handed it to him. 'Go on, ask. What harm can it do?'

'Well, all right.' Leigh keyed the microphone.

'Dispatcher.'

'Is the Sheriff there?'

'He's busy —'

'I have to talk with him.'

'One moment.'

'Sheriff Lafferty here. That you, Young?'

'Yes, sir. Sheriff, I'm on the Rez. Most of the Indians are moving on, but some aren't. Isn't there anything I can tell them that'll make them move out?'

'Tell them they'll get killed if they stay.'

'I did. I said the snouts are going to bomb Bellingham.'

'Snouts bomb us! That's a good one. Leigh, we're going to bomb ourselves, there's going to be atom bombs —'

The radio dissolved in static.

'What the hell?' Leigh tuned up and down. 'Buzz saws. Like we were being jammed.'

'Maybe we are,' Miranda said.

'What —'

'Leigh, what did he mean, bomb ourselves?'

'I don't know.'

'I don't know either, but why would the Army jam your radio? Leigh, I'm scared.'

So far, so good. Jenny watched the big wall screens with satisfaction.

'M minus fifty-five minutes, and counting,' she announced.

'Thank you,' Admiral Carrell acknowledged.

'Melon daiquiri,' President Coffey muttered.

'Sir?' Carrell asked.

'Nothing. Admiral, I have a good feeling about this.'

'Yes, sir.'

'You don't.'

'Mr. President, they say that Admiral Jellicoe at Jutland was the only man in the world who could have lost World War One in a single afternoon.

'Oh. And we —'

'Can lose something more than that,' Carrell said.

'Of course you're right.' The door opened to admit a mess corporal with a tray of coffee. Outside the door were half a dozen military personnel, plus Jack Clybourne, who was doing his best not to look through the door and across the office so that he could see the big battle screens on the floor below. The President grinned. 'Mr. Clybourne —'

'Sir.'

'Let Sergeant Mailey's people act like doorkeepers. Come in and watch the action.'

'Sir?'

'Come in. You've earned a ringside seat.'

'But – well, thank you, sir.' Clybourne stood against one wall.

He blends into it. Like wallpaper, Jenny thought. She turned to wink at him. There was a buzz in her headset.

'Control. Gimlet.'

'Gimlet, this is Harpoon. We have a security breach. We have a security breach. This went out on police radio air four minutes ago. I play the tapes now . . .'

'Launch now,' General Toland said.

'There are people in Bellingham,' the President said. 'A lot of them.'

'All right, so it's hard on Bellingham! Launch! Colonel, tell them to prepare.'

'Yes, sir.' Jenny spoke into the microphone. 'Prepare for launch in five minutes. Launch in five minutes.'

More sirens blared on the floor below.

'Admiral?' the President asked.

Admiral Carrell put his fingertips together and looked across their tops at the situation maps. 'Give me a minute.'

'Not much more than that,' said the General.

'All right. First, the timing is terrible. We'd be launching straight up at Bogie Two, and we didn't hurt those digit ships enough.'

'If they drop rocks on *Michael*, we've had it!' Toland shouted.

'Yes.' Carrell glanced at his watch. 'What are we afraid of? A laser can't hurt *Michael*. A meteor takes time —'

'It could be on its way *now* —'

'And ready to hit atmosphere. All right. I say we wait. Get ready to launch on ten seconds' notice. Wait the full hour if we can, but if Gillespie sees a light in the sky he'll launch. A meteor would flare at fifty miles up, and come in at a slant at five to six miles per second. We'd be twenty seconds in the air when it hit. *Michael* would survive.'

'*Michael* can blow Bogie Two out of the sky,' the General said. 'It's all alone. We won't *see* another digit ship for an hour.'

'We have a plan,' Admiral Carrell said.

'And if we stick with it, we lose! Mr. President, you're betting everything on this.'

'General, I'm aware that it's important.'

'We have to fight the damn digit ships anyway! Go now.'

'And kill everyone in Bellingham,' President Coffey said.

'Better Bellingham than the whole damn human race!'

'Oh, Jesus.' President Coffey stared at the situation screens. 'Admiral Carrell, you're my naval expert. Take command.'

'Yes, sir. Colonel Crichton, get me direct communications with General Gillespie.'

'Sir.' The first three lines she tried were filled with static. 'General Gillespie, sir.'

'Ed, this is Thor Carrell.'

'Yes, Mr. Secretary?'

'There's been a possible security leak. Your local sheriff used his radio.'

'Is that why there's jamming? We can't talk to our own MPs.'

'That's it. General, you're to make ready for instant launch. Watch the skies. The first glimmer up there, and you go. It's your ship, as of now.'

'Acknowledged.'

President Coffey looked significantly at the Admiral.

'Mr. President,' Carrell said.

'I won't take your time,' Coffey said. 'Godspeed, General.'

The sirens were still wailing on the floor below.

General Toland was still frowning. 'All right, God damn it, we'll do it your way.' He turned to Jenny. 'Colonel, get me the MP commander in Bellingham. I want the sheriff's ass in a sling.'

'General —'

'Yes, Mr. President?'

'Have your MPs do what they can for the people in Bellingham. They're Americans too.'

'Yes, sir.'

——————

John Fox heard it first.

There was high wind with a few raindrops in it. Fox was turning the compost heap. He'd managed to make this his own territory; nobody else would fool with it. His pitchfork probed, and he worked around the denser mass he sensed, to keep Roger hidden. Bones showed suddenly, not clean yet – a foot. Fox grimaced and picked up a pitchforkful of compost.

He stopped, cocked his head. There was a sound in the wind.

Motors.

Fox placed his forkful to cover the bones deep. Then he

622

moved briskly toward the house. He opened the door and shouted at the first human figure he saw. 'Navy coming back. Alert everyone. I'll be at the gate.'

The Navy had come twice before, first for the CBs, then for Roger Brooks. Both times they had come in force – but not like this. You could hardly hear the wind for the roar of motors, and they were only just pulling up!

Armored trucks lined the road. It must be a nuisance for them, John Fox thought. All that gasoline. But they know we've got guns, and somebody might do something stupid if there was just a truckful of them —

He counted eight trucks, and more vehicles behind them. New cars, old cars, decrepit civilian trucks, a score of them running out of sight into the rain.

Four men climbed out of the third vehicle and came to the gate. They looked nervous. One was the sheriff, old Ben Lafferty. Three were Navy, and Fox had seen one of them on their second visit: Commander Arnold Kennedy. Kennedy stepped forward and said, 'You know we're coming in. We've been through this before.'

John Fox's worries were growing. Nobody had come out of the house to join him; what did *that* mean? Were they getting ready to shoot it out?

Two more came up. Miranda Shakes, and that deputy sheriff she dated.

'It's all right, John,' Miranda said.

'What is it this time? Who the hell are *they*?' Fox waved back down the road.

'Your neighbors,' Sheriff Lafferty said.

'Civilians seeking refuge,' Commander Kennedy said, 'and you will by God give it to them. 'We're prepared to shoot the top off your house. What we want is the use of your bomb shelter for about two hours.'

Fox nodded. *Orion*, he thought. *Now*. 'How many are there?'

'About three hundred.'

'You're crazy. Even elbow to elbow —'

'And on top of each other too. This is serious. You tell the rest of 'em in there, this is serious. If they start shooting we'll take the house off the top of the shelter. It'll go anyway. Now, you and I are going up to the house.'

They walked around the greenhouse and up to the front door. Kennedy rang the bell.

The invaders trooped through the house and through the 'secret' door and down.

There were storekeepers and Navy and Indians, grandparents and children and infants. Two old men and a heavy middle-aged woman had to be lifted from wheelchairs, carried inside, and deposited in the three decks of bunks. The wheelchairs stayed in the living room, along with everything else, suitcases, briefcases, picnic baskets, even heavy overcoats. The living room looked like a rummage sale. The rug was a swamp. Clara was too angry to scream, but Bill Shakes raged.

'We'll have to tear up the floor to get rid of all they've trucked in! We've got one – count 'em, *one* – bathroom down there, and we'll have to pack people in that too. We'll have to fumigate – Commander, who's going to *pay* for all this? *What are you laughing at?*'

'I'm sorry, Mr. Shakes. You submit a bill for damages. I guarantee you it'll be honored, but you'd better wait an hour before you add up that bill, Mr. Shakes!'

George Tate-Evans felt his insides turning to water. *What were we supposed to do, conduct a point defense against the Navy? We've got enough firepower here to get us killed dead, and not even Jack lost his head quite that bad. Thank God. But they've none of them thought it through . . . The Navy searched us when they came for the CBs, so they knew we had a bomb shelter. Half of Bellingham is trooping through our basement because we've got a bomb shelter, a bomb shelter!* 'Commander, what happens in one hour?'

'That's still classified.'

'Are you out of your —'

'You had a fuck of a lot of radio equipment, and I'm not sure in my heart that we got it all, and the sheriff used his car radio to try to alert the populace! You almost died then, Mr. . . . Tate-Evans. I'll tell you when I can. Really.'

'But what do we prepare for? How long will we be in there?'

'Hours, not days. Without us it would have been days.' Kennedy said. 'We've got decontamination equipment parked outside, ready.'

'Decontam —'

Up the stairs came a riot of noise. People were jammed in the stairwell, all the way to the thick iron trapdoor. 'Something I think we'd better do,' Isadore said. 'Pass out *all* the booze. I mean it, Bill. You heard the commander, the Navy'll pay for it. But that's a supercooled riot in there, and something awful's about to happen, and we'll want them tranquil.'

'Right. Medicine too,' George said. The living room held only Navy men and the legitimate owners. 'Commander, get your men to carrying booze. I'll get the medical kit. We'll set up on the stairs. Force the rest of those carpetbaggers down to leave the stairs clear. And then I'll offer you a drink.'

'Not for —' The Commander checked his watch. 'We've got twenty minutes. And then I'm prepared to drink a toast.'

———————

There were no windows on *Michael*. The control room was buried deep in *Michael*'s heart, between the water tanks, with the towers to shield it too. For Harry and the others there was nothing but TV screens.

Somewhere outside, there were still people to talk to

Gillespie. 'Nothing from the President. If anything comes, it'll be a messenger. We've got a tight phone to the gate.'

Gillespie said, 'If a digit ship changes course anywhere, I want to know it.'

And the tinny response: 'We're getting some action from the ships we attacked, but nothing aimed here.'

'How long?'

'Eight minutes.'

There were cameras everywhere, inside and outside *Michael*. One camera on the wall of the dome showed all of the great ship: the Shell, the placement guns protruding under the rim, six towers around the base; the Brick standing above them, its flat sides hung with smaller spacecraft, shadowed by the overhang of the nose. The dome that had swarmed with activity, day and night, for months, now looked deserted, silent, empty.

Gillespie turned toward the repair crew. 'Five minutes. Close your faceplates *now*.' Then, by intercom, 'Testing. Can you all hear me?'

They responded.

'All personnel outside *Michael*, get to the shelter. And thank you all.'

A dozen crash couches covered the floor. Harry and Rohrs and Gamble and the others were strapped down like mental patients; the only difference was that they could pull their arms free. An umbilical carried oxygen from the wall, and made a cold spot on Harry's chest. Harry was feeling claustrophobic. And elated! Here's Harry the Minstrel in a by-god space suit, waiting for launch!

Rohrs said, 'It'll be rough on the pilots, riding outside like that.'

'At least they've got windows,' Harry said.

Someone said, 'Here we lie, waiting for an atom bomb to go off under our asses —'

'There has to be a more graceful way to say that,' Tiny Pelz said. Dr. Pelz was an atomjack, built heavy and strong. He looked strange with his bushy black beard shaved off to fit him into the pressure suit.

The desks and tables and phones and lines were all gone. The ready room was neat and clean. Padded handholds lined the walls and ceiling.

Harry remembered the men in Kansas who had gone forth to battle the enemy with tanks. They talked to keep their courage up. Harry didn't know these men. Young, strong, healthy – if he told them about his back problem, what would they say? Pelz would understand, or Rohrs, or Gamble.

'One minute,' said a tinny voice, 'and I'm going.'

They watched for bright light in their screens. The snout meteor could fall at any second. The silence grew thick, the tension stretched until Harry could stand it no longer. He bellowed. 'Sancho! My armor!'

The youthful faces looked at him. Some were grinning. He heard Gillespie's grunt of disgust and saw Gillespie's elbow move. An atomic bomb went off under Harry Reddington's ass.

Maintaining a civilization in here was going to be worse than Isadore had thought. He'd *never* seen human beings crowded so close. Miranda and her deputy sheriff shared a bunk. All the bunks held two or three each, and if the supports collapsed the bunks would not fall. There was no room.

He heard, 'Oh, God, it's another meteor!' and wished he hadn't. It could start an epidemic of fear; and it might be true. Bill Shakes was still fulminating at Commander Kennedy who still hadn't lost his temper, quite.

'Hey, Bill,' Isadore bellowed. Nothing less would be heard. 'We always prepare for the wrong disaster. You told us. Remember?'

Shakes turned. 'Well, this idiot won't tell me what disaster we *are* prepared for.'

'Reminds me,' Commander Kennedy shouted. 'Just how did you go about constructing this place?'

'We built it good. Two layers of – why? You crammed ten thousand Indians in here with no deodorant, and *now* you want to know it's safe?'

'I do.'

'It's safe. Two layers of concrete separated by —'

The sound of the end of the world slammed against the ceiling.

For a moment that incredible crowd was totally silent.

Then it came again: SLAM.

Commander Kennedy whooped. 'They made it! They're up! It's —'

SLAM

'It's the second bomb that counts. If the first —'

SLAM

'– first bomb fails you just start over.'

SLAM

'If the second bomb fails, you're already —'

SLAM

'– already in the air. You'll fall. They're on their —'

SLAM

'– way, by God! You can give me that drink now.'

SLAM

CHAPTER FORTY-ONE
BREAKOUT

Heroes are created by popular demand, sometimes out of the scantiest of materials.

— GERALD WHITE JOHNSON

COUNTDOWN: M HOUR

God was knocking, and he wanted in *bad*.
        WHAM
        WHAM
        WHAM
        quiet

'The respite will be brief,' Gillespie bellowed. Harry barely heard him in the silence after the bombs. *How many were there? Twenty? Thirty?*

'Stay in harness and be ready for acceleration.'

Goddam! We made it! The screens showed little but clouds. Harry caught a glimpse of Vancouver Island and the Straits of Juan de Fuca. There would be nothing to see but the Pacific Ocean anyway. Presently Earth was a shallow arc, cloud-white, and beyond it a winking light, *blip blip blip* — 'Digit ship under power, two o'clock high!'

'Roger, I see it,' Gillespie said.

'There's another!' Ensign Franklin shouted into the mike, then lowered his voice and tried to sound like an astronaut. 'Nine o'clock low, far away. Accelerating.'

'Roger. Stand by for acceleration. Fire.'

Harry was shoved back against his couch. In the

moment before thrust resumed, the screens showed lines of spurt bombs leaving their rails on all sides. The spurt bombs looked like fasces, bundles of tubes around an axis made up of attitude jets and cameras and a computer. They moved in straight lines past the rim of the Shell, turning as they went —

WHAM

WHAM

WHAM

The nearer of the blinking lights had gone out. The view in one screen expanded once and again. Something showed dim against the stars. How far?

'Object in view, nine o'clock low.' Franklin had his voice under control now. He sounded like Chuck Yeager in *The Right Stuff*. 'Might be Big Mama.'

'Roger. Acceleration.'

Gillespie sounds tired already. Maybe he's just bored?

WHAM

WHAM

Spurt bombs rained into the blast. The forward view jittered . . . but that distant object was too blunt to be a digit ship. Other cameras swung in arcs . . . and that glare-green star was a digit ship, and it had found them with its lasers.

Harry switched the intercom to local. 'Max, when do we turn the Shuttles loose?'

'Not for a while.'

'But —'

'Just now we can shoot anything that moves.'

'But if we wait too long —'

'Harry, we all have work to do. Ed flies the ship, we watch for bandits.'

'Yeah.' *And when the ship gets holes in it, we go fix it. That's democracy.*

WHAM

WHAM

Harry lost count of the explosions.

630

'Blue fire around primary target,' Ensign Franklin said. He was shouting again. 'Sir, I think they're accelerating.'

'Roger.'

WHAM
WHAM

Harry's universe was a madness of noise and jolts, as if a giant had put him in a garbage can and used the can for a field hockey puck.

Quiet.

Harry waited. Nothing. Then Gillespie's voice in the intercom.

'Looks quiet for a while. Keep your straps on, and take a break.'

Harry opened his faceplate. So did the others in the damage control section.

'I think we took out that first digit ship. The second is receding, it can't slow down in time to hurt us, and the third is around back of the Earth. Odds are we won't see another digit ship for the next hour.

'We're moving toward the prime target. It's running away. We'll give the computers a chance to gather data so we can tell which way to run. God knows, big as that thing is, once it gets started it won't turn fast! When we launch the Shuttles, we'll have to switch over from automatic aiming for the laser weapons. We'll hang on to the Shuttles and gunships as long as we can.'

'Enjoy,' Max Rohrs said. He took out a pack of cigarettes. 'Anybody really mind?' He offered them around.

Harry reached out eagerly.

Ensign Franklin said pointedly. 'There are studies that prove smoking takes ten years off your life. Harry, you really ought to give that up.'

'Well, I don't believe in statistics. What about Max?'

'He's smoked so long it will probably kill him about' – Franklin looked at the wall chronometer – 'now, and I'll be in command of damage control.'

Nobody wanted a second cigarette. Harry tried to relax, half close his eyes, to look like Franklin and his two Navy boatswain's mates. His three personal TV sets showed unchanging views down access ducts within the Brick. Harry began playing with the view. Steam pipes; more steam pipes; outside, looking past the attitude jets into the overhang of the nose shield . . .

'Bandits,' Franklin said. 'Half a dozen pulsing lights, west and a little south . . . more of them . . . start just above the arch of the Earth, you can follow them up to the primary target. They're all accelerating.'

'Got them,' said Gillespie.

Harry slammed his faceplate shut. So did the others, but more slowly, deliberately. The lights were far apart, and they changed with relation to each other.

Don't panic. Calmly and deliberately as he could, Harry adjusted his straps. No one was watching. *Pity.*

Michael's nose was a thick shield, and the butt plate ought to stand up to anything. Turn either of those toward danger and you couldn't be harmed. But if danger came from half a dozen directions —

> *WHAM*
> *WHAM*
> *WHAM*

Michael was pulsing too, and the spurt bombs were throwing gamma-ray lasers. *Death rays! Eat hot gamma rays, foolish Centaurans!*

> *WHAM*
> *WHAM*

One of the pulsing lights went out.

'Another one . . . Bandit, south, just above Europe.'

'Stand by. Maneuvering.'

Harry heard the faint hiss of steam jets. The drive explosions stopped, and *Michael* was turning, before Harry spotted the other lights.

'Bandits to starboard. I think those are missiles.' Tiny flames, wavering against the stars.

'Roger.'

Blam. Blam. After the shocks of the drive bombs, the big antimissile guns were almost gentle.

'Stand by. Maneuvering. Acceleration.'

WHAM

They attack at night. They know us that well. For us it is night. For them it is day. I should have expected this. Do the prey have other surprises for me?

Already the Herdmaster knew that he had been tricked. He had been strapped to his acceleration pad for an hour now, on duty to handle further emergencies; but *this* was not what he had expected.

It pulsed like a digit ship, but more slowly. Half a breath passed between explosions. *We taught them that*, the Herdmaster thought. It looked bigger than a digit ship, smaller than *Message Bearer*.

Four digit ships, the lowest in their various orbits about Winterhome, converged on the intruder. The Herdmaster saw the pulse drive fail on one of them. He watched, and another died.

How did they do that? They're killing my fithp!

'Defensemaster, you lead *Message Bearer* now.'

'I obey.'

There were sounds. The screens showed sixteen mounted digit ships released from their ring around *Message Bearer*'s stern. They formed an expanding ring about the mother ship.

'Prepare. No spin. Prepare.' The Defensemaster's voice was sent through the ship.

Spin decreasing. Digit ships launched, to form a defense screen. And where are the others?

He had lost several himself, an hour ago.

There had been eight digit ships in twelve-hour polar orbits, passing repeatedly over various parts of

Winterhome. Two of those had been attacked by missiles from the sea. Attackmaster Koothfektil-rusp had agreed with his assessment: the missiles were a diversion like the attack that preceded the bombing of the Kansas foothold. The prey had already aimed one missile at the fithp base in Johannesburg. Surely there would be more. Pastempeh-keph had set several digit ships to converge on Africa, ready to fire on missiles aimed at the African foothold.

Wrong! Five, perhaps six could not reach the intruder in time to fight.

He tapped rapidly, summoning knowledge. Four digit ships were already rising from the Moon. Those carried material to wherever the war effort needed meteors. But, though two were empty, though they had risen as soon as the enemy ship was sighted, they would not arrive in time. Still, meteors would be needed. The enemy ship had to come from somewhere.

The ships patrolling Africa: could he use them? Sixteen were in eccentric geosynchronous orbits: dropping low while they moved east, falling outward, drifting west while they arced around and fell back; but always over Africa. Ten of those were in the upper arcs of their orbit, above *Message Bearer*. Lower above Africa, the remaining six were low enough to engage the enemy. The Defense-master was doing his frenetic best to coordinate their efforts . . . and three were not responding.

He eavesdropped . . . The fi' talking to the Defense-master sounded sick, or mentally deficient. He had something like hiccups. '. . . like a laser attacked us, but not like. Heat all through the ship, fuel pressure very high, as if light we cannot see was shining all through the hull. Gamma ray, it may be, but where do they find their power? We were eight-cubed of makasrupkithp distant!'

'Can you fight your ship?'

'No. We cannot breathe, can you hear? Shookerint-buth has stopped. I can't control my digits or my legs. Controls burnt out too.'

Enough of this. *Mourn in daylight*. 'Defensemaster.'
Tantarent-fid broke contact with the sick fi'. 'You will be
certain Attackmaster Koothfektil-rusp is aware of the
situation.'

'Herdmaster, I'm doing all I can. What could he tell us?'

'Possibly nothing. This is your thuktun. I will see that he
is told.' He gestured to one of his aides. 'It is important that
you and the Attackmaster coordinate digit ships for simultaneous attack.'

'It will be done, Herdmaster.'

'Talker, get me Takpussch-yamp.' Be glad even of small
benefits: the mating season was over. 'Breaker-two, is
Tashayamp available too? Good. Send Tashayamp to
fetch Rogachev from the human restraint cell and bring
him to the bridge. You come straight here.'

———

Night. Jeri lay curled against his chest. It was a frustrating
experience, sleeping with a woman in a public place, a
woman who did not care that her daughter knew what she
did with Arvid Rogachev, but who would not let anyone *see*
her behave improperly —

Alien speech sounded. The room tilted sideways. Arvid
felt Jeri's nails dig into his arm.

The others stirred. 'What is it?' Jeri demanded.

She believes I know everything.

Dmitri shouted in Russian.

So does he. 'Wait. What else can we do?'

Presently the door warning light came on. Tashayamp
stood at the entrance. 'Rogachev. You will come.'

———

Takpusseh-yamp moved at a slant. It wasn't exactly a run,
yet it was fast. His body tilted against *Message Bearer*'s
awkward acceleration. *Message Bearer* was losing its spin.

635

The Herdmaster must be preparing for acceleration.

The bridge was frantically busy. The Herdmaster summoned him with a wave, and pointed. 'I want to know what to expect from *that*.'

Takpusseh-yamp looked at three displays of the sky. Black, star-sprinkled, with a crescent of Winterhome showing large – and a black dot that flashed light around its edge. There were sparkles in the flash.

'I am not a technician.'

'How did I know you would say that? Breaker-two, I can learn about that craft. Assume that there are humans in it. Assume a length of twice eight-cubed srupkithp or less, and half that in width. It moves in the manner of a digit ship, but more crudely, probably using fission bombs instead of deuterium fusion. Assume a bumpy ride. Query: humans can tolerate more shock than we can?'

'Yes.'

'Assume at least one weapon which can't describe. Query: what do they want to do with this?'

'Win a war.'

The intruder had stopped pulsing.

The Herdmaster said, 'But of course they —'

'No, *listen*, Herdmaster. This is no demonstration, to give them higher rank after surrender. If there were two of these, they would have sent two. If they know it to be inadequate, they would not send it until they could build two. I am no Predecessor. I guess. My best guess is that this device is expected to set a human foot on the Traveler Fithp.'

'How?'

'You spoke of a new weapon. Remember that the human fithp must write their own thuktunthp.'

At that moment the unknown ship seemed to explode. *Message Bearer* must have looked like this when the digit ships were loosed on the USSR space station. Ships were spreading out around it – 'Defensemaster, how big are those ships?'

'Tiny. No fi' would fit the small ones. They must be automatic. Two or three might wedge themselves into the large.'

Takpusseh said, 'Automatic, perhaps. Perhaps one human each.'

Hardly volunteers . . . rogues, captured, then forced into ships, launched, then expected to perform alone in space and under fire . . . with no similar mind nearby, no contact with the herd . . .? 'No. Ridiculous. These are big automatic devices. We would not have built so large.'

' "Now my digits are whole again," remember? Human rogues may co-operate.'

It was still nonsense. The devices were *tiny*. Even a single rogue man would not fit. 'Take an acceleration pad, Takpusseh. Remain. Defenscmaster, is the drive ready?'

'No, Herdmaster. I need another sixteen sixty-four breaths. The alien device would need sixteen times as long to reach us. We could move if I had kept the digit ships mounted, but —'

'Better to set them free to defend us, yes.'

The doorway opened. Tashayamp entered, with the human. Takpusseh-yamp curled his digits, a private message of affection. She pretended not to see.

'Tashayamp! Excellent.' The Herdmaster gestured her toward his station. 'I will need you to translate. Arvid Rogachev, look at this.'

The human stood tilted, looking about the bridge. He came forward, lurching, gripping consoles and machinery where he could. Screens showed him the intruder pulsing against the dark night side of Winterhome. 'What is this?'

'Man, I expect you tell me that!'

'Lead me.' Rogachev braced himself against a console and continued to watch.

The intruder had resumed acceleration, but more slowly now. The smaller ships diverged on what had to be chemical flame: some toward the two closest of the digit ships now converging from low orbit above Africa; some moving ahead, toward *Message Bearer*. One enemy flared, then became a fog.

Rogachev spoke in the language of the thuktunthp. 'Some fi' placed weapon well. This is a spacecraft carrying smaller spacecraft —'

'We know that.'

'Bombs make it go. Thuktun students of United States and England consider idea long ago, but we make it against the will of the Fithp of Nations. Query: size of these things?'

'The largest is twice eight-cubed srupkithp. The smallest are five srupkithp in length, no more than one srupk thick.'

'Ah. My fithp may ride such small things, but I thought United States fithp be afraid.'

'The device rose from the North American continent,' Takpusseh-yamp said. That was certain; otherwise it would have been seen. 'Rogachev, they have something that is killing our fithp aboard the digit ships. Can you make a device that throws gamma rays in a narrow beam?'

'Not understand.'

'Tashayamp?'

'Shine light like laser at two time eight to minus twelve srupkithp wavelength.'

'Means nothing,' Rogachev said. 'I need tools –' He gestured, tapping on his hand with one finger.

'Ah. He wants the calculating device from their space city,' Tashayamp said.

Why did I not understand that? I was shrewd to choose Tashayamp as my mate. 'Shall I send for it, Herdmaster?'

'Yes. Rogachev, that sparkle within the explosion —'

'I not understand either. Query: the United States build some rogue device? They did not tell us!' Rogachev laughed, a peculiar, hackle-raising sound.

He should not do that.

The Herdmaster stamped impatiently. 'Tashayamp, return Rogachev to the restraint cell.' He turned to

Takpusseh-yamp. 'The fi'-killer has not heard a fithp or human voice in more than sixty-four days. Will he be sane? Will he be amenable to reason?'

'Herdmaster, I do not know. I believe he will be both sane and reasonable, even though such treatment would make rogues of any normal fi'. Dawson understands how machinery may be used in space. Perhaps we can learn.'

We're finally fighting back! No, the United States is fighting back, Arvid corrected himself. *Never mind. What have they got? Can they win? Can they even catch us?* The spin was gone. Gravity was a feather-touch aft. *Thuktun Flishithy*'s drive took time to build power, but it was possible that the ship could simply outrun the Americans.

'Tashayamp. Query: you usually have warriors with you?'

'For this breath the warriors have better things to do!' Her tone was sharp. The fithp could enunciate, could decrease the air escaping with the words, when they wished. 'Here we are.' The key she used was a bar of metal; the lock was magnetic, as Arvid had established long ago. The hatch swung out. 'You have sufficient padding, but acceleration may come from abnormal directions. Be careful. Grip when you can. You will be as safe as any fi' aboard. Now go in.'

The others watched as Arvid swung his body around the edge of the hatch. They saw him grip Tashayamp's trunk, brace his feet, and pull her digits loose from her handhold.

Tashayamp shrieked. Her first impulse wasn't to crush Arvid Rogachev; it was to tether herself. Her hampered digits wrapped around the edge of the hatch. Dmitri leapt from below. He crashed into her like a fullback. Then Arvid and Dmitri were pulling her trunk in two directions, pulling her through the hatch. *And the hatch was still open!*

Tashayamp recovered. Arvid found himself flying. He curled himself into a ball; struck padding; struck again with less force; uncoiled and leapt again. The others had got the idea. Mrs. Woodward and the children huddled in a corner. Jeri, Dmitri, Nikolai looked to be tangled in Tashayamp's digits. Arvid snatched at her harness as he passed, climbed around onto her back. He found the buckle and loosed the harness.

Straps and a pack. Arvid opened the pack and swung. The contents flew wide. Tashayamp was screaming, thrashing, drifting much too near a wall. If she could anchor her feet in the padding . . . He swung around her belly, caught the wall with his feet, and kicked away, toward the middle of the cell.

The fi' seemed to be tiring. Arvid joined the others at her head. 'Push them in here,' he shouted, and grasped a digit that writhed like a fire hose . . .

Five minutes later, a furious fi' female glared at them over the edge of a bag. Straps were tight around her ears. Dmitri moored other straps behind her forelegs and tightened them. He cast loose and studied the situation thoughtfully. 'Is there a reason to betray our true motives now?'

'*Thuktun Flishithy* is under attack,' Arvid replied. He heard Jeri gasp.

'Right on!' Alice shouted.

'By whom?'

'American. One carrier with missiles and smaller spacecraft. Our last chance, Dmitri. The fithp cannot follow us into the ducts. We fight there!'

'I see. Agreed.' Dmitri spoke rapidly in Russian.

'No, what?' Jeri demanded.

'It is State Security!' Dmitri shouted in Russian.

'He wishes to kill this fi',' Arvid said.

Jeri said, 'Hey!'

Mrs. Woodward said, 'You *wouldn't*.'

'Do you think those straps will hold her helpless?'

Dmitri shouted. 'And so do I, but what do we *know*? Kill her. Think of India and kill her.'

'Over my dead body,' Jeri said. She moved closer to Tashayamp.

Dmitri shouted in Russian.

Arvid replied. 'I will think with what organs I choose. I grant you command, but not in this. Think, Dmitri. *Thuktun Flishithy* is under attack.'

'Da.'

'By the time they find the Teacher's mate, we will be beyond their reach. There is no need whatever to kill her.'

'You let women think for you.'

'He doesn't need women to tell him what's right,' Carrie Woodward said.

'I like Tashayamp!' Alice said emphatically.

Dmitri looked about him. Arvid, Alice, Jeri, and Mrs. Woodward were between him and the fi' . . . who had stopped thrashing because of an understandable interest in the topic of conversation. 'Arvid, you may regret this, but it is done. Now let us be gone! Mrs. Woodward, take the children to the Garden. It is never locked, and you should be safe there, if anyone is safe anywhere. Nikolai, Arvid . . . with me. Jeri? Alice?'

'Both of you to the Garden,' Arvid ordered.

'Wes! What about him?' Alice cried.

Dmitri snorted contempt. 'Have you any idea where he is? Forget Congressman Dawson. He is untrustworthy, he has proved it again and again.'

Alice shrugged angrily. 'I don't like you very much.'

'Imagine my concern. You are unreliable. Go to the Garden with the others.'

'Damn right.'

'I'm coming with you,' Jeri told Arvid.

'Mother —'

'You go with Carrie. Arvid!'

Arvid studied her face, and nodded.

'Do as Carrie says,' Jeri said. She slapped Melissa on the rump. 'Now get moving.'

They set Tashayamp spinning in the middle of the cell and left her that way. They set off forward along the corridor. The first grill they passed, Arvid unscrewed the wing nuts and led half the party inside. The rest continued.

CHAPTER FORTY-TWO
THE MEN IN THE WALLS

I don't shoot a man for being incompetent in the Devil's work. I shoot him for being competent in the Devil's work. Admiration for his technique is part of the process.

– LAURENCE Van COTT NIVEN, D. Litt.

Four digit ships were coming near. They were half a thousand miles away, not close enough to use missiles, but close enough to show as brilliant, wavering green suns. That laser light must be boiling away *Michael's* hull. Refrigerators chugged, pumping unwanted heat into *Michael's* heat sink: the water tanks that had been two huge icebergs at takeoff.

The bombs were still going, *WHAM WHAM WHAM*, the spurt bombs were still raining into the blast, but Gillespie was on the radio link. 'Shuttle One, I'm cutting you loose. Gunships one through six, I'm cutting you loose. See if you can damage some bandits for me.'

WHAM

WHAM

quiet

Vibrating through the hull came *chunkchunk* sounds. mooring prongs releasing their passengers. Flames lit and pulled away. The exhausts of the gunboats were bright and yellow: solid fuel rockets. The single Shuttle flame showed faint and blue: oxygen and hydrogen. They swept away to do battle.

Watch for bandits. Watch for damage. Watch

temperature gauges. Listen, watch, and hang on. Constant chatter in the intercom —

'Too many digit ships,' Gillespie said. 'If I can kill a few, I can outrun the rest. Jason?'

'Targets acquired. Fire when ready.'

'Acceleration. Stand by.'

WHAM

'Get on the horn and tell the fly-boys to leave that nearest ship to me. Get 'em away from it. Fire.'

WHAM

'Bandits, eight o'clock high.'

'We're getting an overheat amidships starboard.'

WHAM

'Request salvo —'

'Time problems.'

'I need it.'

'Roger. Say when.'

'Stand by. Targets acquired. Ready.'

The bomb placement cannon *chugged* almost inaudibly. 'Acceleration. Stand by.'

WHAM

'Bandit, eleven o'clock low.'

WHAM

Harry's teeth were clenched. The temperature starboard amidships was falling again. No major hits on *Michael*. A gunship flared brilliant green, held, died . . .

'Stovepipe Five; this is Big Daddy.'

'Big Daddy, this is Stovepipe Four, scratch Stovepipe Five. I say again, scratch Five.'

'Bandit, eight o'clock low.'

'Big Daddy, this is Stovepipe Three, I'll take the new target.'

WHAM

'Request salvo.'

'Roger. Acceleration. Stand by.'

WHAM

WHAM

Three digit ships showed behind them as brilliant green suns.

'Temperature rising, ventral aft four.'

'Steam forming, ventral aft six.'

WHAM

'Big Daddy, this is Stovepipe Three, scratch one bogey.'

Two brilliant suns aft.

'Big Daddy, this is Stovepipe Four, scratch Stovepipe Three.'

WHAM
WHAM

Temperatures fell toward normal. Two lights showed aft. The gunships were invisible, beyond the battle now, living or dead.

'Short break,' Gillespie said. 'They're trying to clump. They want to hit us in clusters. We won't reach the next cluster for a couple of hours.'

'*Thank God!*' Harry eagerly reached up to open his faceplate.

'Sounds like a good time for an inspection tour,' Max Rohrs said. 'Get used to moving around in free-fall.'

'Hey, give us a break,' Harry said.

'I'll suggest it to the snouts.'

Harry fastened the faceplate again.

The ducts were roomy enough. They were square in cross section so that patch plates could be all the same size. What had been ladders, padded rungs welded into the sides, had been left for handholds.

Harry knew the ducts like the roof of his mouth. The trouble was that he kept bumping into the sides. Ensign Franklin stayed ahead of him. Franklin hadn't helped build these ducts, but he'd had astronaut training in a weighted pressure suit in a swimming pool.

'Acceleration. Stand by.'

The ship surged. Gillespie was throwing the thrust

bombs far back, using them less for thrust than to power the spurt bombs. Still, Harry snatched a rung only just in time.

'Where are we?' Franklin asked.

'About the middle of the Brick. That was the midpoint lateral tunnel we just passed. Port water tank below us. Here, this is one of the equipment bins.' He looked in, and Franklin peered past him. 'Nothing shook loose. Welding and cutting equipment, patch plates – same size as the walls, you have to tilt them to get 'em through the ducts —'

'I know.'

'Patches for steam pipes, the valve wheels, lines and cables . . . nooses of the finest hemp.'

'There was a girl who never laid me, but she made me see *The Five Thousand Fingers of Doctor T*,' Franklin said.

'I like her already.'

'Yeah.' They continued forward. Harry tried launching himself from the rungs, bouncing slantwise from the opposite wall. It didn't work. Best move was to parallel the rungs and keep them within reach. 'It's harder to move around than I thought it would be. Tires you out faster, too.'

'Yeah. That's always a surprise,' Franklin said.

The duct expanded into a maze of pipes. Pipes five feet wide flared into cones eighteen feet across. The cones ran through the hull and outside: twelve cones facing in three directions in rows of four each. 'The attitude jets. We're at the upper port corner of the Brick,' Harry said. 'It's all so clean. I'm going to hate seeing it messed up in a battle.'

'When they told me about the steam pipes, I wondered if they'd want me shoveling coal too.'

Harry laughed. 'Shall we take the cross duct and come down the other side?'

'Lead on. I'm lost already.'
'Acceleration. Stand by.'

WHAM

Nikolai led. The gravity was still low enough to let them move in great leaps.

If it gets strong enough, he won't be able to move fast, Jeri thought. *What will they do then?* She wanted to ask, but the last time she'd spoken it had upset Dmitri.

Arvid lets that commissar tell him what to do. Why? We aren't in Russia, and he isn't smarter than Arvid.

It was difficult to keep up. It was also obvious that the Russians weren't going to slow for her. They moved on through the air shafts. Each time they passed one of the ring-shaped robots Jeri felt terror. Suppose the thing came after them, tentacles flailing —

They moved deeper into the ship. *Where are we going?* Wherever it was, Nikolai never hesitated as they went through twists and turns. Jeri caught glimpses of marks by some of the tunnel forks. *Cyrillic letters. Of course!*

'We are here, Comrade Commander.'

Dmitri might be in command, but Nikolai spoke and listened only to Arvid Rogachev. *He must not like Dmitri any more than I do,* Jeri thought.

The room below was filled with cabinets and boxes, but no snouts. Dmitri waited impatiently for Nikolai and Rogachev to open the accessway, then dashed ahead of them to begin opening boxes, flinging their contents out onto the deck.

Tang? And that label says something in Russian! Where are – oh!

Dmitri opened another box. 'Ha!' He reached into the box and brought out a big pistol, then fumbled in the box again until he found ammunition.

'That belonged to the American, Greeley,' Arvid said.

647

'Is there another? The Americans brought several and gave one to me as a gift.'

'Da. There are two.' He brought out another pistol and handed it to Arvid with a box of ammunition.

Only two. I wonder if Dmitri can shoot as well as I can? I don't suppose there's any point in asking.

Arvid loaded the pistol and held it high. 'At last my arm is whole again!' he shouted in English.

And what did the snouts make of that picture? 'Is there anything else? Knives? I had a Walther PPK when they captured me, is that in there?'

'No.' Arvid opened wall cabinets. Spacesuits hung like mannequins. 'Hah. I suppose it is too much, to hope there will be filled air tanks.'

'If these can be made airtight,' Dmitri said, 'will they not allow us to live in vacuum even without air tanks?'

'A few minutes longer. Not more.'

'We can kill many snouts in a few minutes.' Dmitri said. 'Let us see if these can be made to fit us.'

Mrs. Woodward was dithering. 'If I thought we could get to that big slab, the Podo Thuktun – they worship that, don't they? We'd be even safer —'

'They lock it,' Alice said. 'They lock everything but the kitchen and the garden and the funeral pit. You don't want to hide in the funeral pit!'

'No. What are you doing?'

Alice was unscrewing the big wing nuts on a grill. 'I'm going to Wes. Get the kids to the Garden. Hide.'

'Hide? Alice, they won't harm children.'

'Carrie, you don't want to be caught after Arvid and the Russians start their moves!'

'Oh.' Carrie put an arm around each of the children. 'Alice —'

'I'll be fine. Wes needs me.'

Carrie Woodward nodded agreement. 'I'd have gone for my John. God be with you, Alice.'

'Thanks.'

A recorded voice trumpeted in the alien language. 'Take footholds against thrust!'

Alice dove into the air shaft. Behind her Carrie Woodward gripped the corridor's wet carpeting, both children clinging to her.

The pull increased until it was uncomfortable, then increased again. *Like Kansas? More? I don't know.* Alice moved through the air shafts. Somewhere ahead was Wes Dawson.

———

The fithp warriors gestured but didn't speak.

All right, Dawson thought. *They're still trying to drive me mad. Have they done it? How long since I had anyone to talk to?*

There were only two, one before and one behind. *I'm strong like Superman. Exercise. I've walked all the way from New York City to Joplin, Missouri. And they're still elephants. Too damn big.*

I'm as fast as they are. Faster. Jump back, grab that one's gun! But why did they come for me?

No spin. Acceleration, thrust *after all this time. Why am I out?*

To prove I'm a rogue. Wait for me to go for a gun so they can kill me . . . no. Makes no sense. They wouldn't take the spin off just for that.

Damn! I'm a schizzy as Alice. He stifled that thought. *Alice isn't crazy. Maybe she got over it.*

Alice is sweet, and if I live through this, what will I do with her? Carlotta will kill her!

They were in a shallow spiral curve, climbing toward the ship's bow. Thrust had risen to something like Earth normal.

They emerged in a place with windows, a place he had never seen . . . except in his mind, perhaps. A starship's control room, an alien starship. It was dimly lit; half the light was coming from square TV monitor screens. There were no chairs, only pads and recessed holds for the claws of fithp feet. The pads would tilt for spin gravity, but they were flat now. He'd guessed from the change in gravity, and now he knew: *Thuktun Flishithy* was on a war footing.

The warriors were holding back, out of the way.

Four fithp stood together in the center of the bridge. Dawson recognized one. Takpusseh-yamp. A fi' saw them and beckoned. The Bull Stud? Yes, for the warriors immediately brought him forward, digits twined round his arms.

'Dawson,' the Herdmaster said. 'Are you sane?'

He suppressed the urge to roll his eyes up and bobble his finger against his lips. 'Yes. No thanks to you.'

The Herdmaster pointed to a screen. The view zoomed toward a distant, fuzzy object. As Dawson watched, it flared brilliant green, then flared again. Faint blue-green threads played against it from distant digit ships.

The Herdmaster gestured impatiently. 'Look at that and tell me what it is.'

Dawson's lips curved in a smile. 'That is a tape of *Star Wars*,' he said. *We're fighting! Should I have jumped that soldier? Hell, no. This is where they run everything. Stall. Wait for the chance to snatch a gun and —*

'Speak our language, Dawson. We have no time for gibberish. You lectured Fathisteh-tulk on devices for use in space. Lecture me now regarding *that*. If you remain silent, I will return you to your silence.'

'I can't even tell which is which. There's too much going on. That – big blinking thing – is that ours?'

'No, it rose from the United States. It carries a weapon that would be a laser but that it sends an impossibly high frequency. We have no such in our thuktunthp. What can you tell us?'

The last thing Wes wanted was to return to the dreadful silence of his cell. Here was where it was all happening! And he wouldn't be giving away anything useful. 'Gamma-ray lasers are possible. They destroy themselves, you only fire them once. You pump them with a fission explosion.'

The Herdmaster bellowed something.

Takpusseh-yamp spoke too rapidly for Wes to follow. Another fi', one Dawson was certain he had never seen before, listened gravely, then spoke slowly.

'Perhaps. There is nothing in the thuktunthp. This would explain why they use so many bombs.'

'What is the purpose of the intruder?'

Was that a serious question? Wes said, 'They make war.'

'War has a purpose. What is the purpose? Do they seek a not-surrender surrender?'

'I don't understand. They want you extinct. They're coming to kill you.'

'They will kill entire fithp? Females, children?'

'India.'

'India was not all of the human fithp.'

'Unless you surrender, that ship will destroy *Thuktun Flishithy.*'

The Herdmaster didn't seem surprised. He spoke to the fourth fi' in the group. 'Defensemaster, you have heard. Warriors, keep this one there, where he will not interfere.'

The guards dragged him to one bulkhead. They placed his hands against the damp, spongy wall. 'Grip.' Each hand was encircled by tentacles. The fithp warriors dug their claws into the floor.

———

The Herdmaster made certain that Dawson was held securely, far enough away that he could not overhear.

Thrust was steady now. The sixteen digit ships which

651

had surrounded *Message Bearer*, her last wall of defense, were dwindling in her wake. 'Defensemaster.'

'Lead me.'

'Can we avoid battle?'

'Herdmaster, the intruder already has too high a velocity. If we thrust lateral to his path, he will still miss by only a few makasrupkithp. I am thrusting away from him, directly out from Winterhome. He must pass the last digit ships to find us.'

'This is your thuktun.' *Do it your way*. 'Takpusseh-yamp.'

'Lead me.'

'Raztupisp-minz told us that the humans in Africa often demand conditions before foot touches chest. What words did he use? "Not-surrender surrender"?'

'"We took to calling it a "negotiated loss of status." '

'Draft me one to be used if we lose this battle.'

'Herdmaster, is this possible?'

'Probably not. What else are you busy at? You have said yourself that this is their last attempt to break from beneath our foot. When the intruder is gone, then we can let them study how to surrender to us. Meanwhile, exercise your skill. Prepare for us a negotiated loss of status giving them as little as possible.'

'Herdmaster?'

The call came from one of the lesser posts. 'Speak.'

'Camera twenty-eight.'

The Herdmaster tapped two buttons. A screen lit with a view of an air duct . . . and a small, red-haired human female.

'It's – she's just outside the aft control room, watching through the grill.'

'Send a warrior for her. Send another – send *three* to the human restraint cell. If she's loose, they may all be loose. And summon Tashayamp!'

Half a dozen fithp were beyond the grill. They didn't seem particularly excited by what they were watching, and they weren't doing anything but switching the views on their TV sets. One view stayed. It showed a room like this one, but much larger. There were windows, with stars beyond.

There was Wes Dawson, against a wall, between two of the horrors.

And there, suddenly live on another screen, Alice saw herself peering through an air duct.

Time to move on, Alice thought. Forward. Windows on a spaceship had to be at the nose . . .

CHAPTER FORTY-THREE
STEAM

Lord, Thou has made this world below the shadow of a
dream,
An', taught by time, I take it so — exceptin' always Steam

      – RUDYARD KIPLING, 'McAndrew's Hymn'

The big digital timer above the war screens ticked off the
seconds since *Michael's* launch. When it passed six hours,
Admiral Carrell said, 'Try it now.' He put on his own
headset.

Jack Clybourne sidled through the room like an English
butler, silently removing coffee cups and emptying ash-
trays, before fading back against one wall. *Can you type?*
Jenny thought. She touched keys, and gave orders that
flashed across half the globe.

*Somewhere out there a submarine sticks its nose up just
so we can get a report —*

The situation boards had showed few changes in the past
two hours. The missile sites in Georgia and Missouri were
craters now, and a curious pattern of meteoric death,
neither random nor any geometric figure Jenny had ever
seen, had fallen on the South Atlantic. Nothing had hit
Bellingham yet. Harpanet had been badly upset to learn
that the Friendly Snout had been painted on the Archangel
dome. If the digit ships were given leisure – if *Michael*
fell – they would punish that affront.

There was static in her phones. 'Try routing through
Florida.'

'Trying, sir.'

And if that doesn't work —

'Gimlet, we have Nosebleed.'

The computer console identified Nosebleed: *Ethan Allen.*

'He must have gone deep,' Admiral Carrell said. 'I thought we'd lost him.'

'Gimlet, we have Chickenpox.'

Another nuclear sub.

'Two possible links. Good enough. Try to get through,' Carrell said.

'*Michael*, this is Gimlet.' *Oh ye Thrones, Dominions, and Powers —*

Static burst in her headset. She winced.

'Can you put it on the speaker?' the President asked.

'Yes, sir.'

'Gimlet, this is *Michael*.'

Hurrah! '*Michael*, this is Gimlet. Your orders are unchanged. Continue your mission. Godspeed, Ed. Report, please.'

'Reporting. We're 20,000 miles above Africa and climbing, present vel – ' The voice faded.

'Come *on*,' General Toland whispered.

'*Garble garble* but no serious damage. Casualties are light. We have launched five gunships and one Shuttle to assist in breaking through *garble garble* —'

Damn!

'– a formation of digit ships above Africa. At plus one hour *garble garble*its drive. We believe the enemy mother ship is running away. *Garble garble*.'

'They have to catch it!' the President said.

'*Michael,* continue pursuit.'

'– are in pursuit. Estimate we will be in effective range within six to twelve hours. We will have to fight our way past a formation of sixteen digit ships they have left to delay *garble garble*.'

'Hoo boy.' General Toland thought he was whispering.

The countdown timer showed 6 hours, 12 minutes since *Michael*'s launch.

'We have not been attacked for four hours. The next attack may be worse. No missiles so far. We've used more missiles than I like, but we still have plenty, and the spurt bomb supply is *garble blurble garble garble.*'

The static increased.

'Link with Nosebleed has been lost.'

'Should we try for a new link?' Jenny asked.

'How long until we have direct contact?'

'About two hours. Relay through the East Coast in half an hour.'

'Any orders for them, Mr. President?' Admiral Carrell asked.

'You're in charge, Admiral.'

'We'll wait. Hide the subs,' Admiral Carrell said.

'All fishes, this is Gimlet. Run away!'

'Bogeys ahead are at extreme missile range.'

'All right, children, quiet hour is over!'

Harry jumped awake. He had slept! Harry found that amazing. He'd thought sleeping would be as difficult as pissing, which had required two men and fifteen minutes each to open the pressure suits and close them again. He'd slept, and he felt wonderful! Now, what? . . .

His forward view showed sixteen digit ships in a spreading ring. Their light swamped the stars, hellglare green. In their center was a violet-white glare.

It'll be like a single pass through a Cuisinart. But we're gaining on Big Mama!

'Acceleration. Stand by.'

WHAM

WHAM

WHAM

Three kicks in the ass. One of the green suns faded,

then became a fireball. 'How did we do that?' he asked aloud.

'Gamma rays could have set off fusion in the deuterium,' Tiny Pelz said. 'That's a guess. We still don't know just how their drive works.'

'One thing sure,' Jeff Franklin said. 'Hot gamma rays can't be doing their ships any good.'

'Crews either, if they're anything like us.'

'Bandit at one o'clock high is changing color.'

'Roger. Take him, Jason. Acceleration. Stand by.'

                    WHAM

'Good shooting!'

Jason Daniels opened his faceplate. 'Did you get through to Colorado Springs?'

'I did my best. No new orders. They may be missing all the excitement.'

'More excitement coming up,' Jason said. He scratched his nose, then closed the faceplate. 'Missiles dead ahead.'

They showed as a swarm of fireflies. *Bullets would be as dangerous, and they'd be invisible.* Harry winced. At these velocities, marshmallows would be dangerous. They would strike like meteors.

'Rotation. Stand by.'

Steam jets hissed. *Michael* turned ponderously.

'Don't turn a cold shoulder; show your armored ass,' Franklin said.

'And if we don't turn fast enough?' Harry asked.

'Keep the frivolous chatter to a dull roar,' Gillespie said.

Aw, shit! Harry turned his intercom switch to local. So did Jeff Franklin. *Kid looks embarrassed.* Harry did an exaggerated shrug so that Franklin would see it.

TV cameras looked up along the flanks of the Brick, toward digit ships spreading across the sky. The Brick's massive nose would reflect some of that green glare, absorb some too. Some got through. The forward shield couldn't hide them from all sixteen enemies, but turned ass on to the enemy they couldn't accelerate.

Michael's amidships guns were firing forward, assisting in rotating the ship. *My guns. I put them in.* Clouds of shotgun pellets made of spent uranium were arraying themselves ahead of *Michael*. Harry saw bright flashes among the missiles.

Steam roared again. *Michael's* rotation ceased. Cameras on long booms looked out beyond the butt plate, and the ring of digit ships.

The first of the missiles struck. Whatever they carried for a warhead, it was puny compared to *Michael*'s own drive.

'Ten minutes. Then we turn again and accelerate like hell,' Gillespie said. 'Amuse yourselves.'

Yeah. Sure.

'Stovepipes Seven and Eight. Shuttle Two. Your turn. Stand by.'

The gunships cast loose, accelerating to the side. Shuttle Two followed. Harry watched the flames dwindle, then veer, around more oncoming missiles and toward the digit ships.

'It's their last chance at us,' Tiny Pelz said. 'They'll pour it on —'

'Rotation. Stand by.'

Steam jets hissed.

'Hail Mary, full of grace . . .'

Franklin had forgotten the intercom was on. *Don't blame him much.* This was the trickiest part: as they passed through the ring of digit ships, they would rotate to face away from the thickest cluster, protecting themselves with the butt plate, but exposing *Michael*'s comparatively weak sides to others.

The ship turned ponderously. *Spin, you bastard!*

Missiles exploded. Light washed two screens. The ship kicked mildly, *Wham Wham Wham* pause *Wham:* snout missiles exploded under the butt plate.

'– now and in the hour of our death, amen. Temperature rising starboard amidships.'

'Gun turret four no longer reporting.'

'Bandit, nine o'clock.'

'Steam forming, bow section three.'

More missiles. *Michael* trembled to the shock waves.

'You can do it, baby, you can do it —'

A vastly larger shock wave kicked *Michael* sideways. Somebody screamed. Half a dozen screens blinked white and went blank. Tiny Pelz said, 'Oboy.'

'Damage control, report!'

'Stand by,' Max Rohrs said. 'Tiny, what the hell was *that*?'

'We got two! Two digit ships blanked out!' Harry shouted.

'Fascinating. I didn't shoot,' Jason Daniels said. 'Who got them?'

'We're tumbling,' Gillespie said. 'I've got no attitude control. Damage control, do something!'

'I know what happened,' Pelz said. 'I just can't *see* it. Somebody deploy a camera.'

'Gamble, go. Tiny, talk.'

Hamilton Gamble left his seat on the jump. Tiny Pelz said, 'I think we've lost one of the spurt bomb bays. The snouts set off a nuclear missile close enough to pump some spurt bombs. Maybe the whole bay fired! One tremendous blast of gamma lasers. It's not as bad as it sounds – I hope —'

We've had it! The implications hit him. *We're all there was. Aw, shit.*

'Kasanovsky, get moving. I want to know what's happened to our steam jets.'

Another suited figure left the bridge.

My turn soon. Harry played with his own TV screens, switching to internal cameras. Nothing here. Go around the ship. Assume we lost the ventral spurt bomb bay. Move from there. *Ha!*

Something had kicked an enormous dent in *Michael*'s port side. Forward of that, the port pipe room was swirling gray chaos.

'Ham Gamble here. I see it. Look for yourself, channel Alfa six.'

Harry switched his TV monitor. *There*.

The screen lit to show the sky. Digit ships were blurred green spotlights; the stars didn't show at all. The camera swung down.

Spurt Bomb Bay 1 was gone. Only its melted-looking base still stood up from the Shell. The much larger tower that was Thrust Bomb Bay 1 had a chewed look. As Gamble swiveled the camera, their view ran along the flank of the Brick. Meteor holes pocked it. The base was ripped. A stream of fog jetted away.

Max Rohrs spoke quietly, a litany of disasters. 'Port water tank gone. I've got the port fission pile scrammed. We've got no water for it anyway. The whole portside attitude jet system is dead.'

'Slow response to starboard control system,' Gillespie said.

'Nothing from the Stovepipes or the Shuttle. I think they've had it.'

'Overheat, starboard amidships.'

'We're still taking hits,' Gillespie said. 'Max, if you can get a wiggle on —'

'Situation assessment coming up,' Rohrs said. His calmness was a rebuke.

'Okay, I have the picture,' Pelz said. 'It could have been worse. Most of the energy must have gone forward. Better figure we killed all of the ships we deployed, and the two snout ships that aren't firing lasers anymore. We got some spillover energy to the side.'

'Anything coming apart? If we shake and rattle, do we break anything?'

'Not by me,' Rohrs said.

'Stand by. I'll try to stabilize. Jason, get ready! Kill something! Acceleration and rotation, stand by!'

'Wait one. Bombs away – she's yours.'

WHAM
WHAM
WHAM
quiet

'It sure sounds good in theory,' Tiny Pelz said.

'What does?' Franklin demanded.

'Firing bombs off center to compensate for rotation. Sure sounds good in theory.'

The screens showed they were still rotating, but more slowly. *Michael* was the center of a ring of dazzling green lights . . . receding aft.

'We're through, or close enough,' Jason said. 'Their missiles can't hit us, we can't hit them, but this is closest approach to those damn lasers. The steam we're losing – the cooling effect may be all that's saving us.'

'If we don't get attitude control, we've got a big bloody pinwheel! Acceleration. Stand by. Jason —'

'Bombs away. Locked on. She's yours.'

WHAM

'Try again. Jason —'

'Roger.'

WHAM

'Shuttles Three and Four. We may not make it. We have to hit this mother with something. You're on. Stand by.'

'Roger.'

'Max, get me some attitude jets!'

Harry already had his faceplate closed.

Max Rohrs used a light pen to trace lines on the screen. 'There's plenty of pressure in the starboard system, and we have working attitude jets starboard, ventral and here and here dorsal.' The pen flicked across a stylized view of *Michael*.

'The port jets look okay in TV pix, but they won't hold pressure. The electronics aren't much good either.'

No wonder! Half the portside pipes are gone!

'What we've got to do is isolate the working chunk of

the portside system, then shunt steam in there from the starboard generators. We don't have electronic control of those valves – or if we do, we don't have any feedback on what they've done, which is just as bad. What we have to do is start at the breaks and move toward the jets, patching as we go.'

Harry laughed. His screen showed a three-foot pipe with a six-foot section missing. Beyond it was a hole in the hull, a neat oval with a rim that bulged outward. Stars showed through.

Rohrs pointed at Harry's display. 'The merely difficult we do immediately. The impossible we leave for dry dock. You're supposed to use judgment, but get the damn lines fixed! Patch anything you can patch, and use the manual valves to shut off everything else.

'Lambe, Donaldson, go through the starboard system and check it out. Get things set up to shunt steam across to the port system, and stand by. We'll need pressure to test.

'Reddington, Franklin —'

Here it comes.

'Start with the big hole in the port system and work your way up to the jets. Your goal is to make the port jets work with starboard steam. Got that, Harry?'

'Righto.' *All this so I could wear a pressure suit?*

'Move.'

Chunk Chunk: Roy Culzer, in Shuttle Four, named *Atlantis* in a more peaceful era, felt the prongs unlock at the nose. The main tank was moored to *Michael* by the same matings that in gentler times would have gripped solid fuel boosters. Now only the aft matings were still attached, and *Atlantis*'s nose pointed beyond the overhang of *Michael*'s roof.

Jay Hadley had the motors going. Blue flame played

down the flank of the Brick. The aft prongs released, and *Atlantis* was free.

The sky was a hot green.

'Turning. Stand by.' The Shuttle turned as it pulled away. Earth and *Michael* were behind, the violet-white flame of the prime target ahead. Four, five green spotlights sank below window view. 'Okay,' Jay Hadley said, 'now they're only heating the main tank. We'll burn that fuel before the tank blows up.'

For nearly eight hours *Michael* had been in direct sunlight. The pressure in the main tanks was already too high, and rising. *Have to live with it.*

Shuttle Three, *Challenger*, was already lost to sight. Roy caught sight of a gunship's yellower flame just before it disappeared into a missile explosion.

'Maneuvering. Stand by.'

Roy's sense of balance protested as Jay turned the Shuttle. 'What have we got?'

'Missiles. We've got five miles per second on those snout ships. The missiles only get one pass. They can't hit us if we keep veering.'

'You hope.'

'Semper fi, mac. Let me know when you think you have a shot at something.'

'Yeah, sure.' The missiles were in the main compartment, and the big bay doors weren't open.

The ring of green lights dropped away aft. 'Go, baby, go,' Roy prayed. *Talking to the ship. Why not? What else can I do?* 'Maybe we should open the bay.'

'No point.' The dreadful green lights were fading. 'Our missiles can't reach them either. Save 'em for Mommy Dearest. How long before we're in range?'

'Maybe an hour, if we don't get hurt, and they don't get more acceleration.' Roy poked numbers into *Atlantis*'s computer. 'Looks to me like they're pouring on all they have.'

'So are we. Roy —'

'Yeah?'

'General Gillespie said *Michael* might not make it.'

'Yeah. I heard.'

'That leaves it up to us.'

'Well, there's *Challenger*.'

'Heard from Big Jim lately?'

'No.' *Big Jim Farr. Six four, only he managed to lose two inches in the official records.* Laurie Culzer and Jane Farr and five kids were sharing a house in Port Angeles. 'Think he's had it, Joe?'

'I think we act like he's out!'

'Which leaves us.'

'Which leaves us. Maneuvering. Stand by.'

The whole portside structure was hot.

'X-rays,' Tiny Pelz said. 'What they don't go through, they heat up. Efficient at it.'

Harry trailed air lines behind. The tanks in his backpack held an hour of air, but without cooling he wouldn't live an hour. It was already uncomfortable. His trailing air lines were picking up heat.

Sweat pooled. When he jumped it ran down his face, his arms, his legs; when he was still it couldn't run.

'I've closed seventeen-tango,' Harry reported. 'Moving forward. I don't see any breaks in this section.'

'Stand by. I'll send over steam for a test.'

'Roger.' Harry put his helmet next to Jeff Franklin's and turned off the intercom. 'All we need. More heat.'

'Sure hope it holds – naw. Look.'

A thin plume poured out ahead: live steam, absolutely clear up to two feet from the break. 'Kill the shunt,' Harry said. 'We're losing pressure —'

'Belay that,' Gillespie said. 'Reddington, you're a wonder. I'm getting some control.'

'You're also losing steam.'

'Can you fix it?'

664

'Sure, if you take the pressure off!'

'Give me ten minutes.'

'Harry,' Rohrs said.

'Yeah, I knew he didn't mean it.'

'Harry, scout ahead. What's it like on forward?'

'Hot!'

'Sure be useful to know —'

'Max, has anybody ever suggested you change deodorants? I'm moving forward.'

It wasn't easy getting past the plume of leaking steam. Harry took it fast, then waited for Jeff.

The ship surged, then surged again. Gillespie sounded excited. 'Goddam! We're turning. Head for Big Mama. Coming around. Almost there . . . Jason —'

'Ready!'

'Acceleration. Stand by.' Harry grabbed for a ladder.

WHAM
WHAM

Harry slapped on a patch and braced against the bulkhead while Jeff Franklin ran the torch. Metal glowed where Franklin worked. He was almost done —

'Maneuvering. Stand by.'

'Shit, give us a minute!' Harry shouted.

'Stand by.'

Steam leaked from the side that Franklin hadn't finished. *Michael* turned. Harry's head swam.

'Maneuver done. Acceleration. Stand by. Jason —'

'Locked on and tracking. Take that, Mommy Dearest.'

'Acceleration.'

WHAM
WHAM

'Maneuvering —'

'How do you get a transfer out of this chicken-shit outfit?' Harry demanded.

'Well, you have to fuck up —'

'Fuck *up*. That's my problem. All this time I tried to fuck off.'

'Maneuvering. Acceleration. Stand by.'

'Target acquired.'

WHAM

The gauge on his wrist said 40.1 *Shit fire, why couldn't they give me a normal thermometer?* 'Jeff, what's 40 degrees?'

'About 105° Fahrenheit.'

'No wonder I'm hot. That's what my suit shows —'

'Harry.'

'Eh?'

'That's not your suit temperature. That's you. Inside.'

'That thing they rammed up my ass? One-oh-five? Jeff —'

'It's dangerous but not fatal. What we have to do is cool off.'

'Sure. Where?'

'Acceleration. Stand by.'

WHAM

'Incoming.'

'Missiles dead ahead.'

'Target acquired.'

'Acceleration. Stand by.'

WHAM

'This is Turret Five. We have a target. Permission to fire.'

'Let her fly.'

WHAM

'Maneuvering. Stand by.'

Steam poured out through the leak. Harry braced a pry bar against one bulkhead and wedged the other end against the patch plate. 'Hammer —' He felt it in his right hand. He grabbed a handhold with his left, then pounded on the pry bar. 'I got that one. Hit it with the welder. I'm going forward.'

The next compartment held a storage area for welding equipment, and cooling air outlets. Harry tested the air pressure. 'Goddam, Jeff, cool air!'

'Be right with you.'

666

Harry gratefully found a corner to wedge himself into. Presently Jeff Franklin joined him. The ship continued to accelerate.

Franklin talked to the control room. 'We need some time. We're getting goofy with the heat.'

'Take ten minutes.'

'It'll have to do.'

Had Franklin been acting goofy? Harry hadn't noticed. But the cool felt wonderful, as if his skin were drinking a good brand of beer. The air jetted through his suit, and he waved his arms and legs to let it through.

There were no digit ships now. *Atlantis*'s screen showed only the prime target – unmistakably the Mother Ship now, short and wide, as in the last transmissions from Kosmograd, and riding a spear of violet-white light. The drive flame was swinging around.

'Trying to lose us,' Jay Hadley gloated.

The Shuttle's thrust dropped suddenly. Roy started violently.

'Relax,' Jay said. *Chunk Chunk*: the empty main tank was free. Attitude jets popped, and *Atlantis* eased back until the Mother Ship was behind the main tank.

'They can't get loose now. They can't turn fast enough. We're on intercept and in missile range. Let's see what happens. Are you going to open the bay?'

'Not just yet. We're too fragile with the bay open. You know damn well what they'll do when we're in range.'

'They're doing it now. I saw missiles before I turned us.'

'Yeah?' *Intercept*. Roy couldn't make himself feel surprised. *He's going to ram. He didn't even ask me.*

The Shuttle main tank was a green-edged black shadow, growing brighter. Big Mama had its own defenses. The main tank must be boiling —

And suddenly the main tank's black shadow vanished in

667

half a dozen simultaneous flares. Missiles were homing on the explosions of other missiles. The Shuttle turned, and Roy felt the solid *thumps* of fragments impacting the tile shielding. There would be no reentry for *Atlantis*.

Jay reached down to move lever arms that protruded through the floor. These were new: they connected to petcocks in the lower level. Water that had been ice at takeoff was jetting from vents in the Shuttle's nose. The cloud of debris ahead thickened with water vapor.

It might hide *Atlantis* . . . but there was no hiding Big Mama. Her drive flame must be visible across half the world. Jay was firing the EMU motors, the smaller jets that connected to the Shuttle's onboard tank.

'Still on intercept?'

'Yeah.'

'Opening the bay. Let's get closer before we loose the birds. If you did everything right —'

'They'll think we're dead.' Jay laughed.

The gauge showed Harry's internal temperature at 39 degrees. *I've gained some. Not enough.*

'Incoming. Hang on.'

Oh, shit.

Michael shuddered.

'We took something, portside forward,' Gillespie said.

'Losing steam pressure —'

'She's getting sluggish. Doesn't want to maneuver —'

'Something's wrong portside forward —'

'Harry!'

'Yeah, Max, I'm on the way. Jeff, let's do it.'

Progress was slow. As they moved forward, the ship was hotter, and there was more damage. Handholds were missing. New holes punched through.

Some punch. Michael's armor was in layers: steel armor, fiberglass matting, more steel armor, layer after layer of hard and nonresilient soft. Anything coming through that had been moving fast – and hadn't melted.

Harry felt a tug. He looked behind. His air lines were stretched taut. 'End of the line.'

'Max, we can't get further,' Jeff Franklin reported.

'You have to. We're losing pressure just forward of you.'

'Losing pressure.'

'Yeah, the most powerful spacecraft ever built by man is going to fail for lack of steam —'

'Okay,' Harry said. 'I'll go have a look.' He disconnected the line, and now he was on canned air.

Big Mama was close, close. The drive flame, the dark cylinder at its tip —the sudden green flare, the firefly lights of missiles pouring from four points along her flank . . . 'Firing,' said Roy.

'I'll wait.'

'Good. Missiles one through five away. Getting target acquisition for the next group. We've actually got a few minutes, don't we?'

'Say two minutes before the missiles get here —'

'Missiles six through ten, away.' The green light had dimmed. Big Mama's lasers had found more interesting targets: *Atlantis*'s own missiles.

'– But we're heating up. Oh, fuck it. We won't be taking it long. How you doing?'

'Target acquired, missiles eleven through fifteen away, that's all of them. Turn us! Now!'

Motors popped on. *Atlantis* turned, belly toward Big Mama. Roy opened the petcocks again. A cloud of water vapor might slow a missile or confuse its poor brain —

Something slammed them against their seats. Again. 'Reentry is going to be a problem,' Jay said, and laughed.

'It isn't atmosphere you're —'

The Shuttle twisted: an explosion against one wing. Jay brought them back with attitude jets.

'– thinking of entering. I wish I had a view.'

Nothing showed beyond the window save stars and a halo of green. The reentry shield was boiling under Big Mama's lasers. 'Are we still on target? I'd hate to miss after all this.'

'Big Mama's a big target,' Jay said. There didn't seem to be a hell of a lot more to say.

The portside bow was chaos. Steam poured from broken pipes and streamed through the ripped hull.

'Shut the damn steam off!' Harry shouted.

'Maneuvering. Stand by. Harry, if we cut the steam on port side, I won't be able to maneuver.'

'Incoming. Stand by.'

Michael shuddered again.

Max Rohrs was holding his calm, but it sounded like he was fighting to do it. 'Steam pressure falling. We'll try to shunt to secondary water sources.'

What good will that do if we can't get the leak shut off? Harry studied the situation. The compartment ahead was filled with steam and wreckage. He could feel its heat radiating through his faceplate. *If I move real fast, I can just –* 'Jeff, I'm going forward and close that valve. Nine-alfa for the record.'

Rohrs overrode Franklin's answer. 'Don't, unless you can open nine-bravo. We need that steam path.'

Oh, holy shit! 'Roger. Here I go.'

He dove forward. The handholds were hot through his gloves. The ship maneuvered, so that he wasn't quite in free-fall, but there wasn't real gravity either. Ragged metal ends reached out to scrape against the hard upper torso of his suit.

He reached the valve wheel. 'Max —'

Nothing. 'I don't think he can hear you,' Jeff Franklin said. 'Harry, do you need help?'

'Not enough room in here for two. Tell Max I'm opening nine-bravo now.'

The big valve wheel didn't want to turn. There was nothing to brace his feet against, and the valve wouldn't respond to one-handed operation. *Got to move slow. Careful. Think it through.* He placed his feet as careful as an Alpiner on a granite wall. Finally he had both braced, his left foot wedged into a wide crack in one bulkhead.

'Turn, you mother! Got it! Now to close nine-alfa.'

He didn't dare look at the temperature gauge on his wrist. The valve wheel was all the way forward. Beyond it was a smooth-edged hole four feet around. Stars shone through that.

Between him and the valve was a jet of steam.

'Jeff, make them stop acceleration for a moment. I have to jump.'

'Okay. Command, this is Franklin. Reddington needs things stable for a minute.'

Static in Harry's intercom. Then Franklin. 'You can have two minutes, exactly four minutes from now.'

'Roger.' *If I can live four more minutes.* He could hear each heartbeat as a base drum in his head. *Slow down. Calm. Relax* – Relaxation made the pounding sound worse.

There were flashes out there, outside. Shadows flickered through the hole in the hull.

Jeri. Melissa. They never found the bodies. Hell, here I come!

'Stand by, Harry. Ten seconds. Okay – now.'

Harry leaped across the gap. Steam played over him.

It was cooler on the other side. The black outside seemed to suck heat away. 'Got the valve. Turning it. It's turning – shit! Have to brace my feet.'

'Harry, can they maneuver now?'

He sensed urgency in Franklin's voice. 'All right.'

671

'I'll relay warnings. Acceleration. Stand by.'
WHAM

Left foot here. Right foot. Okay. Grip. Turn. Turn. His left foot slipped. Sharp pain ran up his shin. A small plume of steam came out at the ankle. *Steam? That hot in my suit?* He tried to brace his foot again. The universe shrank to a sticking valve wheel —

Behind him the steam plume was tiny, nearly as small as the plume from his suit.

'You got it, Harry, get the hell out of there!'

'Coming,' *Turn, you bastard. Turn.* His foot hurt like hell. Forward was the black of space, cool. *If I wedge in that hole I can get leverage.* He moved forward. *One quick look outside.*

The Mother Ship was far ahead, still too far for details; but the drive flame was a spear, not a dot. She had turned sideways. Trying to dodge. To dodge one of the Shuttles. Harry could see the familiar triangular silhouette limned against the flame, easing forward, past the flame . . .

Flame burst from near the center of the cylinder. *They rammed*, Harry thought, and *They did it right*. Big Mama's drive flame veered, and suddenly there was a brighter streak in the violet-white. Yellow and orange, and the wavering flame was veering back into line, but down the violet-white spear ran a stream of bonfire-colored flame.

'Jeff —'

'Yeah? Harry, get out of there!'

'In a minute. Jeff, tell the boss. Shuttle Four. *Atlantis*. They rammed. They hurt that mother, they hurt her. I can see it did something to the drive. They hurt her —'

'Harry, are you all right? Get out of there!'

'Yeah, they rammed! They damaged her! They damaged the drive! *Now* we'll catch her. Something inside the drive is boiling away, you can see it in the flame. And the impact point, it's a pit, and I bet I can see four layers deep. Big Mama must be built like a Heinlein *Universe* ship, for spin, you know? Layers wrapped around a free-fall axis. We hurt her.'

'Yeah —'

'Tell Gillespie, damn it!'

'You tell him! Come on, Harry —'

Harry shined his light down. The small jet from his left ankle was pink. The gauges showed that he had five minutes of air. It was cool out here, most of him outside the hull. His legs were inside. It was hot in there. Go back in there?

Five minutes. It takes three or four to get through there. And it's hot . . .

'Maneuvering. Acceleration. Stand by.'

WHAM

In there? With acceleration?

'Incoming. Harry, move!'

'Can't move, Jeff. Anyway, I'm leaking.'

'Harry! I'll come get you —'

'Bullshit! Get your goddam hero medal rescuing somebody else.'

'Harry —'

'Incoming. Missiles.'

'Harry – oh, shit! Maneuvering. Stand by.'

'More missiles coming. I think they'll hit,' Harry said. 'Tell Gillespie. We hurt them. Tell him.'

CHAPTER FORTY-FOUR
IMPACT

And there was war in heaven: Michael and his angels fought against the dragon; and the dragon fought and his angels. And prevailed not; neither was their place found any more in heaven.

– REVELATION 12:7-8

Sometimes Jeri Wilson thought she heard – or felt – shocks, but mostly there was the steadily increasing acceleration that had topped out at around one Earth gravity. No one – or no fi' – had been interested in the storeroom. She'd lost all track of time.

'Arvid, we can't just sit here doing nothing!'

'What would you have us do?'

Jeri glared at him. 'You're the damned expert! But we ought to be doing *something.*'

Dmitri spoke sharply in Russian.

'Our commander says you should make less noise,' Arvid said.

'That's another thing. Why is he in charge? You're smarter than he is. You know spaceships. He doesn't.'

She felt Arvid's hand on her shoulder. His fingers gripped tightly. 'You wanted to come with us.'

And you'll send me away? But he wasn't threatening. *Worse than threats. Reminds me of promises.* 'We could – we could go open air shafts. Find a way to vacuum. Threaten the women and children.'

'You are bloodthirsty,' Arvid said.

'No. I hate it. This isn't my game at all. But we have to do *something!* We wouldn't have to kill them, just show we could. Between that attacking ship and whatever we can do, maybe they'd surrender.'

Dmitri spoke in Russian.

'Tell her yourself,' Arvid said.

'It won't work,' Dmitri said.

'Why —'

'We cannot threaten *all* of the women and children,' Dmitri said. 'Without atomic weapons we cannot threaten all those aboard this ship. Thus, why would they surrender?'

'But —'

'We would not surrender,' Dmitri said. 'Not even Comrade Rogachev. So why should the Invaders?'

Jeri huddled in the corner.

'We wait,' Dmitri said. 'We will have one chance. We must not throw that away.'

'What if it never comes?' she asked listlessly.

The ship rang like a great brass bell. The wall slammed against them.

Thuktun Flishithy shuddered with the impact.

Alice picked herself off the duct floor. Her whole body was bruised. There were spots before her eyes. A whistling shriek echoed through the ducts. The gravity fell to near zero, then began to build again.

What the hell was that?

The scream was dying, or else she was going deaf. She moved to the nearest grill.

A horror was out there. An armed snout, floating in the hall, turning. Stunned. Alice didn't stop to think. She twisted the wing nuts loose and wriggled through. The horror still hadn't made a move to anchor himself. Alice kicked toward him.

The tiny impact of a human body didn't wake him.

She pulled the gun from its holster. The stock was short and very wide. Trigger in the middle . . . safety? Did it have to be cocked?

Tentacles wrapped around her and pulled.

Alice shrieked and pushed the barrel against flesh and pulled the trigger.

The gun went whipping down the hall. The snout moved the other way, turning slowly, spraying a cloud of dark red blood. Alice leapt after the gun. *Damn thing would have killed me if I'd had it against my shoulder! Brace it against a wall or something next time. Have to fire with my left hand, too.* Her right arm flopped limp. It was just starting to hurt.

She didn't notice the slanting duct until the second snout came out. The snout emerged like a bomb, caught itself – herself: the harness was a female's – against the wall. She saw the spinning gun coming at her, and Alice behind.

Alice couldn't even flee. The walls weren't in reach yet. The fi' caught the gun, tossed it behind her, and reached forward in plenty of time to catch Alice. The constricting tentacles sent red agony through her arm and hand. Alice screamed and fainted.

The impact had knocked Jeri dizzy. It wasn't just dizziness. She was almost floating. Jeri clutched wildly and found a handful of wall rug. Air was escaping somewhere: *Thuktun Flishithy* screamed like a dying dinosaur.

Arvid had already anchored himself. He gripped Jeri's hand.

Nikolai shouted something in Russian. Dmitri answered.

'The Americans are coming!' Jeri said.

'I agree,' Dmitri said. 'Something has damaged this

ship. It can only be the American ship that Comrade Rogachev was permitted to see.'

Nikolai spoke rapidly again.

'He is right!' Arvid said. 'Dmitri, he is correct.'

'Da.'

'Correct about what?' Jeri demanded.

'The ship's drive has been damaged,' Arvid said. 'You can feel it. The gravity is much lower now, it fell, then builded, but it has not come back to its original strength.'

'Let us suppose the drive damaged, and the Americans in pursuit. The Invaders will wish to repair their drive.'

'Rogachev!' Dmitri brandished his captured pistol and shouted what must have been orders.

'Da, tovarishch. Jeri, we must prevent those repairs. Nikolai will lead us to the engine room control center. We will attempt to destroy that.' Rogachev took out his own pistol and inspected it. Satisfied he thrust it into his belt.

Nikolai was already in the air duct. Dmitri waved frantically. Arvid moved to the shaft.

'Jeri, you will follow me,' Arvid said. 'Let us go.'

Right. Jeri Wilson, famous Amazon, all hundred and twenty pounds of her. The Russians had pressure suits. She did not. *Maybe I ought to think this over?*

———

Fithp soldiers reeled across the bridge. Wes Dawson flailed to save himself, and wound up clutching a fi's harness.

The fi' responded by wrapping digits around him. The grip constricted. The fi' said, 'You saw the weapon. Was it an automatic device?'

Wes had seen it on half the screens and through the window too, in that last minute before impact. 'My fithp have come knocking,' he said.

'I am Defensemaster Tantarent-fid and I assert my right to know! Are your automatics so agile? It escaped our guns —'

677

Dawson grinned into eyes the size of oranges. 'It was an ordinary Space Shuttle. Men! We've rammed you.'

'Man, they died! Are you *all* rogues?'

'Why ask me? Ask your Breaker.'

The fi' hurled him away. He picked himself up and moved toward a wall, reeling in the dwindling gravity, seeking a handhold. No warning this time! *We actually did them some damage!*

The hive was broken and the bees were in turmoil.

One warrior had rolled shrieking across the room, denting a monitor console with his body, damaging himself more. He was getting medical attention. The other had Dawson back in restraint.

'Herdmaster, I have our thrust up to five eighths gravity, but a 512-breath of this will ruin the drive. We must make repairs.'

'We have no more time than that?'

Tantarent-fid spoke into his microphone and listened to replies. 'Herdmaster, I can guarantee no more time.'

After crossing from the Homeworld it has come to this. The alien vessel was aimed directly at them. It flared continuously, and with each flare gamma-ray lasers shone through hull and walls and flesh and bone. Tiny spacecraft had spread from the enemy, and now they hurled missiles to trample him. Tinier missiles leaped from *Message Bearer* to intercept. *That ship comes closer.*

'Dawson! Will they trample us as the Shuttle did?'

'Herdmaster, my *people* will do what they can to make you extinct. This is the cost of the Foot.'

That is no surprise. He would say that in any case, for strength in negotiation. 'Defensemaster.'

'Lead me.'

'Maintain maximum thrust.'

For a moment Tantarent-fid hesitated. 'As you will.'

'Takpusseh-yamp.'

'Lead me.'

'You will assist. We must send messages to' – he struggled with the alien name – 'to the United States. Dawson will assist.'

Humans in Africa had given them six possible loci for the surviving government of that fithp. They would all be the targets of tightbeams. *Now I must know what to say.*

The Herdmaster changed channels. He could have leaned across the corridor and spoken to Takpusseh-yamp, but he didn't want Dawson to hear. The rogue human's thoughts had begun to matter.

'Breaker-Two, do you now have a . . . what you called —'

'I have prepared two versions of a negotiated loss of status, Herdmaster, though I'm sorry to hear you ask. Here, channel 46.'

The Herdmaster read. *I must. That thing will catch us. We may destroy it when it comes near, but it will send fire and gamma rays regardless. Our mates and our children are at ransom here, and what Breaker-Two suggests is acceptable. The dissidents will be joyful . . .* 'Maintain this channel.' He motioned to the warrior, who led the human forward.

'Wes Dawson, I wish to negotiate a loss of status.'

'I don't understand.'

'Takpusseh-yamp?'

'The Herdmaster wishes to offer *conditional surrender*.'

The air went out of Dawson. In full thrust he might have collapsed. He said, 'Speak more.'

'You shall have Winterhome – Earth. We shall have the solar system.'

'Why do you offer this now?'

'You see the screens. Your ship approaches. It can harm us. I would avoid that harm – but, Dawson, your fithp have no other ship, for if they had, they would have sent it.

679

That ship cannot destroy us. It can only harm us, kill females and children. I would avoid that.'

'I wish to think of this.'

Dawson's eyes strayed to the screens. *Message Bearer* had been ripped; the edges of the hole still glowed red and orange. Sun-hot plasma must have roared down the corridors. Against the dark back of Winterhome, a light pulsed. Smaller flames came near, and flared green.

The ship rang to the tune of another explosion. Missiles exploding against the hull made a muffled thump you could hardly hear. But when a missile went off in the scar the Shuttle had left, it was different. Vibrations came from everywhere, with a sound like that of a smashed banjo.

'Dawson, you act now or not at all.'

'I won't send your message.'

A communications console buzzed. Pastempeh-keph gestured to the Breaker to answer. *Not now!* 'Dawson, this is what you offered Fathisteh-tulk! We will depart Africa, all of the Traveler Fithp and the humans who wish to join us. We will follow the paths we both know, reaping the riches of space, trading your soil-grown products for metals and —'

Dawson dared to interrupt. 'Fathisteh-tulk knew me. I see that now. I want the solar system. If I'm crazy, that's partly your doing.'

'You are mad indeed. When we have destroyed the intruder, we will visit *Winterhome* with destruction. That ship was built under the sign of peace. Never again will we honor that. We will trample every place, large or small, that ever displayed that sign.'

Dawson said nothing.

As I thought.

Takpusseh-yamp was finished with his call. He looked smug. *It is his thuktun. He deserves one last play.* 'Breaker-Two. Speak to this rogue.'

Takpusseh-yamp turned. 'Dawson! We have captured

your mate. Pay-kurtank, the priest's acolyte, found her after she left an air duct.'

'My mate is on Earth,' Dawson said.

'Untrue. We know she is your mate because we watched you mating in the ducts.'

Dawson flushed. 'So? We watched you mating in your rooms.'

'We do not speak to amuse ourselves, Dawson! You pretend to be a rogue, but you have a mate. A fi's mate is clearly responsible for him! Your pretense is done.'

'Hell. If we'd known . . . wait a minute. You *captured* Alice?'

The Herdmaster was in a towering fury. 'I would kill you this instant, Dawson, did you not represent your fithp in council. Will you transmit our terms and let your – Breaker-Two?'

'Your President. Dawson, your President surely has the right to hear such an offer.'

Dawson said nothing.

I have him!

'You have a point,' Dawson said. 'But – you had to *capture* Alice? She was loose! They're all loose, aren't they? Where?'

'We will leave your world to heal,' the Herdmaster pressed. He had not really believed this would work. Negotiated loss of status, indeed! 'There will be none of us on Earth, but there will be humans among our fithp. Surely your fithp and ours can survive alongside one another,' he said, not believing a word of it. 'Humans will travel as passengers in our ships. From us you will eventually learn to build your own.' But the losing fithp become part of the winner's. It had never been different.

Dawson's objection fell very wide of tradition. 'Let you leave, huh? And go to Saturn, and repair your ship? And what then?'

'Then . . . I don't understand. Breaker-Two?'

Takpusseh-yamp said, 'We fail to taste your problem.'

681

'What's to stop you from coming back with another Foot?'

'Our surrender, you brain-damaged rogue!'

'Are you telling me that a negotiated —' Dawson fell silent.

Now what stops him? Ah. The red-haired female had reached the bridge. The frail human was nested in Paykurtank's digits. She'd been hurt; she was hugging her right foreleg. She writhed at the sight of her mate.

'Wes! The Russians are loose. I killed a snout!'

'Good! Alice, we're hurting them, we really are. The Herdmaster wants me to transmit a conditional surrender. Trouble is, we can't trust it.'

Alice looked from Dawson to the array of screens.

A female. We know too little. Will she be able to hold him calm? What counsel will she give? Was it an error to bring her here?

The Herdmaster listened as Dawson explained to Alice. Her alien face was unreadable, but the Herdmaster could guess at her bloodthirsty joy as she watched the sparkling intruder come near. When Dawson finished speaking, she said, 'They'll come back!'

'Yeah. Herdmaster, Takpusseh, have you been trying to tell me that a "negotiated loss of status" is the same as a surrender?'

The Herdmaster couldn't speak. Takpusseh-yamp said, 'We give our surrender forever. You know us that well.'

'I have not been offered a surrender,' Dawson said.

'What is it you want?' But the Herdmaster knew, and he was trumpeting in agony now. 'Wish you my chest under your foot? You shall not have that!'

And every fi' in earshot was staring at him. 'Fight your ship!' he trumpeted. 'This battle is not concluded! We waste time. Kill that enemy. Signal the moon base. Trample that planet until its leaders roll on their backs. Dawson, we do not kill without reason. You have given us reason enough!'

'Hey, wait —'

'If we wait, that ship will harm us. When it is close enough, we kill it. Then there will be nothing to discuss. Speak to your President, or return to your cell.'

'Your offer isn't good enough!'

'I have made my last offer. Choose.'

If man and fi' had anything in common, then Dawson was in agony. The muscles of his face looked like digits in knots. His teeth were bared; they ground together.

The female ruined it. 'Wes! Look!'

'My God!'

'Your — ' *Predecessor?* But Dawson and Alice were gaping past the Herdmaster's shoulder. The Herdmaster turned —

Four screens showed four views of the engine room. The floor was awash in blood. The air itself was pink with spray. Nine corpses lay chewed as if by predators: eight fithp warriors and the legless Soviet in his curious legless suit. The remaining three humans were tearing the place apart.

Wes was in agony.

It was Coffey's department – Coffey's thuktun, and the Stud Bull had him dead to rights there. But Coffey would take the offer. Coffey would give away the solar system!

Or Dawson was about to give away the Earth. Could that weird device smash *Message Bearer*? Or was it only coming close enough to die? Would the fithp honor a conditional surrender? *We taught them conditional surrender. Have we also taught them to break their parole?*

'Wes, look!'

Not now, dammit died in his throat.

He'd never seen this room before, but it had that *look*. Machinery took its orders from here. Screens, dials, keyboards with keys the size of a child's fist; and fithp corpses, and blood, amazingly red, hemoglobin for sure, like some madman had bombed a Red Cross blood bank. Nikolai was dead, suit and man shredded by the huge fithp bullets.

Arvid was in a pressure suit. His faceplate was open, and his Cossack's grin would have frightened children. He had braced a fithp rifle against a console and was firing bullets into random controls.

Dmitri wandered about, examining the paraphernalia that made the ship go, shying minimally when Arvid blasted something . . . as if Arvid were a child at play, and Dmitri, the adult, were trying to learn something. He stopped, examined a console; pried the lid off with a piece of steel bar. He began tearing at wiring.

Arvid's rifle ran empty. Arvid grimaced, then smiled toothily into the camera.

Jeri Wilson studied the scene judiciously. Wes wondered if she was in shock. She climbed onto a console to bring her face close to a camera. She shouted soundlessly.

'Put the sound on,' the Defensemaster commanded.

'Negative,' said the Herdmaster. 'Dawson, your response?'

What was the Herdmaster afraid of hearing? . . . Afraid that Dawson might hear? It didn't matter. Wes grinned at the fi'. 'They were in the ducts, weren't they? And they'll be there again, wandering through your air supply. There's a great gaping hole in *Thuktun Flishithy*, isn't there? Maybe they can open more holes. Random death in the life support system!'

The ship hummed like a smashed banjo, twice in quick succession.

The Herdmaster said, 'Dawson. We will leave Africa, we will leave your Earth. You will have your solar system. We will go to another star.'

'You can't —'

'With time and your aid, of course we can. We will

refuel *Message Bearer* and build a new siskyissputh. You will assist. When we depart your system, you will have your own.'

'That word —'

'The siskyissputh is the device we used to cross from Homeworld to Saturn. It takes energy from the main drive and uses the energy to push against interstellar matter. The siskyissputh is your door, not to your own planets, but to the worlds of other stars. Dawson, why did you think we discarded it?'

Dawson, staring, got his lips working. 'Too massive. You could not have reached Saturn.'

'No. Dawson, we came knowing that you might be more powerful than the Traveler Fithp. We came to conquer or to surrender. If we came to surrender, we had the siskyissputh to offer our new fithp. We let the siskyissputh hurl itself at the stars so that you cannot examine it.'

'I had it wrong. That never, never crossed my mind. But you have tapes of thuktunthp —'

'We have the Podo Thuktun itself, rogue! That is the siskyissputh, and the Podo Thuktun's supports are explosive. But if we are to leave your star, we must have another siskyissputh, and you must build it with us. When we leave, you will know how to make another. Dawson, I *know* that you want more than the planets. Take our negotiated loss of status or you will never leave your star.'

'Wes, he's crazy! We'll have it in ten years! Wes, once we *know* something is possible – like the atomic bomb, as soon as they knew it was possible, everyone started working on how to build one —'

The screens flickered. Dmitri jerked backward. One foot was missing. There were holes in the walls. The humans moved to one corner. Jeri Wilson continued to shout soundlessly at the cameras.

Irrelevant. We're all irrelevant —

The Herdmaster said, 'The Predecessors developed the siskyissputh. It took more than eight-cubed years.

Dawson, humans are a herd under siege by their own rogues! You will not survive sixty-four years! And we might yet win this battle.'

Alice was strangling his arm. 'Wes, it's the same thing all over again! They'll come back!'

I wanted to be President! Why? 'Alice, if they win – can they win?'

Her grip slowly relaxed. 'I don't know.'

'I don't either.' *I can't decide this.* 'Give me your microphone. I'll speak to the President.'

CHAPTER FORTY-FIVE
TERMS OF SURRENDER

For a promise made is a debt unpaid.

– ROBERT W. SERVICE

The screens had not changed for more than an hour.

General Toland set down his coffee cup. 'How many snouts does it take to change a light bulb?'

The President wrinkled his brow in puzzlement. 'None. They've invented torches.'

'No —'

'I have something,' Jenny said.

'Gimlet, this is *Michael*.'

They're alive!

Down below all the crews were cheering.

'Gimlet, this is *Michael*. Reporting. We have inflicted heavy damage on the invader mother ship. We have taken severe damage. We have fifty percent casualties. They are definitely running away. We continue in pursuit. Stand by for digital data.'

A picture emerged on the screen below: *Michael* with his whole portside kicked in. One spurt bomb rack had vanished, and the portside propulsion tower was dented and holed.

'Holy shit,' General Toland muttered.

No wonder Ed sounds tired.

More data. A blurred image of the enemy ship. It looked scarred.

'Estimate one hour to interception,' Gillespie said. 'Jenny, is that you?'

'*Michael,* this is Gimlet, Colonel Crichton here.'

'Jenny, tell Linda I love her.'

Jenny looked quickly to the screens below. They flowed and changed as *Michael's* computer dumped in data. *They don't have enough bombs left to kill their velocity. They can't come home unless they win.*

'Admiral, is there anything I ought to say?' President Coffey asked.

'You're the politician, Mr. President.'

'Meaning that it's more important to me than to General Gillespie. Colonel, tell him – dammit. Cut me in.'

'Sir. *Michael,* stand by for Executive One.'

'General, this is David Coffey. I'll give your message to your wife. Anything else?'

'For the record: posthumous awards for civilians. I recommend the Medal of Freedom. Dr. Arthur Grace Pelz. Mr. Samuel Cohen. Mr. Harry Reddington. Military personnel – Excuse me. I'll switch on automatic digital reporting. Mr. President, it's getting a bit thick —'

'Godspeed, General.'

'*Michael* out.'

The screens below shifted: a composite picture of *Michael,* dented and torn. Bombs exploded aft as the big ship accelerated.

Another screen showed a tiny Earth surrounded by colored dots with arrows protruding. Velocity vectors. The Navy would need to learn a whole new way of reading maps if this kind of thing ever became common. The alien invader was a large red spear; *Michael,* in blue, pursued relentlessly; both vectors pointed away from Earth. *Michael's* vector was longer. The dots would be touching within the hour.

Digit ships were orange dots. They swarmed close around the Earth. A few were farther out and tens of thousands of miles away, their orange arrows pointing toward the battle.

Admiral Carrell studied the screen. 'The digit ships are no threat. It'll be all over by the time they get there.'

'Is he going to ram?' General Toland asked.

'He can't come home,' Admiral Carrell said carefully. 'Under the circumstances, what would you do?'

'Damn straight,' Toland said. 'Can he do it?'

Carrell shrugged. 'General, I expect the engineering people will be working on that question. It would be interesting to know what they think.'

'Sir.' Jenny touched more buttons. Jenny Crichton knew: that was Ed Gillespie, her sister's husband, with no more than two hours to live and nothing anyone could do about it. Colonel Jeanette Crichton called the engineers.

'Dreamer Fithp here.'

'Engineering —'

'They're all busy,' Reynolds' voice said. 'So they have me answering the phone.'

'Your projection?'

'I'll give you Colonel Matthews. Al, they want a projection.'

'Matthews here. We don't have a projection.'

Admiral Carrell broke in. 'Colonel, would you care to explain that?'

'Sir. Given the damage *Michael* has sustained, and the defense capabilities demonstrated by the enemy, a majority of my analysts believe the most likely event is mutual destruction of *Michael* and the enemy mother ship. We can't assign a probability to that. A large minority of our people believe the enemy will be severely damaged but *Michael* will be destroyed.

'The Threat Team is nearly unanimous: the enemy will do almost anything to prevent severe damage to the mother ship.'

'What does that mean, almost anything?' Carrell demanded.

'Certainly an offer of surrender.'

'Sincere?'

'Sir —'

'My apologies. You can't know.'

'They'll also go all out to protect the mother ship. Their warriors aren't likely to be less courageous than ours. They'll throw everything they have.'

'No surprise there,' General Toland said.

'Thank you, Colonel. I'll ask you to use screen five to display your projections.'

'Yes, sir.'

On the screen below, *Michael*'s blue crept toward the enemy red.

'Sir. We're getting something —'

'Gimlet, this is Harpoon. We're getting a tightbeam message on the same frequency the aliens used when they sent that message to the President. It's for the President.'

'They want to talk!' General Toland said.

'Put them on!' David Coffey ordered.

'Alert the Threat Team to listen to this,' Admiral Carrell said.

'Harpoon, put them on. Stand by to transmit replies.'

'Roger. Stand by.'

'Mr. President, Mr. President. This is Wes Dawson. Come in, Mr. President. President Coffey, this is Wes Dawson.'

'Am I on?' Coffey demanded.

'Yes, sir.'

President Coffey spoke into the microphone. 'Congressman Dawson, this is President David Coffey. Can you hear me?'

'Mr. President, this is Dawson. I hear you. I have an offer of conditional surrender from the Herdmaster.'

Jenny knew his voice. It was Wes, and he was all right. She could see Carlotta Dawson down on the floor below. Carlotta was grinning like an idiot.

'Surrender,' Toland muttered. 'We must have hurt them —'

Admiral Carrell waved impatiently.

The President said, 'What terms?'

Wes Dawson's laugh sounded half mad. It could have been simply static. 'That's the stumbling point, all right. Here are the terms. We call off the attack. The enemy, the Traveler Herd, will vacate Earth immediately. They'll vacate the solar system as soon as possible. What we'll have to do to bring that about involves building them a – ' Dawson stopped, then seemed to sputter. 'A siskyissputh. They threw their own siskyissputh away while rounding the Sun, so that we couldn't examine it. It's a modified Bussard ramjet. Get a technical expert to explain that to you. It's the key to the stars, and when we've built theirs we'll know how to build one for ourselves.

'The Herdmaster has offered these terms, *not* the formal surrender of his herd. I am not to have my foot on any fi's chest. This was made clear. Do you understand?'

'I understand. Have you a time period for the evacuation of Earth?'

'No. I'm not sure they can enforce it anyway. The fithp can split into smaller herds, and it's possible the ones in Africa won't leave —'

'Dawson! Dawson, come in, Dawson —'

'Africa can take care of itself,' General Toland said. 'Hell, the snouts can't fight with nobody to drop meteors for them. Let the Zulus have 'em.'

'No threat to us, agreed,' Admiral Carrell said. 'Did they cut Dawson off?'

'Dawson here. They didn't want me to say that. They should have let me finish. The ones in Africa won't matter! They'll be glad to call a truce. They don't want Kansas. Mr. President, I cannot tell you what's happening outside. Do you know?'

'Wes, we're in communication with the Archangel. The commander is General Gillespie. They expect to destroy the enemy mother ship within two hours. Certainly we know what's happening.'

'The Herdmaster wants me to repeat the offer. You call off – what did you call it? Archangel? Good name! You call off Ed Gillespie, and they'll use the digit ships to rescue *Michael* and the smaller ships. Everyone who wants to leave Africa will get a chance. Any that stay won't be a problem. They'll tell us how to build an interstellar drive. Mr. President, they're prepared to destroy all the plans for that drive. They've been planning this for years, since before they ever reached the solar system. They planned to surrender the interstellar drive if they couldn't defeat us.'

'Should we take this offer?' the President asked.

'I'm sorry, President Coffey. I don't know enough and it's not my choice. They made a previous offer I decided not to transmit. Mr. President, they'll give you – it's about ten minutes. They say they're mobilizing to fight Archangel, I don't know what with. They say that once they start doing that they will have no reason to surrender.'

'Are they listening to me? Can they understand?'

'They're listening. Some understand.'

'Tell them they will have to wait while I get advice.'

'They understand that, sir.'

'All right. Hang on —'

'They want you to have Archangel stop shooting while you decide. The reason they want to negotiate is to keep you from damaging *Thuktun Flishithy*, because it's carrying all their females and childr —'

'Wes. Wes, what's happened?'

A strange voice, cold, sibilant, spoke. 'This is Teacher Takpusseh-yamp. Go seek your advice. We will listen.'

'Get *Michael*,' Admiral Carrell ordered.

'Can he tell us enough?' President Coffey wondered aloud.

'Whatever he knows, we'll need to talk with him,' Carrell said.

'*Michael*, this is Gimlet, *Michael*, this is Gimlet —'

'Go ahead, Gimlet.'

Jenny motioned to Admiral Carrell.

'General, we're pretty certain our codes are good, but you'll excuse me if I use circumlocutions.'

'Understood.'

'Mama wants to kiss and make up. We live in separate houses, only you have to stop projecting dinnerware at her right now. Great White Father needs a lawyer. You're it.'

'Ah – Roger. Tell Big Daddy we don't have lockjaw yet, but you never know.'

'*Michael*, have you enough dinnerware?'

'We are running short of dinnerware. The family car needs repair too. Can win the case, but cannot stop to discuss alimony.'

'Thank you, *Michael*. Carry on. Gimlet out.' Admiral Carrell nodded, speaking mostly to himself. 'As I thought. If he stops now, they'll outrun him. *Michael* fights on while we decide this.'

'Send for Hap Aylesworth, and get me the Threat Team,' the President said.

Nat had been waiting for the phone to ring. 'Dreamer Fithp, Nat Reynolds here. We've been listening.'

'Mr. Reynolds, your opinion: what do we do about this offer? Accept or let Archangel go for the throat? Bearing in mind that Archangel might not make it.'

The others were crowded close around him, with Harpanet's huge head protruding between sets of shoulders. They all looked like they were ready to jump down his throat.

Nat said, 'Give us five minutes.'

'Take four.'

Nat hung up. 'I'll take a poll. Keep it short. Sherry?'

'They'll honor a surrender. Take the offer.'

'Bob?'

Bob Burnham shook his massive white head. 'It's not a physics problem. Oh, if we let them go, they can go straight for the Moon; then they own us. But whether they'll do it – Nat, you *never* liked my aliens.'

'Right. Curtis?'

'Nuke 'em till they glow, then shoot 'em in the dark. Sherry, you c —'

'*Cool* it! Joe?'

Joe Ransom hesitated, spoke in a rush. 'I abstain. It's too even. I wish Bob Anson were here.'

'We all do. So we don't know. Discussion. One minute each. Sherry?'

'It's not complicated. When they surrender, they stay surrendered.'

'Yeah, but – okay. Wade?'

'No. They'll go back to Saturn, repair their ship, and come back with a fucking moon. We win now or we never do. As for surrender, bullshit, Sherry. The surrender a fi' honors is a foot on the chest and join the herd as a slave. They haven't offered surrender.'

'Joe?'

'By damn, they haven't, have they? But they've been giving conditional surrender in Africa. They understand the concept.'

'Sure,' said Curtis. 'Charnel House Books understands contracts too, but they don't honor them! Sherry, if they don't offer a foot on the chest you can't argue that their reflexes are involved.'

'I haven't heard you commit yourself, Nat.'

'Right. Harpanet? This is a peculiar case. You joined the Dreamer Fithp before you ever heard of a conditional surrender —'

'Not so. I know of such a case in our history.'

'Say on, but keep it short.'

The fi' said, 'There was a war. Others had been fought with nuclear weapons, and so was this. The South Land Mass Fithp evolved a disease that would feed on the edible grasses of the East Land Mass. They demonstrated this for the East Land Mass Fithp and learned that they had evolved something similar —'

'We don't have time, Harpanet!'

'Lead me. The planet was harmed. More harm would come. Maybe all fithp would follow the Predecessors into death. The Herdmasters met and agreed to use the knowledge in the Sky Thuktun to build a spacecraft. The high ranks of one fithp would travel to the nearest star, which was known to house intelligence. When *Thuktun Flishithy* was prepared, the two fithp would gamble for who must leave.'

'Was the agreement honored?'

'It was. We are here.'

'Do you know of any other such event?'

'Ffuff – Within a fithp, such adjustments are common. Between fithp, very rare.'

'Okay.' Reynolds raised the phone. 'Mr. President?'

They barely heard the knock through the thick soundproof door. Jack Clybourne opened it. Hap Aylesworth, fat, bearded, his hair a mess, came in. 'You wanted me, sir?'

'Right with you. Reynolds?'

'We can't agree. It's a good bet they'd keep their surrender. There's even precedent. We don't like the size of the pot.'

'I don't either. Thank you.' The President hung up. 'Hap, I need advice. Have you been listening?'

'Yes, sir.'

Seconds flowed on the big digital timer. 'Six minutes,' Jenny said.

'I thought the Threat Team people would know,' Coffey said. 'But they don't. General. Admiral. You heard. Your advice?'

'The human race won't be safe until the invaders are disarmed,' General Toland said.

The President jerked a thumb toward the big screens outside. 'And if they defeat *Michael*? They could, you know.'

'Unlikely,' Admiral Carrell said.

'I beg your pardon, Admiral?'

'They're closing fast. Unless *Michael* does something stupid, they're bound to ram. I believe you can depend on General Gillespie to detonate every bomb aboard at closest approach.'

'Your advice, Admiral?'

Admiral Carrell raised an eyebrow at the timer. 'I think I would do nothing at all.'

'All their women and children. They came from the stars. They offer an interstellar drive. We lose all that —'

'And keep the Earth,' Carrell said.

'But at what price? Hap?'

'Pass. I know how to win elections. This one's beyond me.'

'Gimlet, this is *Michael*. Big Mama's mad; she's got all the children in the fight. I mean, she's really mad.'

One of the screens below flashed, then flashed again.

'They're really pounding each other,' General Toland said. 'Go for it, Gillespie!'

'No,' President Coffey said. 'Colonel, get me General Gillespie. Inform him that I have new orders. Then get Wes Dawson. We can end this with honor —'

'Mr. President, please,' General Toland said. 'Sir, the risk is just too damned high! Thor, tell him!'

'I've heard your advice, General. I don't need it again. Colonel, if you please —'

Jenny reached for the keys. Her hand moved slowly, reluctantly. Visions of dolls and smashed children came unwanted, and corpses heaped high in a Topeka street, human shapes merging as they decayed. She stood. 'No, sir.'

'Colonel —'

'I resign.'

'Admiral Carrell —'

'No, Mr. President.'

Coffey turned to the door. Jack Clybourne stood solidly against it. 'Mr. Clybourne – you too?'

Jack said nothing.

'I am the commander in chief! Hap, tell them —'

'I'm *not* the commander in chief, David.'

'Colonel, will you at least do me the courtesy of calling Mrs. Coffey?'

Jenny looked to Admiral Carrell. He shook his head. 'Sir, there wouldn't be time to explain anything to her.'

'I'll have you all shot —'

'Possibly,' General Toland said. 'Tomorrow. But just now we have about three minutes.'

'Damn you all! Those creatures will blow *Michael* apart, and then they'll own the Earth!'

'No, sir,' Admiral Carrell said. 'It is you who risks the Earth. We risk only mankind's enemies.'

Coffey sat and buried his head in his hands. After a moment Admiral Carrell lifted the microphone. 'Colonel, get me Mr. Dawson.'

'Sir.'

'Congressman Dawson, this is Admiral Carrell. The President is not available.'

'What —'

'Tell the enemy commander that his offer is rejected.'

———

Steel plates now covered the windows. The sky was alive with green flares and retina-burn-white explosions. Fithp in pressure suits crawled across the slagged hull, towing equipment. *Message Bearer* rang like a smashed banjo, and the Herdmaster trumpeted, 'How are they doing this? Defensemaster!'

697

'The wound in Sector Five is turned full away from the intruder, and has been since before you ordered it. Herdmaster, the tiny ships circle and fire into the wound. They are not using rockets, and our lasers cannot find inert projectiles.'

'Then kill me those flying guns! Takpusseh-yamp, was there an answer from the President?' But he knew. Takpusseh-yamp's digits were rigid across his head. They still strangled the receiver with which he had been monitoring Dawson's conversation.

'Dawson.'

'Say good-bye, Herdmaster. We'll find our own path to the stars, and you won't be there waiting.'

'Could you not persuade —'

'The President's not available. I know David Coffey. He must be dead or dying. Admiral Carrell is in charge now. The Attackmaster. He wants you extinct, and he wouldn't listen to me if I pleaded. I'm not even sure he's wrong.'

'Wes! Did we win?'

'I think so. Hang on, Alice. It's not likely to be long now —'

The Herdmaster asked, 'What would you have of me, Dawson?'

'Two months in solitary confinement, Herdmaster, but I don't think we'll have the time.' Dawson's grip tightened on the wall rug as *Message Bearer* shuddered sideways. Despite the danger, he was standing fully erect.

'Get me my mate,' the Herdmaster ordered.

Safe Room Two was jammed with females and children. The noise was terrible to hear: comforting adult voices, bleating of terrified infants, *the herd is attacked*! His mate cried, 'Keph, what's happening? The children are going rogue —'

'Keph, I want to surrender.'

There was an awful silence. Then the last voice Pastempeh-keph wanted to hear was speaking. 'You would surrender the Traveler Fithp, *you*? Fool rogue, my mate would have had us safely circling Saturn if you had not stripped him of his status!'

'I acknowledge this. You in Safe Room Two must speak for the rest. Will the females consent to surrender?'

'Let me speak to the Defensemaster!'

Tantarent-fid clicked on. Pastempeh-keph listened with half his attention. Damage . . . weapons . . . intruder closing at five makasrupkithp per breath, targeted dead on, able to turn faster than *Message Bearer* ever could . . . 'If we vaporize the enemy, the globules will condense and kill us. If we kill all aboard, the bombs will explode when it is close. Our only chance of escape is for the enemy to guide that ship away from us.'

'Surrender,' said Chowpeentulk. 'Roll on your back for my mate's murderer.'

'Surrender, Keph. We are agreed.'

The Herdmaster stepped – staggered – into the corridor between crash pads. 'Dawson. The ship is yours.'

'I want to see the other humans.'

Screens blurred, then sharpened. Arvid Rogachev and Jeri Wilson stood close together in the midst of carnage and wreckage. Dmitri lay in one corner.

'Give them weapons, and escort them here.'

'I obey.'

'Now turn off your drive. Blow up all missiles in flight. Don't send any more.'

'Agreed. We need your ship alive. Dawson, make haste. Tell your herdmaster. That ship must not strike us.'

'When I hear you give those orders.'

'Tantarent-fid! Destroy our missiles now. Continue to use lasers to stop incoming weaponry. Begin damping the drive.'

'Lead me.'

The Herdmaster could not have imagined how those words would hurt. The eyes of his fithp were all around him. Pastempeh-keph rolled on his back in the aisle.

Herdmaster Wes Dawson said, 'Alice.'

'Wes – did we really win?'

He held out his hand. The frail redhead moved to join him. Dawson took her hand. Together they stepped forward and set their feet on the Herdmaster's Advisor's chest.

LEGACY OF HEOROT

Larry Niven, Jerry Pournelle and Steven Barnes

Civilisation on Earth was rich, comfortable – and overcrowded. Millions applied for the voyage but only the best were chosen to settle on Tau Ceti Four. The Colony was a success. The silver rivers and golden fields of Camelot overflowed with food and sport nurtured by the colonists' eco-sensitive hands. It was an idyll, the stuff of dreams.

Just one man, Cadmann Weyland, insisted on perimeter defences: electric fence, minefield, barbed wire. Against what? Surely humans are the most destructive creatures in the universe? Surely the planet is friendly? Surely it's safe to walk in the fields after dark?

And beyond the perimeter the nightmare began to chatter . . .

'A version of ALIENS by writers who know the difference between Hollywood science fiction and the Real Stuff'
TIME OUT

0 7221 6407 6
SCIENCE FICTION

RAMA II

Arthur C. Clarke & Gentry Lee

RENDEZVOUS WITH RAMA is one of the bestselling
science fiction novels of all time. In this brilliantly
imaginative sequel, another Raman spacecraft approaches
Earth, in the year 2200. Once again, an expedition is
mounted to explore the spacecraft, determined this time
to unveil some of the mysteries which remained when
RAMA left the solar system seventy years previously.
Clarke and Lee build a persuasive picture of Earth two
hundred years in the future, and give a stunning
exposition of the spacecraft that is . . . RAMA II.

0 7088 4833 8
SCIENCE FICTION

FOUR HUNDRED BILLION STARS

Paul J McAuley

Dorthy Yoshida is a telepath and an astronomer. Because of her talent she is sent to investigate the mystery of a small planet orbiting a red dwarf star. Although it appears to have been planoformed, shaped by intelligent life, its only advanced life-forms are creatures called herders. They are known to possess primitive intelligence, while the slug-like herbivores they shepherd have only a rudimentary nervous system.

Could these life-forms really be connected with The Enemy, the unknown entity which fights a savage war with mankind in deep space?

It didn't seem likely. Until Dorthy landed, when her mind immediately detected a dazzling intellect, the intensity of which she had never before felt . . .

'Excellent science, grittily convincing human relationships, precision prose' Lewis Shiner